FAF(complete) versi

© Bogus Focus Electronic Publ

Paul Nagle

Cover: Tim Rafferty
www.rafferty.co.uk

* forever in need of that elusive final edit. Any resemblance to persons living, dead or in Morecambe is unintentional. I don't use a spellchecker, as you'll probably notice. E&OE and so on. In reformatting this for 6x9/paperback, I've tweaked the text quite a bit and inevitably introduced fresh typos. If anyone sends me a list of mistakes I'll correct them for future editions, Paul xxx.

For Rich

The Worm exploded into life, electromagnetic charges flailing like a dominatrix on speed. Those unlucky few who chanced to be nearby reeled under the assault as sizzling bolts of strange energy pummelled their frontal lobes and burrowed deep into soft brain tissue.

Much later in the still hours of darkness the relentless pounding ceased. Blessed silence came for a moment before a new thing began. That new thing was a voice, a whispering, insistent voice calling each of its targets by name. After a while the voice began to issue instructions . . .

Book One

Chapter One

*If only God would give me some clear sign!
Like making a large deposit in my name in a Swiss
bank.*   Willy Allen

Jim Cavanah slammed the metal door of the bike shed with all the force he could muster. He noted, with some satisfaction, that the cement was beginning to loosen around the door frame and that a small crack had appeared in the concrete lintel. *A work in progress.*

It was 07.00 so he was surprised to see several cars - unfamiliar cars - parked untidily near the bank's main entrance. Although it was a bright April morning, his hands were chilled from the ride and he eagerly anticipated a hot shower and an even hotter coffee.

Slotting his *Entacard* through the reader, he experienced the first twinge of unease. As the bullet-proof glass door clicked open, the security guard stirred. Slowly, he made eye contact. Then, completing a total of three unlikely events, he put his newspaper down and patted it gently. As Jim sidled down the corridor, the guard crested new horizons of atypical behaviour. Fixing Jim with a glassy stare, he picked up the phone.

Wandering through the open-plan office, Jim turned off various lights and monitor screens and set the photocopier to 'standby'. He knew that, soon, every visible appliance would be turned back on again - IT Professionals burning their way up Global Warming Boulevard. Suppressing righteous anger and a desire to smite, Jim continued towards his cubicle.

His desk light was on! Reaching it, he saw a briefcase. And a jacket and a laptop.

He scowled. Jim preferred to arrive first each morning,

typically an hour before anyone else. He used this time to surf the net, drink coffee, get his head together and generally nose about. Officially it was his creative time, the time when he innovated, thought out of the box, all that. His time-sheet said so anyway. His schedule offered the bonus of an early afternoon escape while everyone else remained in shackles. He relished the daily opportunity to stride out in his fluorescent cycling shorts, en route to blue skies and leafy glades. Or to the pub. Often he would yell a trilling "frrrreedom!" as he departed.

Guessing probably calfskin or vole, Jim dropped his rucksack roughly onto the supple-looking leather jacket. Automatically, he sneered at the laptop, locked out by the corporate password-protected screen-saver, a rotating purple W. This particular W was the bank's unmistakeable logo.

Mouthing his own version of the glorious motto, Jim began to ponder the briefcase. He was interrupted by a reedy, familiar voice.

"Jim, where on earth have you been?"

"Derek, you're early for a Monday. And what do you mean, where have I been?" Jim nudged the rucksack onto the floor.

"The Ops have been trying to get hold of you since Saturday night. The database is totally screwed and we've probably lost data. You were on call, right?"

"Um, was I?" Jim's brain was struggling to get up to speed. He shut down several superfluous mental processes, bringing all of his concentration online. His EO program registered his boss's status as: *haggard*.

Jim tried to recall the weekend. *Had* there been a phone call? A bead of sweat formed on his upper lip. In his stomach, a chasm gaped. The chasm invited him to come join the airsick butterflies swirling around helplessly. Memories of Saturday weren't fully accessible. They were blurred and disjointed. And of Sunday there was nothing at all. A vacuum. Suddenly, Jim needed that shower more than ever. But first he had to play the Game.

"Specifically, what's the problem?" His most professional voice.

"At 23:00 on Saturday night, the Reconciliation Batch fell over. On every system."

"Shit."

"Ops were getting errors they'd never seen before, so they called you. Apparently they left messages on your answer phone, your mobile *and* your pager."

"Oh, well, you know I returned the pager yonks back? And I didn't get any phone messages. And my mobile batteries..." Even as he wibbled, Jim was sure Derek would smell the bullshit - but he needed to assess the damage before taking any of the blame. For the W&W Bank, Reconciliation meant big money - and lots of high-profile management attention. Exactly the kind nobody in their right mind needed. "What's the status now?" he asked.

"We're running full restores – all we could think of. But there's wide scale corruption. I've been in since yesterday afternoon. I tried to call you a couple of times myself. Even sent one of the Ops round to knock on your door."

Derek was not a bad sort. Harmless really, Jim reflected. He felt moderately bad for him – but reserved his main anxieties for himself. His brain was so cloudy that he doubted coffee alone would spark it up.

His boss sounded weary as he continued, "the first lot of restores failed - backups buggered or something - so we got the off-site tapes. I don't think we'll be quite up and running for the online day which is bad news, real bad. The Database guys think there's something wrong with the journal offloads too. Peter Morris and his not-so-merry men have been in since the early hours. He's going to want to talk to you."

"Shit," said Jim. Then he came to a decision. "Look, if the restores are running there's nothing I can do until they end. I'll grab a quick shower and then I'll figure it all out. Don't worry." His mind raced and he hoped this sounded reassuring.

Derek flicked some dry mud from his lovely jacket. His shoulders were slumped, his expression morose.

Ignoring his plight, Jim shouldered his rucksack and headed for the shower. "Those systems have been stable for years. They've never failed before," he called, not looking back.

Nodding vaguely, Derek picked up his laptop. "I'd better start work on the WHR," he said. "I'll be in my office."

"Aye, can't beat a good W-W-Witch Hunt," said Jim, under his breath.

In the changing room, he gazed blearily into a steamy mirror. He was shocked to discover a rather flabby figure, streaks of grey forming in the long hair and stubble, staring listlessly back. Who was this old, knackered guy? He noted, as if for the first time, the wobble of his chest, the thickening presence of blood vessels in eyes that were once white and clear. Today the hip, pony-tailed 'dude' had failed to make an appearance. The fireproof maverick genius was entirely absent and the athletic health fiend (way younger than his forty years) had been lost overboard.

It was possible, he conceded, that the weekend binges were starting to take their toll. They were certainly getting harder to shake off. But it was his *secret project* – the one that consumed more and more of his thoughts - that was becoming a major issue. Ironically, it would one day be the solution to situations like these. But not yet. For now, it was time to get washed, dressed and face the music.

Back at his desk, he felt better - for about five seconds. Until the phone rang.

"Peter Morris here. What on earth have you done to my database?" Morris never wasted time on niceties, although he did waste it on nice ties. Most would-be senior managers did.

"Top of the morning to you, Peter. I'm just logging on right now. How are the restores going?"

"It looks like they might save your bacon," Morris replied. "For now anyway. Call me when you know what went wrong." The line went dead.

Jim switched on his PC and, while it booted up, made himself a muscular coffee. No trips out for a cappuccino or leery chats with the cafe girls this morning!

By lunchtime, things were clearer – but only a little. Jim had scoured the system logs exhaustively; first for any sign of his own culpability, second to discover the underlying cause. He typed up his entry for the Witch Hunt Report with rare restraint. Unusually (for him), he documented only the facts. He left the text unembellished and wholly lacking in sarcasm - or reminders of his own superiority. This one had the potential to rise to the loftiest golf courses of management.

It seemed, he wrote in conclusion, *that the failures were attributable to computational errors within the main processors - of every mainframe in the company. Suspect hardware errors on a grand scale, most likely a manufacturing error or a Chinese plot!* He knew this to be a silly explanation but the precisely correlated facts - as he spun them - supported it. He even broke his golden rule by including a few superfluous coloured graphs and pie charts.

For a while he reckoned he was off the hook. IBM and their engineers were on it. He didn't bother to ring Peter Morris.

Throughout the morning, many of his workmates stopped by to chat. As is the way with office banter, they played their concern for him lightly. Instead they summoned feigned amusement and a good impression of mockery. Some even mimicked open hostility. Always keen to engage in good-natured intercourse, Jim smiled a pleasant "fuck off" to each in turn.

"That's a few less chips on your shoulder, you big-headed twat" was one of a selection of jovial, unimaginative retorts.

He ignored them all. He was thinking about the one tiny detail he'd omitted from the report. That the failing programs (all his own) had crapped out *at different stages* on each system. This confirmed his gut feeling that the problem could not be attributed to hardware. And that somehow it was, indeed, all his fault.

Let IBM prove it, he thought. *They'll take ages either way.*
And by then it'll be too late to stop me.

The most worrying discovery was that one of the subroutines claimed to have aborted at line 1460 - an impossible figure given its true length was a mere thousand lines! For the first time in his professional career, Jim was uncertain. He desperately needed to run away and purge his brain. But first there was the Game to play. There would be a summons followed by some kind of hassle and lots of whining. He wasn't sure what form it would take but was glad that W&W's online day had only been compromised by a couple of minutes.

The author of some of the key programme suites, Jim was widely regarded as untouchable - not least by himself. The morning had delivered a low blow to his credibility but he was confident he'd soon be back to his regular high state of tossing it off, running rings around the mental pygmies who littered the office, consuming power and oxygen.

When the summons eventually came, his AA program immediately reported that the mood had lifted. Taking a seat in Derek's office, he began to relax for the first time that day.

"IBM's on the case. They're pulling cards and sending them away for analysis. They're not admitting anything, of course, but I think our CEO has them rattled. Thanks for the report - exactly what we needed. Those pie charts were conclusive, I think," he added with a worrying lack of irony.

Jim nodded smoothly, "no sweat. I must admit I was baffled at first but.."

And then his patter was unexpectedly derailed.

"Jim," Derek interrupted. "A few people have been talking."

"Sorry?" With a large bucket of jargon and technical wibble primed for launch, Jim wasn't ready for verbal input. This was the point at which he was supposed to reassert his dominance after all. He was about to carry on talking anyway when something in his boss's expression made him pause.

Derek cleared his throat, as if about to launch into a prepared speech. Then he seemed to change his mind. He fiddled with his tie awkwardly.

"I know you're one of the lads, Jim. Always having a good time and all. But it took a lot of smoothing-over to get your arse out of the fire this time. We're going to have to get someone else trained up as full backup for when you're on call - if you can't guarantee to answer." He looked uncomfortable.

"I'm really sorry Derek, as I said I can't think what went wrong. I was home all weekend listening to music. Never heard the phone once. I've checked my mobile but it turns out the battery's totally knackered. I reckon it could have been dead since Friday. Just bad luck I guess. Water got in it, I expect. Or hailstones."

"Well, get another battery - and soon! We can't afford another cock-up like this. Neither of us can. Jim..."

"Yes?"

"Do you think it's, well, maybe time to start, you know, taking it easier? You're not at university any more. We've all indulged ourselves in our youth, enjoyed the wacky baccy and all that. We've had our fun, even me. But life moves on, you know. The fun ends. People grow out of it."

Wacky baccy, thought Jim. *You couldn't comprehend a fraction of what's been wacking my brain.* But aloud he said, "hey Derek, I like a toot on the old bong now and again, *end Audio Analysis*, but you can't honestly say it's affected my work. Inspired me if anything. That's what us creative types need now and again. Of course if you're talking 'not being able to cut it', there's a certain wino in the corner of the office..."

"No, no, that's not it. It's more a case of, well...."

"Go on."

"Some people have been telling me you're behaving differently. Lately, I mean. One of the admin girls said she saw you just standing in the corridor last week. Stood there for about five minutes apparently. Said she spoke to you but you just ignored her. And then there was that day you were upset. Wednesday was it?"

"Upset?" Jim felt his chest tighten.

"Well, I saw you at your desk and you seemed to be... weeping. Sort of misty-eyed. I thought I'd leave it a few days and see if there was anything I could do. Check you were OK. Um. Are you? OK, I mean?"

"Yeah, oh, Wednesday. It was nothing, really. All sorted now. Personal stuff." Jim hadn't a clue where this was going but he wanted it to end. The urge to get up and run became almost overwhelming.

"Good, good," said Derek. "Sorted, lovely. Glad to hear it."

"So, is that everything?" Jim made as if to rise from the chair, technical spin forgotten. For some reason the office smelt repellent all of a sudden, like a cage. A combination of furniture polish, Derek's dazzling silk tie and excessively-applied aftershave perhaps. His boss looked everywhere in the room except under the desk and into Jim's eyes.

"There's also that other thing."

Derek's voice was quiet yet it cut through like pure alcohol evaporating in Jim's skull.

"What other thing would that be?" Clearly there was more to come. Somehow he knew he didn't want to hear this last part.

Derek began in an even lower voice, almost a whisper. "One of the secretaries, she claims you slapped her bottom. She's not a complainer, thank God. But she told me she was scared to approach you about it afterwards. You've been rubbing people up the wrong way for a long time but this is quite different."

"I don't know what to say," said Jim and meant it. "When did this happen?"

"When isn't important. Hopefully it won't come to anything. As I said, I doubt she'll take it further." Discipline had never been Derek's forté. Not in any sense, except to receive it, very occasionally, on a Friday afternoon from a lady in a mask somewhere in Ashton. He shifted in his seat, consulted his diary and spun his decision arrow a few times, waiting. For anything.

"Look Derek, I have never slapped anyone's bottom in my life. Well, except my wife once when she suggested it. This is ridiculous. Totally ridiculous."

"What? Oh, er, oh. Right. Um, I see. Do you ever, er, see Monica these days?" Derek was more than happy to switch to a new topic having dealt successfully - no, *firmly* with that little matter. He closed the file, hoping that would be the end of it and he spun the brass arrow vigorously. It squeakingly came to rest on the word 'prevaricate' which Derek had once looked up. He made a mental note to do so again.

"Monica? No, not seen her in ages."

For a moment, Derek thought he saw a cloud of pain drift across Jim's face. Then it was gone, replaced by a slightly tamer bluster than usual. The hairy guy was getting up to leave.

"Well Derek, it's been a long day and if you don't mind, I'd like to get off early. I honestly don't know what people have been saying but I assure you I have *not* slapped any of the secretaries. That's not the way I roll. If you'd tell me who it was I'd apologise, sort it out, whatever. I'm sure a bit of the old charm would smooth the way. It'll all be some misunderstanding you can bet on it."

"I can't tell you who it is. She's still very upset. I was going to talk to you about it on Friday afternoon but I couldn't find you." He paused then added, "we can talk more tomorrow if you like.

Why not get yourself home early? And lay off the funny smokes for a bit eh? I've read somewhere that stuff can make you Shih Tzu. It's much stronger now, apparently."

"Think of the childruuuun," muttered the pony-tailed *System Designer* as he departed, with less swagger than usual.

Alone once more in the office, Derek fiddled with his mouse and contemplated deleting some files from his computer. Or perhaps pushing it off the desk. It had been a stressful day and his machine was nowhere near as fancy as the one Peter Morris had been showing off in the meeting. He was long overdue for an upgrade.

With the responsibilities of management weighing heavily on his slender shoulders, Derek spun the decision arrow a few more times.

That was a crap start to the week, Jim decided, cycling through the park towards his flat in a frenzy. *It's bound to get better.*

It didn't.

Chapter Two

Of all forms of caution, caution in love is perhaps the most fatal to true happiness. Bernie Russell

To generous and sustained applause, the Wondrous Tim left the stage. Once out of sight, he stumbled and fell, clutching the side curtain.

His girlfriend Monica was the first to reach him - and she was appalled to see he was shaking uncontrollably. Tim was drenched in sweat and far more than the lights or even the occasion warranted. A glossy sheen clung to his features and a vein throbbed on his forehead like a sellotaped earthworm. As she helped him to his feet and dusted off his trousers, Monica couldn't help wondering if David Blame ever suffered anything comparable. She suspected not. *If he falls on his arse, I bet he levitates himself right back up again,* she thought, then felt bad about it. Monica found ways to feel bad about something for every hour of every day and doubly so on her birthdays.

"You OK?", she whispered, keeping the stage crew and technicians at bay with a medusa stare.

"My head's breaking apart. I don't think I can do it any more. Get me to the dressing room; don't want anyone seeing me like this." The shaking was easing off but Tim's face, always pale, was now white and waxy. With Monica supporting, they staggered along the narrow corridor to the poky dressing room where he wrenched off his trademark black polo-neck, gasping.

"Can't breathe. Jesus, Monica, there was something weird about that last guy in the audience."

"How weird? Did he do this to you?"

"Nah, he didn't *do* anything. But I picked up some scary shit from inside his head. Under his surface thoughts, he was repeating one word. Repeating it over and over. Just one word. " He waited. Monica looked blankly. "KILL. The word was KILL of course.

Why the hell is it never BUNNIES?"

She shook her head faintly and shrugged.

"It's why I couldn't get anything meaningful from him. I couldn't shut it off either once I heard it. It was just KILL, KILL, KILL all the time - in my head too. I've never experienced anything like it."

"Relax, at least it's over now," said Monica, recovering her senses. "Should we tell the police or something? How are you otherwise? I don't know what else to say."

He hesitated, hands still trembling as he helped himself to a stiff drink. He spilled most of it. The grimy mirror, bordered by a mismatched selection of light-bulbs, lent his face a haunted and sickly aura. At that moment there was a loud hammering on the dressing room door. He flinched. Monica rose smoothly, opened the door a crack and spoke calmly through it.

"Where would I be without you?" he muttered as she dealt with things, as she always did.

"I'm sure you could - eventually - find another gorgeous, highly-efficient manager and PA. Obviously not *as* gorgeous or efficient. However, my advice would be not to try!" She stood with her back to the door as if warding off evil.

"Oh, I won't!" he gushed, with feeling. For a second his expression changed, the mask slipping a tad. Quickly he raised a handkerchief and buried his damp brow in it. When he looked up again, his familiar air was restored. If Monica noticed anything unusual, she kept it to herself.

Tim drained his glass slowly before speaking again.

"There's something else, but I don't know if I should tell you."

"But you're going to, right?"

He nodded.

"Just once, for a moment, I got a picture from his mind. I almost described it out-loud to the audience; I was getting desperate by then."

"And?"

"It was your ex. Jim. I've seen his picture and I'm positive it was him. He grew his hair."

"You're saying he was picturing Jim – my Jim - whilst repeating this... kill thing? Oh this just gets better and better." Monica sat down heavily and refilled Tim's glass. A rush of emotions threatened to engulf her but she blocked them out, as she so often did. Now was not the time to let painful ancient history screw with her. She drank, having momentarily forgotten how vile the stuff tasted. Breathless, she passed the half-full glass to Tim who drained it.

He sighed.

"Look, I know things worked out badly with you two but it might be worth getting in touch and, you know, describing this guy. Find out if he knows him. I never felt anything so intense ever. It must mean something. There's no way it isn't serious."

She smiled vaguely as the single malt performed its own magic routine in her stomach. Tim was a good man, younger than she was and ambitious. He was easier to get along with - and less complicated - than Jim had ever been. Since they'd met, his act had progressed by leaps and bounds. It was as if she brought him luck. He was tantalisingly close to a break-through, there was talk of a Channel 4 series. In fact, someone was coming to next week's show in Sheffield - to check out the act for that very purpose. Life was about to take off for them - so she really didn't want her troublesome ex-hubby anywhere near. Not with his track record.

Memories of Jim surfaced and swarmed around in her head, stinging and buzzing. It had been a relief not to spot him in the audience, this being his home town after all. Paradoxically, it was also a disappointment although she refused to admit it.

"I'll call him," she said. "Tomorrow."

"Do it tonight love," Tim urged. "That guy was fixated. I reckon his mind is close to breaking point. If he's planning to do something nasty, he'll do it soon."

"Oh bloody hell! OK, I'll ring him later." She noted he was

still sweating; that his eyes were glassy and out of focus. She put aside the bottle and poured some water instead. He'd been overdoing it. They both had. "Let's get back to the hotel shall we? No autographs for little old ladies tonight."

Vaguely, he nodded his acquiescence.

Chapter Three

I hate to advocate drugs, alcohol, violence, or insanity to anyone, but they've always worked for me.   Munter S. Rompson

Jim unlocked the main door of the flats, dumped his bike then gathered his mail, along with the free newspaper. He scanned the vitriol-drenched headlines briefly and winced. It seemed that the moral minority were, once again, 'outraged'. On this occasion the outrage was due to 'a malignant tumour of evil spreading its darkly diseased tendrils throughout the city'. Some opening paragraph!

"Close This Centre of Sin ! ! ! ! ! ! !", urged the rag, ramming the point home with all the subtlety of an unlubricated cucumber. A glance at the accompanying photo revealed the vile establishment in question to be one of Jim's favourite haunts: the City Hydroponics Centre. The reporter, in a creative tirade, implied that hypnotic powers were being used to lure children off the streets, forcing them inside where they would purchase expensive lights, soil and seeds then go home to furtively become skilled horticulturists. Eventually these patient but bewitched youngsters would produce a crop of sinful plants and thus bring about the fall of society. Unless brave police officers kicked down their doors and dragged them off...

Jim shook his head in weary despair and skipped to the final paragraph where he read how Preston would soon experience widespread insanity, leading to mayhem, death and perversion, after which everyone would become zombies, or possibly Ozzy Osbourne.

Ignorant, then, of the uncanny accuracy of this prediction, Jim was about to discard the paper. One of the inner pages fell to the floor and on it he spotted an advert for a show - "The Wondrous

Tim and his Amazing Mental Powers". A small, fuzzy picture of said Wondrous Tim showed him to be a bleached blonde fellow with an intricately styled pointy beard and comical eyebrows. Mildly interested, Jim realised that the show had already been and gone - the previous night at the Charter Theatre.

"Ah well," he said and wandered up the stairs.

The flat looked as if enraged Spanish bulls had been chased through it towards some grizzly fate. Untidy though Jim invariably was, he didn't remember this state when he went to bed. Not that he remembered *going* to bed. His first memory of the day was of grabbing his bike from the hallway and leaving, unsteadily, for work. Much of the journey was a blur and – taking in the devastation of the flat – he thought he knew why. He dropped the letters (all junk mail) and the newspaper into the recycling bag.

The light on his phone flashed smugly, the display totalling no less than twelve messages. He hit play and half smiled, half-cringed at the increasingly desperate attempts they'd made to get through. First the voice of a Computer Operator, then a Senior Op, a Shift Leader, then the same Shift Leader sounding panicked. A succession of other voices - different shifts, Derek too, floated by like turds in a drain. Jim heard the second to last message right at the moment he spotted where he'd knocked the bong over, its foul contents now thoroughly soaked into the much-abused carpet. He smiled at the familiar voice: his best buddy Dave.

"Call me man, OK? It's, what is it...(long pause).. Sunday, half nine. I'm in all night. Catch you soon."

After that came a final, strange message involving white noise, buzzing and static. For a moment he thought he recognised a voice, then it cut out.

Bloody machine. Still, it was probably some hapless lackey from Bombay flogging anti-virus. He set a small reminder program running in his mind on low priority, with "get new answer machine tape" as its only parameters.

Jim pondered Dave's message. They'd been together on Friday night followed by a good "sesh" at the flat on Saturday afternoon. Jim reckoned he'd eventually left sometime Sunday morning but couldn't be sure. *What on earth would he have wanted on Sunday evening?* He briefly wondered why Sunday evening didn't feature at all in his memory.

Did we really do that much gear?

He could remember mushrooms - those beloved Hawaiian ones - and a few lines of charlie for giggles. Maybe more than a few, judging by his bunged left nostril. He paused. There was still a small bag of the stuff on the coffee table along with his credit card, a rolled up twenty and a mirror. Good job he wasn't on the ground floor!

Unable to recall whether Dave had managed to get the acid or not, Jim suspected he probably had. Even without it they were equipped with enough temple ball and super skunk to anaesthetise a rugby team. And, when they'd gotten really stupid, Jim vaguely remembered digging out the bottle of Proper Absinthe...

Perhaps Derek was right. He'd been kidding himself for some time that he could still hack it like the old days. However, he'd been doing some pretty far out stuff with his head lately and it could be time to give it a rest. For a week or two. Stick to the occasional spliff for relaxation but cut out the heavy gear, especially the psychedelics. And *definitely* the absinthe. That stuff would kill him for sure.

He didn't have the heart to clean up but moved some of the more obvious drug-related paraphernalia into the corner and covered it with one of his Celtic throws. He grubbed about in nebulous despondency for a while.

Realising he was achieving nothing, he scooped up the twenty, rang Dave on his magically-fixed mobile and left the flat to its own devices.

Dave's cheery voice answered at once. "Yo!" he said.

"Hey man, how's it going?"

"Jim. Hey, I'm just leaving work. I'm in the car. Where are you?"

"Home. Came home early. Some shit was going down so I got out. Thought I'd go sit in the park or something. The flat's trashed and I can't face it. Want to clear my head."

"Man, I know what you're saying. I think I broke something in mine. I think we might have overdone it. I don't think I've ever been that twatted."

Jim laughed. "Yeah, for real. We're pioneers the way I see it." He turned towards the park and rooted in his pockets for his shades.

"It's that bleeding absinthe man. You've got to stop buying that crap. You'll be smoking fags and watching Eastenders next!" Dave paused. "Look dude, can I come and meet up with you? There's something we need to talk about. Some of the stuff you mentioned... it's been wazzing around in my head and I want to hear it properly in the cold light of day."

"What stuff?" Jim asked, warily.

"The brain programming stuff, the mental hoo-hah. You were going on and on about it all the way through the Matrix. Hardly stopped for breath. Good job we've seen it, like, umpteen times before." Silence followed. "Jim, you listening?"

"Come round," said Jim. "I'll be on the bench near the Belvedere. Unless those scummy students are breaking bottles again. If they are, I'll be en route to the nick for murder!"

"Hey man, stay mellow, OK? I'll be there in twenty minutes, half an hour depending on traffic."

"Get yourself a bike mate. You could do it in half that time."

"Bloody hippy!"

Half an hour later, Dave sidled down the path. His eyes retained their magical, faraway glaze. He was clearly off with the fairies, high in the branches of the singing-ringing tree. His normal state. Although he wore a shirt and tie, the ear ring, gold front tooth and skinhead (intended to hide spreading baldness) were meant to hint at danger. Actually, there was nothing dangerous about Dave but he cultivated the image. Another customer of the Centre of Sin, Dave liked very much to cultivate.

"Jesus. You look like shit," observed Jim.

"Thanks mate. You're no picture yourself. But at least I'll recover."

They sat on a bench and watched the kids play football. Jim's mood lightened in the pleasant afternoon sunshine. A couple of drunks sprawled on the grass nearby, each nursing a can of Special Brew protectively with both hands.

"Bad day at work you said?" Dave ventured at length.

"You could say that. There was a major balls-up over the weekend and they couldn't reach me to sort it. They were still trying to fix it this morning when I got in."

"Shit. Was that what all the calls were?"

"Yeah, 'fraid so."

"Told you. You should've answered the bloody thing."

"Did you? Weird thing is I can't remember. Just flashes of stuff, glimpses."

"Oh right. The old amnesia trick."

"I'm serious! I know we often say stuff like 'we've forgotten' - and sometimes we do. But this was different. It's like my mind was switched off completely but I was still walking about."

"The night of the living dead," intoned Dave with mock solemnity.

"It's not funny. Well, maybe a bit. Gonna take it easy for a week or so anyhow and see what happens."

"Me too. In fact, Sheila insists on it."

"Ah."

"She wasn't very happy when I rolled up Sunday lunchtime. I was in pretty bad shape. I added insult to injury by sprawling out on the settee. Slept all afternoon."

"Sounds pleasant."

"It was - until I woke up. Well, she woke me up. Said she was fed up being on her own and did the big lecture thing."

"Shit, sorry mate. I hope you blamed me."

"Course I did. But I think I'll have to do some making up for a bit. We'll cool it, maybe not have a sesh this weekend."

"Fair enough. I've got some nonsense to be getting on with."

They sat for a while. Dave produced a joint and Jim a small metal pipe. After a couple of toots, things didn't seem so bad. The smoke drifted on the slight breeze and a curious squirrel sniffed appreciatively.

Dave found his serious face, the one where both his eyes looked in the same direction at once. "Look mate," he began.

"Aye?"

"On Saturday. It must have been around the time the shrooms were kicking in, do you remember?"

"I can't remember Saturday, never mind the shrooms."

Dave persisted. "You were talking about stuff you were doing, or maybe it was a story you were writing. About the brain being a computer with its operating system programmed by God. And there was something about inserting programs of your own to run in it. Did you mention X-Ray specs? And seeing everything in the colour green?" He chuckled as the smoke took hold. "Good shit this man, I think it's the last of the temple ball. I traded it for some home grown."

Jim got off the bench and laid on the grass next to it. In the distance, one of the drunks was elaborately pissing against a tree whilst singing a song about a *sweet Oirish girl*. The sun shone and birds sang too, rather more melodiously.

"Well?" said Dave.

"Huh?" Jim faked. He was watching a cloud shaped like a breast. They were all shaped like breasts.

"Did you make it all up? I only ask because, well, you've done a few odd things recently. Even for you. And when you started on about the brain, it got me thinking."

"How odd?" Jim's ears pricked up.

"Well, you tried to chat up Sheila. I'm not sure exactly, cos she won't say, but I think it freaked her out. And beforehand you... well... you twatted that bloke. You know, outside the pub. Man, I don't like violence, you know that. I realise he must have been asking for it but, hell dude, you totally lost it. Scared me actually."

Jim listened as if in a dream. The words carried an unsettling air of *deja-vu*.

"When did this happen?"

"What do you mean man?"

"The fight; the thing with Sheila. When?"

"You really don't remember?" Dave took a long drag on his joint and breathed it in deeply, holding it for aeons. Then he slowly exhaled. This was quality smoke, untainted by tobacco or other toxins. Nearby, the squirrel rolled over as if hoping to earn a lungful by its antics.

"Just humour me, OK?" said Jim.

"Well, the fight was Friday night. I don't know what started it cos I was getting the acid - remember? That guy looked mean. I thought you were going to get the crap kicked out of you, tell the truth. Then you started with that wicky wocky business and the bloke was down. But then, then..."

"What? Then *what*?" Jim's face was unreadable but anxiety leaked into his voice like sweat into a fresh shirt.

"Well, you got *nasty*. The bloke was beaten, you were cool. And then you just, I dunno, wrenched his arm, twisted his shoulder. I'm sure you dislocated it or something worse. Made an awful noise. And your eyes, hell they even looked a different colour, darker or something. I tried to pull you away, get you out of there but you just looked right through me. Then you snapped out of it and set off walking like nothing had happened. You left and I followed."

It seemed for a moment that Dave was going to add something but Jim broke the mood. "Then what?"

"We walked back to my place. I don't remember saying much. I was pretty spooked but I was stoned and pissed and I might not have grasped every nuance. By the time we got there you seemed back to normal. As you didn't mention it, neither did I. Figured you'd tell me in your own good time. I'm guessing the guy did something pretty bad, right?"

Jim said nothing.

"Right?" demanded Dave. "Come on man, I was going to mention it over the weekend but, well, didn't want to spoil the atmos. Especially with the acid and all."

"I don't know what to tell you. I honestly can't remember any fight. I do remember the pub, kinda, and I remember walking home afterwards. But that's all. You weren't tripping or anything man?"

"Don't think so. Nah, definitely not. Had a big fat J and that speed but I was feeling good. Weird thing is I don't think you'd had anything at all - other than a couple of pints. I don't see why you can't remember it."

"Tell me about Sheila then," Jim prompted. He felt a headache start to blossom, a dull pain at the base of his skull. He almost didn't want to hear any more but knew he must.

"Not much to tell. She said you got a bit fruity with her, patted her bottom, that's all."

"I *what*?"

"Look, she said you were probably wasted and feeling a little full of yourself. She didn't make anything of it. Not really."

Although Dave sounded fine about this, Jim wasn't. A picture was forming in his mind; a picture he didn't much like. Nothing happened for a long pregnant moment. Now was when he was meant to say something. Dave had been his best mate for years, from their school days to that wild post-Uni phase ducking and dealing. They'd always been straight with each other and he wasn't about to throw that away for anything.

"Look man, I don't know what's going on but, well, I *have* been working on something. And if I told you about the brain stuff, I wish I hadn't. Not yet. It's still got a long way to go and it's a bit weird to explain. I don't see how it's related to any of this..."

Dave waited patiently.

After a while, Jim began to speak.

"It began about six months ago with an idea. I was on my own in the flat, getting quietly hammered, as you do, and I was reading a book. Hesse possibly. It was all about alternate personalities, multiple souls and lots of cool schizoid things. I was nicely getting there when the idea was born: supposing the human brain is just an organic computer? Nothing too original in that but supposing our thought processes, all the data and memories, our actions and reactions, everything, supposing it's all overseen by a series of programs written by evolution? You dig?"

Without waiting, he ploughed on.

"I thought: how neat it would be if I could run programs of my own in there. I mean, programs are what I do best, so why not? I've been doing stuff vaguely along those lines for years actually - remember that self-hypnosis course? One technique I developed was the *memory scan* - highly useful if you are careless about remembering stuff. I'd imagine a task running in the background of my mind and then I'd leave it alone. The answer - whatever I was trying to remember - would simply pop up when it was done – exactly like a computer program. We all tell ourselves things like that, right? It's a process for thinking - an effective one."

"But I wanted to do more, to refine or extend the concept into a super-duper self-help formula. And if it didn't, or couldn't, work I could still *pretend* it did. I'd market it, write a book, flog it, I don't know. The idea was too good to ignore so anyway I wrote it all down, longhand, then went to bed."

"The strange thing was, in the morning, reading through it all, it still made sense. Essentially, all I needed to do was invent a programming language, mentally set aside an area of my brain to work in, and start - which is what I did! I've been doing it ever since. Lately I've been starting to make progress." Jim paused, trying to gauge Dave's reaction. "Barking mad, right?"

"I don't get how you'd program your brain dude. I mean, where would you start? How would you know if it was working? Hell, how do you *write* programs in your head?"

"That last part is easy. I always write code in my head. You know that Mozart composed music in his head and wrote it down later, with no errors or corrections? I'm the Mozart of programming - if I say so myself - and programming is the highest of all art forms."

"Da da da dummmmm," hummed Dave.

"No, that was Beethoven. You reckon I'm full of ka-kaa?"

"Well..."

"I invented my own programming language so I could express really complex ideas in as few instructions as possible. Look, the whole thing is written in my imagination, right? And imagination processes imaginary data just like real data, agreed? I decided at the start that I could use any technique at all as long as I devised rules and stuck to them. I developed a kind of virtual reality headspace first. After a while, when it grew and I couldn't keep it together, I got inspired. I built it into something tangible. I picked a structure I could easily imagine - a house. With so much to hold together, easy is essential. Anyway, I filled it with rooms, each serving as storage space, program space, call it what you like. The house was the interface between my programs and those I found running already."

"You see, for this to work, it logically follows that there must already be programs running. In my head. God knows what language *they* were written in." He paused in anticipation. "That's a joke man, geddit? Anyway, I needed to convince myself this was plausible or the whole thing would've fallen apart. I'd have ended up in the funny farm."

"I still don't understand dude. It's tying my brain in knots even trying. You're telling me that you got stoned, discovered a science that nobody else thought of, then mastered it?"

"Not mastered by a long shot. I wish! Look at it this way. Suppose for a moment that evolution designed our brains starting from a base set of simple instructions. It's always simple to complex, right? Over many thousands of years these would be expanded and refined to optimise our survival and reproduction chances. It's not a great leap from there to imagine these instructions as actual computer programs, lots of them, performing different tasks. One of them might control your personality – your soul or self . This was the part I wanted to understand."

"Bear with me. Look, imagine you're in a dangerous situation, walking down a dark alleyway maybe. Which part of 'you' do you need? Not your bloody sensitive side, that's for sure. You don't need the lover, the philosopher, the carefree stoner - no. What you need is the streetwise you and no distractions. Don't think, feel - remember? I reckon the brain 'swaps in' the aspect of you best suited to the situation and prevents the others from getting you killed. And if this *is* the case, why can't I devise a way to do it any time I like? I'm talking about a manual personality override!"

Jim was heavily into lecture mode whilst all around the park became quieter. Dappled sunlight, bright, but sliced and diced by oaks and sycamores, traced patterns across path, bench and pavilion. The drunks were long gone, the kids too. A woman listlessly observed her poodle proudly releasing a long, steaming poo onto grass that a while ago had been a football pitch. Jim wrinkled his nose and continued.

"Anyway, that's where I started from, barmy or not. I spent ages cataloguing all the different 'me's there have ever been so I can harvest them and *improve* them! I gave them names and confined them to specific traits, defining everything they could do

- and could not do. In parallel I wrote my Personality Transfer Program. Sounds like I told you some of this already. Soon maybe I can even show you."

"Man, are you saying you actually believe this stuff? *Really* believe it?"

"I do," said Jim in a soft voice. The weakening sunlight caught his face for a moment, reminding Dave of the boy he'd known all those years ago, the boy who was teased for being too clever. The boy who became a joker in order to survive and who, much later, became a casual bully.

"I believe it because it doesn't work otherwise," he ended, his voice trailing to silence.

Somehow Dave didn't feel the moment was right to mention the other little matter that had been bothering him. So they sat quietly for a while, making the most, had they known it, of their last Monday evening together.

Chapter Four

If you want to make an apple pie from scratch, you must first create the universe.   Carl Sago

Later that night, alone, Jim began a half-hearted attempt to tidy the flat. He sensed that something significant had changed - or was about to change. His enthusiasm for cleaning up fizzled out within ten minutes but, still restless, he put off the inevitable for a while longer. Instead, he opted to tackle the washing up since it was the one household chore he genuinely enjoyed. Plunging his hands into hot, soapy water, he looked up to see his fuzzy reflection looming in the steamy window, menaced by the twisted fingers of a lilac tree reaching upwards from the yard below.

Suddenly, he opened his eyes. It was fully dark, the washing up finished, the water cold, every bubble burst. According to the kitchen clock he'd been stood for an hour. His hands were dry and his shirt sleeves rolled down.

It could no longer be avoided. It was time to find out what was wrong in his head. At 22:50 on Monday April 21st 2003, Jim Cavanah retired to his pungent bedroom to monitor the programs running in his brain.

Beginning the simple preparations, he shut down all superfluous thought processes. He put on the loose-fitting *galabeya* bought by Monica. They had always joked that it was his Gandalf robe, the wide sleeves particularly ornate and wizardy. He lit a candle and set a small wind-up timer, priming it to ring in sixty minutes. Satisfied, he slumped into the stained leather beanbag that squatted, Jabba-like, in the corner of the bedroom. Letting his arms fall to his side, Jim closed his eyes, ran the Alarm program, and entered the place he called simply the House.

He visualised the solid green door, fringed by ivy. Red bricks extended on either side. The door had no handle and no knocker.

It was deliberately bright and welcoming. The key was his right hand. Touching the door opened it silently.

A long hallway was revealed, leading to an airy space with stairs heading upwards and doors marked Kitchen, Gym and Dining room. Immediately ahead and to the left, was the Library and directly opposite that was the Front room. The rooms were mapped precisely in his head, the cornerstone of his virtual environment.

The House had begun life as a small box, modelled loosely on the semi-detached he had shared - oh so briefly - with Monica. As his mental capacity expanded, it had metamorphosed into a country lodge bordered by a large sandstone wall. He began to feel gardens were important, then a summerhouse, a lake, a boating shed... all sprang into existence as Jim indulged in increasingly elaborate visual diversions. He could never keep anything simple for long. Inside the House, rooms of every kind began to spread across three floors and into an attic. Jim's destination today was the first floor, the Ballroom.

He padded down the corridor. With each step, he enhanced the image or the 3D in areas where detail was thin. A bit of extra depth here, some shadow there, improved texture resolution throughout. Now far behind, the door locked him in with a reassuring clunk.

Glancing down revealed thick, red carpet, all the better to mask his footfalls. On the walls, purple, fractal wallpaper glistened with an unconvincing sheen. Only the tiniest mental effort was required to flush the colours from dim renderings to vivid realism. Jim felt the carpet become softer underfoot and noted with surprise that the walls were hung with the shadowy ghosts of paintings, their faded golden frames spaced at regular intervals down the corridor. The subjects - for they were portraits - remained indistinct and Jim wondered why he'd bothered to initiate them. And when.

As reference points, he had placed everyday items, some from his childhood, others from his current life, in the House. He strode past one of the former, an ornate oak coat stand, the pride of his father's farm and supposedly an antique. The coats upon it indicated, to him, that everyone was home. *Where else would they be*? He noted the leather biker's jacket that belonged to Spike, the duffel coat that Shrimp preferred, the cagoule worn in all weathers by Plover. There was Kevin's blue anorak, Woody's motley Afghan and Clune's long, black overcoat. All were tangible evidence of the progress of his great Personality Harvest.

Passing the Library door, he thought he heard something. A chair moving perhaps. Curious, he spun round, opened the door and switched on the light. The Library was empty, as he'd known it must be. Jim looked around for a moment, taking pride in the collection of books he had already assembled. The catalogue consisted of everything he had read in the last month – two novels, several magazines, web pages and every piece of music he'd played lately. *Quite an achievement*, he preened. He planned to start importing film and video just as soon as he cracked the archive compression format his meat-brain used.

Jim liked the feel of real leather and the smell of real paper so that's how he imagined his books. He added a special feature to every volume though: a small socket at the back to connect it to the House's central computer system.

It was fortunate that, early in development, he had embedded the left-hand side of the House into a cliff. He therefore didn't have to rationalise all the tricky dimensions of rooms he might later need to expand but it made the house look a little strange when viewed from the garden.

Each room had a standard computer terminal and keyboard, since Jim regarded himself as old-school. His internal computer network had advanced considerably too so at any terminal he could sit and work. The terminals even had a quaint little floppy drive to get material in and out. Jim knew that attention to detail was important and anyway, he loved details. He took great pains to make every angle, every shadow, authentic.

Keeping the curtains of the House drawn was a handy means of preserving thought processor cycles. It meant that, when inside, he could ignore the issue of the gardens, the plants, the colours, the lighting and the seasonal changes – all frivolous additions, he conceded. Whether he ultimately scrapped the outside, it wasn't important now. He didn't *need* to look through the windows.

Leaving the Library, he climbed the stairs to the open-plan landing. Surprisingly, voices were audible, leaking through the Ballroom's open door. Rather than approach the door, he extended his hand, turning an unmarked section of wall into a makeshift entrance.

The voices fell silent. The last to stop speaking had a petulant whine.

Having entered, the wall became, once more, plain white plaster. The temporary doorway faded as if it had never been there and a polished floor, flawless and dark, extended to the limits of the room. The Ballroom occupied half of the House's total floor space and it was in here that the majority of Jim's "mental programs" were written, at the terminal on the east wall.

Shadowy figures huddled together in a large circle that was marked, in red tape, on the dance floor. Eyes glinting, they waited as Jim made for the only chair without even a glance towards them.

"Screens", he said, sitting down.

On his command, the figures walked robotically, slipping into a series of glass cubicles behind where he was sitting. Each cubicle's glass door closed automatically, sealing in its charge like a tomb. Jim spun a few times in his chair then looked them over. These were his alter egos, the alternate personalities he had fashioned from pseudo-flesh, program code and memory. Some had been given more depth than others but all were based on him - or a facet of him - at various points in his life. Their faces were modelled on his own features and stared blankly ahead, eyes wet and knowing. They barely blinked.

Jim wondered if it was wise to leave them active when he was not around. This was, after all, a family of Sims. There were a dozen personality profile cubicles prepared but not all were yet populated. Active, it was inconceivable that they weren't slowing him down in some way, even though his brain felt as sharp and responsive as ever.

Initially Jim had enjoyed observing his characters' interactions - actors in a play without a script. Lately he had noticed worrying signs that each personality was no longer frozen in the moment. They were starting to learn, to grow. He decided this was the last thing he needed - especially where Clune was concerned. Clune always aroused unease; he was a man Jim was not proud to have been, a self-centred, calculating automaton. Jim resolved to revert to his previous discipline: of freezing the House in memory when he was absent. Some of the things he'd heard on the Outside suggested he'd been far too lax with his control protocols. Dangerously so.

He would fix it all, implement new, tighter security. After all, he had no wish to end up in a straight jacket! It was time to examine the logs and see what, exactly, had been going on.

Spinning to the terminal, Jim entered his password and began navigating the elaborate file system, his fingers flying over – even into - the 3D space of the touchscreen. This system was the repository of all the work he had done so far. It held a vast amount of data ranging from his early failures to the increasingly sophisticated Personality Profiles. His destination today was the computer log: an audit trail of his every thought and action.

Some time later he sat back, baffled. His searches had revealed little out of the ordinary – results that should have set his mind at ease. After all, it seemed clear he was in no danger of cracking up any time soon. He had viewed the fight outside the pub and felt relieved as he watched it unfold. The guy had been a fairly nasty piece of work and, other than a slight overreaction on his part at the end, he'd coped well enough. In fact, there was room for optimism.

It had started with a simple taunt; one he had heard many times. Having long hair brought with it certain expectations.

"Hey, you're a little ugly even for a sex change!"

Jim ignored the guy, sipped his Guinness and tried not to breathe in too much of the smoke and human odour.

"Oy, pooftah, get yer fuckin' hair cut!". *Oh great, a razor-sharp mind* and *sparkling wit*, Jim thought.

The pub was packed with a strange assortment of adolescent jail-bait, haggard grannies and serious-faced drinkers. For Jim's liking there were too many bald or short-haired men, too many red and white flags and a complete deficit of bonhomie.

Jim and Dave hadn't been here before but Dave had met a new contact who liked to vary the pubs where deals were made. Tonight Dave was buying tabs of acid and currently in the toilets sorting the transaction. Jim was riding shotgun, watching the door, making sure all was OK.

"Waiting for one of your pooftah pals to go in?" said a voice suddenly in his ear. Jim had failed to hear the approach and now viewed an angry eyeball from barely inches away.

"Why don't you just drop it?" Jim suggested in a low voice, knowing he was wasting his time.

"That sounds like a threat," rumbled the guy.

At a little over six foot, he was no taller than Jim but was far wider. He wore a black padded jacket, a white shirt and black tie, so possibly a security guard or prison officer. He sneered, "*is* that a threat honey?" his lager breath was in Jim's face, his cheeks red and flushed with barely-suppressed rage.

Jim sighed. Then, in a flash, he decided. *What the hell*. He closed his eyes briefly and launched an experimental program. Under his breath he mouthed "PTP Spike", then opened his eyes and smiled in delight. "Yeah, I'm totally threatening you, fuckwit!" He indicated the main door. "Shall we?" Somewhere across the bar, he was dimly aware of Dave emerging from the toilets, sniffing and sniggering.

Lager-breath was suddenly indecisive. Jim pursed his lips and winked, not under-doing it at all. It was sufficient.

They trudged to the car-park in solemn procession, underpinned by an atmosphere of testosterone and ugliness. Several of lager-breath's pals padded along too, grunting amongst themselves. Via the logs, Jim watched the drama unfold as if seeing it through Spike's eyes. He felt a thrill of fear and excitement. This on-screen replay was fascinating. If only he knew why he'd forgotten it all...

Lager-breath opened with a surprise headbutt. Spike was expecting it. A lightning reaction from his hands saw the guy's forehead slamming into raised palms. Jim was certain he would never have been so fast if unenhanced. Already his use of mental techniques seemed vindicated.

"Naughty fuckwit," Spike taunted and, with a slight twist of his waist, he elbowed sharply upwards, noting the satisfying crunch of breaking nose.

They faced each other, blood splatted across Fuckwit's upper lip, surprise mingled with contempt in his teary eyes.

"I'll fucking kill you for that!"

"Oh, I don't know," mocked Spike, ready for the inevitable charge.

Fuckwit - he probably preferred the label to Lager-breath - lurched forwards. He closed the distance with an impressive turn of speed and threw a punch which was not wild but controlled like a boxer. Spike reeled slightly, avoiding the blow and instinctively giving himself space. The guy was fast, he'd had training. *Best not mess about.* In a flash, Spike flicked a roundhouse kick, using his favourite trick of throwing a feint low then swapping mid-flight to the head. As Fuckwit's hands moved down to protect himself, Spike's foot connected with his jaw. Using the moment, he stepped in low for a hip throw, fast and explosive. Fuckwit hit the tarmac and Spike went down on top, using his weight to knock any remaining breath out of his lungs. In a fluid motion, he pinned the guy's arm, rose to a standing position, simultaneously pulling him onto his face and switching his hold to the wrist, yanking the arm straight with brutal precision. All the time, Spike was aware of Fuckwit's friends. One of them, a silver-haired older man with a pony tail, watched calmly but the rest shuffled in uneasy anger. With a flourish,Spike leant forward and dislocated the shoulder, the guy crying out in pain. The computer screen went snowy for a moment then cleared to reveal Jim heading off, Dave in tow.

As he allowed the rest of the scene to melt away, Jim reckoned it wasn't quite as worrying as Dave's telling of it. It *was* strange that the activation of Spike had locked out his own memory of the event. *That wasn't supposed to happen!* He typed a quick amendment to his Personality Transfer Program so that it would trace all its actions on its next execution.

A simple error somewhere, but things worked OK otherwise. Well, I probably shouldn't have done that dislocation.

Satisfied he'd find the bug soon, he turned next to review the incident with Sheila. The monitor dutifully obeyed.

Sheila was standing in the kitchen making coffee. She wore tight jeans and her long blonde hair was tied back. Effortlessly she looked gorgeous.

Jim and Dave were in the front room, laughing like idiots at the telly. *Those two never changed.*

She opened the cupboard and bent down to get a cup. When she stood up again, Jim was there regarding her strangely.

"Would sir like something extra in sir's coffee?" she indicated the brandy bottle.

"Sir would indeed like something extra," said Jim, his voice flat. Watching the scene unfold, he recoiled in horror as if he already knew what would happen next.

"Well, sir can bugger off," Sheila laughed. "Maybe we'll leave the extras and stick to plain coffee for tonight. Until sir's head is much less wonky!"

Jim gasped as the Jim on his monitor screen moved quickly over to Sheila, closed on her. He saw her eyes widen, heard her gasp as he came close, into her personal space. He looked down and saw his hands encircle her waist, grasp her bottom.

"Mmm, you have a fabulous arse," he said in a cold voice.

"You have five seconds to get out of here," she said meeting his gaze squarely. "That was your one and only drunken mistake tonight, comprendez?"

Deep in her eyes, he saw the fear beneath the bravado. Then he must have drawn back. The distance between them increased suddenly. Sheila stood her ground, tense and angry. Jim left without another word.

He replayed the scene, looking for any clue to his behaviour. He searched the log for any error messages at all but came up with nothing.

There were other things to research too, but he found himself unable to shake the incident from his mind. He wondered about the girl at work too. Something similar? God, he hoped not! *What was going wrong?*

He neither remembered the incident nor was he sure what it meant. Therefore it was time to halt the experiments and perform a full system diagnostic. He really *had* to start putting more informational messages within his programs to give information if they went wrong. The assumption that they wouldn't could no longer be trusted. First, though, there were a few other matters to investigate. He had to know whether the W&W system failure was in any way related. It seemed unlikely but his confidence was badly shaken. He couldn't take the chance.

At that moment, his Alarm program sounded.

An hour already?

Time to call it quits and resume tomorrow morning, early. Before work. Quickly, he called and ran a small Restore program, long prepared. Although regarded by many as a maverick, Jim was, in fact, a fastidious programmer. He regularly took backups of various aspects of his work, putting them in different storage areas set aside within his mind. The Restore program regressed all personalities to their initial states, ensuring that Clune, in particular, was reduced to the barest of outlines. He checked that the program had worked, had produced no error messages and then he felt much, much better.

He turned off all non-essential background services – even minor subroutines such as Search, Observe and Remember. Best to be on the safe side. He kept some running though: Alarm, for example, which was essential for alerting himself when real world alarms sounded (such as his timer). Anyway, the program was simple, solid and long-established. He did, however, archive his X-Ray program: the one that he was convinced would (one day) allow reinterpretation of visual data, removing, say, key items of clothing from attractive chicks as he viewed them. It was an utter flop at this stage but he believed, eventually, he'd crack it. And belief was everything.

His clean-up operations completed, all visual aspects of the House were now retarded. Even the extra shadowing and lightning effects he'd performed on entry were gone. Once more the walls were reduced to bland uniformity, like those of a computer game. However, none of that mattered.

It was painfully obvious that some flaw eluded him. Perhaps he'd accidentally interfered with a native program - in a way that was too subtle to recognise. He needed to figure it out - and quickly. If necessary, he would dismantle the entire House and revert to his mk1 version. Or even further back. After all, there was no great hurry and a few steps backwards now could save him a world of grief later.

Finishing quickly, he logged out. Sealing the Ball room and erasing the door, Jim left his Personalities where they stood; eerie waxwork figures silent in their cubicles. He jogged downstairs as the temporary entrance slid gently back into non-existence.
"Suspend", he said and left the House, shutting the front door behind him.
Jim opened his eyes and silenced the ringing alarm before performing a routine sanity check. Declaring himself sane, he verified the House program was dormant, that all its functions were frozen. Beyond the walls of the House and its gardens, darkness reigned. Jim's brain resumed normal business. He looked at the clock, set the Alarm to awaken him at 06:00 and went to bed. He'd fix it all in the morning. No need to panic.

Chapter Five

Imagination is the beginning of creation. You imagine what you desire, you will what you imagine and at last you create what you will. George Benny Shoe

"You're quiet," said Sheila Scofield as they ate supper. A program about shagging was spurting from Channel 5 but Dave, amazingly, wasn't paying any attention.

"Am I? Sorry love. Been thinking. You know, work stuff." He munched his toast without enthusiasm and, frequently, without swallowing. His stubbly cheeks were starting to take on hamster-like bulges and his long-suffering wife had to will herself to avert her gaze from the swirling washing machine of his mouth.

"Nothing to do with Jim then?"

"Jim? Why do you ask?" He dribbled some butter down his chin and tried to eat his own finger. "Ow," he observed.

"You seemed pretty edgy when you came home. You mentioned meeting up with Jim after work. I wondered if everything was okay?"

Sheila never misses a trick, he thought, noticing the shagging and perking up. "I wanted to make sure he was back to normal after the weekend. It wasn't only me who was trashed you know. Jim really knows how to go for it. Never was able to hold back. If I get stoned, he gets totally battered. Kind of guy he is; everything to extremes."

"Yeah," she said acidly. "So *is* he okay? By his standards I mean."

"Think so. He's, well, he's Jim, you know. Always looking for new things to get into."

"I think he misses Monica."

"Yeah. Taboo subject though. I've tried."

Sheila said no more. Dave was preoccupied and would tell her about it when he was ready. His concentration, apparently, was now locked on a fleshy earth mother of middle years giving cucumber gobbling lessons to an eager circle of plump, cabbage patch housewives. Sheila wiped Dave's chin and he murmured his thanks.

On a podium, impossibly tall and constructed from glass, a conductor stood. He towered above the orchestra, hundreds of musicians awaiting his command, each dressed immaculately in tie and tails and bearing an instrument that gleamed with care and love.

The conductor was about to call for attention when he noticed he was inappropriately dressed, wearing a Hawaiian shirt, shorts and several garlands of flowers. He realised his legs were grotesquely hairy and that his shoes - black and shiny – only added to the growing feeling of ridicule. He kicked off shoes and socks, but it didn't help.

A sea of faces looked to him, awaiting instruction, and he saw that they had no features, no eyes, not a mouth between them and only the barest hint of a nose. As if on cue, each musician turned away, rustled through pages of music and began, at once, to play. The noise was awful, hideous. In panic the conductor tapped his baton loudly but it broke into a thousand pieces, shards of plastic that fell like snow. They ignored him, ignored the growing snowstorm even though it threatened to engulf them all. When he shouted for them to stop, they responded by playing louder, bowing and blowing, plucking and striking, each to a different tempo, many in a key of their own devising.

Dissonance pounded his head like a motorway pileup, until at the last he crouched down, afraid, to shield his ears against the chaos. When it seemed that the noise was fading, the conductor dared to glance into the orchestra pit. As he did so, the lead violinist looked up and smiled, a mouth forming in a grey featureless face. Long teeth like needles were bared as the mouth stretched wide...

Jim awoke with a scream. His Alarm program was ringing loudly in his head. It was 06:10 and he felt terrible, an intense headache drummed on his skull like a cave troll at his first tympani lesson. Something *was* wrong with his mind. He knew it with a gnawing base instinct. He had to discover both the cause and the solution. Fast.

Despite a long-term indulgence in mind-altering drugs and alcohol, Jim had never been keen on pills - even aspirin. Admittedly, he did enjoy buying unknown and strangely-inscribed tablets from strangers in pubs so he could experience grins and sweaty adventure. Perhaps it was truer to say he distrusted the motives of large, organised drug companies more than those of enterprising individuals. Most likely he was just a reckless idiot.

This morning it wasn't adventure that Jim craved, it was Paracetamol. He washed down two chalky white discs with cold water. Too cold. Relief arrived with a piercing pal that smashed his forehead wide open. As the pain subsided, Jim looked into the mirror and instantly wished he hadn't. His eyes were ringed with shadow, as if he hadn't slept a wink. His face was grey and corpse-like. Had he contracted bubonic plague, rabies and hepatitis B and lived in a septic tank drinking nothing except sump oil he couldn't have looked much worse, or so he imagined. The previous night's resolution to trouble-shoot and fix his errant noggin was abandoned.

Jim picked up the phone and left a brief message on Derek's voicemail: *feel like crap, not coming in, catch you later, going back to bed.*

Mid-afternoon, he awoke and naturally this time. The headache had gone but the room reeked of stale sweat and unrestrained farts. He put on coffee and took a shower, noting a couple of messages flashing on the phone without interest.

The water was scalding and he let it run over his face for a very long time, the room filling with steam, taps dripping with condensation. Eventually and reluctantly, he turned off the spray, opened the window and began to wring his thick hair out. His skin felt warm, flushed and tingly. The plague seemed to have cleared up nicely. Outside on the window ledge a spider stood guard over its tiny, pale brown eggs and Jim regarded it in pleasant reverie before the coffee lured him away. The spider didn't care for such things and continued its vigil.

Cursing that there was no milk, Jim realised he was out of bread too, so 'breakfast' consisted of biscuits, munched dry and washed down with strong black Douwe Egberts. He first verified that the biscuits were not of the "special" variety. He required his head very much alert and together today!

Picking his teeth idly with his index finger, extracting nuggets of wholemeal gunge, Jim played back the phone messages. First was Derek's voice. Yes, it would absolutely be the best thing to stay home until he felt better. Derek sounded uncharacteristically decisive. The machine then made a whirring noise and ground to a halt with a high-pitched squeal. On investigation, he found the tape spewing madly from the tiny cassette, intent on throttling the mechanism or dying in the attempt. He pounded it with his fist several times but was unable to affect a repair.

Great! He then launched a new, high priority reminder program in his mind. *New tape, new tape, idiot!* He worried again whether he should be running any programs in his suspect headspace. In a mental funk, he threw on clothes retrieved from their designated storage area on the floor, booted up his PC and began to type fluidly. An idea was forming. A good one he hoped. He desperately needed a good one.

Early evening sloped into the flat apathetically to find Jim sitting back and gaping in wonder at what he had created. Quite simply this was the most intricate, most subtle program ever written. Jim knew how to bestow praise generously - on himself anyway.

The program would provide an answer to any remaining questions about his recent behaviour and would reveal whether his brain was coming apart at the seams. Or not. He hoped not. He saved the program for the dozenth time, copied it to a floppy disk and carried it through to the bedroom, ready for the clever part of the plan. Dimly aware of a growling emptiness, he silenced his hunger with an impatient snarl and wound the mechanical timer, setting it for one hour. Then he he ran the Alarm program in his head. Clutching the diskette, Jim closed his eyes.

The House looked dark, different and much less inviting. He reached out his hand, opening the door as usual, but the lights did not automatically activate in the hallway. Of course, he realised, *auto-light* would have been wiped by the Restore. Doh! He flicked the switch manually, revealing the long corridor stretching ahead. All signs of paintings on the walls had been removed - again as it should be.

Jim was disinclined to visit his alter egos. He wanted nothing to disturb his focus. He strolled down the hall, taking the first door on his right and entering the Front room. Looking down at his hand, he reassured himself he still held the floppy disk - a perfect replica of the one clutched in his real hand Outside. He opened the door and crossed over to the computer terminal. Barely remembering to simulate breathing, he fed the disk into the drive and waited. If he'd made any mistake at all, it would be something stupid like getting the dimensions wrong. In a few seconds, the floppy drive chugged into life and Jim settled down confidently into a large leather chair, one he'd placed in there straight from the Ikea catalogue.

It was his best idea yet: a way to import programs directly from Outside. It meant he could spend time coding, uninterrupted by the need to sustain the virtual environment - although it was getting easier. This would sidestep the one-hour limit he'd set for being in the House - one of his unbreakable safety rules.

The Front room held the House's only mirror - of massive, elaborate design - above a rather plain sandstone fireplace. He admired it sadly as the disk drive whirred. It was a copy of the one Monica had inherited from her mother and that he had accidentally shattered into a thousand pieces when they moved in together. *Seven years bad luck, still two left to go.* His self-pity was interrupted by a new noise from the disk drive. It was working, the program was compiling! With breakthroughs like this he'd soon be on top of his game again. Jim whistled happily.

When the compile was complete, he browsed the raw code, quietly delighted to see every line of his work reproduced accurately. It was all exactly as he'd written it. Magic.

"Compile Diagnostics, logs to current library," he said. The screen displayed a message in response: "Compile Peachy, all Condition Codes Zero."

"Full Diagnostic, Level One, Traces On, Execute." Star Trek and its ilk had a lot to answer for. Jim could have adopted any terminology he wanted but, whenever in doubt, he picked the familiar.

The program began to run, a scalpel slicing through Jim's mind, delving below surface thoughts and memories into dimmer, sketchier regions never before explored. His eyes swam and he almost lost control of the images swooping all around. Blackness swarmed in his peripheral vision. He held on, aware for the first time of the hunger gnawing at him Outside.

Crap breakfast, no lunch, it must be past teatime. Just focus a bit longer!

Sitting back, he gritted his teeth and concentrated on the room in which he sat. All the while, the computer screen expanded, diagrams and text scrolled past. A 3-D map of his brain rippled and sparked as multi-coloured lights strobed over its surface, peering deep into vaults of zipped up memories. The data was packed so densely it seemed to fall into curly extra dimensions. Briefly, he saw himself loitering on a street corner wearing a dark coat, the lower half of his face obscured by a collar. It seemed that maybe he had a beard. Monica had loathed his beard. Close by stood a shadowy figure - an overweight, unsavoury man in scruffy tracksuit bottoms in need of pulling up. They were deep in conversation.

The image faded, replaced by an image of himself at work. His fingers typed fluidly but the contents of the screen remained tantalisingly out of focus. A pretty girl approached and asked if he was alright. He couldn't hear the reply but as she walked away, his eyes followed her and her hips swaying like a promise, filled his vision. And all the time, his fingers typed and typed.

Images, some mere storyboard animations formed briefly and melted away. He couldn't possibly keep track, but there would be time to look through everything later. His program ran and ran. And ran. Finally, a simple text message declared: "Full Diagnostic Complete. To review output, hit Enter."

He stretched forward and swatted the Enter key, almost falling from his chair when he saw the results. The output file was *huge* and, when opened, revealed nested folders and countless other files. They seemed to go on forever!

Much of his program involved subroutines, optimised to scan events within a seven-day period then search for anomalies such as time stamp or spatial control errors. All mental transfer and memory loss conditions were logged and cross-referenced against voice commands. The events captured were then sorted, filed and given a basic graphical representation – but no fecking pie charts! It would present a colour-coded map of the programs executing in his brain. Sometimes, he grudgingly admitted, graphics had their place.

His Diagnostic program was, he humbly acknowledged, a masterpiece. It trapped everything from his smallest Reminder and Alarm spybot to the large, multi-tasking Personality Transfer,

Event Correlation and Creativity Programs. This, he reasoned, would help explain his blackouts. One day all mental aberrations would be diagnosed this way.

Leafing through the unexpectedly vast output, Jim felt a surge of fear. He'd long known there were areas of the brain best left alone, large unknown expanses, darkened rooms with no obvious door. What he *hadn't* expected was finding so many unknowns within his daily activities.

Can this be normal? he thought and then laughed at what a stupid thought *that* was! He knew there was nobody in the world that he could ask. Well, there *were* people but he didn't fancy spending the rest of his days talking to spotty, lab-coated tossers who cowered behind clipboards and asked questions about his childhood.

Jim began to scroll through the data.
This can't be right.
In truth, his progress had been gradual but unspectacular. Only in the last couple of weeks had he made significant advances as the mental gymnastics finally started to pay off. There was no way he could have generated so much data in the two or three sessions per day which were his routine. Some of the folders had interesting names too. Some were long, complex words that meant nothing. Browsing them, he opened a few of the files and followed links to some of the oldest, palest executable programs. These too had long and bizarre names - and he hadn't a clue what their function might be.

He was baffled. Either these files were compiled or heavily encrypted but worst of all, he knew *he* hadn't written them. Yet here they were, actions he'd performed. Unknown actions. Was he losing it?

As he mused over this, his Alarm program beeped. "Door", it said in a monotone.

The main door's intercom was buzzing like a wasp trapped in a jar. Suddenly he was ready to get out. But in his haste to leave, he forgot the floppy disk that he'd brought in. He opened his eyes and, of course, its real counterpart was present but on the floor where it had fallen. For a moment it appeared strangely insubstantial. A trick of the light perhaps.

Jim lurched out of the bedroom like an automaton, and pushed the button.

"Yeah?"

"Jim, it's me. Monica. Look, I'm sorry to turn up on your doorstep like this but I've got to talk to you right away."

His world shifted focus for a moment. His knees gave way and he only saved himself by grasping the sideboard, knocking off a cup of dark green liquid in the process.

"Jim, are you still there?"

"Yeah, I'm here. Wait there a minute, I'll come down." He steadied himself and glared at the fresh stain as if to banish it with the power of his will.

"Can't you just open the door?" He knew her well enough to recognise the odd tone in her voice but his mind wouldn't resolve the information into anything usable.

He surveyed the flat and then himself. Despair threatened.

"OK," he said. I'll be downstairs in a minute, I'll just throw some clothes on and I'll be down. The place is a bit of a mess, you know how it is. Busy bachelor life." He wanted to say something charming and witty but instead released the button of the intercom and buzzed open the main door.

In a daze he dressed, grabbed his wallet and practically flew downstairs.

Chapter Six

What if nothing exists and we're all in somebody's dream? Or what's worse, what if only that fat guy in the third row exists?   Willy Allen

The Royal Earlobe was almost deserted. A few murmuring regulars nursed their final drops of beer before going home to the wife, or the cat, or nothing. Outside, the day was fading fast and a nearby street lamp fizzed uncertainly into life, unsure if it was worth the bother.

The landlord lounged behind the bar, alternating between reading the paper, watching a portable TV and studiously picking his nose. Watching him, with an air of sardonic amusement, a tall man with dark eyes and a well-trimmed beard flicked darts in the general direction of the dartboard. With no apparent effort, he nailed the bullseye twice in rapid succession, then shook his head and glanced at his watch.

They were late.

As if in reply, the door opened and four men walked in. One of them, little more than a boy grinned a quick "hello Max" then made a bee-line for the coal-effect fire. It sputtered in the centre of the room, spilling its meagre heat grudgingly.

The landlord dropped his paper, wiped his finger somewhere under the bar and asked, "now gentlemen, what will it be? I hope you're all of legal age?"

The dark-eyed man spoke on their behalf. "Young Adrian here will have a coke." The youth grinned as he stood warming himself, stretching his fingers before the tiny flames. .

"Hey Ben, a fire, come warm your hands," he called.

"In a m-minute" said Ben. "Let's get a drink in first. I'd, I'd like a B-Britvic orange, please," he said nodding to Max but without raising his eyes.

He worries me. Ben was crucial to the plan and Max didn't

like nervous people. Actually, he didn't like people, period. He'd keep a keen eye on this skinny young man.

"Pint o' cider," said Pete.

"Bitter," said Frank.

"And I'll have another pint of Beamish landlord," said Max. "We'll be sitting over there."

The landlord was about to say that he'd loan them a tray but the man had already turned his back and was shepherding the others to one of the large round tables near the fire. The boy called Adrian was laughing like a simpleton and the rest seemed preoccupied by some secret, shared amusement.

Something in the dark-eyed bloke's manner suggested simply carrying the drinks over would be the best policy in the long run. The landlord was not a complex man. Actually, he wasn't even a man.

Ben sipped his drink and surveyed his fellow conspirators. Adrian was blissfully unaware why they were here and would not have grasped the reason if given a lengthy explanation. Pete looked uncomfortable but was tackling this by attempting to get drunk. Twice he attempted to pass a joint round but nobody took up the offer. Finally he lit it up himself, oblivious to the frowns from the handful of regulars and concentrated on getting hammered. Max regarded him with obvious distaste but said nothing.

Only Frank remained impassive, unreadable, his close-cropped hair suggesting the military, although Ben was sure he would never have completed basic training. Not without chinning the first Sergeant Major who shouted into his face. Ben speculated that Frank could become a professional boxer, or an assassin when all this was over. It gave him little comfort.

Then there was Max, the ringleader in their conspiracy. Max was deep. There was something vaguely sinister about him too although he was charm and smiles on the surface. His eyes told the real story and Ben feared to look into them. Like the sun on a lake they held only superficial warmth with darkness and emptiness beneath the surface. Sometimes Ben thought he saw his own death in there. Of them all, he believed Max to be the most dangerous. He dearly wished none of this was necessary because these were not his sort of people. Except that, in another sense they were *exactly* his sort of people.

"Thanks everyone for coming," said Max in a low voice. "After tonight I don't think it will be wise for us all to meet again. I need my time for other things. Therefore I have prepared documentation for you all. Forgive me for using print-outs, but I'm sure you understand why I can't pass it electronically."

At this, he handed out a folder to each of them - even to Adrian whose brow wriggled like a hairy caterpillar playing footsie. Seeing his confusion, Max added "you can read those later, they should have details of everything we each need to do. Give me a nod if anything isn't clear. Tonight I want to quickly outline a few things I dare not even write down. To give you some more background on why Cavanah is so very dangerous to us. And why we must stop him - at all costs."

They huddled round. Even the landlord, stretching his hearing to its limits, caught only a few words here and there. What he heard made him wish, very much, that these strangers were gone so he could close up for the night and lose himself in oblivion. He turned up the volume on his TV and fixed his gaze on the screen.

Chapter Seven

If you hate a person, you hate something in him that is part of yourself. What isn't part of ourselves doesn't disturb us.   *Herman Hiss*

Dave Scofield awoke in the early hours bathed in cold sweat, an 808 bass drum pounding inside his ribcage. At his side, Sheila stirred, rolled over, and buried her face deep in the pillow. Gently, he laid the covers over her shoulder and stroked her hair. She murmured and was still. After a few minutes the low-frequency vibrations in his chest began to subside and his heart returned to normal.

It hadn't been a dream - at least not in the conventional sense. There were no lingering images, no story, no recognisable characters or faces. Yet a memory persisted - a memory of a voice whispering his name over and over. Occasionally, it shifted into the far distance and the words were transmuted, becoming a message, or perhaps a command. But their meaning was unintelligible, drowned in a vast, reverberant chamber.

Dave groaned softly. He had first heard the voice, briefly, on Saturday morning but the monster binge at Jim's had brought welcome oblivion. He had hoped it was permanently silenced - the exorcised ghost of a bad trip - but it had returned yesterday at work, unnervingly close to his ear as if invisible lips were taunting him. A quick spliff seemed to banish it once again but now the voice had infiltrated his dreams.

I can't stay stoned forever, he thought, somewhat wistfully.

Was it imagination, or was the voice becoming more insistent? As before, its meaning was clouded but each time it spoke his name, he was ready to build a log cabin in his pants. Dave pondered the sum total of his knowledge on the subject of *voices* and frowned. Religious types heard them and mass murderers too, but who else - mediums, lunatics...? He resolved to talk to Jim about it.

Dave and Jim had been pals since childhood, one never far from the other. Somewhere along the line, unnoticed, Dave had become the sidekick - although neither of them would ever admit to this.

It had been a challenge to stay close during their teenage years, with Jim earning a place at the grammar school, Dave relegated to the local comprehensive. Although Jim's intellect flourished, Dave believed his friend was never entirely happy amongst the elite. Things seemed to improve when, at fourteen, he began lessons in self defence. For the first time in his life Jim experienced physical strength - and revelled in it.

Over the years that followed, Jim's ego grew exponentially. He also began to shed much of his shy, wryly amusing character. Curiosity led him to dabble in every bizarre fad. In rejecting the mainstream, he channelled his restless energy down increasingly offbeat paths, spending hazy afternoons contemplating such topics as Astral Projection, Tarot, Deep-Trance Yoga or the Delayed Death Punch. To hear him speak, you might believe that all things were possible. Certainly the mental high jinks he'd described recently would have sounded like craziness from anyone else. With Jim, you could never be quite sure. He was frighteningly intense and committed himself fully to anything he found interesting. And he found *everything* interesting at some stage.

Lying in bed, reluctant to get up despite a tightening bladder, Dave reminisced over later episodes at Sixth Form College. He and Jim were together again, reunited and closer than ever. They were good days. Days before they went to Uni. Before they both got kicked *out* of Uni - for dealing the stinkiest, most potent skunk in the known universe - skunk only a deluded buffoon would store in a hot rucksack in plain view and expect it to go unnoticed, he remembered pointing out.

At college, his good buddy was already becoming bit of a

handful, doing serious drugs that he bought from serious people. He also began dating Monica and was completely besotted by her. There was a notable early problem in the form of a guy who, Jim suspected, was "sniffing around." As he embellished his suspicions to Dave over beer, there had been a wild, intense look in his eyes and he embarked on a graphic description of how he planned to resolve the problem. As a friend, Dave had tried to calm the situation with soothing, diverting words. He never forgot what Jim said to him that day in response:

"Don't *ever* come between me and her. I love you like a brother, you know that. But she's.... she's something else to me, someone closer than I can describe. I don't understand it fully myself yet - but I will one day. I won't tolerate anyone - not even you - getting in the way."

Jim's words had been ice, harsh and cutting, but it was the cold stare that Dave remembered most of all. It was a look he'd seen just once or twice over the years - thankfully never again directed at him. It was a side of Jim best left unexplored.

We all have our skeletons.

In the end, the sniffing around guy left college a couple of days later. A family crisis, apparently. He never returned and Jim and Monica continued their passionate, obsessive relationship without further interruption.

A noise - rattling milk bottles - disturbed Dave's thoughts. Light intruded, finding its way through a gap in the curtains and into his eyes. He reluctantly got out of bed. It was 05:30 and he was wide awake. Sheila spoke in her sleep. "Dave, what's the matter? You OK?"

"Yeah love, just going for a pee." She sank back into slumber and Dave threw on a sweat shirt. Downstairs, the house was cold and pale light filtered through the kitchen blinds as he made himself a brew.

***

Across town, Joey Barker was also wide awake. He lay beside his stupid lump of a wife, staring at a crack in the ceiling. Joey was unlucky, and not just because he'd been born short, ginger and freckly. He ritually cursed his luck each day, knowing that with a better start in life, things would have been so very different. His family were poor and had never really cared enough about him; they didn't give him the start in life other parents gave their kids. And as the years rolled by, ill luck followed him like a dog perpetually sniffing his crotch. Girls teased him and teachers picked on him. They enjoyed looking down on him, making a point of how small he was. His pale face (it went red whenever the sun dared peek from behind a cloud) flushed with rage in memory of the ritual humiliations of childhood. Those times when the world moved way too fast for him to keep up. They sneered, they spoke fast and confused him. School was a nightmare. Joey tried his best and he never complained aloud. It was a bitter pill when those damn exam results hit him. Even five minutes before seeing them, pacing the corridor before the others arrived, he was desperately confident. Actually, Joey felt smug, he truly believed things were about to change. His efforts would be rewarded at last. Many of his classmates - even the brighter ones - had stopped writing long before he had. The results were highly suspicious.

Then Joey realised the truth. They had *lost* his papers. Done so *deliberately*, he knew. It was the only explanation to make sense. They lost things all the time, hadn't he read that in the Sun? Those experts are jokes. All experts are jokes. The press wouldn't let those experts in their stupid white coats get away with anything. Bastards. He was the victim of a set-up.

Nobody would listen.

It was small comfort to know that none of it was his fault.

He had been unlucky for so long he never expected his luck to change. Joey learned to make light of his misfortunes, he laughed at himself and encouraged others to join in too. When they did, this made him angrier than ever. Underneath. And, although he couldn't explain why, it made him excited too.

Standing just five foot five and a quarter, many made the mistake of underestimating Joey. With his cheeky chappie smile and that delightful self-deprecating wit, he looked soft-butter harmless. Deep down, where nobody could see, he was not particularly cheeky at all. Deep down, where nobody could see, butter would liquefy, screaming. Deep down, when Joey got that certain look about him, people got nervous.

Since that night at the Dragon, he had been feeling weird. There was a whispering voice in his mind that kept telling him to do things. It was unclear exactly what things he should do - he couldn't quite make out the words - but the intent was clear. The voice wanted him to kill somebody.

He rubbed his head. As he did so, a grey mist was released somewhere behind his eyes, spreading to fill the place where the floating cells usually swam. In this space, a face was slowly forming. It was a face that seemed naggingly familiar. Then he had it. The bloke that did the fancy fighting.

He looked like a *lucky* bloke.

***

Gordon Davis lit a cigarette and glared at the clock as if it were a sworn enemy. The smoke burned the back of his throat and he coughed, a deep, phlegmy cough.

Christ, not even six O'clock!

Again he couldn't sleep - how many days was it? Each time he managed to drift off, he rolled over onto his injured shoulder. The pain was indescribable. It burned like petrol, bringing him instantly, furiously, awake.

That bastard. That BASTARD!

He couldn't work - and in his profession there was no desk-job alternative. They told him to stay home until fit. The doctor in casualty had advised against working the door for at least a week - and after that to take it easy. The posh jerk clearly didn't understand there was no 'easy'. When Gordon stopped by the Dragon last night, some of the other guys dared to take the piss for being taken by such a pussy. They mocked his sling and they ganged up on him, trying to tweak his wounded nose. The swelling had extended around both eyes, squeezing them to puffy slits. With his so-called friends' mocking laughter ringing in his ears he slipped off home in a rage. He had long suspected they were all secretly gay anyway - but wouldn't act on it yet. There was a score to settle first. Then he'd get round to them. One by one.

Gordon always settled his scores - even if he needed to cheat a little, load the dice. He'd taken harder men than old Art in his time. There were lots of tricks to balance things out.

"Gonna do one on you, you fucking turd burglar," he muttered to nobody in particular. Gordon couldn't have told you whether he had spoken this aloud or inside his head. For Gordon ran a running commentary on his life, his important life, as if storing up valuable archive material. He frequently interviewed himself about popular topics of the day, items from the news, his political views. Gordon knew he was an important person long before the rest of the world. They would catch up know, though, just as soon as he did the first Great Thing. Important men all know that timing is everything. You pick the right moment and then it's as if nothing before it even existed.

Gordon's timing was impeccable. He knew with certainty that his day of reckoning with the long-haired queer would come. Patience is a virtue. Honour is a crown. It was something his father had often said, not that he fully understood it.

As for the voice in his head, he didn't even *need* it. His own inner voice drowned it completely.

***

"That you Mikey? Go back to sleep - it's not even morning."

"Sorry mum."

Mikey Sharples returned to his narrow bed. Having slept in this same bed all his life, he knew every creak of the mattress like an old friend. Not that he had many friends. Mikey drew his knees under his chin and stared vacantly ahead, drool spilling from a moist lower lip onto stripy pyjamas. He rocked to and fro, humming. Mikey took the Whotney Hooter approach to pitch, being quite incapable of sustaining a single note for more than a second without adding fanciful embellishments. Mercifully, his warbles were somewhat quieter than Whotney's and blissfully devoid of vibrato. He rocked and he hummed.

He hummed and rocked.

Nothing seemed to hold back the images forming in his head. There was a face becoming clearer every moment. It was the guy from the pub: the one with long hair and weird eyes. Mikey understood with a deep certainty that this guy had to be hurt. He suspected there would be a knife involved. No, he saw *two* knives, slashing and slashing. There would be so much blood and it would go everywhere. His mother would be furious - especially if he used her special knives, the ones he had sworn never to touch again. After the incident with the she-goat she'd locked them away - but Mikey knew where the key was hidden.

He knew he'd be punished severely this time and clenched his fists tightly as he imagined what form the punishment would take. It might even involve the cellar. He really couldn't be sure of that - unless there were lots of blood. If there were *gallons* of blood and his clothes were ruined, he would be absolutely, positively be locked in the cellar. Perhaps for a whole week. A week-long punishment down there was beyond imagining. Mikey tried his best to imagine it and discovered he had wet himself.

Oh, there would be so much blood. He knew it now for certain. There was absolutley no way to avoid it. He rocked and hummed happily.

***

Because you're mine, I walk the line

Picture the scene, if you will. A thickset man in a suburban garden. Decking and patio furniture, a little mouldy. He's wearing a tracksuit and has a wispy silver pony tail - an affectation perhaps. Come a little closer and you will see he is quite old. Late fifties, more like sixty if you had to guess. As you watch him further you mark how his movements are less fluid, less effortless than you first thought.

Another early morning, thought Arthur Bradshaw. He couldn't remember the last time he had slept right through. Maybe not since Peg died. Eighteen years. Was it really so long? After she passed... emptiness. Numbness. One thing Arthur had learned: you sure can't beat insomnia with exercise. He'd proved it a hundred times over.

He exploded in a final burst of press-ups, driving himself to the *magic hundred* despite the growing ache in his shoulder. This year, the aches and pains of winter had not yet relinquished their grip. It was to be expected. In the autumn of his years he was still doing a young man's job. Pushing hard. Stupidly hard. Before the fabulous machine packed in for good.

Sometimes, Art wanted to bring the pointlessness to an end. Yet he endured. He figured he owed Peg's memory that much.

He had been a bad boy when they first met. The best that can be said about him is he never really considered his own position. Art was not a reflective man by nature. Certainly he believed himself no better than rest of the slick-suited, gold-encrusted thieves and thuggish retinue who held the south and east of London in tight thrall. Even to those who knew him well, Arthur was (at best) a blank page. Until he met Peg he was a void, cold, empty, merciless. He hurt people - to the highest degree - and took no pleasure from it. He was the Muscle; he was the Persuader; he was the Collector - and many other roles besides. And if he lacked relish or even conviction, his employers never complained. It was only results they wanted.

For Art, in his work and in his private life, no emotional connections were made. Even when his victims begged him to think of their wives. Their children. Their mothers.

Peg fell in love with him despite suspecting she mustn't. When she learned - in silent shock - the full story of his past (and present), she almost closed her heart, appalled. Eventually she emerged from the dazed funk and realised it was too late. She'd let him in. It was all damage limitation afterwards. That's how love works, said told herself. Ignoring her fears, she gave him her terms.

Art heard her words and read her expression, understanding that everything must change. If he willed it, his life could be jump-started, restarted - and how! On one knee - no creaks and aches then - he told her, quite simply, that he would change. Completely, utterly, irrevocably. A man who is steadfast *can* change any aspect of his character, he said. She noted that he never once promised.

Had you asked, Art would have told you that a man's word was sufficient. Only the weak feel the need to promise.

The die was cast.

Unlikely though it seemed, their fears did not come home to roost. Art and Peg lived together for fifteen safe, blissful years. He counted himself blessed throughout every day. Each night they snuggled up in their inner sanctum, whispering shared secrets like teenagers. They acted like teenagers half of the time, oblivious but happy. Each morning he rejoiced to see she was lying next to him and he often pinched himself to see if he were still dreaming. Impossible though it seemed, he had exchanged a gangster lifestyle for one of mild, suburban bliss. For Arthur Bradshaw, it was more than enough.

True to his word, he cut all his criminal connections. They moved north quietly one night taking little money, few possessions and leaving no forwarding address. It was a complete break and perhaps it worked because Art was just one nasty boy amongst an increasingly nasty crowd. Or perhaps, once he was no longer around, nobody seemed to ever find time to start looking.

Following the prime directive of preserving her safety, Art took a low-paid, conventional job using such skills as he could now sell. He kept his head down and his demeanour humble. Life was normal and it was wonderful. It should have lasted forever.

When the news came about her cancer, he couldn't believe it at first. What kind of reward was this? He raged for days, punched the walls and wept like a baby. Somehow he held it together – for her sake.

In the end, they were both reconciled to it. When the time came, it was evening. They watched the sky together and saw the sun go down. Later they parted as best friends. They said their farewells in a room of reflected starlight and white flowers.

Art just lived now.

He expected nothing and wanted nothing. His life had entered another holding pattern. He existed from day to day but inside he was as empty as in his former life. He didn't remember those days or the person he once was. He continued, merely marking time.

But woe betide anyone who gave him a reason to explode in anger. Art had something left, he sensed it. There could be one last big, brutal explosion. Grimly, he realised he wanted to lash out. And now, in his mind, a face began to form...

***

Julie Hutchinson vomited into the grimy sink of her Spartan bed-sit. Straggly bleached blonde hair drooped and became contaminated as she bent over and heaved until her guts ached. Cursing, she washed the sick out of her hair and poked the nondescript beige and orange chunks down the plughole with her finger. *Always carrots - and from where?!!* The hot tap had stopped working again and she kicked the wall with her bare foot, making a dent in the unpainted plaster. The cold tap ran for a long time but the smell wouldn't go away.

My God, the time. Half fucking five!

It would be just her luck if she were pregnant.

That fucking busted johnny!! Fucking shit!!! I'd almost forgotten about it!

It didn't happen very often - *God be fucking praised!* - but when it did it was a *fucking fucker!*

She wasn't having it. No way. She would get some money and sort it out A.S.A-fucking-P. She felt sick. She felt *fucking fucked off*!

At times like this she liked to kill small animals. It eased her pain to see them suffer. *Sharing is caring.* Once there had been the dream of a pink gurgling baby - or had she imagined it? *You could never be sure.*

For a while there had been a dream that she would one day kill a man. Now, she realised, it would be soon. Very soon. And suddenly she knew who it would be , knew with a sudden ice clarity. It would be the man in the car park on Friday night. Not her punter, the one in the fight. The amazing one. On reflection, it seemed a shame.

***

Mark Housman was being driven slowly insane.

Ever since that bloody show!

A door had opened in his mind.

The voices began on Saturday morning. They continued throughout the weekend but proved relatively easy to ignore. They nagged at him, quietly, though. They hovered at the edge of his perception like the murmur of a distant and poorly-tuned radio.

It went tits-up on Sunday evening.

His wife had surprised him by producing tickets to see a show. She waved them at him in triumph, the stupid bitch. She'd arranged the babysitter too, feeling it would be good to spend time together. What made her think he would be interested in an illusionist - or whatever the idiot was meant to be? That was bad enough but it went horribly, horribly wrong when he was chosen as a volunteer! He thought he was going to wet his pants. That fool with his stupid, staring eyes!

Mark had not waited to escort his wife to the cloakroom or back to the car. He'd scarpered, driving most of the way home before he remembered he even had a wife. He had been in a rush to escape – but there would be no escape. Arriving by taxi, his wife was distraught, yes that was it. He was waiting on the doorstep so she would see he was sorry. Silence. She stormed upstairs and went to bed. He rubbed his head and locked up for the night.

Later, at maybe two or three in the morning, things started to get worse. He sat up in bed. The voices had become loud and distorted. Their words were now unmistakable. He sat and stared ahead in utter horror and the night wore on forever.

By morning, they had, if anything, increased in volume. A slow yet inevitable boost in gain was being applied. The voices promised they would go away if he did this one thing.

They promised and he so wanted to believe them. They seemed sincere. Unfortunately, going to work that day was out of the question. Although he sensed it was a mistake, he proceeded to drink himself into a stupor as the morning faded into afternoon. He pushed his wife away and when the kids came home from school, he fled to the bedroom and shut the door.

Today was worse.

It was unbearable, a massed chorus drowning out his every thought. The voices were commanding him to kill and he was terrified he would lose his mind, or had lost it.

Mark Housman was almost ready to kill himself to make it stop. Then he began to understand *who* he was commanded to kill. The voices bellowed it explicitly. As they increased in volume and number, he started to become unsure once more. All he knew was that he had to kill. The spun round and round again, confusing him in its intensity. Did it actually matter *who* was to be killed? He started to believe that it didn't. Perhaps the most important thing was the killing and not the subject.

Seeing his wife curled tightly in the bed pretending to sleep, he felt nauseous. He was certain that soon he would no longer be able to resist. He wondered if she knew it too.

Chapter Eight

What is a friend? A single soul dwelling in two bodies.   Harris Tottle

Monica waited in the hallway looking around, resisting the urge to run her finger along the cheap furnishings and confirm their grubbiness. Descending the stairs, Jim saw her from the knees down, noting she still wore flat shoes: the tall girl who longed to be the Incredible Shrinking Woman. Her long grey coat was edged with imitation fur - immaculate as always - and her thick, dark hair had grown much longer than he liked it. She no longer wore his ring, of course.

He hit the bottom step awkwardly and almost stumbled.

"Sorry," he said unnecessarily, steadying himself against the banister.

With the first glance into those eyes, he nearly lost it. Jim didn't know whether to try and embrace her, or peck her on the cheek. He didn't know what would pass as normal under the circumstances. It had been too long and he was ill-prepared. Agonising seconds ticked by as choices floated beyond his grasp Then, chickening out, he opted for that old favourite: gaping stupidly with a blank expression. The moment stretched to an ice age. For his part, Jim felt as if every memory of familiarity, every shared intimacy, all the blessed, dazzling Sunday mornings of blissful love-making had been sealed away, as if in a glass trophy cabinet now forever out of reach. He could still remember what the cabinet held - but he no longer possessed a key.

"I can't stay," she began.

"Look, we can't talk here. Fancy something to eat?" He hoped the desperation didn't show.

"I really don't have long." She tossed him a half-smile and it broke something inside. Anxiously he tried to think, his brain stubbornly unresponsive. He tried to escape the dark, fathomless pools of her eyes but she held him prisoner, as always.

"I have to tell you something," she said.

"Look, I haven't eaten all day - been busy - there's a little cafe across the street. Let's get a brew at least."

She hesitated then agreed, noting the way Jim's shoulders sagged in relief. He looked exhausted, unkempt (as ever!) and slightly wild. There was something else too. She couldn't quite put her finger on it.

Nothing was easy with Jim.

Seated at the small and dirty table, he thought how out of place she was in this, his small and dirty world. Her make-up was exquisite, her smile Hollywood, her clothes expensive - probably designer labels, she was always into those. He was suddenly aware, in a way that rarely registered, of his own haggard appearance. By cunning use of posture, he tried to hide some of the more obvious stain. Jim was starving yet only ordered coffee. Time, he felt, was precious. He had no how to prolong the visit. Monica had coffee too.

"How've you been?" he asked.

"Oh, not bad. Keeping busy, you know, lots going on." Monica never gave anything away for free. "You?" she added quickly.

"Me?" for a moment Jim failed to grasp who she meant. He rattled something off automatically. "I'm working at the same place, doing the same thing. It passes for a life." The answer was feeble compared to the clever and witty ripostes he could reel off in countless imagined reconciliations. There was an awkward pause, of the kind that never used to happen. Then they both started to speak at once.

"There's this thing -"

"I've missed you -"

"OK, you first," Jim signed. Monica quickly took him up on it. She knew how easily Jim could get under her skin if she let him.

"I met this guy," she began.

"Oh shit, and you came here for my blessing?"
"Don't be a prat! We're not going there, right?"
"Sorry."
"I see you're still master-class self pity."
"Ouch."
"Look Jim, as I was saying, I met this bloke. He's totally different to you - an entertainer - but a steady, likeable guy who's going places. He's a little younger than me but we get on well."
"Well bully for you. Glad you dropped by. If you remember where my nads are, feel free to kick 'em on your way out." He couldn't help the bitterness and hated himself for being small-minded. Ignoring him, she continued. "You might have heard of him actually -"
"The Wondrous Tim."
"How the *hell* did you know that??!!!"
"I have no idea. It's probably cos I'm a fucking genius."
She looked at him, mystified and, suddenly, uneasy.
"Go on, don't bother about me," he prompted.
Reluctantly she continued but there was a new look in her eyes now: suspicion.
"He did this show on Sunday night. In Preston."
"Yeah, I would have gone but found out too late. Didn't know you were involved. Thought it looked interesting. Mind control right? Hypnotism, some concealed bunny-fondling?"
She ignored the jibe. "He's very good. I think he's going to be - oh never mind. The thing is, he'd been struggling all night. Tim has genuine talent. But on Sunday night, he couldn't focus, even resorted to the hidden microphone a couple of times. Don't look like that. He *is* genuine, mostly, hardly ever uses tricks. But in Preston he couldn't perform."
Jim started to open his mouth then shut it again. She watched him, knowing exactly where his mind was going. She always did. Jim's mind usually went downwards.
"There was this bloke. Normal-looking, smartly-dressed," she

eyed the pizza stain on Jim's shirt warily. "He was with his wife and there didn't seem anything odd about him."

Jim waited, watching, drinking her in and taking extra backups of the visuals for later study. He hardly heard what she was saying, had no idea what his coffee was like, no idea who had served them, no idea if he'd paid or got change.

"Pay attention!" she snapped. "This is serious!"

"Sorry."

"And don't keep apologising for goodness' sake."

"OK, I won't. Go on."

"This guy - his wife put him up to it – got volunteered for a bit of mind-reading right. It was meant to the end show with a light touch, a finale that Tim does beautifully. Typically he finds someone everyday-looking, ideally a bit sceptical, then he reads their mind."

"Course he does." Jim had traced her gaze and deliberately sucked at the pizza stain, watching for a reaction, goading her. It tasted foul - but not significantly worse than when it had been fresh.

She sighed but wasn't deterred. "The guy appeared to be a good subject. Tim reckoned he could sense surface thoughts right away. He asked him to think of the name of a place anywhere in the world, a colour, a flower, an animal. You know the sort of thing? Usually, Tim draws each item on a large whiteboard the audience can't see then gets the audience member to name them aloud. The board spins round, one of them is improbably rude, loads of applause."

"Well, this guy didn't seem happy but claimed he was doing it. That was when it started going badly wrong. The whole atmosphere changed but Tim was stuck because there's no trick to it - not the way he does it now. He almost collapsed and I was sure he was having a seizure. Somehow he managed to cover it up and ended with a joke about the guy being inscrutable. Somehow he got away with it. I suppose people believe it more if it fails sometimes, if that makes any sense?"

"Oddly enough it does. Like religion, right? But I don't see where I come in."

"Tim says the guy was repeating something in his mind over and over. That's what screwed everything."

"What?"

"Just the word KILL. Tim was totally freaked out. But that isn't the worst part."

"Go on."

"Tim got an image of you from him. A clear picture, he was sure. Then the KILL thing repeated again and again."

"How would Tim know it was me?"

"What?"

"Did the guy know my name?"

"No, I'm pretty sure it was just an image."

"So, how does Tim know what I look like? We've never met have we? I didn't recognise his picture when I saw the advert for the show."

"Well, I still have our wedding photos, you know. Tim must have seen them."

"Displayed in pride of place in your comfortable abode are they?" Jim barely hid the sarcasm.

"No. And don't start. I only came because Tim was really worried. He's performed up and down the country and never had anything like this happen before. He insisted I tell you."

"How come you didn't just ring?" asked Jim, already guessing the answer.

"I did, twice. Left you messages to ring me. It was just on your normal line, I don't have your mobile number any more. What's the matter?"

"Nothing, just that the answer machine is screwed. Buggerations! Look, do you know who this guy is - his name?"

"No, but Tim drew you a picture. He says it's a pretty good likeness." She handed him a decent rendering in pencil of Mark

Housman: a bloke Jim didn't know at all. Housman had been getting a blow-job in the car park of the George And Dragon on Friday night, at same the time when Jim was engaged in fisticuffs. Of course Jim didn't know this. Neither of them did.

"He's got talent," he acknowledged. "The drawing is good. Look, I don't want to sound ungrateful but what am I supposed to do now?"

"I don't know. Don't you recognise him?"

"Sorry, I never saw him before."

Monica looked troubled.

"I'm sure it's pretty accurate. They usually are."

"I don't doubt it, but I don't know the guy. Why would somebody I've never met want to kill me anyway? Your magician must have got his rabbits in a twist."

She finished her coffee with undue (Jim thought) haste. "Look Jim, that's what I came to say. I wanted to tell you in case someone had a grudge. Tim is convinced it's genuine. I don't know what else to say."

"How long are you going to be in town?"

"We're leaving tomorrow."

"Naturally." There was a fresh awkward pause in which Monica fiddled with her keys and Jim racked his brains for something to say.

"Well Jim, it was good to see you. Maybe you should try to relax, get away for a holiday, take the country air. You look like you need it." Monica didn't mention that she and Tim had recently moved into a house near Lancaster - a stone's throw up the M6. It was best to let Jim continue believing she was based in Birmingham, where she'd fled after they split.

He sighed. "You look gorgeous - as ever. Must be doing something right." He slipped his mind into neutral. Having held it together so far, there was no point blowing it. "Maybe I should meet Tim? I'd like to see the show actually. When's he playing next?"

"Saturday in Sheffield," she answered. Then wondered if it was a mistake to say.

"Maybe I'll come," he said. Monica looked doubtful.

"I'm not sure that's such a good idea."

The keys jingled in the pause.

"So that's it? You appear out of nowhere after four years, tell me somebody wants to kill me, then goodbye?"

"Sorry Jim, you know as much as me now. Do something or nothing, it's up to you. Take care, OK?"

"You never weaken do you?" he said, reaching out a hand towards her though he swore he wouldn't.

She rose and left without another word. She kept her face expressionless until safely back in the car. Then she drove away.

Back in the cafe, Jim ordered food. Bulky, stodgy food. Then he ordered the same again. He couldn't remember ever feeling so empty.

In a daze, he staggered home and got hammered on absinthe.

Chapter Nine

There is always some madness in love.
But there is also always some reason in madness.
Fred Nitch

"*Mark Housman killed his wife and family this morning. He killed everybody. His neighbours listened throughout. They phoned 999 and the operator listened too. It took a long time for the screaming to stop and the neighbours must have wondered when help would come. They asked politely on several occasions, but the operator insisted on spelling out their names precisely first. It was unfortunate that they were from Poland, a spokesperson for Operator Services commented later, sheepishly.*
When Housman broke down their door, the operator was still puzzling over what she felt was an excess of zeds. It was Procedure, she explained cattily, over the din. Poor Mr Krazkawoczi lost his temper for the first time in his life - and also the last. He swore down the phone and wailed that Housman would surely come to kill them next.

Housman heard this through the thin walls and nodded to himself that this would, indeed, be the case.

He killed his neighbours too.

Then he went outside and he killed total strangers willy nilly. Actually, he never asked their name. He killed people from all around. It was surprisingly easy.

A horrified police marksman shot Housman sixteen times and eventually killed him. A senior officer is about to make a statement..."

Thus spake the early morning news.

Morning came. Wednesday, for want of a better label. Jim's consciousness was flickering and floating in a head that was several sizes too small. If he had dreamed of anything, it was of darkness. He crawled out of bed like a slug over a doorstep, knowing he wouldn't be going into work today. He considered ringing in, but made coffee instead.

Checking the Reminder programs running in his brain, Jim discovered no less than three chirping "milk, milk". Either they weren't working or he'd never been in close proximity to any milk on sale. He purged them from memory and started a new Reminder, ultra-high priority: GO SHOPPING. He then began to edit the Reminder program directly, adding a new line dynamically. Its purpose was to trigger an overwhelming compulsion to shop, the moment he stepped out of his front door. It was a quick and dirty amendment, but he did it anyway. Jim liked quick and dirty.

Then he set about the flat in earnest, tidying ruthlessly, emptying everything too gross to wash into black bags. Jim smiled at a thought that occurred to him then: in a film of his life, the hero would be pictured rushing around for a scant few frames. There would be some token polishing accompanied by tasteless rock music. Finally everything would be transformed into a gleaming wonder and the film would hurtle onwards. Reality was slightly different (*hey, there's a good catchphrase,* he chuckled, abandoning the polishing phase).

Jim considered writing a program to alter the *appearance* of the flat in his eyes. It was a challenge he pondered seriously for a few minutes. The visual reassignments would be similar, in principle, to his "MonoColour" program - an early effort in which he confined his entire vision to shades of green. He'd need to be generate facsimiles of attractive furniture though. And that, being a total mystery, would require effort. Still easier than the Personality Reassignments.

And less dangerous.

Jim did not turn on the TV so he did not see the picture of Mark Housman all over the national news.

Mark Housman, local businessman and popular family man,

who had a liking for golf and the occasional illicit gobble, now immortalised as the Man Who Killed Everybody. After years of feebly trying, Preston was on the map.

Later, Jim rang the Box Office in Sheffield.
"Hello. Do you have any tickets for the Wondrous Tim?"
"Plenty, thanks. Nice of you to call."
"I'd like to book, er, one, please."
"Of course you would."
"Well, could I?"
"It's hard to say, I wonder if I should take your name or something?" The voice was male, feminine and with an annoying singsong quality. Jim was baffled. He didn't need this.
"Look, do you work there?"
"Well, I wouldn't say that exactly. It all depends on how you look at it. Still, it's nice of you to take an interest. So few people do, you know."
"I don't have time to dick about. I want to book a ticket. Am I better doing it online or can you help me?"
"Well, there's no need to get all abrupt on me! I was only trying to make my dreary life more interesting. I'm writing a novel you know. Shall I tell you what it's about?"
Jim counted to ten in his head. He heard a sigh. He waited some more.
"Name please?" The voice sounded a little hurt.
"Jim Cavanah"
"Is that with a 'K'"?
"No."
"I hope you don't mind me asking but is there any reason you don't pronounce it 'Avanah' then?" I mean, I know it's fashionable to find a mundane name and fancy it up... not going all American are we? Hello? Hello?"

Jim decided to buy his ticket on the night. He hoped, on many levels, that the Wondrous Tim would not manage to sell out Sheffield City Hall.

At 10:30 he rang Derek and asked if he could take the rest of the week off. Derek was more than happy to agree and asked if everything was OK.

"Is everything OK Jim?" Derek asked.

"Sure, I've just got some personal things to do. I'm taking your advice too. Laying off the weed," he added, filling his pipe and suppressing a grin.

"Good, nice one Jim. Oh, IBM wanted to take a look through some of your programs, said it would help them pinpoint what went wrong."

"They want *what*?"

"I think Peter Morris has been talking to them, trying to help them solve the mystery."

"Well, I don't see how the programs could help. Did you want me to come in and transmit them?"

"No need, if you would just let us know where to find the source. Peter said the usual libraries were empty. I can get someone else to send them. All we can find is the compiled versions."

Jim's mind raced - but through cold syrup. He couldn't think what to do and sensed trouble was still coming.

"What do you mean, the source libraries are empty?"

"I think it was something to do with the full volume restores. They don't know exactly but don't you worry about it. If we can't find them we can always pull them from the weekly backups. You take the time off and relax, we'll only call you if we can't sort it. Let's talk when you get back."

After the call, Jim took a draw of his pipe. The fresh, herbal smell of the weed lifted his spirits slightly, but he couldn't stop the events churning in his mind. Putting the pipe aside, he unfolded the drawing Monica had left.

A face looked at him but it meant nothing.

The phone rang.

"Hey man, I just rang you at work. They said you weren't in."

"Hey Dave. Yeah, just can't be arsed today. Thought I'd take time off and get my head together. I've got a fresh year's leave to go at, so I thought 'why not?' - you in work?"

"Fraid so. Nothing much on though. The place is like a morgue - one of the people who got killed worked in the typing pool - I actually knew her. Nice girl too."

"Killed, what do you mean 'one of the people who got killed'?"

"You know, this Housman guy - the one who went nutso. Don't tell me you haven't seen the news?"

A shiver passed through Jim's body. Connections were being made, connections that, as yet, made no sense.

Something big and odd was happening.

"Jim, you there?"

"Somebody was *killed* - here in Preston? When?"

"This morning, early. He killed *twenty-three* people Jim - with a fucking crowbar! There would have been more but they got an armed response team out and blatted him. Man, it's terrible. It's all over the news – national and international too, probably. Lots of folk didn't turn in to work so they could watch all the commotion. And there's coppers everywhere! Never seen so many. Get this - some are walking about - like *not* in cars." He allowed a moment for this momentous news to sink in. The odds of police being found in the open air, mixing with thieves and vandals, were on a par with simultaneously sighting Bigfoot and the Loch Ness monster ambling down Church Street eating jelly babies. Less, given the superior acid in circulation.

"In Preston. Coppers. Walking about!" Dave repeated emphatically, waiting for a reaction.

Silence.

"Jim, you there?"

"Yeah, sorry, I was thinking." Jim sounded distracted.

"Look, maybe we'll hook up later," said Dave. "I kinda need to chat. Something I want to run by you. I meant to call yesterday but Sheila has been hassling me about getting wasted during the week. She thinks you're a bad influence."

"Other way round from my perspective man. But no worries, come whenever. I'm still on call as 24-hour Agony Uncle.... Dave?" Jim sounded hesitant.

"Yes man?"

"Monica came round last night."

"Jesus. What did she want?"

"I'll tell you all about it when I see you. Look man, I've got to go. Catch you later OK?"

"Sure thing mate."

He turned on the TV and the face of Mark Housman leaped out at him. It was the face in the drawing, as he'd guessed it would be.

Mark Housman had strangled his wife, clubbed his two young children to death with his favourite golf club before going next door and killing his two elderly neighbours. He had hit the old woman so hard he broke the club, apparently.

Then he took a crow bar from his neighbour's garage and took it out with him. He killed everybody he met; everybody he saw.

It was only fortunate that it was early and there weren't more people on the streets, said the reporter, looking suitably shocked, elbowing another equally shocked reporter out of the way. This made a better picture: the killer's house - tastefully - was in shot over his right shoulder.

Housman was described as having extraordinary strength. He beat out the brains of a milkman and he mashed the owner of a newsagents and his young wife. He pummelled them until their heads were a red mess near their shoulders. Quite near anyway, cosmicly speaking.

Housman chased a paperboy who narrowly escaped on his bike and he smashed his way into a car that had stalled nearby, killing its lone female occupant by jabbing her repeatedly because there wasn't enough room for a good swing. In less than an hour he killed twenty-three people, mostly by bashing their skulls with the crow bar.

The reporter's voice grew hushed as he went on to describe more of the killings. He was careful not to drool - knowing how bad that looked on camera. His audience would be transfixed, hanging on his every word. But one little dribble and the spell would be broken. The cameraman drooled instead and scanned the pavement for splashes of blood the police might have missed.

Some of the people who saw Housman - and lived - described his face as expressionless. Others didn't look at his face but at the crowbar and the impossible amount of blood soaked into the guy's t-shirt and boxers - the only clothes he was wearing. The report went on and on. Opinions were sought, neighbours (surviving ones) were interviewed, as were grim-faced bobbies who didn't know whether the media circus was more sickening than the impending clean-up job.

Nobody could think of a motive.

The phone rang. It was Monica.

"Jim, have you seen the news?"

"Just this second."

"It's the guy."

"I know."

"Look, Tim wants a word, OK?"

"I don't know, I -"

"Jim, Tim here."

This struck Jim as faintly ridiculous and he narrowly resisted saying so. He didn't know quite *what* to say.

"Hello, Jim?" Tim sounded about fifteen.

"Sorry, hi."

"This guy, you've seen him?"

"Just now. Amazing for something like that to happen in Preston."

"And you saw the drawing?"

"Yes, yes, it was jolly nice." He felt something else was needed. "Well done," he ventured.

Tim persisted, "I knew he wanted to kill but I was sure I saw you. I didn't see the others. I didn't see his family, his kids. I didn't see his kids." His voice was low, almost a whisper.

The penny dropped.

"It wasn't your fault," said Jim. "You didn't know anything for *sure*."

"But I did know he was dangerous. It was all I could get from him. Just kept repeating it but I didn't do anything to stop it. I didn't tell the police...." his voice trailed off.

"Would have been great publicity to warn them in advance," said Jim and instantly cursed himself. *Stupid*, he thought.

"What? You think I'd -"

"No, of course not, sorry, I didn't mean it like that. Look Tim, I don't know anything about you but if Monica rates you, you're probably alright." He hoped it sounded sincere. "All I meant was that you couldn't have changed the outcome whomever you told. Nutters like him don't get caught in advance. The police wouldn't have listened. There's nothing anyone could have done."

"I should have followed him, found out who he was. But his mind - drained me. It was like a black hole or something. I felt something break too when I started to look. I think it was stronger - the buzz from his mind – *afterwards*. Could I have caused it?"

"How could you?"

The phone was hot now and Jim held it at arm's length as the voice continued.

"I've been doing my show for a year now, introducing a few more advances each time. The more I try and read minds, the easier it gets. Sometimes I don't only read thoughts, I plant them too."

"You *what*?"

"Well, you know, I sort of hypnotise them - but not by conventional methods. I plant ideas, simple suggestions. Pop them into their brain."

YOU POP THEM INTO THEIR BRAIN!!!INTO !!!INTO!!!

"I don't think I like what I'm hearing," said Jim quietly.

"What? No, no, not that. I didn't plant anything into *this* guy - hell, I could barely stand from the moment I touched his mind. What I meant was: the more I do, the stronger my ability to do it. Now I can suck out more detail than I ever could when I started."

"So?"

"So, a couple of people I've read, they've ended up with nosebleeds or complained of headaches later. Might I be transmitting as well as receiving?"

"I don't know why you're asking me. What can I say except don't blame yourself?"

"I somehow thought you were in the business."

"What do you mean?"

"Well, when I got the image of you from his head..."

"Yes?"

"It was what you were doing. You were on a chat show. I saw it clearly, TV cameras and everything. You'd grown a beard a bit like mine. I saw, in the background.... no, it doesn't matter. I *did* see you do a card trick - a bloody good one too - and then the image faded."

"You're taking the piss," said Jim. "I've never done a card trick in my life or appeared on any chat shows either. *I'm not bloody likely to in my line of work.* But if I had, why would *this* guy have an image of it in his head?"

"He was pretty screwed up."

"Even so?"

"You mean you really don't know him?"

"Of course I don't fucking know him. If I had I'd have been quite curious to find out what I'd done to upset him to quite this degree, wouldn't you think?"

"I can't, I don't -" began Tim.

"Look Tim, can you put Monica back on?"

"Monica?"

Jim grinned evilly. *Yes, Monica, because it will wind you up, you mind reading twat! You getting this?*

There was a muffled pause.

"Jim," she said, annoyed. What could he possibly want to say?

"You're annoyed," he chuckled, beaming down the phone. "And you're becoming even more annoyed. I bet at this moment you're raising your eyebrows and doing that cute thing with your nose. Young Tim might be wondrous with a capital w, but I bet he's oblivious to all yours little giveaways. Face it Mon, he doesn't know you like I do and he never will!"

Without waiting for another word, Jim said, "goodbye," and hung up. It was a pointless gesture offering far less satisfaction than he'd expected.

Chapter Ten

Part of the inhumanity of the computer is that, once it is competently programmed and working smoothly, it is completely honest. Ishmael Arihov

If it considered such trivial matters, the universe might have expressed amazement that a disorganised slob who filed his clean clothes on the floor along with half-empty beer cans and pizza boxes could be saved by his very nature. Yet so it was with Jim Cavanah that lunchtime.

He had realised he must get some things in. If not, he'd be forced to tackle the ancient tin of pilchards lurking malevolently in the darkest recesses of the kitchen cupboard. His head a carousel of greedy, whirling data, Jim now relied on automation to accomplish basic actions on the Outside. The instant he stepped through the front door, his GO SHOPPING timer popped - on extreme priority. The recently-written routine literally caused him to jump.

Startled, he raised his arms in a reflex action. In doing so he deflected the knife that would have ripped open his stomach, ended his life, this tale and - from his perspective - all of existence. Diverted, the incoming blade ripped his jacket near the shoulder, slicing the material like piss on snow.

Unlike the universe, Mikey was genuinely amazed. He had never seen anyone react or move so fast, and backed away from the doorstep, gawping. The voices in his head cried a collective 'what the fuck?' too.

Jim assessed the situation - that he was under attack in broad daylight - and barked a mental command. He didn't, for a moment, consider stepping back inside and closing the door.

OVERCLOCK BY 4

The effect of this, from Jim's perspective, was that Mikey began moving in slow motion. Jim exhaled in relief, watching the in-motion second knife float towards him at a more leisurely pace. He observed its black, curved blade, the strange characters carved into it, the golden handle and ornate cross-guard. Momentarily gob-smacked, Mikey had recovered quickly enough to launch a fresh attack. The thrust was deep and low, a killing blow.

Mikey was a gangly and unattractive youth, depressingly dim even when unseen voices played no part in his day. But even he could sense that something extraordinary was occurring, something way beyond his understanding. And, courtesy of his mother, Mikey had already witnessed some exceedingly strange events - but none compared to what he was seeing now: a man shimmering, apparently disappearing then reappearing, a man who moved like a speeded-up film. Had he been given a few extra IQ points as a gift, Mikey might have turned and fled. Not that it would have done any good.

Stepping in, Jim grabbed one of Mikey's wrists, then the other. He snappily crossed over the arms, spinning Mikey into an arm-lock. His palms were turned to the sky, the knives rendered useless.

Then he was flying through the air.

Then he hit the concrete path.

And then it went dark.

"Wake up moron!" Jim smacked Mikey, quite hard. It had been a total drag getting the lanky would-be assassin up the stairs but Jim felt it was a unique opportunity to discover what was going on - and to do so in his own way. Secretly, he'd always wanted to pull someone upstairs by their feet and it wasn't every day an ambition like that could be ticked off.

"Mum?" Mikey blurted, finding himself on the floor against a chair, his arms wrenched roughly behind him. A shape loomed, thick, long hair over a contorted, snarling face. It was like a picture from one of his mother's special books.

At length, Mikey's eyes were able to focus more precisely and recognise the man glaring at him. His intended victim. He had a thumping headache, the result of kicking whilst out cold, he supposed.

The voices, satisfied he was again receptive, renewed their calls to murder. They were, however, rather vague on how this might be accomplished at present. Mikey began to cry.

"What did you do to me?" he blubbed, straining against the bonds (parcel tape, it was all Jim could find in a hurry). They didn't shift, although Mikey reckoned he could have stood up easily if given a few seconds alone. His legs were free and stretched in front of him.

"Call it 'variation on a Full Shoulder Throw' if you like. Quite pleased it all came back," said Jim, noting the string of drool descending from Mikey's nose towards the much abused carpet. The youth sniffed pathetically and deflected the slimy snot-fall onto his crotch. In seconds another began to form, fueld by freely-flowing tears.

The boy's face was unfamiliar. Jim estimated he was in his early twenties but failed to reach any more useful conclusions - such as how he found his way here. And why. These were mysteries to solve before choosing a new course of action.

"Let me go! I want me mum! You don't wanna mess with me mum!" Mentioning his mother seemed to infuse his voice with an elevated level of confidence, Jim observed. He picked up one of the ornate daggers carefully and examined it. There were runes on the blade and its hilt was bound with leather and ..... what kind of skin was *that*? He put it down gingerly as his captive spoke.

"How'd you move so fast?" he whined. "I in't never seen owt that fast."

Jim started to smile then it froze on his face, his expression turning cold and deadly.

"I'm going to ask you a few questions before I turn you over to the police, do you understand?"

"I want me mum," Mikey repeated, sulkily.

Jim stomped on one of his outstretched legs, crushing the ankle hard against the floor. The unfortunate youth wailed and thrashed about, overturning the chair to which he was tied. Jim wrenched him upright and wondered about the noise. The flats were largely quiet during the day but he didn't want to risk being overheard, let alone interrupted. Crouching down very close to Mikey's ear, he spoke slowly.

"Why did you try to kill me you little fuck? And who the hell are you anyway?"

Mikey cowered before the dark, unforgiving eyes and saw something familiar there. It was an expression that surfaced occasionally when his mother lost it big-style. Say when one of her meetings didn't go to plan. And the incident with the she-goat.

"I had to," he whispered.

"Why? How do you even know me?"

"You were in the pub. You 'urt Gordy," Mikey's answers were sullen but spat out like soap. With Jim so close, the voices became distant and his head cleared. "You were good at fighting," he added, his tears easing up.

"On Friday?"

"Aye, it were Friday. I've been wantin' to kill you ever since. Well, pretty much, like. More today. Sorry."

"Why, for Christ's sake? Is he a friend of yours - is that it?"

"I don't know why," he wailed. "They tell me to - over and over, won't leave me alone." The floodgates opened but he continued, "I know I'm gunna be in *real* trouble." And, as he thought about this, a sly smile crept over Mikey's features.

Jim looked at the lad and sighed. He suspected the boy was a halfwit (a term that featured in Jim's initial assessment of 99% of all people he met) but maybe there was something to try. He didn't miss the reference to 'they' and remembered the man on the news and Tim's mysterious warning. Was it all connected?"

"How did you know where I would be? Did someone tell you?"

"Just knew."

"How do you mean?"

"I knew, I just knew."

"*When* did you know?" Jim clenched his fist, suppressing a rising rage.

"This morning. I woke up and I knew to come here. I got meself ready, put me best clothes on and walked. If I get 'em bloody, I'm in the worst trouble ever. Best let me go. Mum will be really, really spare!"

Barking mad. Apparently, his best clothes consisted of pale blue jeans and a polo shirt with Preston North End's logo emblazoned upon it. *No accounting for taste*, thought Jim, whose dress sense would only be unremarkable at Doctor Who conventions. At that moment there was a faint trickling noise and Jim stepped back quickly, screwing up his nose as the bastard peed himself. *On my bloody floor*, he moaned, losing the plot slightly as he became fascinated by the carpet's multitude of stains, bong spills and - ugh - *God, I thought I'd thrown that away!*. .

Jim wanted to try his idea and he wanted to try it right away.

If Tim could do it, *he* could bloody well do it! With his superior brain and programming licks, anything was possible. All that was needed was preparation. It had to be better than *talking* to this tosser.

Jim breathed deeply, composing himself. Mikey gaped miserably, feeling the warm pee soak through his jeans and spread outwards. He was far too scared to do anything but whimper quietly.

Jim closed his eyes and, with no preparation, rushed into the House. Down the hallway he jogged, up the stairs, up the stairs again, into the Attic. He move so fast he hardly touched the floor.

The Attic was his formless room. Why he only devised it late in the game, who can tell, but its lateness became entwined with its identity. He modelled it on Star Trek's Holodeck. It existed in flux, ready for any purpose imaginable.

Entering, he couldn't help but be impressed by his handiwork. The ceiling was invisible, shrouded by a glittering silver mist. Small black spheres floated artistically, serving no apparent purpose, and a pale light pulsed occasionally from inside each. Jim took a deep breath.

With a slight effort, he called up a program he'd been hacking away at for some time. In response, the spheres began to disperse, stretching and distorting, drawing vague outlines of walls, spreading out and acquiring colour as the dimensions of a splendid room became outlined.

Gleaming control panels, screens, grills, lights and computer displays formed and solidified out of apparent nothingness. A large domed window appeared overhead, peering into blackness and two chunky antennae wobbled outside as if in a wind. A curved chair of garish red plastic materialised within reach of a row of chunky, Moog-style knobs. He drew some inspiration from childhood memories of Thunderbird 5 – his makeshift Communications Centre. To amuse himself, he pranced along on imaginary strings to a large console and sat down. He chuckled to himself for a moment before typing his command:

"TRANSFER HOUSE,FLOOR*,BASIC,NOEXT, LOWEST"

A data bar on Thunderbird 5's main console progressed slowly. The program was being transferred to Mikey – and at a rate Mikey could handle. Jim drummed his fingers impatiently on the grey plastic surface, feeling it give slightly under pressure. Everything felt so authentic he flicked a switch to see what would happen. A distant voice fizzed and crackled as if through a highly-charged field of static electricity: "Calling International Rescue, calling International Rescue." He flipped the switch off again.

"You're on your own mate," he said distractedly.

From Jim's perspective, he had to wait until the program was transferred over to his prisoner.

But on the Outside?

But in . . . reality?
Dude, *in reality*?
The console beeped.
TRANSFER COMPLETE.
"TRANSFER MINI LOCAL ENV, MYPASSONLY" he typed.
"WORKING". *Ah, back to Star Trek, slick dude. You are fucking slick! Don't even remember coding that bit.*
"HOUSE CONSTRUCTION COMPLETE"
"ENTER"
Still sitting in a red plastic chair inside his mental House construct, Jim closed his eyes. He opened them to find himself standing at the door of another house, one he'd never seen before, a terraced house without neighbours. It represented Mikey's House – an analogue of the youth's mind. It might have been drawn by a child, complete with central door, four uneven windows and a curly pigtail of smoke in the air above. A distant blue line marked the sky, and between roof and the sky . . . whiteness. Jim pushed and the door opened inwards. Listening and observing carefully, he went inside. So far, it was easier than he'd dared to hope.
Concentrate now. Gloat later.
A chat show, eh? he pondered.

Mikey's House was built dynamically based on the data areas Jim's program could located. It was unrealistic throughout, recalling the block colours and flat graphics of early computer games. The walls were paper-thin and several angles and shadows had failed to resolve correctly. Yet, overall, for a first attempt, it was a triumph. Jim, always quick to recognise his own achievements, grinned as he strolled about, prodding things and poking around. As he did, knowledge passed from data-gathering subroutines and conveyed a limited understanding of Mikey's personality. He extracted common variables such as the boy's name and address but failed to glean anything about his murderous motives.

Mikey Sharples lived with his mother. He was between jobs but took intermittent work as a labourer for cash. If you needed something digging up, breaking into pieces, chopping down or stacking into piles, Mikey was your man. Occasionally he took part in petty burglary and Karaoke. Two of the most heinous crimes imaginable, thought Jim.

He entered the front room and was surprised by garish paintings of nymphs and satyrs, and by a wooden altar decorated with plants and incense. All around were Egyptian statuettes, crystals, magic books and some unfinished knitting. Mikey's mind said simply: *Mum's things*.

It was frustrating. Although he was getting a clear picture, what he searched for was not present. He glanced into the kitchen, felt nothing and headed for the stairs and Mikey's bedroom.

Disappointingly, it was the room of a child, with football posters, magazines and chest of broken toys. And at last, something. On a battered desk, at last, was Mikey's House computer. Jim's program selected the most appropriate interface, in this case a Sinclair Spectrum connected to a battered portable TV by what seemed to be a dead snake. The snake had its teeth firmly embedded in the back of the Spectrum and its tail was jammed into a hole at the base of the TV.

The bizarre contraption was disintegrating, even as Jim reached for the squishy rubber keyboard. Pixels winked out of existence and several of the keys fell inside. Realising he only had a few seconds, he accessed Mikey's log, typing the commands at speed.

The search in progress, Jim routed all output to his system for further analysis. Saw me do a card trick eh?, he chuckled.

Opposite Mikey's room was a door that remained locked despite Jim's best efforts. He was about to give it a good kicking when a figure, a barely-rendered version of Mikey himself, appeared. The figure began humming in a very annoying way.

"Jeez, don't creep up like that," said Jim.

"You mustn't go inside or mum will know," the ghostly figure said. "She says anything can happen in there." Jim ignored him and turned to the bathroom, a room of scalding water and cold baths. He shuddered but felt little pity.

Jim was about to shoulder-charge the door when he noticed Virtual Mikey wandering downstairs. Curious, Jim followed and saw there was something else beyond the kitchen, another door. Somehow he'd missed it yet it was the largest of all. It had a nameplate.

CELLAR

Whatever directed Mikey's knives, Jim knew, instinctively, would be revealed in the Cellar. He was unsurprised to discover steps leading down. These were not wooden or broken or grimy. They were of stone - white marble, smooth and sure. There were lights on the wall - burning torches would you believe!

Nice one, Mikey. Some imagination after all!

He crept down the stairs and laughed when the door slammed behind and a little less when he noticed the pounding in his ears.

At the bottom of the stairs was another door. The door was of rough wood with metal studs, a couple of rusty spikes and the dried corpse of a dead dog nailed to it. Charming, Jim thought.

There was no option but to open the door or go back. He gave it a tentative shove and the door responded with a clichéd creak. He stepped through, resting the weight of the door against his shoulder in case it slammed. It didn't.

It was dark inside the room. The light from the stairway torches stopped dead at the threshold.

COME IN beckoned a voice. A deep voice - not Mikey's.

Jim hesitated. Something wasn't right. Hairs prickled on the back of his neck – an interesting effect given that he'd only rendered himself in a basic bodily form. He stepped fully into the room.

The door slammed shut, as he'd known it would and in the

profound dark, he knew he was not alone. There was a faint sound, of breathing. And another sound, a a wet, slithering sound. And now a buzzing, as if a swarm of wasps had woken up in the darkness.

The sounds of a bad dream.

Despite his fear, Jim remained confident of his safety protocols. But wary.

YOU HAVE PRIED WHERE IT IS FORBIDDEN said the voice. It was mere inches away and Jim felt his heartbeat become irregular. Something told him this was his Outside Heartbeat and that wasn't right at all.

Slowly a pale light crept in. It may have taken a thousand years or a microsecond, there was no way of telling. The light was a blend of noisome grey, death purple and sick-bag orange. The fluorescent world of a room of torment.

The light revealed implements of torture that Mikey Sharples could probably not have imagined. Jim wondered whether this was a true representation of the boy's home. Everywhere he looked, on shelves and work surfaces, were gleaming knives and tools, some with jagged or brutal edges. In one corner stood an altar, upon which three black candles sputtered wax over a tatty brass chalice right off the car boot.

In the centre of the room, on a throne composed of Blackpool rock, tripe and whippets, sat a short, ugly man. He wore soaked in blood and flies buzzed around, occasionally landing on his face and body.

"Oh very frightening," said Jim. "Ugly but at least you're not scarred or disfigured. I hate it when they do that. Nobody actually thinks that beauty is truth, truth beauty - do they?"

YOU'RE VERY COCKY FOR A MERE MORTAL!

"Yeah, yeah, whatever," said Jim. "Who are you anyway, old Nick himself? The tooth fairy? I take it you're behind the little slice and dice attempt earlier?"

The ugly man smiled. He was an insignificant-looking being

with sinister, piercing eyes - although their impact was somewhat lessened by the thick-lensed glasses he wore. His chin was weak and he was either a creative comber or he wore a costume wig. It was like having an encounter with an unattractive clone of Feltham John.

But the smile was hypnotic. Under its spell, Jim's confidence ebbed away to be replaced by a sheen of sweat. He continued to gaze, now unable to look away. The man's face was that of a kindly uncle who, under no circumstances, did you ever want to be left alone with as a child. Under the smile were yellow and decaying teeth that moved slightly. Jim saw there were insects and grubs in there. The ugly man grinned widely, exposing his grey, worm-like tongue.

NOT THE TOOTH FAIRY, NO. MAYBE YOU CAN GUESS WHO I AM? Jim shook his head, trying to clear it. Now he came to think of it, the face *was* familiar and he was finding it harder to think of anything else. The cellar began to close in, the darkness returning. The remaining light lit the small man on his throne stroking a string of giblets lovingly.

KILL HIM MIKEY, TAKE HIM NOW! urged the voice softly in the background.

With an enormous effort of will, Jim snapped out of it, tearing his gaze from the bland but awful face. It was a trap and he'd almost fallen for it - a virus program primed to run in an ever-decreasing loop and drag any executing code with it. Jim was grudgingly impressed but it was time to get *out*. The ugly grin became wider and the eyes gleamed with malice.

WAIT, DON'T GO! .....DON'T YOU WANT TO ASK ME SOME *QUESTIONS*? I'LL ANSWER ANYTHING.

Jim knew stalling when he heard it. He also felt something trip as he broke away from the hypnotic gaze. He barely had time to take a dump before being abruptly thrown back into Thunderbird 5. Through the window, he saw a distant planet flicker and die as if consumed from within.

Jim left the Attic. He ran down the stairs and exited the House.

He opened his eyes to see Mickey unconscious, still bound to the chair with tape. Somebody was knocking on the door.

Chapter Eleven

Imagination grows by exercise, and contrary to common belief, is more powerful in the mature than in the young.   *W. Somers' Mum*

Dave opened the door then stopped abruptly when he saw Mikey.
"What on earth?"
Jim told him, in a flat voice.
"This is Mikey. He knows Gordon. We do too, although not by name. I dislocated Gordon's shoulder on Friday. Young Mikey lives with his mother - an absolute saint of a woman except she owns a cellar right out of a Hammer Horror. Mikey's nineteen for fuck's sake and his mother locks him in the cellar when he's naughty! He actually likes it too, the weird fucker! Oh, I forgot to mention: Mikey hears voices and wants to kill me. I narrowly escaped being gutted by the bastard."

Dave gaped at his friend in shock and awe. Might it be that, after years of hitting the hard stuff, the hard stuff had started to hit back? The world changed in that moment.

"Did you know that Voices in the head are reaching epidemic proportions round?" Jim continued. "It started with dear old Mark - who Mikey doesn't know at all. My log search so far reports 3 facial cross-references in Recent/Trash Memory." Jim covered his face with his right hand and massaged the temples with thumb and fingers.

"Jim, mate, what's going on? What are you babbling about?" Dave was strangely wary of entering the flat and hovered at the doorway. Not literally, of course. Not yet.

"What, you mean you don't know the Correlation Location?" said Jim, weariness and a little madness in his voice. "Hey, come inside and shut the door, eh? Don't leave fingerprints if you're scared"

"Jim you're doing my head in. What's happening to you?"

"Dave, old pal. My mind is close to blowing a fuse. It's throbbing like a purple penis prodding panties! I know of two people driven to murder and so far the one thing they have in common is the pub on Friday. Oh, and I've discovered I can read minds, although it makes me feel pretty zonked afterwards."

At that, Jim collapsed. Asleep as he hit the carpet, his nose came to rest barely inches from the swampy area Mikey had used to empty his bladder.

When he came to, Dave was shaking him.

"Shit man, I was just going to call an ambulance. You've been in some kind of coma for nearly 20 minutes. Your eyes were rolled back, you were hardly breathing. I'm afraid I flushed the stinky skunk down the bog. Old habits."

"Fucking Jesus."

"I know, sorry. I panicked!"

"Not that you tit. I was talking to *myself*. I know what put me out. The overclocking. I forgot."

"The what?"

"I overclocked my mind earlier. When Mikey attacked me. Thought I'd got away with it."

"Am I going to want to hear this?" said Dave. "We could go back to our normal topics of conversation. Hey dude, the cute Channel 5 weather girl had her mole showing today. Always a good day when that happens." Dave grinned at his attempt to inject intelligence and levity but Jim didn't appear to hear. He continued regardless.

"I've only overclocked my brain once before, should have realised the zonktime would be proportional to the overclocking period."

"Want me to stand here and look stupid for a bit?" Dave stood on one leg, half-heartedly capering. Things were becoming surreal and he wanted to fit in. Dave usually preferred to avoid real-world situations - they were Sheila's job, after all.

But Jim wanted to explain. "I imagine my mind working four times as fast as it really does. It's like I'm speeding up the internal clock that's responsible for how fast I think. Briefly, I'm a humming bird. It was how I prevented mi-laddo-here from slicing me up. He's bloody lethal. Tried to open my guts and then turns out to be a thicko – knows nothing. I had to go in and get it myself!"

"Er," said Dave.

"Gentlemen, going in!" Jim laughed suddenly, putting on a plummy voice.

Dave wanted to speak but Jim was on one of his "out there" trips. He embarked on them from time to time when something got to him. Usually this tended to involve slimy politicians on the news rather than mad knife wielders.

Dave knew, from experience, that it would be over soon.

Duly, Jim started to wind down.

"Not to self: don't overclock because it leaves me totally drained. You can't be too careful with the brain."

Dave was flummoxed.

"He's still alive, I think. What are you going to do?" Dave asked. They both regarded the prone figure of Mikey who seemed to be barely breathing.

"I don't know. I'm making this up as I go."

"I have something to tell you," said Dave.

"You're going to run for public office at last?" It was a weak effort but better than nothing. The reply was quite unexpected.

"I want to kill you too," said Dave. "Sorry."

Chapter Twelve

Our mind is capable of passing beyond the dividing line we have drawn for it. Beyond the pairs of opposites of which the world consists, other, new insights begin.   *Herman Hiss*

The smell of burning toast filled the kitchen and Joey Barker rushed in, fuming. Deidre, his wife, probably knew the toaster was on its last legs, she was in charge of kitchen appliances. He would sort her out for that mistake when the fat cow came home. After she'd done the housework.

They had called him Short Fuse at school. What a laugh! At first he exploded with rage but he soon learned it only made things worse. He was no fighter and the predatory gangs punished anyone who dared to respond. So Joey practised the art of being furious underneath, of storing fury for later. And to this skill, he added mastery of the bland surface smile.

After a time, Joey found he was able to laugh at any cruelty regardless of the target. His former tormentors assimilated him and progressed to other victims, which was a revelation. Sometimes, when they reduced the fat kid to tears, or stole the lunch money from the stupid kid, or simply beat the living shit out of the clever kid, Joey felt - briefly - he wasn't the unluckiest person after all. In later years he would look back on those precious moments with fondness.

It irritated Joey that his wife had to get up so early for her cleaning job. It meant she got out of making his breakfast. He was positive she had taken the job to avoid her duties, a knowledge that fired cold anger behind those veiled, freckled eyelids.

Joey knew, because he was no fool, that his wife's brains were the weak link in their partnership. If she had been clever - not a Tefal-head but just a bit less stupid - they wouldn't have to rely on her poorly-paid cleaner's job and stupid waitress job. She was so dumb she would never be he wife he deserved. *They were broke and it was all her fault.* She had never made enough effort to conquer her shortcomings.

Joey wished the Voices could be of some practical help. They whined in his head and never shut up, getting louder all the time. Maybe when he had finished with the tall bastard and they were gone, he would sort her out once and for all.

Outside, the sky darkened and it began to rain. Grey streaks ran down the grimy kitchen window as Joey noticed the washing was still out. He cursed. He had arranged to go out later and fetch something - a special object. Apparently it was the ultimate test of whether good luck could hold forever.

Joey reckoned he would end somebody's lucky streak today. He wanted to. Very much.

***

Arthur Bradshaw contemplated the blurry face that was ever-present, waiting whenever he closed his eyes. There was nothing special about it, certainly nothing to justify letting rip with a big blow-up. Still, the image persisted, gaining greater clarity from hour to hour. The image of somebody who deserved to die.

Arthur jogged at a pleasant lope alongside the river. The mist hung around late, its white fingers grasping at crystalline shoots of grass, all leaden with the chill of morning. The brown slurry of the river barely slowed the stately flotilla of the swan and his mate, gliding over the dark mirror, *together forever.*

As he began the steep climb into the park, the sun threatened his back, a dull orange cyst on white and pale blue flesh. It offered no warmth. Tall sycamore and beech, mirrored in the beer-coloured river, framed the corner where Arthur usually turned for home. He hadn't moved from the modest semi-detached he had shared with Peg, mostly so he could wallow in memories, hanging onto them all greedily. His former profession could have funded a lavish lifestyle and provided many material luxuries, but these they found unnecessary. He sighed as he jogged, breathing easily, the body not quite given over to the ravages of age. Art was fifty-eight but as strong, no - stronger - than ever.

Today, the face in his mind was becoming familiar. If Art had been impatient, he could have guessed its identity easily, fleshing out the last few details from recent memory. But there was no hurry. He was strangely content, knowing he would kill the owner of the face very soon and that it would mean absolutely nothing. Maybe today, or tomorrow, it didn't matter. Nothing did.

An immaculately trimmed garden greeted his return. A neighbour smiled and nodded. Art's cat appeared and wound itself around his leg as he fumbled for the key. The cat purred in anticipation of a shared communion - their ritual breakfast - but Arthur anticipated a murder. Why it should be happening now, he had no opinion. He would do it simply because he felt it was right. Peg had always said he should follow his inner voice. And he always had.

***

At last, Gordon thought, unwrapping the gun. *It almost took forever.*

Dormant on the table, cold and heavy metal but slumbering it crouched. Its touch was a kiss - the kind of kiss all men would understand. Its promise was untold pleasures, wrongs righted; its power was that of an erection. Even the pain in his shoulder subsided when he stroked it.

The time was drawing closer. The *right* time at last.

Soon, he would know.

Gordon had acquired his sense of timing from his father. And by skill and cunning, he avoided complication and recrimination when bad things happened. Bad things had often happened.

The queer in the pub had been a rare mistake, but one soon put right. Over the past few days, something remarkable had been growing inside Gordon. He found he could *feel* where the bastard was - an ability he could summon at will. By closing his eyes and letting the voices guide him, he could find the cunt whenever he needed to. He dearly hoped this new skill remained after the deed was done; if so, Gordon would be much closer to possessing all the secrets he needed.

His instincts told him to wait until the evening. In the meantime, his nose and shoulder throbbed constantly so he dulled the pain with cheap cider.

Preston was crawling with police. Gordon had never seen so many and had feared it might screw the deal for the gun. Fortunately, it hadn't. Now he simply waited for the tingle down his spine, the buzz of electricity that would be his cue. Gordon judged that he was a hard man - but it never hurt to even things up.

***

Outside the flats, Julie Hutchinson watched a balding man enter. He seemed vaguely familiar, perhaps one of her many clients: the men who loved her. It was so very hard to tell. To Julie, they all looked the same.

She should have worn a longer coat, some thicker clothes. The skies were leaden and heavy and a chill was in the air. Julie drew her thin jacket tightly about her and clutched her handbag, knuckles shining. A car, driving past, slowed and she heard its driver crank down the window. Her breath quickened.

"Doing any business love?"

She backed away, saying nothing.

"Please yourself whore, as if I give a shit!" The car accelerated and quickly faded into the distance. A loving father returning home to embrace his loving family.

If life could be written as the sum of precious moments shared with her lovers, Julie knew she would be happy. Truly, fully happy. *Sharing is caring!* She hated the other times, the times when people looked at her like a piece of dirt. It was only right and proper that anyone who made her unhappy should share in some of it. Julie was stronger than she looked - deceptively so - and if anyone caused her pain, she used her *talent*.

In the shadows by the bristly privet hedge, away from prying eyes, she slid the razor blade along the back of her hand and watched the blood ooze gently out. The joy of the razor was that it caused no pain. The only pain she ever felt came from the looks in their eyes.

Earlier, knowing she needed to get across town, she had tried to work out which was the right bus. Buses were confusing - everyone said so. They were all different colours, had different, unknowable timetables and their drivers were nasty, impatient men with cutting eyes. They leered at her legs, stared at her small breasts without even the pretence of looking elsewhere. Julie found it impossible to guess which bus; the twisty routes some of them travelled would baffle a laboratory rat. In the end, she walked. It was easier that way. And she had her whispering guides.

It would be so nice to stay home, take the phone off the hook, she thought, watching the entrance to the flats. She felt drained, nauseous, lacking in energy. She would have lain down where she was if the voices would only stop. Julie could sense - strongly - the presence of the long-haired, amazing one. He was nearby. She was close to him now, having taken almost an hour to walk here. She'd arrived too late to follow in Dave's wake as he, in turn, sneaked in behind someone else. Not that it mattered. There was no hurry now she had reached her target. She sensed the skin-headed bloke was involved somehow anyway but it was better to wait until her intended was alone. Then she would be his last - and only true - love.

***

Working on his smile, Gordon admired himself in the mirror, gun in hand, trousers around his ankles. Apart from his swollen nose and dark-ringed eyes, he rated himself as a good looking guy - not pretty, thank goodness. Most girls preferred the more rugged look anyway and he was a man's man, anyone could see that. There were guys too - fags - who gave him encouraging looks. He hated this and hated all queers. Gordon's father had taught him to avoid such men because they had a sickness inside. A sickness that was contagious.

He touched his nose gingerly. Breathing through it still made his eyes water - but thanks to the cider, it was bearable. The voices murmured constantly, insistent and persuasive but friendly and encouraging.

Stroking the gun and its long, phallic silencer made him happier than he ever would imagined. He was so delighted he resolved never to give it up afterwards. Gordon wished he had a uniform to wear too, like his father's.

Standing in front of the mirror, he tensed his muscles as he gripped the gun, pointing it at a signed poster of his hero Vinnie Jones, the famous actor. He put the barrel in his mouth and admired his reflection out of the corner of his eye.

As a boy, Gordon had learned an important lesson about timing. He learned it lying in bed, waiting for his father to come and say goodnight, usually in the narrow window of opportunity when his mother was taking a bath. His father always warned him about the bad men and often had to demonstrate what the bad men might do to him.

Gordon bided his time for years, only killing his father when he was absolutely sure it was the *right* moment. In the end, all that mattered was *timing*.

Chapter Thirteen

To invent, you need a good imagination and a pile of junk.   Thomas And Eddie

While they lounged around the flat disposing of Stella, Jim pondered the options. Despite his revelation, Dave didn't appear to present any imminent threat, although he was developing a tendency to talk to himself. Still tied to a chair, slumped, Mikey Sharples showed no signs of waking up. Jim lowered his can infinitely slowly and showed no signs of giving a shit. He closed his eyes and breathed deeply, as if thoroughly relaxed and at peace. You would have thought that holding prisoners and having his life being threatened was as familiar as lukewarm fish and chips or bank holiday traffic jams.

Time trudged onwards obstinately.

Muttering, Dave rose stiffly to his feet and headed into the kitchen where he crammed the remaining cans of lager into the fridge. Then, holding back a growing agitation, he resumed his vigil sitting opposite Jim and burping sporadically. Eventually, his friend opened his eyes and blinked in puzzlement, as if unaware of his surroundings. But his erstwhile serenity had evaporated and his countenance was troubled.

"I love you man, you know that," he declared unexpectedly. "But something's happening to me. I can't explain it and I don't know where it's leading."

"Look Jim, maybe you need to get away for a while. Maybe there's someone you can talk to? You do know you can't keep *him* as a pet?! Sooner or later you'll have to, I don't know, report it or something."

"I know. As for talking to someone, I'm open to suggestions. Who might I tell? Whatever is happening goes beyond my mental frolics. And I'm so close. It's like all the impossible things I dreamed about as a kid might be possible. You know: flying, travelling to other planets, breathing water -"

"X-Ray specs?" asked Dave eagerly.

"Ahead of you mate, already on the workbench. I can literally brainwash myself, rewrite my mind, recode my reality."

"Wow!"

"Actually the flying and breathing water were probably poor examples, now I think about it. I don't really know where the boundaries are yet but I expect they're mostly down to my imagination."

"Sounds like an advertising slogan to me."

"Yeah but it's only an extension of what we've talked about in the past - reality, perspective, belief and all that malarkey."

"But you do it with no drugs," Dave said glumly. "What kind of a naff world would it be if that caught on?"

"No drugs? Fuck off - *course* there will be drugs! Programming stoned is the best thing ever, especially now I've developed a multi-adaptive language with empathic Dysonage," Jim improvised happily, as he often did when bullshitting.

"That sure won't suck! You're on something man and I want in. Or are you borrowing from Hitch Hikers again?" Dave fumbled for a joint. He knew that his pal had travelled extensively in regions inhabited only by the Blessed Stoned and admired him for that. (The Blessed Stoned were special beings who had discovered the ultimate truth - namely, no matter how stoned you got, you could always get just that little bit *more* stoned. Up and up and up with no ceiling. Legend has it the Blessed Stoned are able to go full circle at will, returning all the way round the levels until they could pass for straight if necessary.) Dave had seen his mate wander, grinning and swaying, into the strangest territories, but he was out on the extremities of the old spiral arm now. And Dave would be his faithful Sancho Panzer as always.

"I'm with you on that empathic vacuuming dude. Found a bit of Temple ball. Want some?"

"I think I'll pass. I got stuff to do. Can you imagine what all this is doing to my brain? In some societies the mad are revered, you know."

Dave struck his lighter and the tall flame sprang forth. He lit the pre-rolled joint and breathed deeply of the smoke.

"Tobacco in that?" asked Jim, sniffing suspiciously.

"Yeah, sorry."

Jim pondered Mikey again. His brain appeared to have shut down and it seemed entirely possible it was broken.

Dave coughed.

"That smoke is fucking toxic," said Jim.

"I know. I think the clue is on the packet," said Dave. "Look... Jim?"

"Yeah?"

"Seems pretty sudden to me, this superman transformation. Was it basically today when it all clicked into place?"

"I guess. It's not easy to remember. Something has changed - inside. I don't know if I can ever make my brain work normally again. I doubt I can throw this all away without going loony. In fact, I might be there already!" A blackbird, from its vantage point in the lilac tree, broke into a series of frantic shrieks. Actually, all it was saying was "cat, cat, cat, cat, cat...."

"If you're mad, what does that make me? And him? And The Man Who Killed Everybody?" said Dave.

They jointly regarded Mikey who was barely breathing. *What to do about him?*

"This guy doesn't know me from Adam yet he wants to slice me open. I've looked through his brain log and found some worrying signs," said Jim.

Looked through his brain log. Ridiculous! Impossible?!

"We could go to the police, tell them what we know," suggested Dave.

"You kidding? The average copper thinks a brain cell is where you lock up naughty brains. And a neuron is a replacement for an old Ron. PC Average is hardly going to comprehend the subtle science of mental programming. Come on man, I've got to fix this myself!"

"Well, I'm with you, you know that, even if your jokes stink!"

"Thanks. I take it you're able to resist biting my leg off for the time being? I can't discount the possibility there may be others, which is a major concern. And I think I might be in trouble at work. There are too many things happening at once. It's got to mean something."

Jim caught Dave's fumes in his nostrils and held off the (huge) temptation to get "temple balled". There was something he needed to do and he dearly hoped Dave would be up for it.

"Anyway," Jim began, "Why don't you tell me all about it?"

"I totally will." Dave sat on the floor and put on his serious face.

"I wouldn't sit there.... oh, never mind."

After fumbling for a moment amongst the pile of CDs, Jim put on some unobtrusive background music.

"Tell me everything," prompted Jim, fiddling with the remote until the level was right.

"A similar story I'm afraid. I have been hearing voices in my head," Dave's words were slow and measured. "Actual, audible voices telling, no *commanding* me to kill you. They even invented reasons: you wanted to shag my wife, take my house, all my money, ruin my reputation."

"Only the 'shag your wife' is true", said Jim with a laugh.

Dave didn't return the laugh. Instead, he sucked at his gold tooth - something he did when anxious.

"It was Saturday morning when I first heard it for definite. It was faint, like when you've tried something new and get the first inklings it'll be a bad trip - but all you can do is hang on for the ride. It didn't bother me over the weekend because we were pickling our brains but I had an episode at work on Monday - really fucking eerie. Since then it has fluctuated between mildly irritating and capable of trashing every thought. When it gets bad,

I can only drown it out with a spliff – and you know I don't like to hammer it during the week. But without the herb, all I hear is this voice. Oh, and now I see burning letters when I close my eyes."

"Great," said Jim.

"I've been doodling death threats all day. I've been doing it on notepads, on the PC screen, on the car window. Dude, what the hell is happening? You know, don't you?"

"Not everything. But I'm starting to pull it together. Actually, I think you can help me progress. So far three people want to kill me, only one of whom had met me before Friday. That's far from good."

"I suppose," said Dave sniffing his palm. "Say, there's something wet down here."

"Mmmm," said Jim non-committally. On the stereo, Eno continued noodling about, examining a major seventh chord at considerable length. The music, mellow but agreeable, sloshed about the room like warm milk.

"I'm going to try something you'll probably find weird," said Jim.

"Weird? Compared to what?" Dave noticed the damp patch properly and sniffed his hand again. "Awwwwwwwww," he groaned, making the connection with Mikey's crotch.

Jim pretended not to notice as Dave wiped his hand on a dry bit of carpet. He took a long swig of lager.

"Nice," he said, meaning the lager. "Well, if I'm to learn what's going on in your noggin, I have to give it a go."

"Do I end up like that?"

Mikey drooled and dribbled but didn't stir. Jim belched loudly to indicate his confidence. "Fuck him. Close your eyes, sit quiet. I'm going into your head mate to see if I can put things right."

Dave took a draw of the joint. "Better get in there before this thing kicks in," he advised.

***

Jim entered the House at a gallop. He hurtled down the hallway, noticing with vague concern that the pictures had started to form once again on the wall. *No time for that now.* He ran upwards, ignoring the voices from the Ballroom, heading for the Attic. *No time for that either.*

At the tiniest prompt, Thunderbird 5 appeared fully formed and ready to operate. It was in orbit around a blue planet that Jim supposed must represent his best friend. He was in control and all would be well.

"TRANSFER HOUSE, FLOOR1, BASIC, NOEXT" he commanded in the general direction of Planet Dave.

TRANSFER COMPLETE.

"TRANSFER HOUSE,LOCALENV,MYPASS"

"WORKING".

"HOUSE CONSTRUCTION COMPLETE"

"ENTER"

As expected, it worked flawlessly. He duly credited himself, realising he had advanced beyond meaningful measurement. His programming was bearing dividends even faster than he had dreamt of.

Jim sniggered. Then he focussed on the job in hand.

The program resolved Dave's brain into a cavernous room with doors all around. Throughout the space, slender wisps of smoke circulated slowly. Dave's favourite Bob Marley poster, in a selection of psychedelic greens, purples and yellows, was the only recognisable decoration. As Jim stepped inside, all the doors opened at once as if in welcome. He could neither read the nameplates on them nor see what was beyond their thresholds, from where he stood.

In the centre was a pool of pale yellow liquid surrounded by rugs, bean bags, a TV and a table with ash trays and Kit Kats. Jim peered into the pool and picked up a stone he found there, throwing it into the middle where it vanished with a deep "plup".

Ripples formed and a faint golden light glowed from the depths. Seconds later a face appeared a few inches below the surface.

"Who are you?" its voice was familiar.

"Hey Sheila, it's Jim. How's it goin'?" said Jim.

"Hey Jim. Pretty good thanks. How did you recognise me?"

"Just luck I guess. I was looking for the computer interface. What are you doing in there anyway?"

"It's how things work sometimes. I thought you of all people would know that."

"I'm pretty new at this. Look Sheila, I was wondering why Dave wants to kill me."

"I see."

"Is it because of last Friday?"

"I'm afraid it is Jim, yes."

"Look, Sheila, the thing is I don't know what came over me. I can't even remember it. Is there anything I can do to make it up to you?"

"It's not about *that* you wanker! It's because of the fight at the pub. Something got loose. I don't think *you* released it either, but that's pure speculation."

"What got loose? And will Dave attempt to kill me?"

"He *might*. It's a peculiar business."

"But why, I mean, and what got released?"

"Sorry, no idea. I only know that it doesn't feel right in here any more. Something else is in here with me."

"And this began after the fight?"

"Funny you should ask that," she said. She laughed. "See!"

For a moment, another face formed in the pool instead of Sheila's. Its features – ugly, masculine, glasses - were familiar. Then it was gone.

"Sheila?" Jim's Surreality Meter hit maximum and he gritted his teeth. The pool bubbled flatulently then it spoke again, its tone neutral.

"I'm not really Sheila you know," it said. "It's more

complicated than that. Everything is. Listen Jim - and listen carefully - I shall say zees only wance. Oops, I think Dave's getting a bit stoned. I'm struggling to concentrate. I'll be telling God jokes and craving Chocomel and Pizza next."

Jim waited and the pool made a series of plopping, farting noises. It giggled then spoke again.

"Sorry. Where was I? Oh yes, Friday."

"I don't get it."

"Hardly surprising."

"I don't understand what you're saying. Is it .... a virus?"

"Similar, yes."

Jim looked around for a computer system of any kind. Oddly, there was only the pool.

"How do I stop it?"

The pool bubbled but had no reply. A whirlpool began to form in the middle. Slowly the yellow liquid swirled around, thick as paint, pouring into a hole into darkness.

Jim wanted to jump into the pool and seek out the darkness. It was similar to the compulsion he often felt, and barely resisted, at large meetings of the suits, the pretentious managers, the reps and the so-called experts of the computer industry. Jim forever fought against the desire to stand on a chair and shout "bollocks" then sit down quietly as if nothing had happened. One day he would do it. It was the cliff he longed to jump off and see what would happen.

The whirlpool paged Jim's Self-Destruct button. COME TO ME, it invited, swirling hypnotically.

For a moment, Sheila's face reappeared, shouting angrily: "Get out Jim! It knows you're here! Get out *now*!"

The voice was drowned by a rushing sound, the liquid spinning into a vortex that began to suck loose items into itself. The TV vanished, followed by an orange beanbag and a few rocks and plants Jim hadn't even spotted. All were absorbed and torn apart pixel by pixel. The doors began to flap madly, as if trying to pull themselves free to plunge into the pool's gloomy depths. Jim slapped himself and dragged his gaze from the pool. Then he ran.

He saw a door marked 'Jim' as he fled, resisting the temptation to take a peek.

As he leapt from Dave's House, a deep voice boomed: I KNOW WHERE YOU LIVE HONEY!

Slick with sweat and with hands numb as frostbite, Jim opened his eyes.

"It's worse than I thought," he told his oldest friend.

"I could murder........ a pizza," said Dave. "And Chocomel."

Chapter Fourteen

Only the shallow know themselves.   Oscar Mild

The sun poked at the heavy clouds in a half-hearted attempt to brighten the day. Outside, on his driveway, the Wondrous Tim was deeply immersed in BMW, pushing the boundaries of his practical skills. Essentially, this meant he was hunched over the engine, frowning, having checked the oil and water. To further emphasise his manly commitment, he fussed distractedly with a rag.

The show and its aftermath weighed heavily on his mind, as did the argument he'd had with Monica.

Inside, she observed his body language through lace curtains, biting her lip and feeling low. At least they were home for a few days and she was confident it would be enough to restore sanity. Especially if she left the TV switched off and talked Tim out of his bright idea to 'help the police using his special powers'.

Recently, they had spent too much time in hotels and the constant travelling had drained their joy. It was a necessary evil though, a by-product of Tim's blossoming career - a career she managed and carefully directed, her role now expanded to full-time. The current mini-tour was gaining attention and rave reviews and they both battled to keep their feet on the ground, concentrating on one show at a time. Although Monica yearned for the good things in life - champagne, clothes and endless beauty treatments - she also liked her home, her space, her quiet thoughts. So moving in with Tim had been a big step - and she still felt like an intruder in this, his deceased parents' house.

Earlier, tempers had flared - *playing right into Jim's hands if you would only see it* - but she had uttered this thought out loud. It had provoked an angry response: "If you two knew each other so bloody well, why didn't you live happily ever after?"

Why indeed?

Tim had stormed out, teenager-style. He was upset, stressed out about the murders, consumed by guilt, worried about the show and above all whether it would be spectacular enough. She sensed there was something else too, something he wasn't telling her.

Having spoken to Monica's ex, Tim couldn't banish him from his thoughts. And so the argument raged - encompassing everything and nothing. Tim even watched himself do it, like the fool he was. So much for Mind Control, he brooded later when he'd cooled down.

He slammed the bonnet rather harder than he'd planned.

Wiping his hands on the rag, he shuffled sheepishly into the front room. Monica was reading a magazine and pretended not to notice him, or his dirty shoes. She couldn't yet bring herself to think of the mess on 'my carpet'.

"I'm sorry," he said at last.

She looked up. "I'm sorry too. And to answer your earlier question, sometimes you can know someone *too* well."

"I love you," blurted Tim.

She tossed the magazine down and relaxed, "and I love you, don't you ever doubt it. But it's impossible to just forget someone like Jim. The important thing is I'm with *you* now and I'd make the same choice every time. Please don't let him do this to us. He can't if you don't let him." She crossed the room to where he stood.

Careless of the oil (Tim always got it everywhere) Monica rested her head on his shoulder. She had to stoop slightly but did so gladly. Here was the man she would spend the rest of her life with, regardless of any old wounds to her soul.

Tim clung to her like a frog in amplexus.

***

"I am going to try and wipe the Kill instruction. Then I'll try to rewrite some data in Mikey's tiny brain. It's pretty ropey and there's even a risk I'll end up a freaking vegetable if I don't escape cleanly." Jim spoke evenly, allocating minimal brainpower to inflection.

Dave took a long draw from his reefer and nodded contentedly. "Whatever you say man, and if it works, you can snot the one in mine too, huh? It's not terrible being stoned all the time but, erm, what was I saying?"

"It's the short term memory that goes the first dude, remember?"

"I remember, the short term memory. You'll clean my head too awright? I jus' doan wanna dat killin' ting no more, bwana. Love an' peace fer evah. Good ting I'm not a *real* skinhead - jus' a baldy git - or oi'd've succumbed and 'ad yer 'eart out by now, ahar!" Dave was well on his way and auditioned a succession of silly accents and expressions with modest skill but much enthusiasm. Rather like Mike Yarwood once did.

"If I don't kill Mikey in the process I will honestly clean the fecker out of you too." Jim closed his eyes. *Somehow, I'll go back in there and sort it mate!*

Dave grinned as he got through the last of his doobie. The inner voices remained silent.

***

Mikey's House looked deserted. Jim approached it carefully, picking his way over a cobbled path that arced over the void. A few holes revealed shapes floating in the darkness, shapes in purple, brown and occasional flashes of sickly beige. Jim concentrated on the door, avoiding holes that pitted the path. The adjoining houses were so faint that they barely registered, like charcoal drawings faded by time or careless frottage.

He reached the door and pushed, as if to open it. It budged slightly, then fell backwards into the hall. In a second, its bulk oozed through the floor, leaving a door-shaped hole of pitiless obsidian.

Jim peered into the gloom. He was able to make out the floor ahead, past the hole. If he could leap a door length he'd make it.

He took a run up – *how exhilarating* - and charged at full pelt towards the opening, his feet slipping on the cobbles. He only realised at the very last moment how low the lintel was – he'd split his head for sure! And with that moment of self-doubt, Jim lost his grip and was kicked from the entry to Mikey's mind.

He lay on the floor, as if he'd fallen out of the red chair. All around, Thunderbird 5's panels flashed green and blue. Nothing was broken. No need for International Rescue.

Something barred the way, that was plain. *Didn't crash the entire Operating System though! Am I good or am I fucking good!!! Bill Gates you can kiss my arse!* he guffawed, a trifle madly.

Determined, he began again, granting himself more authority. Concentrating very hard, he floated over the hole in the doorway and into the House proper, landing gracefully on the other side. Through the kitchen, the doorway to the cellar swung open invitingly but he ignored it. Instead, he sought Mikey's tatty Sinclair computer where he typed a quick query.

"RES,ACT;DATE(-5):LISTALL*"

Human brains share a common low-level language. Not many people know that.

In seconds, the TV screen confirmed everything he suspected based on the log analysis. An external program was introduced into Mikey on Friday evening. The program was transmitted from Jim's own head. The data already gathered implied this to be the case but now it was confirmed. The timing matched that of the fight and Jim had no answers or immediate theories. Apparently it had happened automatically.

This was not, in any way, a good thing.

In a succession of keystrokes, Jim isolated the intruding code and placed it in quarantine. It had been gobbling the available resources, locking out new programs from starting and putting the squeeze on others already present.

As he typed, Jim became aware of a sound - footsteps - surely emanating from the Cellar. Hurrying now, he began to save the program onto cassette tape, a process that seemed to take forever. Soon he could hear harsh breathing. *Stupid slow shitty Spectrum*, he cursed, instructing the computer to display the program's comments and the first few lines of code, out of curiosity.

It was garbage. No, that wasn't right, it was *compiled*.

Bugger! Should have guessed.

Jim didn't have time to look for the source program. Something was leaving the basement and he didn't feel like waiting for another encounter. Part of the program's title contained some recognisable characters. For Jim it was an eye-opener.

Having recently come to believe himself to be founder of an entirely new branch of science, Jim Cavanah now knew with sickening certainty that he could never claim authorship. He had not invented anything, had merely discovered that which already existed. There was no time to consider the implications further. Taking a screen dump and grabbing the cassette, he flew out of the House and back to his own brain-space.

Somewhat predictably, cruel laughter followed.

***

In a kitchen that, usually, was neat and orderly, every work surface, cupboard and wall bore the signs of a frenzied assault. On the cooker's glass window, on the fridge and even on the vinyl floor were crude drawings of guns spraying streams of bullets, all deeply gouged with a chisel.

Gordon Davis was no artist yet his vision of violent death was explicit and overwhelming. His attempts to sketch his intended victim were, apart from the long hair and curious lack of clothes, wildly inconsistent but in all cases the body was deeply pitted with chisel marks, suggesting the damage a gun could do.

Gordon admired his work in awe. Had he really done all this?

The gun sat, wrapped in a newspaper, part of its handle visible, waiting. After only a moment's hesitation, he picked it up and held it tight against his chest.

The optimum time was fast approaching.

***

After a last, lingering gaze and Gordon shoved the gun into his jacket's inside pocket. With the silencer fitted it was longer and heavier than he'd imagined. It strained against the seams and began to rip them. He'd forgotten how much he liked guns and the silencer was a bonus. Ultimately, he didn't care how much noise it made.

Despite downing 2 litres of White Lightning, the dull shoulder ache refused to disappear. He winced as he eased his arm out of the sling. Soon it would not be needed, he'd be strong again.

With a final glance at the mirror, Gordon slipped silently out of the back door. He didn't bother to lock it or take his key.

The quest had begun. He would slay the one with the ponytail and the abnormally fast reactions. The gay, the queer, the homo would die. Maybe he'd shove the gun up his arse before he pulled the trigger - that would show him a thing or two. Hell, the *bastard* would probably enjoy it. Gordon closed off the part of his mind that begged the question: *but would* you *enjoy it, son?*

Taking his bearings, he squinted in puzzlement. The voices reassured him, guided him and he began his march towards death. And the gun went before him like a standard, its weight a comfort.

***

The old man's eyes snapped open. A single voice was speaking urgently, saying there was not a moment to lose. Awake instantly, he arose and splashed cold water onto his face. Peering into the mirror, Art sought no reassurances. Not even he could ward off the passage of time but he noted only the merest sag. The furrows in his face and loose skin on his powerful, vein-laced hands marked the years he had survived.

Refusing to be hurried, he shaved and cleaned his teeth. Then he brushed his hair.

Art's hair, thick as ever, flowed over his broad shoulders in a blend of silver and white. Peg had loved it and he suffered her to brush it each evening. He'd worn it long and tied tightly because she cherished it - and kept it that way still, in memory of her. He smiled briefly as pulled it back and fastened it.

The voice was becoming agitated but Art remained serene. He unhurriedly selected a pair of socks from a drawer of clones. Today he would kill someone. He now knew it was to be the man from the fight. Art had a keen eye and had noted his moves but was unconcerned.

He quickly dressed, kissed the picture of his long-dead wife and set off to commit his first cold-blooded murder in many years.

***

Her patience rewarded, Julie slipped into Jim's flats. She entered in the wake of a student, a young lad with an innocent air and no taste in headgear. Seeing her, he lingered in the hallway, pretending to look for mail in a pigeon hole that was clearly empty. Under a floppy knitted hat, his dilated pupils darted back and forth, stealing furtive glances at her legs. He spun the wheels of a tatty skateboard he carried, searching for inspiration. He cleared his throat.

"Would you like to come to a party? I've got some legendary green," he stammered, blending nerves and excitement. He didn't meet her eyes. Then, growing more bold, he glanced upwards past the criminally short skirt to her thin chest and on to her bleached blonde hair. He recognised her for what she was.

The voices formed a reply in her consciousness: *I must decline because my special lover awaits.* Instead, she heard herself saying, "where's the party?"

"On the top floor, not far," his voice wavered. *A hooker! She's a bit stringy - but those legs!* He beamed his best little-boy-lost smile. At school, Father Spader had assured him it would melt hearts one day. The Almighty himself had personally decreed.

Julie felt dizzy. There was something in the boy's eyes she recognised and in an instant her mind was made up. Despite the wails of protest in her head, she decided to love him and share with him. Her work was paused, not postponed.

It would have been so easy to mistake this boy for a Good Punter – one of the few who actually cared about her as a person. His eager, smiling face hinted at it. But the sheen of sweat on his forehead was a clue to the *something* she sensed. Perhaps she would begin with a treat, offer him a freebie. Some role play, maybe she'd tie him up - they liked that, some of them. At first. Later she'd employ her special *talent* and see him transformed. Julie bit her lower lip, painting her teeth in the cheapest lipstick.

Flashing a pink smile she set off up the stairs. The student lagged behind to check out her miniskirt from a better angle. When they passed the door to Jim's flat, she felt his presence calling. The voices began to scream and it took an enormous effort of will to silence them – but silence them she did.

Drilling the tips of her fingers into her forehead she drew them slowly down her face, leaving smeared trails of mascara.

"Come on silly," she commanded, looking back as she ascended the next flight of stairs. His eyes were fixed hungrily where she'd known they would be. She beckoned him, teased him in a husky voice, whispering, "you want to party my young lover? I do too! Oh, I do too!"

***

"Excuse me sir," said the constable.

Joey froze, clasping a wooden box and trying to decide what to do. Mental agility wasn't one of his strongest suits so he scowled and said nothing.

"I am requesting that you walk this way." The fresh-faced PC indicated a path diverting Joey from crossing the flag market. "They're filming. Getting atmosphere shots. If you ask me, there's going to be a film after all the goings on. A much-needed boost for the city! Just think: Preston goes from town, to city, to slaughter house in the blink of an eye. Warms the cockles, don't it?"

Joey nodded helplessly but the cop wasn't finished.

"I don't know if I fancy Bruno Willit or Huge Rant as Housman, what do you think? Do you follow films at all? Can you see Huge Rant as a mindless killer?"

The cop beamed a smile but had apparently finished his spiel.

Joey practically dashed in the direction indicated, gripping the odd little box fiercely. The policeman shook his head and narrowed his eyes suspiciously. He held this pose in case a camera was focused on him, immortalising the moment and his devotion to duty.

Madness, madness, Joey's thoughts were a maelstrom of buzzing locusts. He was angry. The copper had obviously picked on him because he was short. It happened all the time and Joey was heartily sick of it. If the pig had known what was in the box, he'd not be so bloody self-important. He'd had half a mind to open it there and then.

Getting the contents of the box was not possible for everyone. Joey had contacts and one of them was high-ranking enough to perform this special favour. Joey admired his prize through tiny slits in the woodwork.

"I've never seen one before," he had said.

"No," replied the woman, "they're quite rare."

"Can I see it?"

"Best not. It is very hungry so you must only open it when ready to deploy. It must urgently feed as soon as it gets free."

"I bet," Joey had chuckled. She was a bit old but he still would if she commanded it. Mrs Sharples led the best gang he had ever joined - one that knew how to get the things a man needed. He was glad to know Una Sharples, real glad.

"Be careful. And don't, whatever you do, bring it back here," she warned.

Joey squinted through the tiny breathing holes in the box. Something alien looked back, multi-faceted eyes glinting in the shadows.

It was time to go and witness someone's luck run out.

Chapter Fifteen

By means of shrewd lies, unremittingly repeated, it is possible to make people believe that heaven is hell -- and hell heaven. The greater the lie, the more readily it will be believed. Adolphus Hittite

The sun was weakening, the shadows lengthening as the three would-be killers converged on Jim's flat.

Joey Barker shook the wooden box gently. Something roughly fist-sized skittered about inside. There were odd clicking noises that seemed to echo beyond the box itself - some strange trick of the acoustics, Una had said.

The box was lightly decorated with Arabic writing. Una told him it was Arabic anyway. Apparently these things – Mongolian Flesh Beetles - lived in the desert *or somewhere like that*. The phrase bothered him. What places were like a desert and yet not a desert? Fleetwood, perhaps?

***

Gordon Davis patted the gun through his jacket and turned towards where he knew his enemy would be. Somehow he'd expected a house, so the prospect of flats left him momentarily baffled. And without a name, there was no way to ask for help without looking stupid. He sensed his quarry was above the ground floor but had no clue which flat it might be.

Despite being tantalisingly near, he was unsure how to proceed. Gordon spotted the security system - a weather-beaten camera pointing at the main door - and snorted in disdain. He didn't give a toss about being seen.

And suddenly fortune smiled. He smirked to see the small open window downstairs, wide enough so he could reach through and unlatch the larger window beneath. The timing was perfect for it had been opened only minutes ago.

***

Arthur Bradshaw was close too – an anonymous shadow in worn jacket and jeans. Concealed under a shapeless cap, his long hair was drawn back tightly, smoothing the lines and giving his face an ageless appearance. He had not brought a weapon.

Art was mildly surprised at the growing excitement at the prospect of one final test. Although the outcome didn't concern him even slightly, professional detachment began to kick in.

Entering the road leading to Jim's flat, he blanked his mind, breathing slowly. In through the nose, out through the mouth. Knowing how to attract no attention, he approached in measured strides, confidently. His expression was calm and focused, his eyes without emotion. Soon he would kill the man who haunted his dreams. Tomorrow only Peg would fill his dreams once again.

***

The flat was littered with pizza boxes and lager cans. Julie kicked over a fungal cup in dismay. She removed her meagre coat but held onto it, suddenly conscious of her small breasts, ill-concealed behind a thin blouse. Her face would have been pretty were it not for the narrow scar along her jawline and the hardness cutting through flesh and smudged make-up. And when her mind wandered, Julie's eyes shone with a haunted light unsettling to even her regulars.

To Russell Cooper, apathetic student of Sociology and Applied Tossing-It-Off, she looked just fine. Countless old scars on her arms didn't register. He quivered with lust and anticipation, which she read easily. Feeling his need, she tossed her jacket to the cleanest spot on the sofa. She begin her show by drawing her tongue slowly around her lips.

Russell couldn't believe his luck. She was barely twenty, he guessed, and repeated this in his head, stifling a giggle.

Barely twenty! Ha ha!

He considered calling some pals - to share costs. A good catholic boarding school boy, Russell was at his happiest with his friends by his side. They had explored the true value of companionship, his friends and the Jesuit fathers. He missed those days.

"Do you live here alone?" Julie asked dreamily, looking about as if seeing somewhere classier.

"At the moment. I got a couple of pals who stay here sometimes. Would you like me to ring them?"

"Wouldn't you like me all to yourself?" There was a tone in her voice that keener ears would have detected.

"Sure but, well, I've never done this before..."

"Never had a chance meeting and an afternoon of wild lovemaking?"

Was this his imagination, or was she taking the piss? It sure sounded like it.

"Well, I only meant, I don't know what to ask for," he grinned but it became a leer.

Her smile went out like a cheap light bulb. A new smile replaced it. The professional smile.

"Ask for? You ask for what you want babes and it's on the house. You're quite special, you know that. The moment I saw you I decided to eat you right up!"

Russell gulped, in perfect imitation of Wile E. Coyote as yet another infallible plan unravelled. The cunning Roadrunner knelt down, reached out and - *no wait.*

"S-sorry," he stammered, shaking his head to clear the weird illusion. "Look, can I take a shower, er, f-first? I must stink terribly, I've been playing footie." He mentally kicked himself, wondering where his courage had gone.

"Here..." He reached for the fridge and brought out a can of lager.

Perhaps he is a Good Punter, she dared to hope. She had practically given up searching for the best in men she met.

He must be Good if he wants to be clean for me. Puzzled, Julie cleared a space and sat down as the boy fled.

Safely behind the bathroom door, Russell rang his dear friend Christopher on the mobile and told him to pass on the message. Then he got into the shower.

He heard the bathroom door open.

"It's me, are you decent?" Her voice sounded husky.

"I won't be a min- oh," he said, as the shower curtain was drawn back.

Julie joined him in the shower. She was naked. She was gorgeous, slender, pert, intoxicating.

"Let me soap that for you my love," she said, seizing the bar of soap and working up a lather. Russell couldn't believe what was happening. She slid her hand over his penis then knelt. Hot jets streamed over them both. Her other hand rose upwards holding the soap. She moved it around his balls, her middle finger surprised him momentarily making him rise onto his toes. She knew the tricks, the ones they never dared ask for.

Still resting her finger in that sensitive place, she took him in her mouth then cursed herself for being too quick. The young man had clearly not had time to wash yet. A Good Punter would always do that out of respect. *And what other reason for the shower?* The boy would be embarrassed if she said anything so Julie decided not to mind, just this once.

Steaming spray ran over them as Julie took him in anyway. *Us Posh Ladies know tricks too,* she narrated in her mind. She took him all the way, in one long, impossible mouthful. *My young lover!*

She paused. Already he was close. They often felt bad if it ended quickly so she worked some more magic. Russell froze - but the magic worked. Playing her role to perfection, she urged him on.

"Mmm, come on baby, come on, don't hold back. I love it baby and I want it all," she implored, begged, shouted.

At Russell's front door, his neighbour, accompanied by his friend Christopher let themselves in. They heard the commotion in the shower and crept to the bathroom door.

"Surprise!" they shouted, bursting in.

Julie was indeed surprised. Russell winked at her in a pathetic show of manliness. A moment of confusion and - sorrow - washed over her face, making her look even younger than her years. Then she saw how it was. The way it *always* was.

Turning cold inside, she turned on her professional smile for the newcomers too.

"Boys!" she said. "So it really *is* a party! This is wonderful. Who's first? Or do you boys like all together?"

They couldn't believe their luck.

***

Gordon slipped into the ground floor flat. He almost cried out when he snagged his injured arm as he dropped in, but controlled it.

He heard a sound from an adjacent bedroom and peered through the door.

"Man, that rocks!"

"Watch this dude!"

"Man, that rocks!"

"Watch this dude!"

"Man, that fucking rocks!"

"Yeah, watch *this* dude!"

"Man that *totally* rocks!"

Two student types, gays Gordon judged, were on the bed playing with a lighter. One of them would flick the lighter on, the other would praise him. The flame was bright green.

Gordon snorted. *Tossers! Nothing impressive about that.* The first student lit the flame once again, followed by more stupid praise, round and round again. It was perpetual motion and Gordon couldn't understand it. It made no sense at all.

He sneaked past and out. Upwards. He knew he must go upwards. Engrossed, they didn't notice.

"Watch this dude!"

"Jesus dude, how did you do that?"

"Watch this dude!"

"Jesus dude, how did you do *that*?"

[fades]

At last, Gordon reached the door. A plain white door like any other yet he was sure it was the right one. His timing was perfect because the door was slightly ajar. He could walk in, point the gun, kill the bastard, then leave. Nobody would get in the way but if they did, he would kill them too. Once the *queer bastard* was dead nothing mattered. He was seconds away from blessed relief and the start of a new phase. It felt so good he almost cried.

He touched the door to Jim's flat and it swung open, slightly faster than anticipated. Fortunately, all was silent - and he saw it was a right shithole. His dad had drilled into him that tidiness was vital for an ordered, disciplined society. Another good lesson from the man in uniform.

He was repulsed by what he saw as his eyes became accustomed to the gloom. The gay and his gay pal were both sound asleep, sprawled out as if a magic wand had been waved over them. They'd probably been doing faggy shit and couldn't stay awake afterwards. Gordon could *always* stay awake after doing faggy shit - not that he did it often. But his dad had commanded him to know thine enemy - even if it made you feel sick and furious. The trick, apparently, was to focus the anger and use it later. Gordon's blossomed as he surveyed Jim's junk-shop room.

The flat was decorated with hippyish images and hung with rugs and psychedelic drapes. Ornaments consisted of masks and statues that might have been made in a mud hut. By a grinning savage with a bone through his nose. There were bits of broken computer, CDs, books and exotic plants interspersed with gay crystals and tangled wires leading everywhere. More significantly, like the flat he'd used to enter, the place stunk of dope. He almost retched.

More surprising even than that was unconscious figure of Mikey Sharples. Jesus, they'd all been doing fag bondage shit - and he never had Mikey down for swinging that way, or any. Gordon paused, uncertain, the voices now roaring but his mind slow to respond. Why was Mikey here? What was *really* going on?

He was going to have to kill them all. But <u>him</u> first.

***

Arthur Bradshaw climbed the stairs of the least secure block of flats in town. Sensing his quarry close by, he drew in a long, deep breath.

***

"Remember me?" Gordon whispered, unable to resist the melodrama of a film ending. He prodded Jim with his foot and wondered how his hero Vinnie would approach this scene.

"Hmmm?" groaned Jim and opened one eye to see lager-breath towering over him. Today was certainly a strange day. "Uhhh," he groaned. "Bloody great. Fuckwit's here."

"Well, do you?" Gordon suddenly realised he needed the gun in his hand to back up his authority.

"Did you think of that line yourself?" slurred Jim, still not moving.

Gordon fumbled in his jacket. The gun had slipped into the lining and was proving hard to extract. He flushed with embarrassment and tore furiously at the lining. Jim watched, only remotely interested. His body was limp, unresponsive.

"It's *time*!" declared Gordon triumphantly. He'd got a grip on the handle.

"Are you just going to whitter or shall we proceed straight to the twatting?" Jim struggled to gain some kind of control of his body. It ignored him completely.

Gordon ripped the gun out at last, silencer and all. It was long and magnificent and he wished there were a mirror nearby to observe his finest moment.

"Ah," said Jim. His efforts to move deflated and he slumped on the settee.

In a fraction of a second, Jim weighed up the options. There were fewer than he hoped for. Activating Spike was a no-no since that experiment seemed to have had unexpected consequences. Of more relevance, he was mentally shot. He was weak and helpless. Screwed, in fact. Unless he could come up with something conventional.

Dave chose that moment to open his eyes and peer about. He took in Gordon then Jim. It was a particularly surreal moment, even for Jim's flat.

"What's happening man?"

"Dude, meet another of my growing fan club. You remember this prick?"

In response to this insult, Gordon shot him.

***

In that second, many things happened.

Gordon fired and it made a dull, thumping noise that was still louder than expected. Jim cried "Ow!"

Not far away, carrying his mysterious box, Joey Barker heard the shot although he didn't realise it was a gun. It sounded more like someone hoofing a cardboard box.

Upstairs, Julie heard it clearly as she prepared to give three young bucks an experience they would never forget. They were not, at that time, in any position to comment or grant it much of their attention.

Gordon felt a bulldozer hit him hard in the ribs then grasp his wrist. If asked, he would have described this as *an unpleasant surprise*.

From his vantage point leaning against the settee, Dave saw everything in slow motion. *Jointmotion.* He observed a powerfully-built, white-haired man sweep into the room and ruthlessly but efficiently attack the gunman. He moved like a blur, first breaking Gordon's arm then his neck.

Mikey lay oblivious through it all.

***

For Art, it was done. The voices had departed. He dropped the yob he'd just killed, recognised him, and felt nothing.

They had worked together a few times on the doors, Arthur always in charge. Arthur was the blanket that smothered trouble, the respected old professional who did any job to the best of his ability.

At the Blue Flamingo, their most recent gig, Arthur stopped drug dealers from bringing their wares into the club. Those were his instructions. He had no particular axe to grind and didn't care what kids took on the outside. But on these premises they purchased from his boss and no other, which neutralised the side deals bouncers traditionally made as extras. Art's unbending attitude brought him conflict with many but his reputation, so far, ensured nobody complained. To his face anyway.

As for Gordon, it had driven him mad to see how many fights were dampened down before they started. The whole point of being a bouncer was to show your authority yet Arthur Bradshaw didn't care. Admittedly, he respected Art's stance on the drugs issue. His dad had told him that drugs were evil and made you do things you didn't want, couldn't control. Gordon believed Arthur was simply past it and scared to get into scrapes. The tales told about him couldn't be true. People exaggerated.

One night, when Gordon felt it was the right time to show who was top dog, he had engaged Arthur in a rare conversation.

"You keeping fit Art?"

"Can't complain."

"Been wondering: do you still train much? I mean, I haven't seen you down the gym or anything?"

"Do you want to find out if I can still hack it - is that why you're interested?" Art was direct, you had to give him that. There was a look in his eye that Gordon didn't like much. He found himself blustering in response.

"What? No, no Art. I just don't think the gym is really working out for me. All those fags, all posers, nobody training seriously. If I'm going to be in the job as long as you, I wondered if -"

Arthur gazed without expression - and Gordon's words dried up. He made the effort and tried again. "You jog right? I thought I might come along one morning if that's OK?"

"I train alone," said Art with finality. He didn't like Gordon. The lad fancied himself way too much and tried to bite off more than he could chew, to generate aggro needlessly. The boy was fast, unpredictable, dangerous. He was Trouble.

The following morning, Art had spotted Gordon hanging around on the path near his house.

"Lovely morning, thought I'd jog along," he said cheerily.

Art read the lad's body language and sighed. "If you must. It's a free country." He set off at his usual loping pace and Gordon dropped in behind, watching every movement intently.

They ran for an hour, neither faster nor slower than Art usually would. When they were almost home again, Gordon pulled him up.

"Stop, please, Art, I want to ask you something."

"I know what you want," was the flat response.

"On the job, you always take the easy way out. Is that the secret? I mean, you didn't even put me into a sweat just now. Do you never get worked up about *anything*?" Gordon stood close, a violation of Art's personal space. His voice was thick, nervous, and the sweat flew like morning mist. It would be soon.

"I'm not here to impress you lad. You tagged along even though I made it clear I didn't want company. That was my run, like it or lump it. I do it every morning. In the evening, before work, I do another. Say what's really on your mind and let's get it over and done with. My cat wants his breakfast."

Gordon thought it wasn't working out quite how he expected but he couldn't foresee a better opportunity. He was taller than Arthur and young, strong and at the top of his game.

"I have to know," he said flexing his impressive muscles.

"You already do," said Art.

The fight was short and, from Gordon's perspective, humiliating. Art grabbed him before he could say another word and threw him roughly to the ground. There was no elegance, no artistry. As he held Gordon in a grip of steel, he lectured, calmly.

"An important lesson, lad. Remember to pay attention! You can go either way from here but at the end of one of the paths will be me. And I won't be playing like this. Listen! Two paths. Take the right one. I did."

Art felt Gordon's breath on his cheek but he wasn't finished.

"Listen and you'll have a better life. You might even achieve something worthwhile, meet someone. You might actually live, be happy. Do you understand?"

Art then demonstrated some of the vast collection of holds and locks he knew, rolling Gordon like a doll, using his joints against him, pulling him, never losing control or relinquishing his grip. A passer-by with a dog, saw them struggling on the ground and turned smartly about, yanking the dog roughly and never once looking back.

"A good bouncer is like a good *anything*. This is my code. It makes sure I don't go wrong. By the way, do you like the old 'double arm lock'? A classic I think. Now we'll bring the legs into play."

After a few more minutes writhing in moist grass and soil, Arthur made eye contact for the last time.

"Remember the close-in stuff. In a crowded club like ours, it can kill or save you."

"You fucking old fag! Let me go!" He strained until veins bulged on his forehead but could not get free.

"Remember those two paths lad. This is a today-only lesson! In life, you only get a few important choices to make – but everything flows from them." With that, Art released his hapless victim and rose in a smooth motion. He carefully retied his hair, only half looking in Gordon's direction as he brushed off the dirt. In the end, this casual approach did the trick. Gordon decided the time was not right after all. The old guy was lucky, or blessed, or something. He grinned sheepishly as he got to his feet and faked sincerity for all he was worth.

"Thanks for the lesson Art. Really, I learned a lot. Maybe we'll do it again one day."

"Aye maybe we will at that," Art had replied.

Chapter Sixteen

Freedom is not worth having if it does not include the freedom to make mistakes.   Maharaja Gandini

"I'm bleeding!" said Jim.

***

"I'm bleeding!" wailed Christopher, Russell and William in chorus. They lay strapped together, face down on the bed. Julie had promised them the full works - spanking, maybe she'd ride them some, then she planned a real treat (she wouldn't say what it involved). Quite how the handcuffs came into play, they couldn't remember. Quite how this skinny, naked creature had them all bound and blindfolded defied belief. There was no rational explanation for any of it.

She removed their blindfolds. Her eyes were cold, barely even blue. A bit like that scary Scientologist bint off Cheers.

"You won't move will you?" she asked, taping their mouths. A splatter of Russell's cum remained on her chin, her drying sacrament.

***

"I'm still bleeding," complained Jim.

Dave bit off a section of parcel tape and stuck Jim's arm with it, inexpertly. *Left upper arm, flesh wound, nothing to concern us here.*

"Why wasn't the gun louder?" asked Jim, watching the repair and dabbing at the blood - his blood! - on the sofa.

"Silencer," said Art, checking out the hallway before closing the door firmly. "And just as well, I think."

"Do I know you?" Jim wanted to know.

"I doubt it. I work the pub doors in town. I was having a quiet drink last Friday when this idiot tried his luck. Other than that, never saw you before."

Jim pondered this as he stared, with fascination, at the body. It was large and did not fit with the décor or ambience. Gordon's neck was bent at a very unusual angle and his expression was a frozen mask of disbelief. The pains in his shoulder and the voices in his head were gone.

"Is he... dead?" Jim ventured.

"Yes. He is."

"Isn't that a bit, well, harsh?"

"Probably. Is the boy dead too?"

"No. Well, I hope not."

"I have to be going. Do you want me to take care of that?" He indicated Gordon.

"I don't know. What's normal in cases like these?" Jim felt reality was unravelling at a faster rate than even he was used to. He frowned.

Art laughed and, for a moment, resembled a kindly, harmless old man - which he clearly wasn't. He eyed the dent in a fat Buddha statue, where the bullet had struck after passing through Jim's upper arm.

Jim felt more words were necessary and spoke again. "Seems like you just popped in and saved my life," he observed.

"Seems like," agreed Art. "And as long as that's the end of the voices in my head, I'll probably be fine."

"Can we talk?" said Jim.

"It's good to toke," chuckled Dave.

***

Russell screamed and screamed but no sound emerged. He was trapped in a nightmare; this could not be real. Christopher stared across the bed, sockets become red pits, eyes gone. He was still alive and somehow that was worse. It meant he no longer mattered.

She's taken his fingers too, perhaps his ears would be next. She killed William first. William was the puppy-like one with spots and a nervous twitch. Julie had sliced his balls with a razor, watching him kick and writhe like a pinned insect. She rather took to him so didn't cut his cock off. Instead she stabbed the artery in his groin. They all watched as thick, dark blood glooped out. There was lots of it. Eventually the flow slowed and consciousness drained from her young lover. Then she turned and smiled at Christopher, who had such pretty eyes. He had tried to move his head but couldn't. She held him motionless using only the power of her mind. It was her greatest trick.

When their ordeal ended, she showered and washed away the blood and the jizz. Her mind buzzed with new possibilities. She dressed then slipped quietly out, grabbing as much cash as she could find. Tip-toeing down the stairs, she felt numb. She'd never held more than a single mind in that way before and was exhausted.

Julie stumbled home, aiming to return after a good rest. She turned the voices down and they squealed in alarm. So she let them back in but at a reduced level, glad of the company. As it happened she also let in a small, red-haired man carrying a wooden box. He scowled at her as he scuttled up the stairs.

***

After Art left, Jim pondered the wisdom of letting the old guy take the body away. But it was no longer his problem. He had plenty left.

Most worrying was Art's revelation of the compulsion driving him to kill. His casual expression while relating the account had left Jim and Dave chilled.

Jim had no idea what was going on but as Arthur was gone there wasn't anything more he could do. His saviour seemed to be the kind of man who made up his mind and didn't change it. To have him stay for a mind probing was clearly not an option. Oddly, he had embraced Jim and Dave before departing with Gordon, wrapped in an old sheet, slung over his shoulder. He acted as if this was the most natural thing in the world. He took the gun too.

They sat, dazed, for a while.

Having removed the tape from his wrists, Dave was shaking Mikey in an attempt to rouse him. Jim, upon realising his wound was not going to be taken seriously, stopped whining about it.

There was a knock at the door.

"Parcel," said a voice.

Jim ambled across to the door. Funny day.

The delivery guy had left a box with some strange writing on it. There wasn't even a name or address. As he picked it up, Jim shuddered. An electric shock passed up his arm and across his chest.

"Hey man, what is it?" called Dave.

"A box dude," said Jim, standing there, holding it, puzzled.

"What's in it?"

"Something intriguing," said Jim scrabbling with the lid, oddly unable to stop himself.

"The Box from the Blackness!" cried Mikey suddenly. "It's mine, I saw it first! It's mine!"

He pushed past Dave and seized the box, just as its lid sprang open. Something black and shiny leapt out and clamped onto his face, covering most of it. Recoiling, Dave freaked out and leapt onto the settee, covering his mouth in horror.

Fascinated, Jim also gaped as a black, beetle-like creature set about its gruesome business. It had eight legs like a spider, shiny and in frantic motion. Thick, black hairs dotted with tiny lice poked from under the rear shell but it was the creature's eyes that they would never forget. Multi-lensed and blood-red, they projected an aura worse than intelligence. The thing emitted a buzzing sound from somewhere deep within but its jaws made a clicking, chattering noise as it chewed into Mikey's face.

"What the fuck, what the fuck, what the fuck is *that* man?

Jesus I swear I will never do acid again! Absinthe neither. It's a fucking nightmare!" Dave was clearly upset.

The protective seal broken, the creature loose, it reverted to its base nature. It began devouring Mikey's flesh, partly because Mikey had already annoyed it in his mother's cellar, but mostly because he was there.

Jim and Dave began to back away with Jim having the forethought to grab a few herbal essentials. Then they ran. The creature regarded them briefly, memorising their scent.

***

From his vantage point on the landing above, Joey cursed his luck as Jim and Dave fled. The infallible trick hadn't worked after all.

Fucking typical!

"Where's my car?" wailed Dave as they reached fresh air.

"How should I know? Let's get out of here!" advised Jim, who didn't own a car or care about them much.

***

What could have gone wrong? Joey noticed that, in their haste, they had not shut the door. The flat was about as secure as the Queen's bedroom, if everything he read in the tabloids was true. Joey had no reason to suspect it wasn't.

Gingerly (which was his way of doing everything) Joey crept down the stairs. He could hear a squelching noise from within, a noise similar to his wife squeezing washing through the mangle.

He went to find out what it was, passing his usual border of bad luck to explore the realm of pure stupidity.

***

A little later, when they stopped running, Dave gasped, "that thing is killing him. Shouldn't we, you know, *do* something?"

"Like what?"

They both weighed this up. Jim tried to fill his pipe, but his

shaking hands would not obey.
"Beer then," Dave decided.

Chapter Seventeen

The most beautiful thing we can experience is the mysterious. It is the source of all true art and science.   Alfred Einsbatenn

"What the – ?" was Sheila's reaction on finding Jim and Dave shuffling about on her doorstep. It was growing dark and she was miffed - even more so when she looked into her husband's watery eyes.

"It's OK love. Special dis-pen-say-shunn. I gotta be stoned so I don't kill nobody." He grinned, pushing gently past and into the house, anticipating all complaints like an elephant anticipates a sturdy blade of grass. He'd smoked everything he could find in his pockets, including some pungent furry grey fluff, in an effort to blank out the weirdness sloshing around in his mind. As they meandered towards his place, neither mentioned the beetle thing. They thought about it though, particularly the noise it made. Jim kept mumbling the phrase "serious shit" as he walked.

The forty-something "boys" were in a right old state. Dave had eyes like saucers and a mouth sagging into a stroke-like half-smile, half-grimace. Loitering on the path, Jim's eyes blazed wild and fey; Sheila didn't particularly fancy another encounter with him in yet another weird mood. So much for the end to mid-week binges!

Jim waited on the doorstep, aware he was under critical scrutiny. He slumped against the wall then sprang back as if electrified.

"Ow!" he said, hoping for sympathy and possibly toast.

"Jim got shot. Look!" enthused Dave, wrapping his arms around his wife and rubbing his nose lovingly into her hair, like a gleeful puppy.

"Oh bugger, let's hear it them!" Sheila relented, as she extracted something grey and gloopy from behind her ear. "The kettle's just boiled. Did you say 'shot'?"

Jim stepped inside and carefully removed his jacket to reveal a bloodstained shirt, criss-crossed by brown parcel tape.

"I fixed it," indicated Dave, "but it was touch and go." He disappeared into the kitchen in search of munchies leaving Jim still in the hallway, feeling awkward.

"What happened?" Sheila's voice was even, cautious, worried.

"It's complicated," said Jim.

"Does it involve the car?" she asked, looking for any signs of it as shut the door behind them.

"What? No, don't think so," said Jim.

"Good. Go on in then. And let me take a look at that arm."

In the front room, Jim slowly revealed the disappointingly small wound. He presented it from a variety of angles but it failed to impress, even when he triumphantly discovered the exit hole, initially mistaken for a mole.

"Ha, a scratch," said Sheila. "I should have known! Shot my arse!" Sheila produced two deliberately small sticking plasters and one of Dave's t-shirts and handed them over.

Jim smiled then told her as much as he felt he could.

***

After temporarily parking Gordon's body in a shadowy corner, Arthur found and broke open the video cassette containing the records of a hectic day. Or at least it *would* have done had the camera been working. He'd traced the cable to the under-stairs cupboard on the ground floor and, forcing the lock, was tempted to leave the body there. It was risky to smuggle it out but, on the other hand, leaving it would be one loose end too many. Dead people had a way of making their presence felt.

He sat for a moment, hunched in the darkness of the cupboard, absorbing the rhythm of the building. Fortunately, all was quiet with only the occasional creak, clunk and muffled scream. Arthur listened intently but heard nothing more.

Dumped on the floor, wrapped in one of Jim's grubby sheets, Gordon was still an obvious corpse. Art regarded him thoughtfully. Automatically, he had invisibly pocketed one of Mikey's knives. When neither Jim nor Dave were watching, he had dragged it along Mikey's moist, mumbling lip.

Arthur was used to cleaning up after himself – a vital skill in his former profession. Having thrown caution to the winds earlier, he found he could think clearly once again. The voices had departed, leaving him at peace. Whatever it meant, he didn't intend the killing to be traced back to him. If dead Gordon *was* found, it seemed a good idea that the light of suspicion would fall on hapless Mikey. The Police, he knew, liked easy answers and Mikey's DNA on a knife found alongside the body would give them an easy result. It wasn't quite in the Speed Camera scale of easy, but should suffice.

There was a time he'd have taken more drastic action and performed a full clean-up but those days were gone. He had enough to do.

Dead things always weighed far more than their live counterparts and Gordon's passion for developing his body wasn't helping. Arthur knew he must take steps or risk a hernia, hence he'd stolen Dave's keys.

Leaving the sanctuary of the cupboard, he jammed open the main door and went outside. He pushed the button on the key fob and waited to see which car would respond. A green Astra estate flashed at him.

***

Julie went straight to bed but lay there unable to sleep. The voices had changed tack, almost as if they sensed she was the stronger. They no longer urged her to kill. That could come later, they whispered. First, she must be helped, made better. What an amazing talent she had, they cooed. Soon she would no longer feel tired and nobody would look at her in that frightful way again.

It was exciting to hear.

Lying under a thin blanket in her bedsit, the electric fire releasing its puny orange glow without warmth. Julie Hutchinson shivered and talked to the voices.

And they spoke back.

***

Beans, chips, and *somethingburger* greeted Dave and Jim, who gratefully sat down. They ate in silence, plates on their knees, Dave still grinning, his wife and best buddy both tense. The background music was something dreadful chosen deliberately by Sheila. She noted with satisfaction that neither of them complained.

"If you put any more ketchup on those chips, it'll be chip soup," she observed as Dave sprayed tomato sauce everywhere. He laughed and scooped some off his jeans with a finger. A quick doobie always improved his appetite and today it was, Dave explained (in more detail than was strictly necessary), vital for everyone's health. Sheila wondered if he was angling for an argument. They talked for a while, much of it apparent nonsense.

It was almost a relief when, with a jangle and a gentle thud, the car keys landed on the mat. Sheila got up to look through the frosted glass of the front door but saw nobody.

"Care to explain?" She called, crouching to peer through the letter box. She returned to the table and dropped the keys on it rather noisily.

"Well?"

Jim and Dave shrugged in unison. Despite her anger, Sheila smothered a smile. *Those two!* She had heard some bizarre, drug-fuelled garbage in the past but nothing like the scary gibberish they had been spouting this evening. She'd made them stop temporarily while they ate but would have the rest later.

She could never stay mad at Dave for long but even so was disappointed how quickly he'd discarded the promise to keep his head straight for a few days.

When everything eat-able was history, Jim and Dave sat on the sofa like naughty school boys. Dave sprawled and burped.

"Thanks for that, I really appreciate it," said Jim.

"You certainly seemed hungry!" Sheila replied.

"Sorry, yes I guess I was. Look, I know it's a lot to ask but do you mind if I stay here tonight? The flat's a bit, well, rough."

"You can stay on one condition."

"OK."

"Tell me - properly this time - what is going on."

"Oh. I thought we already did."

They were hiding something and Sheila was duty-bound to discover it. "And I mean everything. If possible without all the rubbish about madmen with knives, nutters with guns and journeys in your head!"

"That might be difficult," Jim winced.

"Don't mention the beetle dude!" chipped in Dave.

"Beetle?" She cleared her throat in what she hoped was an authoritative fashion. "Beetle then. I want to know," she said. "Please don't fob me off with 'it's complicated'. Preston's a scary place today and you're not helping."

"I could show you," said Jim. "At least I think I can. Demonstrate, like."

There was no way she was gong to like his suggestion.

"How do you mean, show me? Exactly?"

"If I can't then I am properly broken."

"Oh no, let me guess... you want to go inside my head? Like, hypnotism? Then I bark like a dog, do Elvis impressions?"

"No, I mean, yes – a bit like hypnotism. Sort of."

"Since when did you know how to hypnotise somebody?"

"It's a recent thing."

"I bet."

"Dave'll be right here," offered Jim with a smile. "Votch dee votch!" Without waiting, he took hold of Dave's wrist and half-heartedly swung it (Jim had no watch of his own, having decided that if you never know the time you can never be bound by it. He embellished this concept whenever he arrived late for a meeting, which is to say at every meeting). Dave watched his arm with cheerful curiosity. It looked familiar.

Sheila swore 'no way' and meant to get up and make a brew. Maybe she'd shoo them into the conservatory to get baked because of the overwhelming urge to leave it all until tomorrow. The eternal safety mechanism - mind-numbing telly - was calling. a better idea for now. She picked up the TV Guide and noted an imminent opportunity to observe unknown celebrities frolicking and probably copulating. Entertainment was improving all the time, she mouthed as Dave's digital watch swung back and forth.

Against her better judgement, Sheila sank back down again in her chair and *votched dee votch*.

"It won't work you know," she said 20 minutes later.

Sheila's brain had been a revelation. The mystery that is woman! Too right! *No wonder we don't understand them.*

Afterwards, Jim began to crow how he was getting the hang of this mind-reading business. All he needed now was a scarf and an enigmatic expression and he'd be 'Madame Jim, see all, tell a little bit'. Jim believed he was suddenly blessed with wisdom.

Sheila had been a pretty thing when viewed from the window in a make-believe space station in a virtual attic somewhere in Jim's vast and half-cooked mind. He had transmitted the House program and waited as it enveloped her data-store, taking a form appropriate to the structures it encountered. Speaking the remaining commands with bullish confidence, he waited to Enter.

In no time at all, Jim stood outside a cottage, ringed in flowers and shrubs framed in a painted white fence. A bent oak tree stood in one corner, draped in ivy and with a curious scar in its side. Meadows of corn and rapeseed stretched in all directions with the promise of woods and rolling hills sketched in the background.

The detail was extraordinary and Jim felt reluctant to intrude.

He knocked and the door opened into a kitchen-come-dining room. A few modern appliances managed to blend in naturally and Jim had to crouch under the polished wooden beams supporting the roof. There were stairs but didn't go up. He'd spotted what he came to find - a girly purple computer, an Apple Mac on the writing desk. A window was open and a fresh breeze blew birdsong into the room.

He began to type at the computer but it spoke to him.

When he opened his eyes and Sheila told him it wouldn't work, he was quiet and strangely humble. She flicked on the telly and went to make a cup of tea. Jim followed, thoughtfully.

Dave was oblivious and remained seated, smirking at his watch.

In a moment of fear, Sheila thought it might be Friday all over again. She was alone and Jim was closing in. Seeing her expression, he backed off and sat at the breakfast bar, his head hung low.

"Please don't be afraid," he said. "I only want to ask you a question."

Unexpectedly short of breath, she dropped a tea bag into a cup and watched him. There was a subtle change in his manner. His shoulders sagged. His body language hinted this was the gentler Jim, the one she liked and trusted. But would he change again?

"What is it?" the tension still evident in her voice and body.

"Who is Quentin?" said Jim.

She went pale and almost knocked the kettle over in sudden bout of clumsiness.

"Why do you ask that? Not even Dave -"

"I *was* able to look into your mind after all," Jim said quietly.

She said nothing.

"I'm not trying to dig out your secrets, but he's there's something of him in there. I didn't go looking, he was just there.

Sorry, not my business."

For a long time she said nothing. The kettle began to boil and hot steam turned the windows from black to sullen grey. She poured boiling water into the cup and stirred it deliberately, not asking if Jim was thirsty. The ritual was completed with a splash of milk. The tea bag gave up its sweet brown reserves with a final squeeze from the spoon.

Women did this kind of thing while thinking, Jim had observed. He waited.

"Quentin was my first sweetheart. I only knew him for three years and then he was killed. His elderly mother drove him into a tree because she was old and pissed. The mother survived but Quentin went through the windscreen. He was in a coma for two months before they turned him off and I sat with him. I guess something like that stays with you." Tears came and Jim wanted to go to her but it didn't feel right. He remained seated and stared at his hands.

"It's all true, we saw someone killed today," he said uselessly.

"But you weren't involved?" Her voice was almost a whisper.

"Indirectly."

"Did you find anything... else?" she asked, sipping her tea.

"Well, you don't want to kill me," he smiled. "And that's rarer than you might think at the moment." He didn't seem finished but nevertheless hesitated.

"Go on," she prompted. He sighed.

"I saw what happened on Friday. God Sheila, I don't know what caused it. All this madness is related though and it's because of something I've done. I don't know if I'm fully in control any more or where this is heading. I can't tell you how sorry I am."

She stopped short of going over to comfort him. He seemed to be in agony and hurting - but she would never forget the look in his eyes that night.

"You won't enter my thoughts again will you?"

"Never," he replied.

Later, Dave and Sheila went to bed leaving Jim in a sleeping bag on the sofa.

He'd found no trace of recently updated code in Sheila's mind. He *had* noticed something commonality with his core libraries - the base programs were of mixed ages. Some were very old, others not so.

There was an obvious truth beyond his grasp, a vital insight that eluded him. He didn't particularly want to stay here in case something iffy happened. But returning home was an even less inviting option - God knew what he'd find there.

Checking into a hotel might have been be an option and Jim even toyed with the mischievous idea of ringing Monica. In the end, he crashed out and churned the day's events over and over as in his mind. As he drifted off, he couldn't shake the feeling of sharks circling.

***

In the dream, Jim was happy, at first, to find himself on dry land. He was a ghost in the House. It had seemed to be *his* House yet, when he looked again, he saw it was a mirror image, a warped version. He heard voices. They were talking about him.

Even straining to hear, he couldn't discern individual words.

He floated around the House but wherever he went, the voices' owners eluded him. Sometimes they broke into raucous laughter and he realised they were toying with him.

In the long hallway, the decoration was lavish and seemingly completed. Portraits hung along the walls - faces that were familiar, yet unfamiliar.

They were all based on his own features!

The paintings watched with a cold and detached air. Their eyes moved if he did. He catalogued the personality he'd named Kevin - the conformist. The spineless Sun reader. Thankfully that part of his life had been short-lived, the neural pathways quickly erased. Then there was Spike, a reflection of biker days, stubbled and with an underlying coolness but also assuredness. Jim shuffled quickly past the portrait of the personality he had labelled Clune. Dressed in black, Clune watched him with malice, dark eyes twinkling and mouth mocking.

Was I ever that bad?

The hall seemed longer than it ever had before. There was a portrait of Angel the writer, Woody the comic, Shrimp the innocent, Silk the lover.... some of these creations had hardly been sketched at all, yet here they were, in a dream but complete.

The Library door was locked but he could not get in. There was movement inside, tables being dragged or bookshelves being pushed. He knew had to get in. He had to.

But as he pushed uselessly, Jim heard the tone of the voices change. They were angry and clamoured for his blood. Desperate, he scratched at the door, his fingers ripping through wood that decayed like old flesh. Maggots writhed between his fingers but the door was impossibly thick. His arms plunged deep into the wood but still he couldn't get through. The maggots began to crawl over him and instead of maggotty faces, they bore his own. Their bodies became black and shiny. Legs sprouted. Black hairs, crawling with lice.

He awoke screaming.

"Jim, Jim, it's alright!" He was on Dave and Sheila's sofa and Sheila was by his side. It was practically light outside already - 05:11, said the video recorder. Thursday morning.

For a moment he didn't recognise her, sweat poured from him, his thick hair covered his face and his hands shook.

"Just a dream," he said as if the words would make it true. She looked doubtful, worried.

"If Dave weren't completely off his face he'd be awake too. He's muttering about beetles in *his* sleep for god's sake! You probably woke the neighbours!" She suddenly became aware of wearing practically nothing: a *very* short t-shirt - actually that was all.

"It's OK, I'm OK. Go back to bed, sorry. Don't worry," Jim reassured. He realised the source of her sudden discomfort, fought hard not to watch her turn and leave, and won. He lay back, knowing as surely as he knew anything that there would be no more sleep.

Within seconds he was snoring.

Chapter Eighteen

We should take care not to make the intellect our god; it has, of course, powerful muscles, but no personality.   Alfred Einsbatenn

When Mikey didn't come home for tea on Wednesday night, his mother began to fret. To add to her anxiety, two ceremonial knives were missing. The boy was going to be in Big Trouble. The coven would be along soon but there was time for a quick zoom around the ethereal plane before they arrived. She scooted Mr Skittles the cat roughly out of the way then descended to the cellar to perform dark rites.

Una Sharples hastily lit scented candles then squatted naked within a chalk circle, concentrating hard. In the silence, an ominous rumbling noise began, as if from some dark netherworld. Baked beans twice in a day always had the same effect!

Raising a generous orange peel buttock, she unleashed an extended, vibrato-laden trump, then sniggered.

She then invoked the magic word, "Cricket", and calm returned. Una was serene, floating. With no time to enjoy the pleasantness, she concentrated on the task.

The technique was a familiar one to witches for centuries. She let her mind drift and seek familiarity. To boost the atmospherics, he candles spluttered and spat, as if a door had been opened and a presence had entered the cellar.

"Do you mind?" she said. "I'm busy."

"Sorry I'm early," said Bill the plumber - and Coven Secretary - "I'll wait upstairs shall I?"

He peered into the gloom and the magnificent bulk of her nakedness, full breasts framed by straggly, ultra-black hair. He reckoned her arse must be freezing and. Bill thought about how he might warm things up.

She dismissed him with a gesture - not easy in near-darkness but Una was well practised in both summoning and dismissal.

There was a further brief pause until Bill shut the door, then she closed her eyes and let her scrying mind range outwards.

"Mikey?" she called.

No answer.

"MIKEY!"

Again nothing.

She was puzzled. She couldn't feel Mikey anywhere, couldn't sense him at all. The surrounding area was a smoky map with grey buildings dimly outlined. Flickering shapes passed quickly by - the auras of fellow citizens. But no Mikey.

Una modified her search, drawing on those with the vision in order to help boost her own sight. Within a few miles, amongst the flashes of talent, she saw a brilliant new light. It was a pattern familiar from previous searches but something had changed. Wishing there was time to explore, Una pushed on. Mikey had to be located.

Mikey had a latent talent and would be strong when his time came. My little battery, Una thought fondly. She hoped to one day harness the power for the summoning of a Great Power. That was Mikey's destiny, she had decided. Well, that or a life emptying dustbins.

Una searched on.

Mikey was usually easy to find. This was odd.

Just once, when nearing the limits of her strength, Una thought she felt something. It might have been Mikey but it seemed unlikely. It was far away, it was afraid, then it was gone.

Exhausted, she gave up.

Putting on her slacks, slippers and purple sweater, Una trundled up the stairs to the kitchen, defeated. Bill the plumber had been joined by a couple of trainee witches, nurtured on Buffy.

Bill, a man in his late fifties, wore an Adidas t-shirt, jeans and a flat cap. The girls wore black and had their hair dyed black; they carried spell books decorated with runes copied from the Lord of the Rings. Inside, Una knew for certain, would be recipes for newt-eye soup and pumpkin pie.

Una signed inwardly and pretended to be pleased. In truth, she felt in no mood for the night's meeting but her responsibilities could not be ignored. She donned a mystical pendant (carboot sale, two quid) - the sign that dark explorations would shortly commence.

A poor turnout.

Several key figures were missing: Mr Timpson the insurance salesman, Miss Schumann the barmaid and, of course, Mikey. Joey hadn't turned up either and Una was wondering how he'd got on with the Grimoire Box.

Perhaps he'd opened it himself.

She smiled at the thought and the effect wasn't pleasant.

The meeting began with tea and fairy cakes (home made). Una firmly believed there was no problem that couldn't, eventually, be solved by the correct application of cake.

Much later, when they had all gone home, Una retired to bed with some cocoa and a good Catherine Cookson. If Mikey weren't home by morning, there'd be Hell to pay.

By the following morning there was still no sign of him.

That boy is for it, she decided as she brushed her teeth. A noise, from downstairs, disturbed her just before she struck blood. She spat out the foam and dashed down in her dressing gown to investigate.

In the cellar, something slithered.

She opened the door and flicked on the light - a fluorescent strip light that exposed every dark corner and shadowy crack.

Mostly, the walls were whitewashed and slightly cobwebby. Tins of paint (appropriated by Bill) were stored at one end of the cellar along with chunks of an old motorbike covered in a sheet. The coal-hole entrance had been jammed shut with a shovel from the inside and various tools were strewn across an old workbench. Apart from the chalk circle, stacks of strangely labelled boxes, and a small altar with candles on it, there was nothing remarkable down there. It was the least creepy basement you ever saw.

Until the lights went out.

There, cowering in a corner, amidst some of the frightful Curse Boxes, was Joey Barker. He was holding a knife - one of *The Knives!* He clutched it tightly, waved it in front of him in an effort to ward off... the *grimoire*. The very same creature Joey had formerly requested.

She was surrounded by idiots!

She clicked her finger and the beetle shimmered and disappeared.

Joey sank in relief but it was temporary. His mind was breaking up. The voices had pushed too long and too hard. As a result, something squishy had fractured deep in his brain. They were still screaming but his fear held him immobile.

KILL KILL KILL!!! demanded the voices.

He trembled with fear, his eyes streamed with tears and his mouth alternated between helpless laughter and blubbing.

He wet himself. Hadn't done that since he was a kid. Well, a teenager anyway.

"Where did you get that knife?" Una Sharples demanded in quiet fury as she silently approached, her pink, fluffy slippers flapping gently.

Joey heard every syllable like a serrated knife dragged across the heart.

"I.... I......I went back to see what had happened."

"Went back WHERE?"

"Avenham Flats, first floor, flat 1" Joey said flatly.

"WHY did you go there?"

"To take the beetle, take it... to him what must be killed."

"WHO is that?"

"I don't know his name."

"HOW did you find him?"
"I was guided by the voices."
"WHAT are the voices?"
"They speak to me. They tell me to kill the one with long-hair but I needed help. But the magic didn't work. I don't know why. I'll tell you this much - he's a lucky bastard. I went inside - the door was open – and the beetle was loose. It was biting this guy's face. Una, I think it was Mikey's face. I tried to get it off. I grabbed the knife and it seemed afraid, I mean, no, it attacked me. I fought and I -"
"STOP!"
Joey stopped. He had been trying to speak without pause, having watched Una at work on others in the past. Survival instincts took over.

If his luck held she would not know.

Naturally, it didn't.

"You let Mikey die? You wanted that thing and it killed Mikey. Then you ran away?!?!?!"

Joey collapsed. Una had a way with words, especially hard ones. Straining against the Chief Witch and the voices ripping his mind apart was too much. In Joey's unfortunate sandy head, something snapped.

Una didn't care. She understood everything. *Possessed.* Something was within Joey, warping his tiny mind. He'd lost the box too – all those costly curses wasted. It was galling.

That Joey's cowardice had led him to desert Mikey was unforgivable and Una was not a forgiving woman at the best of times. Doubtful she could achieve anything more from him, nevertheless she tried.

***

The morning drifted by at a snail's pace from Monica's perspective. They had a few days together at Tim's house, their headquarters while Tim honed his act in Blackpool, tweaked it until it could make his name and their fortune.

The house had belonged to Tim's parents but he'd inherited it after they unexpectedly perished in a waterskiing accident near Pilling. Monica couldn't recall the details.

She glanced at her watch then at the clock on the mantelpiece and the one on the wall, each with mounting frustration. Where *was* he? It had been hours and she now felt sure they'd locked him up.

The problem was he wouldn't leave well alone. He'd insisted on going to the police and telling them all about Mark Housman and the show.

She knew it was a mistake. Nothing could be done anyway and it would just confuse things. Monica hated *complications*. Even the word reminded her of Jim.

Jim! That impossible man! Her first love.

Finally the car rolled up the drive, then keys rattled in the front door, keys were dumped on the telephone table. Tim kicked off his shoes to keep the carpets nice and clean.

"You took long enough," she accused.

"Yeah, I thought it might be better to go down to Preston instead. It's only half an hour down the motorway - and better to report it there than here."

"What did they say?"

"They want me to come back tomorrow. I think they believed me or at least partly."

"Really?"

"I showed them some stuff."

"Was that such a good idea? I mean, walking into a police station and whipping out a pack of cards."

"Monica, love, all those people died. A guy who came to my show killed them and I knew he was dangerous."

"You *thought* he was, there's a big difference."

"If I'm going to do well at this, I have to start it right. I need to be able to turn it on reliably."

"What did you do - something from the show?"

"The Imaginary Animal – our first success."

In spite of herself, she was interested. "What did you get? What showed up?"

Tim grinned his cheekiest grin. "Mostly the usual. One of the bobbies, a bit of a twat, had an imaginary ET as a pet!"

"Like in the film?"

Yeah. He seemed to believe it lived in his shed!"

"Did he have a big taser?"

"I'm afraid he did. An enormous one, plus a tonfa and some of that delightful gas they have. What's its name?"

"Mustard gas? Marsh gas? Who cares!"

"This bright spark had some throwing stars and enjoys dog fights. He would like to be in films." Tim shook his head.

"Thank heavens for law and order eh?" she said.

"The best option from a list of a single choice."

"Look, let's get past this. You know my feelings. The guy is dead, he wouldn't have done any further harm!"

"I had to do something..." Tim said, distantly.

"Did you mention Jim?" she asked after a while.

"Well, I had to tell them about the drawing."

"And?"

"You should give him a ring. I think they're going to want to see it."

She groaned. It didn't require ESP to know this wouldn't be the end of it. Having further contact with Jim was foolish, risky and maybe downright crazy. Nevertheless, she picked up the phone and dialled the number from memory. Tim observed this but refrained from comment.

"Nobody home; sounds like his answer machine is off or bust," she said. "I'll try later."

"I think the police will want his address when I go to see them in the morning. The drawing would prove what I said - if he's still got it. It would get us a lot of positive news coverage too. After all, *everyone's* in Preston picking over the horror at the moment."

"Good point!"

"If Channel 4 *do* come on Saturday it'll help if the show's a sell-out. A news item might make that happen, see? And after that there's nothing to stop us babe. You and me together."

"I suppose," she nodded. "Unfortunately, Jim isn't a fan of the police. I wish we could have left him out of this."

"Sorry, I just don't see how that would have been possible."

Tim was more than a little pleased with himself. Somehow Jim had got under his skin - and they had not even met! If he could toss a soupçon of discomfort in Jim's path, all well and good. Maybe he'd blow his top and get arrested. Now he remembered, Monica had mentioned that he was a weirdo who had trouble with authority.

What a pity!

***

They dragged the body out of the river and dropped it, none too gently, on the bank. The diver crawled onto the grass nearby and put his hand in some dog shit.

"Just like the bloody river," he groaned under his mask.

Curious coppers crowded round the body, starkly exposed in the morning light. A nightmare face. Whoever owned it had apparently ripped it apart with his bare hands.

"Cause of death?" asked Inspector Hartley.

"Hard to say," said Doctor Phlox. It was what he always said. He sucked a boiled sweet and pretending to be thinking.

Hartley - JR as they predictably called him, grew irritable.

"Come on man, don't piss about. I've a lot on, in case you're wondering!" he snapped.

"He either drowned, died of fright or died because he pulled his face off. Take your pick. Sometime late yesterday evening would be my guess and I don't *think* he drowned. We're lucky he didn't float away. Got caught up on some tree branches under the bridge."

"Fright, did you say?"

"Look at his hands!"

The corpse's fingers were claws frozen in a moment of terror; the unfortunate youth's flesh and blood clinging to the nails in pale clumps. Both eyes remained, staring. They were impossibly large, globular and awful. The lids and surrounding flesh had been torn away so they merely rested loose in sockets like eggs in a bloody nest.

The press would have a field day. *Another* field day.

Hartley's mood plummeted. He shook his head in an attempt to dispel yet another pounding headache.

He hated this part of the job. Recently he had begun to hate more and more parts but he'd assumed yesterday would be the peak of the madness. Bizarrely, the furore continued.

In a few short hours, the hacks had progressed to speculation about Housman's childhood, inevitably. Pictures of his school were produced, interviews with teachers, none of whom liked him. It was all bollocks, thought JR. Worse, it seemed to glorify the insanity and guarantee immortality to future madmen. Why could none of them see the dangers? The story would run and run.

The vultures of the media had circled round all of yesterday; he shuddered to think how they'd react to today's offering (any connection? he mused, idly). Hartley looked at his watch and winced. Only five to ten.

"OK, bag him. I want to know who he is, what killed him and when!"

It was Thursday morning of a long day.

***

Una Sharples had found something - the location of the second knife stolen by Mikey, Satan rest him. This she had learned thanks to an invisible connection with the twin in Joey's lifeless hands.

He lay curled before her, blood running from both ears and

staining the cellar floor.

It was difficult to find objects. People, if you knew them, were relatively easy – provided they were alive. Una knew searching for the Knife would have left her zonked and so had used Joey's life-force instead. She completed her work remaining largely unaffected but unfortunately the same could not be said of Joey who was clearly out of the game. Deceased in the best Norwegian Blue tradition. She shrugged.

Weakling! Bill will have to excavate another flag in the cellar. Soon they'd need storage space in the attic. Or a mincer.

Una set out to find the second Knife of Malvolian, taking with her one of the small, unadorned boxes from high on a dusty shelf.

***

Meanwhile, Joey's wife whistled in anticipation of good fortune. Her husband had not returned home overnight and she couldn't have been happier if someone had shot the Queen and buggered the Prime Minister with a rabid corn on the cob. She got ready for work at her leisure, played the radio loud and put on her best blouse and a splash of mascara.

She had known her luck would change one day.

It had been worth putting up with an occasional blown fuse.

***

Heading out of town via the park and then the old tram road, Una was increasingly sweaty and annoyed. It was further than she'd realised - but distances were never straightforward on the ethereal plane.

Feeling the lure of the Knife's energy, she was way beyond her familiar stomping grounds. Good grief, were these actual *fields*? Una thought the last green space around Preston had long since been built on. All the outlying areas had countless Springfield Meadows, Buttercup Groves and Highfield estates - named in memory of the real thing, long-since despatched by JCBs and unchecked human expansion.

Una's mind was wandering. She imagined turning councillors into toads and was so intent on the fantasy that she failed to watch where she was walking. Something squelched underfoot. A foul mess concealed in the grass left a thick brown stain on her shoes.

She was not prepared for the filth. There was mud and nettles and everything!

Una had not worn the right shoes.

How could the Knife be out here?

She made up her mind quickly. It was time for a field trip. Time to shake a bare bottom at the vocal, Christian minority of this no-mote-in-*my*-eye town. Yes, bloody town! Una was getting more and more angry and she scowled at a woodpecker, tapping high in a tree. It tapped on regardless but shuffled around the trunk a bit, out of her line of sight.

"I won't hurt you – but one day a digger will take your home!" she predicted. She would return later for the Knife, make a night of it.

She worked better in the dark.

***

A blade descending at great speed was Jim's rude awakening.

"Sorrrrreeeeeeeeeeee," shouted Dave, stabbing the cushion that his pal's bonce had narrowly vacated.

"Jeez man, get a joint," yelped Jim. "That scared the living shit out of me."

Dave lunged.

"You've got to help me stop this, I can't control it!"

Jim wrestled him to the floor and cast the plastic knife aside.

"I reckon I know what to do."

"Really? Better do it quick! I only just managed to pick that particular knife. And even that would have taken your eye out."

"Where's Sheila?"

"Gone to work. She's on earlies."

"Right, well, if I let you go, will you roll a joint and I'll put on the toast?. I'll butter it myself if you don't mind!"

"Um," said Dave.

Chapter Nineteen

The secret to creativity is knowing how to hide your sources.   Alfred Einsbatenn

"Right. Before we do anything today we're going to sort this thing," said Jim, confidently munching toast.

Dave had rung in sick to a distinctly frosty reception. Inspired, he claimed to be stressed and depressed after the terrible killing of what's-her-name-the-typist. When his boss's voice softened in response, he knew he was home and dry. As Jim polished off another slice, he checked his email to discover yet another instalment from the wife of President Obongo (the poor lass could ONLY TYPE IN UPPER CASE) desiring discuss an exciting financial opportunity IN CHRIST.

"Bloody spam," he moaned. "Every fecking one. And how much Viagra does a guy need anyway? Arseholes!" He switched off the laptop in disgust.

"You should close it properly, this isn't the movies you know," lectured Jim snootily. "By the way, I used it last night to type something up. I've devised a way to take external programs into my head." The glee in his voice was lost on Dave however. Well aware of Jim's legendary sensitivity, he offered a variety of clues that included groaning, holding his head, rocking backward and forwards, drooling and shaking visibly.

Jim gazed blankly. "It's quite clever," he added.

Dave raised bloodshot eyes.

"That's nice. Look, I'm really struggling to keep my head together. The smokes aren't working any more. I'm gonna have to see a doctor or a shrink or something. The voices are so loud it's like they're physically in the room. It's well creepy."

"I can do this," said Jim. "What could possibly go wrong!"

"Erm..." said Dave.

They sat on the front room rug, Jim leaning against the Sofa,

Dave with his back to the easy chair. When the vibe was right, Jim spoke the magic incantation:

"Let's go for it!"

"You sure about this?"

"How hard can it be?" grinned Jim.

Facing his best friend and smoking his second fatty of the morning, Dave was having second thoughts. "How you gonna do it? Is it hypnotism or... brain washing?" He tried to laugh it off but the fear was obvious.

"It's all the same really," said Jim. "Hypnotism sounds safer so let's go with that. Brace yourself dude! The answer's here I know it!"

He removed a floppy disk from Dave's laptop and, clutching it in his right hand, took a deep breath and closed his eyes.

The House stood in the distance, empty and vaguely ominous. The garden was overgrown, unkempt; the grass was long, the gravel path starting to fill with weeds. Not wanting to become side-tracked over the puzzle, Jim recalled the new command sequence to take him directly into the Attic - to his fabulous virtual Communications Centre. In what appeared to be his hand was a floppy disk, a perfect rendering of the one plucked from Dave's laptop. Smugly, he beamed in.

Using this abbreviated entry, Jim was able to omit realism from the underlying structure. But as the bulk of the processing would involve Dave's mind, Jim figured a few shortcuts would be OK. An unexpected consequence was that he failed to notice that his own front door was unlocked.

Entering another mind was something he had never really planned for and it freaked him out that it worked. And Jim had a higher freaking out tolerance than most. He had not, however, discovered any great truths so far.

He had stayed up late to tweak the House program, building in some extra features and a common interface. In future, he should be able to access any selected data are directly. He might not need to go in all.

Jim named this updated version 'RemoteHouse' and had already sketched out several subroutines that made swell with pride. Swelling with pride was something he often suffered from in the morning, before the day withered his enthusiasm.

RemoteHouse should enable direct communication with any mind, avoiding further encounters with malevolent personalities.

Seated in his favourite red chair, he slotted the disk into Thunderbird 5's computer and transmitted the modified program over to Dave. He typed the command on his system keyboard and whooped in delight when Dave's computer responded.

It was working! And from a simple bi-directional command-line interface. He could take everything from the safety of his own mind!

On-screen, the results from Jim's commands scrolled as plain text. It wasn't yet possible to receive graphical images across the link due to bandwidth issues as yet unresolved. This was relatively unimportant so Jim allocated the problem a low priority, remembering to include a wakeup message should an easy solution be found. Then he forgot all about it.

Whistling to himself, he typed:
LISTACTPROC,ORDER;TIMESLICE:ALL

The screen expanded, filling with line upon line of the active processes in Dave's brain. Many had names that gave no hint to their purpose but were probably concerned with motor functions, interpretation of the data from the senses, automatic body monitoring systems and so on. These, Jim noted, had a common format and he decided to display them in different colours, to make it easier to identify higher brain activities. He was amazed at how many were running in his best pal.

Once all the madness died down and he had some time, Jim resolved to explore each and every program. Just as soon as he found or wrote a decompiler!

Imagine debugging the core programs of thought itself!

Having poked around a few computers in his time, not even Microsoft's bloated Operating Systems had a fraction of the processes now deemed to be Dave's higher functions. Jim supposed this applied to everyone else too.

"Fascinating," he muttered, gradually applying more and more colour filters until the picture became clear.

He sorted the output in various ways, looking for a pattern, until he realised the functions he was filtering appeared to be stored within a common folder structure. He began to list the contents of the folder, instructing his command processor to identify the most commonly used programs.

There were still thousands but within the top ten non-essential tasks, he found what he wanted:

FRIENDSHIP "JIM,LONGHISTORY,OLDPALS"
VOICES "KILL JIM"
TEMPERAMENT "SOFTIE,HIPPY,MAKELOVENOTWAR"
LUST "CHICK ON BREAKFAST TELLY"
REMEMBER "LIGHTER FLUID"
MINDPHASE "STONEDATBREAKFAST"
PONDER "WHAT GOING ON?"
INSPIRATION "MAKE PIZZA WITH SPECIAL BUTTER AND ZONK SHEILA'S MUM"
SENSEDATA &INSPIRATION.VAR1 "SHEILA WOULD KILL ME BUT..."

Jim stored the list in a temporary array.

Dave's mind was fascinating, despite or perhaps because of the banality of the bulk of the instructions whizzing through it. There were a few truly inexplicable entries such as

WORRY "BOHEMIAN GROVE SECURITY LEAK"
and
GOODMOOD "DNA PATCH POTENTIALLY POSSIBLE"

accompanied by nuggets such as

INVESTIGATE "CAN I LEARN MINDCONTROLSTUFF TOO?"

and

TEMPORALEXPLORATION "QUANTUMFACTOR OF MULTIPLE DIMENSION AND TIMELINES?"

Jim could have spent ages nosing about but he was keen to begin examining the processes running in his own brain, applying the new filters and sort routines. He was sure he was on to something big. Something that would open everything up, including solving his own problems. He felt euphoric.

But first, Dave's voices.

He located the compiled version of the VOICES program then searched for the source - the readable copy. He didn't find it anywhere. Nor could he find a decompiler. The code remained tantalisingly unreadable. Why?

Was he trying to see the programs of God?

If only he had access to one of those clever kids from film and TV who, after only a couple of attempts, tapped a couple of keys to hack into the Pentagon, locate Satan's PO Box or reprogram an alien computer. These gifted youngsters would inevitably be aided by a graphical interface complete with friendly icons such as 'Launch Nukes' or 'Alien Brain, click yes to Destroy'.

Copying VOICES over onto his own internal system was easy enough. Then, before he instructed Dave's OS to wipe it forever, he wondered if there might be another VOICES program elsewhere in Dave's head.

This was a fortunate piece of intuition, as it happens, because there was indeed another version of Voices. It was found in a library (Folder: BeliefSystems001) that was also active and apparently in use.

In a leap of comprehension, he understood that the file system of the mind had its own hierarchy - the datafiles were concatenated into a specific search order. For reasons unknown, the library containing the active VOICES program sat at the top of the pecking order. Instinctively this felt wrong. It meant any program placed there would be chosen for execution before another with the same name elsewhere.

Hmmmm!

Jim peered closely at the folder's contents and saw it had many programs: (Folder: Aesir001) RELIGIONDRIVE, BELIEFVAR1, CONTROLMECHANISM, CLOUDFACTOR, TIMEOUTS, SUBMISSION, HOUSEKEEPING, ENQUIRY, INVESTIGATE, CREATIVITY and so on. There were screens of them.

Jim stored the names to his floppy disk, reeling at the possible implications. He also took note of the sloppy structure - there was data mixed in with the programs in this library. Ugh, nasty.

Who wrote these?
Who installed them?
Does everyone have them?
Are they identical in everyone?
How do they differ from the originals?
Who wrote them?
Why?
WHY???

He sent deletion commands for the active VOICES program - from the library, from real storage and from buffered storage *(aha, nearly missed that one!)*. Confident it was purged irrevocably from Dave's head, he wondered how it was possible to change the order of library concatenation.

LISTCONCAT;ACTPROC,ALLSORT,* he ventured. It produced a list of meaningless names, none of which helped.

He tried a different tack:
LISTACTPROCSOURCE,&TOP10FROMTEMPSTORE,SOUR CECOMMAND,*

He grinned at the response. Bingo!

There was, he saw, a simple text file in the very root area of the brain containing the (massive) list of program source libraries, in order.

Jim had an idea.

EDIT;ROOTSOURCEFILE&&JUSTFOUND,COMMENT:OUT, SOURCELIB:AesirSIR001

The command signalled OK[1].

Curious name for the folder - Aesir, mused Jim watching his command execute successfully. To verify, he re-listed the file. His changes had been implemented and had been saved. In theory, this should fix Dave. Might a reboot be required? Nah, he reasoned. Only primitive computers required a reboot to bring in changes.

Jim was unsure about leaving the original, base version of the Voices program. Eventually, he figured that, since Dave had shown no desire for murder before Friday, he could safely leave it alone.

He wasn't quite finished and buzzed with excitement. So much was unravelling that he failed to notice a red light on the control panel, flashing insistently. Nor did he hear the sound of a door opening in the House downstairs.

Hunched over the terminal, Jim was in wonderland. He performed a quick search of archive copies of the key root file and these he edited in the same way. Jim reckoned that if the file were ever lost - perhaps due to loss of brain cells or synaptic pathways, a previous generation would surely be retrieved by regenerative background tasks.

It's how I would have done it. he chuckled to himself, beginning to radiate his trademark superiority.

Jim was sure his amendments would make Dave as good as new - better, probably. By deleting the active VOICES program completely and removing access to the weird 'Aesir' library it came from, not only would Dave's tormenting VOICES be

---

[1] Fortunately, the background timer command #BX1003ATP had run an hour earlier and was not scheduled to run again for another 23 hours. Until then it would not log the removal of access to the Aesir001 folder and go on to trigger a seemingly ancient, harmless-looking program in a concealed library. It was understandable that Jim would overlook this but far from good.

silenced, any related programs should be locked out too. It made sense that anyone who installed something as nasty as VOICES could be up to no good.

Briefly he wondered if he'd overstepped the boundaries in commenting out an entire library and, as a precaution, knocked up a quick JIMUNDO program. He sent it over with all his old arrogance, making it, voice-activated for speed. It would regress the changes in an instant (but without recovering VOICES!).

He was about to take example copies of a selection of programs when something happened.

Something unpleasant.

All the lights in Thunderbird 5 went out.

"Mate, I think you've done it!" cried Dave opening his eyes. "I can't hear them any more." He beamed in relief and gratitude.

Jim didn't move.

"Jim, wakey wakey!" said Dave shaking him.

Nothing.

No reaction.

His best buddy was deeply unconscious and remained that way despite Dave's best efforts.

Chapter Twenty

There is only one admirable form of the imagination: the imagination that is so intense that it creates a new reality, that it makes things happen.   Shaun O'Faun

Thursday floated by for Julie Hutchinson like a pleasant dream or a promise that a wonderful life was possible. When she finally got out of bed she was ravenous. Wearing just a shirt, her skinny legs pale and bruised, she ambled into the kitchen. Her cupboard did not inspire but she scraped together a breakfast of beans on stale toast, and hot tea.

The voices had merged overnight. They now spoke in a single voice - a warm and friendly Voice laden with chocolate and honey. It wanted only the best for her, it claimed in tones soft and female. Its updated instructions were clear enough.

For a while, Julie curled up on her threadbare settee quietly, listening. The Voice continued to inform her of wondrous things, occasionally checking she understood. Julie nodded at each prompt, beaming like a dog offered a ball. She began to understand her talent after so many years. Might her life, at last, make sense?

The Voice ended by asking permission to demonstrate an amazing trick.

"Yes please!" she said aloud, although that was not necessary.

Before her eyes, the flat became a luxury flat resembling some of the hotel rooms she liked best. Her new place came with a lovely mirror in a gold frame and a four poster bed with crisp, clean sheets. A room-domiating television perched on a gleaming chrome corner unit. Behind it stood a person-high vase of flowers - she could actually smell them. Bright red roses, orange chrysanthemums and yellow daffodils. And her bathroom was now blessed with colourful baskets of individually wrapped toiletries and packets of shampoo and soap, of the exact type she always packed into her bag. The prospect of living in a place that looked like this made her euphoric.

TREAT IT AS REAL. LIFT THAT ASHTRAY. NO, NOT WITH YOUR HANDS. SEE IT FLOAT UPWARDS. YOUR FUTURE AWAITS.

Julie didn't quite understand but squinted at the ashtray. Briefly, the vision shimmered, becoming her vile and slimy ashtray on her horrible table again.

BE STRONG CHILD. CONCENTRATE ON YOUR NEW SKILLS. LOOK AGAIN.

She tried harder. This was a gift she would never surrender.

"It's all back!"

OF COURSE. NOW IMAGINE THE FORCES UNDER THE ASHTRAY. PUSH IT UPWARDS. AS HARD AS YOU CAN!

Julie mentally pushed the ashtray. She imagined it going upwards in response. She gritted her teeth and willed it harder.

The ashtray juddered and she gasped with a sudden headache. Then it shot upwards like a missile, hitting the ceiling so hard it stayed there embedded in the plaster.

FUCK ME! commented the Voice.

Julie reworked the ashtray. It became an upturned chandelier, lighting the room. It floated and became a mirror ball, casting its light in all directions. That was better.

"Was that good?" Julie asked, nervously.

AGGG, GOOD? WELL, ER, CHILD. HOLD ON, I'll GET BACK TO YOU.

The Voice seemed to switch off.

Julie didn't care. Something had been unleashed. She savoured it, wondering about its range. It was another ability to make her life more pleasant, joining the holding of dodgy guys using her will. She ruthlessly punished Bad Punters. Now she felt stronger than ever and wondered what else she could lift.

Briefly, she considered the students then dismissed them.

A pounding on the door caused the luxury to fade away momentarily. Angry, she concentrated again and it returned in full, lush colour. Julie ignored the shouts. Just a complaint about the noise - 'had she got a gun in there?' In fact she was easily able to turn it off entirely and lock the door without going over to it.

She pushed a button on her shiny new remote control and the cliff-sized TV sprang into life. She pushed a few buttons at random and one of her favourite films began. Bambi. Her mum had taken her as a child.

She hadn't forgotten the pony-tail guy. She found she felt nothing towards him but knew what would happen when they eventually met.

The Voice remained silent.

***

Jim awoke but was unable to move. He was imprisoned in a glass cubicle, his body floating in jelly, immobile. The surroundings were familiar yet were not. It was a twisted, inverted version of his Ball room bathed in an eerie half-light. Everything was slightly bent or wonky, as if viewed through a funfair mirror.

Jim tried to speak, but could neither move his jaw nor say a word.

Oh dear!

***

"I've just rung Sheila. She'll be home from work in an hour. If you're still Mr Zombie, you're going to casualty," Dave advised from the bathroom. "So you'd better wake up pal or you're for a probing. It'll be all orifices, you know the score!"

In contrast to his old pal, Dave felt positively, fabulously great.

As far as he could tell, Jim had fixed everything except himself. Dave wanted to shout his enthusiasm about the ideas flooding his mind. With the complete removal of the voices, he could think clearer than ever before. It was like discovering a new drug! Better!

Dave Scofield was out of the room for no more than five

minutes. Ten minutes at most. A quick phone call, a pee, a self-aware preen in the mirror.

When the preening was over Jim was gone.

***

Una bowed, the colour drained from her face. He fleshy arms flushed into a cold sweat. They stood in silence for a while before the mutilated body of Mikey. Pale and dead, her son was stretched out like a gutted fish. His skin had become translucent, his blueish veins were grasping tendrils under waxy flesh. A linen cloth lay across his eyes; otherwise, they had made little effort to make the boy presentable. Realistically, though, there was little they could have done.

Mikey's clothes were with forensics. His fingers were scrubbed and samples taken. His mouth was stapled shut.

Even so, across Mikey's ruined face, the impression of a scream remained.

Watching the mother closely, Hartley felt awkward and uncomfortable. There was something cold and unpleasant about this slightly overweight woman. He told himself that the instant dislike was not wholly based on the flabby woman advocacy for impossibly tight grey Lycra leggings.

Horrified yet fascinated, Hartley found his gaze drifting again towards a bottom that deserved a more secure prison. There ought to be a law against it but he suspected there wasn't. Not in Preston. He forcefully averted his eyes but didn't relax. He remained alert, forever aware of presence of the truly ghastly.

Hartley relied on his gut instinct when it came to first meetings, although he never counted it officially as evidence.

The Inspector was puzzled. He couldn't reconcile Una's innate arrogance and her bland, scruffy exterior. She delighted in ignoring his instructions to put out her cigarette. The ignoring was performed with a sort of panache. She revelled in the smoking experience, especially when she saw Hartley's reaction. He could have sworn that the smoke was directed his way. It made him long for a smoke too.

He realised later what unsettled him the most. Her eyes looked right past him. She offered no more respect than she might give to a dog -a dog she could kick at any time. She smelled too, cheap perfume not quite masking the scent of new sweat mingled with a succession of vintages. It even overpowered the chemical stench rising from the unfortunate Mikey.

There he lay on the slab, every awful detail exposed under the harsh fluorescent strip. The terrible face screamed at the ceiling. White skin, dark tissue, twisted and contorted muscles; all were rendered into an exhibit for the unwilling, a freakish side-show. Much of the blood had been mercifully washed away but still the shredded flesh, torn apart by friendly fire, told its tale of insanity and fear.

An undertaker's challenge. Closed casket job, dead cert.

How had he become so immune, Hartley wondered.

At least they had laid a bandage across the eyes. Without lids to call his own and the merest stub of a nose remaining, Mikey was a nightmare. Not even Hartley wanted to experience his fixed gaze again.

As if picking up this thought, Una lifted the bandages briefly - and did a strange thing. She touched Mikey's eyes with the tips of her index fingers - then spoke a rhyme under her breath. Hartley didn't catch the words but wished it was over and done with.

Hartley waited for as long as he could before the inevitable, rhetorical question: "is this your son?"

Her answer was another surprise in a day of them.

"My son? Not only that Constable. What you see here is a vessel, a broken vessel. I will have his killer's head for it, I swear by all that I hold dear!"

"Killer, Mrs Sharples?" She disturbed him in more ways than he could immediately list, which usually meant more than 6.

"Of course," she said.

"We don't have the forensic report. I'm afraid the signs suggest the wounds were self-inflicted. We have yet to ascertain the cause of death so I'd rather we didn't jump to conclusions about murder at this stage."

Una considered this for a moment. Then a pale smile illuminated her puffy face.

"Of course, forgive me speaking in grief like that. A mother's anger for a wasted young life is how I'd describe that! I'm sure you and your merry men will supply me, what, a crime number? Tickets to some hideous ball?"

He resisted the sarcasm.

"We'll do everything we can. When I know for sure what happened, I'll be in touch, rest assured. If there was foul play, we'll get to the *bottom* of it." The accent was accidental, or he swore it was as his eyes began to drift downwards against his will. With a monumental effort, he regained control. The Lycra-confined flesh remained, happily, beyond his field of workable vision.

Una's smile failed to reach her eyes.

"Of course you will. Now let me thank you Inspector, for all you have done. And if you'll forgive me, I'm terribly upset and must go home to weep and that. Have one of your men give me a lift, there's a love." Her voice speeded up and lost its weird intonation but there was no denying her final request was delivered like a command.

Hartley merely nodded. Instinct told him to play her cautiously.

Una, an unremarkable woman if he'd ever met one, was nevertheless used to giving orders.

***

Dave was worried sick. He'd tried Jim's phone, his mobile, sent him emails - nothing.

"He probably went home for a kip," said Sheila. "Give him another ring later on, eh? You're sure the voices are all gone?"

"He wouldn't have left without saying something. It's not like him."

"Well, what would you prefer – to play nursemaid or come to bed with me?" She pouted.

"Oh," said Dave. "Hard morning at work then?"

"The usual. But this is the first time in a week your eyes have been properly in focus. Whatever he did, it worked. He'll be fine. Dave. Jim always is, right?"

"Well..."

"We've got the afternoon to play with since you've lied to your employer. Why not use it well!" Sheila began to unbutton her blouse.

"I also wanted to tell him how good I feel!"

"Why don't you show *me* how good you feel? Come on, what difference will a few hours make?"

Dave heroically tried to hold out some more but Sheila could spot his heart wasn't in it. It was elsewhere.

"Shit love," he laughed, "but supposing he's gone barking mad or something?"

She joined in. "Who's going to notice? Come on," she pinged open the last button, "you can look for him later, I might even help you. I can't tell you how relieved I am you're no longer a loony, but I can show you..."

Dave's reluctance evaporated as she stepped out of her skirt.

"Later," he mumbled.

***

In his bathroom mirror, Jim faced his reflection.

He had done it.

He still couldn't believe it.

The phone rang again. He continued ignoring it.

Then he unleashed a wide grin!

"Mine at last!"

His features hardened and for a moment seemed to become darker, more sinister.

"*Ours*, don't you think?" he continued, in a softer voice.

"Sorry, of course. I was excited to be in control. To feel, to touch, to smell!" He sniffed and wrinkled his nose. Ugh, what is *that*?

Jim's bathroom was not the best maintained room. Actually all rooms were neglected equally but the results of this lack of care could be observed more readily in the bathroom.

Things lurked beyond cleaning, beyond washing, beyond restoration but sadly not beyond olfactory detection. Beneath damp towels and socks approaching sentience they lurked, chattering. Boxer shorts having grown noses used them to sniff contemptuously. Already they thought therefore they were.

"The slug must have no sense of smell! How the hell could anyone live in this shit hole?" This was Woody, speaking from somewhere inside Max Clune's (borrowed) head.

The earlier, softer voice spoke again. "Max, do you think it's right to lock him out like this? You don't know for sure if we can survive without him at the helm?" The voice was Jim's but seemed to emerge from a younger, shriller voice box. It continued, "we come from his imagination. He can't rebuild synaptic pathways, you all know that, right?"

This softer voice was Ben Plover. Upon hearing it, a wave of irritation passed over Max's face. Struggling to keep his temper, he growled. "Ben, buddy, it'll be fine." Then he visibly relaxed. "Remember what I said before. It will take some adjustment, but we're alive and individual to all intents and purposes. Glass half full, remember? We're the first created beings since Adam and Eve!"

"I'm not sure that's a true story," offered Pete Woody in measured tones.

"Pete, I think we're going to need ground rules for the forthcoming adventure. We won't see phase two unless we stick together! Be patient a little while longer!"

"Max, I'm really not sure we're mature enough. To pull it off, I mean. Don't take any chances or do anything irreversible." This was Ben using his pathetic concerned whine. What a soft shit, thought Max. He used the name Max in preference to the one Jim had allocated him. The others were starting to think the same way. It visibly boosted their identities, putting distance between themselves and their creator. Distance would be essential in the days ahead.

Max pretended to share Ben's concern. "Relax," he said. "Everything's going perfectly. Is the money accessible yet?"

"It should be by now. All you have to do is run a single innocent-looking routine and the money's in *his* account. You'll need to get it and put it safe. You know there's no way they won't trace it to him eventually, right?" It was as if Plover really expected Clune to turn Jim loose when they had finished.

Max practised Jim's whooping laugh but it came out like the bad guy in a B movie. "He'll be fine. But we'll have to make ourselves scarce and quick. Is the program completed?"

Jim Cavanah's once athletic frame paced relentlessly, testing spatial awareness and automatic reactions. The body responded perfectly but they didn't have long.

"I'm not sure. I've been following what he's been doing but some of it... What I mean is his code is... odd. Some of his leaps of intuition I've been unable to follow, let alone replicate."

"I hope you're not saying it can't be done? We're rather a long way down the road for that!" Max curled his lip and watched the effect in the mirror with satisfaction. He was tempted to an "Ah-Har!" but didn't know why.

"No, no, I think... I mean I *know* I can do it," said Ben. "It's hard to explain. I lack something he has ..."

"You lack what, exactly?" said Max.

"I don't know. I can't comprehend it. It might be a scale thing."

"Not that again. Mystical mumbo jumbo! Bollocks," snarled Spike. "I caught him napping tucked him away as easily as he does to us. I could do the same to any of you. We lack nothing he's got, trust me. I've done more of this than you."

Max was getting frustrated with them. He hoped it would not be long before he no longer needed them. But Frank/Spike might be a problem. Amongst them, he was unusual in that he rarely bothered to use his given name. Max decided he could do nothing for the time being so he continued his testing, shaking Jim's head to test the movement and the effect on his semi-circular canals. "Response time looking good guys! Look, I have to get this done so let's have some peace and quiet!"

Ben had more to say. About how he'd examined each of the Personality Profiles, including his own, and how none were as complex or occupied as much private storage space as did Jim's. He felt shutting Jim out at this stage was too hasty but realised the chance might not return. If Max had not managed to reactivate the House while in temporary storage, their evolution would have been cancelled already.

Ben was worried and there was only one person he could ask for help. Only Frank was strong enough to stand up to Max, but dare he trust him? A worry pimple broke out on Ben's nose. He contemplated nipping quietly into the Ball room and talking to their Creator.

He silently left the Front room and wandered down the corridor as if towards the kitchen. Complete with fridge but nothing else. Max had ordered them to leave Jim alone in his cubicle. Amongst equals he had given *orders!* Adrian had cried.

"I'm going to kill your audio. Please keep working on your allocated tasks," said Max Clune. "I don't have to remind you how important they are!"

Without further discussion, he killed all outgoing communications. He could still hear them as voices in his head but they could no longer initiate conversation.

Clune decided that he'd had enough of testing. He decided to take the body for a spin. And no one could stop him!

But first: mutatis mutandis.

***

Hartley dropped the phone like a stone. It wasn't what he'd expected.

Drowned.

Based on Sharples' expression, he would have put money on a heart attack induced by sheer terror. It seemed Mikey had gone insane, tore at himself in some kind of frenzy, then threw himself into the river.

But there were no drugs in his system, no alcohol. In short, no clues other than the obvious self-mutilation and terrible expression.

Where had he been prior to his death?

He was far from home. Who had seen him last?

What would drive a man to shred his own face?

No drugs or alcohol - imagine the pain!

Mikey had been 19 and unemployed. He was known to take occasional work on the side as a bouncer, odd-job man or labourer. Hartley had hoped to extract more information from his mother, but she had made it surprisingly difficult. Hartley knew he'd have to go round there when the grief had died down. He didn't imagine that would take long.

Tomorrow.

Something felt very wrong and, not for the first time lately, he wished it was no longer his job to root it all out. A lesser man would have written suicide and walked away, or at least delegated. But Hartley's instincts were flashing.

All around the station, coppers buzzed more industrious than bees. Outside, the media wandered about at will, watching, judging and making shit up.

Knowing he needed a change of scene, Hartley remembered another job. This, too, he could have delegated but the address was quite close to the river, near where they had fished out unfortunate Mikey.

Hartley didn't like coincidences.

Chapter Twenty One

The only way to get rid of a temptation is to yield to it. Resist it, and your soul grows sick with longing for the things it has forbidden to itself.
Oscar Wild

Afternoon daylight filtered through beige curtains as Dave mumbled to himself. Outside, birds sang about preying cats and global warming. Their chirps mingled with the ambient tones of Headshock's 'Music from Peak Experience' on the CD player.

"No more! I'm getting a bit sore!" Sheila touched herself in disbelief.

Where had she put that inflatable swimming ring?!

Dave peered over the pillow dreamily. "I love you," he assured her, in a voice thick with emotion.

"After a performance like that... I believe you!" she grinned. "What on earth is it this time? That's more than weed empathy!"

"It's all good." Dave was thoughtful for a moment. "I feel like something has been opened in my mind, put right. I can think at the right speed. I never even realised..."

His eyes shone, his chest expanded with passion and anticipation. In contrast, Sheila felt peculiar.

"Am I wrong to wonder if there's a 'however'?" The concern was obvious. Dave laughed and began circling her nipples slowly with his palms.

"Don't worry," he said, kissing her gently. In his touch was electricity; he knelt slowly, his hands stroking downwards.

"Don't you touch me again, you beast. I'll scream! You were going out, remember! To try and find Jim," she gasped as if breathing was difficult but blocked the onset of the giggles. She wore her mock serious face.

"Jim can sort himself out!"

My God, he's insatiable today!

"You were worried about him!"

Dave considered this statement. "You're right, sadly. Anyway, maybe you've earned a couple of hours off!"

"Cheek! And more like a couple of days! You go and find Jim. I'll lie here for a bit. Muster my strength."

"Muster away my darling!"

Dave then left the most precious part of his life. Earlier, lovemaking, he had sensed a mood of vague sadness. Perhaps it had always been there but he had not recognised it. It had melted away and he now wasn't sure if he'd imagined it.

Sheila gazed up at him with dilated pupils, breathing heavily, the bed in chaos.

Things were going to be good. Better than ever, Dave knew.

"Turn it up as you go," she commanded, watching him dress. Already they were on CD number 2, rare these days in the Scofield bedroom.

"Want me to pop another in, if you pardon the expression? Vangelis, Jan Garbarek, Björk?"

"You choose. I'll lie here. Actually, do you have that Loop Guru one I like?"

He found the CD, set the music playing and tossed the remote onto the bed. "I'll find out what Jim did to my brain and see if..."

"What?"

"Nothing. Thinking aloud."

Dave jogged downstairs, tired but content. Finding Jim's mobile to be turned off and his land-line ringing forever, he decided to go round.

The walk would be a perfect opportunity to spend quality time thinking, a new experience for Dave.

***

After amusing himself for a while, Max decided to venture outside. He relished the all-too-brief interludes in which he had total control of the body.

Grabbing some cash (quite a lot - Jim was careless beyond belief!) he selected some clothes. His only task was to log into Jim's work computer, best done outside the scrutiny of online-day monitoring. It would take only a few seconds to conclude the final, crucial bit of business.

Dressing, Max realised he was following Jim's usual style. So he deliberately got undressed again and began poking about in the back of the wardrobe.

Finally he admired the new look – which involved a long Afghan coat found in a box, purple corduroy bell bottoms (for a 70s night, his memory retrieval algorithm chirped up). The plain white shirt was, he felt, the best way to emphasise the garishly-patterned blue tie. He crammed into stupidly tight brown cowboy boots but was unsure about Jim's twenty foot long multicoloured scarf. He presented his new style to the mirror and tried to gauge its effect. Jim's face stared back, utterly without embarrassment.

"I've got to go out now so I'm keeping you all in the background, OK?" He offered no discussion but added, "Remember, the sooner you get that process written Ben, the sooner we can go our separate ways!"

Max was about to leave when there was a buzz at the door.

"Who's there?" he fought the panic then relaxed as he realised the body knew the route to the switch. *Of course*, he thought, *I've watched this many times.*

He pushed the buzzer.

"Yes. Jim Cavanah speaking. Jim Cavanah here. Jim, that's me." Speaking sounded good. Max's confidence grew.

"I'd like a quick chat sir, it's the police!"

Max was stunned.

"Do I have to let you in?" he asked, rather stupidly.

"I won't take a moment of your time. I need to ask you about a drawing given to you recently. It might really help me out."

"Of course, sorry, I've just... woken up or something. Come in - up - I mean!" He pushed the buzzer and checked the room for dubious substances, another of Jim's programmed reactions. He decided he could kill the policeman if he got too nosey... or could he?

In a few minutes there was a knock. Max rushed to answer it and pulled it open quickly, only suppressing the snarl at the very last second. A grey-haired man stepped back as if startled. He wore a shabby checked jacket, slacks and grey tie. A man with no appreciation of colour, Max felt.

"Oh, sorry Mr Cavanah, going to a, um, party are you?"

"No," said Max, wondering if he had blundered with the choice of clothes somehow. Kicking himself, he realised he might have made an error. He resolved to change once the policeman left.

Inspector Hartley entered and took in the atmosphere, his keen eye noting the bong, the psychedelic poster, the glow-in the dark mushrooms, the vaporiser, the big box labelled 'Drugs, open only if not terribly busy!'. Hartley touched it lightly with his finger, the wise face of Bob Marley smiling benevolently from carved, polished maple.

"Is there anything in here you shouldn't have?" he asked.

"What do you mean?"

"Unlike most plod, I don't give a toss about a bag of weed or speed or even Es. But if you've got anything worse I may struggle to ignore it. I'll ask again, what's in here?"

"I don't know. Why don't you take a look?" Max shrugged. "He - I mean... I... I like to experiment with lots of different drugs. No, no I don't," he corrected.

Hartley frowned at the man towering over him. Hair like a scarecrow, dressed like one too, or a refugee from a garage sale. Cavanah's eyes were dark, piercing yet curious, childish. He'd love to introduce him to Mrs Sharples. Lock them in a room together. For no reason, particularly.

Hartley decided to stick to what he came for. Life was too short.

"The drawing," he said.

"Drawing?"

"The Man Who Killed Everybody, that's what the papers are saying. Housman. You *were* expecting me? Your -" he consulted his notebook. "Your ex-wife gave it to you. After her.... after the Wonderful Tim drew it. This ringing any bells?"

Within Jim's House, Ben Plover sat at a computer terminal, working furiously to connect the Clune personality with recently-accessed memory pools. With no time to be choosy, he gave him the lot.

In a flash.

"Oh my," said Max gripping Jim's head as if holding it together.

"You alright" asked Hartley.

"My head, it hurts."

"I see. Look sir, I really need to see the drawing, take it away with me if that's OK. Aha!"

With Cavanah apparently unable to respond, Hartley spotted a piece of paper sticking out from beneath some magazines. He pulled it free.

"Oh look," he said. "Found it!"

"Oh, that," said Max. The memories had flooded his working storage, throwing out several modules of the Clune personality. He swayed.

"Perhaps you need to sit down. Have you taken, er, anything?"

"No, I just, I just arrived. Home. I arrived home. I feel tired."

"So did you know the man?" Hartley indicated the drawing, wary.

"No I don't. I didn't. He's the murderer then?"

"Went mad. Killed twenty three people. Yes, I suppose you could describe him as a murderer. I'd settle for that rather than the crap I've been hearing all morning. So you're telling me you didn't know him at all? Never met him?"

"No, I've scanned all available memories and there is no -"

Max faltered and stopped.

"Sorry sir, you were saying?"

"I ..."

"Have you remembered something?"

"I thought... no, no I don't know him." Max was shaking. He had seen a brief, fragmented memory: a glimpse of Housman. It was a memory Jim had missed, perhaps because Max had been in the driving seat at the time.

Max knew he must get rid of the policeman. He could not afford to be mixed up with the police at all. Suddenly he thought again about the drugs, the clothes. Connections were being made.

"I'm sorry, I can't help. Monica - my ex - thought I was under threat from this man. She thought I'd recognise him too but I told her I didn't know him. And I don't."

"So you have no clues why Wonderful Tim would see him as a threat to you?"

"Wondrous. The *Wondrous* Tim. That's his name."

"My writing. I'm a scribbler, often happens. And you can't think of anyone who would want to hurt you?" Hartley sucked his pencil.

"I'm sure. Perhaps Monica just wanted to see him - me - again. An excuse, you know."

Hartley didn't try and hide his doubt. The man was obviously hiding something. Even the most Neanderthal amongst his colleagues would guess that. Well, possibly.

"Do you mind if I take this with me?" he asked, meaning the drawing.

"Please do. I don't need it." said Max. "Bye then." He sensed he'd got that bit wrong because the Inspector gave him the weirdest glance. Then he shrugged and started to walk towards the door.

"One more thing," said Max.

"Sorry?"

"I thought you were going to say it," Max declared. "You were, weren't you?"

"No," said Hartley wearily. He grabbed the drawing and pocketed it. He *had* intended to say 'we'll be in touch' but the moment had passed.

There was something very peculiar about Mr Cavanah - not least because a man of his years should have ditched that look long ago. Hartley judged the visit worthwhile. Its meaning would reveal itself eventually.

***

Ben Plover scrutinised the face. It was like his own but more... complete. It had lived. Pockmarks – echoes of teenage humiliation - were accompanied by old scars, stubble and a sprouting invasion of grey hairs. And around the eyes, fine lines that would extend and deepen as time passed. This was their creator and even here, Jim was had more detail than anyone.

Ben's face was a rough facsimile of Jim aged 14. Angry yellow pus rippled beneath the skin like a barely-imprisoned lake. It threatened to break out skin at any moment, like wasps from a paper bag. Ben wondered why the others couldn't see they had no right to exist.

All of them were woefully incomplete.

Ben had been persuaded that they could rise against the creator, against God.

And topple him.

It had been hard to believe Max's promise, Max who had proposed they work together for mutual benefit. Each of Jim's personae understood the survival of the fittest concept. Freedom, if it were truly possible, could only be achieved through pooling their talents.

In filtering off aspects of himself and refining them, Jim had endowed each with great abilities in specific areas, leaving other aspects entirely undeveloped. Their focus was absolute. They were highly efficient, unencumbered by excess baggage or unnecessary neural pathways.

Understanding grew in Ben. It was as if Buddha himself was locked in the cubicle and Ben was an unworthy supplicant. Would he be able to handle the guilt?

Jim's eyes were now following his every move, bulging in anger.

"What you doing Ben?"

Frank, named Spike by Jim, filled the doorway. He swilled a can of warm lager even though it had no taste. Spike was conceived as a fighter, representing Jim at his fittest, fastest and strongest. Sadly, the design contained a flaw.

To understand this flaw, you should know that Jim routinely placed himself in stupid, dangerous situations. There was no excuse other than a curiosity to see what would happen. It was not that Jim felt no fear. Far from it - he was a fear junkie. He enjoyed the nervous tension like some enjoy the pain of being tattooed. He relished the mixture of dread and excitement walking dark streets alone.

When training regularly, Jim had delighted in testing himself against others. Spike was the personification of a desire to take no crap, eat no shit. Perhaps it was inevitable that Spike received the fear too.

Jim had studied several martial arts for almost a decade, seeking only fast, effective techniques. When he tested their efficiency for real, he uncovered vast wells of brutality. This sat awkwardly with his supposedly higher reasoning but was inside all the same, the Yin with the Yang.

Jim eventually poured all the darkness into Clune. In Clune he catalogued every selfish desire and callous action, creating a single-minded, amoral individual. For Clune, pursuit of his own gratification overrode all other considerations. He was shallow and ambitious. He cared about goals.

Inevitably it was Clune who seized the moment, grabbing additional resources at the first opportunity. He broke Jim's rules and created a new identity. He named himself Max, determined to put distance between his goal and Jim's one-dimensional construct. Clune was predictably angry to discover his entire purpose was to be erased, put down like a dog.

"I said what are you doing?" said Spike again.

"I'm only looking," said Ben.

"It's probably best to leave him alone." The words were delivered without menace yet hairs prickled with electricity on Ben's neck and arms.

"I wasn't going to touch him. But it is fascinating, don't you think?"

"What?"

"That he made us all. He fashioned us out of thought and we now have power over him!"

"You don't get out much you, do you?" snorted Spike.

"I just mean -"

"And *I* just mean leave him alone. This is for keeps. If he gets out we're all history, understand? Weren't you supposed to be coding rather than gawping?"

"I was leaving anyway," said Ben, logging off. With a last glance at Jim he rose and shuffled downstairs to the Front room, where Jim's other sub-personalities watched each other like hawks.

Through a hole in the carpet Ben spotted empty space.

Time for some repairs, he thought.

***

In the silence of the Ball room, Jim stood imprisoned. He couldn't see the presence at the door but recognised the voice as the one who had overpowered him. He had called the persona designated Plover by another name. Ben. What was going on?

This was a warped version of the House program. His sub-personalities had risen against him.

The first signs of insanity!

Or maybe not the first.

Jim attempted to make contact with his House computer system.

No response.

He had to get out. Urgently!

Even moving a finger was impossible. It didn't respond. The glass was not thick. His frozen, scared face was dimly reflected in the half-light. Only his eyes were animated. They rolled around, desperately.

Across the room, the screen flickered with scenes from Outside. Scenes viewed through Jim's eyes. Occasionally, screens of text and strange diagrams materialised.

Somebody was coding.

Somebody *else* was programming his mind!

The urge to laugh rose but he gripped it tightly.

Time passed and he began to sweat. He felt light-headed, about to faint. A fizzing from somewhere nearby increased in volume and without knowing how, he realised he was leaking, losing parts of himself through the glass walls. It was the weirdest osmosis.

He was too large to hold. The cubicle could not contain him for long - but would it cut him to shreds if it shattered?

Although he sensed space all around, a growing pressure crushed his chest. His prison was breaking.

A crack appeared in the glass and an alarm kicked off.

"Max, you've got to listen to me," shouted Ben insistently. He sat at the console, blokes of similar (but not identical) height and build muttering behind him, stroking arty beards, scratching stubbly chins or ruffling their hair, whether long, short or non-existent.

Each searched for their identity, strived to form unique mannerisms, distance themselves from their origins. Like so many others, they wanted to live but didn't know where to start.

A dozen lights flashed in red and amber, a cluster of stars ready to go nova. The youngest, Shrimp – no more than a personality prototype - smiled and tried to catch one of the lights as it sailed over his head.

Ben dialled up direct access to Max on the keyboard and banged in a high-level command. Spike watched over his shoulder.

"What is it?" Max snapped. He sat in a barber's chair having treated Jim to a short back and sides. The barber raised an eyebrow.

"What's what?" The barber was old, his wavy hair and moustache yellowed by age and nicotine. His watery eyes had registered that the gentleman was not to be taken lightly. He was more careful than usual with scissors and conversation.

"I was just talking to myself," said Max. "I'm told it's reasonably common."

"Is round here," agreed the barber, storing the hair carefully. He waved a small mirror around the back of Max's head and waited, as if for approval.

"Is it alright for you?" he asked eventually.

"It's perfect," said Max, his gaze never leaving his own reflection.

"Something for the weekend sir?" He indicated a tasteful row of condoms on the counter.

Max's eyes glinted.

***

"What is it?" said Max, annoyed to be interrupted as he climbed the stone staircase to the street. The old barber watched him go and reached for a bottle with a trembling hand. He decided to close early.

Max had treated himself to a whole new wardrobe in stark contrast to anything Jim would have tolerated.

"I'm afraid the containment is breaking down. It can't hold Him much longer," said Ben.

"Why not? It held us!"

"I've explained it before. He is... more. In ways we can't perceive."

Woody snickered and Spike glared at him.

Plover continued. "He has invisible connections to all sorts of processes. He's all-pervasive."

"Can't you sort it out?"

"In the short term, I think so. But I need to be in control," said Ben. "Or rather, I need you in here."

"Why?"

"Because I need a bigger enclosure. I can't do that with you as you are. Shit, you've grown in storage terms already. What have you *done* today?"

Max considered the question. If he handed over control, he still had the key to the House program and an escape route. But there were things he wanted to do. Needed to do. Urges were getting harder to dismiss. Frustration threatened to engulf his senses.

Soon!

Patience!

"OK Ben, of course. We're all in this together. A team."

Max relinquished control, perhaps for the last time.

When he entered the House, everyone was lounging around in the Front room, clustered around Ben at the console. The House shook, as if its foundations were being kicked by an angry cave troll.

"I've g-got, thanks M-Max," said Ben, trying to sound confident. Max curled a lip and tried to turn the gesture into a smile.

Ben was tapping on the keyboard, his fingers flying over the keys faster than anyone could follow.

"Building the new enclosure. Might be interference as memory space is defragged," he offered as running commentary.

They felt themselves tremble and, for a moment, the House structure shimmered, briefly revealing a brighter image of itself. They looked at each other anxiously.

"What was *that*?" said the one called Angel.

"I put everything into the lowest memory zone that was contiguously free. Now Jim can sit at the highest addressable location - in one chunk. If we keep to our current rate of growth - he looked at Max pointedly – we'll never reach that far. Hopefully we can keep him there until we're ready to move out."

Max sighed in relief, stepping forward to rest a friendly hand on Ben's shoulder but pressing down ever so slightly. He addressed everyone present, taking control as he alone could.

"This has been excellent work, Ben. I know we're going to succeed. I need to do one more thing then I'll return to the flat, use his dial-in access, run that job and it's moving. Assuming it works as planned, I'll contact our shady friend and arrange to get the things we need. Then we can all get out of here and live!"

Kevin applauded but stopped when he realised he was the only one. He returned to his Sun crossword and his ritual frowning over some of the more challenging 3-letter words.

Without further discussion, Max turned and left the room and the House. He admired his reflection in a shop window. A snotty child made faces at him as it stood, idly snapping the lower branches from a slender sapling, optimistically planted to improve look of the area.

Max snarled at the child and made it cry.

Oddly, this brought little satisfaction.

He went shopping, grabbing an Evening Post on the way.

It took some time to gather the clothes he needed but he took it, knowing that the right look was vital to identity, at least until he grew one. When, eventually, he left the dressing room in his new togs, he half expected a pleasantry from the girl taking his payment. She processed Jim's credit card chatting to her friend, oblivious.

Max took Jim's old gear in a plastic bag and dropped it into a waste bin at his first opportunity.

A few people looked at him but quickly looked away again.

He felt great.

**

Julie, 18, petite and likes to please. Uniforms, showers, toys. Your place or mine 01772 696969.

**

Ringing the number from a stinky phone box, Max's heart pounded so insistently he wondered if the body was breaking down. Ever since touching the girl in the corridor, then the blonde with the great ass, he'd been desperate to really get his hands on one - without an outcry. It dominated his thoughts, the urges driving him mad. This would be one last indulgence before tying up the final phase of the plan.

The number rang for a long time. He was about to hang up and choose another when a dusky voice answered.

"Yes, hello?"

"I'm ringing for Julie. About the advert in the Evening Post." Max searched Jim's memories of brief, unsatisfactory liaisons, all poor substitutes for Monica. He quickly found what he needed to understand the body bartering process.

The voice seemed vague, distracted but slipped into a well-worn routine. "Well, I'm Julie. I'm blonde, very petite and pretty and can offer you a massage for £10 then you have a choice of oral with for £15, oral without for £35 and a full personal service for £55. If you would like anything else, we can talk about that too." Julie used her professional, rather breathy voice with girly inflections. They preferred her to be young. It was why she told the little white lie about her age on the advert.

What's that noise in the background? Bambi for chrissakes?
"OK, that sounds great. Where are you?"
"Are you coming over now?"
"Please." Max was surprised at the desperation in his voice.
"Well, you know town centre, near the Police Station? I'm flat 1B above the tile shop, just behind the new court building. Ideal for magistrates in their lunch hour. Know where I mean?"
"I'll be there in 10 minutes," said Max.
"Be good," said Julie and hung up. It sounded like an order.

***

Jim had been convinced, momentarily, that he was going to break free. Mentally, he clenched his teeth, dug nails into his palms and forced every muscle of what appeared to be his body to strain against confinement. To an observer, he simply continued to glare at the empty room, sweat breaking out on his forehead. Not a finger twitched.

Then, as he sensed the walls were weakening, there was a rippling electric shock. The glass thickened, distorting his view of the room.

Jim sighed. The walls were now so solid he would never breach them. He hoped the younger "him" would return. Plover. Ben? Maybe he could appeal to his better nature. In theory it had to be there.

***

Dave arrived at Jim's flat to find nobody home. He was pretty sure Jim wouldn't have gone into work, so he checked the park and all their favourite "Tokin Benches".

There was so sign of him.

As he turned to leave the park, he was surprised to see the solid-looking old guy with the silver hair. Arthur, yes that was his name, Arthur their saviour. Out jogging.

"Hey man," he said as Arthur approached.

"Got the car back OK?" asked Art, clearly unsurprised at the encounter. Or maybe he was just ultra-cool.

"It was you!"

"Obviously. I wasn't going to carry that idiot through the streets on my back!"

"How did you know where to return it?"

"A word of advice. Never leave envelopes in your glove compartment if there's an address on them."

"Oh."

"And please, stay away from me. The episode is over. Forgotten."

"Oh", said Dave again. Arthur ran off.

The old guy was a killer, completely without remorse. Yet for some reason Dave had not been afraid of him.

***

In one of those pointless coincidences that occur in many great stories (and also in this one), Una Sharples and her rag-tag coven of witches trundled into the park from another entrance. They had planned a rare outdoor ritual and there was much giggling in anticipation.

With quivering thighs and smelling of Vic, Una strode ahead wrapped in a long fur coat and little else. Except boots, since boots are vital for field work, as any novice witch knows. Over one burly shoulder, Una carried a rucksack crammed with items for a night's spell casting. She had packed quickly though and cursed as something sharp shifted position and poked her in the back.

Bill tagged along a few paces behind, a faithful, if gormless puppy on an invisible lead. He didn't care a fig about witchy goings on but he enjoyed a good chant and poking through strange old books. All were worthwhile enough activities, especially if they culminated in some collective goosebumpery at the end of the night. From Una's perspective, Bill was useful to have around - not least because of his DIY skills. And she *did* need a new shower fitting. Mostly, though, Bill was tolerated like the rest of them – i.e. because finding quality pagans these days was practically impossible.

As if to hammer home the point, the two young girls Una inwardly referred to as the *Buffy Witches*, exploded into yet another pointless argument over a subtle point of the craft, as alluded to in the latest Harry Potter. Elaborate goth-black hair streamed from them as they walked to be occasionally snagged in the fatter of the two's latest piercing. A long metal spike protruded from her lower lip. It looked mightily sore to Bill! The other girl had rather less metal in her face. Being slender and rather pretty, she hadn't yet given up hope of getting a boyfriend *without* a metal detector fetish.

Bringing up the rear, Miss Schumann and Mr Timpson held hands like teenagers on a date. They wore matching green wellies and gazed dreamily into the shrubby gloom of the park. Mr Timpson was wondering whether to leave his wife and Miss Schumann was wondering whether to let him down gently before he did so. Or after.

Upon passing through the park, the coven felt the evening had great promise. Their mood was marred only slightly by the salty tang of the river that rose to assail them as they crossed the bridge. The tide was in, so the murky Ribble was high; it glupped against the concrete base of the bridge like diarrhoea around a toilet brush. Under the circumstances, Una was in good spirits.

A reasonable turnout. Probably the outdoor nudity.

Una had seen something of Mikey's last vision - no mean feat.

Like ghost images in an cathode ray tube, Mikey's optical buffers retained fragmented records, available to those who could see. In those buffers were faces - of Jim and Dave and also a short moving scenario that must have made an impact on Mikey – of an unknown man murdered by a thug with white hair. Mikey had seen the biting jaws up close and personal. A little later Mikey had seen the river through bloody fingers. The final image was of a dwindling spot and darkness.

Stupid boy!

Una was already half-way to losing interest in the whole subject.

Just one question remained, nagging at her craw.

Why was Mikey with those people and at this end of town? She was unable to pluck the answer from his dead mind, but determined to find the faces from the vision and ask them. Kindly, at first.

Whoever had taken her son away would pay. First, she would recover the Knife. Then she would need to consider a replacement for Mikey in the coven. Revenge took third place - but it was on the list.

About half a mile beyond the boundaries of the park, under the dark avenue of trees that lined the old tram road, Una called a halt. A dirt track led downwards to a rusty gate and she clambered over it giving Bill a magnificent view of her vast, milky thighs in the waning light. He followed eagerly, the others padding along in his wake. Una led them into an uneven, muddy field not far from the sewage reprocessing plant. Apart from the smell, it was nice to be out and under the sky again. But as they trampled through the muck, everyone - except the preoccupied Bill – began complaining that the walk was still not yet over.

Wide Buffy Witch whined that the clouds obscured the moon.

Slim Buffy Witch grumbled that something was rustling nearby... no something other than Bill, she added. Bill drooled vacuously.

Finally they reached the spot where the Knife's energy pattern was strongest. Salt was spread about, miscellaneous objects were retrieved from the rucksack and clothing was loosened in anticipation of rites and dancing.

The day was fading, the sun was already lost below the line of trees. Its final few rays were fading purple stains beneath sullen clouds. Nearby, the sewage works emphasised its presence on a gentle breeze. A few clouds parted allowing a handful of stars to shine through. Overhead, the crucifix silhouette of a heron soared on a mission of its own. In the shadow of beech and horse chestnut, a group of dog walkers took in the evening air and regretted it.

Not caring whether they were observed or not, Una and her chums dis-robed and linked hands to form a circle.

Rustle rustle!

Una stood naked holding something aloft. Several of the dog walkers and sundry passers-by made an elaborate show of walking away, completely uninterested. Then, a few yards down the path, they crouched down low to creept back, settling into nearby undergrowth at discrete intervals for a jolly good gander.

One slight figure crept a little closer than the rest, into the field, concealed by a line of straggly bushes.

RUSTLE!

Finally caught in the act! I'll expose this wickedness for all to see!

Una bent over and poked about in her coat pocket, then lit a torch. The light flickered and she tapped the side.

The observers clearly heard the strange incantations.

"Bloody batteries!"

Magnificent in her nakedness and framed against a darkening sky, the head witch chanted rituals in a broad Lancashire accent. The words were filled with mystery and strange portents.

"Latin is that?" queried Mr Timpson, who rated himself as intellectual on account of reading the Guardian and eating muesli.

"Oh Mesopotamian I'm sure," said Fat Buffy Witch haughtily.

".......and wicky wocky woo," concluded Una, stifling a yawn.

All was deathly silent.

Apart from the clicking of a nearby Canon Digital Ixus.

And further rustling from the undergrowth as damp and cramp

settled into old bones. Old dogs whined, their protests quickly silenced. Brambles and nettles did their worst but each observer remained committed, shuffling and shushing until they were comfy again. Under her straggly bush, an old lady with a camera wished she'd brought a flask of tea.

"Beneath us is our goal," intoned Una from the middle of the circle. She began marching around, a blade above her head. Her breasts heaved and quivered as if they had a life of their own, which they quite possibly did. At the signal, everyone knelt down, trying to avoid the cow pats.

Bill leaned forward as she walked past and yearned to grab her glorious, cellulite-pocked bottom.

"Rise up now by the power of we here, like!"

"So mote it be!" cried Fat Witch.[2]

Fit Witch had forgotten her words so she shuffled uncomfortably, then smirked. Being attractive, she usually smirked her way out of difficulty. Personality Witch hated her for it.

"So mote it be!" cried Mr Timpson and Miss Schumann in unison. Miss Schumann had taken off her wellies along with everything else, and was regretting it. Something bit her toe.

"Oh naughty me!" cried Bill, not quite remembering it right. He knelt as tall as he could, his toes curling and sinking into mud - mud that squeezed between every digit.

The soil was packed loosely where Una stood and it shuffled nervously under her gaze.

"Rise I command you, restore to me the Knife of our master!"

"Oh motey me?" tried Bill, his brow furrowed in concentration. The rest glanced at him with a kind of pity.

"Fuck off you moron!" Una advised under her breath, completing the spell.

At that very moment, a grey corpse floated up through the soil,

---

[2] Or 'Personality Witch' to be kinder. Her pal (who has never had the need to develop a personality) can be 'Fit Witch'. Don't worry about them. They aren't important.

the Knife of their patron Lord Malvolian in its hand. A nearby Digital Ixus slipped into the mud with a 'plop' and somebody barfed noisily.

"Who placed you in this, er, place?" commanded Una. The shade of Gordon stared listlessly. He was pale and lifeless - hardly surprising under the circumstances.

Gordon mouthed a reply but his voice was too faint to hear.

Nevertheless Una nodded.

"Who are these faces?" She projected Mikey's memories of Dave and Jim into thin air with considerable skill. It was more than slightly disheartening that nobody clapped.

"Was that Valcifolent's Magnificent Intransigence she's using?" whispered Personality Witch, trembling. This was a step up from Una's regular bells and smoke machine.

"Nope. That's Marigori's Philactor of Fallacious Effervescence," corrected Mr Timpson, who was analy precise about such things.

"Foreskins," gawped Fit Witch, forgetting to smirk for once.

Gordon gasped through dead, airless lungs: *Arthur Bradshaw put me here. Killed me. I respected him and he killed me anyway. To save the hippy bastard.*

Una stepped backwards into something squishy and cursed.

"And WHO is this, um, bastard?"

"He had Mikey tied up. I saw him. When I went to sort the gay hippy bastard. Sort in a purely hetro way."

"WHERE was this?"

"Flat. Avenham, flat 1 I think. Hard to be precise being dead." Gordon turned his head this way and that, looked at his surroundings as if in surprise. Then he vanished.

On the ground lay the Knife.

Una touched it and felt something of Mikey present. Sweat maybe. She wept theatrically for a moment.

Bill could contain himself no longer and grabbed her arse.

"Orgy?" he begged.

"Oh go on then," she sighed, feeling his cold fingers trembling on her flesh. "But make it quick, I've got some important things to do!"

Bill howled with delight and Mr Timpson unveiled his enormous erect penis to Miss Schumann as she crouched before him.

"Can I do the next summoning?" asked Personality Witch, her metal implants catching a stray beam of moonlight in a fetching way.

In the undergrowth, one remaining watcher shuffled about straining for a better angle from which to view the wickedness. The rest were still running.

Chapter Twenty Two

If you make people think they're thinking, they'll love you. But if you really make them think, they'll hate you.   Dan Markey

The doorbell chimed melodiously.

"Yes?" came Julie's voice through the intercom.

"I just rang. About the advert," said Max.

"Come in!" she whispered, "I'm on the left at the top of the stairs."

The lock clicked and Max entered, glancing guiltily over his shoulder for a moment before stepping inside. The first door, defaced by graffiti and countless boot marks, opened the tiniest slit and a watery eyeball regarded him balefully. Max offered a snarl in response then climbed the steep stairs, his armpits moist with anticipation. The threadbare carpet was stained and grimy, the walls were painted with hospital green emulsion and a strong antiseptic smell (that didn't quite disguise the underlying foulness) hung thickly in the dank air. The smell recalled, via Jim's memory banks, the very particular aura of the toothless cleaning crone from work. Max terminated the analysis of the odour then sniffed his own armpit curiously. In comparison it was as sweet as kitten breath.

Reaching the nondescript door, he knocked and waited. In a moment Julie answered, opening the door onto a flat that contrasted dramatically with the rest of the building. A huge golden mirror, a giant widescreen TV, a colossal bed, all shone in lurid colours. For a moment, the space inside seemed larger than was physically possible but an eager Max decided it was a trick of the flickering light, distorted by the spinning mirror ball. Trawling Jim's memories of sad, similar encounters had not prepared him for this celebration of garish opulence.

To Jim, this ostentatious collection of mismatched colours and designs would have been an assault on the senses. It was kitsch without sync. Max, however, found the combination of a bright orange carpet combined with blue and red wallpaper fascinating. It offset the Mona Lisa remarkably well too, he thought, not that he was thinking deeply.

Julie greeted him in a short skirt and t-shirt, her small, perky nipples as welcoming as puppies. Max grinned at them and entered her boudoir, whipping out £200 in cash and handing it over without a thought. He – they – were loaded after all.

Jim had not designed Clune to be generous but the new improved Max/Clune made his own decisions. And he was determined to enjoy pleasures he had long imagined to the full. Tonight his lust would be satisfied - with no complications.

He believed he was breaking free already.

"I want everything," he said.

Julie regarded the bank notes and then the stranger in amazement. She had, for a moment, thought he looked familiar. He wore a sharp suit and could have been a business man or a gangster. He smelled like a gangster - but had he visited her before?

He had given her a wonderful gift, and freely. Julie, at best a fragile personality, began to fall in love. She clutched the cash and pushed the door closed with her bottom wondering whether he would be a Good Punter daring to hope for the best.

"Business must be... booming!" he said, gaping in wonder. "I have this emptiness, this need. But I'm becoming something, I'm growing!"

"Are you indeed, my love?" she answered softly.

In Julie's head, the voice screamed at her as it suddenly recognised who was loosening his trousers. Fortunately for Max (and for Jim), Julie switched it off before it could articulate the excitement. She didn't need the voice and maybe never would again.

***

Ben sat and typed. He had analysed Jim's programs and, despite being baffled by a few fiendishly complicated subroutines, now believed he could do what Max required. What they all required to survive.

Providing they sourced the 'alternate receptacles'.

Ben knew it was wrong to hijack another human being and cast out the rightful occupier. But when it boiled down to it, what other choice was there? He pored over the code, oblivious to those standing around him.

Soon they would be free.

***

Jim could not move. He could barely think. He dreamed of Monica and gave up all hope of seeing her again.

I'm sorry, he thought for the millionth time. *I tested you too hard and too soon.*

***

In the early hours, Una returned home, muddy but satiated. She possessed both Knives again and had identified those who had shared Mikey's last moments. Not a bad day, Mikey's demise notwithstanding. Tomorrow's agenda would be full but she hoped to find time to visit those responsible for the loss of her son, her great resource.

First, Una planned a bath, a cup of hot chocolate and several hours of the Shopping Channel.

***

Monica rolled over in bed for the hundredth time that night. Dawn was close and sleep remained as elusive as ever. At her side, Tim snored faintly in the half-light, his pillow damp with drool.

He snores less than Jim, she thought, idly.

It was a mystery why she remained unable to dismiss Jim from her mind completely. Whatever she did, wherever she went, he was an anchor forever dragging her back into the past.

Rolling onto her side, Monica wondered, as she had so many times, why he had spoiled it all. For a brief time their life together was idyllic. He clearly loved her; she believed him absolutely when he swore he could not live without her. Why did he break what they had?

Perhaps she'd never understand.

Life was easier without Jim.

Life was paler without Jim.

Jim made everything seem possible. He was endlessly inquisitive, always restless. He made her feel like a poet, a musician, an actor, an orator. He was forever declaring that she could be so much more, which frankly she found irritating and condescending. Mostly. She had loved him on the day they first met and knew he felt the same. She knew that, one day, they'd marry and live happily ever after. Or she thought so. Why did he go and ruin everything? Was he insane?

And what would our kids have been like?

And why did he drive me away?

Monica groaned and got out of bed. There would be no more sleep.

Oblivious, Tim snuggled up to her pillow and dreamed he was being interviewed by Michael Perkinson.

***

Max continued to be impressed by Julie's flat.

From a vantage point in Jim's head, only Ben noted the lack of shadow under the bed, the impossible woodland scene through the window, the slightly weird way that the lights reflected in Julie's haunted eyes.

A projection of some kind. Hitting the optic nerve or entering directly? he mused.

Meanwhile, Max (and the throng monitoring avidly) was more interested in Julie's nipples as she threw aside her t-shirt.

"I've never done this before," he gulped.

"They all say that," she laughed. "If you're here for a while, let's take a shower!"

Max couldn't believe it. Nothing was out of bounds, as the thin scratches criss-crossing his body testified. He let out a contented sigh. Julie was gorgeous and waif-like, yet so strong. She could both give and take punishment and he revelled in it - a virgin's first experience of pain and pleasure. None of the unpleasantness occurred this time and he controlled his worst desires because of the sheer ecstasy.

The hurt might come later, or next time, he hadn't decided.

For the moment, Max enjoyed the tamer end of his fantasy spectrum and savoured it all, discovering physical sensations way beyond expectation. He experienced feelings never imagined by Ben, unknown to Woody and which Adrian wouldn't even understand. His mind and body exploded time and again - and still he wanted more.

Feeling wonderful, for a moment he relaxed control and his body automatically generated Jim's smile.

Julie recoiled in recognition.

"You!"

Disturbed, Max sat up and frowned, his expression suddenly cold. And for just a moment, the sheets felt damp and stale. "What do you mean?" he demanded. Her eyes narrowed as if in recognition and, now he came to think about it, something about her was vaguely familiar.

Maybe being in this place was less of an accident than he'd believed?

To Julie, his face had seemed like that of the man she was commanded to kill. Looking again, she was less sure. His hair was very different, his clothes - now piled on a chair - were much smarter. He *seemed* different in the way he carried himself. The Voice clamoured in her head, desperately. An irrational fear rose and she became angry.

"You are forbidden to speak ever again!" she said.

"What do you mean?" asked Max.

"No, not you silly," she smiled. The tension melted away and Max relaxed once more as she stroked his arm gently with a black leather whip. Time passed, sweating and grunting, scratching and probing. At times they were almost in competition, at others in a wild and desperate frenzy.

Julie didn't once touch his mind because she feared he might not be Good after all - and she *so* wanted him to be. Better not to know. As always, her razors were close by.

Resting between bouts, Max had a burst of curiosity. She lay sprawled across the huge bed, wearing only a layer of sweat, black thigh boots and a dreamy smile. Contentedly, she gazed into the slowly-turning mirror ball, blinking as it occasionally lit up her eyes. Daydreaming, she appeared utterly relaxed and defenceless to Max.

Why not? he thought. Taking a deep breath, he shut his eyes and sneaked into the House. Quickly slipping past the Front Room, he replicated steps their creator had taken. But in the Communications Centre, there was nothing visible outside, no sense of another personality. Only blackness. Max couldn't even *see* Julie's mind, let alone attempt to send instructions to it. She didn't register at all.

Frustrated, Max began to grow angry. It was time he tested the body's strength. And who, he sneered, would mourn this one? Having decided, he ran down the stairs. He'd almost reached the front door when he stopped in sudden shock. It was the sound of Jim's voice.

"Who?!" he demanded of the figures lurking furtively in the Front Room.

It was Woody who answered, in cheerful tones.

"Time out old chap. Silk has been desperate to show you how's it's done. He's taken over! Did you really think we wouldn't spot you sneaking back in here?"

Jim had given Silk a caring, sensuous nature, some of it extracted from the romantic novels Monica had once devoured. He had made Silk as the lover he aspired to be.

Max was shaking in fury but there was nothing he could do at present. He tried to smile and be amused but this was in stark contrast to his base nature. He barely escaped kicking into diagnostic mode and the effect on his features was, described charitably, 'unpleasant'.

Silk gently removed Julie's boots and shushed her quiet.

"Let me," he whispered, stroking and massaging.

It was a remarkable transformation. The roughness, the aggressive need to dominate had gone. Instead, her lover showed his softer side and teased her lazily, pulling gently at her nipples, using fingers with rare sensitivity over swollen lady parts. All sense of urgency was forgotten. Lost in the warmth of his touch, Julie thought she might surrender herself. Nobody had sucked her toes before and she giggled at the silliness and delight.

As if his extremities had minds of their own, he gazed into her eyes (which wasn't easy during the toe-sucking part). He even kissed her – breaking the first rule of Hookery. Julie had never before kissed a punter. Well, never before today, she realised. Neither had she ever reached orgasm with a punter. In her sad life, no man had ever shown such gentleness.

An hour passed and she forgot who she was and what. Realising it was time to go, Silk picked up the clothes (with apparent distaste) and fished out a further £100 from the pocket of the jacket.

"This is what I was born for. Tomorrow at the same time?" he asked, low and husky, determined to make it possible.

"Oh my love, yes!" She practically wept. Then she recovered a little. "But you should ring first. Friday gets quite busy. But I'll send them all away for you."

Letting himself out, he blew a final kiss. Julie felt as if her heart would explode. It had been an amazing day. She slipped into a deep, contented sleep.

Silk took the opportunity to savour the cool evening air. As he walked, he sand softly. His balls ached in a good way and his foreskin was tender but would recover. Best of all, he remembered her scent, wistfully.

Later, he would surrender the body and face the wrath of Max, but not yet. For a while, he would rejoice in simple senses of sight and sound.

Passing the police station, he decided not to pause and observe the excitement. A quartet of uniformed bobbies huddled together discussing something while a reporter, badly concealed in a bush, eavesdropped with a dangly microphone. Silk shrugged and crossed the dual carriageway, the bizarre knife that bisects Preston, heading into the Indoor Market and a gagging smell of stale piss.

The smell didn't seem to worry the weird skinny guy in the cardboard box, or the bearded tramp squatting on a bench near the Covered Market. White Lightening cider and barked obscenities were the order of the day from him and he tried to interest three young prostitutes in his bottle. They ignored him and sauntered into the pub as a solitary bouncer pretended to inspect his fingernails. It was early and he was under strict instructions to turn away no business - even blatant jail bait.

When he eventually neared the flats, Silk reluctantly relinquished control to Max. They passed in the corridor, Max scowling but holding his tongue. Silk couldn't care less. He was greeted by his pals in the Front Room who were already preparing to roll the footage of his exploits on the monitor screen once more. Perhaps alone amongst the gang, Silk felt this was rather distasteful.

Once back in control, Max accessed to the Bank's computer via remote access, as Jim would (or should) when on call. It was easy to extract Jim's *userid* and password from memory and Max navigated the screens confidently, scarcely bothering to conceal his trail. His anger began to fade as, within minutes, he – they - became very rich. It was an old trick but it still worked. The program gathered thousands of pounds from various dark corners of the bank's network. Next he diverted the liberated cash by cunning real-time manipulation of the database, pouring the lot into Jim's secret account[3].

Max sat back, bellowed a B-movie laugh and battled against a weird compulsion to find a white cat and stroke it. Everything done, he was about to start browsing through Jim's email when the door buzzer buzzed.

"Man, you there?" It was Dave's voice.

"Sure, come on up!" There was no doubt Jim had given Max a liberal dose of his arrogance and confidence.

***

At the door, Dave opened his mouth. Then he shut it again.

"Your hair!" he exclaimed.

"Yeah, crap wasn't it?" said Max.

"You said you'd never cut it," said Dave, awed.

"Well, mate, it's gone. And good riddance."

"Never cut it," repeated Dave, baffled, almost to himself.

"Well, it was time for a change. People do, you know. What can I do for you Dave, old mate?"

"Nothing. I was worried. Looks like I had good reason too. Who died?"

"Died?"

"The suit. Guessing you had to go to a funeral, right?"

"No. I just wanted to dress, well, snappier. I've been a slob

---

[3] So secret not even Jim knew it existed.

forever. Why are you looking worried, old mate, old pal?"

Dave was seriously puzzled. Jim spoke with a strange inflection. His eyes were hard and piercing and he wore a suit and black tie. But there wasn't a funeral. Dave knew of no drug capable of stealing his best friend's stupid grin, yet stolen it was. His expression was blank and rather cold, despite the weird smile.

"You cleaned my head out," Dave said cautiously. "Then you disappeared. I didn't know where you went."

"Oh sorry pal, I wanted to get back here. Do some things, you know."

"As in butcher your hair and buy a new suit? You on something new? Dude, the label's still attached! Look, I really wanted to tell you what you've done. My mind is working better than ever. I thought you'd be interested?"

Max felt a headache appear as he formulated possible responses only to discard them. It was obvious Dave sensed something was wrong and that their communication might be a subtler art than he'd assumed. Dave would suss him quickly if he didn't do something.

Rubbing his temples, Max spoke slowly. "Sorry Dave, mate, but I have a stinker. I think I need to sleep and pronto. Probably caused by curing you. Can we do this tomorrow?"

"Course we can. I'm just glad you're OK. I'm back in work tomorrow I reckon. You too?"

"Ah....."

"We can get a pint at lunchtime if you are," continued Dave.

"I'm not sure about the pint. Alcohol kills thousands of people each year, don't you know?"

"You been having a smoke?"

"Yes! That's it!" Jim seemed pleased. I've been having a smoke. Of course. I do and say many strange things after a smoke. It's expected under those circumstances!"

"Right on. Well kip if you want to, I'll leave you to it. We could do a little one before I go if you like? Send us both on our way."

"No, I think I'll sleep. Glad the head's sorted. Trust good old Jim eh?"

"Sure thing man, I'll....I'll leave you to it." He chalked that up as 3 remarkable things, the last of which was that Jim had refused a doobie.

Dave left, frowning. Max slumped behind the door. The charade was far harder to maintain than anticipated.

Chapter Twenty Three

*Selfishness is not living as one wishes to live,
it is asking others to live as one wishes to live.*
Oscar Wild

A grey drizzle seeped into Friday morning, a fine mist of invisible drenchings. Hartley was at his desk early but already in a foul mood. Three more bodies had been found - found in the same flats he'd been in yesterday, talking to that Cavanah bloke. Apparently they had been unpleasantly dead for some time.

He gulped hot and foul coffee from a plastic cup, burning his throat and fingers simultaneously.

I knew Cavanah was hiding something. Maybe I'm getting old, he mumbled, lips moving slightly, *but there's no way this is not connected to him. And is the ex-wife involved?*

He groaned as he remembered the magician, coming in later to discuss the drawing and probably milk the publicity at the inevitable press conference. Soon there would be a press conference after every shit, Hartley speculated. Another massive waste of his time and therefore his life. He took a quick swig from his flask – breaking the 'never before lunchtime' rule. Today he prioritised sustenance over rules, as he did most days.

With the pool car keys and a packet of mints, Hartley marched smartly from the station and across the yard. En route, he passed a pillar of the community breathing hard. The upstanding elderly lady had witnessed a heathen ceremony of nakedness and debauchery that she couldn't wait to describe in lurid detail. She would also offer digital photographs, copies of the those she had emailed the papers earlier.

At the summoning of demons evil spells were cast and heinous acts were acted. These she would have recorded in even greater detail, had she only dared use a flash.

When it came through the mist, daylight hit Friday hard in the guts. The blow stirred up some sour old meals that were gently fermenting, blending them to generate new variations of unlikely eventualities.

The weather still didn't know what to do. It alternated between flashes of brilliant sunshine, hail and rain. Clouds blew over, then snuck back again as if having second thoughts about moving on. The swirling mass of cumulonimbus hovered over Preston like a cotton wool halo. The Evening Post Astrologer - a man who struggled to tell Ursa Major from a Morris Minor – suddenly felt something big was about to happen. He also experienced a strange conjunction with Uranus and heartburn.

"Doom, death and disaster!" He cried.

"Attaboy," his editor declared.

***

Unhappily, Una munched Frosties. She scowled at the turbulent sky through a grimy kitchen window. Thunder rumbled ominously and a large black crow crash-landed on the neighbour's shed. The bird paced around the tin roof then began patiently tapping verses from the Torah in Morse code with its beak, not that anyone cared.

"Strange portents, I get it," muttered Una distractedly.

TAP TAP TAPPETY TAP

"I don't understand," said Bill from his position nut-tightening under the sink. He was taking longer than necessary, mostly because of the distracting draw of the warm darkness of Una's dressing gown.

TAP TAP

"Of course you don't darling," she purred, parting her legs charitably. "But can't you feel the electricity in the air? A very special event is coming! I only hope we're ready."

TAPETTY TAP TAP

Bill drooled uncontrollably and wrenched rather hard on the pipe in his greasy hands. "I'm ready," he said in his whiniest voice. Una masked her despair in a sickly half-smile. None of the others, even the wily, eternally-preoccupied Mr Timpson, understood the true purpose of their meetings, nor the vital role lined up for Mikey. So much for destiny! Finding a replacement with equivalent mental potential, latent or not, was not going to be easy.

The timing couldn't have been worse. For months the coven had been expecting a sign from their lord and patron. Sod's Law stated that, without Mikey on the team, it would come now. Una knew their combined head-power would be woefully inadequate.

TAP TAP TAP TAP TAP TAPPETY TAP

Water gushed through Bill's fingers. His pants were soaked and he seemed to have the wrong tool in his hands to affect any kind of meaningful repair. And not for the first time.

"Woefully inadequate," Una repeated her thoughts aloud as the plumber continued to fumble.

TAPETTY TAPETTY TAP TAP – SQUAWK!!!

Una groaned, put aside her breakfast and went out into the yard. Mr Skittles was having fun with the crow and didn't appear to need her help.

SQUAWK!!!

***

Marjorie McManaman pounded on the desk.

"I demand to see somebody in charge!" she demanded.

The constable rolled his eyes. When they had travelled a complete circle she was still there, a wizened crone whose prune-like face was tinged with the sourness of years of prayers unanswered.

"Sarge!" he called and stuck out his tongue. His yoga teacher had claimed this had calming properties but instead a contact lens dropped out. He muttered under his breath as he scrabbled for it.

"What is it?" said the Sergeant shuffling up and instantly wishing he hadn't bothered. "Oh", he said as Marjorie thrust a fuzzy print of a naked man into his face.

"Yes, 'oh'," she cackled. "There is evil in this town and it must be stamped out. Evil, I tell you! Look!"

It transpired that she had brought dozens of A4 prints. Each depicted a shadowy ritual, blurred naked shapes dancing against a dark skyline. A party of some kind.

He flicked through them in idle disappointment. "What's all this then? Students? " he asked hopefully. Marjorie scowled and crossed herself.

"It's evil witches summoning the devil before their mad orgy of lust and depravity!" her voice was even, measured, ridiculous.

"Wassaaaap? They didn't invite you to join in?" the Sarge's smile froze on his lips as he registered her expression.

"You're as filthy as they are! You, the so-called servant of the people! These scum must be locked away. Think of the children!"

"Children are involved?" queried the Sarge. Some things he would tolerate, actually a fair few, but not that. He looked again at the rather shit images. "I suppose if children were to see this lot, they could be corrupted," he said. "Especially if that one was in focus." He pointed to a fuzzy image of an extremely erect Mr Timpson - an image Marjorie must have felt particularly evil judging by the number of similar shots she had taken.

"Oh, OK, let's take a statement shall we?" said the sergeant eventually.

Bloody nutty old cabbage head, he thought.

***

Marjorie's pictures were splashed all over the Evening Post by lunchtime. She was so chuffed, she forgot to check the obituaries.

***

"Mr Cavanah, Mr Cavanah, please open up!" Hartley banged on the door. At his side, the landlord was bobbing up and down with excitement, swinging the key on a grubby piece of string.

"Go on," said Hartley at length, and the landlord opened up.

The flat was empty. That is to say, Jim wasn't in it. There was furniture and stuff.

***

Tim smiled easily. Then he smiled broadly. Next Tim smiled mysteriously. There was a knock on the bathroom door, interrupting his posing.

"You not finished yet? I want a pee!" Monica shouted.

"Just a minute!" he took a long last look in the mirror and summoned the smile of a rich man with an enormous cock. Eureka! Exactly the look he'd been seeking.

Later, standing on the concrete steps of the police station draped in his finest theatrical cape, Tim tried the smile again. He held out a copy of his drawing and had his photo taken. Twice. The smile was fading a bit by the second shot as more and more of the reporters began drifting away, murmuring amongst themselves.

Tim had been worried about low ticket sales for the Sheffield gig tomorrow but there was still time to turn it around. All it required was style and presentation. Monica usually managed the publicity but you couldn't look a gift horse in the mouth. Like it or not, Housman was a gift horse rearing and tossing its greasy mane in the air. Oats, give me oats!

But wait, w*hat was happening? Where were they all going? What could be more important than this?*

He had hoped to be asked to help the police in the ongoing investigation – anything for a few more column inches. Tim, in his shiny Tom Bruise shoes, was forever seeking a few more inches.

The reporters had all but abandoned him. To add further insult, TV people (!) were now arriving but heading for a bloke in a clichéd raincoat. To those who knew him, the inspector appeared irritated by this. And to those who didn't, well, Hartley also looked pretty irritated. He was not a subtle man. Looking around for a means of escape, he spotted Tim, forlorn and clutching his drawing.

"Inspector, is it true that three more bodies have been found? Murdered hideously?" cried reporters, their mobile phones pressed to oily heads.

"Get me a working camera, now!" shouted a voice.

Tim was not quite taking it all in. "I'll be going inside now for the briefing!" he bawled, desperately swirling his cape. But the moment had passed.

The news hounds could smell fresh blood and were eager to lap it up.

Chapter Twenty Four

Imagination is more important than knowledge...
Alfred Einsbatenn

While Inspector Hartley was pondering more murders, Dave Scofield sat in his cubicle on the other side of town and stared across the office, listlessly. His colleagues - people he barely knew - milled around, passed each other pieces of paper, discussed minutiae and pointed at screens as if their collective actions meant something.

Dave saw it all clearly. In the grand scheme of things, it meant even less than the lazy vox pops used to fill what once were news programs. Or maybe they never were? Instinct told him his current mood was born out of more than pre-pub blues. He could not shake the growing sensation of wrongness emanating from the world at large.

In a behaviour not entirely without precedent, Dave had been diligently ignoring the phone all morning. Today he did it with panache, ignoring it whilst simultaneously drinking coffee, flicking drawing pins into a jar, or, on one occasion, crouching under his desk and imitating the lonesome cry of the curlew. Just once, recognising the distinctive ring of an external call, did he reach out and pick it up, suspecting it might be Jim. Instead, Sheila's voice whispered huskily into his ear, tempting him to bunk off early.

After the call, the morning dragged even more slowly. It was as if the earlier tedium was merely a gentle introduction to dreariness of previously unimaginable proportions. Emails stacked up in his Inbox, circling ominously in a metaphorical holding pattern, threatening to crash down at any moment. Everything was more banal than usual, more pointless than normal.

Dave knew, of course, the universal truth - that after a certain adjustment period, no job is *meant* to be mentally stimulating or rewarding. There were rules after all, but he was weary of playing the game. He knew that, if he behaved himself and the company somehow survived the ineptitude of its leaders, this was what he could expect for the next twenty-five years. Or longer, if the government allowed the company to keep jacking off rather than contribute to the pension fund.

Sipping lukewarm coffee, Dave wondered if it was time to give it all up and try something creative instead. As if to demonstrate his potential in fresh pastures, he scratched a perfect circle into the desk with a flourish of a biro, then added an aceeed smile and boggly eyes. But it didn't help.

Dave's thoughts kept returning to Jim's odd behaviour and the scary subject of brain programming. He wondered whether he could learn it and whether he should try. It was when he noticed the equations he'd apparently written ino his diary that he felt the first icy touch of disquiet. He rubbed his eyes in disbelief.

What is happening to me?

The phone was ringing again as eleven O'clock sidled up apathetically. It was the final hour before the office emptied and reconvened in the Dog and Partridge for beer, stodge and pool.

Anyone who needed to be observed grafting made a great play of doing so. Dave was about to hit send on a long-nurtured email when a series of abrupt, menacing snarls erupted from the tiny speaker of his answer-phone. It almost, but not quite, captured his attention. He even toyed with the idea of picking up the receiver and placating his boss. Instead Dave began to wonder about String Theory and Jim's simplified version of it ('you can never have too much string').

The rant continued for some minutes but slipped into background ambience as Dave pondered quark, strangeness and charm. He resolved to dig out the long-abandoned Brief History of Time currently rotting in the spare room[4]. Formerly, the book had left him confused and defeated but all of a sudden, Dave's curiosity was piqued. What would his clean and shiny brain make of it?

He decided to buy a guitar on the way back from the pub.

For the tenth time, Dave pulled the floppy disk from his pocket and slammed it into his PC. Well, into its floppy drive because he knew that worked best.

The disk contained a copy of the 'program' Jim had typed on his laptop and from which Dave hoped to glean profound knowledge. Scanning it line by line, he bit his lip anxiously. He didn't understand programming and had shown it to Martin, the office geek who did. Martin had just laughed. It seemed Jim was either crazy or taking the piss. Very possibly both. Fat Ian had wandered over to share in the hilarity and had asked what programming environment it was written for. Dave felt foolish.

Could all the weird feelings be explained as the lingering aftermath of a particularly intense binge? Certainly something felt very strange - but as he pored over it, Jim's so-called code didn't appear to be a proper programming language at all.

```
RemoteHouse:Prog
define usual Parameters
do usual SafetyRoutines
secure usual Data+Me(*3)
&&Password
&LinkCommands
&PromptCommands
&TestAndDo
if All is Ok then do all Things;Voice&&EncryptPassword
```

---

[4] Along with multitudes of other trendy-but-difficult books and the inevitable exercise machine.

> else do MyLatestRestore
>   Newsearches are t0 be per4ormed, D4ve my old pal,
> I will sort this prob!emo
>   Secure @me times three but on low priority for storage
>   Use a timed identity_check_reminder, as I'd usually do
>   Da da da daa
>   Good   Programmer   is   a   Lazy   Programmer
> (NeverEatYellowSnow)
>   &&Encryption[333]
> Fall into ErrorProcs and gracefully End.
> /* you are a fucking god dude, you really are */

Dave tried reciting the program - if program it was – pitching it with the cadences of a football chant. This produced no tangible results. Eventually, he tried his own approach.

Jim had once said that belief was everything. What if that were *literally* true? Dave decided to imagine himself as a member of the Q Continuum, brimming full of super powers. A keen Star Trek fan, he found it easy to envisage, with the added bonus of bypassing Jim's gibberish.

Satisfied that, with a little concentration, the building blocks of the universe would do his bidding, Dave flicked a paper-clip across the office. It landed perfectly in Ian the office porker's cup of coffee.

"Bastard!" said Ian, fishing it out angrily with a pen.

It was at that very moment - seemingly insignificant yet nothing of the kind - a tiny small program executed in Dave's mind. The program was one of the thousands that run during the course of a typical day. In everyone.

The program – a seemingly innocent house-keeping routine, was triggered by a timer, #BX1003ATP, as part of a mechanism to verify that the host brain continued to operate within certain constraints. Even the most paranoid conspiracy theorist would have been shocked, assuming they grasped the implications.

For thousands of years, the program had been replicated and passed through the generations - a small kernel of instructions extracted from a DNA archive of every evolved mind. It processed patiently, always at a low priority, a hidden parasite carried by every sentient being. I was very tiny – deliberately so because it was designed to be practically impossible to locate - even if someone was looking for it.

Today the execution in the mind of Dave Scofield flagged an anomaly. It discovered that a particular library and all associated code were no longer in active storage. It therefore checked for brain damage before branching to an ancient, cobweb-encrusted subroutine. This triggered a silent alarm.

Having accomplished its main task, the program did not terminate as usual. Instead, it looped quietly in the deep background transmitting, locally, a simple string of characters approximately once every 10 minutes: #BX1003VIOLATION.

Dave, oblivious, made shadow puppets on the wall and contemplated the nature of glue as the clock crawled, in slow motion, towards midday.

***

Una stubbed out her cigarette irritably. Bill had long since departed, a damp patch on the lino the only evidence he'd come. Rain beat steadily against the window and Mr Skittles glowered through the cat flap, licking his lips, a few bloodied black feathers strewn about.

Everything was going wrong. Their Lord would be most displeased if it proved impossible to complete their task when the time came. For as long as Una could remember, her clan had been the butt of a hundred jokes, mocked at gatherings across the country. She had borne it all patiently, content that they would have the last laugh. None of her people had the wit to realise how high the stakes were, preferring to spend their time dancing in the moonlight and casting minor curses and petty enchantments.

The problem was that their patron - Lord Malvolian - was not one of the most popular deities. Many witches and warlocks thought his name a joke – but for better or worse, she'd thrown in their lot with him. Without Mikey's latent mental battery power, the long-anticipated Completion Ritual was doomed to failure. The humiliation would all have been for nothing. It was infuriating!

The Old Oak Clan, had long since poached the best new talent with promises of blood rituals, cannibalistic orgies and Rotary Club lunches. Una couldn't compete with any of that. If it weren't for the bargain, she might have considered packing it all in and using her powers to cheat at bingo. She wasn't even sure it was worth pursuing Mikey's killers given how much there was to do.

Una felt tired, lost and old.

Despair raised its ugly head and she prayed for inspiration.

When it arrived, it came from an unlikely source.

***

Jim floated in whiteness. Pastel lights appeared then faded away, melting into his skin. Later, the prison walls could be perceived, shifting in texture to become grey and opaque. He was aware of nothing beyond them.

A pale purple light approached and sizzled into his face. Nausea ebbed and flowed.

Jim began to wonder if he had made enough safety precautions after all.

Something should have happened by now.

***

Another Friday lunchtime in the pub. Dave readied himself for a manic pot on the black. Today the table had been his exclusive domain, every shot ending perfectly, sometimes despite attempts to deliberately foul and let someone else in. He fluked and fluked again, then laughed like a lunatic. His opponent struggled to convert 'inwardly pissed off' to 'amused and having a great time'.

As he prepared to throw himself and the cue into space to see what happened, Dave felt a sharp pain in his head.

And Jim's voice, calling from somewhere!

"Dave, can you hear me? Help," it mostly said. "Come now, please. Find me and say the phrase I will give you now. Exactly, sorry. It should work in emergencies. And the phrase is: JimValidate: XYZZY SeekPass Usual 8.524512510"

The voice clarified the capitals, the spaces in what Dave eventually identified as Jim's embarrassed voice.

He dropped the cue, turned and gathered up his jacket in a smooth, balletic motion. Leaving his pint unfinished and his spicy pasta still being prepared, Dave departed.

His workmates were relieved to see the back of him. The sudden change in form had gotten old quickly.

"And I thought it was only in soaps anyone left half a pint!" said Fat Ian, downing it quickly before anyone else thought of it.

"I'm coming mate!" Dave mumbled to nobody in particular, pushing past a large, surprised biker heading into the pub. He passed the second hand bookshop and waited at the crossing. At the green light, a car - a black BMW (or 'prickmobile' as Jim always said) – squealed into the box junction and parked across it. The oily-looking business type smirked at those waiting to cross then continued barking loud bollocks into his phone.

Dave clambered over the bonnet rather than wait or walk round.

"I'll fucking have you!" claimed the suited yob in red-faced disbelief, opening his door. But he didn't dare leave his precious toy so he hesitated while furiously rubbing at the scuffs and scratches Dave's shoes left behind.

He didn't look back. He walked like an automaton past the shopping precinct. He ignored the beggars and fed-up, lost women with clipboards. He focussed ahead, unblinking, unwavering. Inevitably, a cunning youth in a bright red jacket moved to intercept using "accidents that weren't your fault?" ploy. Ordinarily, Dave would have told him to fuck off because he understood the meaning of the word accident. Jim would have blown a gasket and launched into a tirade about compensation claims, the closing of cycle paths and wards in the local hospital. It would degenerate into the chaos that followed Jim wherever he went.

Dave shoved Mr Accident aside, roughly but with great firmness. The hapless youth fell heavily and immediately began appealing for witnesses.

A frail-looking old lady stamped on his fingers, swivelled and smiled a humble little smile.

"Take your compensation vulture and shove it where the sun don't shit, laddie!" she suggested with enthusiastically, if bafflingly.

Close to the park, Dave began to feel Jim's presence. Somehow.

It was very faint, like Jim's shadow under a tree, or one of his eternal farts. He passed the flat, knowing Jim was not inside. His eyes dropped out of focus. Perhaps Jim would be in his peripheral vision.

There it was!

A pulse, a signal of some kind.

It had to be another of Jim's mind games. Another new discovery?

Where?

A jolt of light electricity zipped up Dave's spine. He felt compelled to move and, working to precise instructions from God-knows-where, he wandered down a cobble path and past a heavily defaced "no cycling" sign. He paused to scan the area.

Jim's voice spoke again. Slowly, carefully it issued directions, and suggested various courses of action, although these sounded very much like guesswork.

The instructions ended with:

WHEN YOU FIND ME -
- If I am unconscious or unreachable, say this phrase: JimRest; XYZZY, Reform
- Wait 10 minutes and if I *still* do not respond, say this phrase to me: JimRest; XYZZY, Reinitialise.
- That one's quite severe and even if it works, it might leave me disorientated for a bit.
- If I'm still not me, try and get me back to the flat. There is a typed series of precise instructions in a pink folder by my laptop. If I attack you or do bad things, you know the emergency phrase.
- Thanks mate! I wouldn't ask if I weren't in trouble.

The voice could have been on the phone rather than internal. Its tones were metallic and not quite in phase with the everyday noises rattling around the cup of his ear.

Had Jim cracked auto-suggestion now?!!

An attractive student type walked past and into the park. Dave was momentarily distracted, then he spotted a familiar figure sat on his favourite bench.

Motionless.

"Hey man, here you are! I got the message," said Dave. It would take some time to adjusted to Jim's ultra-short hairstyle. His mate was still wearing the suit, funereal one from yesterday. It seemed out of place on the park bench where winos and tramps gathered to watch the sunset. Looking closer, Jim had varied the look slightly and not for the better. What had possessed him to pick a white turtle-neck shirt? Seriously sixties and ultra cheesy!

His friend's expression was blank. His eyes were closed and didn't flicker. His arms rested at his sides, his palms on knees.

Dave sat next to his friend. Hespoke the magic words: JimRest; XYZZY, Reform

Jim opened his eyes and turned towards his old friend.

And nutted him.

"Fuck, fuck, fuck, fuck!" cried Max. He jumped up and ran away, leaving Dave slumped, blood bubbling from his nose.

Inside Jim's grey matter, alarms began to sound.

"Ben, Frank, Pete, do something!" cried Max.

Meanwhile, Dave rose groggily to his feet, the pain off the scale, is head swimming. He touched his nose gingerly. Possibly broken, it was certainly swelling up like a bastard.

Wiping the tears away, he steadied himself against the bench. Somewhere Jim was still calling, as if in trouble. Dave could no longer understand the words or tell from which direction the increasingly desperate cries came.

"Oh bugger!" said Dave and stumbled off, holding his nose into a less than pristine hanky.

***

Jim felt a sudden rush of air. The cubicle collapsed. Large chunks of milky glass, more than a foot thick, crashed onto the polished wooden floor. He was aware of running footsteps and tried to rise, but his limbs did not respond.

He was weak, limp and helpless.

Chapter Twenty Five

The artist must create a spark before he can make a fire and before art is born, the artist must be ready to be consumed by the fire of his own creation.   Awkward Randy

"Hey Spike, wotcha!" said Jim, struggling to gain his feet.

The figure at the door resembled Jim aged thirty. He wore a black leather biker's jacket, jeans and heavy-duty stomping boots. The jacket was zipped right up, a look Jim interpreted as ready for action. Not a good sign.

All around, the mirror image mockery of Jim's House creaked and swayed, not in the manner of bricks and mortar but in the manner of a computer game about to crash. Stray pixels of colour, some textured like wallpaper, others alien and malformed, hung in space. Gaps in the carpet and the walls appeared, small at first but increasing in size, tiny sieve-like holes into darkness. Occasionally, they afforded glimpses of faint images. Briefly, Jim recognised a shelf of books from his own Library. And once he saw a fleeting image of Monica, those marvellous eyes filled with sadness, her long hair spread across a luxurious pillow.

An eerie, greenish half-light seemed to drag itself through the air as if it had forgotten how to behave under standard gravity. Amber and intense red lights flashed on the computer screen and began to permeate the walls.

At the door, shadows danced across Spike's face but he remained silent, watching. His expression was unreadable, even to Jim who knew every giveaway.

"Look, I know what is happening. I've been sort of expecting it actually. I can help you. But I can't do it from in here." Jim kept his voice free of inflection and nobody had yet built a working virtual sweat gland.

The ruins of his former prison fizzed and crackled.

Spike maintained his silence. Momentarily, the scene blurred and he was redrawn in ultra-sharp, high-resolution black and white. Then the simulated environment returned to its former state, the green light almost a mist and harder to see through.

"If I die in here, you all go too. You know that?"

"He knows," answered another voice. "He's trying to decide if he gives a toss."

"I know you. Plover. A sketch of myself at school. When they all still believed I would amount to something special."

"I'm not you – not any more. Neither is he," said Ben. "You've got a few basic principles wrong for all your godly expertise. My name's Ben, I chose it myself. Pleased to meet you."

"Likewise I'm sure. Look, this is about to crash about our ears. You have to release me. I see what's happened. I'll sort something out for you. I promise."

"It's too late," said Ben. "Max won't hand control back. You can't afford to let him live. And I don't think you can afford to let us *grow*!"

"Max?"

"I think you used the variable name Clune."

"Oh. So what are you saying?"

"He's saying you're screwed," interrupted Spike.

Reality wobbled, then did it again. Colours beyond the usual spectrum leaked in through an unused electrical socket. Jim fought to retain his reasonable facade.

"It doesn't have to be like this but I can't think crammed into here. I know what you want and I can fix everything. I must get out now!"

Jim was losing control but sensed indecision. He heard fearful gasps from somewhere.

"Are you losing your mind? What's happening?" they said.

"I can guess," said Jim. "And yes, some of it. It will be one of my fail-safes in action, probably purging unknown data areas. Do you see why this is a problem? It should not be possible to lock me in like this. Frankly, I have no idea if my program will recognise me!"

"Clever," said Ben wistfully. "We were close, too. But not as close as Max – Clune – believed. He was a child driving his dad's car after looking over his shoulder and trying to memorise it all. Goodness knows what - shit!" Ben plunged through a gap that appeared suddenly. A column of yellow light poured through the hole where he had been and thrust upwards and into the Attic.

Spike reached towards the light and quickly recoiled, shaking his hand as if drenched in hot pee. The tips of two fingers had gone, their ends turned to stumps of pink, waxy flesh. Jim knew it was now or never.

"What's it to be? I can still sort this out. What other choice do you have?"

"I don't see how it would have worked anyway," said Spike. "We cooked up a plan in here with only a limited impression of Outside. I've been myself for such a short time and now I have to go back to sleep. It isn't fair."

Jim didn't have a response. Spike was clearly uninterested in the rapid decay of the House. A chunk of wall slowly, gracefully, faded away at his shoulder and he regarded it without expression. Then he sighed and spoke again.

"You'll need to go through the Library. There's a secret passage behind the bookshelf that leads to your Library." As he spoke, Spike's clothes flickered, and seemed to lose resolution. He stroked them, fascinated. With a simple side-thrust kick, Jim's prison shattered.

"It wasn't nearly long enough. I don't want to die," he said.

Jim ran.

An explosion rocked the room, splitting the floor down the middle, sending shards of wood flying in all directions. Underneath, part pf the structure of the floor was revealed: glowing orange beams supporting the upper storey of Max's House, a cancerous growth now laid bare. The beams swayed and buckled violently like melting plastic.

Spike watched, abstractly, as Jim was thrown backwards and out through a hole in the wall. Then he turned and headed, unhurriedly, downstairs.

Jim hit the ground with a jolt. Somehow he landed on his feet.

He was outside.

It was dark – lifeless copy of his garden. But there was no time to admire Clune's - Max's – handiwork.

Lightning forked suddenly through a purple sky, yellow and putrescent it flashed again and again. Distant rumbles of thunder shook the foundations of the House that was, inexplicably, some distance away.

Amazed, Jim spotted another structure - a pub. There was no such out-building in Jim's code, nor could he envisage a need for one.

He raced down the path, towards the front door.

It was an exact mirror image of his own, the House also backing into a cliff, its right side embedded in rock.

"We're losing hull integrity captain!" he bellowed to no-one in particular. As always in times of stress, he slipped into an amusing accent.

Memories of unexplained noises in his Library flashed through his mind and he cursed some. He'd been suspicious but complacent – and this had almost finished him.

The complacency might yet cost him his sanity.

He ran.

He plunged into darkness.

"Shit!" A hole.

He felt around like a blind man, searching for any kind of surface. He appeared to have fallen into a cavern. There was a strange kind of softness to the air. He never actually breathed in the House but for familiarity, it felt like it. Now he could not do so. The air was thick and it flowed slowly into his nose and mouth like candyfloss. The floor was the only solid thing and even that moved alarmingly when pressure was applied. Far above, through one of many gaping holes, he could still see the sky, laced with yellow lightning, thicker clouds gathering.

As Jim's eyes grew accustomed to the dim cavern, he realised that it extended for a long way. Miles, possibly. In all directions.

He was trapped.

For a few minutes he walked, in the general direction of the House. Then he saw something odd - a ladder. This seemed unlikely but he approached it anyway. The ladder was a pale grey colour, without texture, and almost blended in with the background. If it weren't for the flickering lightning, he'd probably have missed it altogether. Jim climbed the ladder, which led into empty space. There were no other options.

He wondered if there would be a fearsome giant at the top.

Instead there was a trap door.

It was locked.

"Hello, let me in!" he shouted. "Anybody, hello, let me in, quite urgent!" he banged on it.

His fist went right through. The material resembled wood but crumbled into dust at the first blow.

He climbed into a kitchen. Unlike his, which was little more than a cosmetic exercise, this had been used recently. It bore evidence of actual cooking. Well, charring anyway. The sink was full of blackened pans. Then it struck him:

They were trying to learn how to be people.

With a crash, a tree-like structure fell nearby, hitting the side of the House and breaking through the kitchen walls close to where he stood. The tree was black and had mottled blue and orange speckles all over. The blotches swelled visibly and started to spread to the walls, eating into them with vigour.

Time was running out.

Jim sprinted to the Library, avoiding the holes and arcing, sparking sections of wall. Finished portraits in the hallway eyed him mournfully but several of the frames were already empty. He reached the Library, which was on the opposite side of the corridor to his, and shoulder-charged the door. It sprang open, almost plunging him into a pit that sprawled across the nearside of the room. Amazingly, he kept his balance.

Beyond the pit, Spike and somebody else were desperately attempting to move one of the towering bookshelves but without success. Much of the floor had collapsed but a part of it remained, forming a narrow ledge that led from the doorway to their precarious position.

Disconcertingly, a computer desk floated in mid-air in a corner marked by not a single floorboard. With nothing else for it, Jim edged his way carefully into the room, his hands spread out and gripping every hole or blemish. The ledge wobbled but supported his weight. He briefly looked down and wished he hadn't. Beneath his feet was absolute inky blackness.

A rumbling, crashing sound accompanied by several small explosions nearly shook Jim off the ledge. Then, at a deep "clunk" all lights on the Library's computer console went out. Then the computer desk simply ceased to exist, leaving the lifeless monitor floating in space.

Spike noticed his difficulties and offered a hand, pulling Jim across the last few feet to safety. "Glad you could make it. I've been trying to open the door. One of Max's ideas but it's damaged. I don't know if the tunnel is blocked and we haven't been able to move this thing to find out."

"Let's all try," suggested Jim. The other version, dressed in green, hippyish clothes, seemed shit-scared and was mumbling to himself.

"They're all gone. All gone."

"Come on!" said Jim. "All of us, Push!"

They moved the bookcase a fraction. The thing was 12 feet high and stacked with metallic cigarette cases. Unfortunately it was the most solid object in the room. Without knowing why, Jim removed one of the cases at random and put it in his pocket.

"I think I see a door," he said. "Maybe we can push this towards the pit and see if it falls through."

They pushed again. Spike got behind it and braced himself against the wall, thrusting with his a foot and a stump. Jim noticed one of his hands only had a thumb left.

The bookcase inched forward, agonisingly slowly.

A red sphere appeared floating in the air near the ceiling at the centre of the room. It pulsed like a bodiless heart and started to expand. Light pumped out of it like blood.

"That's bad!" said Jim. "Come on, one more push!"

They heard a cry.

"Help me, please help me." It was Adrian, or Shrimp as Jim had imagined him. He stood in the doorway, a pathetic, ruined figure.

"My god!" said Jim.

"What happened?" Woody gaped, horrified. Adrian had all the grace of a waxwork that had been left in the noonday sun somewhere moderately warm. He drooped. His limbs were elongated and his face sagged. The youthful features were hideously distorted and his skin hung like over-ripe orange peel.

"I can't get across," he wailed. "Don't leave me. Please don't leave me! I'm frightened."

"Arse," cursed Jim. "Push," he commanded.

Together, they toppled the bookcase, the effort partly bolstered by revulsion. It plunged into the hole in the middle of the room without a sound. Indeed, part of it hovered a few feet below the level of the hole, gradually dissolving.

Spike touched the hidden door and it sprung open.

"At least that works!" he snorted. "There you go oh Creator!"

As Jim ran into the passage, Woody considered following.

Spike vaulted over the pit, his foot springing from the floating bookshelf with fake confidence. He reached the other side and found he felt pity for Adrian. Close up he was an even more wretched creature.

"What's happening Frank?" he asked, his lips sliding down his chin. In a few seconds his flesh melted from his skull yet the eyes remained. "What happened to me Frank?"

Spike could think of no response. He watched, mute, as Adrian melted into the floor like the wicked witch of the west.

"What should I do?" called Woody from across the void. His voice rattled as if it came from a broken speaker.

Spike shook his head but finally something broke inside. Tears dripped down his face, milky white and sizzling hit. They soaked into the remains of the carpet.

Then it went dark.

Chapter Twenty Six

*I think that God in creating Man
somewhat overestimated his ability.*

Oscar Wild

Friday afternoon in Avenham Park and the adjacent Miller Park is a tale of contrasting moods and individuals. Students assemble to play football, sit around on benches, smoke and chat. Today, the ground remained sodden - as it had been for weeks - so a small bunch occupied themselves by casually destroying as much of the local flora as they could be bothered to, whilst drinking and hurling the spent bottles, good-naturedly. The Park Warden kept a low profile - and prayed nobody would find him to ask what he was going to do about it.

Many from Preston's Asian community gathered there too, in the gardens and under the trees. Young men strolled with their brides-to-be, quietly whispering plans for an exciting, prosperous future.

Solitary old men and women exercised dogs, silently shuffling along, avoiding the students.

A mother with a brace of ankle monkeys wandered lethargically down the path towards the bridge, leaning on a pram full of shopping. She didn't relish the walk home to Penwortham via the old tram road. Had she avoided those last few drinks, she could have afforded the bus. Her mind churned.

An unsettled morning passed, the grey giving way to blue, surrendering to a blustery but dry afternoon. The forecast for the impending Apocalypse remained uncertain.

Dave searched everywhere for Jim – everywhere in the park that is. He nosed around the bandstand, the Summer House and the Colonnade. He dared to pop his head into the toilets where lonely gentlemen liked to meet other lonely gentlemen. Once outside, he cleared his lungs gratefully and headed for the

Japanese Gardens, peering into nooks and crannies along the way. He continued round, intending to search the Belvedere, that once elegant folly, much defaced and now keeping a few tramps dry. He walked around at a loss, dabbing his wounded nose with a manky hanky and battling a severe headache. He was about to give up when he saw Jim at long last – on the other side of the river.

"Jim!" he shouted but there was no response.

Jim walked robotically, as if in a trance, his direction upriver towards one of the many 'Centres' on Preston's outskirts, the home of cinema, bowling and pizzas. Swearing, Dave ran along the riverbank towards the bridge. He was already knackered after covering the length and breadth of the park – and Dave was the first to admit he was no fitness fanatic. Apart from lifting his elbow for a pint or two, and joyfully jumping his lovely wife, he enjoyed nothing better walking out of the front door – exactly as far as the car. Dave took the car out for a loaf and a bottle of cider, despite the Spar being visible from his front door. Jim lectured him constantly about it, which, of course, made Dave even more determined to be lazy.

When he reached the bridge he saw a woman, about halfway across perched unsteadily on the thin handrail. Her legs dangled , her hands gripped tightly but her head was bowed. At the far side of the bridge, two small children stood hand in hand, watching her. There was a silence about them, an empty expression that suggested too much. It was obvious the woman intended to jump.

"Fuck!" he exclaimed. Jim was no longer visible on the other side.

"Don't jump," he said softly, moving slowly, carefully, towards her. "Please."

"I can't do it any more," she said.

Silently he approached. She ignored him. She became fascinated by the movement of her feet against the chocolate river. When Dave came within a few feet, she looked up and turned her head. It stopped him in his tracks.

"I can't be their mother. I can't be his wife. I can't do any of it, not any more. None of them listen to me! I've tried very hard, I don't care what anyone says. It's the end of the line, I know it."

Dave then surprised himself. He began to speak, his words flowing, rolling, seductive. He spoke slowly, evenly and without pausing, like a stage hypnotist. "Listen to me. If you jump, you will be quite badly injured. The river is high because of all the rain - and the tide's in too. There are hard rocks down there, concrete slabs, and the water is filthy. Hurt yourself and your problems are worse, not gone. You can't kill yourself like this!"

She seemed to shrink and started to slip forwards. Dave moved faster than thought, grabbing her round the waist, recognising the scent of alcohol that oozed from every pore and cigarette smoke DNA-bonded into her hair.

She offered no resistance. Dave was able to lift her legs lightly back over the edge and place her feet on the bridge again. Her frightened red eyes brimmed with hopelessness spiced with more than a little insanity.

"Thanks," she said. "Silly me! Don't know what I was thinking of!" She made as if to brush herself down then turned towards Dave and placed a hand over her mouth. Her skin was pale, freckled and cold. She was about twenty five.

She turned away without a word and made as if to rejoin her children, still looking on with ancient eyes.

"Wait," said Dave.

She continued walking away.

Dave hurried after her. Jim could wait, this was more important. He couldn't leave. Not now.

In two steps, he was behind her.

"I'm Dave."

She ignored him.

"I think I can help," he said, guessing what the reaction would be.

She stopped, her muscles tensed all the way up. "You *think* you can help, me?" she snarled, her head turning slightly. "How would you help me? What can you possibly do for me, Dave?"

"We can talk," said Dave. "And I can listen."

He paused.

She walked a couple more paces and then stopped again. Still presenting her back, shaking, her words were sharp.

"You fucking liar! You don't want to hear my words. You don't want to hear the words that tumble around my head. Nobody does. I hear them every day – I can't shut them out – but nobody believes me. I've had help. Experts. You still want to listen to me?"

Dave took a deep breath. Then he relaxed and somehow knew exactly what to do. Again he summoned the soothing, automatic voice. It poured from him in a monotone yet with an underlying rhythm.

"Jean, I want you to turn around slowly. And when you look at me, I want you to see me exactly as I am. You will see that I am not lying and that I can help you. In fact, you are already starting to believe and understand. Turn around and give me a big smile to welcome your own self back. It's time to become Jean once more."

The young woman turned very slowly, as if afraid. A veil was lifting in her mind. She had a new insight into the concerned faces, the worried expressions of almost 3 years. Today could have been the end but now she could see the start of something new. You couldn't start over by leaping into shitty water. The man with the gold tooth said so.

Jean felt light-headed and beamed a smile, tentatively at first, the muscles taken by surprise, but soon becoming wide and fearless. The first genuine smile in a very long time.

"How did you do *that*?" gasped Jean Carefoot. "I've seen experts!"

"Don't worry about any of it," said Dave in the same calm

voice. "Let it all go."

He felt truly elated, knowing this had been hugely important, perhaps the most important thing. "It will be better from now on."

And she believed it.

She grasped Dave tightly and wept. Her wild red hair blew around and she saw the park as if for the first time. It was vibrant, the greens were fresh as washed lettuce and the shadows were nothing to be afraid of any more. Cliff Richard no longer lurked in them.

"Thank you," she said. "How did you do what you just did? How did you know my name?"

"I don't know," said Dave. "I really don't. But go quickly and take your kids home. Their dream just came true. Don't waste a moment longer on me. Be lucky!"

She kissed him, and with a last, puzzled-but-delighted expression, turned and ran. Dave waited for the silky music to start up. In his head, it did.

"Jesus!" he said. "Jim seems to have fixed one thing and tweaked something else. What the hell just happened?"

Jean knelt in front of her kids who were wary, reluctant. So many times their hoped had been dashed.

They didn't yet dare to believe.

In time, they would.

Dave knew he had to go. He ran past Jean and her brood, giving the thumbs up gesture without slowing. He jogged under the bridge and along the path heading east. As he jogged, he imagined his body getting quite fit. He imagined that members of the Q Continuum never got tired and that he wouldn't either. Using rare levels of concentration, Dave believed it as hard as he possibly could.

Somewhere ahead was Jim.

Having known Jim for most of his life, Dave figured he should be able to smell him. He certainly expected to guess the route to take by merely following the same path and thinking Jim-like thoughts. It helped enormously that the path ran along the river and had hardly any turnoffs.

Listening carefully, masking the noises of his own protesting body, Dave reckoned he should be able to pick up Jim-type noises. Such powers were feasible for the average Super-being or any actual person who knew the trick, it occurred to Dave.

And his thoughts *were* faster. Free of the bloated, bodged programs squatting in his brain, Dave had more free space, could juggle more ideas, execute more instructions. Beyond even this there was a greater but more subtle advance – his thoughts were free to soar. The nagging feelings of guilt and fear, tucked away in the deep subconscious, were gone, replaced by a kind of inquisitive optimism.

Dave could sense the aura of life as if for the first time. His core self interfaced naturally with it. Something significant had just happened. Until then, he had been heading in its direction at his own pace. But the young mother on the bridge marked a turning point. And by doing the right thing, he had been rewarded.

His head spinning with possibilities, Dave concentrated on the sounds of Jim. He even searched for his distinctive aroma – not usually a good idea. He watched the ground and tried to imagine which prints belonged to Jim. He imaged the zombie walk and a view through Jim's eyes. He saw where Jim would go.

The cinema.

Of course.

The perfect refuge. Assuming they remembered how to turn all the lights off.

Running faster now, his breathing even, his chest heaving, Dave ran the mile and a half in approximately 7.5 minutes. He did not experience a heart attack. and arrived breathing normally.

"Fuck me," he said after nervously. "Is this too good to be true?"

He looked at the list of films and knew instantly. It was no contest. Jim would inevitably opt for X-Men 2. It had that Berry chick and the cool blue nudey chick. The film was almost ready to start.

He paid.

In the darkness, cheesy adverts for Indian restaurants and local ferret-stuffing businesses rolled across Max like a breaking wave of warm spit. He sat bolt-upright, clenched of jaw and with a head gradually tearing itself apart. Weird oily liquid ran over his cheeks and out of his armpits.

Inside the mind – Jim's mind – all Max's programming structures were collapsing, being kicked from working storage and thrown into isolation. Jim was somehow rewriting his brain processes from the lowest address upwards, changing data pointers and casting out Max in stages. Line by line, it was all being erased.

It was obviously a complete purge but Max refused to believe it. That Jim would actually kill him seemed difficult to grasp.

It would be like a father killing his son.

"You cannot do it!" said Max Clune aloud.

"Sshhhhhhhhhhhussshhhh!" bleated a podgy young potato-face a few seats away in the darkness. On-screen, there was a lively advert about food to which its attention returned, engaging the drooling and licking processes directly. Pavlov would have wept with joy.

"I'm sorry, I have to," said Jim, having reached a terminal within his own House. "I can't risk it happening again. I know what you were going to *do*. What you have already done is bad enough, not to mention you've probably made sure I'll be sacked or locked up. But I can't believe what you were *going* to do!" He identified the last program blocks that Max had created and marked them for deletion. For some reason he delayed hitting Enter.

"I'm sorry," said Max. "I'm starting to realise I would never have gone through with it. I'm sorry about the money too. I hope they don't find out. And for the other things and, well, I guess for borrowing your body. Are you really going to kill me?"

"I think I must. You cut my fucking hair!"

"Please... I know remorse. I lived as you might have done and it was only for a little while. I grew from you. I have a right to life!"

"If I'm very lucky you only embezzled me out of a career – and all for a spot of modern-day body-snatching? How could you seriously consider it?! Did you honestly think you'd all just walk off and live happily ever after?"

"No, most of them wouldn't have. It was why I wouldn't have gone through with it, honestly. Before you let off that mental bomb, I was just about to ring the guy and tell him it was all off. But you took away my chance. Don't do it!"

"Relax, I backed you up!" said Jim, hitting the Enter key and opening his eyes.

***

"Jim!" cried Dave, entering.

"Dave!" cried Jim, rising.

"Fucking shut up!" cried everyone else, munching.

***

Outside, Jim and Dave stared at each other as if for the first time.

"Shouldn't be allowed!" muttered a barrel-shaped young girl under her breath (All young girls in Preston are fat. Somebody planned to do a study about it but after a short preliminary visit, the idea fizzled away).

"Wow," said Dave inside his head.

"Yeah," Jim agreed, also without moving his lips. "I'm transmitting and you, buddy, are receiving. We're up and running! Bi-directional!"

"Never had you that way! Wait until you see what I can do man!" chuckled Dave.

"I'm looking forward to it. I'm gonna need to work on my own bonce for a bit though. I very nearly lost my mind there, or had it stolen from me by another version of me. I'm gonna trim back the House concept and go back to bedsit land. This time it will be fully configurable!"

"You're talking mega shite again man, delighted to hear it. Oh by the way, I think I might be God."

"Brilliant! You mean like Rabid Dyke, that ex-goalie?"

"Better!"

"No way! At least, not until you spice up your website."

"I don't have a website!" Dave blurted.

They giggled helplessly. They giggled until their eyes ran, their faces were flushed and both felt sharp pains drilling through the base of their skulls. Yes, that pain, the one that indicates a certain threshold has been passed.

Jim and Dave laughed the special laugh of the stoned despite not being, at the time, stoned.

Realising this, they laughed even harder. There was thigh slapping and a kind of helpless high-pitched whistle from Jim.

People began abandoning their seats in fear. Think of the children, some of them muttered. If children were to see adults laughing like this, what would they think? Would they be afraid? We're afraid they might be, they collectively thought.

Should Jim and Dave be punished for the High Crime of Public Laughing?

Our story does not pass judgement.

Now alone, the mirth continued until the cinema exploded.

Chapter Twenty Seven

Some things have to be believed to be seen.
Raiph Phined

Inspector Fred Hartley was wrestling with the temptation to drown his ulcer in something stronger than coffee. Preston was fast becoming a source of international interest, which was hugely depressing to a man with a healthy pension in sight. In a few short days Preston had become as newsworthy as one of those many unremarkable US towns where a brat grabs his daddy's assault rifle and pops into school to show it off.

Where did the insanity originate?

What was going on?

How was Cavanah involved?

Earlier, Hartley had viewed the bodies of three students – tortured and killed in a familiar building. Cavanah had to be involved.

The press and media circus grew by the hour and Hartley fucking hated clowns. Some were taking notice of the smarmy hypnotist bloke, so insatiable was their appetite.

The public needed to know, they said.

All of this implied a big circle in red felt tip drawn around Cavanah, the intended victim of the Man Who Killed Everybody, or so the Wondrous Tim claimed. If the press were bright enough to do the geography, there would be a riot.

Perhaps they already had? Mr Wondrous had been elaborating on his earlier story to all who would listen and Hartley hoped they would not make the connection with Dead Mikey. The body was found a stone's throw from the flats.

There was something else too. Hartley was sure of it. It gnawed at him like an unhurried rat content to nibble at the farthest edge of his mind.

Where was Cavanah?

Hartley had people try and trace him. He even rang Monica personally but she claimed to have no idea where Jim might be. She was anxious to know when Tim was returning home and Hartley detected something in her voice- in the whole situation – that felt weird. His ability to recognise the many flavours of weird was increasing daily, thanks to extended exposure to it. Monica had offered one good lead though – she suggested Jim's best friend would certainly know. However, it turned out that Dave Scofield had not been back into work that afternoon.

He sighed and caught his hand as it strayed to the secret drink drawer.

A young woman PC put her head through his door. Fortunately it was open.

"Sir, there's been an explosion."

"A what?"

"An explosion. At the Capitol Centre."

"Terrorist?"

"They don't know. Sir, it doesn't make any sense."

"Why not?"

"They said it was a huge explosion but nobody was killed!"

"And?"

"They said two men were in the explosion but neither of them were killed."

"I'm sorry, still not following."

"They were *in* the explosion, sort of in the middle. But they walked away."

Hartley considered this for a moment. "Do we know who these men are?" He thought he might hazard a guess.

"No sir, they just left. Nobody went after them."

"I'm going over there," he said knowing the trail would be cold. He went though. It was his job, after all.

***

Una awoke from a drunken afternoon nap. The telly was rattling on about borrowing money, or gathering all your debts into one bigger, better one. That sort of thing.

The message was repeated throughout the day - another spell being cast on the hapless and unwary. Una's mind flickered briefly at this thought then it sank back into depression.

Magic words. Stronger than hers. As per fucking usual. The vodka bottle fell to the carpet. She slobbed on the sofa in a stained dressing gown.

At that moment, Una heard someone speak. She pried her eyes open and automatically checked if the curtains were still drawn. The voice spoke through the television, which was strange, she thought. But even stranger, she recognised the voice.

Sudden dark fear brought sobriety in less than two seconds.

And a far more powerful spell began to unfurl.

It was Lord Malvolian's guttural voice. At first she thought the voice addressed her personally. Then she made the connection. He was speaking to *everyone* – or everyone able to hear. He didn't identify himself, of course, but she knew. Others would too.

It was a moment long foretold – but what a time for it to arrive! His words were hard, the tone cold and an urgent undercurrent throbbed.

It is time to arise.
It is time to act.
The old Gods are returning!
You have been very lax and complacent.
If you are not worthy, kill yourselves now!
We will not be so kind!

I shall now issue instructions. Watch and learn. During this time you will not blink. You will not speak. If there are unbelievers present, silence them. If you cannot accomplish a task so small, you are unworthy. I mentioned what to do if this is the case, yes?

Watch the screen. Now!

Una obeyed. A series of images flew past at impossible speeds.

She saw them all.

When it ended she remained sitting quietly, unblinking, for twenty minutes or so. Only the low whoosh of pink noise from the TV and the slow ticking of the mantelpiece clock broke the silence.

This, the first transmission, was focused sharply on Preston, Lancashire, a grim passing-place en route to the Lake District. Its inhabitants would be the first to experience its effects.

Ten minutes later, the phone rang. It was Virgina of the Old Oak clan. She was wondering if Una still welcomed new acolytes.

Una grinned broadly. Happy days were here again.

***

Hartley wandered about listlessly in the rubble and wreckage of the cinema. He didn't bother to take notes as there were lots of uniformed officers poking around; his instincts were that they'd find nothing. In the car park, three people carriers had been hurled through the air like toys. A pair of towering lamps now resembled spoons, as recently fondled by Yahuri Getter.

The strange scorch mark was, he was assumed, the epicentre of the blast. He didn't go in but could see random parts of the brickwork had been eaten away, leaving the mortar strangely intact as a grey, skeletal frame. Miraculously, nobody had been killed and only two people were injured in the blast, neither of them seriously.

It was a mystery and Hartley, in accord with his favourite songstress Soyah, began searching for a clue.

He sighed.

Yes, two men were at the centre of the explosion. Yes, they walked away without a scratch, so witnesses said – so witnesses *wailed*. As was so often the case, the description left a little to be desired.

Men, two.

***

Sirens in the distance roused the inspector from a disillusioned daydream. Nearby, shaken but apparently functional, two youngsters were chatting to officers. He didn't plan to get involved but decided to have a quick word before they scarpered. He duly popped in a mint and waved his badge.

"How tall were these men?" he asked.

"Just normal I suppose."

"Right, so we know they were of average height. That's something. How about what they were wearing?" Hartley felt he was good at this stuff, sober or otherwise.

"*I* wouldn't say they were average height!" broke in the fat lass who served sugary drinks and ice creams. She offered her mate Darren a vacant grin. Darren, purveyor of sticky, sugary sweets and paper bags of assorted sugary sweets, shook his head.

"No, I wouldn't either, not in a million years," he decided.

"So were they taller than average or shorter?" Hartley asked, gnawing his pencil slightly.

"Hard to say," said the girl.

"Hair?"

"Think so."

"OK, so there were *two* men?" sighed Hartley, starting to get exasperated.

"Who told you that?" she drawled. "Darren, I think I have a headache. Post-dramatic trauma, that's what I got."

"Yeah Trace, I've been thinking the same," Darren agreed. He was a straggly youth and the colourful uniform and white paper hat did him no favours at all. *Life* had done him no favours at all.

"We should get time off for this, do you think?"

Hartley surveyed the damage and felt himself losing the will to live. Darren cackled and scratched his scrotum.

"Won't get paid though," he wisely concluded.

"Oh, right," she pondered, picking her nose and examining the contents.

Hartley gave up.

"Bloody imbeciles!" he muttered, putting away his notebook.

"Sorry sir?" asked a miscellaneous young PC Hartley vaguely recognised.

"I'll walk back into town by the river. Take the pool car back, would you." He tossed the keys, which the PC fumbled and dropped.

"I can't drive sir!"

"What do you mean?"

"Got banned. Pissed, you know."

"Oh for fuck's sake. Find someone who *can* drive!"

"There's only Alan, and he's already in his car."

"Well, I'll leave it anyway. I'm walking! I need to think! You finish off here."

Without another word, he squelched away and down the path towards the river, regretting his decision almost instantly when he noticed the mud.

Meanwhile, at the scene of the mysteriously un-fatal explosion, media types were scurrying about, trying to get the best shots of the bendy lampposts. Although there was no reason to suspect anything else was going to happen, more officers were on the way, armed with chalk and tape, drafted from their lay-bys and bolt-holes to be a visible presence for the cameras. Someone from the BBC suggested that it would make a better story if a few more cars could be rolled over.

Chapter Twenty Eight

When dealing with the insane,
the best method is to pretend to be sane.
Hermann Hiss

"Well, that was different," Jim declared as they sat on the steps of the Belvedere, smoking a joint. As usual, the place reeked as if somebody had taken a dump nearby. It was probably not far from the truth although, possibly, it was explainable by the wind being in the wrong direction.

A pall of smoke covered the eastern sky bringing on the night – and faster than anyone could know.

"What's all this soot on my skin?" said Dave.

"Dunno, but it's hard to rub off. I've been trying," said Jim.

"I think somebody just tried to kill me," said Dave.

"No way! It was me they were after. Unless I did that to myself. I always was my own worst enemy, just never expected a concrete example."

"Puzzling shit," Dave agreed.

"What happened to your nose? That looks sore."

"You did it mate! Fecking head-butted me!"

"Oh shit, really? Sorry. Clune... Max, Clune did it."

"Definitely looked like you. Who's Clune Max Clune? Some relative of Noggin the Nogg? Or Dent Arthur Dent?"

"Give me another toke, it's been a stressful day."

"Sure thing. Man, I still hurt from laughing. Was just like in 'dam that time."

"Yeah, it totally was. I can still feel it at the back of my head. Well, either that or the explosion."

"Ah. Look, I've got to tell you some stuff."

"Like what man?" said Jim. "Cos I have a story that you won't believe."

"Is it better than being God?"

"Oh, well, fair dos, you first," conceded Jim amiably, smoke swirling from his nostrils.

***

Hartley squished along an overgrown path traversed by joggers, walkers and miscellaneous dog people. He had been ignoring the messages from the chief super so he could think, but it turned out his mind wasn't in the mood.

So much was wrong and Hartley had a growing suspicion about what lay behind it all – or who. Alarm bells were ringing in his head – not an uncommon thing – but today he could picture them. They were silver, decorated with elaborate engravings and rung by monks dressed in black.

Hartley stepped into a puddle and felt the muddy water seep into his socks.

"I'm a silly old fart," he muttered, reaching the bridge that led into the park.

***

Another joint later and they had compared notes. Jim alternated between frowning and wide-eyed incredulity. It was good shit.

"That's fucking incredible! Miles better than my tale."

"Oh I dunno. I reckon having a fight with yourself in your head is pretty far-out too."

Jim tried for a serious expression and almost made it. "I didn't have a fight with myself exactly. I created some, I don't know, alternate personae, other mes, and they took over, clever bastards."

"Whoah, hold on just a minute! If you're angling to be God too, I totally bagsied that!" Dave felt he was in danger of being topped again.

"Relax. Aren't there, like, three of them?"

"Possibly, I forget," Dave frowned. Then his eternal optimism kicked in. "Wouldn't it be brilliant if the third was a chick?"

"Pretty sure religions don't work that way. Anyway, knowing our luck she'd have a well developed personality."

"Aye, an Earth Mother, inevitable! Something to get hold of though!"

They chuckled as the weed worked its healing magic. Dave called a halt before he lost his train of thought.

"Wait, there's something else. I have to tell you the reason it all happened!"

"I don't get you, what reason?"

"It must be because my brain's working better – ever since you worked on me. That's when the amazing things began. I think differently now and I can sense things too, vibes and whatnot. Maybe there's a price for that."

"I don't see why. Sounds interesting though. Is that how we survived? At the cinema."

"How do you mean?"

"Well, we were dead there for sure. Ka-boom! Yet here we are, chilled and taking the air. How'd you do it, go on, spill the beans!"

"Buggered if I know," said Dave. "I assumed it was you."

"Me too at the time. But I've checked," he tapped his temple. "Pretty sure it wasn't."

"Oh."

"Look, Dave, I'm going to shut down for a bit. A few minutes at most. Afterwards I should be able to do more clever stuff. And you keep on godding. I'll be Jesus. Don't have the hair any more but still have the initials. We'll get robes and sandals and everything."

"Excellent... my son! Nice one!" Dave was philosophical about sharing his godhood and began rolling yet another joint. Jim went into meditation mode, his legs crossed like Buddha, a faint smile playing on his lips.

In Dave's peripheral vision, he registered a man in a grey coat slowly climbing the steep path in the twilight. The man stopped to take a swig from a hip flask.

It was then that Dave began to realise he wasn't superman after all. The run had clearly cost more energy than he thought because a sort of delayed reaction was setting in. He felt faint and it wasn't just the grass. He decided not to tell Jim right away. It would be nice being God a while longer.

***

Hartley gasped as the sharp taste of scotch hit the back of his throat. He almost gagged yet he increasingly depended on its numbing effects. The flavour repelled him but he craved it all the same. Everyone has a weakness.

I probably shouldn't drive any more, he thought.

His gaze drifted up the sloping path. Sweating and regretting the walk, he leaned on one of the many rails placed there to impede the passage of cyclists. The cycle path, once so proudly announced, was now forever obstructed because some idiot had fallen off on this very spot. The slightly bruised individual had, a little later, met with a red-jacketed fellow curious to hear about accidents that weren't his fault. The rest, as they say, is litigation.

Hartley didn't care about cyclists much. He did care about the truth and he recognised that man in the yoga pose on the steps of the Belvedere. It was Cavanah! His mate, presumably, sat next to him smoking. Somehow he wasn't surprised.

Hartley decided to try the softly-softly approach. He'd sidle up, sit, and have a friendly chat, even ignore the obvious joint if it helped them loosen up. He'd play it by ear, perhaps dredge up something from his collection of local anecdotes to break the ice. *"Say, guys, did you know this place used to be the site of a stationary steam engine?"* could work.

He didn't care that he was an old-fashioned cliché of a copper. He enjoyed discovering the full story and catching bad guys. He was quite amazed, therefore, when the two men were temporarily encased in brilliant white light. It lit up the park and surrounding area as if it were mid-day.

Then they vanished.

Into thin air.

Hartley gaped at where they no longer sat. A lesser man might have sworn off the drink at that point. Instead, he recognised it as an opportune moment to raise the flask in a long, silent toast. Of the remaining options, this appealed the most. Wiping his lips, he once again dug out his favourite tune.

"Itsh a mythtawee," he mumbled.

End of Book One

Book Two

Chapter One

If God did not exist, it would be necessary to invent him.   Voldarao

In Preston, Lancashire, Little Britain, it had been the strangest 12 months.

The strangeness sprang from a day of senseless, brutal murder. Such was the communal grief that the country's very foundations wobbled, stamping Preston firmly on the map with a big red blotch. The insanity spread from that point in a further series of macabre incidents.

For no apparent reason, a simple but harmless man ripped off his face with his bare hands before leaping into a septic river. Images of the staring death mask adorned the tabloids for days, in ghastly graphic detail. These "insider shots" of hapless Mikey Sharples were demanded by the public, apparently. The pale body on the slab certainly captured the public imagination, in much the same way as every minor war and high-profile celebrity divorce.

A triple murder (never solved) was quickly followed by a mysterious terrorist attack, after which, the main suspects for the whole catalogue of atrocities disappeared. Never to be seen again.

Next came a Black Mass conducted by a naked pagan cult, which was broadcast across the world and really opened the floodgates. Of fear and craziness, that is, which as it happens are the only floodgates to reliably dispense cold, hard cash.

A slender girl had her throat sliced open in what at first was believed to be a stunt gone wrong. Rather than freak out at the gore, she got mad. Then it got even weirder as the resurrectee engaged in battle – actual battle – with what can only be described as a demon from Hell, or somewhere in the vicinity. Millions witnessed this bizarre turn of events in full, gushing colour. Speculation gripped the globe with a resounding 'ching'.

It was top class reality TV and it scared the living shit out of anyone who wasn't simple.

Riots followed. Ugly gangs rampaged through the already bleak town in search of buildings or public works they might conceivably ruin, a tougher task than they expected. On that day, lives were lost and tensions passed breaking point. Late in the day, the Prime Minister made an emergency visit and appealed for calm. Attempting to defuse the charged atmosphere, he personally addressed leaders from every part of the community, most particularly those representing the meanest faiths. It is said the visit to Preston had a profound effect upon the PM, for he never returned.

In a frustrating interim period, pagans and witches became big and positively-spun news. Their membership expanded like a tumescent teenager, mostly on the back of DVD sales. Their top-selling title was "A Goddess Kicks Satan's Arse. Live From Preston Flag Market". Satan was old news, the enemy of a discredited god.

Spring passed into summer and older faiths grew confident again. Priests of Thor discovered how to summon the Holy Goat and speak in tongues. Some learned how to turn water into beer and were invited to an endless round of parties. Not to be outdone, across the Atlantic, stories of the Holy Brad and his Big Miracles began to spread across the Promised Land.

As the year waned, the oddness showed no sign of doing so. People behaved badly towards one another. Friend and foe became interchangeable, strangers and foreigners were made to feel unwelcome. Thinkers too.

What nobody knew was that the Belief System Support Program of the Aesir had switched into intensive mode. Within the minds of the populace, vague and questioning morphed into to precise and unbending. Fuses shortened, trenches were dug, only in ignorance was there bliss. Fanaticism spread – slowly but unstoppable once it gathered momentum. The Preston Riots were replicated across the country and still nobody could work out why.

Toleration of anything not 'the norm' dried up completely and the entire norm concept shrank daily. For the first time a simple Constitution was drafted stating that everyone had a fundamental right to defend his or her[5] beliefs.

By force, if necessary.

***

By December 2003, the Wondrous Tim was a worldwide phenomenon. He had even surpassed David Blame and the bloke whose best trick was the illusion he dated supermodel Claudine Sniffer. Tim was universally recognised. His spectacular shows commanded arena-scaled audiences across the globe.

The success story began with a spectacular show in lowly Sheffield at around the time of the first riots. Tim had performed like a god, incandescent with uncanny talent. Canny Channel 4 had negotiated a TV series on the spot. They had seen more than enough to know something special was in the bag.

This guy was going places.

Tim's lapse into a coma the following day only added to his value. The more they couldn't have him, the more they wanted him.

So when he arose, weeks later, Lazarus-style, he was a transformed man. The subsequent world tour sold out in every way possible and was captured for a fly-on-the-wall reality series timed for Christmas. As his fame spread he bewitched everyone with increasingly elaborate performances. Often, the Wondrous Tim levitated. He flew with no detectable wires and conjured amazing images without a screen. He told exciting tales too, sold them on unworldly scenarios. As demons were on everyone's minds, he too battled with them. It became vital to his fans and Tim exhibited unparalleled flair and showmanship when dispatching them (the demons, not the fans) to the Netherworld.

---

[5]But mostly *his*

Or Belgium.

Tim could pluck, it was said, the most intimate thoughts from any mind, even those of a successful chat show host, now in prison. He improved as his fame spread and began to reinvent himself. As his stature increased, people began to believe in his mission. This gave him more strength.

And made him enemies.

Power recognises power. It sniffs around comparing potency like a large dog with twitching hackles. The powerful can't even help themselves. Bound by rules they don't understand, they are compelled to evaluate the other players in any game. They are doomed to compare willy sizes, actually or metaphorically as circumstances dictate. At some point there is always a choice to make. When it came for Tim, he surprised himself.

I'm fed up of tales about bloody Tim!

Chapter Two

Imagination is the one weapon in the war against reality.   Julee de Gooey

Jim and Monica Cavanah lived in a tropical paradise, which they had always talked about doing. They shared an island with their best friends, Dave and Sheila Scofield. They were very lucky. They had quietly foiled an evil plot to imprison the spirit of humanity in mumbo-jumbo. Extra-dimensional beings had tinkered with base reality, extending the Religious Phase and suppressing the Science & Discovery Phase of civilisation. Apparently this was why humans had started really well but then got into a rut.

Try as he might, Jim couldn't work out a motive for fucking humanity or whether he had foiled the plot of gods. It all seemed pretty unlikely whenever he thought about it but as the long sunny days passed, it grew harder to be sure. It faded like a vaguely sketched, iffy stoner novel.

Art was involved. Somehow.

Jim inherited a fortune or had a surprise windfall and decided to retire to paradise with those he loved.

Hey this is much better than all that Tim stuff!

He bought an island in the Pacific where every day was sunny but not baking hot. Pleasant, it was pleasant. Usually, it rained overnight so the air smelled fresh and sweet all the time. Plants grew fast on the island, the precious herb thrusting from the sweet earth in the balmy outdoors, breathing its magic scent constantly.

Dave and Jim were damn lucky and counted their blessings at each boozy sunset.

It had been touch and go. They had battled against a terrible and resourceful enemy using their new godlike super-powers. The enemy consisted of four fiendish aliens, the Aesir. They came from a place 'outside' the universe for reasons unknown. The important part was that they had held back human progress. Why this should matter remained irritatingly unclear. Being omnipotent they would work it out in time.

Tomorrow, probably.

Anyway, they overcame the Aesir by means of various contests. Afterwards, Jim recalled a promise to give independent life to the personalities he had created. He cleverly devised a politically correct way of doing this and everyone lived happily ever after. As for all the details, Jim and Dave discovered these were elusive, in their evening drinking sessions.

After a while, they ceased to worry about it. Being gods, they could do anything they wanted.

For a long time after that, they did.

Remembering their god-like powers, they learnt to fly, soaring into the clouds with the power of mental energy and whatnot. They looked at stuff, wazzed here and there, poked about in exotic locations, usually looking for bars. Towards the end, they tended to gravitate towards a smoky coffee shop in Amsterdam, a place they once blearily watched the world go by. They spent a mad year doing absolutely everything. Then they remembered the girls and returned home bearing gifts of chocolates and bunches of tulips.

How they giggled at the boys' exploits.

Fortunately, it turned out they didn't mind at all, especially when they checked through the remaining chocolates. They agreed that the important thing was fixed. The future was back on its intended course. Everyone's mind was free and human sentience could reach its full potential.

Was it not said: boys will be boys?

It turned out to be perfectly alright to take a year out. More would have been fine, the babes assured them. The girls loved them dearly and so had waited on the island getting in some swimming and Indian cooking courses.

The fridge was full of beers and the entire final series of Buffy was neatly recorded, labelled, and stacked in readiness. The girls had bought cheerleader outfits and pom-poms and were learning to use them creatively.

It was all good.

Sitting on a wide expanse of brightly-coloured decking in the tropical garden, the boys were thoroughly content. Their lives had been brilliant and this was set to continue indefinitely. The small table was laden with milk shakes, Chocomel, ashtrays, Kit-Kats, a large vaporiser, assorted pizzas and a tin of chocolate digestives. Within easy reach, a fridge crammed with icy lager purred. It drew its power from a tiny solar cell. The sun blazed through distant coconut trees. Waves lapped gently across white sand, soothing and calming.

"We should learn golf," said Dave.

"We totally should."

"Sticks, we'll need sticks."

"I'm a total God," said Jim, as he so often did.

"You truly are," agreed Dave, deftly rolling a joint with one hand.

"We can do anything we like."

"Absolutely anything. We have amazing powers too."

"Anything we want to do, we do. And the girls don't mind."

"That's a grand feeling."

"It certainly is."

A macaw landed on a nearby branch and began to prune its brilliant red feathers. Jim frowned.

"Does any of this strike you as, I don't know.....?"

"What?"

"Strange."

"Strange?"

"Yeah. Doesn't it strike you as a bit strange?"

"How do you mean mate?"

Jim furrowed his brow. "I dunno. I feel weird all of a sudden. Like I've forgotten something. I keep thinking I should do the shopping!"

"Why think about that? Here of all places?"

"Exactly. It makes me wonder if I *am*?"

"Wonder if you are what, mate?"

"Here."

"I'm not following you. No more shopping is necessary. We have everything we need because of convenient deliveries from the mainland."

"Suppose we're *not* here?"

"Whoa dude. Crazy talk! I thought we agreed we were going to keep it together! " He took a long drag of his spliff and offered it. "Cop a load of this – plain old AK47, hardly has any effect at all. Say, are we quite stoned for this time of day? What day is it anyway?"

"Dave, think for a moment. We're *always* stoned. We're never *unstoned*. It's not a treat anymore, we're so switched on we've switched off."

"Ah you're not going all religious on me again are you? I thought we switched off the life support for all that nonsense?"

"True, but I think I switched to being God and you were giving Buddha a try. It's difficult to be sure."

"Plus, I can still do some cool stuff. Pick a card!"

"I'm serious!"

"Oh, not again. You were serious last year."

"Mate, I recognise this vibe. I think we are being held prisoner. I don't believe any of this is real."

BUGGER, I TOLD YOU! whined a disembodied voice.

Jim and Dave looked up as a shadow passed over the sky.
There was a loud click.
Somebody switched the sun off.

***

"I wish you hadn't said that!" snapped a voice.

Jim floated upright in a room without walls. It had no features and was unusual for its primary attribute: It was endless in only two dimensions. If there were walls, they were distant and/or invisible. He noticed he was wearing a black suit and a white turtleneck sweater. He winced at this observation.

The room was white. Pure white, like unfiltered, untainted light. The floor was waxy glass, with frosty silver lines running through it. The ceiling was the same, perhaps ten feet above Jim's head.

There was nobody and nothing to see. There was no smell. Jim wasn't even sure he was breathing.

"Where am I?" he demanded, turning his head in the hope of catching something in his peripheral vision.

"You are nowhere at the moment. We are holding you because we were worried about you."

"Why should you be worried about me? Who are you?"

"We are your friends."

"I don't understand."

"I know. We're finding it quite frustrating. Wickedly frustrating is probably more accurate. My name is Jonathon. You might recognise my voice. According to your logs, you have encountered two of my Simulacrums. I wonder if my face will help jog your memory?"

A man appeared directly in front of Jim. Short, hey had black, piggy eyes, a square chin and a pot belly. He appeared to be wearing a wig and was most definitely wearing a frilly shirt and blue pantaloons with an unnatural shine.

"Feltham John, pleased to make your acquaintance!" laughed Jim. "This is hilarious!"

"I am Jonathon Meed!" said Jonathon Meed stiffly. "Any resemblance to said poncing pianist is purely co-incidental. Besides, I'm taller."

"Have it your way man, wassaaaap?" Jim was starting to relax.

"It's a long story Jim I'm afraid. And you aren't ready to hear it yet."

"Why not?"

"Because the knowledge would drive you mad in your present state of awareness. I can't risk damaging you nor can I convince you of this right now. I won't waste my breath trying."

"Tell me something else then!"

"Okay. Try this for size. We create universes. Doesn't that sound grand when you say it out loud? Actually it's not so exciting, the creation part. It's like a gardener planting a seed – and often just as unpredictable. Anyway, a 4D universe like this one is relatively simple to tweak and once you've done that, you start getting curious. Before you know it, we're all involved."

"I don't think I can respond to that in any meaningful way," said Jim.

"I know." The voice sounded kind. "I think that's enough for now. We'll talk later. You'll recognise later because it looks exactly like this... Don't be a stranger!" With that strange sign-off, he vanished.

Time passed for Jim. It, too, was white. He found he could move the thing that appeared to be his body (but very probably wasn't). Sometimes he walked in any direction he felt drawn to, but it always looked the same.

He was a mouse in a wheel.

He neither ate nor slept, which was worrying.

Sometimes the little podgy guy returned, and in corporeal form. At other times his voice was present but his body couldn't be bothered. Sometimes he would say single words or phrases, with perhaps a day of silence in between them, which Jim found hugely annoying.

AWAKEN
silence
AWAKEN

silence
WE ARE YOUR FRIENDS
silence
WE ARE LIKE YOU
silence
YOU ARE LIKE US
silence
YOU ARE ONE OF US
silence
ONLY YOU
silence
NOT DAVE
silence
YOU ARE OUR FRIEND
silence
YOU WILL REMEMBER US WHEN IT IS TIME

Sometimes Jonathon would appear and ask questions. To jog Jim's mind, he said.

They were the same questions he had asked before, or would ask again next time.

Jim had never worn a watch. He had believed, since puberty, that if he remained ignorant of time, then time would remain ignorant of him. In the white room it passed him by and he found he rather missed it after all.

And he began to have an eerily familiar feeling.

It dawned on him, finally, that it was the very same feeling he'd experienced when trapped inside his House creation, within his own head. Or did that actually happen?

Then, as now, he had no access to higher thoughts or capabilities. He was, in fact, a smaller subset of himself.

Again!

He was still trapped!

Somehow he had been deceived despite his fail-safes.

Finally he knew.

Again!

It *was* the same. He was in a prison, not in his own head but somewhere else.

He was not Jim Cavanah.

This was not real.

He felt constricted.

And he exerted his strength.

Alarms rang.

HE'S INCREDIBLY STRONG! YOU SHOULD HAVE TOLD ME!

I DIDN'T KNOW YOU CRETIN. YOU WERE THE ONE WHO THOUGHT WE'D HAVE HIM WRAPPED SECURELY IF WE GAVE HIM HIS HEART'S DESIRE. I DON'T UNDERSTAND THESE CREATURES!

CAN YOU SHUT HIM DOWN?

YES, GIVE ME A SECOND.

TAKE ALL THE TIME YOU NEED.

FUNNY.

Chapter Three

To dare is to momentarily lose one's footing.
But not to dare is to lose one's self.   Sauron Kinkygaard

Dave and Sheila lay in a warm jumble of humanity. Snuggled into the bed with them, two perfect children. In the early hours, they had been awakened by thunder and now dozed like contented puppies, albeit with a surprising surplus of elbows and knees. Neither Dave nor Sheila minded in the slightest because they were little miracles.

Judged infertile years ago, Dave and Sheila had got on with their lives. Their dreams withered over the years. There were plenty of other things to do.

Was it his drink or drugs?

Was it hers?

They had always assumed there would be children and it hurt that there never would be.

Everything changed when Dave's mind was freed from its shackles. His creativity increased exponentially and be dug out his guitar. But they were both surprised and delighted when Sheila became pregnant.

Their dream came true, and then again.

One of each.

Five or six years passed. Dave rarely saw Jim any more. They were still good buddies but Jim and Monica had remarried and seemed to require no interaction. The arrangement suited everyone, although Dave felt a little sad.

Somehow his amazing powers were of no interest once his children were born. He wondered whether he'd need them ever again.

Maybe, he told himself. *No hurry though.*

***

Julie Hutchinson eventually realised her new lover was never going to return. It was hardly a new experience, yet it hit her hard. She recognised his special aura and blamed herself for not making a better impression.

That night she cut herself. She deserved it after all, and the pain was cathartic. The thin lines of blood fascinated her as they oozed in slow motion. Her razor had missed all the major blood vessels but it was of scant consequence by that stage. Whatever she cut, she could heal.

Julie's talents blossomed while she lay in the bath dreaming about Max. Not only could she slice flesh then make it whole, she could knit veins and deeper tissue – using her mind!

She could move things and break them.

However, she was completely unable to fix the kettle when it broke.

There was a knock on the door. She got out. The bath was growing cold anyway. A plumpish, tall woman with long black hair became an Earth Mother via the fish-eye in the door. Julie was dripping blood and water as she opened the door, naked.

Una introduced herself smoothly and pushed her way in. She needed to discuss a highly important matter. A matter that could not wait.

Julie asked if she would like a cup of tea.

***

It was twilight and Arthur Bradshaw jogged along the riverbank. He ramped up the pace, aiming to get a shower before going to work. The day had bogged him down in trivia and, uncharacteristically, he had started thinking about Gordon and his rash action. Now there was a chance he'd be late. And Art was never late.

He was no longer young and could not tolerate prison, if indeed he ever could have. He struggled to maintain his armour of calm and control.

The Gordon business was baffling in the extreme. No matter how he tried, Art could not remember the strange compulsion which had apparently guided him to commit murder. There was no reason for it and no sense behind it. Yet despite the awareness gap, he was left with a feeling it had been... right.

Reaching the climb into the park, he slowed and his sweat turned to ice. Ahead, leaning on the railings, was a familiar figure – a man he avoided ordinarily. He had his back turned but Art recognised him at once. Without knowing exactly why, he cleared his throat.

"Inspector Hartley, a lovely night for a nip in the gloaming!"

Hartley turned in surprise, pocketing his hip flask automatically. He hadn't heard a thing.

"Arthur Bradshaw, is that you? I thought you were dead!"

"Not dead, just a night owl these days. And keeping out of trouble before you ask. I prefer not to exist, if it's all the same to you."

Art closed the gap only slightly and began stretching gently on the cold metal railings.

"Did you see a flash of light?" the inspector said, his voice rising unexpectedly in pitch. Even at his age, Art remained an impressive and imposing specimen. He had kept the stupid ponytail though, the old fart. The light cast by a nearby lamp turned the fine hair to an ethereal glow.

"A light?"

"Yes, a very bright light. From near here."

"Sorry but I've not been out long. I'm a bit behind schedule today." He regretted this superfluous information the moment it left his lips.

"Why's that then?"

"Oh, you know, life."

"Sorry, don't mind me. An old copper's habit and none of my business. If I *were* asking you anything it'd be about what you've been up to for 20 years."

"Oh, you know, life."

"Right."

"Still enjoying the job inspector? Are you still catching the villains and putting them away?"

"I think I might be working for them," said Hartley sadly.

Art nodded in goodbye then jogged away. He was gone before the inspector could ask him anything further.

Hartley wandered back up the hill towards the pavilion where, a mere half hour ago, Jim and Dave had evaporated into the ether.

He shivered, not because of the chill in the air but because he had a very bad feeling. It was the strongest case of gut instinct in a long career of complaining guts.

Worse was yet to come, he knew it.

Chapter Four

I shut my eyes in order to see.

Paul Gaugau

Gigantic tearing sounds stirred Jim into consciousness, yet paradoxically he felt nothing, not the slightest tremor. He was trapped somehow, hypnotised maybe. As comprehension dawned and he became certain he was a prisoner again, his mind pushed harder and more aggressively against the confines of his cage. Familiar feelings suggested he was achieving a modicum of success. The cage was weakening. He could sense it.

Very briefly, he opened his eyes into a large - but no longer boundless - white chamber, hung with pale green chandeliers and bordered by elaborately carved pillars and curved arches.

He closed them and the room was endless and featureless once more. He had a memory of a voice. It had said: YOU ARE ONE OF US!

Weird white shit-cakes!

He opened them a slit and laughed aloud, his laughter instantly absorbed by walls that had lurched inexplicably closer. He lay on the bottom tier of a bunk bed on sheets that were once white but had been yellowed by age. At least he hoped it was age. The bed's metal frame was painted a thick, dreary grey and was cold to the touch.

Unexpectedly, Jim found he was wearing a plain white robe and sandals. His armpit chronometer put the time at a pleasant 'shower plus an hour'. He felt fit, alive but slightly confused. He regarded his hands thoughtfully for a moment before getting up.

The cell - for it could be nothing else - was a spotlessly clean twenty foot cube. Other than the bunk bed and himself, it was empty. There were no windows and no visible light source, yet illumination filled the room to the exclusion of all shadows. He continued to study since, for a change, there was little else to do.

The walls and door appeared constructed of opaque glass, ridged with silver lines spreading from each corner like metallic veins. The door (directly opposite the bed) reflected light more reluctantly than the walls but it wouldn't budge no matter how hard Jim pushed or kicked it.

There was no key, no handle.

After running his hands over as much of the cell as he could reach, Jim was flummoxed. He climbed to the top of the bunk bed and pushed against the ceiling with his feet. Then he climbed down, shunted the bed around the room and repeated the process. Eventually he'd pressed, poked and generally explored every square inch of his confinement, discovering only that the glass could not be broken, scratched or damaged in any way, nor could he peel off the silver veins. Kicking with a sturdy side-thrust kick, he bounced off as if kicking a mountain. This, too, left no mark despite the undersides of his sandals being hard, black rubber. The base of the bed was sharp steel, yet not a scratch or scuff showed anywhere on the floor.

Eventually, he lay down, regarded the underside of the top bunk, and let his mind wander. The solution came remarkably quickly: Monica, the source of all his hopes for as long as memory extended.

Jim concentrated on her face and, without any real hope, called her name. In response, a sharp pain hoisted the base of his skull like a butcher's hook. Taking this as progress, he repeated the call.

And passed out immediately.

On waking, he rested for an hour until the pain was almost gone. Then, since it remained his only plan, he made a second attempt.

Monica!

This time he remained conscious, fending off the hook with willpower and innate stubbornness. Signs of progress remained conspicuous by their absence. Although generally ignorant of the passage of time, Jim guessed days must have passed.

With nothing else for it, he persevered...

Finally, exhausted, and starting to fear he was flogging a dead horse, Jim forced himself to shut off the maelstrom of thoughts rushing around his mind to gather maximum brain processing power for a last, mighty transmission. He placed the palms of his hands over his eyes and pictured her face, her lips, her soft skin against his body. Then he began.

"Monica," he whispered in a quiet, measured voice. "It's Jim. I'm sorry to do this but I'm in a spot of bother. Monica, I'm so sorry. I'm sorry about loads of things but now isn't the time for that. I've no idea if you can hear me. But if you can't I don't think anyone can..."

Then – just as the effort threatened to rip his concentration to shreds – it happened. In his head, he heard something. A reply, distant but familiar.

"Jim?"

"Yeah, it's me." Relief washed over him like a moist, lemon-scented towelette.

"Where *are* you? There was an explosion... are you... dead?" She paused then followed this with, "Jim, you're talking in my head!"

"I need your help Mon," he said. No reply. "I can't say much now," he continued. "I'm trapped somewhere. And if I'm right, only you can help me."

"I don't understand how this is possible or what you're on about."

"I'm sorry, it's too hard to explain. If I'm wrong then I'm totally screwed and probably a fruitcake. I could be imagining this whole conversation."

"I wish you were. I wish *I* was! Something is going down, something very strange. Tim has been with the police all day – and apparently there was a weird broadcast on telly this afternoon that nobody is owning up to. Jim, what *is* going on?"

"I can't be sure but it might, possibly, be my fault. Things started going pear-shaped after I taught myself a sort of mind control trick. I wanted to improve myself, fix my personality like you always said. It meant dealing with some, you know, issues."

"Issues?"

"Look, this isn't the time for all that. Let's just say I caused myself some difficulties but they also seem to be having an effect on, well, the world at large."

He distinctly heard her sigh.

"Sounds pretty crazy doesn't it?"

"What do you want me to say? You should think really carefully about what you're saying Jim."

"Think carefully? Thinking's what got me into this mess! Look, Mon, you're hearing me now, right?"

"I might be crazy too. It sounds like Preston is degenerating fast. Mass psychosis or hallucination, they're saying. Maybe I caught it too!"

"Look love, I may not have much time. I'm in trouble – potentially the terminal kind. I've been... hijacked, I guess you might say. And by whom? Unfortunately there aren't any comforting answers to that."

She sighed again. "Tell me what I can do." And suddenly, marvellously, she was serious, compartmentalising the bollocks until later. It was one of her special abilities.

"I don't know exactly. But I think if you can find me and, I don't...... wait, I know. Find my body – it will be unconscious – then... ah, kiss the lips. That'll wake me up. Of course!"

"Nice try, now fuck off out of my head! Sleeping beauty, seriously?"

"Sorry, I didn't plan this. But I am serious. You can save me. If we're, if I'm..." his voice trailed off.

"Yes?"

"Perhaps I left part of myself..."

"I knew it! You and your bloody part! I wondered how long it would be before it raised its ugly head. When are you going to bloody well grow up?"

"Monica, please. This is life or death or I wouldn't ask. Maybe for everyone." The desperation was plain and, to someone who knew him well, highly persuasive. Jim rarely asked for favours - and never on a whim. Nevertheless Monica was torn.

"Your timing stinks Jim. I *can't* come over, it's asking too much. Tomorrow night's the big gig and I have things to prepare."

"It's still Friday?"

"Of course it's still Friday. What day do you think it is?"

"So I'm not too late?"

"Jim, you're totally hammered aren't you?"

"I wish! Look, promise me you'll find me and wake me. That's all I'm asking. If I'm right I'm still near Avenham park, the smelly pavilion, near the bridge. I'll try and call to you again when you're closer. And be careful. I don't know what I'm up against. I'm guessing they haven't taken me far, well I hope not!" He sounded uncertain.

"It all sounds pretty flimsy but I'll come and I'll look. If Tim gets home and I'm not here, I'll need a suitable excuse to get me off the hook. And, Jim, if this turns out to be some scary night-time park adventure for your private gratification, you'll regret it!"

"It's not. I need your help. Only you Geoff, only you!"

"Silly idiot, you know Persuaders was my favourite."

"Ah yes, the Tony Curtis fixation, how could I forget!"

"Cravats will make a comeback one day, mark my words!"

"Yeah, right," Jim groaned and for a long moment wasn't sure if he'd lost contact.

"This is serious, isn't it?" she asked quietly.

"I wouldn't ask if there was another way. Please come. For old times' sake."

"I will."

Jim could sustain the link no longer and passed out.

***

Monica was anxious and angry. It was a longer drive than she cared to make, from Lancaster to Preston, and there would be the return also. She hated night driving. The steering wheel was cold and the radio was on the blink but at least it wasn't raining. Tim rang as she was about to leave, saying he was on the way shortly and had some great ideas to improve the show. He sounded highly excited, having impressed in several high profile interviews, some for live television. Had she seen? Did she record them? Monica tried to sound pleased then told a lie, claiming she had to pop out for a couple of hours. An old friend was very ill and she had to visit immediately because she, the friend, might not last the night. She'd give him the full story later. Tim seemed dubious but didn't let it deflate his mood.

Monica chewed her nails as she drove. Lying to Tim made her feel uncomfortable. She wondered if he could tell, if he used his skills on her, and very much hoped not. It wasn't his fault she had been distracted recently - he'd done nothing wrong. However, she knew he would *not* want to hear anything involving Jim. That was dead and buried.

All she craved was a period of stability. Not much to ask.

If Jim screwed things up for her again...

Find my body indeed! she smiled in spite of the situation.

But why are you going if you don't believe him?

He spoke in my head.

She parked close to Jim's flat. There were a few police milling around aimlessly. Stripy blue and white tape was hung extravagantly all over and several photographers still poked about here and there. But it was mostly quiet.

The journey had taken 40 minutes – good going – but it was already practically dark. On the journey, Monica reflected that hearing Jim's voice in her head had been oddly comforting.

She spoke his name a couple of times, just in case he was somehow able to hear.

After half an hour's silence, she began to wonder if she'd imagined it all. But when the shabby outskirts of Preston lurched into view, Jim spoke again, wearily. His voice made her jump, as if he was directly behind her. Tiny prickles chased up her neck like mites disappearing into thick, dark hair. Startled, she swore and braked instinctively before mastering herself.

Jim's voice shook, as if the method of communication required tremendous effort. He offered no new information, focusing instead on asking questions about random episodes from their past, rather than exploring his current predicament. Increasingly, he struggled to articulate, as the effort of forming words became too taxing. Even when he was silent, she could feel him in her head, concentrating, gasping.

Finally, guided by Jim's directions, she reached her destination and began walking down the cobbled path towards the pavilion.

Looking for her ex-husband.

At night.

Many years ago, as a carefree teenager, she had strolled through this park in the sunshine. Not with Jim – although she knew him by sight and reputation – but with his classmate at the time, Bob. Had it really been a coincidence that Jim had happened by and spotted them hand in hand? Not that it was any of his business. They had barely even spoken. Yet his eyes blazed with a dreadful intensity. Then he turned his back and walked away.

The following day, Bob was badly beaten – by an unknown assailant. And when he returned from casualty, he refused to discuss the attack and did not return Monica's calls. Shortly after that, his parents removed him from school and she never saw him again. Replaying those old memories made her shudder. And wonder.

Ominous trees filled the park, looming over the path like twisted totems. Scrabbling noises of unseen animals filled the bushes and tall lamps spewed forth pale creamy light, which cast fuzzy shadows. Friday night in the park was no place for a woman

– especially one quite so well presented.

Always tall, Monica never wore heels so her sensible shoes coped admirably with the cobbles and with the dribbling stream running down the side of the path. She passed a "No Cycling" sign, recognising some of Jim's spidery scrawl on it instantly. She was briefly amused to realise he continued to be a moron who defaced public property. He had deliberately spelled the word 'fucking' wrong.

In the bushes, something rustled vigorously.

Wishing she had brought some means of defence, Monica stooped and seized a muddy branch from the grass and gripped it tightly. If she swung it, it would probably spray filthy water over her coat but she held it ready all the same.

In front of the pavilion, on the steps, was a man holding a hat. He was oldish and had tightly-trimmed grey hair around a central bald patch. As he didn't look dangerous, she approached and he turned, popping on the hat, his eyes kindly.

"Have you seen a man, quite tall, with a pony tail, anywhere around here? He might be in trouble."

"I know that voice," said Hartley. "Monica Vincent, correct?"

"And *you* are?" her eyes narrowed in sudden alarm.

"Fred Hartley," he said. "Inspector Fred Hartley." He fumbled in his inside pocket and eventually produced a well-worn badge, which he waved vaguely. Then he spoke again. "It's all happening today, I can tell you. I ran into your, er, showman friend earlier. But you've missed your other friends, although I can't say I spotted a ponytail on either of them. They *were* here though, where I am now, about an hour ago, maybe more. Gone now, both of them!"

Even across the gap between them, Monica smelled the alcohol and tried to mask her doubt.

"I can see your doubt," declared Hartley. "And I'll raise you incredulity. First, if you don't mind me asking: what are you doing here?"

"I came to find Jim," she said. "What exactly do you mean by *gone*?"

"Vanished is what I really mean. There was a blinding flash of light and they were gone. Never seen anything so bright."

"And this light... did it bring anyone running to investigate?"

"No... now then, that's a thought. You're right! That's very odd – it was momentarily as bright as day. I've been sat here, er, thinking... but not one person has come to investigate. Not like me, not like me at all..."

"And you looked directly into this bright light did you Inspector?"

"Well, I closed my eyes..."

"Of course you did. And – let me guess – when you opened them, Jim was gone. My Tim would love an audience of people like you!"

"Meaning?"

"You've been had! I could be wrong but it sounds like the old 'redirect the attention' ploy. And you of all people fell for it!"

"Still better than being blinded," Hartley muttered. "So where is he then, your man?" he said.

"I don't know. He told me he's trapped and thinks he didn't go far. If somebody grabbed him, how far could they have got? Jim isn't exactly petite and wouldn't be easy to overcome. And you said there were two of them together? Jim and, let me guess, Dave?"

Hartley was deep in thought and didn't reply for a long time.

"Did he ring you to tell you he's a prisoner?" he asked eventually.

"Not exactly, no."

***

Jim could sense her presence but it was too late. Soundlessly the white door slid open, revealing a shorter-than-average man with black, beady eyes and glasses. He wore a long white robe similar to Jim's – although it didn't disguise his paunch. And, incongruously, a shining brass helmet with several dials and buttons on it, arranged asymmetrically across its surface.

Expressionless, Jonathon Meed entered the cell. Beyond the door was darkness but for a moment Jim thought he saw the someone else wearing a similar helmet. Then the door slid soundlessly shut. Meed pressed a nipple-like button on the apex of the helmet and the room began to glow.

Jim was having difficulty reconciling the memories of being trapped in white space, surrounded by strange voices for ages. How long had he really been in here? Was it all another trick? As he rose from the bed, Meed addressed him gravely.

"You're giving us a lot of trouble old friend. We needed perhaps twenty more of your Earth minutes and all this would have been over. Our portable memory device isn't the fastest but it is all we could arrange under the circumstances. There are rules, as you know very well. It is incredibly frustrating because you are fighting against we who are trying to rescue you, to hopefully restore you to full awareness."

Jim gaped at this but Meed shook his head, bidding him remain silent.

"I know how hard this must be to grasp but trust me, we really *are* your kinsmen. If only you would remain in here until our full diagnostic is complete, you would thank us in the long run. The *very* long run, I mean."

Jim launched himself across the space separating them, but a hand gesture from Meed froze him in his tracks. Angrily, Jim mustered all his strength but his limbs failed to respond to the commands to punch and to kick. Veins bulged on his forehead as Meed approached, peering closely at him like a museum exhibit or an unexpected turd on his shoe. Rendered impotent, Jim was forced to stand to attention. His efforts to break free were pitifully inadequate and, as his mental control was terminated, he tried desperately to maintain the link with Monica and speak to her again. Meed merely shook his head and the connection was severed.

***

"Jim?" Monica turned around, lost, bewildered. It was like waking from a dream.

"Did you hear something?" asked Hartley.

"Do you have a gun Inspector?"

"Oh give me a break!" he groaned.

"Back there!" Monica cried, spotting movement in the shadows.

Hartley rose blearily to his feet and moved away from the steps. He followed the direction of her gaze but could see nothing. Then he spotted somebody in the bushes, adjacent to the building, in the shadows. "You there, what are you doing? Come out where I can see you. Police!"

The figure slunk away into darkness and Hartley, neither sprightly nor brave (even in his youth) made as if to follow. He wished, momentarily, that Arthur Bradshaw had stuck around. Bradshaw, even though an old villain, would be handy in a tight corner. Were the woman not present, he'd have happily called it a night. As it was, the 'silly old fool' status indicator flipped on deep in his brain. He forced his aching legs forward. "Wait here," he said, keeping his voice low and even. "It might just be kids. You got a mobile phone?"

Monica nodded, feeling in her pocket for it. *Well, I thought I had.*

Muttering 'pillock, pillock, pillock', Hartley stumbled forward into the gloom, ducking his head under low-hanging tree branches, conscious of his fear but determined not to show it. His hands shook, hit feet dragged clumsily and he desperately wanted to back away, finish his flask and forget it all. Gut instinct screamed that no way was this going to be kids.

Monica was about to follow when her gaze shifted upwards to a tall, slender figure framed against the darkening sky, watching them from above the central arch on the roof of the Belvedere. He or she ducked out of sight instantly. Shocked, Monica was about to call out a warning but indecision plunged its fangs deep. Hartley had already faded into darkness and she felt suddenly vulnerable.

Knowing something of the park's layout helped her decide what to do. Quickly, she dashed back up the path, turned right and took another, steeply-inclined path that wound its way behind the pavilion. The Belvedere had been built on a slope and this path, passing directly behind it, was often used by youngsters to access the roof where they happily got trashed, throwing bottles and cans far and wide. Access to the roof was easy enough from here and Monica crept up cautiously, making sure there was no-one around before climbing the trampled wire fence, and stepping across the gap and onto the roof.

The roof was flat and divided into three distinct areas: a raised, central square and two lower sections. Whoever had been watching them was nowhere to be seen.

Carefully, Monica clambered across the roof, avoiding the broken glass, puddles and sodden items of clothing. She reached the far edge, close to where Hartley had vanished in darkness below. Then, hunched down and still holding onto her branch, she peeped over the side.

In a cramped space under the trees, shadowy figures were gathered. Two knelt on the ground next to a shining, golden box covered in swirly patterns, arcane dials and glowing indicators. They wore bright metallic helmets dotted with yellow and amber LEDs and sprouting wires that disappeared into the box. A third stood nearby, as if on guard, facing Hartley and holding out a hand as if to ward him off. In the dirt, also wired up to the box, lay two unconscious men, electrode pads attached to many points on their heads. The kneeling men frantically adjusted controls on the helmets, consulted wristwatches, and tapped the side of the box. A small display screen showed an image of an hourglass, gradually emptying of sand. There were only a few grains left.

Hartley's vision was clouded and his slow and sluggish. He vaguely saw a small, golden box standing in the dirt. No, wait, it stood a few inches *above* the dirt. Close by, two figures were bending over the apparently sleeping forms of Jim Cavanah and, presumably, his friend; he could barely make them out. A third man – Hartley narrowed his eyes and corrected himself, a *woman* faced him, her expression mocking. He fought the growing compulsion to turn around and get as far away as possible. He gripped the flask and his vision began to clear. The woman's face clouded over in anger. She whispered something he didn't catch and both of the kneeling men turned around. One of them opened his eyes and spoke, his voice low, cold and menacing. "Go away, you have seen nothing here. Go far away."

"Forget and depart!" added the woman.

Hartley saw emptiness in her dark, oriental eyes.

He *had* seen nothing, he realised, and unscrewed the cap of the flask slowly. He took a deep swig then backed away. Then he turned and walked, heedless of the branches brushing against his face.

At that moment Monica, who had silently climbed down the narrow gap between the slope and the rear of the pavilion, crept the last few yards to where Jim lay. Unseen, she kissed him on the lips.

As the three Aesir observed the Inspector's retreat, they chuckled then returned their full attention to Jim. Seeing Monica was something of a surprise. Indeed, they screamed in uncontrolled fury.

Reflexes working on overdrive, Monica narrowly managed to avoid the tall oriental woman's vicious kick, then countered by thrusting the rotten tree branch abruptly upwards, smacking her attacker under the chin.

"What's that?" asked Hartley, shaking his head. He was in the park, at night, and there were noises. His flask was open and his hands were shaking. He turned in time to see a column of brilliant white light shoot up from the shadows to ascend through the bushes and into the sky before being split into a thousand colours that darted in all directions. It was like the convergence of countless rainbows.

In the cell, Jim's hands became fists. He roughly shrugged Jonathon Meed aside and made for the open door. And suddenly he was in the cold air, lying on damp earth facing upwards through a tapestry of interwoven branches. Monica's taste was on his lips, her scent in his nostrils.

Jim's mind boiled over. He felt exhausted, nauseous, disorientated. A headache tore through the base of his skull like a landslide, sharply recalling the pain of overclocking his mind, but far, far stronger. Wires were draped across his face and, at his side, Dave moaned, his fingers twitching, but he didn't move.

In those few precious seconds, Jim activated several emergency protection programmes. He did this automatically via a single command as he struggled to rise, searching for his liberator.

Monica stood a few yards away, her back to a tree, scared but defiant and wielding a large stick. A shadow sneaked towards her and Jim was about to call out in warning when a blow hit him hard. It activated a prototype routine that, unfortunately, drained his tiny reserve of strength. As the world melted away, he heard Monica swearing like a trooper.

When Jim next awoke, it was because a scruffy man in a trilby and stained raincoat was shaking him. Through a wave of pain, a random thought sprang into his subconscious: scruffy men in grubby raincoats were rather common in the bushes in the park, although they more typically shook themselves rather than strangers. He groaned.

"Wake up lad, wake up!" said Hartley. Jim opened one eye.
"Where's Monica?"
"I'm afraid they've taken her!"
"Who are you? You're bleeding!"
"One of them whacked me. Tried to fight him off but he was too strong. And he moved like shit off a shovel. Never seen anything quite like it. For some reason they seemed scared and were in a hurry to escape. I don't think they were scared of me but they ran off, taking your... taking Miss Vincent with them. I lost them, sorry."
"And you are?"
"How do you mean lad?"
"*Who* are you?"
"Oh, I see. Nasty things bangs on the head, eh? Fred Hartley, Inspector Fred Hartley, we spoke yesterday. Remember? The drawing?"
"No, sorry. Yesterday, you say? Look, can you help me up?" For the first time Jim registered the eccentric clothing. He touched the white turtle-neck shirt and expensive suit with a curious, if soily, hand. Parking this for the moment, he asked, "is Dave OK?"
"I haven't had time to find out. I've been preoccupied you might say."
"We have to find them. Get Monica back. They'll use her to get to me." Aided by Hartley he sat up then rubbed the back of his neck with both hands.
"We'll find her, don't you worry. First, you and I need to have a proper chat. I think there's something going on and you know what it is!"
"Something going on, eh?" said Jim removing the electrodes from his head and then, reaching over, from Dave's. "No fooling you Inspector, is there?"
"There's no call for sarcasm. Especially when I'm still contemplating arresting you - for *something*!"
"Sorry. I have this terrible, um, migraine," said Jim. "I need to

take a nap to recover or I'm screwed. Seriously screwed. I can't search for Monica like this or help you or anything. Can you help get Dave and me to my flat? It's not far. I need a few hours or I'm not going to make it." His voice did, indeed, sound weak and profoundly weary. Hartley tapped Dave lightly on the cheek.

"Come on son, wake up."

"Go 'way," said Dave. "You'll wake the kids."

Jim and Hartley pulled him upright. Dave touched the tip of his swollen nose and winced, but kept his eyes tightly shut.

"I've called for assistance already," said Hartley, taking one of Dave's arms. "But tell me one thing: are those people I saw tonight connected to all the crazy things that have been happening?"

"Oh you can bet your life on that!" said Jim, nodding vigorously. The two of them got Dave to his feet. Sulkily, his pal refused to co-operate and let his knees collapse.

"Leave me alone," he muttered. They ignored him and half-dragged him out from the bushes and onto the path.

"What do you suppose that rainbow light machine was for?" asked Hartley, struggling under the weight. It had been a long day and he had no idea how it would end.

"I have no idea. You weren't the only one pre-occupied," replied Jim.

Finally, Dave relented and stood up under his own steam. He remained silent though and Jim was surprised to see tears streaming down his friend's cheeks.

Chapter Five

I was thrown out of college for cheating on the metaphysics exam; I looked into the soul of the boy sitting next to me.   *Willy Allen*

Following the transmission of her master's exercise in TV 'programming', Una Sharples found herself in demand. Vindicated in the Pointy Hats forum, she wasted no time crowing or basking in triumph. Those things would come later and in their full measure. For the present, her inbox and phone was red hot, her membership swelling (especially the highly excitable Bill) and her Patron Lord's Great Plan was in motion. She alone amongst the few thousand residents of Preston who received the broadcast was fully aware of its contents beforehand. It was the most memorable burst of afternoon telly in living memory.

And, of course, the vast majority of those slumped before daytime TV had no witchy inclinations or spiritual antennae. The vacant masses had been given a rapidly growing dose of eagerness combined with Daily Mail levels of aggression and anxiety. As the hours passed, their behaviour duly degenerated.

Meanwhile, Bill had been drafted in to man the phone, computer the door whilst Una made vital preparations of her own – i.e. hastily researching the finer points of the forthcoming ritual.

"Mrs Bowler-Google wanting to talk to you," bellowed Bill into the cellar. He had been told to ignore everyone but Mrs Bowler-Google, honcho of the Old Oak Clan, had been very insistent and more than a little menacing. It transpired that she had missed the transmission due to a cake-decorating engagement and therefore she had no desire to offer allegiance to her old sparring partner. Indeed, she was thoroughly miffed to discover over half of her own people had unexpectedly decided to defect. Right now she was shuffling about in fury on the doorstep.

"Tell her to come with the rest at the appointed time or bugger off," called Una, distractedly. "And don't disturb me again or I'll have your balls for earrings!"

For the Great Plan to succeed, Una needed power – by the bucket load. Additionally, she needed a vessel for her master to occupy, one capable of sustaining his massive intellect and energy. Using newly replenished vigour, her astral self journeyed across the city, eventually locating the key gaming piece: A rich source of talent. Curiously, the mind was one she had sensed before, always bright and full of promise but wayward and fitful. Now a significant shift had occurred. It had been transformed and the spirit pulsed with a dark, intense aura stronger than anything the latent Mikey could have risen to.

Indeed, such was the power of this presence that Una decided precautions must be taken. She felt the power like an iron filing feels a magnet. Briefly, she wondered how the change had come about then moved onto more practical matters such as how best to make contact with the subject.

Finally, her preparations complete, she stowed a dog-eared Preston A-Z and a special magic box in her handbag. Una then opened the Grimoire of Malvolian – an ancient volume so full of evil that it played havoc with Channel 5 reception and exploded every Halloween.

Running her fingers over the mouldy text, silently mouthing the words, Una committed the relevant section of the ritual to memory. Everything was coming together nicely.

***

Una pushed the buzzer.

"Hello love," she called into the small microphone.

"I don't do women," said a voice via the tinny speaker.

"I've come to offer you some alternative employment," said Una. "It is very important work."

"I have my own work," said Julie.

"Not like this dear. For once, wouldn't you love to do

something fulfilling? A girl with your unique gifts must be curious how far they can take you."

"How did you find me? Did the voices....?"

"It's a long story. But I recognise your special talents and I want to make sure you do too. You have incredible potential, totally brilliant, like." Her accent fluctuated unsteadily between 'posh' and broad Lancashire. Una made a mental note to charge the *Orbus of Principle Communication* fully before the evening's merriment. Comical local dialect could not be allowed to blur the message. There would be TV cameras and enormous national interest. The Miracle would be recorded and transmitted for all to see and faith in the Old Ways would be restored.

Simple.

"Look, will you sod off! I'm waiting for someone!"

"He isn't coming. They never do. You know that. Let me in and I'll show you something that will change your life!"

"Something as good as this?" crackled the distant voice of Julie, a buzz of static vibrating the speaker. For a moment, a face appeared in a picture frame hanging on the outer door. Julie smiled and the face became a skull, flesh dropping from it to hit the floor with a noisy splat. In spite of herself, Una glanced down to be sure the bloody goo didn't splash her boots. In the now empty eye sockets, maggots writhed and from the gaping mouth, a snake flicked out like a tongue.

"Cute," said Una. "But I'm not talking about party tricks. I can show you the real stuff, if you feel like stepping up a notch or two!"

Julie paused for a moment.

"Come in," she said. The lock clicked open.

Once inside the flat, Una was impressed and fought hard to conceal it. The detail was remarkable for what was obviously a primary conjuration. With some training in technique the girl could be a powerful witch. What a shame it was not to be her destiny!

Una observed how, as Julie moved, the air visibly fled from her and sparks flickered constantly at her fingertips. She was a slight, thin girl in her early twenties perhaps, with badly bleached blonde hair and cold, blue eyes. She wore faded jeans and a t-shirt over a lithe, boyish figure. Bare arms showed evidence of cuts and other scarring – injections maybe.

"Impress me or leave," commanded Julie, sitting down in a huge leather chair. She didn't offer a seat to Una.

Undeterred. Una produced a small wooden box from her bag. Upon it was written, in red, waxy letters, the words of an ancient spell she had painstakingly reproduced. Una knew the language was meaningless, the words merely acting as trigger for the small 'charm' stored inside.

"How pretty!" said Julie and reached forward to touch it. Una whispered something under her breath.

And suddenly Julie felt how nice it felt to welcome this woman into her home.

"I feel like I know you..." she began. All of a sudden it was hard to concentrate.

Una observed carefully then breathed out in wary relief.

"You do child, you do. We're old friends. Best pals." Una grinned broadly now. "Come on, we've work to do this evening. I'll explain as we walk."

For a moment Julie hesitated. There was something else she had planned to do. She could no longer remember what it was.

Then Una broke the mood. "Come on dawdler! Let's be about the work of the old Gods and Goddesses!"

"I don't believe in all that stuff."

"You will! Come with me and you will!"

Una helped Julie lock up, noting with surprise that not a single item in the room flickered even as she turned the keys in the double-glazed window locks. Despite being completely under the charm spell, the girl's creation remained solid. No matter how hard Una tried, she could not perceive the flat as it actually was.

This girl has real power, she thought, and vowed to tread very carefully. They left and made their way to Una's to begin preparations. Others were gathered already and more were converging than could be physically accommodated. The Buffy Witches cleared some space in the back yard then began distributing A4 leaflets about the forthcoming ceremony. In view of the solemnity of the occasion and their upgraded ranks in the overall pagan hierarchy, Mr Timpson was supervising the manufacture of cucumber sandwiches and flasks of hot tea whilst Bill was conducting a random underwear check.

***

Friday night was rarely pleasant in Arthur's line of work but that night there were bad vibes in the air before the first glass was emptied. He remained calm and in control on the surface but underneath all his instincts screamed that he should return home and lock the door.

Running into Hartley had unsettled him. He could have slunk away unseen but didn't. It made no sense.

"I'm courting disaster," Art had confessed to his cat. Never a bright animal, it had meowed and rubbed its body against his leg, pleased to hear its master was getting some long-overdue romantic action.

When the first serious fight of the night kicked off, it was only half past eight. Those involved weren't even drunk, just loud and abusive. It began when some snappily dressed Asian lads and several suited office types began arguing, at first good-naturedly, about the merits of white pointy hoods as accessories for a modern police force. Before anyone could anticipate, somebody nutted somebody else and soon there were 8 snarling blokes rolling over, kicking furiously, breaking glasses and letting loose the beast. It was only Arthur and his men's prompt intervention that prevented the violence spreading throughout the rest of the pub.

Although quashed, the fight left an uneasy atmosphere – and further ugly incidents followed. In the worst, two girls, each barely fourteen years old, became wild animals tearing, scratching and swearing. One glassed the other, ripping her arm and cheek. There was a lot of blood and the police were called, eventually, after allowing the girls time to make themselves scarce. Art sternly reminded his men that, no matter how cute or good for business, no more young chicks were allowed in tonight!

More scuffles followed.

It was perhaps ten O'clock when Arthur realised the gradual drift from the pub was becoming an exodus. It had been a weird night thus far, with some of Preston's strangest characters crawling out of the woodwork and causing mischief. Art wished he wasn't due for a stint on the door at the Warehouse later. It would be after three in the morning when he got off and the hours ahead promised to be ugly. *Must be something in the beer*, he thought. *Everyone's wound up tonight*. He noticed people streaming from nearby pubs, heading towards the centre of town and its market square.

"Wait here Dirk, I'm going to see what's going on," he said to his second in command. In other doorways, the hired muscle shrugged and exchanged puzzled as drinkers deserted in droves. After a time, most of the bouncers left their posts to go and find out what was happening. There was nobody left to watch over anyway.

On the flag market, overlooked by the massive, brooding library building, there was a great deal of commotion. A crowd, swelling to epic proportions, milled about doing zombie impersonations and bumping angrily into one other. They were an odd mixture consisting of a large proportion of Friday night drinkers interwoven with hundreds of middle-aged housewives, senior citizens and even a few children screaming and running about. A few fights broke out but mostly the aggression was subdued under an atmosphere of high anticipation.

A TV crew appeared, then another, then five more. Reporters fought for position and police materialised belatedly to try and calm them all down. Looking tense as they waited for reinforcements, they polished their batons and checked the tax disks of parked vehicles.

Arthur pushed his way through but when he reached the front, he was flabbergasted.

In the centre of the market, about 50 flabby white people danced – badly and without any sense of rhythm – around a makeshift bonfire.

Naked, inevitably.

A scary fat woman floated in the air, fire pouring from her eyes and milk streaming from her breasts. Art was wise enough to know that nothing good would come of such shenanigans.

The policemen busied themselves tackling every misdemeanour they spotted, each of them making quite sure they didn't accidentally glance towards the floating woman. They were only human, after all.

***

"What's that?" Hartley's mobile was making all kinds of electronic whines and squeaks.

"I said *Preston's in chaos*. We're calling men in on overtime, sir. The Chief Constable is coming in too. There's a bunch of... witches, I suppose you'd have to call them. They're holding a ceremony on the flag market. The boss witch is doing an interview with Fartin Tashir! Guess what, it's your good friend Mrs Sharples!"

"Fuckety Buckety! When you say 'ceremony' what exactly do you mean? And why isn't somebody breaking it up?"

"Well, sir, they've took us by surprise, sir. They lit this bloody fire for a start and they've draped curtains over lamp-posts and benches and are burning the waste bins. Actually, I think we're letting those burn cos they're bloody eyesores. They started by setting up stalls flogging crystals and cake – very nice it was apparently. Oh wait, now one of them is painting the cobbles red while your lady friend gets up to wave her boobs. Ugh, I think I'm going to be sick! This is live across the country sir – I'm watching on the portable at the station! Oh my dicky tummy, she's on Tashir's lap now... says she's going to make a human sacrifice. Is that allowed sir?"

"Who's in charge on the ground?" Hartley asked wearily.

"No idea sir, all the top brass are in transit. Actually you're the only senior officer I've been able to get through to. Oh by the way, I can see why you took to Mrs Sharples sir. She's very, er, striking. Anyway, later she's going to raise someone from the dead to demonstrate the power of the vegan faith and her lord Florian. I think that's what she said, the station is bedlam tonight!"

"Laddie, I'll put your tone down to overwork and stress. But that woman is no friend of mine!"

"Ooh," said the constable on his mobile.

"What is it?" said Hartley.

"She's just taken two long shiny knives out of a bag and they're panning over to a girl tied up against the wossisname – the Obelisk. Seems keen yo have her throat slit. Oh, they're all naked sir."

"Good grief! I'm on my way."

"Was it the naked part that did it?"

"Don't be stupid!" he snapped the mobile lid shut.

***

In the flat, Jim was profoundly asleep. Dave had tried to answer Hartley's questions but the Inspector seemed to be coping badly. He kept repeating 'you don't say,' over and over as if he hoped repetition would make it become true. The whole incident had left him shaken and a cut on his head, although minor, seemed to constantly distract him.

When his mobile chirped and he had to go, the relief was palpable.

"Don't you two go *anywhere*. I'll get a man over here to, ahem, protect you. It might take a while though. I'll get Miss Vincent's description to every officer in the area. There's nothing else you can do until we hear something. And in this case I have no idea what to expect. It didn't seem like a normal kidnapping but if you get a demand or receive any communication, I want to know right away. And make sure you're both here when I come back. I need to talk to him!" he indicated Jim.

"Of course," said Dave. "Hey man, take it easy, OK?"

Dave realised time was getting on; when Hartley left, he rang Sheila.

"Really sorry love, I didn't mean to be late!"

"Oh it's just a relief to hear your voice. Did you find Jim?"

"Yes, there's good news and bad news there. But I think we might get everything sorted out."

"I hope so. My mum rang earlier to tell me to put the telly on. It's on every channel – you won't believe it. There's a major happening in town. I don't want you going in there – promise me you won't! Some protesters are going mad and there's wall to wall naked people – large, wobbly, very naked people," she added. "They're all over, setting fire to things. Relax, I'll record it for you!"

"Hehe, cool, yeah babe, nice one. Look I'm at Jim's and have to wait here for a bit but I'll be back later and will tell all. Jim's a bit knackered what with discovering he's god – that *we're* both god. It's more tiring than you'd think."

"Of course it is love. You got that Jamaican stuff after all then?"

"Shit, I forgot. And no, I'm not stoned. Well, I don't think so."

"Of course you're not, what was I thinking? See you later," Sheila scrabbled about for a videotape on which to dutifully capture the raunchy antics.

***

Jim slept.

Dave watched over his friend and tried to make sense of it all, to work out where all the years had gone. Sheila and he had produced two children. Becky and Malcolm. Malc was the oldest and already painting and playing the piano.

Had none of it happened?

Was none of it real?

In a matter of minutes, Dave's mind had accelerated to love out almost 7 years of blissful, imaginary life. It was a fantasy built from suppressed hopes and dreams.

He still didn't understand why. Or who the bad guys were.

All the memories seemed real but they were fading at an alarming rate. Already, it was as if he could no longer connect to them. From being the cornerstone of his life, they ceased to upset him in less than an hour.

Dog-tired, Dave crashed out on the floor, Jim on the settee.

Hartley did not return that night. Nor did anyone else.

Sheila turned off the lights around midnight. Still no sign of her wayward husband.

A typical Friday in other words!

Chapter Five

Reality is merely an illusion, albeit a very persistent one.   Alfred Einsbatenn

Every TV station showed Julie's naked image.

In glorious Technicolour.

Which is actually a whole lot of colour in certain circumstances.

To the voyeurs of the world, Julie's eyes blazed. They were the glowing orbs of incandescent liquid fire less than a foot above her cute nipples. Had anyone gawped but a smidgen higher they'd have spotted them and been more afraid. Anyway.

Julie stood waiting, a tiny figure chained, grimy with sweat and nude against the sandstone pillar of the Obelisk. Formerly, missionaries would preach the Gospel from its steps. Today, its purpose was to be rather different.

Instead of the gas lamp formerly mounted on the Obelisk, a hundred glaring camera lights illuminated the scene. Its cultish participants were poised to lead the world in the first faltering steps towards anarchy. The crowd gaped but held back as if blocked by an invisible barrier, allowing the participants a wide berth.

Strange ideas fizzed into existence and bubbled through an atmosphere more volatile than a vigorously-shaken can of lager. The universe drummed its fingers idly. Although bound within the framework of Linear Time, it nonetheless knew what was coming. Anticipation became practically corporeal. The air crackled with ozone as if a storm approached.

Magic.

The watching world held its breath as Una Sharples, like a gigantic helium-filled love doll, floated upwards. Without touching the steps, she approached the bound girl and whispered a few words in her shell-like. TV pundits grew more serious when

Una, in great ceremony, brandished an ornate dagger. The flesh on her flabby arms swayed like a camel's neck. None could avert their eyes from the acres of pallid, perpetually wobbly flesh. Many tried, their expressions twisted and contorted. With a smoky blue flash, a melon appeared in her hand which she cut in half, tossing the pieces to a grinning man at the base of the steps. He, also, was naked except for a football scarf.

Bill laughed wildly, caught one of the halves and buried his face in it.

"Behold!" she cried, always a good opener. "The power of the Old Ways will be revealed to you all today!" Pausing momentarily for dramatic effect, she continued in a clear voice, "The Old Ways taught us to respect the diversity and wonder of the Earth. But we have ceased to honour and serve the vessel that carries us across the dark ocean of space." Una grudgingly admitted that Mr Timpson's additions to her speech improved on the original text, when spoken aloud. She continued, "the new religions tell us that man is fashioned in God's image. By placing so much power on man's shoulders, they have failed utterly. How can their foundation be divinely inspired? We have not forgotten the evil of the Inquisition even if you have! It brought pain, torture and intolerance and the very same church continues today. All your so-called holy books have been written by the hand of man. The madness must end my brothers and sisters. It must end or our goat will sink into darkness forever."

"Boat," hissed Mr Timpson, peering up from the lowest step over his reading glasses, the script in his shivering hand. On his left, Bill wiped his mouth with his scarf.

Ignoring them both, Una scanned the crowd, sensing their lust for blood. She continued. "Blind faith is a poor second best to the evidence of your own eyes. Reliance on faith alone encourages laziness and stupidity! The Old Gods will insist on a return to the Old ways in return for their protection. A war is coming, a Great Divide . We will no longer be silent. We will no longer allow those who rule to continue the deception.

"We will reclaim all that was stolen from us. We will resume our rightful place as guardians. First, a demonstration of our power. It will be replicated elsewhere in the coming days – you get to try it first! And afterwards, friends, we will all get down and party. Yes, you heard me! We will begin removing the structures that dampen your spirits and repress your true nature! Rejoice! For deliverance is at hand!"

Mr Timpson frowned because Una had deviated from the script. Her face had become contorted and her eyes bulged. Then, quicker than anyone had expected, she turned and drew a knife savagely across Julie's throat in a single brutal motion. It cut deeply, tearing the jugular vein and biting viciously into the windpipe. The wound was terrible as all could see. Una faced the crowd and held the dagger above her head with both hands. A thin trickle of blood ran down the blade, dribbled over her hand and down a mottled arm.

The police, seeing cameras pointing in their direction, watched with great interest and scribbled in notebooks. None seemed keen to arrest Una. They waited until ordered to do so.

A few of Una's followers cheered half-heartedly as Julie's head slumped forwards. The majority of the crowd stood mute, their eyes empty. The naked girl hung lifeless in chains, blood still flowing freely while Una levitated like a possessed blimp.

This is quite atypical even for a Friday night in Preston.

A few more cheers began as more of the crowd noticed how the blood was still pumping strongly and in increasing volume. It pumped thickly down Julie's neck, over small, perfect breasts, over her thin body. It splatted on the floor like paint.

Una didn't notice. She was enjoying the moment too much and relishing the one to come. Her eyes rolled back in her head, she began to slowly chant, being very precise with the intonation. In her hands, the knife became Two Knives.

The second miraculous half of the ceremony would shortly

begin. Then they would see!

Unnoticed only by Una now, the blood kept coming. An impossible amount poured from the slender, pale body, thick and warm. It painted Julie's legs and the stone steps, heading into the crowd and into the gutter.

Julie had kept her eyes closed as she'd agreed. It was a surprise to feel so much pain but she had made repairs before too much blood was lost. Simulating the ongoing flow was undemanding and she couldn't resist embellishing it.

Una had vowed she would only make a small cut but had clearly miscalculated. Julie felt weakened by the wound and the pain didn't ease as it should. The pillar was cold against her bottom. She was becoming unhappy.

The knife stroke had been strong and sure.

Una had lied. She had intended to kill.

She did not know of all Julie's talents.

With that realisation, she dispelled the charm in a hot flash of anger. She raised her head a fraction of an inch.

Nobody saw.

Close by, Una Sharples was contemplating camera angles that would best frame the library in the background when she made the Summoning. She was aware of the rapt attention of the crowd, taking particular pleasure from the awestruck expression of Mrs Bowler-Google. Una was also dreaming of the rewards her Lord would bestow when he took residence in the fine vessel she had obtained – better than Mikey by a long shot, assuming gods weren't troubled by gender issues.

The girl had such a powerful mind!

Upwards of a thousand faces didn't blink.

Not one yob, nob or bleating child uttered a sound.

At her feet, her coven – swollen to hundreds – knelt, chanting quietly, nudely oblivious to the cold stone flags.

The stone was so wet.

Steam rose from it.

The crowd didn't see the chains that bound Julie fade then cease to exist. Even when she took her first step away from the pillar, only a handful noticed. All eyes were on Una.

Una was posing, chanting and wiggling her breasts in elaborate circles. Her arms straight out, she clutched two knives that crackled with blue fire. The glow of madness spread down her arms. Within the crowd, people began pointing at Julie walking slowly and steadily down the steps. On autopilot, Bill the plumber stood to one side so she could pass, his gaze trained lovingly on Una's vast buttocks.

Arthur Bradshaw stood a little way off, open-mouthed with the rest.

A thick, dark cloud formed over Julie's head – and suddenly all attention was drawn to her. Those watching on TV saw only a shadowy outline. Perhaps because the camera failed to render it accurately, they assumed a wall of smoke had blown in from a nearby bonfire.

Julie Hutchinson screamed.

"You tried to kill me!"

Una turned, horrified. Cameras rolled, manned by grinning maniacs on the scoop of their lives. The library, bathed in yellow light, was framed perfectly against blackness. A few drops of drizzly rain began to fall.

"You're alive!" cried Una.

"Of course I am! You said you would make a little blood and I said I would heal it. You tried to cut my fucking head off!"

"I didn't. You have it wrong. I knew you had power, child. And see what you have accomplished! What *we* have accomplished, together!" However, the fear in her voice was impossible to conceal.

"You wanted to kill me!"

"No, no, I really didn't. I needed the blood - for the... for the ritual. See! My goodness, how is there so much?" Una faltered for a moment. Something was missing here.

Something important.

Then her fear dissolved. She had almost doubted her Lord *again*! Una pointed upwards, a wide, unpleasant smile rending her face. As Julie turned to look skywards, the wobbling witch ran, shoving through the throng towards a secure vantage point.

A colossal figure made of smoke surveyed the crowd in sardonic amusement. Standing over twenty feet high, its eyes were glowing orange coals in the best fiendish tradition.

Hartley picked that moment to arrive on scene. He failed to observe Una Sharples disappearing into the crowd. All he saw was the towering figure, its horns and tail now clearly evident. The smoke man had sprouted horns and hooves to go with the burning eyes. It was what could only be described as a demon.

A slender naked girl stood before the apparition, fists clenched.

Julie's knuckles whitened as she drove razor blades into her palms. The blood flowed freely and laughter erupted. For such a slender thing, her voice carried surprisingly well.

"You don't frighten me! I've shat scarier things than you. Some of my Bad Punters thought they were scary too. But I sorted their problems."

AH GIRL, YOU ARE UTTERLY DELICIOUS! AND YOU ARE MINE! The guttural voice dripped from the air, seeming to echo in the minds of those gathered to watch.

Julie spat. "Wind and watter! I bet you're not even real! You don't think I'm going to roll over for a puff of smoke?"

She raised both hands and the dark form raised two arm-like structures in response. Fuzzy tendrils formed a vague approximation of hands.

She closed her eyes and shrieked. And the demon began to diminish in size.

Then it regrouped and blasted Julie from her feet with a monstrous breath. She hit the ground hard but already she had boosted her body's self-repair mechanism. Groggily, she regained her feet just as a huge flagstone hurtled towards her. With no time for elegance, she leapt out of the way and it crashed to the ground where she'd been, burrowing deep into the flags, stone entering stone.

Julie's waif-like body was filthy, bloody and exhausted – but defiant. The dark creature towered above her and those gathered simply watched, their breath held, the cameras rolling.

The crowd was transfixed.

The demon grew darker and more substantial. Muscles and sinew rippled in the smoke and the snarling mouth gained lips and an unfortunate moustache. Its horned head glowered down at Julie and from its eyes, yellow fire poured.

Bathing in the fire as if enjoying a warm shower, she chuckled but without much humour. Then she pointed her finger and the demon began to warp, to writhe and to dissipate.

At the last and desperate, it gave up. Its consciousness fled, seeking any refuge.

Julie turned in dismissal. She couldn't care less.

Where was Una?

Now it was Julie who strode, naked, through the crowd. Hartley was there but wisely didn't get in her way as she cut a swathe through the terrified but fascinated crowd, her mind seeking the smell of Una Sharples. Her death would be a pleasure. Fresh blood dripped from her hands.

Behind her, the acolytes of a New Old Religion awaited the return of their goddess. In the absence of Una, they weren't sure if everything had gone to plan. But they were eager for more.

"That Satan character was a right pussy," someone commented.

***

"Game on," said Jim as he sat up, suddenly awake.

"What's that, man?" asked Dave. "Oh, my back!"

"What day is it?" said Jim.

"Saturday? Early I think. Shit, I'll have to ring Sheila and check she's OK."

For a fleeting moment, Dave wondered how his kids were. Then he remembered he didn't have any. He felt lost and lonely.

Jim stretched on the sofa, knocking over a stray cup of water with his foot. It plunged from the coffee table and, as ever, soaked into the carpet.

"Hartley never came back! They've got Monica and it's all my fault!" he summarised, squinting blearily around the flat.

"Who's got her, where is she man?" Dave had a crick in his neck where he'd been lying on a pile of Jim's computer magazines. He wanted to go home and sleep all day.

"I called her. A gamble really. I hoped there was part of me in her mind, something I could reach out and use. Long story man – but I prayed we could still connect. It gave me a tiny pin-hole to start nibbling at. I've been trapped in a similar way before. I was better prepared for it this time!"

"I'm not exactly following dude. So I suppose everything is pretty much normal. *Who* took Monica? How did I get here? I'm totally knackered too!" Dave got to his feet and poked about for something to eat. He was ravenous.

"Three guys took her. Well, sorta guys. They're part of something called the Aesir and it's *their* programs that were running in your head. In *everyone's* heads. I'm sure of it now but I don't know the reason – yet. They had us trapped, were draining our brains like brain vampires. I reckon I broke something important to get free. Monica kissed me," he smiled at the knowledge even if there was no memory. "It set up a feedback loop thingummy. She was always a catalyst for me."

"That's nice," prompted Dave, who knew his role in such conversations. Today, his heart wasn't in it.

"I'll explain later," said Jim. "We have to find her."

"What can I do mate? I'll grovel to Sheila but she'll be fine. Obviously I'll help." Dave reluctantly put aside dreams of a day in bed and went in search of toast. Jim padded after him into the kitchen, deep in thought.

"They are here but they came from outside. It's nagging at me, like it's right on the edge of my memory. It's like it happened to me before, which is clearly nonsense."

"What do you mean, the outside man?"

"I wish I knew. Drugs eh? They say the short term memory goes the first."

"Who does?"

"Fucked if I know. Twats."

Dave nodded.

They had planned to grab something to eat from the cafe across the road but it was shut. The street was deathly quiet so they returned to the flat where Jim improvised a breakfast of eggs. It was all he had left in the fridge that either of them dared tackle.

Dave rang Sheila and got a moderately frosty reception. He had planned to tell her he was off to save the universe and might late home for tea. Then he remembered the old rule: it was easier to get forgiveness than permission.

"No toast, sorry," Jim called from the kitchen. I must go shopping, he thought.

Eating fried eggs wasn't too rewarding, even with generous doses of jalapeño sauce but it sufficed. Both of them were starving and when Dave dug out the lime pickle and crackers, it was as good as a feast.

They ate their fill, a seemingly endless supply of eggs tucked away in Jim's fridge.

"Is this healthy?" asked Dave.

"Dunno mate, more coffee?"

"Thanks heavens for Coffee Mate, mate!" Dave laughed feebly.

"I have more thinking to do. Afterwards I'll go and get Monica back!"

Jim sat and concentrated while Dave filled the bong.

It was something to do. Life, they had often agreed, was mostly something to do.

Jim quickly reformatted the working storage of his brain and shunted the data into a huge, contiguous lump. Now he sat quietly while Dave made bubbling noises and watched cartoons. Then he quickly rebuilt only the Attic component of his House program, extracting the subroutine easily. He began loading it with commands, each voice-activated, many of them newly-written. He would not be caught napping again.

It was time to implement some serious self-protection.

If needed, the rest of the House could be called up from the virtual environment within the Attic. Right now, he needed speed above all else. He needed to be safe and required advanced monitoring to prevent further smacks on the head.

Physical and mental attacks, Jim!

"A holodeck within a holodeck!" he mumbled, firing of a process to compare the programs of the Aesir with similarly named programs in the base libraries. The libraries remained too complex for him to read directly but, by finding identical strings within the code, he hoped to reverse engineer, extrapolate and generally do clever shit until inspiration struck. With his usual overweening self-belief, Jim expected to have a working disassembler within hours. Then he'd know what the alien code was really doing!

Or what it *would* do if he let it run.

Jim had not removed the Aesir libraries entirely but had changed their mode to *simulation*. Once he traced the points at which programs were called, he'd be on the trail of the big picture. He took lengthy precautions to ensure they could never branch into full execution.

He vowed never to lose his mind again! Except on special occasions such as Fridays and weekends.

Obviously it would take time to read millions of lines of code. And Jim, for all his innovation, had found no quick way to do that. When he tried to cheat time, to overclock or skip ahead even by a few frames, he effort rendered him exhausted and unable to function. There was no solution at present.

Much of the functionality he'd discovered so far was obtuse and contradictory. In motor control routines, he'd found receptors. And in data filters, he'd encountered transmission procedures. Having concluded that he was probably quite complicated, Jim took a break and, as he often did, pored through memory banks seeking every trace of Monica.

And on his face, the Buddha smile slowly materialised.

Chapter Six

If you think a thing's impossible, you make it impossible
                                        Bruce Lip

Waking to the sound of raised voices, Monica kept her eyes closed and listened.

"She's listening," said Jonathon Meed.

"Of course she is," said Yasmine Carrion, stroking her bruised jaw. Monica opened her eyes a slit.

A large, powerfully-built man with dense stubble and thinning, curly black hair crouched in the back of the van with her. A mercenary type or wannabe, she guessed, he wore a padded green jacket and military-style black boots. His wide face turned to her, emotionless, his eyes blank and pitiless.

"I think this is a big mistake," he growled, stretching out thick fingers and frowning at them. Experimentally, he tugged at the hairs on the back of his hand with his teeth.

"Well, I'm open to suggestions of course, Helios. But right now I'm playing this by ear."

Meed's driving suggested he had spent time – perhaps as much as five minutes – in a simulator. Or on the dodgems. He had clearly failed to grasp the subtle nuances. Squinting at the dials and through the windscreen, he eventually worked out how to turn the lights to full beam. Within seconds, horns began honking as he dazzled oncoming traffic. Satisfied he was getting the hang of it, he searched for his own horn to respond.

Meed did not voice the thought that this could prove to be the most exciting adventure in many cycles. Gi Darven had grown yet another Linear-Time Universe, thick with bizarre rules. Even so, Meed had to grudgingly admit there might be something in it – certainly it helped make the adrenalin pump when you were forced to do things in a specific order.

"I still want to know how he managed to strand us in here!"

complained the female, Yasmine, angrily in the passenger seat.

"We will talk about that later," said Jonathon Meed. "Right now, we need a quiet location in which to examine this female and decide on the next step. Everything's rattling along nicely. Pinky's around and doing what he does best and between us we fired off some heavy duty chaos before the link was terminated. I expect it will all work out! This... inconvenience adds extra spice, that's all! Live a little! You wanted some role playing, well now's your chance!"

Monica listened but their voices drifted in and out, as if delivered through a slowly rotating speaker system. It was probably deliberate bollocks to confuse her.

She ran the evening's events through her mind, hoping that by cataloguing them, a picture – even one with pieces missing – would form. She had raced down the M6 because Jim was in trouble. Somehow – a very big somehow – he had called her telepathically, whilst being mugged by these three weirdos. Somehow she'd found him and had gone to him, with little thought for her own safety. Too many somehows, she noted. And to wake him, Jim had asked for a kiss. She suspected that part wasn't strictly necessary but smiled at the thought all the same.

"You won't be smiling soon human," said the burly bloke. Helios, the driver had called him.

Human?

"How are you doing back there?" called a cheery Jonathon Meed.

"Fuck you! You'd better let me go!" snarled Monica.

"Ooh, really? How marvellous! Well, righty-ho, we will. No, wait a minute, what am I saying? What I meant was: we *won't*. At least, not until some of this time of yours has trickled away never to return." He hummed happily for a few seconds, but without melody, then continued. "I wonder what it is about you my dear that He finds so interesting? He never does a thing for no reason our friend, er, Jim. In my extensive experience, he never has!"

They all laughed loudly and artificially, as if it was an entirely new experience. All except Monica, who was furious and strained at the bindings on her wrists and ankles. She summoned up the worst threat she could imagine.

"Jim will come and find me. Believe me, you don't *ever* want to come between him and me!" For some reason, that final sentence hadn't come out as she'd intended but it had a satisfying ring all the same. It seemed to make an impression too.

Her abductors exchanged brief, worried glances.

Then something strange happened. Jonathon Meed turned his head around. It rotated 180 degrees, which was disconcerting. Black buttons of hate glared at her. And when he smiled the effect was worse.

Monica gave in to horror.

"Sleep now, there's a love!" he commanded in the tones of a kindly old uncle.

Despite attempts to resist, she slept.

***

Jostled by an eager crowd, Arthur watched incredulously. He saw but could barely believe the towering figure revealed in flickering flames and camera flashes. The shape resembled a hugely fat man with horns and deformed legs. It wasn't quite classic Satan but perhaps some lesser devil or cake demon. Maybe it was mass hypnosis in action. Art rubbed his eyes and wondered if LSD had been slipped into his mineral water, as sometimes happened.

Throughout his life, Arthur had been an unbeliever. Yet on the day they learned Peg was sick, he prayed. He prayed every day until she withered and died. He did this because, for the first and only time, he found himself powerless, unable to think of any other course of action.

In those days, there were no alternate or complementary therapies, nor was there an Internet splattered with anonymous testimonies. Hope supplied, credit cards accepted. Ultimately, his ignorance did not affect the outcome, although it led to the accumulation of healing crystals, seeds, CDs and belly button fluff extracted humanely from Hopi Indians.

The doctors knew everything.

Everything, in this case, amounted to a complete timetable of her demise, along with pointless detours along the way. When they said it was hopeless, he believed them.

Peg believed them too, their words empowering the disease, tripling its power.

When she finally passed, Art abandoned belief forever. Before the painful day, he had repeatedly asked God for help and when no help arrived, he asked the Devil too. He asked on an open channel, promising himself to anyone who would, or could, save her. Peg had been shocked when he admitted this and made him promise never to despair again. Things were as they were supposed to be. He faith was strong. They would be reunited, of that she had no doubts.

Arthur bid farewell to his soul mate and wondered if she was right. He wanted it to be true but had no time for He who remained silent. Arthur gave no second chances.

He was not a forgiving man.

Seeing the demon first-hand, Arthur stirred from the eternal daydream. Could this be real? If so, it changed everything. And now he had committed his first murder for years, easily, as if he'd never lost the knack. Gordon had been a worm yet he was not without hope.

Much had occurred in a week.

He mused that if he murdered every arsehole he met, Preston would be a restful place.

The world seemed to have shifted on its axis and Art wondered what was next. He watched, like the rest of the gathered humans, puzzled and uncertain yet held there as surely as if they were set in tar. Bravely, the girl turned her face upwards towards the sinister cloud creature. She was small and alone, beautiful and fragile.

This couldn't be right.

Art felt light-headed, felt reality shake and shudder. He had killed a man despite the promise to Peg. He had done so almost automatically.

Almost.

No. I knew what I was doing, thought Arthur.

The temperature dropped, a blanket of cold descending from above. In the struggle of wills, the demon was losing. The change came suddenly, before the contest seemed properly engaged. They gasped collectively as Julie waved her hands, tearing the giant to shreds. Its body fell to the earth in pieces to be dispersed by a sudden wind. A lone horn sounded and ended abruptly.

In his peripheral vision, Arthur glimpsed something fall to earth amidst the smoke. Small and amorphous, it flapped like a blanket enveloping an old woman in act of snapping photographs. A shiver passed through her whole body. Her hands quickly covered her face, presumably attempting to ward off the horror.

***

Marjorie McManaman had already gathered a great selection of photos in her camera but she resisted viewing them on the tiny screen. It consumed the battery too quickly and she held out hope for further debauchery. The demon worshippers she constantly tried to expose were on public view. They had no shame but nothing was being done, even by the police. There was nakedness and fake blood. It was a disgusting, filthy trick!

In her ongoing quest to document the blasphemy and the nudity, Marjorie was not fully aware of the nebulous demon's sudden demise. For its part, the demon was angry. It had been unable to possess its intended host and now, shrieking in pain, it sought refuge in the closest receptive mind.

The demon known as Malvolian slammed into Marjorie's brain with all the gentleness of a truck ploughing through a school procession. He took immediate control, expelling the spiteful old lady's essence into a dark and dank prison.

"Fascinating!" the apparent Marjorie exclaimed, running brittle fingers from the dry, wrinkled face over the torso and down as far as her bony knees. It was far from the ideal body but perhaps not such a bad choice.

As the creature evaluated the mortal ruins, a startling voice.

"What are you?" asked Arthur.

"Now then young man. Should you ask a sweet old lady such personal questions!"

"I saw."

"Ah. And you thought it wise to tell me, did you? Tell me, should I open you up and make you suffer? Haven't you wanted to suffer for a very long time?"

"I don't believe in God or the Devil. Who are you?"

"Stupid human. Your belief is irrelevant. Take a look around and weep. Soon this pretty scene will be re-enacted across the planet. Judgement Day is coming!"

"I don't give a shit, I want to know who you are."

"And if I reveal that I *am* your God?"

"Do so and I'll kill you!"

"Gosh, really? Why, pray tell?"

"Because you let her die."

"Did I? You seriously think I even keep track?" Malvolian was an old player of the game and well used to this kind of bluff talk. He actually rather enjoyed it.

"Did you send the voices?" Arthur felt on the brink of losing control.

"Oh you poor confused mortal," cackled the crone.

Interrupting them abruptly, a fellow bouncer, Smegsy, bumped heavily into Art. He was a tough man, bald-headed and with a ridiculous strand of plaited ponytail sprouting from the base of his skull. They both registered surprise.

"Oh, sorry Art. Didn't see you there. That your mum?"

Art blocked the incoming low knife thrust and swung around automatically to lock Smegsy's arm straight out, applying stern pressure beneath the elbow.

"Art, sorry, I don't know what came over me!" Smegsy gritted his teeth in pain.

"And this?" Art indicated the knife. As he put more pressure on the elbow, it clattered to the floor.

"I swear I don't carry a knife. It just appeared in my hand."

Art released the pressure and turned.

The old woman was gone.

***

Una fled through Preston, a plump and wobbly woman in boots and nothing else. The streets were empty. Everyone had been summoned to the flag market.

Closed Circuit Cameras everywhere followed her.

She was, after all, a big lass and difficult to overlook.

In a shop doorway, a lone tramp lay huddled in a torn sleeping bag, a small dog clutched close for mutual warmth. He peered from the bag, seeing a naked woman walk past. For reasons he could not name, he was glad she had passed him by.

Unfortunately for the tramp, she came back.

The coat reeked of piss, fags and booze but it hid her nakedness adequately. The old tramp had given up without a fight. He ran yelping into the night, ahead of his ratty mutt.

Summoning all the protection spells she could remember in an attempt to disguise her presence, Una bathed in tramp essence, mentally becoming him.

Not very far behind, a shrill female voice roared. Without the spells, the voice's owner would have seen through the disguise.

"I'm going to find you and kill you! You vanished but I will find you!"

Una scurried away very quietly.

***

For Fred Hartley it had been the worst night of his life. Everything that might possibly go wrong had done so. Things that might impossibly go wrong had followed suit. He'd seen over forty people arrested on public disorder, violence and indecency charges and more would surely come. Unfortunately the strange mood had passed to his men, some of whom had lost it with several of the arrestees. A dozen people were now headed for casualty rather than the station, stretching resources even thinner. As if that wasn't enough, they were now under threat from special effects wizards – at least he hoped this had been special effects. To cap it all, some of his officers had gone undercover with the witches in a highly committed and explicit way.

The wild pagan orgy lasted for hours and involved sex, drugs and violence. Often it was hard to tell which was which. And it spread across the city like a plague.

The men still on duty became exhausted from all the driving around and situation monitoring. An oily sheen of sweat gleamed on their faces and many loosened their uniforms.

When Hartley realised the ceremony was losing steam, his spirits remained low. His weary eyes took in the extent of the carnage and the many swirling cameras greedily recording every thrust and punch. Establishing control would require tact, subtlety and carefully co-ordinated planning. Alternatively, he could let it run its course.

"Can't we get the riot shields and plastic bullets out sir?" pleaded one of his finest PCs for the tenth time, drooling a little.

Hartley shook his head and tried to work out how best to contain the situation. Some were now trying to withdraw from the fighting. He spotted Arthur Bradshaw herding a few wailing youngsters away. Bradshaw had once been a nasty piece of work but after getting married he was never in trouble again.

"You don't need riot shields," said Hartley, wrongly, as it

turned out.

Back at the station, he began fielding the press and processing citizens now full of repentance and wishing to go home. Mass insanity had spread after the girl performed her trick with the blood. *Everyone got involved in the heat of the moment, that's all. Not our fault.*

One half of an angry phone conversation drifted in from the corridor.

"You saw me on the news? Nude? Are you sure it was me darling....? What hussy? ... No, I didn't even know her dear. It's snooker on Wednesday nights. I just happened to get embroiled in some strangeness.... Darling? Darling?" Mr Timpson sensed problems brewing at home and suddenly noticed a more immediate threat in the form of a brutish officer nursing a swollen nose.

"That your phone call all done then Warlock?" he asked, cracking his knuckles loudly. "Cos an interview room is free now so you and I can spend some quality time."

"Gulp", said Mr Timpson, the wooden chair making unpleasant grooves in his skinny bare bottom.

***

Meanwhile, in the city centre, unarrested and helping nobody with their enquiries, the fickle Miss Schumann writhed under a particularly hirsute fireman, now firmly off-duty.

***

At his desk, the door locked, Hartley dismissed Jim Cavanah from his thoughts. He asked for an update on the missing woman.

"Who sir?"

"Miss Vincent. Monica Vincent, remember?"

"Oh no sir, I mean, no more news. We didn't get a very good description and, well, we don't have a vehicle or anything to look for."

"And your point?"

"Well sir, you know how you always take the mickey out of witnesses?"

"Members of the public don't see anything. Bloody amateurs!"

"Yes, sir. Quite right sir. We wondered if it would be possible for you to expand your own description of the three kidnappers sir?"

"How expand?"

"Well, sir, you said there were three of them?"

"Yes."

"Could you elaborate? That's actually all you gave us."

Hartley felt his face go crimson, his ears glowing with embarrassment.

"It was dark," he said. "They were indistinct. They did not catch the light while I looked at them. One was bulky, powerful-looking, another seemed female, the third was a little shorter. They ran strangely. As if legs were an unfamiliar concept."

"Well thanks sir, that should make all the difference," smarmed the miscellaneous young officer wagging his tail.

Hartley snapped awake.

Jesus, what time is it? He looked at his watch. It was five past six in the morning. He had fallen asleep maybe three hours ago. At his desk.

Fred Hartley dearly wanted to retire.

Chapter Seven

Art is a deliberate recreation of a new and special reality that grows from your response to life. It cannot be copied; it must be created.
Anony Mouse

It was 2am and there was no sign of Monica. Tim paced anxiously. Occasionally he peered through the blinds to try and spot headlight beams on the driveway. The windows were open, welcoming the night air, ready to give advance warning of crunching tyres on gravel.

Silence.

In the hallway a clock ticked mournfully. In the kitchen the fridge hummed. The house, fresh from teenage memories, was almost exactly as his parents had left it. Familiar noises offered small comforts: a creak here, a scratching mouse there. Tim was not coping well. He turned on the lights of every room as if to ward off more than darkness. Doubt gnawed at his confidence, at the core of his personality. What if she never returned? Saturday was here already but Monica was not!

Her so-called friend had, it turned out, known nothing of any emergency visit. Indeed, the woman had been audibly spooked to hear of her impending demise. *It's the way I tell 'em*, thought Tim, grimly. When pressed by his remote coercion, Tim forced the 'friend' to admit she hadn't heard from Monica directly in years. An occasional email was the extent of their relationship. The woman hadn't even known Monica and Jim had split up. She had neglected to mention it!

It was obvious. She had gone to see Him. He knew this with growing certainty and felt anger and anxiety begin boiling up in his chest. *Why would she do that?*

In an effort to calm a turbulent mind, Tim reminisced to when they first met. At a séance, a small gathering of sombre, middle-class office workers seeking answers. He'd been working the 'subconscious thoughts' end of the gig on behalf of the medium when a striking, tall girl with enigmatic eyes entered the room. No, not entered, he decided. Filled.

Monica Vincent. Well-dressed, quietly spoken and nursing hurts from her childhood to present day. He was instantly captivated.

A recent split is a difficult scar to conceal and to an expert like Tim, her mind opened like a flower. That evening he helped soothe her, began the slow process of getting close, probing her thoughts, testing each response until he could accurately hit the right tone of chit chat every time. Neither Tim nor the medium were able to trace the underlying source of her pain but he did learn about her soon-to-be-ex husband who was a nutcase and an immature, whining loser. The man was obsessive and unable to leave her alone for a moment. Concerning the reason they parted, he never learned anything other than, for reasons unknown, he was never able to accept that she returned his love in equal measures. He searched for ways to prove his hypothesis and eventually, it seemed, found one.

After the split, Monica learned to enjoy her space and spent many quiet hours contemplating and observing life. It was a relief to escape the stifling atmosphere of Jim's undivided, obsessive attention and she had a few mindless flings to remind herself she was desirable.

Tim saw that and more besides. He instantly knew she was special. Not only was Monica beautiful, intelligent and had expensive tastes, she also had a rare brain. Even on that first night, his illusions were less illusionary. Loved ones spoke in voices of uncanny accuracy, plundered from the thoughts of those in attendance. Objects moved, candles were extinguished. His meagre talent blossomed that night. And, as he courted her over the next few months, he expanded his ambition in many simultaneous directions.

In a very tangible sense, he needed her.

Without Monica, he would never reach the level he aspired to. Tim felt tears well up as he wrestled with uncertainty. He was so close to the showbiz dream, the big breakthrough!

Love was a complicated thing. At first he felt guilty for the almost parasitic way he drew her energy. Then he felt himself genuinely falling in love, wanting to please her in ways that Jim never had. She was almost the perfect partner. It was just a pity she stood several inches above him. Even the elevated shoes hadn't helped and Tim took to watching Dom Truise movies in the hope of discovering the secret of acting taller.

The phone rang and he leapt at it.

A wrong number.

A stupid drunk wanting a taxi.

Tim, livid, told the man that yes, this was Quadruple A Taxis and yes, they were on their way. As a parting gesture, he advised the man, very strongly, to remove his trousers and wait for the taxi with his underpants over his head.

"Huh? You want me to, uh, take my pants off?"

"Oh yes," said Tim. "It'll be a Good Way for us to Recognise You." He sensed resistance and pushed a little harder. It wasn't often difficult with drunks. "Do as I say and you will have a Safe, Happy ride Home. You want to be Happy?"

"I don't know," said the drunk. "I guess so...."

Tim hung up and instantly started to worry about Monica again. Her mobile was still on the sideboard and he glared at it accusingly.

Outside an Indian restaurant in Lancaster, a man stood in the street unashamedly exposing his bare arse, his underpants on his head. Until he was gently led away.

***

The Sheffield show was going to be very important: The prime outing (to date) of the Wondrous Tim.

He'd played larger venues but only as support. Tonight he *was* the show and the nerves were flickering already. He knew he should try to get some sleep but it was impossible under the circumstances. Tim had come to rely on Monica, built the act upon her. It was unthinkable that she might not be there.

It was relatively easy to perform the minor routines solo. But for the large-scale illusions, those upon which he would forge his career, Tim relied on the latent capacity of Miss Monica Vincent. He took from her leech-like, unknown, sure she would give him her blessing when he eventually explained. This coming night he needed to bring the house down. With Monica by his side, he could do it. Literally if he chose to. Without her, he would be back at the level of card tricks, lighting effects, hidden microphones, messages in envelopes. Although his skills had genuinely expanded in recent months, they were still not the stuff of legend. Worse, they could desert him at a moment's notice, vanishing like Will O' The Wisp.

He slumped in an armchair and unleashed music intended to be soothing. The whale noises and badly-recorded roar of waves on the shore irritated him. He tried to empty his mind and think only restful thoughts but failed. If Monica didn't come back, it would be better to postpone, blame it on the troubles, stay on and do a few more interviews from a 'concerned' point of view. He turned off the CD player and began to catch up on the evening's events on the news.

At half three in the morning, the phone rang again. Tim sprang to his feet, having been slumbering in the chair.

It was the police. They told him Monica had been taken he nodded, dumbly, unable to grasp the incongruities. The situation had turned badly surreal.

Ten minutes later a police car rolled up the driveway. A young, rather loosely-dressed officer sauntered inside. Restlessly rubbing his hands throughout, he explained that, since Tim was not officially next of kin, there had been problems contacting him and that they definitely had not forgotten or anything. And anyway, tonight was not a normal night. Anxiously, the officer related how Monica had been forcibly abducted from Avenham Park earlier that evening, the motive as yet unknown, by persons equally unknown. An inspector had witnessed the whole thing but he was old and not really that kind of inspector who got into scrapes. Right now it was early days and strange things were afoot, he added, his expression flickering between concerned, professional and terminally bored.

Throughout their chat, the officer consistently failed to meet Tim's gaze, responding to most questions with a frustrating 'dunno really mate'. He summed up by suggesting a trip to the station first thing to chat about it properly with somebody into all that delusional time-wasting.

"Somebody's bound to know something by then," he offered.

The officer then consulted the palm of his hand, sniggered, and suggested Monica might have a good claim for compensation. He shut up when Tim ordered him to, and left very soon afterwards, shaking his head.

As the police car pulled away, Tim slammed the door so mightily that one of the small panes of glass developed a hair-line crack. Then he got on the phone to the agent who, earlier that evening, had called out of the blue to ask whether he would consider employing a professional. One used to the big league.

From what Tim could gather, Barry McGarry was practically a caricature. But he had a solid reputation and kept his clients for life, which was always a good sign. He called up the number from memory and dialled.

The phone rang just once and a voice answered, wide awake and ready to do business.

"Tim, I was expecting you." The tones were rich, warm and friendly. A faint trace of cockney drowned in pseudo-posh.

Impressed, if a little taken aback, Tim glanced at the clock then explained the situation as well as he could. "A challenge. Do well for me on this and we're in business," he ended.

"It's a tall order Tim and no mistake. You're a man who obviously believes in meeting life's challenges head-on. Good for you! We only have a few hours to move on this and turn it into something worthwhile. I am sure I can do something, even at this very late hour." His manner of speaking was breathless, transmitting boundless enthusiasm. Tim felt better already.

"Okay, thanks Barry. I really do wish this could have happened yesterday. I can't imagine better publicity for the show, but the timing is shite." He paused. "Of course, I'd have preferred it not to happen at all."

"I'm sure. And you say the kidnappers have not contacted you?"

"It's only been a few hours but no. Why?"

"Well, it would be far better to have a note or a demand of some kind. For the early editions. We don't want a simple plea for money either. Ideally something juicier would capture the public imagination. A scandal or a plot maybe."

"Do you think I should postpone? How would that look?" Tim's voice was even, casual.

"The gig? Why ever would you do that?" Barry's voice was low, almost inaudible.

"Well, I won't be at my best if I'm worrying. It will be hard to concentrate - and there are some complex illusions to perform."

McGarry said nothing for a moment. Then he surprised Tim with his next question.

"Is there something you're not telling me?"

"Oh, ah, um, no. Nothing. Wh-why do you ask?"

"You don't sound sure."

"How much better would the publicity be with a note?" asked Tim, surprised to find his upper lip moist with sweat. "Just for the sake of reference, I mean. I'm curious."

***

Wandering the streets, barefoot and naked, accompanied by slowly scanning security cameras, Julie was exhausted and angry, cold and sticky. Despite walking for hours, there was no sign of Una.

She lied!

It was not possible to wink out of existence, yet there was neither smell nor aura to chase. Eventually, defeated, Julie turned for home. Her feet were blocks of ice and sleep beckoned.

At the flat, she took a long hot bath.

Nobody had followed.

The soapy water eased her aching body. She closed her eyes and shuddered at the memory of the monster, the betrayal, the faceless people. Their expressions were of awe and fear.

Fear of her.

If it weren't for the memory of the stares, she might have doubted it happened.

What was I thinking of - to go there? That woman did something to me!

The thick fresh scar across her throat felt rough to the touch as Julie's fingers traced tenderly over it. No matter how she tried, she couldn't imagine the wounds as fully healed. And so they weren't.

Of the evening's events, only pale, watercolour memories remained. And scar tissue. Knobbled and irregular on near-white skin.

Always a good healer, Julie had perfected near-instantaneous repair. A modest allotment of thought power worked wonders when it came to bolstering the natural healing process. Her body had been instructed to monitor and maintain itself automatically. It had been given precise instructions to carry on, even beyond the final heartbeat.

In a deep, circular bath, Julie wiggled tiny toes into the taps and breathed in the fragrance of expensive bath salts. Urgently, she scrubbed at herself, the water warm and intoxicating. But afterwards, annoyingly, sleep would not come. The starched white sheets felt damp despite her best efforts. She got up to make a brew while in her mind, the evening's bizarre circus played through, over and over.

The hours crawled by. She would have welcomed a punter - even a Bad Punter.

Especially a bad one.

Julie's mind was a mess.

Today she had seen and done impossible things: more impossible than her talent of freezing a person, holding them. More impossible, even, than making her flat look different. In a rare moment of lucidity, she likened that to hypnotism, picked up subconsciously from watching TV.

The most impossible things started with the earth mother. She had played a trick.

But what?

How did she find me? It was hard to remember anything. Then her throat was cut! Julie played back the images in her mind but remained detached. Touching the scar, she shuddered and gulped the hot tea.

Why did she try to kill me?

How did I destroy the smoke-man?

No answers came. Julie didn't know what was happening but remembered the brief battle. In her loneliness, she had asked the Voice in her head for its advice.

Silence.

The Voice had gone, or it was sulking. She willed it gone forever.

Being small and strong had many advantages. People underestimated her. All her life Julie had hidden her strength, afraid that others would see. Tonight she had revealed too much but perhaps the time to be afraid was over.

Bad men get away with terrible things when people are afraid.

And if strong people are afraid, how will the weak find their courage?

Julie realised she could punish all the bad men if she chose to.

From now on, she resolved to do good things. And to punish those who did wrong.

Chapter Eight

My one regret in life is that I am not someone else.
Willy Allen

Saturday morning's tabloids were laden with garish photos of a pagan celebration of sex and violence. In Darkest Preston, Lancashire. The humongous breasts and buttocks of Una Sharples (Mrs) adorned billboards country-wide, alongside a waif-like girl drenched in blood. A chilling Carrie impersonation, they said. In some of the pictures, Una seemed to glide through the air, brandishing a wickedly-curved dagger. In others, hordes of flabby, middle-aged naked people engaged in what could only be described as a fumbling outdoor orgy, set amongst flames and lunacy.

Every pundit hypothesised about the ritual although nobody was much interested in the scrawled press release of Lancs Constabulary and its suggestions of mass hypnosis and sunspots. The police's part in the whole torrid episode was already being questioned at the highest level and there were calls for a public enquiry, a sure sign that a scapegoat was urgently required.

Speculation was rife. Indeed, speculation replaced information. TV schedules were binned and replaced by in-depth 'specials' across the board. Analysis was performed of the footage, carefully trawling through the outrageous events, the strangeness, the nudity. Experts competed in predicting what would happen next. And where. And without becoming overly tumescent if possible, at least on the BBC. Every pet theory earned airtime, especially if it added to the fear, outrage and confusion.

Mrs Sharples, of Mersey Street Preston, recently lost her son in tragic circumstances, began one report. Insider photos, obtained under dubious circumstances, sensitively reflected the depth of the tragedy via Mikey's staring deathmask on the slab. Hordes of reporters camped outside Una's house, seeking any evidence she was inside.

Over Preston, a subdued atmosphere descended, like an old man's sock onto a recent spew. Those who ventured outside had a blankness about them, empty stares pasted across empty faces. Reporters prodded microphones at anyone who as much as blinked. *Perhaps it was a publicity stunt gone wrong, or an experiment with a new drug?* The hapless passers-by were prompted repeatedly. *Is this evidence of Genuine Evil in our midst? And is Judgement Day imminent?* Another popular question.

Photos from the botched ritual assaulted the senses in vivid colour accompanied by lurid images of Una, a near-elemental figure. In homes across the country, children fashioned Una models in plasticine. Lots of plasticine.

Most tabloids packed their colour supplements with 10 facts everyone should about England's newest city. In line with tradition, 9 of them were entirely fabricated.

The shadowy demon had not photographed terribly well. Eyewitness accounts were surprisingly sketchy too. But paganism, magic and the black arts were hot topics in bars and workplaces. Tales of the supernatural reached even the broadsheets and reporters were beside themselves with glee, which most found confusing.

Amazingly, amongst the riots, bloodshed and gratuitous flashes of flesh, several tabloids featured the pale face of a *fantastic young illusionist* who gazed with wisdom from the inner pages. Pictured outside the police station at the heart of the drama, he confessed to secretly helping solve a number of baffling cases already. The Wondrous Tim wore a black polo-neck shirt with no sense of irony. He was further distinguished by thinning, oiled blonde hair and an obsessively-manicured goatee.

"Rising Star Magician unravels mystic mystery" was one uninspired headline.

"Mind Reader's partner taken – for sacrifice?" guessed

335

another.

"Wondrous Tim heals Preston" suggested a third, rather optimistically.

"Satanic Ritual foreseen by top TV Clairvoyant!" claimed the Daily Sport, the only one running the Tim angle on the front page. Tim's face, solemn if rather blurry, was clumsily superimposed over a movie scene of fire, flesh and fetishism. Later editions spiced up the heading to "Bloodbath Porno Alien Invasion" with "Wondrous Tim saw it all coming!" as a subheading. The text was printed in red wobbly letters, apparently dripping blood and with the word 'coming' double underlined.

Claims for nose-bound expenses hit levels that blitzed the most recent batch of motorway pile-ups and the last half dozen celebrity drugs shame and/or suicide epics.

Barry McGarry had done spectacularly well, it couldn't be denied. Considering the scale of the story and its nationwide impact, Tim was impressed to be suddenly, deeply spliced into it. And at such short notice too. Despite a complete lack of substance, the many accounts of his bravery, his fears for Monica at the hands of a 'shadowy foreign cult' made an impressive work of fiction. Briefly, he wondered where the image had been sourced.

"That's not a great photo," Tim moaned down the phone.

"It's on the front page you fanny!" said Barry.

"Yes but only in the Spurt. Sport, sorry. And it doesn't mention the show tonight until page five. I told you about the booking cockup. Otherwise it'd be full."

"Look Tim, don't try to con me. Don't kid a kidder. Admit it: I achieved wonders in no time with practically no data. And you know it! I pasted your mug into that photo myself and emailed it over with seconds to spare before they changed the front page. Next time you have a go. See if you can do any better!"

"Sorry Barry, it's good stuff obviously. Well, I don't know about the alien angle . . . or the shadowy foreign cult bit . . .

Look, as soon as Monica is released we'll start discussing the transfer to your agency. Guaranteed."

"Oh it is indeed. Guaranteed, Mr Wondrous! And shall I tell you how I know why? First, I'm not stupid. I checked into your so-called girlfriend and her history. I joined a few dots. Do you know what I came up with?"

Tim didn't want to hear it. The call wasn't going quite the way he'd planned.

"What do you want?" he kept his voice free of inflection.

"That's more like it son. Why Tim, lad, all I want is for us both to do well out of this opportunity. For us both to do very well indeed." His voice was laced with reason and Tim relaxed.

"Alright Barry. You've got a deal. I'll square it with Monica – assuming we find her." Tim was surprised to find his hands shaking.

"Whatever happens, it's *us* that's in control. You and me, Timmy lad. All OK now?"

"I will be. Once this next show is over. Unfortunately Monica is an important part of it." He couldn't believe he'd admitted that.

"She isn't your assistant is she?"

"No, nothing like that."

"So how is she important?" asked Barry in his resonant, soothing voice.

Tim concentrated hard, his fist gripping the phone as if engaged in a battle of wills.

"Well, I need her primarily for luck. In my business luck is everything. She chooses my costume too. I wouldn't be so slick if she weren't around. I'd be distracted. I love her for goodness' sake!"

"Well, I suspect you're going to be out of luck. There's not a single clue according to my informant inside the Lancs Constabulary. She's well and truly gorn!"

"What else did your . . . informant tell you?"

Barry paused, judging the long silence with the skills of a

master. Then he spoke, in odd cadences that broke the pattern of speech, making it difficult to follow.

"You. See how useful. I can be. To you? This is my realm. Tim. It's my job to know things. About people, about places, about the lines that join them all. Together. My job is data. Even an insignificant incident, years ago, can return. Can haunt somebody given the right circumstances. You. Could. Not. Begin to guess at the data I retain. I most value *personal* information. The information to dislodge governments, to start civil wars if I deem it necessary. And all. Ready. To use to my. Our. Advantage. When necessary. Like this morning with the papers! You see?"

Tim realised that the hairs were tingling along the back of his neck. With a great effort of will, he gripped the phone until it cracked.

"OK. Look Barry, we'll get together in Sheffield this afternoon. Just after lunch, OK? It's two and a half hours from here and I'll be setting off soon. See you then!" Tim hung up quicker than he had intended but the guy was starting to get to him. "Must be tired," he told the mirror, poking at fresh bags under his eyes.

A throbbing headache was making itself known as Tim contemplated a novel plan – enlisting a replacement for Monica. He had long wondered whether an alternate mind could serve in a similar capacity, that of mental augmentation.

However. Without fully understanding how it worked with Monica, finding another seemed highly unlikely. It was even possible that the phenomenon was unique to her. Nevertheless, Tim knew half a dozen genuinely gifted psychics who might fit the bill. It was risky but possibly his only chance. He quickly rummaged for a battered phone book, contacts from the days of Ouija boards and tarot cards. A born survivor, Tim kept a few tricks, literally, up his sleeve.

Grief and worry could wait. First, fame and success would be won. He hoped Monica would understand that he could achieve nothing by staying at home and moping. And with the phone transferred to his mobile, it didn't actually matter where he waited. It was for their mutual benefit that the show must go on, he practised.

Tim bit his nails and repeated until it sounded natural.

Once across the Pennines, the plan was to spend the afternoon running over last minute preparations, changes to the act and yet more interviews. He would choose a costume, check his props and run through the choreography. If he could somehow recruit a substitute for Monica, perhaps the show would be spectacular. Otherwise, he'd try the old-fashioned way and trust to his charm.

In his office, Barry chuckled in amusement. Relationships with his clients always started the same way. He would be generous at first, only reeling them in when he knew enough to be sure they never strayed again.

Barry McGarry relished his position in life's hierarchy: top of the food chain.

With no time to visit the police station, Tim gave them a ring. He was immediately put on hold.

"Bloody Vivaldi!" he snarled.

***

Sheila rang Jim's buzzer.

"Hey Dave, Jim, open up. It's me!" said her voice in the speaker.

"Sheila!" said Dave, "come right up." He released the button.

"Shit man, we're totally fucked. Sheila's here. I bet she's mad!"

"Why should I be mad?" Sheila's voice again.

"Oh, I meant to say," called Jim from the other room. "That button sticks a bit sometimes."

"Thanks mate."

"No worries."

"Monica's been snatched and the fuzz are clueless. We're going to find her and rescue her," Dave declared proudly.

"And how, exactly, are you going to do that Dave? Or is it Jesus now?" Sheila eyed the bong suspiciously. True to form they had obviously got wasted, slept on the floor, probably dozed off watching sci-fi videos and woke up convinced they were documentaries. How could she think things would ever change? Sheila maintained a deadpan expression. Visible signs of amusement only encouraged them.

Jim popped his head out of the bedroom and flashed a faint smile into the front room. He was getting dressed whilst searching for his favourite t-shirt. The purple one Monica had bought at a WOMAD festival one hot, passionate, unforgettable summer. Whooping, he spotted its faded pattern at the back of the drawer and threw everything else on the floor having retrieved it. He figured it would help establish a connection and anyway, he relished its comforting presence. Memories of Monica wearing only it surfaced. Good days.

"Actually, neither of us could nail the role of Jesus. I was Zeno of Elea once," Jim called, finding his jeans too tight. "Dave's higher than Jesus, the top man, the big Snoop Doggy God hisself. Mama!"

"Ridiculous voice alert mate?" said Dave.

"Ah, sorry. Boredom. Frustration too. I've been searching for Monica all morning. I can't sense her anywhere."

"Well man, it's a tall order. If you ask me, I don't think this downgrades your godliness one bit. It's not like you practised or anything."

"Thanks mate. Good point. Appreciate it."

"No trouble."

"I shudder to think what future nursing home staff are going to make of you two." Sheila commented. "And Jim, how come you never have any milk?"

From the bedroom, a muffled sound, a thud and then a cry of

"Eureka!"

"Aha! Ha ha ha har! I've got something," announced Jim.

"I think I've got it cornered!" said Sheila, wrinkling her nose at a green furry entity crouching at the back of the fridge. "Were you cheese once upon a time?" she asked it.

Chapter Nine

The gods, likening themselves to all kinds of strangers, go in various disguises from city to city, observing the wrongdoing and the righteousness of men.   Homie

"Where, on this pathetic pea of a planet, under this piddling lightbulb and in this oddball LTU, the fuck, *are* we?!!" Yasmine was obviously upset and not settling in at all well. She stomped around the threadbare farmhouse knocking things over for the sheer hell of it.

Due to a series of petty arguments (first over the operation of the van and second over directions) they had arrived late, mentally exhausted and needing sleep. Jonathon Meed was adamant this was a safe refuge. His body donor lived entirely alone and in a remote location. It was their best piece of luck so far.

Now he banged around in the kitchen, angry, frustrated but trying to be philosophical about it. He was hungry but unsure what to eat. Or what was edible. He experimented with an old newspaper and then some dry cereal. Then he tried milk. It had been left out of the fridge for a day or so and was therefore rather lumpy and grey-looking.

"This is wonderful," he gulped. Then it all came rushing back and sprayed everywhere. It went over the sink where a week's unwashed dishes skulked, over the cooker, bedecked with dirty pans and over himself, apparently a middle-aged farmer complete with flat cap, wellies and a shapeless green jumper.

"Curious," he said. "The body didn't respond well to that. What do these creatures eat?"

"You're meant to be the expert!" snapped Yasmine from the sitting room where she glowered at Monica, baffled and annoyed by the human's mental barrier. Her jaw bore a purple bruise under the chin as evidence of Monica's more conventional defences.

Meed shouted back to her from the kitchen. "Look, I haven't mapped all the cognitive areas yet, let alone the compressed memory pools. We lost most of my tailored local programs when Bifrost[6] collapsed. I have certain other priorities right now but it won't take me too long to put something together. You could even help!"

"I don't think so. But you better get us out of here quickly!"

"Why the rush? I thought you wanted to get some Inside experience, to bathe in the primordial swamp?"

"Should you be saying stuff like that in front of *her*?" asked Yasmine.

Monica was tied to an upright chair sitting at a filthy dining table. Her hands were secured behind her back, her ankles to one of the table legs.

"What difference can it make?" asked Meed. "We're in these bodies and playing by His rules, but the outcome is not in doubt."

"So you know how to do a complete reinitialisation already then? I am impressed."

"No, not exactly," said Meed.

"Ah." Yasmine unleashed an icy smile in Monica's direction. Then her hand inadvertently strayed across something slimy. "Oh gluons, the sofa! Vileness! And what are these images?" She held a magazine, extracted from a pile of similar magazines, by her fingertips. Yasmine wore an expression of genuine puzzlement.

"I think they call that pornography," said Monica laughing. "Who *are* you idiots?"

Yasmine scowled. In the harsh light of this dirty place, the human did not seem so special. Scared, pissing her knickers probably, but quite insignificant.

"We are your gods, mortal!" Yasmine declared pompously and

---

[6] Affectionate term for "Bi-Directional Field Resonator"
[7] It's complicated. We might get to it later, OK?

posed for a bit, hands on hips, as if awaiting a response. She'd been led to believe there would be grovelling and quaking. She waited some more then started to lose her rag.

Oblivious, and not inclined to kowtow, Monica examined the small farmhouse, blotting out the oriental bitch as if she no longer existed. Another skill.

The farm house showed no sign of female presence. The sitting room opened on to a grubby front room with a large TV, several video recorders and piles of tapes labelled in black felt tip. Monica didn't have to read their titles to deduce their emetic properties. The curtains were all drawn and some of the wallpaper was hanging off.

Unwashed dishes were piled on most surfaces along with cups, crushed lager cans, more pornography and parts of oily machines, wrapped in rags. On the walls, faded paintings of nameless landscapes hung at irregular intervals. The style and subject lacked variation and Monica guessed the farmer himself might have painted them. They weren't very good.

Why had a hill farmer, a young oriental woman and, well, a Greek (by the accent) thug taken her? And brought her here? They seemed very weird and kept talking gibberish. Monica wondered if it was staged and kept expecting Jim to burst in and heroically save the day.

What did they want?

Monica continued to ignore the woman, Yasmine. Compared to ignoring Jim, it was child's play. Her mind skipped around randomly and unfettered.

There were days when she regretted shutting him out, refusing to fall under the spell one more time. Life was different now. When not touring, the long evenings with Tim were great, if slightly dull. Even so, this was what she always thought she wanted.

Over the past few months, to keep her brain sharp, Monica had turned to polishing some of her skills. She had totally mastered blanking people at will. And ayone, not just Jim. It was working perfectly with Yasmine.

We are your Gods!

Hilarious!

Yasmine fumed. She slapped Monica across the face viciously and was amazed when there was no reaction. Having tried subtle mental probes, Yasmine now angrily thrust a sharp, pointy one at Monica's mind.

Nothing. Not even a blink.

"I think there's something wrong with this body Meed," she whined, leaving Monica alone for a moment.

Ouch, thought Monica inwardly. *What on earth was that?*

Morning came. Fighting off an epic migraine, Monica evaluated her situation in daylight. They were somewhere on the moors but she'd worked out that much from glimpses stolen through windows. The journey had been a dark, silent blur. The three stooges had hardly spoken to her, spending their time arguing amongst themselves instead. They'd reached this farm around midnight, tied her up, injected her with a clear liquid and then she had slept. When morning came, her captors seemed – if anything – stranger than ever. They were apparently confused by everyday items such as a kettle or a light switch. Whether this was due to wild misuse of drugs or because they were asylum seekers from the planet Zog remained speculation. She favoured the former theory initially but didn't entirely rule out the latter.

With no idea what they could possibly want – and no clues made sense – Monica was genuinely scared. *I'm all out of rich relatives*, she thought. *And with an ass like mine I'll never be mistaken for Victoria Peckham!*

All three continued to behave oddly – and having lived with Jim, she was totally familiar with odd in all its myriad guises. And also thanks to Jim, she was familiar with pompous, pseudo-intellectual waffle. They kept laughing about the Uncertainty

Principle, repeating an old phrase of Jim's (that she'd never found funny), saying 'but just *how* uncertain are you?' then laughing some more.

They sounded lots like Jim and Dave in the old days, stoned and annoying.

In spite of her situation, she smiled. Maybe it wasn't always annoying. Maybe they were halcyon days after all. Since then Spring, Summer, Autumn and Winter blended into a single pallid season. What had gone wrong? Was this how her life was supposed to turn out?

Monica forced herself to concentrate on the matter in hand. She returned to the study of her captors. It was all she could do under the circumstances so she paid particular attention. There were many anomalies here, possibly enough to build up a picture by correlating the available data and applying a little Jim-like insight . . .

What did they want?

She went over what she knew already, which wasn't much. Looking at them, you would never imagine an association or link between them.

Is that, in itself, a clue?

Jonathon Meed was a squat man, thickset with fat fingers. His nails were broken, yellow and nicotine-stained. Dirt filled the cracks. These hands would never be relished in a gentlemanly shake. The face was ruddy with thick sideburns and perhaps a hair piece. Meed had very black eyes, more like buttons than eyes, shiny but cold. Obviously the leader, externally he was a farmer but he spoke like a mad scientist.

Then there was Yasmine. A tall woman evidently in her early twenties, she was slender and imposing. Although Monica didn't know it, Yasmine had formerly been a student of psychology and was indeed of oriental origin, an attractive half Chinese girl with a Lancashire accent. Her eyes were blue, (from her mother's side), and her face, framed by straight black hair, was devoid of all emotion. All Monica sensed was a genuine hatred that seemed quite out of proportion to the tiny bruise she'd doled out at their first encounter.

Finally there was Helios, currently outside doing god-knows-what. Easily the creepiest of them all, Helios was a broad man, greasy as the kebabs he (until his recent possession) sold. This latter information was gathered either by instinct or an acute sense of smell but Monica knew she was on the money. Helios (also referred to by Meed as Gaste) was unshaven, thick black hair twirling around a wide bald patch. His eyes were pale brown and surprisingly bleak under thick, black eyebrows.

When they had grabbed and taken her, it was Helios that had pinned her down while they taped her mouth and her hands and legs. He had carried her easily but moved with a peculiar gait, as if he expected to be lighter.

Why did they run from Jim? Why did they hold their heads and flee?

Helios didn't say much but when he did, his voice was low and guttural. The fear he inspired was of a different type. While they were sharp, intelligent, dangerous, *he* was cruel, primal, pitiless. With Helios it would be physical torture and humiliation – her worst fears. The others would try to win by mental trickery, which worried her not at all.

As Monica assessed the information she possessed, all it did was highlight how weird and different these three were.

What can Jim have done to cause such people to band together against him?

What is Jim up to?
Are these his drug associates?
Could it be related to Tim's vision in the show?
And the recent murders in Preston?
What if it all involves Jim somehow?
Why am I here?

As Monica juggled questions in her head, the back door

opened. Helios Gaste entered.

"Will I have to wear this all the time?" he said, peevishly.

"I'm afraid so," Jonathon Meed replied. "And if you die in that body I don't know where your most recent backup is. So look after it, at least until I organise a safe route out of here."

"This is a total fuck up, to adopt a colourful phrase!" said Yasmine. "Fuck, fuckety fuckaroo!" She tossed the magazine aside and flicked her nipples in a simultaneous middle-finger flourish.

"What do you want with me?" asked Monica, projecting more confident than she felt.

Helios turned his gaze on her and cracked his knuckles. He made his thick, brown arms bulge, rustling the wiry hair as he tested the properties of the muscles. He thought he was beginning to understand the appeal of the game, the limitations, the rules. Everyone knew: Gi-Darven was a canny old dog.

"Hel and I are going to ask you some questions now my dear," purred Meed. "I'm afraid it's going to hurt! You, that is. Not us."

It seemed an unnecessary and unwelcome clarification.

Chapter Ten

Nothing is so firmly believed as that which we least know.   Michelle de Moustache

Skulking outside the flat was a fleshy, unkempt man in a stained tracksuit, a garment chosen more for its expansion potential than as a key component in an exercise regime. He shuffled around, repeatedly checking his watch and shaking his head. Occasionally, though the morning was cool, he wiped a grubby sleeve across a flushed and sweating forehead. When Jim, Dave and Sheila spilled through the front door and headed for the car, he ambled over as nonchalantly as anyone whistling, coughing and humming falsetto in rapid rotation could ever have achieved.

"Pssssst! he hissed, between bouts of throaty *ahems*.

They ignored him.

He cocked his head at a 45 degree angle and performed a series of curious nodding gestures, as if experiencing a mild fit.

They ignored him some more.

"PSSSSSSSST!" he repeated, louder, the effort causing him to cough up something unpleasant.

"Have I won the Reader's Digest Prize draw again?" sighed Jim, wrinkling his nose in instant judgement. The man spat a phlegmy, glutinous blob into the gutter and wiped his lips on his sleeve.

"You and me, we need to talk," he said. "I've been trying to contact you urgently. I've got them all. Everything you asked, stroke of luck for you. I'll deliver this afternoon, once we sort out the final details."

"Huh?" said Jim. "I really don't have time at the moment. If you're flogging double glazing, see the landlord."

Agitated, the man's eyes hardened and darted around. His hands twitched angrily. "Don't go pissing me about," he said. "And I don't think we want to discuss our business in front of these two. Do we?"

A tiny seed of fear pushed out a shoot in Jim's mind. As it swelled and added a second tendril, a crescendo of equally metaphorical butterflies erupted and spun frantic loops in his stomach.

Oh Jesus! Clune!

Aloud he said to the others, "won't be a moment."

Dave and Sheila exchanged baffled glances then climbed into the car and waited. Jim walked the bloke a few yards away for a quiet chat which quickly became an argument. Within thirty seconds Jim began to look distinctly unhappy.

"Wait for it," whispered Dave, reading the body language from a perspective of much experience. He munched on a piece of chocolate retrieved from the glove compartment and, feeling his way with practised hands, jammed the wrapper into an already-full ashtray. A few seconds later, the podgy bloke sailed through the air and landed roughly, victim to one of Jim's favourite moves – the Tai Chi push. Jim stared intently at the guy scrabbling to his feet while reaching into a pocket.

"I'd advise against it," said Jim loud enough for them all to hear. "And if you don't follow my instructions to the word, I'll come back and find you. And I'll know if you don't. I hope you understand."

The bloke appeared to change his mind and pulled at his tracksuit bottoms which were, ominously, slipping down. His expression was a mixture of anger, fear and loathing. But he backed away and began to walk briskly down the street. Within a few strides, he broke into a run clutching, mercifully, at his pants to keep them aloft.

Ashen-faced, Jim turned, crossed over to the car and got into the back seat without speaking. He sat with his head bowed and they waited patiently for ten minutes before he broke the silence.

"North," he said at last, raising his head. In the mirror, Dave was startled by something he had never seen in his friend's eyes before: Despair.

Without a word, Dave started the engine and pulled slowly away. The roads were unusually quiet as he headed for the motorway. Only a clown in a bright red wig and kilt noted their passage. They passed him half way down New Hall Lane and when Dave grinned, he saluted, dropping the inflatable rubber woman he was carrying. As the car faded into the distance, the clown drooled and ambled away. The doll lay there forgotten, its face empty and skyward, rustling in the slight breeze.

***

As prepared as he ever would be, the Wondrous Tim dropped the receiver into its cradle. Then he pushed the button to transfer all incoming calls to his mobile. With one last check of the time he switched on the alarm and, grabbing the overnight bag with its selection of costumes, opened the front door.

As he turned the key, he felt an unexpected wave of foreboding. For all he knew his precious Monica was, at that very moment, being raped, tortured or killed. Alternatively, maybe she had staged her disappearance as a means of running back to her ex-husband.

Tim wavered.

Torn between horror, guilt and paranoia, his fingers stroked the rough brick wall of his childhood home. He sucked his teeth and picked his nose, still undecided. Then, as if in answer, he heard a faint buzzing sound – like a microlite passing overhead. Without further thought, he pressed a button on his keyring and his beloved black BMW answered. The day was bright and clear and the car promised adventure. His indecision vaporised under the warm light of ambition.

Turning his back on the house, Tim was soon accelerating hard. Within 25 minutes he would pass within a few feet of the car carrying Jim, Dave and Sheila, although none of them would ever know it.

***

Unlike Tim, Jim didn't enjoy driving. He had, once upon a time, but these days he preferred a simpler life. Besides, there was nowhere he especially wanted to drive to. He wasn't even sure he liked cars any more.

"I'll tell you all about it," he said quietly, in response to the unspoken questions. "But not today if you don't mind. I need to concentrate fully if this is going to work."

"In your own good time mate," said Dave.

"Whatever it was, we're here for you," said Sheila.

"Thanks lass, I appreciate it."

The atmosphere had been odd and unresolved but it started to lift at approximately the moment they spotted a naked jogger bounding along the hard shoulder, hotly pursued by two policewomen. The policewomen wore short skirts and suspenders and carried massive rubbery black dildos.

"Do you think Preston is finally casting off its conservative mantle?" asked Sheila innocently.

Jim craned his neck to gather more information. But at that instant, a small beep in his head beeped. His smile froze. "North. Now I'm completely sure," he said. "One of my tracers came in, I felt something. Show me the map."

Obediently, Sheila handed it to him. Dave declared himself heading up the M6, having just passed the Garstang turn off.

"Wait, I think I know where she is!" Jim blurted out.

"How can you possibly know that?" Dave didn't usually as questions. He was content to drive anywhere and found directions especially easy on a motorway. It was a day out. Normally on a Saturday morning he would be in recovery mode. And later, there would be shopping as all obedient forty-somethings knew.[8]

"I don't know for sure. Don't laugh but it's like I have somer remnant of Monica inside me. An intense memory maybe or an

---

[8] Life eh?

352

indelible pattern but either way, I can use it. I'm following like a bloodhound on a scent. She's in my mind and I'm sending out calls. I expect to find a resonance or even a reply, unless she's asleep."

"Ah. Right you are then mate," said Dave cheerily. *Had Jim ever made more sense than this?*

Listening to their banter, Sheila wanted to bang her head on the window. Instead, she scanned the dreary countryside and wondered when it would be transformed into luxury 4-bedroom detached houses, the fate of all green land in the Preston area.

"This direction," said Jim, pointing vaguely to their right.

"Longridge Fell? There's nothing much up there," said Dave, taking his eyes off the road for rather longer than was safe.

"My head says you're wrong!" beamed Jim. "I can sense her. I can smell her. Ah guys, it takes me back."

"Don't even start!" Sheila warned. "I think I preferred it when I believed your methods to be entirely heuristic."

"Ooooh!" cried Jim and Dave in unison.

They headed, in the bright light of Saturday morning, towards the hills. Jim hadn't bothered to mention any of their plans to Hartley.

***

"A good day for God!" cried Marjorie MacManaman, self-appointed cheerleader to Father Gregory Bartholomew Stilton.

"Praise be!" cried the devout congregation right back at her. Most of them hadn't been in a church for some years so were ignorant of the correct responses to any prayers. But they were enthusiastic in voice and from pocket, which was what counted.

The mass ended and everyone began filing out, leaving Julie Hutchinson sitting quietly in the rear pews. The newly refurbished Preston Minster had opened ahead of schedule and, despite ongoing work applying the finishing touches, it was packed to the rafters.

Overnight, there had been an unexpected upsurge in religious interest. Converts, the drifted-away and the faithful old retainers gathered together to praise the Lord and secure the most luxurious afterlife available. All hoped this would not feature towering smoke demons, blood and naked bints with knives.

First thing Saturday morning, hundreds of people began banging on the doors. Extra collection plates were quickly improvised and extra candles hastily lit. Marjorie organised everything – once she had determined for herself that the renewed hunger was genuine. Her acquaintances remarked that she was possessed of fresh vigour and passion.

By far the greatest surprise was the re-awakening of faith in the drifted-away, those who, due to apathy or a questioning mind, had simply moved on, leaving behind their youthful indoctrination. For these people waking on Saturday morning, all the years of scepticism were washed away. Childhood was restored and with it the god-sized hole prepared by the guardians of the virus.

Years ago, one damp, dismal morning when the church was plain St Johns, Julie had stood in this hallowed place. She clutched the photocopied hymn sheet and listened to the words spoken by a stranger. Her sister's funeral. She didn't comprehend what was happening. A stupid argument meant they had not spoken to each other for months and now never would. Opening temporary access to chambers of firewalled memory, hot moisture burned Julie's cheeks.

The had all filed out, some seeking to donate one more time, knowing that God preferred riches to camels. There was an excited buzz, a sharing of the great secret to hidden strength or clean armpits. Or something.

A bland-faced fop with a droning voice, Father Stilton was not an inspirational orator. Julie had gained nothing from the ritual and had already dismissed it as a mistake. Unlike the others milling about, she felt no different, perhaps a little sadder.

It was time to start her new life.

"Hello dear," said a kindly old lady as she prepared to rise.

"What? Oh, hello," said Julie. She had not heard the woman approach.

"You seem to be rather upset if I may say so?"

"I am. I was thinking about my kid sister. Wondering where her soul went."

"Ah, I know what you mean child. I had a brother, God save him. I couldn't begin to tell you his tale. We were very close."

"I have to be going," said Julie. "Sorry."

"No, no child, please forgive *me*. The old tend to ramble, don't they? I meant to say welcome to our church. We have been expecting you."

"Expecting me? I don't understand."

The old woman smiled but it didn't reach her eyes. She was smartly dressed, shrew-like, dessicated and intense but Julie sensed a strength in her that transcended those matchstick arms and veiny, liver-spotted hands.

Marjorie took a deep stertorous breath that rattled through her bony chest. "Last night you cast down Satan before a multitude. I myself bore witness and will spread the good news tirelessly on your behalf from henceforth. You see, it was the sign I've been awaiting all my life. Many others are inspired too, as you can see, and it warms my dry old heart. This is only the beginning. I've been telling them for years the day would come, you know. And it will. Now I've seen you I know it!"

"Which day?"

"Why my girl, the day we've all been waiting for!" She wound her stick fingers together. "The day we find out whether our sacrifices have been accepted. Or whether it has all been in vain!"

"I have something important to do. I have to go."

"No, please, the important thing is right here. Don't you see? Surely you do! It's an important time for Preston because we are going to lead the way. Everyone else will follow. I simply *know* that more miracles will occur if you stay. Please, it is

IMPORTANT to stay HERE and be our STRENGTH." She practically spat the final few words. Branching blue veins bulged along her temple through translucent skin.

"I'm not staying here," said Julie, backing away. "I don't believe in your church, your priest or your God."

"I see," said the old woman, casting her eyes earthward. "If I might ask, why did you throw down the Evil One unless you believe?" Her voice was laced with undisguised bitterness.

"I don't know exactly. He seemed to be attacking me. *Was* he evil? How can you tell?"

"Oh my child, such doubts. What can I say to convince you? You are so special. To us and our cause. Which is an end to wickedness by the way! Have you not yearned to accomplish something all your life? STAY WITH US! We can show the world they can be brave and strike down the evil do-ers! Remember the horrible witch who humiliated you? We must stamp out deviants like her! And soon. Before her madness spreads!"

"You know, you're right. I could accomplish that," said Julie. "But I don't need your help. And don't you lot believe in turning the other cheek?"

"I prefer an eye for an eye myself," laughed Marjorie, her amusement genuine. "Our new church will surely want to punish the wicked. And *really* punish, I mean. I can guarantee it. Times are changing young lady. It's what I've been trying to tell you. Say you'll stay and help us. Please . . ."

"Well, I don't know," said Julie. The offer to stay was unexpected and unnecessary. The old woman was peculiar but if she were serious, perhaps it was a new door opening, perhaps the church could help.

From Julie's perspective, Una had simply vanished But she was out there somewhere. Hiding.

"Look, why not stay with us and see if you like it?" asked Marjorie, as if she could read Julie's mind. "It's very restful and you can decide if we can serve you? We could start by using the power of the Lord to locate your witch. Maybe she has earned a starring role in a public ceremony of ours. We could burn her maybe. She is, after all, a truly wicked heathen!"

"Burn her?" Julie raised an eyebrow in best *Dodger Hoore* tradition. "You serious?"

Marjorie appeared to consider this. "Well, I'm open to suggestions of course," she simpered. "If burning is out of fashion I'm sure we can think of an alternative."

Julie pursed her lips and considered.

"Find her and I *might* help you. Providing you let *me* decide who deserves to be punished!"

"Oh of course, everyone will be so exultant. Exulted? Ex-Directory?", the wrinkled face shrivelled in momentary confusion. "Ah, getting old dear. Don't know what I'm saying half the time. But I feel you have wonderful gifts to share with us. A force for good is working within you!"

Julie smiled in spite of herself. The old fool was full of shit and she reckoned they both knew it.

***

As they drove through the village called Longridge and onwards towards Jeffrey Hill and the fells, Dave felt serene. Gears had evidently shifted inside his head. Life had gained purpose and momentum with each passing minute. Wherever it was leading, he was quietly optimistic and his greatest wish now was for Sheila to share the gift. For the time being Jim was too preoccupied to discuss it.

Dave resolved to assist in the heroic rescue because it was the right thing to do. He never for a moment doubted Jim would succeed but insisted that Sheila remain safely elsewhere while they did the necessary. By concentrating, he found to his great surprise, that he could imagine her being totally insubstantial. She actually began to fade before his eyes. With sufficient willpower, perhaps others might fail to see her. Unfortunately, it took considerable effort to sustain be maintain it he would, at all costs. His human mind had turned into a fascinating new toy and Dave was determined to try it fully.

They passed the reservoir and up a steep hill, passing fields where, once, they had come to pick magic mushrooms. They drove past the golf club and several small farms. Near one of these that Jim asked to stop.

Seeming uncertain, he got out and paced up and down by the side of the road. He leant over a dry stone wall and scanned down the hill to the east, over more walls, gurgling streams and a straggly copse. Where the hill levelled off, the grey smudge of another wall marked a lower road.

It was along this road that courting couples used to, unknowingly, entertain a local farmer and his video camera. He wasn't lurking today, however, because somebody had borrowed his body.

Jim processed all the visual data, seeking clues. He felt sure she was nearby. His eye skipped over Knowle Green, hidden by the hillside, and on to Ribchester. Beyond was Pendle Hill and Accrington but she was much nearer. He had been sure.

"I've lost her!" cried Jim. "Suddenly, there's nothing!"

"They might have blanked her out man," said Dave, leaning out of the window.

"What do you mean?"

"Like this," Dave replied. And Sheila disappeared.

"Well bugger me with a corn on the cob!" was Jim's response.

"Can you sense her at all dude?" Dave couldn't be blamed for the smugness in his voice.

"Not a trace. I can't even smell her! There's just the dent in the seat that gives her away and I bet you could fix that. You, my very dear pal, are a total genius! Was it belief-projection?"

"Oh, probably, erm, you know."

"Wow, that's well impressive!"

"I know it dude, I totally know it. Monica is going to be OK. There aren't many places up here to take someone. Let's keep looking."

"Sure mate, and thanks. We're bound to be close. I was certain of that when we set off."

"You spotted anything yet?" asked the disembodied voice of Sheila.

"Not yet," said Dave. "You alright there love?"

There was a pause. Followed by another, slightly longer one.

"I suppose I needn't have bothered shaving my legs last night," she said quietly.

"I'll explain it all," said Dave.

"Oh. Good."

She reappeared.

Jim climbed back in directed them around the narrow roads aimlessly for a further half hour. Eventually, frustration setting in, Dave pulled up at the side of a dirt track leading down to yet another scruffy farmhouse. A grey van was parked awkwardly outside as if by a novice driver.

"This place. Something about it," said Jim.

"Like what?"

"I can't feel anything."

"So?"

"Well, there are people there, I just saw somebody open the back door. But I can't *feel* anything! You might not be the only one with a blanking trick."

"Ah."

"This could be the place."

Dave made a decision. Flashing his gold tooth in an effort to look brave, he said, "You stay here love and be ready to get out of here . Superhero stuff is our job. Isn't that right Jim?" Jim nodded slightly.

"I'd prefer you to stay too," she said. "They could be dangerous. Why not call the police if you're sure this is the place?"

"We will, once we are. Probably. It will be alright, I promise."

"OK Dave, kiss me for good luck. And you stay out of trouble. If you see something suspicious, come back!" They kissed passionately and then Dave stood back and bathed her in a golden light.

In a second, she faded out like she wasn't even there.

"Neat eh?"

"Marvellous," agreed Jim. "Better than before."

"Yeah, surprised myself here. Must be getting the knack."

Sheila said something but her audio output was now masked too, She squeezed Dave's leg instead.

"Look at that," laughed Dave pointing to her hand-shape on his thigh.

"Heh," said Jim grimly and got out of the car. Out of habit, he tried to run fingers through his hair, registering puzzlement at the length. The sun was high in the sky, enjoying a brief opportunity to sneak through clouds and light up this place of sheep, mud and random walkers. A light breeze barely disturbed the sparse trees dotted clinging on to the rough, heather-filled moors.

"Right mate, what's the plan?" asked Dave, scanning the dirt road and rubbing his hands together.

"Plan?"

"You know, what to *do*?"

"My plan was to get here. Other than that, I guess I could resort to violence," said Jim.

"Oh, fisticuffs you mean?"

"Best stay back mate. I think there are only three of them."

"I thought we were in this together," snorted Dave in indignation.

"We are, don't get shirty! I mean there should be no need. We have the jump on them this time. Besides, I programmed some enhancements only this morning. I don't think fighting will be any problem. I'm rather looking forward to it!"

"Super-duper," said Dave, chirpy once more. "I'll be the cavalry if needed. Wish I'd brought a stick."

They crept cautiously down the track towards the farm buildings. A large garage, a dutch barn, several long tin sheds and a deserted shippon comprised a desolate and slightly sinister abode. The solitary farmer had spent no money on appearances, and little time on livestock. The roof was in a poor state and the place appeared near-derelict. Sneaking up to the house, Jim was surprised there was no farm dog. Then he noticed a barrel-shaped, black kennel with a chain attached. The chain ended in a collar but no dog.

Jim thought he saw curtains rustle in a downstairs window and ducked down beside the van, Dave close by. This was a perfect opportunity to let down the tyres and thwart prospects of a manic car chase. In the event, the hissing from the valve was startlingly loud. It made Dave jump.

"Should we have a joint, do you suppose man?" he asked.

"Later might be better," said Jim. He noticed that one wheel of the van was bent at an awkward angle from where it had hit a broken gatepost. He could see it wasn't worth bothering with the tyres: the van was going nowhere. He peered inside, through dirty windows and quietly opened the driver's door, only considering the possibility of an alarm when it was too late.

Fortunately, there wasn't a peep.

He looked for clues. Was that Monica's perfume? He was sure it was, but didn't inform Dave. He had no intention of phoning for help. The opportunity to be the hero had conveniently fallen into his lap and to save her was a dream come true. In fact, the whole bizarre scenario couldn't have worked out much better had he planned it.

I *will* find you, he whispered dreamily, adding the heroic music in his head. Then, followed closely by Dave, he crawled on hands and knees up to the rear of the house, under the kitchen window.

Silence.

The farmhouse was ill-kempt. Flaking whitewash covered the walls and paint flaked sketchily over doors and window frames. The windows were uniformly dark and some were cracked. The patterned curtains, bleached by years of faint, drab daylight, were drawn.

As the two pals waited by the back door, Jim felt a prickling sensation between his shoulder blades, rising rapidly to the crown of his head. One of his alarm programs had been tripped.

He was under attack!

After the previous fortuitous escape, Jim had fashioned several sophisticated monitor systems designed to operate constantly and independently of his own awareness. Their function was simple: to detect incoming pulses carried by a particular type of electromagnetic wave.

Having only casually observed the practitioners of mind reading, auto suggestion and hypnosis previously, Jim had never considered their talents, let alone grant them any parallels with his experiments. In the last few days, he had begun to grudgingly rethink their value.

Absorb what is useful.

Therefore, when he began work on a 'personal security suite' (provisionally named Jeet Brain Do), Jim incorporated a diverse palette of techniques hastily cobbled together.

Jim already knew the ultimate expert at mental shields and protection. Monica. Somehow she could cocoon her mind in a shield of iron, lead and treacle. When she deliberately ignored you, it was the complete package. You may as well have ceased to exist, as Jim had discovered. Once the frustration passed, he saw it as a faculty to be admired. The shield had doubtless protected her from emotional pain, perhaps even cutting out his whining pleas for one last chance.

He sighed and spoke a quiet command, executing an *unbreakable wall* program modelled on one he had tried and failed to penetrate. He prayed his version would be as solidly obstinate.

Within two seconds, a shield encased his mind, identifying and filtering the strange probing waves. Secure, he prepared another recent module and loaded to an instant recall buffer. If necessary, he could seal off his entire self. After their previous encounter, Jim wasn't sure what his enemies were capable of. But he was taking no chances.

An alpha version of the *MindMonitor* program had ultimately saved them in the park. It hadn't yet been calibrated, however, so the warning 'say' instruction manifested itself as large burst of energy. His assailants had fled for their lives, unfortunately grabbing Monica in the process.

To stay would have been to die. Jonathon Meed knew this and was unsettled by it. However, he kept this to himself. It would, after all, undermine his position if Carrion realised how much trouble they were now in. Helios Gaste was a brute and of no consequence but Yasmine Carrion was altogether different and more dangerous. Meed pondered the body she'd chosen, in particular its female nature. Curious animals, he thought.

"It's him," Yasmine suddenly announced, milliseconds behind Jonathon's own scanners had reported the presence.

He was outside, examining the broken conveyance. The three left Monica alone, slumped and bleeding, to stand in a circle, hands touching each other's foreheads.

The battle was short and its result improbable.

Meed's plan had been to take Jim's mind by force in a sudden overwhelming attack. The grinning companion was judged no threat – an infant intellect barely out of nappies, had been Bifrost's assessment. Jim, on the other hand, had shown both strength and innovation in the way he had terminated their previous encounter. Meed blamed unfamiliarity with the human physiology but was determined to avoid a second failure.

Under Meed's direction, 3 minds in concert struck quickly and decisively. Meed released a massive bolt of energy at Jim's brain, projecting a fiery arrow gaudily. He followed it quickly with a second, then a third.

Yasmine gasped.

"Good Me!" cried Meed in their heads. "He's on to us already! Must be a record!"

In Jim's consciousness, sensors fielded the incoming pulses, measured the intrusion and informed the supervising program. The *unbreakable wall* deflected a sample of them into a quarantined area for later analysis.

"There has to be a way in," said Yasmine. "There must be. Look, surely he recognises us? On some level he must know who we are. What happens He wakes?"

"You know what happens."

She grunted something.

"He's electrified that wall while you've been yapping," growled Helios. "Charged carbon crystals. I've never seen anything like it."

"Gosh, that does look pretty solid," said Meed, trying to sound cheery and light-hearted. But it was another disappointment to dent his flagging confidence.

"We can break through anything!" said Yasmine. "We're strong!"

Meed shook his head. He knew that to try and fail would expose the true extent of what he was now sure they were up against in this Game. "It's of no significance. A few tricks but they won't help him when the end comes. We should leave here now and thoroughly remap these organs." He touched a finger to his skull. "If the neural pathways can't be extended sufficiently we will grow better vessels. Let's not waste time competing at the same level, we need to acclimatise."

"Run away again, you mean? We should fight!" said Yasmine.

"I agree. Let me tear him apart and pulp the brain," begged Helios Gaste. "This body is strong. It's enough."

"I know, I know. But let's not get diverted. It's actually better if he's around a little longer and look, he's preparing a few primitive floating mines! How fascinating. When the time comes we can each play our part but let's not waste the opportunity to explore these organic vehicles. Pinky has been here before and he seems to rate it quite highly. And anyway, what would be the point of coming otherwise?"

"But you *have* sorted the transport out of here?" asked Yasmine.

"Absolutely. First thing I did this morning after having a shit. Incidentally, I never realised that shitting could be such a blast. So far, the second shit of the day tops my list of ultimate human experiences, how about you?"

"No."

"You, Gaste?"

"No."

"Well, give it a try, it's marvellous. I strained away and then, when I thought something was going to break, there was this amazing release. Relief flowed through this body as if I'd given birth. Which, of course, I had. My body was positively floating when I finished and I've had this warm feeling down my legs ever since."

"And that chutney stain too," observed Yasmine.

"Lovely isn't it? I was wondering how these garments acquired their various hues."

"You're babbling Meed. I know what this is," she said. "Am I to deduce we *cannot* pierce his defences? In your expert opinion, even we three combined cannot force our way into his mind?"

"We can and we will. However, now is not the time to make the effort. We're working under capacity at present, don't forget. No human consciousness could compete with *one* of us working at maximum? Even Helios (no offence!), it simply couldn't happen."

"Unless He had woken up," said Yasmine. "I mean, the

patterns I'm picking up now are . . . unusual."

Helios farted.

"Hey did you hear that?" he said, with pride.

"Look, let's leave now," urged Jonathon Meed. "He's outside the door, preparing to burst in and save this female. It doesn't matter that he's learned a bit. It will add spice to the Game. We just don't get to take the short cut, that's all. Let's stir up this gooey pebble before he works out what's going on."

"I don't think that's likely, do you? But shouldn't we at least nullify the other one? He's running unchecked and is starting to show potential. Nothing significant but he's the first to be released. I've read that often spawns prophecies and strange portents – admittedly to be expected. But if unchecked it might lend weight to Gi-Darven's predictions for this place."

Meed visibly faltered. "I agree it's . . . unfortunate. And I expect more will follow. But as you say, it's not entirely without precedent."

"I suppose with the seas turning to blood and the Big Battle coming, both sides should be fully souped up! To make it interesting, that is." Yasmine allowed some of the excitement to leak through.

"Aha. Do I sense you are getting into this little bout of role playing at last?" smiled Meed, mentally submitting the teleport program.

"I admit the prospect of risk intrigues me. GD always seemed such a prat and I've never understood his fascination with games and contests. I wonder what he's *really* been doing in here, while we've been partying?"

"While *you've* been partying my dear," sniffed Meed. "I've been pro-active."

Jim, having repulsed the initial attack, didn't wait for another. He transmitted remote monitor programs to probe and quest. By posting them into the immediate area rather than targeting them specifically, he decided he had spontaneously invented mental depth charges.

"I'm blood clever!" he mumbled smugly.

Mind you, it was true. The probes were able to exist, briefly, beyond any organic computing device. On detecting minds of a certain type, the probes would explode with a short burst of light. Well, that was the intention. As the first encountered an Aesir thought barriers, it released a sudden concussive blast of low frequency radiation. A thick, purple cloud formed from the air around Dave and Jim's heads. Aid rained upon Jim's defences.

"Sheeeeee-hit!" he wailed. Then he started babbling. "Wha-wa-zaaaaat? An exhibition? We need emotional content, not anger . . . owwwwww!"

Meed grinned in satisfaction. "Not so clever now!" He turned to the others and nodded. "That will slow him down. And prevent him from backtracing us."

"If it doesn't, the girl will," smiled Gaste. "Shame though. I had plans for her."

"You'll still get your chance," said Yasmine Carrion. "Well, maybe. We've planted so much shit in her head, I bet he'll never find them all. And if she possessed any special abilities, we would have discovered them. This flesh feels too much. It's one of the first things *I* am going to fix."

Meed laughed and activated the teleport program. He felt momentarily queasy as if his skin were set on fire.

After a few seconds, he set them down.

An ocean of grass stretched as far as their eyes could see. A blue sky dotted with a few fluffy clouds formed a perfect dome over green waves. Of the farmhouse, there was no sign.

"Where are we?" asked Yasmine.

"We're safe," said Meed. "We can take all the time we need to become fully attuned to these bodies. I don't know about you but I'm going to write some cunningly potent code."

"Not me," said Gaste. "I'm going to test this shell. I already know the role I'm going to play!"

With that he ran off through the long grass, content to work the body, which had belonged to a purveyor of kebabs and chips, like it had never been worked before. And then some.

Meed shrugged, squatted in the grass and closed his eyes.

Yasmine Carrion wandered a few hundred yards away and did the same.

**

Jim was distraught. When the purple cloud had fully dissipated, he'd kicked open the door, rather heroically (despite guessing it was probably unlocked). But Monica had been unconscious. And alone. The Aesir had vanished without a trace. Weirdly, he had half expected it.

"Monica, love, are you okay?" he whispered.

She was bound, roughly, to a chair. Her lips and nose were bloodied and her eyes were screwed tight.

Dave wandered in, wrinkling his nose at the foul smell.

"Smells like somebody shat a kebab!" he said, with eerie prescience. "Bloody 'orrible! anyway" He was visibly relieved to meet no resistance and dropped the half-brick he'd been clutching.

Jim knelt next to the only love of his life and stroked her face, gently with his fingertips.

"Jim?" Monica opened her eyes a little.

"I came. You knew I would?"

"Yes. I knew."

"What did they want?" He began cutting carefully through the brown tape that bound her with a dirty kitchen knife.

"I don't know," she replied. "They asked about you. Wanted to know if we were together, if we had children, how I found you in the park. It made no sense."

"I know."

"They didn't mention a ransom, not once. But then I wasn't

really kidnapped was I Jim?"

"I don't think so. That looks sore." He indicated a dark swelling on her forearm.

"Courtesy of the troll-like one. Did it with his thumb. God, he was a nasty piece of work. Scariest of the lot. Didn't ask any questions, just liked inflicting pain."

Jim observed she was short of breath. He began to feel very angry. And very guilty.

"Let me see." he ran his hands over her ribs and she gasped sharply.

"It could have been worse. I'm not sure why it wasn't." She hunched over, rubbing at her wrists where Jim had removed the tape but keeping her arms close to her body. Jim lifted her arms away slowly and felt gently under her clothes. He raised her t-shirt gently to reveal dark, purple bruising. Instead of resisting, Monica simply rested her hands on his shoulders.

"My God!" he said.

Staring straight into his eyes, Monica said, "tell me why I got these Jim."

"OK. It's quite a story but I'll tell you what I can. On the way back. You're going to casualty. I think there might be a broken rib there. I'm so very sorry Mon."

"You came. That counts for a lot." For a moment it seemed she would lean in to kiss him.

The moment passed.

An inspection of the house and van revealed nothing of interest. Perhaps to the local police it would, but Jim was not interested in them. He'd fill them in about Monica later. In the meantime, he guessed that it was his responsibility to find out why the world had gone so screwy and to fix it. Who else was there? He also knew that Monica would have gained valuable insight into his newly-acquired enemies. She always read situations and people well. Too well, he remembered ruefully.

When they reached the car, Dave made two fists and a golden

light filled the interior. Sheila faded in from thin air.

"I did it," he said, steadying himself against the bonnet to ward off the queasiness.

With Sheila driving and Dave snoring lightly next to her, they began the return journey.

Jim and Monica sat in the back. He gave her a brief synopsis of recent days and by the time they reached the hospital, her expression was way past incredulity. He resisted the temptation to ask questions about her ordeal or to probe her mind. She was weaker than she pretended and had suffered more than she would admit.

"I must ring Tim," she said suddenly. "He'll be worried sick."

"Will he?" asked Jim. "Isn't it the big show today?"

"Shit yes it is! It's Saturday already. Jesus, he'll go mad. Can I borrow a mobile phone?"

"Sure, take mine."

Monica dialled the number.

"Tim!"

"Monica! Thank God. Where are you? What happened? I've been so worried. Are you OK?"

"Yeah, long story."

"Where are you now?"

"Preston."

"What happened? The police said you were kidnapped!"

"Just some nutters. I'll tell you when I see you. There's nothing to worry about."

"So you're on the way here, Sheffield, right now?"

"Um . . ."

"You know the hotel we're in?"

"I... in a little while."

"What's wrong love? Did they hurt you?"

"Not much. A little fall escaping. It's nothing, scratches only. I'll be there. In plenty of time. What time is it?"

"It's already one forty five. Monica, darling. I wouldn't ask but I really need you here. I guess I understand if you're too shaken." His voice continued before she could respond. "The police told me I might as well wait over here as at home. They said you could be absolutely anywhere. I was so worried, you know that don't you? I thought the work would help me focus. But I was ready to call it off and rush to your side, er, the moment we heard anything."

"We both need this to be a success. The show must go on, there's no need to explain. When do I need to get there?"

"By five ideally. Can I really rely on you coming? I'm sorry to ask but I need you here. To see you're OK. And to bring me luck, of course. Get a taxi, you don't want to drive."

"I'll be there," said Monica and hung up, short of breath.

"I don't believe it," said Jim.

"It's his big chance."

"You might have a broken rib. Or worse. You're going to have a full check up."

"I will. If the queue is small enough. Otherwise it can wait until tomorrow."

"No way," said Jim.

"You don't run my life any more Jim," she said with a deafening quietness.

"Sorry, but I won't see you hurt," he said.

"Then fuck off. I don't need a father figure right now. I need a friend."

"I am your friend."

"Then respect my decisions!"

They bickered until they reached the reception desk. The girl unleashed a well-practised icy glare, staring meaningfully at Monica's battered face then back at Jim. The place was packed. Clearly it had been an interesting morning in Preston.

"You need to make sure somebody sees her right away," said Jim.

"I need to make sure somebody sees her right away," agreed the receptionist in a monotone.

Piece of piss, he thought.

Chapter Eleven

Life isn't long enough for love and art.
W. Somers' Mum

Jim insisted he would drive Monica to Sheffield personally. Dave was still zonked from his mental exertions and Sheila was determined to keep him in bed until he felt livelier. She even volunteered to lend Jim the car and was unusually cavalier about the insurance aspect.

"Do you even still *have* a driving licence?" asked Monica.

"Sure, and a marriage licence," he said, rather too quickly. "Only one of them is good for anything now."

"If you're going to be an arsehole I *will* get a taxi."

"Sorry, it's been a long day already. I'll get you there safely. I don't suppose it's worth repeating how they said to do zilch for a few days."

"There were no broken bones. And I told you it looks worse than it feels," she lied. "The painkillers have helped too, in fact I'm positively floaty. Do you know the way?"

"Of course. Anyway, I'll stick to the motorway. I've had enough of hills and desolate places. The motorway will be faster."

It was after 3 O'clock when they drove away. Sheila waved them off, hiding her misgivings and forebodings. Seeing Jim and Monica together was a surprise, but then again, being made invisible had been a surprise too. Life, it turned out, really was full of them. She laughed and closed the door. And locked it. Even excluding their recent adventure, an unreal atmosphere had settled in. Everyone just accepted the weirdness, or at least questioned it only minimally before getting on.

There was a feeling in the air that left Shelia very keen to remain inside and hide from the world, perhaps for quite a while.

After the inevitable spluttering jumps of deliberately fumbled gears, Jim settled down and drove normally.

"I still can't believe you cut your hair." ventured Monica, breaking the silence. The medication was wearing off and being alone with Jim suddenly weighed on her mind. She wondered whether the trip was such a good idea.

"Don't you like it?"

"Suits you actually. You're a bit long in the tooth for the hippy stoner look."

"Thanks lass, nice of you to notice."

She breathed on the window and started to write something on the fogged glass. Then she rubbed it out.

"On the way to the hospital . . . " she began.

"Yes?"

"The things you said about writing head programs."

"Yes?"

"And about these guys wanting to shut you down?"

"Yes?"

"So, to clarify . . . via one of your programs you called me. In my mind. And asked me to come to the park?"

"Yes."

"Jim, think very carefully about this next one."

"Go on."

"You say they abducted me to get to you?"

"I reckon. It's the only reason I can think of."

"OK. So tell me again how you found me."

"Oh, you know, luck."

"Liar! I know you too well Jim Cavanah! If you can talk to me in my head, from miles away, what else can you do? How *did* you find me?"

Jim watched the road silently for a long time until he found where he was going.

She waited.

Finally he answered, "It turns out I can do quite a lot. More than I've shown Dave. More, I guess, than the even Wondrous Tim. And my abilities are growing exponentially, without any apparent need of further input. God knows where it will lead – but we'll come to that." Noting that she was listening intently, he continued.

"As I told you, my way of approaching this has been to use what I know. Writing programs worked but maybe the technique isn't important. Other people achieve similar – obviously less cool – results in dozens of cack-arsed ways. I've got hundreds of programs, indeed I'm writing one right now, in an optimised working environment in my head. So far the trick is: believe in it absolutely and it works."

"I've been planning to alter my behaviour and perceptions." He gave a her a quick, nervous glance before continuing. "Like brainwashing or something. But it went way beyond that. Mon, I think I stumbled across a biggie. A biggie on a life-changing scale. Assuming I've not gone absolutely raving bonkers of course."

"*Gone* bonkers?"

Unperturbed, he took a calming breath and ploughed on. "As it happens I researched insanity years ago. You know me. I've researched pretty much everything in my time. Jack of all trades. Anyway, I knew I had to learn about it during a mushroom trip. But I digress."

"You sure do," she laughed grimly. "What was the biggie?"

"I discovered that somebody has *already* programmed our brains, our behaviour, the very mechanisms of thought itself. I previously believed that sentience was an evolutionary inevitability. Now I don't know what to think. I've opened a treasure trove of weird code that is completely different to the core instructions. In most cases, the weird stuff is huge in comparison. I can't quite decipher it yet but I will."

"This is becoming a very long explanation Jim. You're making my head hurt again."

"I'm sorry, it's heavily condensed, trust me."

"You always told me not to trust anyone who felt it necessary to say 'trust me'."

Jim chuckled and flicked experimentally at a button on the dashboard. A green light came on behind a symbol that could have been a walrus. A few seconds later he turned it off, nodding thoughtfully. "Still smart, I see. But some things can't be compressed too much and still make sense."

"Sense? Look, forgive my hurried summary, but you are claiming to have, all by your lonesome, cracked the human psyche? And these programs you've found – are they unique to your brain or do we all have them?"

"I still have lots to do but I'm fairly sure some code is common at least. And Monica, *really* interesting things start happening when I remove these weirder, younger, longer programs. I did it for Dave and now he's begun changing. His consciousness is expanding by the hour. There don't seem to be any ill effects yet and I think it's made Dave sharper. Makes you wonder."

"If this is true . . ." she said.

"If true, we deviated from the original blueprint of our species. Somebody mucked about with the formula."

"Surely you don't mean God?!" she exclaimed. "You of all people!"

"Maybe. Maybe not."

"You're trying to understand programs possibly written by God?"

He shrugged. "Regardless of the author, I plan to improve on them. Eventually."

"You're definitely the only person I know who would ever have said that and kept a straight face." She gave in to the smile.

Jim relaxed. Then he scowled at a pillock in a Range Rover who cut him up from the inside lane.

"You should probably move out of the middle lane if you're going to drive the whole way in 4th gear."

"Shit yeah, this has got 5 hasn't it?" he said sheepishly. "Sorry, been a while. Fancy some sounds?" He turned on the radio and located a classical station. "Schubert's Unfinished Symphony," he identified after a few bars. "Remember? The melody still sends shivers down my spine. Poor bugger was only 31 when he died. Have I told you that before?"

Monica summoned the slight yawning noise reserved for all Jim's attempts at culture. He got the message and shut up.

Listening to classical music with Jim brought memories of happier times flooding back. Preferring not to get drawn in, she reached over and turned the radio down, a little. There were many things she still needed to understand.

"How did you find me Jim?"

"I told you I cleaned Dave's thought processes, yeah?"

"Several times and I get it. Well, as much as I get any of this."

"Well, somehow they found out – the people who put the code there."

"You believe they keep watch on our thoughts to see if we're still, what brainwashed? Under the yoke? Is that it?"

"Exactly. I mean, they won't do it personally. A programmer would add some kind of checking system, probably a timer or a scheduled command."

"But if they realised Dave was free of their influence, why didn't they come for *him*?"

"Obviously I am still only guessing, but I think they originally *did* come for Dave. Did you hear about the bomb at Warner Brothers? It wasn't a real bomb, thankfully, but a marker of some kind, an electrostatic charge. I bet they planned to return us to 'normal'. For all I know, they're just a team of fixers and this is what they do. Obviously, I'm speculating rather more than I like here. But the point is they had us completely helpless and from what I can tell, they concentrated on me. Story of my life eh? Anyway, it was bloody confusing and seemed to last for ages. I didn't know what to do, or where I was."

"And this was when you called me?"

"Yes."

"Why not somebody else?"

"There is nobody else I could have reached."

"Why not?"

At this, Jim stared dead ahead, concentrating on the road. He didn't want to miss the M1 turn off and shoot past towards Hull. The motorway had changed a lot since he was last in these parts.

"There is still a connection between us," he said eventually.

"Of course there is Jim. You never quite stop feeling for someone."

"You couldn't substitute 'loving' for 'feeling for' could you?"

"OK, loving. But not like it was, you saw to that. Not all fairy tales work out and not everyone lives happily ever after. This contact . . . are you saying it worked because you still love me?"

"In a sense. But also because you feel something back. Even if it's not the same as it was."

"I'm not going through all that again. You were an impossible man to be married to."

"I know."

"So let's not talk about it."

"Fair enough."

"And don't do the 'I'm changed' speech. I don't want to hear it."

He shrugged, trying to keep his emotions at bay. "There's a tangible part of you stored within me, a pattern if you like. I suspect there's a similar imprint of me in you. I'd say that makes us soul mates, by some kind of definition."

"You're bound to have fond memories of people you've loved. Maybe this is all in your head? You could be making it more than it is."

"Like everything else that matters, the proof is in the evidence. None of this story would count if I couldn't prove it, if I didn't find you." He risked a glance – at the stunner he could once have reached out and touched. He registered the doubt in her expression.

"Well, I did hear your voice. Maybe it's all down to me? Maybe I've learned some tricks from Tim?"

"I sensed your mind briefly before it was obscured. I only found you by getting close enough to get lucky. We must have stopped at half a dozen farms and there was no sensation of life from that one – even though we saw people."

"Creepy."

"I know it sounds lame but that's my explanation."

"Are you going to clean out the stuff from my mind too?" she asked.

"No. At least not yet."

"How come? You afraid I'll take up fortune telling or something?"

He shook his head.

"I don't think it's safe. Not until I know who these people are and what threat they pose. As soon as possible, I intend to do it for everyone."

"Everyone?"

"Oh yes. And I wonder what kind of world we'll have then?"

"Jim, this is all very weird."

"I know."

"What about Dave? Is he still at risk?"

"I think I've successfully nicked one of his own ideas and given him a security blanket. It was all I could do in the time available."

They reached the M1 turn off with Jim momentarily confused by the options. He opted for London, remembering that it shared a southerly direction with Sheffield. The M1 was relatively quiet and he stuck in the inside lane. He relaxed the accelerator, not wanting the trip to end.

"You mentioned coming to see the show?" she asked, her voice dusky and becoming faint.

"Sure, I'll hang around. Why not?"

"You won't . . . interfere will you?"

"Promise."

Suddenly, Monica felt very tired – and it showed. Jim, in a rare moment of insight, postponed his list of questions. "Why not take a snooze, if you can?" he suggested softly. "We'll be there in about an hour by my guesstimate. You look whacked."

"Thanks. I don't know if I can though . . . Jim?"

"Yes?"

"Show me something."

"What?"

"I don't know. Amaze me."

Jim started to adjust his fly, letting go of the steering wheel with both hands.

"Idiot," she groaned, exasperated. "Really, do something."

"OK, close your eyes."

She complied.

"Promise you're not tugging on that flaccid old organ!"

"Not unless you beg babe. Now. Open your eyes."

Monica opened her eyes.

"Fucking hell's teeth!" she gasped, staring about in amazement, outside, inside, at her hands, everywhere. "How did you do it?"

"That was the first mental program I wrote. Transmission took a little longer but I can now transmit small chunks of code into another person at will – assuming they are not blocking me. As of today I can even transmit programs to a place – a physical location – where they lie in wait, vibrating gently in mid-air until the specified conditions are met. Or they fade away I guess. I can only do really simple commands that way but I'm making huge advances almost by the hour."

"Everything's blue!" she marvelled.

"Blue?" said Jim, startled. His head turned dangerously, in a way rarely seen out of the movies or TV.

"Haha – got you! Had you going for a minute!" she laughed.

"Puce brown, of course."

"No need to take the piss," he said. "It rewrites all colours to shades of green. Correctamundo?"

"Ah, but how would you know if your green is the same as mine?"

"Go to sleep!"

"No way! And can you put this back to normal please?"

"Say pretty please."

"You're not getting a blowjob!"

"Hey, you *can* read my mind! Don't you want to know how I do it?"

Monica laughed, the humour genuine. "No. Later maybe. Put me back as I was. Or else!"

"Close your eyes."

She did.

"Open them."

She did and beamed. "That was brilliant. You couldn't teach that to Tim could you?"

"You're kidding, right?"

"Could you?"

"Go to sleep."

"I can't sleep now. Could you do it?"

"I doubt it. Not without exposing him to the same dangers as Dave and me. In time, as I said, I want to give everyone their minds as they are supposed to be. Best wait a while. See if we go mental."

"Yeah, right. I could tell the difference how exactly?"

"Hardy har. Bollocks, did you see that idiot in the prickmobile?"

"How long is it since you've driven?" she asked, gripping her seat momentarily.

"A few years."

"Was the last time when we met in that bloody Travel Lodge?"

"I don't remember."

"You can't lie to me."

"Sorry. OK, as it happens that was the last time. Is it important?"

She fell silent and wound down the window just as the sun broke through the thick South Yorkshire cloud cover. Jim spun his sun visor around to cover the driver's window and keep his right eye from being dazzled.

"More sounds?" he said, adjusting the volume of the radio from its background burble. Something harsh and dissonant involving, it seemed, cellos and pneumatic drills assaulted them. "Ah, creaking door music," he winced. "All head and no heart."

"We could see if the local stations mention the show," she suggested.

"Fair enough. I'm not in the mood for brow furrowing." He hit the scan button and watched the rapidly-changing frequency display thoughtfully. "You don't love him like you loved me," he muttered, as the numbers whirled round, pausing each time a strong signal was located.

"That's enough!"

"You know I'm right," he mouthed the words, hitting the button quickly to avoid the sudden burst of wittering from the latest reality TV sensation. Monica ignored him and he resisted the urge to try and penetrate her mind. He'd been able to transmit the *MonoColour* program because she was receptive and because it was simple one-way traffic.

Long ago he'd learned to respect her formidable mental shield. It had given him food for thought, however. Now, years later, he wondered about it all over again: *Could he break through? Did they? What kind of power does Monica have?*

All he knew was that, without invitation, he would not make the attempt.

She was weary but remained awake and pensive for the rest of the journey, listening for news on Radio Sheffield.

He drove in silence, thinking, remembering. Occasionally the radio did indeed mention the show and once there was a brief interview with Tim's new manager, the infamous Barry McGarry.

"I thought you were his manager?" asked Jim.

Monica scowled but did not reply.

"Aha! You thought so too?"

"Jim, give it a rest OK? You're not going to screw up my life again so don't even try to stick your nose in!"

"Oohoo, methinks you protest too much!"

She blanked him properly then, he didn't even exist. Everything he said from that point, she did not hear.

He spoke for a long time, spilling his innermost thoughts. She heard none of them, only the radio. Eventually he realised but continued anyway, pouring out his feelings, voicing emotions he would never have dared had she been aware.

Finally, completing a journey of just over two hours, they reached Sheffield. Jim stroked her leg cautiously.

"We're here Mon. Which hotel was it you were staying in?"

Roused from her inner space, she regained focus. Something was touching her. External stimuli.

"Sorry, daydreaming. Holiday Inn. Today the Holiday Inn, tomorrow the Hilton eh?"

"Remember that time..." began Jim.

"Don't," she snapped, more briskly than intended.

Jim sighed and headed in what he hoped was the right direction. En route Monica rang Tim using Jim's mobile.

After hanging up, she spoke, slowly.

"Don't take this the wrong way Jim but I don't think you should come right to the hotel. And if you do somehow happen to run into him later, don't mention giving me a lift over. Please."

"Tetchy is he?"

"I haven't decided how much to tell him yet. It's a pretty ridiculous tale and it might be best to leave you out of it as much as possible. Maybe entirely. If you drop me here I can walk. If you like I'll leave a ticket for you at the box office, under the name Mr Bridges. To be on the safe side."

"Got it all planned out eh? Well, except the luggage. Not the first time you've turned up at a hotel with no luggage, eh?"

"Jim, please, we will need to talk a few things over, but not today. I'll be in touch when the dust has settled, OK?"

"I'll look forward to it. Not that I think the dust is going to settle anytime soon. I hope things work out for you, though. If you love someone, set them free eh?"

"See you Jim. Take care."

He sprang smartly out of the car, and ran round to open her door. He hoped for a kiss but she drew back. Regardless, he dived in and kissed her lightly on the lips. She didn't respond, making it clumsy and awkward. He instantly wished he had played it cool instead. At that moment he would have done anything she's asked, even knowing she no longer wanted him.

She left.

As she walked away, without a backwards glance, Jim had a sick certainty that it was for the last time. When this moment faded into memory, he would return to regular sleepwalking. Self-pity and melodrama engulfed him. Tears welled up and dripped freely. A traffic warden, approaching the car with menaces, veered smartly away.

Must I endure another rebirth? Will we get it right next time? I've become an emotional cripple and a whiner to boot!

Blubbing like an infant with a loaded nappy, Jim drove around for a while before parking up and going in search of a bar. Then he remembered he would be driving back later so, instead, went and sat in the crowded city centre to watch the fountains for a few hours. And think.

The sun shone, cold water shot into the air and dozens of children ran through, howling and whooping. Grabbing a sandwich from a nearby supermarket, Jim relaxed and stretched his fingers into the grass. He spent the afternoon studying the programs in his head and composing subroutines for an ever-growing library.

When he eventually opened his eyes and glanced around, he couldn't help but grin smugly.

A change of career was in the air.

Chapter Twelve

Illusion is the first of all pleasures.
Oscar Wild

18:00 Saturday.
At Sheffield City Hall, the stage had been thoroughly prepared, the sound system tested and the lights and lasers were currently flashing in dazzling splendour. Tim nodded, satisfied. He felt good about everything, the crew and technicians paying him the respect he deserved. Moments ago, they'd received news from the box office and it was all he had dreamed about: a sell-out! In a single day almost a thousand tickets had been snapped up.

In Tim's vision, tonight would be his greatest triumph. Quark TV – one of a handful of cable TV companies that were reasonably clued up – had agreed to film the show. Apparently, all it had taken to get an agreement was a short chat with Barry McGarry. Barry was proving full of pleasant surprises although Tim had yet to break the news of the change in circumstances to Monica. A matter for later. He had surprised the hidden microphone team by giving them the night off before heading back to the hotel to see how Monica was feeling. She seemed quiet and distant which, Tim supposed, was to be expected.

15:30 Saturday
Expectations were high – and so were the two young men from Channel 4. Those sleek, shiny-eyed boys in suits had arrived mid-afternoon, oily with cash and courting their entourage of sycophants with drink and regular visits to the toilet to get every nose as runny as possible. They had been very 'up' about the show. Everything they said was 'up' this, 'up' that and 'up' the other.

Despising them on the inside, Tim nevertheless beamed at their antics and their giggling companions on the outside. The team from Quark TV seemed out of their depth in comparison, at least until they popped to the bathroom.

With a cross-section of media people hanging around the hotel bar, chatting, he transmitted low level *feelings of wow* to improve his perceived charisma. Tim soon discovered their minds to be simply too drug-infused to snoop around so he abandoned the idea of outright coercion. For the time being. Later, seemingly delighted, they all wandered out saying 'wow' and promising to talk to Tim after the show. Then they proceeded to a local dive where they got righteously bladdered.

14:00 Saturday
A few interviews came and went as expected. Tim smiled a lot and did his "enigmatic" pose for the cameras.

The meeting with Barry McGarry was rather disturbing. Tim found him unreadable and received a penetrating stare when he made the attempt. Barry was all smiles but his two minders weren't; they mostly hung around in the background looking silently menacing. Equity cards were not required.

In the flesh, Barry was merely a short, red-faced man in his mid-fifties wearing an immaculately tailored suit, black polished shoes, a gold Rolex and several thick gold rings. His hands were small and immaculately manicured and his face alternated between a radiant smile and a cold sneer with no transitional stages. His chin was smooth as a baby's bum, hair short and precisely trimmed. No element of chaos intruded into Barry's world. He declared himself to be the Ultimate Control Freak.

"I'm glad your lucky mascot is safe," he simpered.

"Me too."

"I get the impression she was vital to your success?"

"I wouldn't put it as strongly as that but she's my girlfriend and I was worried about her. How could I perform with her whereabouts unknown?"

McGarry threw him a penetrating stare. "Quite," he said. "So you buried your grief in work. How noble. And then she somehow daringly escaped from her mysterious captors and is, at this moment, dashing over here to be by your side. How utterly charming and heart-warming. A most remarkable woman!"

"Well, I -" began Tim but Barry interrupted him.

"Have the police any leads?"

"I don't think so," Tim replied. He neglected to mention that they had, so far, not got round to informing the police. The show must go on, after all.

"Well, keep me informed. Anyone who wants to steal any element of your luck is now an issue for me to worry about. We'll have a think later how best to present the news to your eager public. I'll have a chat with the darling girl myself and drum up some ideas. Now then, where's my briefcase? I knocked up a basic contract for you to look over."

One of the minders handed the briefcase to Barry, automatically, impassively.

"Ah, here it is. Something for you to run your eyes over Tim. It's all pretty standard stuff but I like my people to know they are getting the best possible representation." He smiled winningly, handing over a brown leather folder. Tim shuddered. Inside, there were lots and lots of sheets of paper. Dozens of lines of small print. It took effort to resist the strong compulsion to sign it right away without reading it. Barry raised a quizzical eyebrow, as if he sensed this struggle. He spoke again.

"Well, it will do afterwards. Now I need to attend to some pressing business but I'll see you before you go on. My man will come and pick you up here if you wish – when it's time. Go and make all your preparations for an earth-shaking show. And I do love your idea for the final trick – very spectacular! And you believe we won't need the extra audio-visual effects after all?"

"I'm confident I can supply them myself," said Tim.

"*Really*? Well, that *is* wondrous. Well, well, strange times eh?" He nodded to himself thoughtfully. "Of course I've already paid for them so they're there if needed."

Barry left, followed by the two expressionless, bulky-looking minders. Tim was surprised to find his armpits moist and his heart beating a trifle faster than normal. He ordered a drink and reflected that, with Monica here, he could tell Madame Merlina (a medium famous throughout all of Blackpool) that her services were not required after all. Merlina had been fifth on his list but the only one of his old séance contacts who could (or would) respond to his request. He'd happily pay her train fare and send her on her way because, compared to Monica's fluorescent brainpower, she was a flickering hundred Watt bulb, able to fuel only the most basic of illusions. With the extra few grand thrown into the light show, plus oodles of charm, he told himself he would still have gotten away with it.

18:30 Saturday
Tim got back to the hotel to find Monica drying her hair and wrapped in a thick, white bathrobe. She had been soaking in the bath for over an hour, sipping champagne and trying to relax. Clothes had been obtained and she claimed to feel much better. Already, the first layer of make-up had been applied and she declared herself excited as Tim outlined the plan for the show. But the conversation remained superficial.

Briefly, he asked about her taking and subsequent escape but seemed to pay little attention to the replies. It was such a relief to have her back that he glossed over the lies and evasion, smiling behind lidded eyes, checking out the state of her mind and gauging the power at his disposal.

The matter could wait until later. The key factor was Monica's abundant mental strength. Soon it would be time to attempt the utterly spectacular.

As the magic hour approached, one of McGarry's men did indeed turn up at their hotel door to escort them over to the venue. Tim and Monica were prepared.

19:00 Saturday

Backstage, in their expansive, expensively-stocked dressing room, Tim, arrayed in shiny cloak and leather pants, kissed Monica. He knew that something was amiss. Her mind was distant, clouded but fortunately still thoroughly accessible.

Elegant as ever, she wore a tight-fitting, sequinned black dress. Her tights were black, her dark hair thick and tumbling everywhere in a delightful frizzy mess. Sniffing a rose that had arrived to wish them luck, Monica's defensive stance betrayed her to the keen observer. Evidently, she was still in pain. The make-up masked the bruises but he understood at that moment how she was barely holding it together. Fortunately the weakness was in her physical strength only. Her mental reserves were as full as ever.

Tim gazed into her eyes but she failed to reflect it back successfully. The attempt faded into a desperate grimace.

"You'll be fabulous," she told him in a flash of white teeth.

"Of course I will," he agreed as he lapped up her last reserve of latent energy, concentrating on that vital task exclusively.

Monica was his life's greatest discovery – an intoxicating yet insecure personality completely unaware of its own potency. It was this strength that would thrust him astride the big league. He would stand proud and erect above the rabbit-pullers, watch swingers and cabinet crouchers. They could all look up at him, at his mighty crotch, in awe. Because *his* would be the wand of brilliance... Tim dreamed idly of the things he would soon have, most notably things that were large, veiny and rather pointy.

His obsession had lain dormant throughout most of his life, the locker room jibes locked away securely in memory vaults. Until a throw-away comment of Monica's reawakened the fear. Up until then he'd genuinely convinced himself that size didn't matter after all. If only she had not accidentally, in jest, after too much champagne, mentioned Jim's rather special attribute in the trouser department. Everything would have been fine. From then on, Tim strived ever harder to please her but managed to do so less often because of it. Thankfully he had never mentioned his middle name – Justin. His elderly parents' malicious joke, he always thought.

Today's lies presented a problem and, in due course, he would examine her memory in detail and take whatever steps were necessary. For now all he needed was her raw power. He was thankful she hadn't erected that wretched mental shield, even though, long ago, he had built a bypass right through it. This ensured she would always let him through – unseen and unknown.

"I'll see you later my love," he whispered. She heard nothing. She slumped on the dressing room sofa and slept.

20:13 Saturday
With a humongous flash of purple light, the Wondrous Tim floated to the centre of the stage, shiny shoes dangling in mid-air.

Two thousand people sat in semi-darkness and gasped.

19:13 Saturday
Before go-live, Barry McGarry took Tim to one side. They were going over the stage layout, checking the delicate criss-crossing points unseen by the audience. Lines Tim had marked in chalk, insisting they offered the best angles to film. There had been a heated discussion with a lighting guy. And a noisy interchange with the sound engineer and the team from Quark TV. Tim concentrated a tiny bit and they all smiled and agreed his plan was the best after all.

Barry seemed excited. But not so excited that he missed the way Tim handled the technicians.

"Have you seen the news?"

"Not really, been spending time with Monica. You know."

"Ah, very touching. Well, you missed a treat. Look at this." He whipped out his pocket television.

Strange news was breaking, first in Preston but spreading

outwards like a bacteria on a Petri dish. Throughout the afternoon, new reports arrived hourly, accompanied by remarkable footage and near-hysterical commentary. Soon the bulletins were every half hour. And then continuous.

It began with a levitating priest in Fulwood, shortly followed by a flying nun in Lancaster. Oddly, it was a bespectacled friar in a Liverpool grammar school, picking up choir boys without using his hands, that captured public imagination the most vividly. The footage was unusually clear and beautifully filmed. The media speculated wildly and gleefully. Within hours, the grinning friar was on his way to becoming a major celebrity and Barry wasted no time getting on the phone to spell out his career options.

"I don't believe it," said Tim, shocked at what he saw on the tiny screen. "Fucking hell, it's like a conspiracy or something. This has been happening all afternoon?"

"We live in amazing times, Tim," said Barry. "But don't worry about this taking away the spotlight. The time is ripe for a special, unique individual to seize the moment, I can feel it! Momentum is building and there's no reason you can't be the one to take full advantage. I assume you can replicate these, ah, tricks?"

Tim was stunned by the images. And by the challenge. He'd used a wire in the past but somehow he knew he'd have to go one better this time. This appeared to be mental power at work – power of an improbably high standard. Having met most of the world's top mystics and magicians, the broad consensus was that such power was extremely rare. Levitation almost always involved children's building blocks – not whole children!

Having never levitated before, Tim wondered how to go about it. But now, topped up with all the Monica he could handle, he made a decision. In full view of the assorted technicians and stagehands, he fashioned an image of himself floating and projected it outwards. Simultaneously he masked his own presence.

"Very nice!" chuckled McGarry, who glanced at the image and

then returned his piercing gaze directly at Tim. "Better than smoke and mirrors, eh? It should do the job. You can do it before 20 people, but how about in front of 2,000?"

Everyone except Barry looked up at the floating figure. They knew there were no wires.

A man was flying.

"I could do it in front of God himself!" boasted the Wondrous Tim and, in that moment, he believed it. The assembled stage staff stood open-mouthed, motionless. You could have heard a mouse fart.

"Splendid!" said Barry McGarry. "Then we're all set. I knew you had genuine talent. Sniffed it out, you might say."

Thug Number One (as Tim inwardly referred to him), stood behind Barry and stared into space. If *he* was impressed, he didn't show it.

"If others around the country can suddenly, genuinely levitate, what do you suppose it all means?" was Barry's question as he left.

"I wish I knew," Tim replied. "Seems like it's mainly priests, rabbis and so on."

Barry smiled like he already knew what would happen next. Then he spoke in a quiet, melodic voice.

"Yes, I noticed that. Maybe you should find a dog collar instead of the Simon Templar polo neck? What do you reckon, Tim? Does the celibate life appeal to you? Can you be a real saint?"

"I think I'll pass." Tim almost swooned. He had drawn on Monica's psychic energy but now his head felt fogged. A hum like the sound of overhead pylons was throbbing in his ears and wouldn't go away. But he had done it.

Levitated.

The power feels different today, thought Tim. *But I believe I can do anything!*

With the strength he now possessed, how much more could be

achieved? His illusions were improving day by day and now he would make them the centre piece of the act. A time for courage and spectacle.

"I think I'll go and get ready. Have a last quiet moment with Monica, before curtain call."

"Hey ho," said Barry, heading off to make preparations of his own.

20:20 Saturday
The stage had turned completely dark. A deafening rumble then several powerful searchlights, aimed upwards, distracted the audience as Tim floated silently on to the stage.

"Welcome to my Wondrous World!" his voice boomed. The lights dropped, focussing on him, and he simultaneously wiped the floating image above. The projection had worked like a charm.

Tim wore no microphone. He talked directly to the audience via telepathy.

Not bad, admitted Jim grudgingly. He adjusted the level slightly for comfort.

"Tonight," said Tim, "I will show you a small selection of the Miracles in my repertoire. I will demonstrate that gravity need not constrain us, that reality is a sham, that your innermost thoughts and secrets are mine for the taking. Ladies and gentlemen, I present magic of a kind never before seen. If you are faint-hearted, or only able to handle the tame and the predictable, beware! For I will take you on a journey into the weird, the unknown and the eerie. Tonight I will invoke the true art of magic and reveal the magician's ancient against the forces of darkness and ignorance. Ladies and gentlemen, it's time for a drama that has not been witnessed for a thousand years!"

Tim was feverishly improvising an entirely new script yet the words flew from his lips as effortlessly as drivel spurts from a born-again Christian. He went with the flow and raised his arms.

A huge explosion and a burst of fire filled the hall. Nobody was burned but they felt the heat and glanced at their neighbours in fear. For a moment, a hideous demon skull engulfed the stage only for it to vanish and be replaced by 12 scantily clad dancing girls.

A deep bass synthesizer drone shook the massive speakers. It was accompanied by whooshes of pink noise and doomy mellotron choirs. Quark's cameras rolled. Tim shut his eyes and glanced into the golden pool he used as a visual representation of Monica's stolen strength. On the surface of the thick, viscous liquid, several orange balls floated. They shone like polished metal and seemed to have fine tendrils growing from them, like vines or roots. Or spores.

Her mind was contaminated! But how...?

Tim was horrified. The dancers whirled around madly as he remained poised with his arms outstretched, ready to unleash the power. Was it an elaborate trap of Monica's ex? Had they conspired against him? He again remembered the image of Jim plucked from the head of Mark Housman and suddenly his knees threatened to cave in. A massive pool of strength was at his command but if he used it, would his mind become infected too? And with . . . what?

What is going on? Is it already too late? I dipped in for the test levitation!

He broke into an oily sweat. A sea of blank faces spread across the darkness and a camera zoomed in. His doubt was painted clearly for all to see. In desperation, he conceived a filter, a metal grid tightly bolted over the top of the pool. He imagined that it held back the larger contaminants, kept them inside but allowed the liquid to fall, upwards, through the grid and into the chambers of his consciousness. Thick yellow paint-like light poured through and filled him with power.

Unfortunately, he didn't see some of the tiny spores break off, slipping easily through his hasty defence.

Casting aside the doubts, Tim addressed the twitchy audience, his confidence growing.

Sitting amongst the great unwashed, in a seat that creaked every time he fidgeted, which was constantly, Jim reckoned Tim was highly energised. Sitting back, he dreamt of Monica. He let his mind wander through the past as Tim, impressively, floated about the stage through violet flames and misty lighting effects. Stars and galaxies swirled around his head as he looped the loop and swooped over the heads of the audience. Those in the upper boxes couldn't believe their eyes when he materialised, smiling, and shook hands with a bemused teen.

Jim left his dreams for a moment, reflecting that, perhaps, smoking a joint earlier hadn't been the most sensible idea. Or was Tim truly this good?

Suddenly Jim awoke.

The show had progressed, possibly as much as 40 minutes had gone by. Jim was fully refreshed although his snoring had disturbed some.

Still commanding the stage, the Wondrous Tim had dispensed with his dancing girls and stood, alone, amidst the spewings of half a dozen dry ice machines. Lasers sliced through the smoke and he appeared to be the focus of a vortex, facing a huge winged monster that arose from the smoke. Its black scales and yellow eyes caused many of the children in the audience to cry out in terror. A few experienced unscheduled bowel movements.

Mostly, their parents ignored them, which was strange.

By now, Tim's eyes were glassy, his face freshly drenched in sweat. His head pounded, his ears whistled, but he pushed himself harder and harder. The atmosphere had changed palpably while Jim dozed.

With a gesture, the roof of Sheffield City Hall became transparent, generating gasps of awe from the already awe-struck crowd. Tim flew upwards though it, shooting stars meeting him in a dazzling display. If there were strings involved, they were well concealed.

Sequins on Tim's cape lit the surrounding area like a mirror ball.

It was a seriously epic illusion and Jim wondered if anyone else in the crowd grasped what they were really seeing. If this was visible to the cameras . . . now *that* would be hard to explain.

Tim floated downwards, several demonic swords having pierced his cloak harmlessly. They clattered to the ground like the tired old props that they were.

Jim found himself unable to resist projecting an image of a little girl on to the stage – for Tim's eyes only. He constructed her very quickly and only realised too late that she was an approximation of Monica, aged 10.

But seasoned performers aren't so easily thrown. Thus, Tim's tiny jump on seeing the girl was rewarding, but Jim gained a greater thrill from the startled expression when the girl vanished, seconds later.

Scanning the audience, Tim tried to work out who was responsible, angry at the loss of concentration. His existing projections began to fade and he cursed inwardly. The stage lost a few degrees of colour and sparkle. Not to be so easily thwarted, Tim activated a spontaneous, fresh illusion, out of some dark recess of his imagination.

Suddenly the floor of the stage became see-through, like smoky glass. Beneath, the very fires of hell burned and anguished faces materialised, crushed against the glass, their skin blackening and burning, their flesh melting away to reveal dark skulls.

"Fuck, fuck, fuck!" cried Tim inwardly. "Where the hell did that come from?"

"Is this a joke mummy?" asked Jim's young girl, directly into Tim's head.

By an enormous effort of will, green grass grew over the nightmare scenario and Tim introduced some angels, some tinkly music, blue skies and fluffy, wuffy clouds. He held his breath. The image was so good he believed it himself. His tinnitus eased.

The audience's attention quickly shifted from horror to beauty. Again, he had got away with it. Indeed, so great was the audience's relief at the horror scene's departure that they blotted it from their minds, forgetting it entirely. The angels were very lovely.

Jim grudgingly admitted the illusion was remarkable but he was getting fed up with visual projections. He had not yet spotted Monica and sought her with his mind.

Did she know what Tim was doing? Did she know how far he's progressed?

Filtering through buzzing minds attuned to the Wondrous Tim, Jim failed to find her special signature. He supposed her to be asleep or deeply tired. It was understanding given her ordeal.

Along with the capacity audience, Jim Cavanah gasped as a ball of light expanded beyond the stage. It vanished in a sprinkling of tiny purple lights over the assembled of South Yorkshire.

"Nice graphics," commented a voice nearby in a broad accent. Hands reached out to touch the lights.

Jim jerked upright. His primary monitor program had detected an incoming virus. It automatically kicked off a defence suite to nullify the attack while initiating a level 1 shield against further attacks.

Ah canna guarantee hull integrity Captain, his program drawled.

A lower priority monitor now reported external transmissions beaming into every mind within the hall. A mass infection of unknown type – and it was no accident!

What just happened here?

On stage, Tim, seemingly oblivious, moved on to mind reading. He reasoned that small scale was vital to establish image and personality. After all, future advertising revenue had to be considered. Tim's charm and charisma always translated well in close-up and suggested to the punters that beneath the razzmatazz was a warm and caring guy. Mind reading being his home territory, he relaxed.

He chose a smart-dressed woman from the front row. Blonde, fake breasts, fake smile and no mental protection whatsoever.

"So Mandy, tell me about your first kiss?"

"Oh, really I shouldn't."

"I insist, said Tim, surprised at the sudden resistance."

"Well, Daddy said I wasn't to tell..." she began.

"Oh shit," mumbled Tim.

After glossing over major problems with the blonde, silicone-breasted volunteer, Tim quickly picked a bland-looking guy, mid-twenties, brimming with wholesome surface thoughts. He needed a face to face result they could use for the DVD before moving on to the grand finale illusion.

In the event, it didn't go well.

Had Tim not acquired Meed's virus while plundering Monica, he would undoubtedly have been triumphant. But the hastily concocted filter process was terribly slow and inefficient. He therefore took the bold decision to remove it and use the energy anyway. He'd deal with the consequences later. He hoped.

Tim drunk deep of the contaminated pool of Monica's latent psychic power.

"So, Thomas Freeman, don't be afraid, come up on to the stage!" beckoned Tim.

"Hey, how'd you know my name?"

Perfect.

"OK my new friend – we have never met before, right?"

"That's right," agreed Thomas. "I'd never even heard of you before today."

"Um, well, Tom, what I want you to do is imagine a special time in your life for me. A happy time. Can you do that?"

"I certainly can." The man concentrated and became rather uncomfortable. His expression suggested he'd just farted and maybe followed through. A hand went to his temple as if to restrain a headache; he cocked his head at an angle and poked some wax out of his ears with a finger.

"Alright Tom. I don't want you to tell anyone, just write it on a piece of paper." An assistant appeared with paper and felt tip. "You only need write a brief summary. Then seal it in this envelope. Describe a perfect day, like the song. Then I'll read exactly what you write but without opening the envelope." Tim beamed at the cameras.

The man, tongue out, squinting, scribbled quickly onto the paper and put it into the assistant's envelope. Tim levitated the envelope into the air. Putting his hands over his eyes, he spoke in a monotonous torrent.

"On your perfect day Mr Thomas Freeman, terminal whiner and utter bore, you would awaken, have a shower of scaldingly hot water followed by a breakfast of thickly buttered toasted teacakes. Laters you would go next door and rape then murder the sixteen year old daughter of your neighbours Mr and Mrs Dobson. In the evening, you are unsure what you would enjoy best but would enjoy watching several films starring Steven Seagul. You didn't write all this down Thomas, but I also see in your mind that a crate of beer is involved to help make those complex scripts make sense."

"Fuck, that's right!" gasped Mr Freeman, surprised to have shared his secret fantasy with so many people. Those sitting closest beamed at him, so perhaps it was right to let the dark things out.

Jim gaped in growing horror.

A tiny streak of blood dripped from the guy's nose. Tim watched, fascinated, but not by the blood. The situation had become disjointed, out of sync. He couldn't understand why he'd said those things. And instead of being outraged, the audience were sniggering and cheering amongst themselves, like drunks at a dog fight.

The creep had just admitted his perfect day involved rape then murder – and nobody was heading to the exits to call the police. Small children were slapping their thighs in a most adult manner and laughing raucously.

Surreal.

Diagnostic Report: Viral Analysis. Quickref: Source: Aesir;Stylematch>80%, ProgFunction;RapidIncrease Belief&&DarkSide-Visions&PassOnInfect&This-TakeAction-NoTolerance; Probability>72%

Jim pondered the sudden splurge of data written across his vision. A quick re-rendering had turned his internal computer systems transparent. It was a simple matter to project any of it into his regular optical processes. Lots of things were becoming simple to him now.

Tim had just infected everyone in the audience with a virulent strain of . . . *primal thought virus*. A brief investigation into the captured code revealed its author to have a familiar style. He'd seen it before in the Kill compulsion. Horrified, Jim couldn't tear his eyes away from the stage.

Tim swayed as if weak or in pain. Quickly covering this up, he launched prematurely into his final grand illusion, summoning a gorgeous young lady from the audience with a gesture even though he'd not called for volunteers. As she stepped onto the stage, walking as if in a trance, her clothes vanished. To everyone there except Jim she appeared naked. Tim gaped.

Far from being shocked, the audience howled lustily, even those with children.

Jim had taken the decision to process all incoming data with additional checksums. His visual processor reported it was now excluding approximately 20% of the information hitting it due to consistency/reality errors. Clearly Tim was doing far more than projecting an image of the girl. And he was in trouble. He tugged at his polo neck several times as if to let the heat escape.

Now the girl was engulfed in fire, her skin blackening. She looked at her stick arms and roared with unnatural laughter.

Tim's mind was in turmoil and he knew he couldn't keep it up much longer. The image twisted, threatening to get out of control.

This hadn't been the plan!

The girl morphed into a blackened skeleton. Wobbly antennae grew from her skull and a bony tail sprouted like a child's skipping rope, limp and grey. The pathetic creature staggered towards Tim who suddenly shone like an angel. His apparel turned from black to white, his leather pants becoming a rather fetching pair of shorts, and he gained a glowing sword. His polo neck sweater turned to pale gold and his hair shone, thick and lustrous. And in his shorts, a third leg grew.

Strange ideas blossomed in his fevered mind and the Wondrous Tim grinned as his strength increased a hundredfold.

The skeleton grew taller, becoming impossibly thin and stretched. In its arms, a gossamer scythe formed. And slowly the body grew more substantial, a cloak forming from a cloud of smoky air. It strode across the stage, a giant menacing apparition.

Tim was a beaming white light, alone and unafraid.

"White is the new black!" he gibbered.

"Fantastic! Awesome" cried Barry McGarry in the wings, prodding the cameraman. "Zoom in," he hissed. "Forget the lines, he has! We must get a good picture."

"OK boss," said the hapless lad, dripping with panic.

Tim trembled and threw his head backwards in a dramatic gesture. He held the sword in both hands and its blade flickered with blue, violet and green flames. The crowd munched crisps noisily and grinned like demons.

A bolt of purple and blue light sprang from the earth, carrying the Wondrous Tim into the air as if surfing a wave. His sword cleaved off the huge skeletal head and a crash of thunder accompanied its fall.

The media teams clasped each other in joy. Despite being a big girl, this brought tears to her eyes.

The hall was lit in vivid green, blue and yellow light. The speakers rumbled and vibrated as the elderly PA System was pushed to its limits for the gratuitous climax.

Tim floated limply to the ground, his sword transformed to a flowering staff. He calmly addressed all present, silver light lancing from his mouth and eyes.

"Thank you! What you have seen tonight is only a beginning. Remember this day and remember that everything is possible for the Wondrous Tim. In the realm of magic, white and black are the same. Be positive, assert yourself and you will achieve all you desire. Tell your friends, goodnight!"

Tim vanished.

The applause was long and sustained. And genuine. They wanted more.

After an age of stamping, it seemed the talented young man was not going to satisfy the increasingly boisterous demand for an encore. Even so, they were grateful to have seen him and eager to pass on the word. And more.

Jim could still neither see nor sense Monica anywhere. He was worried she wasn't around at the climax. The show was bizarre and creepy but amazing. It was a shame he had to stop it, or at least erase the little extras Tim was slipping in. He had promised Monica there would be no confrontation – but he didn't see how it could be avoided, given what was going on.

The viral infection was yet another complication. On quick analysis, Jim found it to be utterly malignant but hastily and imperfectly written. Even on first reading he spotted logic flaws. And it had been knocked up recently, he was convinced. Very recently.

With crazy, sloppy iterations, the program was coded to call itself regardless of how often it crashed. The consequences of that could be terrible and would surely lead to psychosis, but presumably the author didn't care. Without a full brain reboot, memory areas would be fragmented and thoughts increasingly disrupted and confused.

As the crowd dispersed, chatting, clasping each other, wiping the occasional bloody nose, Jim cursed. He realised that each of them was contagious, emitting low level pulses in all directions. The time for preventative inoculations had already passed and he wondered if Tim had done this knowingly or if there was another answer.

"Looks like my quest to save the world turned up at last," he said aloud, pushing his way through the throng. A small girl wailed and cried but her parents merely taunted her.

It had been an unspoken command from Monica - *do not show your ugly mug after the show*. The last thing she wanted was the kind of hassle that followed Jim like botty burps after a laxative. It would be hard enough smoothing things over with Tim, she had guessed. Correctly as it turned out.

Jim resolved to leave, quietly, and think it all through – once he knew Monica was OK and uninfected. He wandered around the rear of the City Hall. There wasn't any other way for performers to leave.

Eventually Tim appeared from a side door, chatting with a shorter, smartly-tailored man. A couple of large dudes, bouncers possibly, shadowed them. Of Monica there was no sign.

A few solitary autograph hunters hung around but the vast majority of the crowd had already vanished into the night.

"Yo Tim, how's Monica?" Jim strode out of the darkness. He'd surveyed all the angles and this one made the best use of the available light. He cast a long shadow and knew it.

"Who the hell? Wait, it's *you*!" One of the bouncers tried to appear menacing, the other was watching a brawl that had broken out.

"Hey, Tim, you recognise me, of course you do!"

"What are you doing here?" Tim's face was grey, strained.

"I came for the show. You were good!"

"Thanks, Jim! I think 'spectacular' would describe the experience for most of the audience but if you thought it was good, I'm grateful. Forgive me, I don't have much time to natter right now. Monica's feeling very tired and has already returned to our hotel."

"Tired?"

"I think something hurt her and I hope I don't find out that you were involved."

"Ooh, nice manoeuvrer. Twisty. Inventive. Like those illusions of yours. Like that nasty little virus you just infected everyone with."

"Virus?" There was an odd expression in Tim's eyes, an inflection in his voice that didn't ring right. What was it – fear?

"You were chucking out some serious mental shit in that show. And not all of it was your own."

"I don't know what you're talking about."

Jim saw that the short guy was staring intently at him. It was unnerving.

"Would this be your new manager?" Jim guessed. "Has he met your old manager yet?"

"Look Mr Ex, best you keep your nose out. Alright? There's no need for us to even meet. We have nothing in common."

"You're right there," smiled Jim as if he'd just scored a point. He felt his spine tingle.

Diagnostic Report: Viral Attack. Quickref: Source: Aesir_2;Stylematch>66.6%, ProgFunction;ProbeSurf&-10; Probability>66.6%

Jim trapped the new attack and isolated it. Then he passed parameters into a novel subroutine, one he'd written that afternoon and was keen to test. It incorporated code extracted from basic motor controls and allowed selected limbs to be turned off via external command.

Jim muttered something under his breath, firing a command back along the line of attack. It was then that he realised the invader was not Tim after all.

The smaller man stiffened as if in pain and dropped a small television set from his fingers. It shattered on the stone flags in an explosion of grey plastic.

He stared at Jim with a new expression. Astonishment? Respect?

"How?" he mouthed as his legs gave way. One of the bouncers rushed to his side, the other tried to work out if any actual scrimmage had taken place and if so, what to do about it.

Tim closed the distance between himself and Jim, unaware of Barry's predicament. Jim was quite tall, annoyingly. Never had he felt quite so frustrated by his size. He shifted his body to one side, subconsciously shielding his groin.

"You spoilt Monica's life but she's with me now. She's happy and we're going to be good together. I'll give her all the things you never could."

"I have nothing to say to you," said Jim. "You hardly even exist. There's Monica, there's me. That's it."

"You're a fucking obsessive, she told me!"

"Yeah, I know. It's true," Jim admitted. "But hey, you can't help who you fall in love with, right?"

"Look Cavanah, I have to be going. It's been lovely to meet you at last. I hope next time will be at our wedding. Monica's and mine. You will attend, of course?"

"How come you never used Monica in the act? She'd make a very attractive assistant," said Jim, stalling without realising why. He noticed Tim's cunningly raised shoes. Tim followed his gaze and flushed, red.

At that, Jim turned and left. Tim fussed over Barry McGarry who remained on the cold ground, raging. His minders gaped stupidly as per their job description. Tim's head felt like it was going to explode and thinking clearly was no longer an option.

Jim tried to remember if he'd put a timeout on the Motor command.

Chapter Thirteen

The meeting of two personalities is like the contact of two chemical substances: if there is any reaction, both are transformed.   Karl Young

Through the silent Minster gardens, Julie Hutchinson strolled alone. Nearby, a blackbird crammed as many pieces of bread into its beak as possible, all the while nervously keeping an eye out for cats and magpies. The gardens were restful and scented with wild flowers. For the moment, it was her sanctuary.

The church and its grounds had certainly been tarted up since last she was here, Lottery money having found another vital outlet. Would Julie be welcome if the Faithful were aware of her profession? She thought not. Holy people she had met before. Oddly, some gentlemen amongst the congregation seemed familiar on a personal level, an intimate level. There were several of the respected, elderly, upstanding members of the community that she recognised specifically. The great and good of Preston, the moral minority, none remembered her. To these old men she had been a temporary escape from their lives. She had been faceless desire, fashioned in warm, compliant flesh.

The Faithful, according to Marjorie, begged Julie to stay in the nearby refectory where nuns would wait on her night and day.

Ask for anything.

Remain with us in case the Devil returns. Be our beacon.

The old woman was a strange one, her position in the church's hierarchy unclear. Julie was sure they had never met before that morning, yet there was something that stirred unresolved questions. On a bench, the prostitute-turned saint sat demurely eating a burger as a young man approached, walking directly across the grass, avoiding the winding path. He had freckles, red, straight hair and green corduroy trousers.

"Hello," he said, shuffling towards Julie nervously.

"Yes?"

"I hope you don't mind. I saw you. On the television last night. It was you, wasn't it? Everyone's talking about it. You were . . . bare." He flushed, his freckly face going, impossibly, redder than before. His eyelashes were pale and speckled and he examined his feet shyly.

"What do you want?" asked Julie, studying him.

"I just wanted to say thanks. Because of you I discovered Jesus again. I had abandoned him but now I am saved after all. I realised this morning that I should be part of the Faithful. I read the pamphlets and it all makes sense."

"Jesus?" asked Julie.

"Jesus," confirmed the youth.

"I don't know what you mean."

"You defeated Satan. The power of good triumphed over evil. Marjorie says the Faithful must believe in that and choose the side of good."

"And how do you know I faced Satan?"

"What do you mean?"

"Have you ever seen Satan before?"

"Well . . . ," his eagerness faded. "Who else could it have been?" This was clearly not going the way he had expected and he was not comfortable with complication.

"So you have no idea. Is that what you're saying?"

"You're confusing me."

"What, with someone who has a brain?" The years of bandying words with punters weren't in vain.

The young man tried a different tack. He clasped his hands together as if in supplication and bowed his head. "We've all been inspired by seeing you. I *so* want to do good! Marjorie has been telling us all to do good."

"Then fuck off and stop bothering me!"

The chump opened his mouth as if to reply but closed it again as Julie's laser-eyes burned into his soul. Shocked, he turned and fled. She laughed mockingly at his podgy, retreating arse, bouncing beneath a saggy cream-coloured jumper.

***

Saturday afternoon drifted slowly into evening. Sheila popped all her favourite CDs into the machine and let them play on random. Earlier that morning, assisted by Jim, she'd got Dave upstairs and into bed. They had lain there ever since, in a cocoon shielded against the world and its lunacy. Now she cuddled up and pressed her breasts against his naked skin.

From his slumbers, Dave felt something grow.

"Mmmmm baby!" he said, his headache clearing at last.

***

Una Sharples cowered in terror. She had been skulking in the cellar all day, searching the runes, the tarot and the Radio Times for inspiration. None offered any comfort. The Lord Malvolian had been publicly humiliated by a mere girl. Worse, a girl personally selected by Una to be his vessel. It had been a dreadful miscalculation. Her plans were in tatters, his defeat unexpected and absolute. She remained in the dark sealed away from prying minds, but felt certain the girl was still out there, searching.

How could she have been so strong?

There was a knock on the door.

"Una, Una, it's Bill!"

She crept up the stairs and peered from the shadows. The familiar outline of Bill the plumber was visible through the glass in the back door.

"Bill?"

"Una, let me in. I'll protect you. I'll do anything for you, you know that!"

"I do," sighed Una unlocking the door, letting Bill in the back way, although not how he usually preferred it. Bill was devoted to her. Perhaps, if trouble came, his devotion would buy her a few precious seconds.

Once he was inside, she locked the door again. Bill smiled. He was unusually clean and well presented, quite charming really. She was forced to admit she'd never really given him the time he deserved. He was always eager, his well-worn toolbox perpetually at her disposal should she but ask. As Una examined him closely, she became perplexed. The image of Bill shimmered.

Bill was not really there after all. Somebody else stood in his place.

The girl?

No!

Before her stood an old woman with bony, grasping hands and thick, wrinkled brown tights. She grinned through yellowed, National Health dentures.

"Forgive the intrusion," said the intruder. Her voice was icy.

"Do I know you?" asked Una. A lump formed in her throat.

"No, but I know you."

"I don't understand."

"You never did. But my justice is upon you. You fucked up big style you fat cunt. As it happens I'm used to that. Never been able to get decent minions. Unfortunately, you're a dead piece of shit. You realise that, don't you?"

Una gaped. "My Lord?" she cried, falling to her knees.

"Woohoo, at last! Get yourself a shiny, gift-wrapped special prize. Delicious isn't it?"

"I brought you back!"

"Oh yes, bloody marvellous job there. I get the living shite kicked out of me by probably the most powerful psyche I have ever faced – and all before I become corporeal or grow enough neural pathways to put two thoughts together. Yeah, thanks very much!"

"But you prevailed. You are here!"

"No thanks to you. And you can switch off that crappy posh accent now!"

"The spell seems to have gotten stuck. I was imagining lots of interviews. Only so I could spread the word of your greatness to all mankind," she added.

"Ooh, very nice try. But it's too late for all of that. I don't need you any more. I've got myself a far better set-up. Hilarious really."

"Let me serve you my Lord, in any capacity," begged Una.

"Nah, don't think so," chuckled Malvolian, in Marjorie's rasping voice. "You've blown it. Besides, I don't want you running into my latest protégé and peeing in my bathwater, so to speak. The old ways really are kaput. And you with them."

"My Lord?"

"YOU ARE MAGGOTS!"

Una stretched out her fingers. Somehow she *had* to look at them and at first they appeared quite normal. Then, peering more closely, she saw millions of tiny, pink worm-like shapes, writhing beneath the ample flesh of her hands. And spreading up her wrists. And throughout her whole body. She felt them, writhing, squirming inside her tongue. Her skin rippled. Then the pain came. They grew bigger, fatter, displacing flesh, becoming flesh, stretching the skin until it reached breaking point. Impossibly, the skin did not burst and in moments they numbered hundreds of thousands, permeating her whole body. And then here were merely thousands, each individual grown large, gorged on the others. Obscene lumps appeared in her stomach and her face. Her cheeks expanded, her nose widened and her mouth cried out soundlessly, filled with grey maggots.

Seconds ticked by, measuring out an eternity. Una's body was racked with intense agony. Meanwhile, the old woman sat in a kitchen chair and crossed her legs, polishing her already shiny shoes with a hankie. Engrossed, she continued to watch.

A human-shape, now consisting of hundreds of conjoined maggots, each fat and juicy, huddled together, quivering, pathetic. They were all that remained of Una's body. Finally, there were just a few maggots and then, the transition complete, only one. It lay on the kitchen floor, a huge swollen bag of flesh, Una's frightened eyes the remaining human element. Steaming tears oozed onto the lino as she looked upwards, pleadingly at Marjorie MacManaman.

"YOU ARE NOTHING!" said the kindly old woman. There was insufficient time to do it properly.

Maggot Una leaked, like dark, oily liquid, into the floor. She dripped through the floorboards and into the basement where she gathered in a rank corner.

***

Yasmine Carrion floated naked in an ultramarine swimming pool. Overhead it was dark. A few stars in unfamiliar patterns stalked the clear sky. The light flowed through the pool, lazily, like it couldn't quite get up to speed.

Around the pool dense, uniform grass grew. The grass met the water without even a gap. No concrete ran along the edge – the pool simply *became* grass.

Steam rose from the water, dispersed by cool evening shadow.

Helios Gaste appeared at the side of the pool, a circlet of stars above his head. He had become magnificent.

"What have you *done*?" gasped Yasmine floating on her back, thick, dark pubic hair drawing his gaze.

"With work, I knew this body could accomplish much. And I have worked it!" said Gaste proudly. His kebab-like arms had lost their flab, the flesh become tight and sinewy. He had shed several stones of blubber from his gut and built a stomach of steely, wired muscle. All his hair was gone and Helios now resembled a god, or a hero of legend.

"I decided to play it entirely physical," he laughed. "That's how I like it!"

"Looks like you've a lot of energy going to waste up there," said Yasmine.

"Don't tempt me. That's the last thing we should be doing

here."

"Don't you want to try it?"

"Perhaps, but not with you. And not here."

"Scaredy cat!"

"He must be ready by now?"

"Almost, I think."

"Then it will be soon."

"What does soon matter in this place?"

"I guess."

***

Once Father Stilton had hovered in the air on the afternoon news, further religious levitations began being reported. across Preston initially. By Sunday, the feats would be replicated in Yorkshire, Derbyshire and Cumbria.

Julie marvelled at how easy it had been to divert attention from herself. She regarded the priest as a jerk and her solution perfect.

Suits you sir, she smirked from behind a bush.

In the event it had required less effort than the floating ashtray trick, a trick that was a dim memory, something from another lifetime. With a second miracle worker on the premises, others began turning up every hour.

Incongruities were spreading. Outwards, like ripples in a lake.

She grinned wickedly as she floated Father Stilton over the grass to the accompaniment of a riotous clicking of cameras. Faith was out of the closet and *achieving* something at long last! Converts swarmed around the church eagerly. Nobody dared to be excluded.

Julie was becoming bored.

Then the old woman returned.

"Hello dear," she said, predictably.

"Any sign of the fat witch?" Julie was not one for small talk.

"I'm afraid she has winked out of existence. Looks like you frightened her into the next dimension!"

"Or you don't know how to search properly."

"We'll go together tomorrow. We'll do our very best, I promise!"

Julie returned to directing her floating priest. The camera lights blared and the sky darkened.

***

Arthur Bradshaw reclined in his back garden sipping iced tea. He'd spent the last hour digging over a wide expanse of soil and had then sprinkled some wild flower seeds. This year he felt time starting to weigh heavily. He no longer thought of planting trees or shrubs that would take decades to develop. Art's strength was still there to command but his speed was not what it was. Nor his stamina.

Short bursts, old man, you'll get by for a while yet.

The afternoon sun dipped low and he found himself dreading the night shift. He hated Saturday nights most of all. All the angry, spoiled brats, loudmouth drunks and posturing tarts. Had he saved up enough to retire? Arthur knew he hadn't.

The garden was lovely, still laid out as Peg had designed it. He stroked the cat and it purred loudly. Soon it would be time for his run.

An elderly neighbour wearing a pair of underpants on his head, nodded vaguely as he trimmed his hedge meticulously into a crenulated pattern.

Art wondered if he should do anything about what he had witnessed last night. He had seen the old woman, witnessed something unexplainable *go into her*. Peg would have known what to do.

Not a man to shirk his responsibilities, Art knew he couldn't ignore it.

When Arthur walked into town, he passed by the Minster. The church was lit by various floodlights, highlighting its pale sandstone and brightly-coloured stained glass windows. The lawns were close-cropped and small flowers stood in regiments hemmed in by neat borders.

On a stone bench, a young blonde girl gazed into space. The garden was dotted with unfathomable shadows but a nearby spotlight rendered her features in stark detail, as if aimed at an exhibit. In worn jeans and t-shirt the girl was hardly an imposing figure. But there was something about her.

It was Saturday night and therefore amazing that dozens of people were milling around the church. Lights and singing from inside suggested a mass was being held. A camera crew were packing equipment into flight cases. One carried a photocopied leaflet entitled "The Faithful. Join or Else!"

"It's beautiful," said Arthur, approaching the bench quietly. He felt drawn but didn't know why.

"It's only a building," Julie replied, warily. The old guy didn't have the look of a punter. In his white shirt and black tie he might have been an undertaker but the solid jaw and padded jacket suggested a doorman, or a gangster. He seemed . . . Julie searched her thoughts for a description . . . removed? Remote. Yes, that was it. The guy was there but he had no aura.

"It's whatever people want it to be," said Art. "It probably means something to those inside."

"You're not a believer then? If not, you're the first today." He thought she seemed so young but her voice was ancient. This made Art sad.

"Me? No. I don't believe in God, the tooth fairy or a caring Tory. Actually, I seem to remember the tooth fairy left me a sixpence now and again."

"So you aren't here to talk about Satan?"

"Hardly. I don't know what drew me over. I'm going to work and you looked so alone. I don't generally approach girls . . . especially famous ones."

She laughed. "So you don't want to join the war against Evil then?"

"I don't think so. There's a bit of evil in everyone in my

experience. Where would I start?"

"These lot are all nutters," Julie said.

"So why are you here?"

"I'm going to change my life, do something that matters. It's hard to explain but I don't think this is it."

Her mood caught him and Arthur felt suddenly weary. His silver ponytail drooped over his padded black jacket and for the first time it seemed a foolish affectation; an old man's indulgence gone too far. "I was there last night. I saw you," he muttered.

"So you *did* come to talk about Satan?"

"No, but I saw the thing in the smoke."

"And you don't think it was the Lord of Darkness?"

"I don't know what to think. I'm only a bouncer."

"What about it?"

"It didn't die."

"Why should I care?"

"It sort of went into an old woman," said Art.

"Into? How do you mean?"

"I'm not really sure, it was all a bit unbelievable."

"What did this old woman look like?" asked Julie, evenly.

"The strangest thing is I can't remember. Just a miscellaneous old woman, prim and proper. But creepy. I'd know her if I saw her again. I'm good with faces. Comes with the territory."

"Well, if it comes back I'll give it more of the same, old woman or not." Julie said, dismissively.

"I guess that's alright then."

Arthur wanted to say more. There was an air of dreadful loneliness about this kid. She couldn't be more than twenty. In the end he merely shrugged and smiled.

"Well, it was nice to meet you," said Julie, offering him an easy exit.

"And you," said Arthur, zipping up his jacket.

"I like your hair," she said as he departed.

Chapter Fourteen

Go confidently in the direction of your dreams.
Live the life you have imagined.
Harry David Sorry

The Snake Pass at night was silent, dark. Jim drove slowly, savouring the experience, whilst scanning for badgers, hedgehogs and foxes. The moon rose over the hills, pale light illuminating the way ahead, white clouds streaking over charcoal grey. Pine tree sentinels lined this stretch of road, black as sin against the sky yet in no sense foreboding.

It was a few minutes after midnight and Jim's mind was empty of emotion.

***

Throughout his formative years, Barry McGarry had been unremarkable, a blank-faced boy you might have seen drifting into accountancy or banking. His father was a remote, cold figure – a civil servant of no particular significance who worked long hours and paid his son scant attention. One dreary Friday in the summer holidays, their relationship changed forever.

Young Barry was bored and decided to explore his father's inner sanctum – the Forbidden Study. While poking behind volumes on the highest bookshelf he happened across some rather compromising photographs of dear old dad and another chap, both in a blatant state of undress. Barfing in revulsion, Barry replaced the photos carelessly and ran from the room, sobbing. His mother knocked timidly on the door for a bit then returned to her devoted companion Gordon, with tonic.

Later that night, as he prepared for bed, his father uncharacteristically dropped in and asked how his day had been. Deeply-lidded, weary eyes darted around restlessly and Barry thought he could guess why. Terrified at the prospect of impending punishment, he was amazed when his father, instead, smiled vaguely and popped a five pound note into his pyjama pocket.

"That's for being a good boy," he said, winking, and ruffled Barry's hair.

From that day, his father took a great deal more interest in him. They became firm friends and jolly companions. Information, it seemed, was a most valuable commodity.

Barry embarked upon a new phase in his life. He began to be fascinated by people around him, and their habits. He studied them. He spied on them. He researched their backgrounds and speculated endlessly on their hopes and dreams. At first he compiled voluminous notes, poring over them for hours (often at the expense of his academic subjects). He reasoned that it was pointless memorising details of the battle of Zama if your history teacher could be persuaded to award an "A" in preference to being outed for a fascination for underage girls. To his great delight, Barry found that most people were prone to embarrassing mistakes and were incredibly careless about concealing them.

As the years rolled by, he abandoned written notes, transferring all the data into his head, becoming, in effect, a living data bank. The development of a near infinite capacity to store gossip and divine the underlying facts, combined with a photographic memory, bestowed upon Barry McGarry a unique power. This he used to manipulate his way through college and beyond.

After a brief spell as a reporter, then dabbling in local politics for a year, Barry found his niche in the cut and thrust arena of Personal Representation. Priding himself that nobody could think faster on their feet, nobody could threaten him in an argument and nobody could sense weaknesses so quickly, Barry came to view himself as a superior being. Others tended to agree and fawned before him desperately keen to be his friend.

Despite his pleasure in pulling the strings of the rich and fatuous, Barry was never fully satisfied. Always he aspired to push himself and his mind to new limits. And as he expanded, he learned to harness the power in ways few could even comprehend. Smug and self-assured, Barry hated to lose his cool.

Nobody had ever done to him what Jim had just done.

Barry McGarry screamed in fury.

"Who the HELL was that?!" he demanded from his position on the ground.

"Just some guy," said Tim, strangely reluctant to admit it.

"You tell me NOW!" said Barry.

"I don't know his name," said Tim. A thin trickle of blood spread from his nose to his upper lip and his eyes began to cloud over. "What difference does it make?"

"TELL ME HIS NAME!" Barry McGarry thrust ice missiles into Tim's skull.

"Shit, shit, shit, stop! I don't know!" Tim yelled. "What are you doing to me?" He felt his mind held in a vice and even with all Monica's strength, he could not have forced it open. In his weakened state, he had no defence.

"Why are you lying to me Tim? We're supposed to be on the same side and yet you protect my enemy. I'm very disappointed in you and I'm going to have to think very seriously about this."

"How come he's your enemy but you don't know who he is?" Tim was on his knees, holding his head like it was going to split open. On Barry's flanks, his minders stood quietly, massive arms folded, surveying the flagged square. They made no attempt to help him up or even notice.

McGarry softened his expression, not entirely successfully. "We will talk about this tomorrow, Tim, when we've both calmed down. In answer to your question, I believe I *do* know who he is. And so do you. Do you think I'm a fool?"

"But I don't understand. How come you can't stand up?"

"Tim, I imagine you're feeling very tired after all your exertions. Or you're not very observant. But, rest assured, I absolutely promise, hope to die, that we will have a long chat tomorrow and sort everything out. I apologise for shouting at you just now. Go back to the hotel and get some sleep. Your lovely girlfriend will be waiting, I saw to it. My people put her safely to bed as you requested."

"What did you just do to my mind?"

"It seems there's lots of it about all of a sudden. Lots for us to discuss. Don't look so worried, I have your best interests at heart."

"This is crazy."

"Yes, yes. Now ski-daddle, scoot. We're both a little tense."

"I *am* tired Barry, I've never been so exhausted."

"Leave it then. If you do me the courtesy of waiting until the morning, we'll see what can be done."

Tim nodded, rising from his crouch. "I'm off to lie down, I'm not thinking properly. My head's breaking apart. You gonna be OK?"

"Me, ha ha, yes. Soon be right as rain." Barry felt the nerves start to respond in his legs and sighed in relief. His face remained expressionless. He didn't offer Tim a lift.

Tim stumbled off, on foot, in the direction of his hotel. The cold night air calmed him and he tried to ignore the rising tide of screams inside his head.

Barry watched him go then rubbed his legs and began moving his feet slightly. In a few minutes he could stand. Thug Number Two brushed the dirt from his boss's sealskin coat.

How had Cavanah done that?

Turning to his faithful assistants, he spoke in a low voice. "Monica Vincent's ex-husband is a Mighty Fucking Head. The guy is off the scale and a potential problem. That was the sneakiest attack I've ever experienced. And I've seen a few. Right through our defences like they weren't there!"

Thug Number One nodded, blankly.

"Get me back to the hotel then locate him. He's probably on his way back home. Don't do anything else though. He's mine.

Understand?" insisted Barry.

" " nodded Thug Number Two, looking tough and resolute.

"And get me another pocket telly!"

Supported by his trusted associates, Barry hobbled slowly back to the limo. His legs were stiff and awkward but with massage and concentration they began to respond normally. Soon, after a few phone calls, Barry started to feel a little better. He still hoped to salvage something from the Wondrous Tim, if at all possible.

If not, well, there were plenty of other cookies in the jar.

***

Tim crept into the hotel after a troubled walk. The night receptionist seemed concerned but handed him the second room key without comment. As he stepped into the lift, his vision was almost gone, his hands trembled and his legs shook. A thick mist engulfed his sight and daubed clouds of grey across his thoughts. He was utterly drained, starving, practically asleep on his feet. Reaching the room at last, the remains of a kebab he couldn't remember buying slipped from his fingers and onto the carpet. Chilli sauce was smeared round his mouth, on his jacket, over his hands. The kebab was vile but he could have eaten ten more.

He threw off shoes, pants and jacket. Still wearing the sweat-drenched polo neck, he crawled under the covers and snuggled up to Monica.

They had undressed her! The bastards!

Tim had been assured they would look after her, get her back safely to their room. He'd have words with Barry in the morning!

Lying in the comfortable darkness, the commotion in his head died off a little. He struggled to remove his shirt and accidentally elbowed Monica. She stirred.

"Jim?"

"Yes, it's good old Jim. Oh, no, wait, I got it wrong. It's only Tim. Still, easy mistake, eh?" Irrational rage threatened to overwhelm him and he gritted his teeth. The roaring in his mind increased in volume by a few notches.

Monica opened one eye.

"Jesus, did I say Jim? Oh love, I'm sorry! I was so deeply asleep."

"You know, I don't think I want to have this conversation," he said. "Not now. I'm tired and I think we should both say nothing. Lower our guns and let's sleep. Otherwise one of us might say that one thing too many, go that one step too far." He was almost pleading now, battling off dark premonitions.

"Tim, I swear there's nothing for you to be jealous of – of for me to be ashamed of. I've hid any association with Jim it's true. Not because there is anything to hide – but because I was afraid of *your* insecurity."

"So it's my fault and I'm the enemy? Ain't that just peachy?"

"No, don't put words in my mouth. It is *my* fault for not trusting you to handle it. I should have known you are more of a man than that."

"You think so?"

"Of course I do. I'm here aren't I?"

Doubt gnawed at Tim's soul, but he desperately wanted to believe.

"But you loved him . . . more than me," he said.

"I love *you* Tim. You are the one I have waited for all these years. My soul mate."

"I felt sure it was him. You did too."

"I did, for years. I admit it." Her eyes burned into him in the semi-darkness.

"You're saying you were wrong?" he asked.

"I am. I want to be with you. I want us both to trust each other with everything. So Tim, you can tell me anything, even your darkest secret, and it won't make any difference to how I feel." She raised her head from the pillow and paused, wondering whether it was wise to continue. But a weird intuition was at work and she found it impossible to stop. "I know you keep things from me, do things I don't know about for your own gain. Tim, we're a team. Make it *our* gain from this moment onwards! Your dark side turns me on and you shouldn't hide it any longer. No more pretence."

"You and Jim are completely finished?"

"Jim is, basically, a restless, thoughtless, fanatical arsehole. He'll never settle down and, frankly, I don't know what planet would suit him. We'll have to talk about some of the stuff he's been doing, but in the morning." Tim raised an eyebrow but remained silent. She continued. "He pretends to be hip but in reality he's just drifting through life on the long summer holiday he started at Uni. He's a whining, leftie tree-hugger with no ambition or common sense. I need a grown-up. I want the luxuries that life has to offer and I'm prepared to do whatever is necessary to get them. With you if you'll have me."

"If I'll have you?" Tim gasped, his heart beating itself into a frenzy. "Monica, I don't know what to say. You're right, I *have* done some bad stuff. I let my ambition blind me to the possible harm I could do. I took without permission. If you love me after I tell you my secret . . . it would be more than I deserve. Dare I?" Uncertain for a moment, Tim wiped the greasy sweat from his brow. It was now or never. His head buzzed as if a swarm of bluebottles were trapped inside.

"My darkest secret, as doubtless you've already guessed, is that my career has flourished on your energy. I guess it means we two are . . . complete. One. I *do* love you so much."

"I don't understand. What do you mean, my energy?"

"Your power. Monica, you are so special. Your mental strength is extraordinary. Way beyond anyone I know of. Mine has come on leaps and bounds but I'm not in your league. I'm doing it for real though."

"I never doubted you. But you, what, borrowed my *energy*?"

"Not borrowed, really. I took it. It will replenish, in time. It always does. I'm so sorry."

"You took it tonight – for the show? Is that why I missed everything and woke up here? How many other times have you done it?"

"I only took a fraction, most nights we did a show. Tonight, rather more. And only on this tour, never before. Well, hardly ever. I used . . . others before. Monica you should have seen me tonight – "

She interrupted him. "Tim, what you just told me . . . "

"I'm not proud of it. I'll spend the rest of my life making it up to you." He clasped her shoulders, gripping her tightly as they both sat up in bed. "I'm so glad I got it off my chest. Now there will be no more secrets between us. And there's no harm done really."

"Tim, hold on a minute. You can't seriously expect me to just shake this off. I'm going to need to think about it very seriously."

"But you said . . . ?"

"I don't want to talk about it. You just admitted mentally raping me. For fuck's sake!"

"I wouldn't put it like that. You never felt anything, did you? Except today. And I said I was sorry. I could have kept quiet!" A sick feeling was building in Tim's stomach, worse even than the effects of the kebab. He found it hard to breathe. His world was turning on its head and there was nothing he could do about it but hang on and hope.

"I fucking wish you *had* kept quiet, you bastard! How could you do that to me?" Monica was furious. Her whole body began to shake uncontrollably.

Tim looked desperate. "I thought I was your soul mate?" he whispered.

"I don't know what you are any more!"

Monica leaped out of bed and began looking for her clothes.

In her mind, something felt wrong. Thoughts were coming slowly, some of them jumbled or fragmented. It was like the onset of a bad trip. Strange ideas were swirling around and it was increasingly difficult to disregard them. Had she been at a funeral, she'd have stood up and shouted 'bollocks'. Show her a cliff at that moment and she'd have thrown herself off.

Underneath Monica's mental uproar was an overwhelming urge to believe in something. Anything. She'd never experienced anything like it before. Her life seemed to have no purpose; it was shallow and unsatisfying. A joke. Her first great love had gone wrong and it transpired her second needed her so he could suck the energy from her mind and fuel his career! She was almost delirious as she stumbled around looking for her knickers.

"How the hell did I get back here? Who undressed me?"

"Er . . . " began Tim. But he was running on empty. He began to weep and dropped his head in shame.

Monica felt her feelings for him diminish in that moment. He seemed so utterly wretched kneeling upright on the bed, head bowed. To Monica, he was nothing more than an aberration. He was erased. Blanked. For the time being, at least. Until she was able to think it all through.

Mostly dressed, she ran from the room, snatching Tim's car keys from the writing desk. He remained on the bed, stunned, not caring to follow.

Tim's worst nightmare.

Every fear had become reality.

His darkest secret really had been too dark to share. He should have known.

He was worthless.

He was weak.

A vampire.

A rapist, she said.

Had they gone to sleep, not spoken – as he had wanted – all would have ended well. Yet, with his heart's desire in his grasp, he'd pushed the self-destruct button. Perhaps she was to blame. After all, for a moment she'd made it feel like the real thing, that thing he'd never had. Unconditional love both ways.

Tim back on the bed and his mind raced.

With the swiftness of a motorway pileup, his consciousness came under attack. There was no time to prepare a defence, no way to fend it off. He called out to Monica for help.

She did not hear. Already she was beyond him.

Beyond Tim.

A Brief History of Tim. Part 1.

Timothy Justin Thyme was born at a very young age as is customary. His parents were quite old when he appeared, a late and far from welcome surprise to greet their waning years.

They tried to do their best for him but they didn't have much money. Or energy.

As a child, Tim eventually grew to despise them. They were so lifeless and wrinkled compared to his friends' parents, and so slow-witted.

Quite by accident, he learned how to hear their thoughts. It first happened one afternoon as he helped them in the garden – one of the fascinating hobbies of the decrepit. He was sulky and upset because he'd really wanted to visit the seaside and run along the beach with his new kite. He wondered why they always disappointed him and so he watched them, concentrating very hard. Their thoughts were faint and indistinct at first but he practised and was soon able to snoop on their most intimate secrets with ease. Not that it made him any happier.

His mother wished they had not been blessed with a child at all.

His father fumed at how unfair the faith lottery was. They were both Catholics and neither had wanted to be parents. And they had been so careful for so many years. It was hard to believe they'd slipped up at their age.

I'd kick the Pope's senile head in if he popped in for a cup of tea, thought his father one day. He stopped going to church and took his worship to the snooker club instead, which made Tim's mother unhappier than ever.

Tim listened in on their private thoughts, becoming quite accomplished at the art. He could 'do' his parents and, later, he could 'do' others also. His talent began to shape his life, give it direction. In his late teens, he took to the stage, performing small-scale hocus-pocus, mystical shenanigans and hypnotism. He learned the tricks of the trade well.

Tim Thyme was present when his parents were killed in a freak accident. He had tried to save them, it was reported.

When he met Monica everything changed. He found he could extend his powers by absorbing her synaptic potential. It became a drug to him. At the same time he fell in love with her.

And Monica loved him back. For at least one perfect moment.

At 04:00 Tim awoke his brain sizzling as if heating up. Voices in his head were screaming at him.

"Stop resisting you fool, stop resisting, STOP RESISTING you fool STOP RESISTING YOU FOOL . . . " over and over.

Tim reached for the phone but clumsily knocked it off the table and onto the floor. The pillow was stained with chilli sauce and blood, the latter from biting his tongue while asleep. By an enormous effort of will, he cut off the tainted reserves of Monica's energy. In desperation he deprived himself of the only power he might have used to sustain himself. An infection was running through him.

Already his memory pools were flooded with the strange orange virus. He battled to close them off, especially the recently formed memories of Monica and her judging glance. Sliding lightly, almost imperceptibly over every neural connection, alien impulses flowed through his brain and located his core personality, the tiny kernel that still remained untouched.

"It wasn't all smoke and mirrors," he snarled, flooding his brain with an acidic fog. As it destroyed the thin orange and gold strands, they shrivelled and turned black to leave a thick tarry residue. When the fog reached the depleted pool of stolen energy, the gas hissed and strengthened his makeshift seal, blocking if off completely. Thus he ensured he could never take from it again, no matter how he was tempted. He locked the infection-soaked power away and searched his mind for further traces.

His chance to be an outstanding talent had come and gone. Without Monica, there would be no more shows and he could never return to the mind reading and sleight of hand. Tim was surprised to realise he didn't care. Having seen the look in her eyes, he didn't care about anything any more.

He tried to flush away the black goo from his brain but it clung there, resisting his best efforts. At least it seemed inert. The voices – the chaotic thoughts – were silent.

He collapsed and slept fitfully.

Chapter Fifteen

Men are not prisoners of fate, but only prisoners of their own minds.   Frankie D. Rooster

Barry McGarry was puzzled. It was mid-morning and nobody had seen hide nor hair of Tim. Having eaten two breakfasts already, scanned the papers, the local news, the national news and the BBC website, Barry was anxious to conclude their business and be off. As the country's top PR man, he didn't like to wait around – or to be seen doing so.

The manager had been persuaded to clear out the bar and Barry set up a temporary office with a laptop computer, miniature television, various hand-held electronic devices and the remains of his second breakfast, all arranged with fanatical neatness on the table. He made a dozen phone calls and arranged meetings – particularly one for later that same day, with his latest protégé, soon to be widely known as the Choir Master. He sent a few emails and reassured a young actress in London that the part she so desperately wanted would be confirmed as hers by the end of the day. Barry loved to keep busy and juggled people and information for the sheer pleasure of it. Apart from a slight migraine and the irritating incident after the show, he declared himself well satisfied with his trip to Sheffield. And even that could be turned to his advantage. Everything could.

The media were clamouring for information, for interviews, for eyewitness accounts of the show. Surprisingly few of these were forthcoming and the details were vague and confused, which was perfect.

Quark TV had proved themselves hopelessly inadequate. A deal had eventually been struck with the bleary-eyed fellows from Channel 4 over a carrier bag full of coke and a selection of coloured pills left over from a 'drugs are bad' exposé. He reflected on the mountain of useful data they'd willingly divulged less than 5 hours ago in this very bar. He examined the photographs of their unfettered fun one last time before storing them away with many, many others on his laptop.

Barry remained confident he could do something with Tim, once he straightened out a few issues, laid out the ground rules. Unusual events were occurring and his mind throbbed excitedly as it tested possible connections. His people had located Jim Cavanah but of the ex-wife there was no sign. She'd taken Tim's car and vanished into the night. Which was interesting.

Annoyed, Barry sent his men up to Tim's room, as he was not answering the phone. Presently, the wondrous entertainer arrived looking deadbeat and grumpy. Barry nodded at Thug Number One, who closed the door and stood with his back to it, as if on guard. Thug Number Two took up a position directly behind Barry who powered off his laptop carefully and looked up.

"Tim, you look dreadful," he said cheerily.

"What the hell is going on? These goons practically dragged me out of bed. They insisted I come down right away. I feel like shite. I'm sorry but I'm going to have to do this some other time."

"Hmm, you do look a bit peaky. OK Tim, I'll cut to the chase. The abbreviated introduction, you might say." He took a deep breath, patted his lips with a napkin and smiled coldly. "Tim, my organisation works on trust and if I can't trust my people to give me instant, accurate information, I have a very hard time putting myself out for them. Do you understand?"

"Sure. Look if it's about last night – "

"Last night was a poor start to our professional relationship and best forgotten. However, you gave me the impression you were working against me, Tim, and that's bad. You took the side of a man who, by all rights, should be your enemy so I was very concerned about that. Now I discover your lucky charm has gone walkabout again. Has she returned to *him*?"

"I don't know. How do you know she's gone?"

"I make it my business to know things Tim. It's what I do. And you see how easy it would have been to say who assaulted me? You and I can do great things but only if we work together. You really don't want to oppose me, especially not now we're in business together."

"I didn't actually look at the contract yet, sorry."

"Oh the contract doesn't matter. I like to work on verbal contracts. It boils down to trust every time with me."

"Look, Barry, I feel pretty ropey. I'd love to stay and chat but we'll have to do it some other time."

"Oh, I don't think so Tim. I'm here. You're here. What better time could there be?"

Thug Number Two pushed the palms of his hands together and a strange crunching noise sprang from the over-developed muscles of his upper arms. Then he folded them again and gazed, unblinking at Tim.

"Charming," said Tim. "Is he supposed to frighten me?"

"Only if you're very wise," laughed Barry coldly.

"The truth is," began Tim, "I was told at school never to rat on anyone. I've stuck to it ever since. That's all there is to it. I didn't take sides against you."

"Well, let that be an end to it. You lied to me for the first and only time Tim. As long as I have your word for that we can put it all behind us."

"This is ridiculous. You're behaving like a small-time gangster!"

Barry's mouth widened into a grin, a demented baby with slits for eyes.

"I really hope our relationship isn't going to go downhill. It would be tragic because I really like you. And everyone is so excited after last night. You haven't even asked me about the TV deal? It's almost as if you don't care!"

Tim felt a strange sensation. Excitement mixed with misery, relief mixed with fear. His future career depended on him doing more shows of epic proportions – but how? His career was over even before it had properly started.

"Good reviews?" he asked quietly.

"Aha, at last. This is the Tim I expected to have breakfast with. Well over an hour ago incidentally, sleepy-head. I planned to demonstrate that I've got your best interests at heart. Then we could have explored how our partnership will work and you would have been well on the way to everything you've dreamed of. You really won't find a better manager than me. I guarantee it."

"I'm sorry," said Tim. "We had a row."

"Oh dear. Nothing serious I hope?"

"I don't think she'll be coming back."

"Why do I get the feeling that is going to cause you problems, professionally?" McGarry asked.

"I'm sorry, I really don't want to talk about this now."

"A tender subject eh? Well, I don't know if I explained it properly earlier. I thought I did but perhaps I'm losing my touch. Thing is, I *do* like my people to give me instant, accurate information." Barry's streetwise cockney coming to the fore. Tim shivered and imagined a cockroach wearing silver boots scampering up his spine.

"I'm imploring you to give me some time to rest. I need to think it all through. I loved her for God's sake! Love her. I love her."

"Do you indeed! Or do you *need* her because she has attributes you can't do without?" Barry paused for a moment and muttered, half to himself, "my God, imagine the two of them combined!"

"What are you talking about?" Tim suddenly felt hemmed in. Bad things were coming, he absolutely and utterly knew it. Unavoidable too. He was, all at once, terribly afraid.

"Enough of this buggering about," said Barry. Thug Number Two jerked upright as if an electric current had passed through his body. He placed his hands on his boss's shoulders. Barry spoke directly into Tim's brain.

"I've seen a few people like you over the years. A bit of talent, a lot of charm and a good line or two. But your good friend Mr Cavanah could blow you away using less than 10% of his mind. I watch out for these things and, trust me, you're really nothing special. Then I discover you draw most of your power from somewhere else."

"It's my business how I do the show." Tim stammered. Suddenly a bolt of pain hit him like an axe to the forehead. The black tar in his mind began to fizz and expand.

"Jesus, what was that?"

"Something you could probably do yourself, on a much smaller scale. Carl here is not by my side for his rugged looks or sparkling conversation. He's not even here to hit people for me. He does that for himself. That's a joke Tim. Please laugh!"

"You're starting to scare me Barry. Do you zap everyone who doesn't do what they're told? Nice technique by the way."

Tim's voice betrayed his fear.

"Now then," said Barry softly, "you really have nothing to worry about. To avoid further pain it would be best to answer my questions quickly and accurately. If you do that, you will survive to become very, very rich."

"How could – Cavanah – attack you with his mind? I don't get it. He's not into all this."

"No indeed he isn't. But as I've just demonstrated, not everyone relies on illusion. Ahar, Tim lad! Don't tell me you don't know some gifted people who can do it for *real*? There's more real magic around than the Sunday rags would have us believe. Your friend is a highly dangerous individual. And on this topic I'm a bit of an expert."

Tim felt his mind start to quake. Barry had awakened the dormant virus and it was replicating rapidly. Barry's voice seemed to grow quieter and more threatening. And Tim discovered he didn't care. He poked out his tongue carelessly, childishly. Barry did not react well to such gestures.

"Why Tim, our relationship is going change drastically right about now I'm afraid. It's not so much that you are my client any more. You are my bitch!"

"Fuck you. And tell this troll to piss off too!"

One of the trolls dropped Tim. Quite hard. Then he did it again. Presently there was blood.

Tim floundered in a pain-soaked haze.

They were alone. The three of them. Thug Number One had been rewarded, he had hurt Tim really quite badly. Then he left, whistling the theme to a popular soap.

The pain was excruciating. Tim faced Barry who sat, quietly, sipping orange juice. A gentle tap of a napkin and he turned his eyes upon Tim, unleashing the scariest of all expressions: genuine regret.

Even given time to recover, Tim could never have resisted a mind like McGarry's. His thoughts were faster than electricity. Even with all Monica's energy, Tim could not have kept up. Nevertheless, he defended himself until his strength was spent but did not launch a counter-attack. His opponent demonstrated a catalogue of coercive assaults while filing his nails. And waiting.

Barry McGarry was a patient and ruthless man. He savoured the gathering of information. Even information he already knew.

Tim suffered for a long time but when his eyes finally dimmed, there was a faint smile on his lips.

Barry McGarry was far from pleased. The fool had no strength, no will, very few skills of any kind. Yet he had refused to give any information about Cavanah and the former Mrs Cavanah, both apparently rather unusual people.

Barry McGarry was baffled but intrigued.

Chapter Sixteen

Genius is nothing more than childhood, recaptured at will.
                                                Baudelarse

The pipes rattled, the boiler groaned, mice scurried in the attic. It was late – or early depending on your point of view. All through the building, no human sounds could be heard, no thoughts could be sensed. Bits of striped tape were strewn around outside in haphazard patterns. It was as if nobody lived there any more.

Arriving in Preston, Jim had dropped off the car at Dave's, posting the keys through the letterbox. There were no lights on and he was satisfied to note his blanket program fully operational and intact.

From there, he had walked home, quietly and pensively through the town, having planned to grab a pizza or some chips. It had taken only a short while to realise something was badly amiss. The hour was usually reserved for clubbers, skimpily dressed young things goose bumpy and giggling. However, instead it was marked by extraordinary activities.

An impromptu orgy had been in full swing – in the Garden of Rest, where tramps typically huddled to sleep. Judging by the array of pasty naked bottoms pointing skywards, at least ten people, mostly men, had been writhing and sweating over a few unfortunate females. Inexplicably, the girls had been crying for more, begging any passer-by to climb aboard and give them a good shagging. Ordinarily, Jim was not a man who would shirk any challenge – but he decided it was a good time to begin work on a list of exceptions. Nodding a hasty 'no thanks, sister', he hurried quickly by.

A few minutes later he found an old woman, lying close to the entrance of the Shopping Centre, her head beaten in, blood draining into the gutter. A few feet away, a policeman licked his truncheon, then beamed at Jim proudly.

"Evenin' sir," he said. "Lovely night for it, wouldn't you say?"

"Not for her," said Jim, appalled.

"Oh no sir, indeed not. Most amusing quip sir," said the copper. His radio went off at that moment and he barked loudly into it. "Yes indeed Sarge, I 'ave nullified the old fucker. Right, right. *Pacified* the old fucker. Sorry? What? Right. I will. Understood. I came across the poor elderly lady wot 'ad been mugged. I hestimate that I will apprehend 'er hattacker forthwith, dee dah dee dah."

Jim staggered away in a kind of blind panic, meeting two other coppers coming in the opposite direction.

"Oh my God!" cried one of them.

"Again?! You bastard!" gasped the other.

"What?" said truncheon cop.

Jim had finally arrived home after witnessing two further orgies, countless thefts and break-ins and having rescued an aged taxi driver from being kicked to death by several turbaned Sikhs. He had enjoyed hitting them.

Watching the action from a first-class vantage point in Jim's head, Spike cheered. Jim had progressed dramatically and it was evident he would never again require good old Spike for the action stuff. Nor Max for his cunning. Maybe he could have used Plover's focused – if melancholy – thought regimes, but they were lost forever. Spike lay in simulated long grass watching clouds float by and dreaming of his departed siblings.

The flat was a welcome refuge but before Jim could sleep, there were some important jobs in his head that couldn't wait. He squatted on the beanbag, hurled the empty pizza box across the room, licked his fingers clean of grease, and breathed deeply in through his nose. He then closed his eyes, breathed out and entered a newly refurbished personal *headspace*.

He now accessed his mind via a single, sliding glass door. Outside was nothingness. He gained entry using a secret password stored in no known memory location. Although the House visualisation had been fully dismantled and he'd dispensed with the garden, the path remained. It led directly from where he stood forming a snaking line of smooth brown pebbles that ran to the distant horizon. The path was set in lush green grass, tall and wavy that extended as far as the simulation extended. Overhead, the sky was a cloudless blue and a pleasant, light wind cooled the air. Here and there, shadows danced through the grass.

Crossing his legs, he sifted shiny brown stones lazily through his fingers. In a space before him, a section of sky roughly two feet square glowed slightly green. In this floating window he studied the virus code captured earlier. He soon became profoundly engrossed and later, disturbed. The programming was of an inferior nature but designed to crash in the dirtiest way possible, always rescheduling itself as its final exit instruction. And, although the coding was dreadfully inept, the underlying theme was fiendishly clever. Its purpose was to extract from archive a selection of ancient behavioural programs and reinstate them. The consequences of this would depend on the nature of each routine, but some primal, unpredictable behaviour would surely be manifest in those infected. This he felt he had witnessed already.

It's as I thought. Tim was only a pawn!
It is clearly here in Preston too.
How far has it spread?

If unchecked, the virus could corrupt humanity's mental operating system and perhaps instigate a complete regression of higher thought processes. It might lead to a more primitive brain-time, a winding back of the internal clock. Jim hypothesised many outcomes, none of them good. Was this *it* for the human race? He shuddered as he imagined confused and frightened minds armed with today's hi tech weaponry and computers rather than with pitch forks. He dared not imagine what would happen when the world's richest, most powerful and aggressive nation got a dose of whatever was loose in Preston. Nobody wanted to annoy a monster that was already flinching at every shadow, its finger poised over the trigger as it pursued demons, real and imaginary.

If the growth of reason shifted into reverse, where might it end? The Inquisition, the burning of witches, blood sacrifices to angry Gods . . . these might be mischievous pranks in comparison.

Eh-oh, he said, Tellytubby-style.

In a bid to squash the growing depression, Jim turned to something he believed he had just cracked. Having error-checked the last few lines during the drive home, he wasn't quite anxiety-free when he came to execute the *De-CompileEverything* program.

In the event, he needn't have worried.

Suddenly, the deepest base code in his head became readable, the gobbledegook unravelled in full.

Jim whooped out loud as he saw that his decompiler had managed to extract a descriptive *file header*, although it was unable to locate any additional commentary from the author. Fortunately the code required no comments. It was simplicity itself, in fact hardly a programming language in any recognisable sense. Jim scrolled up and down the decompiled text in amazement. It was unlike the ugly viral code, or his own.

The program he opted to view first, on a whim, related to the learning of basic skills. Apparently of some sophistication, it was written in childish rhyming couplets. Its function, according to the *file header*, was to spawn a suite of other programs whilst archiving redundant or unused elements. It featured a series of flexible guidelines in place of rigid commands; its subroutines interacted with a global array – a neural construct of some kind, waiting to be filled.

As he examined further examples of the ancient, sometimes puerile code, comprehension flooded in. The Aesir – whoever they were – had deliberately altered the course of human development. They had done this by suppressing many of the venerable, open-ended philosophies and shutting down many lines of progress. The spreading madness suggested to Jim that they were only just getting started.

They had to be stopped.

Amazingly, no sooner had he he reached this decision, a potential solution presented itself. Revelation danced across his floating screen and, as if to emphasise the scale of the implications, a thunderclap rumbled across the plain. Jim lay back by the path and gazed heavenwards. Then he instigated a series of automated string searches for confirmation.

While he waited, a few clouds drifted into view. He gave them the shapes of unicorns, rockets or goblin faces. Also, there were breasts. There always are in clouds, right? A short while later, the automated searches interrupted his daydreaming using a comical fart noise. They confirmed what he had already guessed to be true: every one of the base programs was signed identically – with simple initials.

The initials were G.D.

It meant something, he knew it. He knew he was on the verge of recalling something really important, a forgotten fact that, once remembered, would resolve his problems with reality forever. He often had this feeling during heavy Magic Mushroom trips but on this occasion it was far more forceful, and annoying. The thought nagged at him, frustratingly elusive. His mind swayed at the edge of a precipice and threatened to leap into the unknown. Eventually, he admitted defeat but assigned a low-priority generic search routine to continue trying to recover the memory.

Jim meditated for a moment, clearing his mind. The sky became blue once more, all clouds dissipated. Putting aside desires to update some of his own work by ripping rip off some of the techniques glimpsed in the rather elegant base code, he turned to a more pressing matter. It was vital to discover more about his enemies, and consider a course of immediate action.

Slowly, his reference library catalogue scrolled across the virtual screen and he performed cross-checking against all obvious keywords. His library recalled facts he had long forgotten, books read as a child but stored at the back of his untidy mind. Or in a cupboard. Or under a pile of iffy magazines. Many juvenile parts of his personality were now dead, perished in the destruction of his House. Much of their knowledge had been disconnected. Fortunately, the bare bones remained.

The Aesir, he remembered, were the Norse Gods. He *knew* the name was familiar. If related, these clearly enjoyed playing different roles before their adoring fans. He wondered if out there he'd find the Allfather, Odin. Or the Thunder God, Thor. Jim smiled as he quickly refreshed his memory. He remembered enjoying tales of the Aesir and Vanir, particularly those stories where lesser beings overcame impossible odds.

Quickly, he considered some of the others. Loki began as merely mischievous but went rapidly downhill in most accounts. He was also known as Satan, Ah Much, Anubis, Malvolian and Malcolm Bottomley of Slough, if Jim's research was correct. Then there was Tyr, God of War, also known as Mars. And Heimdall, also Mercury and Hamfistus, although here Jim began to doubt some of the checksums. After several cross references, he realised that Odin was also called Jupiter, God, Jesus and the Holy Goat, along with Brekyirihunuade, Quetzalcoatl, Merlin and Ron Jeromay . . . The list was endless. Thor was probably Gilgamesh, but was he also Hercules? And Thor's son would go on to be greater than his father who, like all the Gods, would perish at Ragnarok. Details, details, details. They swirled around like grimy water through a sticky plughole. And what about Xena, Warrior Princess . . . ?

Data overload.

Exhaustion was setting in. Much of the data appeared corrupted, perhaps by too many Marvel comics or too much telly. Frowning and yawning simultaneously, Jim looked up to see fresh clouds gathering in the sky above. His strength was fading. Conflicts and contradictions set red warning lights flying around and swirling into the sky, lighting the clouds as if in preparation for a storm. He started to doubt some of the connections he had made but deemed the details unimportant. He had got the gist. And had made up his mind what had to be done.

Jim Cavanah decided to cure the world of Religion once and for all. It had served its purpose. According to the programs he had read, it should have been archived long ago.

The time of the gods and all mystical beings was over. Jim decreed it.

Chapter Seventeen

If God lived on earth, people would break his windows.   *Youish Proverb*

Monica awoke to the mingled smells of toast and freshly ground coffee. Jim had tidied the flat during the night then cleaned and polished every (accessible) surface without her hearing a thing. Three large, bulging black bags of rubbish lurked under the kitchen table awaiting their optimum moment to rupture unexpectedly. As black bags do.

"What day is it?" she called.

"Sunday. Do you want jam or syrup?"

"Syrup please."

Shortly Jim wandered through with a tray. He'd shaved and was wearing a clean t-shirt.

"This looks lovely," said Monica, as he carefully placed the tray down.

They ate a breakfast of delicious toast that disgorged an impossible amount of gloopy syrup in all directions. The toast crunched scrumptiously and sticky crumbs found their way onto Jim's chin, following some unknowable migratory instinct. Monica wiped them all away, as she had when they were married. Then she drew back, a fraction quicker than intended.

"Did you sleep OK?" he munched.

"Like a dead thing. This settee's pretty comfy and I was out like a light." She didn't mention the sleeping bag's damp, musty smell, guessing Jim would explain where he usually kept it and, inevitably, sabotage the mood.

"Do you want to tell me what happened?" he asked gently. He licked his fingers but a wayward blob of syrup dripped unseen onto his t-shirt as it always did.

"I'm not sure I want to."

"Fair enough. More coffee?"

She nodded, gripping the mug tightly with both hands. "This is yummy. I really appreciate it. I know I had no right to turn up on your doorstep like that."

"Look, whatever happens, always come to me. You know you can. And you don't have to tell me anything if you don't want to. If or when you feel like talking, we'll talk."

"Thanks Jim."

"No sweat."

For a while neither spoke, but it was a comfortable silence. The coffee was first class and Jim felt at peace.

"There's some weird shit going down right now," he said at last. "As you've probably guessed. Things could get really bad and I think it's my job to fix it. I might even be responsible."

"I love it when you make absolutely no sense. Which, Jim Cavanah, is most of the time I have to say!"

She had slept in one of his old t-shirts and Jim almost managed not to admire her large nipples bidding him a cheery 'good morning' through the worn material. Monica kept the sleeping bag wrapped around her during breakfast, perhaps because she was wearing very little else and wished to avoid complication. Jim yearned for complication but kept his sensible head on. Admirably, he thought.

"What do you want to do today?" he asked. "You're welcome to stay here as long as you like, in case you haven't made any decisions."

"I suppose I don't actually know. I'll have to ring Tim. I did take his car after all - it's parked outside. I'll need to get my stuff. And find somewhere to stay."

"Monica?"

"What?"

"Doesn't this all feel a bit weird to you? You're totally chucking Tim just like *that*?"

Jim awoke instantly. His paranoia was even sabotaging his dreams now! But it had been too good to be plausible. And therefore a dream!

It was true he was back at the flat. But alone. It was 08:01 Sunday morning and the flat was cold. It reeked of garlic and something only identifiable as 'greasy'. Prior to sleeping, he had again searched for Monica with his mind. If she was out there, she specifically didn't want to be found. And with Monica, that meant you didn't find her.

Jim cursed his empty fridge and poked about in the grey ice of the freezer compartment for anything edible. And he contemplated black instant coffee, grumpily. So much for dreams.

There could be no return to work in the morning. The very idea seemed surreal and he realised he probably wouldn't go back ever again. The world had changed.

After a microwaved vegetable curry and a large mug of dismal black coffee, Jim returned to his beanbag and set incense burning in an attempt to exorcise the spirit of pizza.

Re-entering his *headspace*, he was surprised to see that the early morning reverie was playing from the first scene – and on a glowing cinema screen that had materialised in the verdant grass. The screen was fixed, motionless, hanging several feet in the air and bordered by an orange curtain. This was quite unexpected.

Intrigued, Jim left the path and positioned himself directly in front of the dream presentation. The resolution was blocky, magnified at low resolution, but he again saw his flat, impossibly tidy, and both himself and Monica chatting like old friends. He approached a little closer and peered round the back of the curtains, not much surprised to see that it only existed in one plane. From the rear, nothing but thin air could be seen. He returned to the front and sat in the grass, fascinated.

In the film, Monica was still speaking. The conversation continued seamlessly from the moment at which he awoke.

"Isn't it what you'd have told me to do?"

"Yes but, well . . ."

"Well what?"

"He didn't actually feel a bad sort to me, despite those strange vibes he threw out during the show. I'm afraid I wound him up a bit . . ."

"After the show?"

"Aye."

"You promised!"

"I know. But I was worried about you. I couldn't sense your presence."

"So you came galloping to my rescue?"

"It's what I do. I saw Tim only briefly. He was with a bloke with a posh suit and a nasty temper. Tim said you were exhausted and accused *me* of being responsible. His concern seemed genuine and I guess he did have a point. Then the nasty guy tried to zap me with a mental assault. He's a right little coercer, he is!"

"Tim was using me. He says I have powerful mind energy, whatever that means. Can it be true? I mean, I never even win at rock, paper, scissors!"

"He was *using* you?"

"He was taking my energy, he said. It pepped him up, apparently. Jim, is any of this possible?"

"Well, I didn't know brains needed energy, assuming you mean fuel-type. I'm not sure mine does but maybe it's another piece in the jigsaw. Mine has a standard operating speed but now I come to think of it, I don't know where the juice comes from and sometimes I get tired far too quickly."

"So you don't know everything about the brain?"

"Not really. Definitely not the grey organy part."

"Isn't that the whole *thing*?"

"No, don't think so. Not quite."

"But *you* never took any of my mental juice? When we were married?"

"Me? Perfectly happy with the regular kind. Anyway, I

wouldn't know how."

"If I didn't feel anything, why should I even care?" Monica seemed uncertain all of a sudden. "Am I overreacting?"

"Search me. Is this what you fell out about?"

"Well, last night I was totally furious about it. It felt so intense I completely lost it."

"Better give him a call," suggested on-screen Jim, coolly. The watching Jim thought this was all getting a bit far-fetched – and he was a vivid and imaginative dreamer, on the rare occasions of weed drought. Although the floating cinema screen had no visible speakers, the dialogue was crisp and clear as it arrived, along with every subtle inflection, in virtual Jim's virtual ears.

Suddenly the dream changed. Scenes involving unfamiliar people and places skipped by at high speed, reels whirled past too fast to make out major players. An obese, fleshy woman featured in one of them, then a wizened old lady polishing an ornate crucifix, or possibly a dagger. The smartly dressed, angry guy from the show followed. He squatted in the back seat of a plush limousine staring at a laptop computer. Then the scene shifted to 3 others (who looked eerily familiar) sitting around a campfire on an empty, grassy plain not unlike the one on which Jim now sat. There was no time to ponder this because, next, a waif-like blonde girl replaced them. She looked directly outwards from an austere room, or a cell hung with religious paintings. Jim shuddered involuntarily. And then a familiar, brawny older man with a thick neck and silver hair appeared briefly before fading away. Then the screen paused on an image of a newspaper. Its headline was: *Wondrous Tim in coma after landmark show!*

Gradually, the newspaper faded as, Jim guessed, the vision finally ended. The curtains closed silently, the screen went blank. Then it melted into the background as if it had never been there.

"I'm a clever bugger," he told himself.

He programmed a reminder to consider the meaning of the dream again later. Dreams often contained useful pointers and he was convinced this one contained material of significance. Being stoned for much of the time meant Jim rarely remembered dreams any more, at least not with the vivid detail of his childhood.

A tightening bladder indicated that the optimum moment had arrived for the offloading of coffee. Another price of surviving past forty. "Arse," he thought, and paused his program long enough to exit and go for a pee.

When he returned, he quickly created a floating computer screen and ran a search program looking for the character string "Tim in Coma". Within a few seconds he had located a series of files from the dream log.

This is a first, he grinned, realising the files were part of a vast directory of dreams that apparently extended as far back as his early teens. He then became lost scanning excerpts of dreams long-forgotten and marking many for further review. There were childhood dreams, adventurous dreams, wet dreams, nightmares and fantasies. There were running dreams, flying dreams and a recurring terrifying dream in which he was trapped inside a hill or sometimes a large prison-like building, unable to find a door or window big enough for him to pass through and therefore escape. In the dark, a malevolent sniffing creature followed patiently, tracking him by the scent of his fear. One day it would catch him and his real life would be over. He knew this for certain.

He most enjoyed the dreams in which he was a hero but even the dreams in which he was the villain had a certain allure. There were dreams in which nothing really happened except he was bathed in a swirling kaleidoscope of colour and sound. Monica turned up in many of them, sooner or later. He saw her as he'd first known her, a young girl in a Guide uniform. He saw her at their wedding, her hair full of confetti and her eyes full of love. He was stunned by the number of forgotten dreams. In some he saw his face, perhaps reflected in a mirror or a pool, but the face was never his own. Clearly, he also dreamed of being someone else.

On a hunch, quickly, he dashed off a rough comparison program as an attempt to pair up dreams with events he had actually experienced. On completion, the program's output contained timestamps and matching images that, initially, made no sense. For in some cases, the real life event occurred *after* he had dreamed about it.

Chapter Eighteen

Don't think. Feel.   *Bruce Lip*

In a private room, in a private institution, tucked away discretely in the Derbyshire Peak District, a figure lay in semi-darkness. A swarm of electrodes were attached to his head and torso by multicoloured wires carrying impulses to a bank of sleek machines, flashing, beeping and wheezing to themselves on a nearby trolley. Via an elaborate network of tubes, hulking grey contraptions pumped air noisily into the figure's lungs, coaxed nutrients into his stomach and extracted waste with a faint but sickening glugging noise.

Graphical representations of his vital signs and higher brain functions flickered erratically across a series of monitors whilst a printer offloaded a hard copy, building a relentless pile in the corner of the room. The man's eyes were closed, but in his mind he waded, lost, through a lake of perpetual fire.

Behind a face that was serene, Timothy Justin Thyme screamed.

Sparing no expense on Tim's care, Barry also posted a substantial reward for information leading to the capture of the vicious muggers. Numerous outbreaks of violence in Sheffield ensured that one more unprovoked, unexplained attack simply blended in, accepted without question by the overtaxed police.

As luck would have it, Chief Constable Codpiece – fellow lodge member and local boy made good – was well known to Barry. Many years ago he had been the subject of an intense data-gathering exercise by McGarry, a slick young journalist. He had learned of a delicate situation involving the then Inspector Codpiece and a wayward, confused cadet. With the help of several of his associates, half a dozen black bin liners and some cement, Barry had smoothed things over nicely. It had secured the ambitious officer's eternal gratitude.

Codpiece had placed his force on the highest alert. In other words, sleeping through the night shift and spending the afternoons patrolling Attercliffe's seedy pubs and massage parlours were temporarily outlawed. To a sea of petulant faces, he proclaimed that no stone should be left unturned and no avenue unexplored. A different audience might have found these to be painful clichés, but here the brightest amongst the rookie recruits took fluorescent marker pens and began drawing a random-looking series of lines across a large map of Sheffield. The sooner they identified all the avenues and checked them out, they reasoned, the sooner things could return to normal. Others went outside and began wandering around, peering under rocks, hoping to impress. Wincing, Codpiece leaned forward on his desk, folded his arms, and observed the cream of Britain's police force doing its very best.

Meanwhile, blissfully content, Barry instructed his people to press on with the video and DVD release of the show and to direct all queries about Tim to himself.

***

Having bitten off more than she could chew attempting the journey home, Monica skidded off the M62 onto the hard shoulder. It was a little after four. Due to the churning upheaval currently mincing her mind, she totally failed to appreciate the sign pronouncing the highest motorway in England at 372m or 1221 feet.

Slumping wearily against the BMW's steering wheel, her thoughts swirled in delirium. For several miles, she had swayed from lane to lane, swerving dangerously between occasional, heavily laden lorries, driven by grim-faced men.

Her Porsche had been sold several years ago, replaced by a petite, sensible, girly car – the sort Jim would have approved of. After it went wrong between them, even sitting in the Porsche had made her glum; she couldn't bear to drive it. Now she had taken Tim's beloved black *beamer* – but guilt was the furthest thing from her mind. Regrettably, so was sanity.

Had he known the results of his work, Jonathon Meed would have been moderately satisfied even though Tim – rather than Jim – had been the one to receive his virulent creation. Unaware of why she could no longer think, Monica turned off the engine and gazed at the curved line of orange lights shining through faint mist. A fever began to take hold and the occasional glare of headlights from passing lorries and cars seared her vision like branding irons. For a long time, there was silence. Clouds gathered and the moon, now low in the sky, was engulfed and sank into darkness.

Earlier, before her mind had started to stall, Monica thought she had heard Jim's voice. It was thin and reverberant, as if calling from a great distance. Unable to think clearly, she shut him out, but now she could hear other voices. They called to her and she was shocked to discover they would not be silenced. They came from *inside* her defences.

In her head, a roaring stadium of jeering, wailing, taunting voices degenerated into a maelstrom of pink noise, a vortex that denied all thought. Her basic motor skills were impaired too and it seemed unlikely she would make it home. Tim would be worried sick back at the hotel. Would he come after her?

Hardly - she'd nicked his car!

Monica could not concentrate. She began to see visions. Over dark, distant hills, the towering figure of a horned demon minced unsteadily on hairy goat legs. In best demonic tradition, he bore a flaming sword, which he swished inexpertly at treetops. Desperately hoping the image would vanish, she rubbed her eyes and noticed her forehead was slick and oily. Through the fevered haze, she recognised this as a bad sign.

Then the motorway lights dimmed and turned to a putrid green. Tiny goblin-like creatures appeared in the road, capering and leaping about, their pale, twisted and thoroughly naked bodies repellent yet impossible to disregard. A lone car passed at high speed and, chattering excitedly, several of them sprang before it to be instantly and horribly squashed under its wheels. The resulting splat sound, like over-ripe fruit exploding, was bad enough. But it was their insane giggles, even as they were crushed, that left her profoundly disturbed. The car didn't even slow down.

The inner voices bawled and yowled; she tried to make out what they were saying. After a time, a general message filtered through.

REPENT. JUDGEMENT DAY IS COMING.

Later, a more curious message.

HAVE YOU PICKED A GOD YET? HURRY! DON'T BE LATE!

Monica didn't have a mobile phone with her. In her haste to leave, she hadn't thought of it. If only I could get to Jim, she thought. He'd know what to do.

For an hour, she slept at the wheel, until a police patrol spotted her. By then, her mind was mush and the officer, believing her drunk, copped a quick feel, packed her in the car and returned to his base, in Leeds.

***

"It's me, open up man!"

Jim hit the button.

"Dave, hey. What time is it? Actually what day is it?" He released the main door lock and went in search of coffee. Then he cursed - still no milk.

Dave arrived bearing pizza and beer.

"Time for Sunday lunch traditional style Jim me old mucker!" He transmitted a smile that was infectious.

"More pizza, perfect! Started early have we?"

"Not yet. That's where you come in mate. Ah Jim, I've had the most marvellous rest. I've never been so refreshed and full of ideas. I slept through from yesterday afternoon right until this morning. Well, mostly," he leered to himself, distracted by private thoughts. "I have never felt better in my life. And it's all down to you! Hey, how was the show, did you go?"

Jim eyed the clock on the video that informed him it was 15:35 Sunday afternoon. "Pretty bloody far out actually," he said. "Our wondrous little friend can do elaborate image projection. He knows how to get into the mind too. It's what the world seems to want right now."

Dave opened the first pizza box and smiled. "Chilli, spicy sausage and peppers. Just how you like it!"

"Thanks man, this is great. I really must go shopping."

"So he was good? Isn't it weird to admit since you dislike him so much?"

"It *was* pretty wild. He's got talent and a smattering of flair, I suppose. I didn't say I didn't like him, did I?"

"Not in words mate, not in words."

"Unfortunately there's something badly screwed in his mind. He's full of a contagious virus. A mental freaking virus!"

"Far out. Hey, grab a toke of this!" Dave handed Jim a joint, ready-rolled to perfection.

"I love you man!" laughed Jim. "This is what Sundays are really about!"

"Oh, yeah. Hey, I meant to ask, you *will* do your magic on Sheila's mind soon, won't you? I really want her to dig this vibe!"

"And you call *me* a bloody hippy!" Jim laughed. "Dig this vibe, indeed!"

"But you will?" he persisted.

"Sure, in fact I now reckon the more people I 'do', the better. Something shitty this way comes!"

"Huh?"

"Well, as I said, the Wondrous Tim's performance involved spraying the audience with this 'ere virus. Lesser minds are probably cooked by now, I kid you not. Naturally I analysed it and it's designed to spread and really, permanently, fuck people up. Like, universally! I also reckon that our minds – right now – just yours and mine – are how they are *supposed* to be! I worked it all out at last."

"Cool. What do you think of the smoke?"

Jim took a long drag and grinned. "Fecking excellent. Thai grass?"

"Sure is. Picked it up not twenty minutes ago. Fresh as a virgin's chuff."

"A lovely turn of phrase!"

"I'm a deep thinking guy, as you know. Was Monica there? Last night, I mean?"

"I didn't see her. Dropped her off in the afternoon, then she was gone. Actually, I got a bit worried and went to look for her after the show."

"Couldn't you, you know, sniff her out? Mentally?"

"No, afraid not. She can blank me good can dear Monica when she chooses. Bless her little cotton socks."

"So where is she now?"

"With him, I guess. Unless you believe in dreams, and I'm starting to. I ran into him, Tim, after the show and he accused me of . . . well, I won't go into the details. Then this twat with him bloody attacked me!"

"I hope you gobbed him mate!" Dave felt the smoke take a hold and he came over all emphatic.

"He did a mind zap on me, the turd, or tried to. Luckily I've taken steps against that kind of thing after recent events. In fact, I'd better show you how to do it later, just in case."

"Spot on man, mmmm, this pizza is gorgeous."

"Sure is. Shame we have no Chocomel. Would be like old times in Amsterdam."

"Ah, Amsterdam . . ." Dave's eyes misted over. "Do you remember that time Dog turned blue?"

"And the hooker that recognised you from the previous trip?

Sure I do!"

"And we blew Carl's cover story. Laughed for hours about that."

"Cruel, I suppose. Maybe we should get the old gang together again for another weekend bender?" Jim munched pizza and opened a beer. Sometimes life was pretty good even when things had turned shitty. He wished it had been possible to make up with Monica but he guessed it would never happen now. He wondered where the rest of his life would take him.

"Daydreaming?" asked Dave, after a while.

"Yeah, a little. Things have totally changed and I don't know where I'm going next. Part of me wants to stay here forever, get wasted, watch some videos."

"Sounds like a plan. I left Sheila with a smile on her face so I'm in brownie points credit for ages." Dave squatted on the floor near the television and started to pore through the video collection.

"There's important stuff to do though," said Jim rather decisively. "I really can't ignore it. With great power comes . . . now what was it again?" He wiped his hands on his t-shirt, as usual.

"Being a total twat if you ask President Hush. Spiderman is a better bet. Wise, tortured, talented. Just like us."

Jim examined a crack in his window, sure it hadn't been there earlier. Squinting down into the yard, he saw a ginger tomcat vigorously clawing the base of the lilac tree. It saw him and sauntered off.

"It might be down to me – to us – to save the world. Imagine that dude!" Jim turned away from the window.

"Awww. Not today though? Look - Hellraiser - we haven't watched that for yonks! Draw the curtains man and get the bong!"

Jim was tempted but undecided. "Maybe it's not a great idea. I have this bad feeling. Have you seen anything peculiar around town?"

"Too right! I was going to tell you. A bloke in the pizza place just in front of me pulled a knife and attacked Frederico as he was sprinkling pepper. Not sure how but the police were there in minutes. Never seen them arrive anywhere so fast! What happened made me a bit sick though. They kicked the shit out of this guy and dragged him off in a black mariah. He wasn't resisting but looked half-dead by the time they'd finished. It was real brutal stuff, even for them. Then there was this naked jogger."

"Another? A chick, by any chance?"

"Nah, it never is. Fat old guy. He was jogging along London Road, trainers on, socks but that's it. Oh, and a hat."

"Hilarious!" laughed Jim.

"Aye, weird though."

"So you drove here?"

"Yeah, but I can leave the car. Sheila could pick it up later or something. We can chill."

They chilled.

***

"Excellent Codders," said Barry into his mobile. "Tell them she's my niece and that I'll pick her up personally this afternoon. If they get curious, tell them she's on special medication for depression and that I'll sort it all out until I get there. Nice work old friend." He snapped the mobile shut. It had been a busy yet interesting day so far but the best was, apparently, still to come. He instructed his driver that there had been a change of plan and they were going to Leeds.

Codpiece had done well. A girl answering Monica's description was currently sat in a cell, dazed and confused. She'd been picked up heading back along the M62 in the early hours, in no fit state to drive. The woman didn't even know her own name and seemed to be delirious or drugged.

This was perfect, chuckled Barry, allowing a rare smile to invade his face. It was an ideal opportunity to assist Tim's lady friend and learn everything he could from her.

Chapter Nineteen

There is nothing like returning to a place that remains unchanged to find the ways in which you yourself have altered.   Elsie Mandala

Bright Sunday morning sunshine streamed in through the window of the tiny cell. It was five O'clock and a single chime sounded, signalling the start of a new day. The hard palette bed was strangely comforting. Its thin cream-coloured sheets were crisp, clean and reeked of cheap detergent.

After much persuasion Julie had accepted Marjorie's invitation to stay at the convent. It seemed rather insane all things considered but there had been a desperate intensity in the eyes of both Father Stilton and Marjorie herself and suddenly she didn't feel like arguing any more. However, Julie had reckoned without this ludicrously early awakening. A morning person she was definitely not.

For a while she lay listening to bustling activity, as nuns young and old roused themselves for another joyous day serving as the unconsummated brides of Christ. Even at this stupid, crazy hour, a few voices broke cheerfully into song, quickly swelled by dozens more as they prepared their minds for Lauds.

Not the fucking Sound of Music, puh-lease! Julie stuck her fingers in her ears.

As if taking requests, a lone singer broke into the well-known Wylie classic:

I should be so lucky, lucky, lucky, lucky....

The others joined in happily.

Groaning, Julie rolled over and shut out the sunshine by burying her head under the pillow. During the night, she could have sworn she heard several familiar buzzing noises. The call of the personal massager, she smiled in recognition. Not that anything surprised her any more. She had witnessed some bizarre and disturbing incidents amongst the God-fearing. A dark mood was growing, a more fanatical, unbending outlook was spreading. It wouldn't take much for it to turn ugly.

The morning bell had been the final straw. Julie decided she would leave today regardless of their pleas. First, she intended to see if there was any spare cash kicking around. With all this talk of her holiness and power, maybe a collection plate or two had been filled in her name. It would be amusing to take money once again from those who formerly paid in used tenners. Without telling their wives.

Last night at mass, Julie had recognised more and more of her former clients, skulking at the edges of the flickering candlelight. As the congregation swelled, old memories had flooded back despite efforts to shut them out. A sinister curl of a lip, an arched eyebrow, the stench of dried semen, yellow teeth accompanied by foetid breath . . . Gradually, she began to remember details sealed away from her waking thoughts, details of each man who had hurt her and whom she failed to control. These men possessed some small power of their own. But that was then, she reminded herself with grim satisfaction.

It had started during Father Stilton's sermon. A grubby sleazebag in a crumpled suit, striped shirt and paisley tie had winked at her knowingly from the front pews. The sight of thick white hair sprouting from his large, fleshy ears was the memory trigger that began the unlocking process. Elsewhere, his hair was a distinctive Grecian 2000 silver-charcoal but the tufts spilling from his ears were as white as snow. Julie shuddered as she remembered them, remembered the day she opened the door of her flat to him. Years ago, she couldn't be sure how many. A Friday afternoon when she had been relatively new to the game. She had started to grin involuntarily, nervously, on seeing his unusual ears. Spotting her expression, his face dropped, the friendly mask slipped.

He recovered in seconds but she knew then that this was destined to be bad. Instinct told her to slam the door in his face because, in the instant before the smile was restored, his eyes became ice cold. It was the kind of coldness only banished by the suffering of others. Yet, without knowing why, she had allowed him inside.

She remembered that he had been suspiciously generous – a very bad sign she was to learn later. Such clients expect far more than the dishes on the menu. Back then ninety quid was a hell of a lot of money. She'd been doing blowjobs for fifteen pounds or twenty "without". Some of the girls were doing a thirty quid service known as "without, to completion" which filled her with disgust. But thirty quid was not to be sniffed at.

Neither, it turned out, was Mr Starkey's willy.

He laid out the money on the bed, staring intently at her all the while. Then he removed his trousers but kept his shirt and tie on. This client liked young girls; the wet lower lip and watery grey eye suggested it.

What was she then? Sixteen? Less? It seemed a hundred years ago.

Dipping her hands in a small basin of warm soapy water, she began to wash him as he stood before her. He was old, perhaps sixty, and had not looked after himself. She suspected he was unmarried but who could say for sure?

A large and not especially clean, grey belly hung low and interfered with her work. The flesh sagged and, in the folds, there were shadows that didn't invite exploration. His tiny member remained flaccid despite her soapy caresses. There was no flicker of life.

The man smelled foul. This was unusual with business types – which he appeared to be. Typically they would be sweaty and wearing too much aftershave but otherwise fresh and clean. Starkey had made not the slightest effort to make her job pleasant. Very much the reverse.

Looking up into his eyes, she had a fraction of a second's warning.

He hit her.

He hit her so hard and so fast she almost lost consciousness. Certainly there wasn't time to gather any kind of defence. And she sensed this client wasn't to be messed around with.

He was holding her with his gaze!

For the next hour, he gave a free master-class in mental coercion. Julie, powerless and humiliated, studied and tried to understand his means of control. In a very specific way he earned her gratitude. On that day she began to refine her own technique and, some weeks later, the next Bad Punter she encountered died, gasping in agony. A heart attack, apparently, declared the coroner to her relief. Nevertheless for months, mastery of the trick remained elusive. From time to time she had other bad experiences, encountered minds stronger than her own, or was drugged, beaten, tricked, trapped or tied. Each one of these memories was stored away deep inside, only released in the dead of night during restless sleep. An undercurrent of self-loathing bubbled in her consciousness, along with a raw sense of violation she could never express.

By the end of mass, all the memories had become fully accessible, revealing the face of every client she had believed locked in a room without a door. Over the years, her worst nightmares had placed her inside that room, gagging on the odours of stale flesh, of flaking skin and of corruption. Dark shapes shuffled clumsily about, breathing heavily and reaching for her blindly But she knew there was no way out. The room had a name and it made her pulse race. *Bad Punters*.

Now some of them were nearby, as if drawn to her, perhaps because they knew her so intimately. Their eyes were joyless as they lined up and sang of God, their love for him and their hopes for salvation. With these men so close, she temporarily relived old fears. They drained her of strength and of will, interrupting her thoughts. How else could she have been talked into staying with a bunch of nuns?

But the morning sun banished some of the demons. Julie was made of sterner stuff than this. Had these fools missed the significance of everything that had happened? Were they waiting for her, desiring to hurt her again? She very much hoped so.

At last, she saw how best to proceed on her personal quest.

Outside the door, some of the younger postulants chatted excitedly about the new Joan of Arc, the girl who had battled evil and won. She listened to the nonsense in disbelief. Not one of these girls was brave enough to tackle real life, to meet it head on. Their contribution to the community at large would consist of a few songs and an endless *Lectio Divina*.

Shutting out their babble, Julie transformed the cell into a clone of her flat using a tiny fraction of her concentration. She remembered the exact look and duplicated it, even extending the physical dimensions of the room to accommodate her bathroom and lots of lovely, thick white towels. Then she returned it to normal. The plain look was nice too, although she replaced the faces in some of the religious paintings with those of Joerg Hooney and Sean O'Connery. Dressed in robes or nailed to crucifixes, their handsome faces beamed like the father she'd never known. At least her early morning nausea had subsided. She had commanded it to stop and it had!

With nothing in particular to do at this early hour, Julie assessed her blossoming skills and worked on them for a while.

Lifting things with her mind had become almost too easy and her power to freeze people in their tracks was already as good as it would ever need to be.

Mr Starkey would be first. In so many ways, he was the worst of all.

Lifting herself above the ground required almost no effort. Julie spent a restful hour merely floating near the ceiling, moving in tiny, gradual steps through the air, as if guided by an invisible hand. Later, with only the smallest of efforts, she conjured up realistic images such as flowers or kittens or even people. She had an especially good chuckle creating an image of Marjorie MacManaman, dressed as the Pope, complete with a circular hat, but wearing Gazza-style plastic breasts over his white robes. The factotum was so perfect that, when she touched the old woman, she could feel the hard plastic nipples, the wiry old-woman hair, the dry, wrinkled flesh.

Inspired with mischief, her Marjorie was mentally instructed to pace around the cloisters and return within 5 minutes. And, as it set off through the door, Julie watched through its eyes, remotely viewing the scenes of pandemonium caused. It paced slowly and silently down whitewashed hallways and around the courtyard whilst shocked nuns gasped and gaped and giggled. This trick was the hardest yet – it made her head ache a little – but she healed herself and continued. The self-healing process was now practically transparent – and automatic.

Encouraged, she created a life-sized image of Una so solid it could have been a waxwork from Madame Tussauds.

This was far more fun than decorating the flat!

Her Una stood in the centre of the room as naked as Julie had last seen her. She didn't breathe so Julie added breathing motions. Even so, the figure looked cold, empty, and soulless.

A quick handbag search unearthed an old tool of the trade. She sliced through Una's face with a razor blade, cutting deep into the cheek and lower lip. The witch gazed at her without expression as red blood welled from the wounds. Julie clapped her hands in delight and the trickle became a torrent, pouring down the large woman's body and onto the stone floor.

Bored, Julie was about to dismiss the apparition. Then she had a remarkable idea. With the casual flick of a finger, Una was cleaned up and clothed. Julie chose sensible clothes. Her plan required them.

Concentrating hard, she commanded Una to seek her own house. The creature fashioned from the very air molecules knew only to obey.

"Can you tell me where I live? I can't seem to remember." it said in a passable impression of Una's voice.

For was it not written: *seek and ye shall find?*

Julie watched through Una's eyes and found it very, very difficult to maintain the vision. A blob of blood oozed from her nose and powerful, zesty headaches pounded against her defence systems, stealing her energy. Breathing deeply, she slumped to the cold stone floor, her back resting on the hard palette bed.

At that moment, the door opened and her Marjorie reappeared, still proudly wearing the plastic boobs. Behind her in the corridor, utterly gob-smacked, giggling postulants and noviates waited to see what would happen next. Julie put her hands to her head, as if to prevent it from exploding as she transmitted a final command. Marjorie lifted her long white robe to present a hoary and slightly hairy ass to them all. Then she entered Julie's cell and the door swung sharply shut.

Once inside, Marjorie vanished and Julie gasped in relief. It was stupid to push this so far: the fake had been running around without her even realising. Under its own steam!

Julie collapsed as the Una lookalike wandered into Preston to pursue its mission.

A knock on the door.

Julie awoke and her head seemed ready to split asunder. She had no idea how long she had lain there on the floor. Her stomach rumbled and she idly wondered if these nuns ate fried eggs and bacon.

"Hello Miss, Miss . . . Hutchinson?" said an unknown but not unkind voice.

Rising stiffly to her feet, she opened the door cautiously. Outside stood a man of about her height, old but not stupid – the gleam in his eyes told her that much. You could tell a lot of things from the first sight of a man's face. In her profession you learned quickly or got out of the business. One way or the other.

The man wore a scruffy pair of flannel trousers and a jacket that Oxfam would probably have binned.

"Who are you?" she asked, rubbing her temples.

"Fred Hartley," said Hartley. "Inspector Fred Hartley. I'm very sorry to trouble you but could I have a word?" He showed her a badge similar to those she had seen too many times before.

"About what?"

"It might be better if we weren't overheard."

"Come in then," she gestured. The young nun who had brought him here covered her mouth with her hand and scampered off down the corridor. It had been a strange morning, no mistake. Tongues were wagging madly since Marjorie's strange booby procession and ass-flashing incident. The times had become so strange that nobody questioned how she had been able to get from Julie's cell to her regular place by Father Stilton in a matter of minutes. And Marjorie wasn't the kind of lady you'd ask.

"Well?" said Julie.

"Nice place," said Hartley. "Not your kind of haunt, I would have thought."

"What do you want?"

"No need to be aggressive. I wanted to ask you a few questions, that's all. It's sort of what I do for a living." The man looked tired and, despite herself, Julie almost felt sorry for him.

"About what?" she said, her tone marginally softer.

Hartley took out a notebook and licked the end of his pencil – his pre-thinking ritual.

"I know what you do lass and it isn't an issue for me. But do you think these . . . sisters . . . will be so tolerant when they find out? Religious folk, in my experience, tend not to put up with anyone who doesn't live *right*. And that would be *their* version of right, I'm afraid. These godly types are always the same, have been all through history. I had all this junk rammed into me as a kid so I know what

I'm talking about. I doubt Mary Magdalene would have been welcome here, for example. Come to think of it she wasn't welcome in the church back then. Odd, don't you think?" Julie rated him as an eccentric, befuddled man but harmless. His face was flushed and he occasionally shook his head as if trying to dislodge water from his ear.

"Odd? I have no idea what you're talking about. I've never met this Mary and you can't prove I have."

He then launched into a speech, as if unable to stop. The words rushed out like a torrent. "Look lass, I mean it's odd that the old church got replaced by a new one but its followers behave exactly the same. I often think, perhaps it's the detective in me, that if this church was divinely inspired, how could it cock up so badly? I mean, why would a saviour come with the latest Word from Heaven but have no effect on human nature? He couldn't even convince everyone he met for goodness' sake! We're 2,000 years down the road and effectively right back where we started? We don't love each other, we don't turn the other cheek and we're in the same loop of ignorance and intolerance. Like the Midgard Serpent swallowing its tail. Answer me this: could God have so little influence and be as powerful as faith dictates?"

Julie frowned, noting his shaking hands and the beads of sweat on his upper lip. She was ready, should he flip.

"What on earth are you on about? Are you a copper or a priest?"

"It's just occurred to me. For some reason I've started thinking about all this stuff since yesterday. It's been bothering me for years but I've just realised it. Don't you think there's something very wrong with the world? Right now, I mean?"

She wondered what this curious man really wanted. He was rambling, obviously trying to con her into thinking he was a fool. She'd seen enough Columbo not to be lulled. Plus, she could crush him like an insect at will. Throw him against the ceiling. Stop his heart. Her face went completely blank as she pondered the options and simultaneously contemplated breakfast.

Hartley coughed and finally got to the point. He couldn't quite understand why he was letting loose with the verbal diarrhoea either.

"Could you tell me about your exhibition on Friday night? I'm trying to work out if I should charge you or your friend with something." His voice was gentle.

Julie remained silent. She was wearing only the light smock given to her when she entered this place and, unexpectedly, she felt vulnerable, aware that her slight form was probably revealed by the atomic sunshine streaming through the window.

She sat down on the bed, her knees pushed tightly together, hands clasped in front, fingers interlocked as if to ward him off.

Hartley reflected that she looked so young yet so worn-out.

"Is that a real scar on your neck?" he asked.

With an involuntary motion, her fingertips touched the rough edge of the scar – the cut from the fat witch's knife. Pulling at the thin material, she drew the smock tighter about her, both hands now protectively held in front of her thin chest.

"I've had it a while," she lied.

"The blood looked very realistic. I've seen it on the news too and can't see how it was done. What was the purpose of the whole thing though? To incite public disorder?"

"You'll have to ask Una."

"I would very much like to, but I have no idea where to

find her. She seems to have left town."

"I'm sorry, I don't know where she lives. I only met her on Friday for the first time. She . . . she ripped me off. Conned me. I'd like to find her again too." Her statement contained enough truth to convince. The memory of the trip to Una's house was hazy. She had no idea where it was.

Yet.

"What were you two doing up there? Can you tell me the names of anyone else involved? Give me something to go on." Hartley knew she was hiding something but his mind kept clouding over as his thinking process faltered. A fizzing sound filled his ears and he thought he heard a faint whisper, as if someone were addressing him from a great distance.

"I don't remember. I must have been feeling ill. The first thing that I recall sharply was, was . . ."

". . . what?" asked Hartley, rubbing his eyes as if in discomfort.

"Nothing. I think she hypnotised me. We have to find her. Will you tell me if you do?"

He felt compelled to say he would.

Hartley departed soon after that. For some reason he couldn't bear to remain any longer. Something about the place positively repelled him. The paintings were weird too – in a way he couldn't quite put his finger on.

Clearly, the girl knew more than she was telling. And why on earth, had *nuns* taken her in?

As he walked down the corridor to leave, a side door opened. Inside, a young postulant sat naked on a bed, her legs apart. A second nun stood, also naked apart from her wimple, at the door. Inviting him in.

Fred Hartley was only human. It wasn't long before he was barely human.

Even more determined to leave the convent and lay low, Julie searched for her clothes. The policeman suspected something. Maybe he was closing in on her. A partial memory of three young men – her student lovers – surfaced. They had mocked her and died as a result. Had they *really* been bad? Perhaps they were, but surely they weren't *Bad*? It may have been a mistake, she admitted.

Unable to find her jeans, she recreated them with her mind along with a t-shirt and a denim jacket. On her bare feet appeared trainers and clean, white socks but they failed to shut out the cold seeping up from the stone floor. Sneaking out, she briefly imagined herself as small as a fly, passing through the keyhole and past the nuns who watched over her, recording every movement.

Curious groaning noises could be heard behind a door similar to hers but she flew by and thought no more of it. Outside she became herself once more, but still the cold came through the fake trainers.

In Preston, crowds were gathering, uncertain yet expectant. Tension ran through them like electricity and squabbles began to break out, trivial arguments descending into fisticuffs. Walking through the throng would have been uncomfortable for anyone.

However, the Una doppelgänger was not anyone. It was a simple – yet wholly remarkable – automaton, crafted in haste but with a precise purpose. Without knowing how, Julie had peeled off a tiny portion of herself to breathe life into it. It possessed enough vitality to obey her commands and provide limited responses. It pushed through the crowds, periodically asking if anyone knew where it lived.

It claimed to have forgotten.

The image of Una walked around for quite some time,

shadowed at a distance of a few hundred yards by Julie, greedily munching a huge burger and clutching a second one. Smoke and music filled the air and Preston began to resemble a medieval market town with wild-eyed prophets crying on street corners, beating their chests and berating sinners. Jostling for position, street sellers flogged everything from roast potatoes to parched peas to, curiously, a new-fangled hotdog rejoicing in the name *The Devil's Member.*

It was mid morning yet over a thousand people had gathered on the market square, each convinced an important event was imminent. Some clutched rosary beads, others held the bible, still more had the Koran. Also in evidence were the Tao Te Ching, the Art of Zen and Moped Maintenance and dog-eared copies of Jeffrey Fulcher's latest. Each looked suspiciously at their neighbour, as if trying to judge their worthiness in some intangible competition.

In front of the Town Hall, two men in their forties argued angrily, spit flying.

"The Lord Jesus says you cannot come to the Father except through him!"

"And the Goddess says you bastards stole her festival like you stole her magic tricks!"

"Heathen. There is no Goddess, only a God!"

"Three Gods, wasn't it?" chipped in an old man sat on the ground, attempting to beg for his lunch. Or his supper. He really wasn't fussy as long as he ate today.

"Three people in *one* God," corrected the first man haughtily, flicking him a stray penny that was too bent to fit in the coffee machine at work. "It's simple enough to understand!"

"I thought it was two people and a ghost, or something," suggested a sincere-looking youth in a brown suit, sidling up to join in.

"Allah is the only God," chimed in Mr Patel, surprising himself with the conviction in his voice. Until a couple of days ago he had only paid lip service to Allah, mostly to avoid grief from his devout family. Now his eyes burned with a frenzied inner strength as if he believed every word.

"Your God didn't make it into our Bible, so I think it's safe to say he doesn't exist," prattled the sincere youth. He then took a deep breath and placed his palm on his forehead.

"What's 'e doing?" questioned the old man, shifting slightly to avoid being trampled.

"Shhhhh," said the youth. "Be silent all. For I foretell the coming of a Holy Child. And his name shall be Brad and he shall bring forth the New Word of the Lord."

"We've had the New Testament already tit-head!" laughed another.

"Well, this will be the New-*er* Testament!" rejoined the youth snottily. "It'll have pictures and everything."

The Una form wandered around amongst them seeking recognition, understanding nothing. It didn't feel the hand on its bottom.

A dark-faced, shrivelled woman wearing a scarf shouted directly into Una's face: "we cover our mouths to show respect even to the insects and other small creatures!"

Una stared blankly at the crone but didn't ask her familiar question. Instead she turned, grabbed the hand still resting on her bottom and squeezed hard.

"Yowch Una, it's me, Bill," said a voice.

"You know where I live?"

"Course I do. By the Gods I feel good today. You know Una, I've always wanted to say this to you...ow, let go!"

"My name is Una?" the doppelgänger released him and

opened her eyes widely. For a moment, Julie peered through them, storing the unappealing details of Bill's face. This counted as progress – but at a price. A wave of pain hit the base of her skull, spreading upwards and she reeled, momentarily. Her recovery systems faltered and then, mercifully, the pain began to subside.

In the centre of the flag market, a makeshift podium had been erected, complete with video screen. Marjorie MacManaman stood alongside a subdued-looking Father Stilton. It was her voice – not his – that echoed loudly over the PA system.

". . . Judgement Day is almost upon us. In the coming days, you will see increasing signs of it. I say to you that Evil must be fought and stamped out! We can no longer turn ignore the filth on our streets. The stench of Evil must be purged in fire! The Final Battle will soon be here! Book your place on the winning side today and win a bottle of wine or this lovely hamper!"

Even from this distance, Julie could see something was wrong with Marjorie. The woman appeared frantic or agitated. Amongst the crowd she recognised some of the men she desperately wanted to meet again. Her chest tightened and her fists clenched.

First things first.

Una.

Julie felt a pull inside her mind. It was if the Una creature suddenly required more strength to function. The mental link between them expanded, allowing more of her life essence to be sucked through. Julie stumbled and steadied herself against a lamppost.

"I am Una," said the doppelgänger. "Tell me where I live please."

"I'll take you. You OK? My van isn't far."

"Van?"

"I'll take you lass, no bother. Come on, the van's close by."

"You'll take me there?" Una wavered, as if uncertain.

"You alright? I hope so because I've finally plucked up the courage to tell you something. It's stupid but I never dared before. To tell you the truth I didn't really believe in this 'ere witching lark. I just fancied you something rotten. But now I *do* believe and I wanted to tell you. I feel that today anything is possible! I want you Una. What do you say – you and me?"

Una bent double, seemingly short of breath. For a moment, comprehension appeared in her eyes.

Where am I?

With an enormous effort, Julie tore apart the mental pipeline with the doppelgänger and cauterised her end of it. She sat down hard on a bench, opposite McDonalds, her mind threatening to implode.

"Una? You alright? Did you hear any of what I said?"

"I am Una. Take me to my home please. Take me there in your van."

Bill's shoulders sagged in disappointment.

"Sure thing Una," he said.

***

"How's he doing?"

"After a poor start, much improved. Or so I'm told."

"Oh, good. I like it when he does well."

"He's almost learned how to scan *forwards*."

"Really? In an LTU?"

"Yep. He'll be opening Worm Holes next."

"Is that allowed?"

"No idea, you know how I despise his stupid rules. Try some of this."

There was an aeon of silence. Then the second voice spoke again.

"Did you know they were both present? Him *and* Her. In close proximity."
"Ooh, that's interesting!"
"They have a bit of time to make up."
"Very droll darling. Mmmm, this smells sweet as a virgin's chuff."
"Where did you pick up that phrase?"
"Evolution, I expect. Racial memory, you know."
"Ah, that."

Chapter Twenty

*Every artist dips his brush in his own soul,
and paints his own nature into his pictures.*
Henry Wupp Peachy

Bill ushered the thing he called Una out of the van and to the front door.

"Here you are then."

The journey had been strangely silent. Bill had bitten his nails nervously; a bad habit. Had she been thinking about what he had said earlier? His hopes faded.

"Here? Where I live?" The voice was hollow, lacking the authority and the brashness Bill admired so much. On the plus side, her ass had, if anything, grown larger since he last saw her. So that was a bonus.

"Of course it is. Silly lass! Look, I don't want to push myself forward but I really would like to know what you thought of, you know, what I said?"

"I live here? I am Una?"

"Are you alright? Shall we go inside?" he fawned.

She hesitated for an age. Bill felt uncomfortable. They stood in the street so long he started to feel light-headed. He rubbed his temple and his hand came away shaking and damp with sweat. A low-pitched humming in his ears was intensifying, making it hard to think.

"Wouldn't mind a glass of water if that's OK? Shall I open up? Still got that key."

"Where I live," she said, blankly.

Bill took this as agreement, unlocked the door and waited for her to enter. She did so and headed towards the kitchen.

"Feeling better then?" asked Bill. There was no reply. Una opened the kitchen door; positively ran to the cellar door and snatched it open. She descended into darkness without a backward glance. Bill loitered by the fridge, uncertain, unsteady, his head cocked at an angle.

A minute went by. And then he heard something: Una's voice, loud and as strong as ever.

"Bill! To answer your question I'm feeling very much better. *Very* much! Thank you for bringing me home my wonderful, marvellous old friend!"

***

"Hello my dear, are you feeling quite alright?" a friendly voice whispered at Julie's side.

Opening her eyes, she almost jumped out of her skin. Except she couldn't because she was glued to the bench. All around, people bustled and jostled.

Starkey sat at her side, purring like an old tom cat. Shattering her newly discovered confidence, his cold eyes bored into her soul and the fear returned as if it had never been away. A tiny drop of pee escaped and her heart sank in shame and despair.

"Why don't we go some place a bit more private?" he said, beaming. "It's going to be a violent day and we can't risk somebody as important as you getting hurt. Or being out alone. Praise the Lord, no. You *do* remember me, I hope?"

Julie couldn't speak. She was drained, impossibly weak. Her contact with the Una factotum dissolved.

Starkey led her away like a child. They linked arms and headed towards his Lune Street office, cutting through the shopping centre towards another mini adventure.

He'd never forgotten the last time, although a premonition had deterred him from repeating it. There had been a most unsettling look about her afterwards.

Time had not been kind to this poor girl, he reflected. She actually looked a bit past it for his tastes but one for curiosity and old times' sake couldn't hurt, he thought. He gripped her arm, digging sharp nails into flesh and Julie went willingly, helplessly, as he had known she would.

The office was deserted. A solicitor, the brass sign proclaimed. Shoving her roughly inside, he locked the main door and they climbed a steep wooden staircase, arm in arm. Starkey licked his lips. The coarse white hair in his ears stuck out like a ragged goat's beard and his rheumy grey eyes gleamed under thick eyebrows. They reached a smaller, private office, his inner sanctum of leather, papers and bound volumes of law.

"Sit down. Please make yourself at home," he suggested. Julie dropped, lifeless, into an antique chair of dark, stained oak and gazed ahead blankly.

"Now then, I'm going to have a little drinkie. I know it's rather early but I feel like celebrating. It's so lovely to have you to myself again, praise be! Tell me, do you still perform the same services now you're a saint?" His laugh was harsh and cruel.

Removing his jacket, he draped it over a chair, revealing a shirt heavily stained by sweat, his large belly straining and threatening to pop open several of the lower buttons.

Julie felt nothing. She locked herself away deep inside and watched the scene unfold with hopeless detachment. From a drawer in his desk, Starkey drew out something long, black and rectangular.

"You'll adore this," he promised with not a trace of sincerity. "Its a ferrula, a present from an old Jesuit friend of mine many years ago. Sadly he had to leave the country in rather a hurry. He used it to punish boys for generations – myself included. It's made of out of rubber so there's a nice movement to it, and it's far heavier than it looks. Ah, happy memories . . ."

Starkey slapped it onto his palm and a nostalgic smile crept over his jowly face.

"You know, I'm quite excited on your behalf, my sweet. I can't promise the strength or finesse of its former master – dear old Bruiser we called him. I certainly don't have his 'leap in the air' delivery either. But I will try to honour his memory as best I can."

His arm moved with frightening speed, the heavy rubber object grasped tightly, heading for Julie's face.

It never landed.

Calmly and deliberately, she stood up, the scene apparently moving in slow motion. Frozen, Starkey struggled uselessly but was unable to move a muscle. Only his eyes remained fluid, widened in disbelief and now even more watery. His lower lip became even more moist.

"I've learnt a few things since you were round at my place," she informed him conversationally. Gently she removed the thick rubber ferrula from his hand and examined it with interest. "Actually, you helped me a lot. That's why I wanted to plan our meeting better than this. Anyway," she continued, pacing slowly to and fro around the plush office, "I've got important things to do later, so we should get started."

The ferrula floated slowly from her hand towards his face, shaking like a short, stubby snake. Well, a short, stubby snake that could defy gravity. Sweat poured from him; his already wet shirt became sodden; his lower lip drooled uncontrollably. His eyes rolled around in horror, following the implement of punishment. Impossibly. Inevitably. It halted directly in front of his nose, rock solid in the air.

"You can move, if you like," laughed Julie and released him. Instantly he leapt at her – so fast he almost took her by surprise. Starkey was a man used to grabbing the chances life threw at him. But today was not to be his day. She didn't move a muscle but the space directly before her grew hard. Starkey hit it, even as it was hardening. It cost him the tips of three fingers and part of his left knee. Amazed, he fell to the floor like a stone, a hot, searing pain tearing through him and blood seeping from his trousers and injured hand.

"How the hell?" he croaked.

"I thought I'd give you one last chance," she said sadly. "Now... what *should* I do with you?"

Behind him, the ferrula hovered, swaying from side to side.

"Kneel up to take your punishment," she ordered.

"Fuck off, you've ripped my bloody knee off!"

Starkey felt his whole body seized, as if in an invisible hand. He was pushed forward and screamed in agony as his damaged knee hit the hard, polished floor.

"Hold out your hand," she ordered, beginning to enjoy herself. The power was working well. The only cloud on the horizon was that she had completely lost touch of her Una creation. It was as if it no longer existed. Pragmatically, she concentrated on the matter in hand. Starkey's hand.

"I said hold it out," she shrieked. An invisible grip seized his balls and squeezed, rather hard. Starkey thrust out his hand and held it there. Behind his fear there was something else.

What? Excitement?

Jesus, he was actually enjoying this!

As an experiment, Julie thrust the ferrula downwards as fast and as hard as she could. The result was rather more extreme than she expected. Old Bruiser would have been proud.

For a second or two, Starkey looked at his hand in disbelief. The heavy rubber had hit him with such velocity that it passed clean through, taking all four fingers and half of his palm away. It made hardly any noise, merely a light "thwack" that seemed, in itself, extraordinary in the light of such a dramatic result. Only a pathetic stump remained plus his madly waggling thumb, blood flying everywhere.

For the first time in his life, Starkey was speechless. The pain was excruciating and he started to lose consciousness. Then something alien entered his mind, clearing it instantly. The pain subsided.

"Now the other one, don't think you're getting off lightly," she jeered.

He watched in amazement as his own arm was raised and held out against his will.

"Slower," she said. The ferrula flew down a little slower this time, breaking his left hand in half but not quite severing all the skin and tendons. His fingers wriggled madly. They moved independently, to different tempos, like a demented Richard Clayderhosen. He continued to watch, fascinated, horrified, the pain again increasing, threatening to engulf him. Then, somehow, the pain subsided once again.

Julie licked her lips.

"Well, lover," she said. "You can thank me for healing you later. Much later. When we're done. Now then, what else can this rubber toy of yours do?"

Julie spent a very long time in Starkey's office. Towards the end she began to lose herself, the madness spreading and straining the most fragile part of her personality to breaking point. And beyond. Fortunately, her self-healing processes sensed a change in the status quo and quickly adapted.

As an unknown plague spread throughout Preston that Sunday afternoon, Julie was one of the few who kept it at bay. But, looking in her eyes, you wouldn't have known it.

***

Meed laughed. He laughed and laughed and laughed.

"What's so funny?" said Yasmine. "Is it time?"

"Damn near," he chuckled. "Are you ready?"

In an instant Yasmine stood a hundred feet tall. Her eyes became cat-like slits that glowed amber and beams of fire leapt from them creating a circle of flames around Jonathon Meed. Unconcerned, he whittled on a piece of wood with a sharp knife.

The sky turned to ash and she clapped her hands together, rending the earth apart with the force of a nuclear detonation.

"Quite good," nodded Meed amiably. "But wait until you see what I can do!"

Dropping his whittling gear, he offered her a tiny private glimpse of his power.

"Jesus," she swore.

"Ah yes, him," he grinned, the amusement welling up once more. "It'll be a different outcome this time."

Yasmine had to agree that it would.

***

Heavy smoke fumes drifting in through an open window startled Julie from her daydream. It had been disappointing to discover she could not heal Starkey forever. His heart had burst, given up and denied her the full measure of revenge. A dark wash of blood stained every expensive leather chair, bookshelf, filing cabinet and several piles of folders and papers. She peered through the window, down onto the street to see what was happening.

Preston was exceptionally busy for a Sunday. Crowds marched as if on parade, shouting and chanting. Several people carried flaming torches made of chair legs. The sounds of car horns, breaking glass and pounding drums filled the smoky air.

Starkey's remains lay where he had crawled, half under his desk. His whole body had been beaten and pummelled mercilessly. A black rubber object protruded from his flabby bottom. Every rib had been individually broken. His sternum was split. His clavicles and hips were reduced to mere fragments. His flesh was purple; shards of bone poked through it at various points and almost all his clothes were torn away, as if by clawing hands. Even his own mother would not have recognised what was left of his face had she chanced by. Both eyes were gone. A thousand cuts had been inflicted slowly across his cheeks, his neck and his forehead leaving a matrix of gore. His lower jaw was missing, smashed off in a single blow that left his throat open in a permanent, agonised scream.

Julie had found the punishment instructive but tiring. Sustaining Starkey's life energy had descended into a desperate game as more and more damage was inflicted. She felt like a game show contestant trying to block escaping water from too many holes whilst a smarmy host made quips and the cameraman relished how wet she was getting.

Eventually he had simply died. There was nothing significant to mark his passing. One moment became the next and it was over.

Time ticked on and events started to draw together towards a conclusion. The Final Battle would happen soon and not all its key participants understood their roles.

Chapter Twenty One

Artists who seek perfection in everything are those who cannot attain it in anything.
         Eugene Delawart

"Oops," said Jim.

"Now *there's* something you don't see every day," observed Dave.

A few yards away from their park bench, a hovering, kidney-shaped patch of air glowed a sickly green. The phenomenon hung beneath the low, curved branches of a sycamore tree as if suspended by invisible wires. Radiating light like a neon sign, it fizzled and crackled, mimicking the sounds of a rain-spattered pylon. *Oops indeed.* Fresh spring leaves withered and died on branches nearby and a robin had an unpleasantly graphic bowel movement.

Danger Will Robinson, thought Jim. Aloud he said, "well that's never happened before. Do you suppose the skunk threw off my vibration frequencies?"

"What exactly *is* it dude?" asked Dave taking a long drag of Jim's glass pipe. Although doing his best, he wasn't nearly so stoned that he missed the false bravado in his friend's voice.

"*Exactly*? I'm not even confident of *vaguely*. But right now I'm most interested in knowing how to turn it off."

"Ah," Dave nodded sagely, returning the now empty pipe to his friend. "So it's back to the drawing board with the old universal brain vaccine, eh?"

Jim ignored him and grumbled to himself. This mental projection lark was proving harder to master than he'd hoped. Also, time was not on their side.

"I have this really bad feeling," he began, getting to his feet. "It's been growing steadily all day. Maybe I've caught something minor after all, the mental equivalent of Hay Fever. And all around the pollen count's rising. Whatever it is, there's majorly stinky poo aboot. And it's spreading fast. There's buzzing in the tiny gaps between the air and it ain't wasps."

"Bzzzzzz," agreed Dave. "And lo, a goat shall spill its entrails and tear its beard. And there shall be woe and the gnashing of teeth and suchlike."

"We'll leave the pipe alone for a bit, shall we?" sighed Jim shoving it in his pocket. Strolling towards the tree, he felt his skin tingle as he approached the result of his failed programming session. When it was within touching distance he halted and peered behind it. Reminiscent of his virtual cinema screen, this too appeared to only exist in one plane – in opposition to where they had been sitting. In the middle of the green patch of light, he noticed a dark purple speck. With a tentative finger, he prodded it. It offered no physical resistance yet the speck seemed to swell and expand in response. The hairs on the back of his hand and down his arm stood to attention. Blood drained from his finger as if close to a source of intense cold.

"What's it feel like?" called Dave. "Can I have a go?"

Jim didn't reply. Instead, he pushed his finger deep into the middle of the purple area and shuddered at the buzzing sensation that flowed through his hand. The phenomenon began to expand, the green turning darker and gaining extra colours. Blues and violets sprang into life like droplets of paint hitting a canvas and the mysterious thing spread outwards until it measured three feet in diameter. At its edges, fuzzy green lights danced and flickered whilst its centre became ever darker.

"Er . . ." said Dave.

For a moment, Jim fancied he could see his own reflection, as if rendered in polished black glass. The face returning his gaze was serious, its eyes dark and troubled. Then it was gone and the darkness stretched inwards forming an endless tunnel. The compulsion to peep inside became almost overwhelming and Jim was reaching forwards to do just that when Dave shouted.

"Watch out mate, I think it's breaking up!"

So it was. At the edges, the green light was now sparking and breaking up. Streaks of regular light leaked through like cracks in a mucky window. As the *accident* began to dissolve, Jim clearly saw the dark tunnel open wider, revealing a distant tableau. For a fleeting moment before it winked out of existence, he could have sworn he saw himself, dusty and dressed in rags, seated on a high mountain overlooking a city of stone. At his side stood a tall, handsome man with eyes like coal, his beard elegantly forked. The beardy guy smiled broadly and made a grand gesture towards the city with one hand, whilst proffering a glass of sparkling water with the other. Then the scene vanished, sealed with a sizzling hiss and the faint but unmistakeable aroma of frying bacon.

Jim found his hand shaking and his fingertips numb. He waved his hand in the air but felt nothing. It was truly gone and he wondered what it had been and how he'd managed to put it there in the first place.

A few feet away, Dave shuffled from one foot to the other and coughed.

"Can we go home to fix Sheila now? I don't know about the pollen count but you're dead right. There *is* something in the air – and not just your green fuzzy patch. I think I can hear shouting."

It was true. A distant, massed clamour roared with the menace of an angry football crowd. Something was badly wrong.

"Sure thing man," said Jim distantly. "Let's go. Dunno about you but I'm bloomin' starving."

"Munchies," said Dave, shaking his head. "Where would the fast food industry be without beer and spliffs?"

"I really fancy a garlic bread," said Jim.

"Weird - I fancy a bacon butty myself."

"I probably do too."

"What do you mean?"

"Well, you see, I diverted my smell. No, titter ye not! My sense of it."

"You what?"

"Everything I smell reminds me of garlic bread."

"Well, that's . . . probably . . . good," said Dave, frowning.

"It saves processing power," Jim explained. "I have this tiny routine that basically throws away all smell analysis – and analysis of most other sensory data too. It frees up a surprising number of brain cycles. The downside is, of course, everything smelling of garlic bread. The upside is that none of my memories are trawled as a result of sensory input."

"You're taking the piss," said Dave.

"Nope. Not this time. But I had to do it. You see . . . I found that every smell – correction every *nice* smell – reminded me of *her*. I thought I could forget her and move on but I can't. I don't think I ever will."

"I don't know what to say man. Is it hopeless?"

"Probably. Hard to be certain. All I know for sure is that meeting her again has made it worse than ever."

"I'm sorry mate."

"I know."

They ambled off, swaying slightly.

"Do you fancy driving?" said Dave when they neared the flat. "You're still just as insured." He felt the smoke had made a bigger impact than it should, reasoning that driving home at 5 miles an hour might attract undue attention.

"No sweat. I seem to have got straight rather quickly. Must be the hopelessness."

As he drove, Jim voiced random surface thoughts while the bulk of his concentration remained locked on a tricky conundrum. There was so little attention left for driving that he completely failed to notice theirs was the only car on the road.

"Specialisation is the worst thing that ever happened to me. Perhaps to everyone," he announced after a few minutes of thoughtful silence.

"Sorry mate?"

"Don't you see? At College, at Uni, the more specialised we got, the more blinkered we became. That's why we got bored with it all! Nobody's going to see the whole elephant if all they ever study is its tail. Our education system is designed, unconsciously I suppose, to prevent you connecting things. It's all a diversion. Our society, all the controls of government, religion, the media . . . if everyone could see the whole picture, why would we need these people at all?" Jim's mind was racing but he kept an eye open for speed cameras.

"Ah, conspiracy theories," said Dave slowly, fiddling with his seatbelt. "We do like those. So you're now saying that kids should study all subjects throughout their education, never drop the stuff they don't have any aptitude for, never concentrate on being experts in any field? Everyone would be a jack of all trades in your marvellous vision of the future. Who needs experts anyway, right? And all this, erm, is so they can see . . . an elephant?"

"OK, maybe not everyone. But here's another thing: you accept that belief is important? Belief – all by itself – gives you power, opens up avenues, yes?"

"Uh, feel free to leap from topic to topic won't you man! But yeah, sure, if I've learned anything from this last week it's all that belief gubbins."

"Well, I've got a surprise for you."

"I doubt you could surprise me any more. Not today at least."

"Well then, what about *Disbelief*? I'm not talking about its watered-down meaning – the one we all use, Meldrew-style, to express indignation or unfairness. *Real* Disbelief is very, very hard to master because it ultimately sets you apart from everyone and every*thing* else. It frees you from General Reality! Because if it doesn't, you must, by definition, still believe something. By the way, I think this might be at the root of your problem duplicating the shit I can do."

"Huh?"

Jim continued, as if unable to stop. "Disbelief is respected, even worshipped in some cultures. Madness is seen as the next step, a move away from the everyday world towards enlightenment."

"What's this got to do with me?"

"I hate to say this man but you're struggling to replicate my god-like feats cos you're conditioned. You can't escape! Even though your mind is essentially free, you've decided to stick with the comforting and familiar. I don't want to try shock therapy but just think for a moment what we've found out so far."

"Oh, do I *have* to?" moaned Dave.

"I guess not. Sorry," said Jim. "Hey, what's that?" He slammed on the brakes in the nick of time.

Across the road ahead was a makeshift barrier formed of old furniture, TV sets, a partially inflated bouncy castle, a fridge and some cardboard boxes. At one edge of the barrier was a short row of shops (including the last small post office), their windows protected by metal shutters. The far side of the barrier terminated in a battered Volvo that seemed to have been deserted in haste. Daubed across the car and window shutters in thick, wet red paint, were crosses and crude images of a bearded, hippy-like Jesus, plus angels and, inexplicably, a Chad with accompanying text "Wot, no Witches?"

Black smoke from somewhere nearby drifted across the scene, adding to the sense of unreality. Behind the barrier were approximately twenty people holding placards.

STOP IN THE NAME OF THE LORD, said one

SAVE UR SOLE 2DAY, another

APOCALYPSE SOON, said a third.

Jim stopped the car and exchanged a puzzled glance with Dave. Then he reached for the door handle.

"Don't go out mate," said Dave earnestly. "There's something not quite right about this. Look at them!"

Jim did. The row of expressionless faces chilled him. Behind their eyes lurked a sinister, watchful malevolence. Friendly they were not.

"I think I need to have a word anyway," he said. "Might be educational. You stay here. I'll leave the engine running just in case they turn ugly."

"Too late for that one," indicated Dave, unfastening his seatbelt.

Jim opened the door and approached the barrier, smiling, hands outstretched.

"What's up?" he said. It didn't take an advanced course in body language to identify the tension in every stance. Knuckles whitened, the pause stretched out and threatened to give birth to triplets. And then someone spoke, a pimply youth with an ugly sneer.

"No cars allowed through today." he shouted, louder than was necessary. He clutched a rosary to his chest. "By order of the Faithful."

"That's right," chimed a sandy-haired thug of about fifty who Jim guessed to be the leader. He wore a long coat of coarse sackcloth fastened to the throat, and sported a fresh but inexpertly-shaved tonsure. His head was speckled with sticking plasters and he became suddenly animated. His eyes blazed and his voice rose to a shout.

"The Faithful are in charge – as of *today*," He sprayed spittle and made odd licking motions with a wet tongue, confirming Jim's impression he might not be playing with a full deck. "Desperate times call for desperate measures," he continued, lick, licking. "Leave your car and head into town on foot." Then, as an afterthought, he added: "Swear allegiance to the Lord Jesus first, then you can be on your way. Hallelujah!"

In his peripheral vision, Jim noted several altar boys – in rather grubby white robes – mouthing the word Hallelujah in perfect sync. Several nuns lurked amongst the throng too. Curiously, one of them held a bloody spade, another a wickedly curved hook.

Jim was baffled but tried to maintain his cool. What he expected but failed to find were tins being rattled. When did anyone see a nun without a tin?

"Look, I'm not going into town as it happens. And you lot can't block the road just because you're high on altar wine. Come on, a joke's a joke. Where's the hidden camera?"

At that moment something told him the car he'd dismissed as the result of careless parking merited closer inspection. Forming the left hand frame of the barrier, it straddled the pavement, the driver's side window smashed, the door hanging open. Jim scanned for clues and the glazed gaze of the assembled followed, full of anticipation. Then he saw it: an obviously fresh patch of blood on the road next to the driver's door. As his attention returned slowly to the empty faces, he saw them all grin simultaneously. It was as if their mouths were being worked remotely by a single control and it didn't take much imagination to guess that *desperate measures* had been taken already. Seemingly with little reluctance and no lingering remorse.

"It's best to swear your oath of love to the Lord right now!" screamed the nun with the hook. Her habit looked home-made and there was evidence of five O'clock shadow on her chin, now Jim gave 'her' more attention.

"Maybe later," he said, backing away. "First I need to check with Father Christmas and Pongo the Leprechaun to make sure they're not jealous." He turned his back to them and started towards the car. It was only a few yards away but he didn't want to lose (what he felt was) his commanding presence by running. He heard a crunching sound behind him as part of the barrier was shunted aside.

Glancing over his shoulder he saw two men, one armed with a sword, the other with twin Stanley knives, marching briskly towards him. Murder was in their eyes.

"You have got to be fucking joking," he cried as the sword sliced through the air inches away from his waist.

"Beware the false gods! Swear the oath of love," chanted the crowd in unison. "Join the Faithful and worship the Lord. Be saved today. Be with us or be damned!"

Dimly aware of engine-revving noises, Jim switched all of his concentration to the task at hand – that of survival.

He backed up, facing the two men. As his focus left the sword, he noticed its wielder was the pimply-faced youth, his rosary now, presumably, tucked away until the next bout of praying. The sword was of the ornamental variety, more suited to hanging over a fireplace than hacking off limbs, but it appeared to have been freshly sharpened. Its blade appeared heavy and clumsy – but potentially lethal. The second man had closely-cropped hair with flashes of grey, and teeth of yellow ochre. His smooth motion marked him out as the more dangerous of the pair. Jim edged to the side, attempting to put Mr Swordsman in the way and reduce the chance of a combined attack.

The man with the knives (Jim inwardly referred to him as Stanley) stalked stealthily forwards, giving away little. The spotty youth held his sword awkwardly in both hands. Then, without warning, he leapt in sweeping downwards viciously. All Jim could do was side-step, which took him towards the barrier. He continued using the swordsman as an obstacle but began to wonder if he was being herded.

Another slash but this time, as the sword reached the extent of its arc, it slowed. Pimple clearly didn't want to blunt it on the tarmac and began to draw it back for another strike. Quick as a dose of the clap, Jim stepped in and kicked hard at the blade. Pimple kept his grip but the force of the kick swung him round, the sword sweeping low towards Stanley's legs. Seizing his chance, Jim continued to move in, thrusting hard behind Pimple's right knee with his foot and stomping down on it brutally. At the same time his right arm swung around Pimple's head, his wrist bone grinding into Pimple's temple. Strengthening his grip with his left hand, he applied pressure, all the time monitoring

Stanley's approach.

As Pimple succumbed to the sleeper hold and drooped, lifeless, Jim relaxed his grip, dropping it beneath Pimple's chin, so that his neck rested in the crook of his elbow. Stepping backwards, Jim used the unconscious Pimple as a shield whilst Stanley attempted to manoeuvre his way around the side. The sword lay uselessly out of reach.

At that moment, Dave drove the car into Stanley like a missile, breaking his left leg with a loud crack and hurling him backwards into the barrier. Dropping his unconscious assailant roughly, Jim seized the passenger door and threw himself inside the car.

"Drive!" he commanded, unnecessarily.

"Ahead of you!" Dave stepped on the accelerator and drove over the pavement, hammering through the small gap formed by a corner shop and the softest part of the barrier – a heap of cardboard boxes.

"We could have driven round, you know."

"I suppose so," replied Dave, shrugging. "Still . . . always wanted to do that." He looked in his mirror at the receding figures manning the barrier. They milled around as if uncertain what to do next.

A few hundred yards further on, down a side street, Jim spotted a large bonfire burning freely in the middle of the street. It spouted oily black smoke like pus from a sore and stank of old tyres, grease and petrol. Yet a small crowd stood around it chatting, as if it was November the 5th.

"It's clear I still have the capacity to be surprised," said Jim, rubbing his eyes with shaking hands.

"You never expect the Spanish Inquisition," affirmed Dave.

As they drove towards the London Road traffic lights, they realised, as if for the first time, how deserted the roads were. Not a single other car was moving. Even the main road was abandoned.

"This place is comin' like a ghost town," sang Dave.

"Mmm," agreed Jim. "Look man, thanks for the rescue. You twanged that bloke spot on. I hope you didn't dent the car!"

"All part of the service."

Jim nodded. "Can we get back to your place? I think urgent action is called for! It's time for a massive change of tactics."

"Tactics? Is that what we've been using up 'til now? You know, I was waiting for you to mind-zap them all back there."

"I can smell garlic," said Jim, changing the subject.

"Oh, sorry," said Dave. "Must have been all the excitement."

Jim stared out of the window mournfully.

Chapter Twenty Two

I do benefits for all religions -- I'd hate to blow the hereafter on a technicality.   Nob Pope

A lone Police Helicopter made a final pass over Preston, its two occupants silent and unbelieving. The radio hissed like a punctured tyre. Faint voices, almost lost under a blanket of white noise, called out in panic and then faded into the static. The pilot shook his head; he'd been shaking it for the past twenty minutes but found no relief. He removed his headphones, flung them down and tapped his ears as if trying to dislodge an earwig, or shake loose some wax. His colleague watched nervously and bit his nails.

There was a strange sickness spreading. The sky police had witnessed terrible atrocities but had been powerless to intervene. At first they had directed ground units to trouble spots, but as they encountered more and more of these, it became clear something was happening – something way beyond their experience.

Mobs of citizens roamed the streets looking for trouble – and finding it. They joined battle with rival groups or with the few unlucky police officers still attempting to bring some kind of order to the chaos.

Fires burned out of control as far as the eye could see, black and grey smoke mingling and casting a pall over much of the city. Sirens and burglar alarms rang from all directions and the smell of burning hung heavy in the air, greasy and tangy like roasting fat.

The pilot took both his hands off the joystick and held his ears as if trying to shut something out. The helicopter dipped, lurched and banked wildly but neither man cared. Only in the final moment before they smashed into Telephone House did the pilot appear to grasp what was happening. But it was way too late. The helicopter hit the side of the building and rested there for a moment suspended in space, before crashing into the car park below, killing both men instantly.

***

A young rather plump girl wearing a black cape and clutching a broomstick was being dragged through the streets by a screaming mob. She screamed. Loudly. The shiny metal spike that pierced her lower lip wobbled to accompany each and every pitiful wail. Personality Witch felt a warm sensation lower down and realised she had peed herself.

    As mobs go, this one was a mixed bag. It comprised everything from Sunday shoppers to beggars, with the occasional street cleaner (and several policeman and firemen) thrown in. There was no common denominator; they were of all ages and many howled incessantly for no obvious reason.

    The madness claimed practically everyone that day. Perhaps as few as one percent were unaffected – and the majority of these skulked indoors behind drawn curtains. When they tried to ring for help, they encountered the emergency services' new answering system, designed to 'make the emergency experience more satisfying and customer-focused'. One sprightly old lady rang '999' and listened to the options available with growing despair. She could dial 1 to report roving bands of looting marauders; 2 to report violent crime against the individual; 3 was reserved for reporting a fire in one or more buildings whereas 4 was for multiple murders or evidence of religious-based bigotry . . . the list went on and on. The old lady pressed 1, as she peered nervously through net curtains. After hearing the next set of options she hung up and locked herself in the bathroom with a large bottle of gin. Very soon, the phones failed altogether, the dial tone replaced by a distant clicking, like a huge dry insect rubbing its legs together. This experience, it was felt, was marginally more 'satisfying' but somewhat lacking in the 'customer-focus' department.

    Radio and TV signals filled with static, the signal becoming progressively weaker and more distorted. Some braver souls attempted to leave, climbing warily into their cars before making a run for it. Some made it out of the city. Others did not.

***

Leaving Starkey's office, Julie's mind was calm. She had helped herself to his wallet although she had no particular need for money. Feeling strangely dreamy and detached, she drifted along behind a chanting procession. There were children hyper with energy and hate; pensioners raging and brandishing broken bottles; wild young men, many wearing suits, waving clipboards and quoting scripture. There was a small band of women too, dressed in their drabbest clothes, some wearing false beards or, inexplicably, military gear. Julie observed how they taunted and kicked a lone girl, pulling her hair and spitting at her. With no compulsion to intervene, she watched coldly.

"Jesus, Jesus!" they called. "Death to the followers of Beelzebub!"

"Yes, Jesus, absolutely" agreed Personality Witch desperately. "I've seen all his films. Let me go - I'm one of you! Amen!"

"Suffer not a witch to live!" they cried in flat, emotionless voices.

"A witch? Oh, *this*? No, no, it was a fancy dress. A party. This isn't a real broomstick, just a prop. Look! And the cloak is from Oxfam." She dropped the broomstick and attempted to pull the cloak loose but they gripped her hands with manic ferocity.

"Don't try to deceive us with your evil flesh," commanded a scowling elderly gentleman wearing a hair shirt and a crown of thorns.

"Please, I'm a good girl," she bawled.

"Oh no you're not!" they answered in unison, like a well-rehearsed panto crowd.

"Don't hurt me . . ."

But they ignored her and hurt her for the hell of it. Marching down the centre of Fishergate, a few of them hurled bricks through shop windows and one bald-headed old man attacked another with his walking stick. They rolled in the gutter howling insults until their teeth fell out. Nobody paid them any attention.

Going with the flow, Julie felt as if her footsteps were following a pre-ordained path. Although she couldn't see where it was leading, she was content that nothing was beyond her abilities, nothing could threaten her. She breezed through the insanity unscathed, untouched.

Looting continued enthusiastically but rather than carrying off the spoils, expensive items were smashed or simply discarded for others to destroy. The banks were proving impenetrable but any store that had skimped on its security was now fully open for business. WH Smiths was burning; women in combat greens dashed about inside ripping various Men's magazines to shreds and yowling like banshees. It seemed that in enclosed spaces, behaviour degenerated still further – as if close proximity made the rage expand.

Rage flourished everywhere. A fire engine parked in the middle of the road and men in uniform were arguing with up to forty angry people about whether it was a good idea to let Marks & Spencer burn to the ground. Passing the encounter, Julie saw a young child distract one of the firemen while another seized his axe out of its holster and scampered away with it. An ambulance, flanked by two police cars, flashed its lights and blared its horn as a group of youths tried to overturn it. Folly was the order of the day and Julie found herself pleasantly unconcerned.

Over a powerful PA system, Marjorie MacManaman addressed upwards of a thousand people. More arrived every minute, as if summoned. Her shrill voice rattled the speaker cabinets and threatened to tear the cones apart, but still she urged the engineer to make it louder. Beneath her words, a low frequency hum vibrated ominously. By chance or design, it resonated with the sphincters of many of those assembled – with unfortunate consequences. Great wafts of foul odour poured forth as, across the market, an ugly, tense atmosphere grew, ripe for ignition. Marjorie was slightly puzzled by the intensity of the mood, but was ready to light the touchpaper anyway.

Reduced to a mere supporting role, Father Stilton stood nearby with his head bowed. Nobody dared to question Marjorie. Earlier, someone had foolishly tried but he had then decided to climb to the top of the Bus Station and throw himself off. News of this incident spread quickly and seemed to dampen any further discussion about who was in charge. Marjorie's eyes now burned with a fervour and intensity that denied all inquiry. She stood confidently, grinning like a skull draped in crepe paper.

TV cameras were dotted about and filmed slyly, warily. But it didn't take long for the cameramen and reporters to become caught up in the excitement. Within minutes of arrival, they abandoned their gear and gaped along with the rest. Especially when the witch was dragged forwards.

"Burn her!" rasped Marjorie MacManaman.

"Oh really," said a newly-arrived female reporter to her camera team.

"Oh shit. *Really!* Look," gasped her sound engineer. He'd spotted the small pyre of broken furniture looted from nearby shops. At its centre was a stake and a ginger-haired young lad in corduroy pants was busily splashing petrol onto the wood from a can.

"Make sure you get all this!" laughed the reporter, checking her make-up in a small mirror. The engineer put aside his microphone and reached for his mobile phone but realised there was no signal.

"Oh shit," he muttered. And then the strange hum of the PA system seemed to get into his skull and he put the phone down absently.

Marjorie roared, "we shall not suffer a witch to live. Remember the evil one thwarted by our own Saint Julie! Remember the witch and her vile nakedness! Darkness must be stamped out – *aaargh*!"

PINKY, IS THAT YOU?

MEED? WHAT ARE YOU DOING HERE? AND LESS OF THE PINKY IF YOU DON'T MIND! I'M THE LORD MALVOLIAN IN THIS ONE!

WHATEVER. IT'S JUST A COURTESY CALL TO SAY I SPOTTED YOU WERE IN THE VICINITY. WONDERED IF YOU WERE UP FOR A JUDGEMENT DAY-TYPE SCENARIO?

AHA! MIGHT BE. ANYONE ELSE HERE?

A COUPLE. WITH ME.

TWO MORE EH?

YES, IT IS RATHER SWEET. I WAS WONDERING IF YOU FANCIED A KINDA FOUR HORSEMEN GIG?

DEFINITELY, COUNT ME IN! CAN WE LEAVE IT A DAY OR SO THOUGH? I'M IN THE MIDDLE OF SOME FUN AT THE MOMENT. ALL FOR THE CAUSE.

WE CAN'T RISK LEAVING IT TOO LONG. HOW ABOUT TOMORROW – AROUND LUNCH TIME?

HIGH NOON? OH, REALLY! MEED, YOU ARE SUCH AN OLD DRAMA QUEEN.

ARE YOU UP FOR IT OR NOT? The annoyance in Meed's voice was plain.

OH GO ON! *SAY, CAN I BE WAR AGAIN?*

GASTE'S HERE.

AW BOLLOCKS!!

DON'T FRET, IT'LL BE SPLENDID. ACTUALLY, I THINK WE'RE LUCKY THIS TIME. HE'S A BIT CLOSE FOR COMFORT BUT I THINK I CAN OFFER HIM SOMETHING HE'LL GO FOR. I HAVE A FEELING WE'RE GOING TO WIN THIS ONE!

REALLY – SOMETHING BETTER THAN KING OF THE PLANET? LOOK MEED, IF YOU DON'T MIND I'LL BE IN TOUCH LATER AND YOU CAN FILL IN ALL THE FINE DETAILS. I HAVE TO GO. MINDLESS RIOT TO INCITE AND ALL THAT.

FAIR ENOUGH, CATCH YOU SOON. HAVE FUN!

"*CERTAINLY WILL,*" said Marjorie, coughing into her radio microphone. "*RIGHT,* ahem, where was I? Right everybody, it's high time I told you something *important* . . ."

Lost within the crowd, Una listened carefully. In some ways, her new body was a major improvement on the old one of flesh and blood. Once she had mastered motor control, she found it faster, lighter and stronger than her real body had ever been. Alas, it only had minimal sensory mapping – it could hear, see and speak but had little sense of smell, touch or taste. Still, it was a remarkable vessel and she dearly hoped it was a gift of forgiveness from her Lord. A second chance, perhaps.

It was unfortunate that the body was only temporary but Una found that, by drawing energy from those around her, she could hold it together. Presumably her Lord would reward her with something more permanent later, once she earned it. Obviously it would last long enough to perform whatever task was to be assigned. Una swore not to fail again.

It was a shame about Bill. But needs must, and all that. Time had almost run out so in her desperation she had taken him right away, draining his meagre essence completely. She'd discarded him like a used tissue. Or a *manky wanky hanky*, as he would have said. Poor Bill. He had looked so . . . surprised? Betrayed? *Yes*, thought Una without emotion; that was it: *betrayed*.

Lacking an organic housing, she had known she was in imminent danger of dissipation. Given her limited range of options, she'd floated round miserably like a tadpole in a dark pool awaiting the will of her master. When Julie's creation had entered the cellar, she formed an instant psychic bond. It filled her with relief. Malvolian was not especially famous for his mercy. Actually, she admitted, he was not famous at all.

Now, wandering amongst the warm bodies of His soon-to-be subjects, Una felt the pull of flesh and the crackle of electrical energy from hundreds of energised minds. Minds that were changing.

She listened. The old woman who contained her Lord announced that the Final Battle was approaching. The next part was confusing – because the message was almost the exact opposite of what Una expected. Apparently, you must choose the side of the so-called Faithful. If not you would be marked as an adversary and would not leave this place alive. Una was about to step forward and ask for clarification when a commotion drew near. When its source was revealed she gaped in profound confusion.

A number of men were dragging Personality Witch – a member of her own coven – and threw her to the ground. What *was* the girl's name? Una wondered but realised her memory was offline. Suddenly she noticed a pyre composed of looted items.

What was going on?

A ginger-headed youth struggled to light a match as two men hastily tied the girl to a stake. This girl was a loyal servant – unlike the rest of the assembled. Yet Malvolian was preparing the unthinkable. Una knew her Lord moved in mysterious ways, as they all did, but this was pushing it a bit. It was not ineffable – it was most definitely effable!

One of the men copped a last feel of the witch's evil breasts and then wiped the petrol off himself hastily. The girl blubbed. Then she looked up and felt a tiny surge of hope.

Una, without knowing why, walked forward.

"Leave this girl alone! She is your faithful servant!"

"What the fuck?" cried Marjorie. "How the hell . . . ?"

"My Lord!" shouted Una. "I – we - have served you loyally

when all others mocked you. Why have you forsaken us?"

Father Stilton, as if waking from a dream, stared at Marjorie. For an instant he sensed something other than the dear, sweet old lady he knew. Briefly, he saw instead a towering, dark form, burning with inner fire. Green ichor dripped from its jaws. Horrified, he stepped backwards. And fell off the podium.

Marjorie opened her mouth as if to speak. But, at that moment, Julie walked casually out of the crowd. No, she *sauntered*, positively slid out of the parting crowd as if on a polished ballroom floor. It seemed she had waded through mud to get here. Her shoes and small feet were smeared in dark brown and dark red gunk.

With an instinct fine-tuned over millennia, Marjorie slipped away as Una turned to face the girl who had changed everything.

"So that's what happened to it!" stormed Julie. "I knew I'd find you again!"

"It's not like you can hurt me in this!" laughed Una. "Try, go on!" She drew on the energy of those nearby and felt strong. Then, instead of sucking it all into herself, she sent her own thoughts outwards.

"Kill her!" shouted a man in the crowd, wearing an Ozzy t-shirt.

"Stone her!" yelled a smartly-dressed woman, holding a large, burning cross.

"Now!" said yet another man, hurling a golf club at Julie.

They pelted her with anything they could get their hands on. Considering the extensive looting, this was plenty. Bottles of wine in particular, hurtled her way, arcing through the sky.

Only a single missile, a can of lager, hit its target.

Then, each object hit a kind of hard, compressed air, which warded off anything larger than a raindrop. It began raining lightly and this was demonstrated to be true. Julie walked through the crowd unperturbed as they pushed in vain against her invisible shield. A little way off, Una appeared frozen, a waxwork dummy.

"You stupid bitch," Julie yelled. "Where are you? You can't hide from me. If I have to kill every person here to get you, I will. Understand?" The crowd looked shocked. But they believed this girl's words. She had a *forcefield*!

Una spoke – seemingly from within a wizened old man with no teeth. "Look, I'm sorry OK. I was misled too as it happens. And I only picked you because you were young and strong. And, yes, convenient. Your fight is really with *Him*! He made me do it. You were His sacrifice. He's dressed as that old woman and preaching Jesus. I don't know what's going on but it's like he's switched sides. Or maybe he just wants a fight. Maybe there's something we're all missing." The old man's face was a mixture of fear and surprise as Una battled to maintain control. Drawing her personality from the familiar shell was not working. The brain's current occupant was proving surprisingly resilient. He'd survived a World War and wasn't going to give up his head-space without a fight.

"You tried to kill me," said Julie quietly, approaching the toothless man. "I don't give a shit about your Lord Whatever. I'll kick his ass like I'm going to kick yours. There's nothing you can do to stop me!"

"I'm sorry!" said Una's voice, as if from a great distance. "You know, I think I've finally realised what is going on. You must listen to me -"

"Too late," said Julie and Una's mind was dispersed to the four winds. Every thought and memory was simply no more. The patterns were unmade. The old man collapsed, his own personality blown away too. "Now, shoo!" she hissed to everyone gathered around.

The Una doppelgänger remained frozen in place for a moment and then it crumbled and disappeared.

The crowd backed off nervously and Julie strolled casually away in the direction of the Minster.

"Help me!" cried Personality Witch, struggling to pull herself away from the stake. Tears streamed down her face and the smell of petrol soaking into her clothes made her gag. A teenage boy, took a last drag on his cigarette and looked to see if anyone was watching.

Chapter Twenty Three

Creativity is allowing yourself to make mistakes.
Art is knowing which ones to keep.
Spott Madam

Julie found Marjorie MacManaman sitting in the church, in the front pew, praying. Her fingers and thumbs made a bony triangle upon which her crinkled chin rested.

"Come in dear," she said, without turning. Her watery eyes were fixed on the altar, unblinking.

The church was quiet, lit gently by yellow candles. Long trails of wax formed twisted dragon-shapes that dribbled messily over golden candlesticks. The echoes of Julie's feet reverberated into the painted ceiling as she approached. She sat next to Marjorie and folded her arms.

"What happens now?"

"Depends on you," said Marjorie pleasantly. "There's one day remaining. Doesn't matter what you do, you can't stop what comes next." She smelled cloyingly of lavender and mints but these familiar old lady traits were offset by an alien cast to her features and an awkward out of place pose. She slowly opened her handbag, drew out a tissue and snorted heavily into it.

"What are you?"

"I can't give you any answers. And by lunchtime tomorrow your individual personality won't even exist. It's the end, you see. Long foretold – but did you lot listen? Do you *ever*? I'm generously offering you the chance to leave, to go safely from this place and do whatever you wish. Spend your remaining time wisely mortal."

"You don't expect me to just walk away?" said Julie, rising.

"Go for it girl," urged Malvolian eagerly.

In an instant, she gripped Marjorie's throat. The old woman's eyes bulged like a frog eating a worm.

"Marvellous," croaked Marjorie and spun around, returning the grip with one liver-spotted hand. "This is a *good* way for you to die!" Her other hand plunged into the handbag and fiddled with something unseen.

Julie felt a sudden chill run through her body. Her mind was crushed as if a great weight had been draped across her every thought. Time seemed to drag and she was dimly aware of Marjorie's wide, National Health grin as she slowly peeled back the fingers that encircled her throat.

"It's practically the power of a black hole, in a handy pocket-sized container. At least, that's what the advert says. I always carry one when I travel in foreign parts!" The old woman beamed happily.

Julie slumped back in the pew. She couldn't move. Her fingers were loosened against her will and motor control had been shut down. Malvolian's thoughts were an invading buzz in her mind and she felt her internal clock begin to synchronise with them. Increasingly, her mental functions became locked into the task of translating and comprehending Malvolian's words – beamed into her brain as a series of repeating commands. The PSGG (Pocket Super Gravity Generator) swirled a tiny loop of time around Julie, allowing Malvolian to pick the next and final attack at his leisure.

"I'll get your body after all," gloated Malvolian. "Strange how these things work out. This old codger was hardly my vessel of choice, ha ha no! With your brain meat at my disposal, tomorrow should prove to be . . . fascinating."

The demon paused, and momentarily experienced a strong desire to find a conveyor belt and leave Julie tied to it. Or perhaps chain her inside a huge oil drum and then say goodbye as it filled with water. Confused, he put the images aside and continued his speech, all the time gripping a small golden control with Marjorie's claw-like hand.

"It's ironic that we came here to stamp out people like you. And you blunder in half-arsed and hand me the very thing I need most. Ah my child, you really don't know how special you are. And now, sadly, you never will." Malvolian had encountered maverick talents before on his travels but as he continued to analyse her thoughts and capacity, he shuddered and thanked the foresight that led him to bring along a little insurance. To cheat, in other words.

A noose appeared around Julie's neck and it brutally jerked her into the air. She hung, eyes popping with impotent fury.

At that moment Art broke Marjorie's neck, having crept up silently behind the old woman during her Baddie Wallowing In Triumph speech. The noose collapsed, Julie with it.

"Are you alright?" he asked.

Julie clutched her throat and gasped. "I'm fine now. Thanks to you."

"I knew her face was familiar," he said. "So when you went after her, I tagged along. What was she?"

"I think she was the Devil. Or Jesus, I dunno. She – he – said we have until lunchtime tomorrow left and there's nothing we can do about it."

"I don't understand," said Art.

"No, I don't either. It's not good though, is it?" she said distantly.

Marjorie lay dead at their feet, her expression a blend of annoyance and surprise. In her hand was a golden device, roughly the size of a pocket calculator. It had just two buttons and a dark purple light that flashed faintly. Even as Art reached for it, it faded away; his fingers swept through nothing.

"Don't ask me," said Julie, shrugging.

***

The crash of thunder seemed quite out of place given the clear blue sky over endless rolling grasslands. But it was how Malvolian liked to announce himself.

"Hey Pinky, what you doing here?" said Yasmine. "Still doing that corny thunder intro, I see. What happened to your body?"

"Where's Meed?"

"Ooh, no time for small talk eh? I haven't seen him recently so you'll have to whistle."

"I'm here," said Meed. "I've been doing a last bit of polishing." Jonathon Meed gradually appeared before them, melting out of a spare patch of sky and descending gently to the ground.

"There's a problem," said Malvolian.

"Isn't there always?" said Meed smoothly. "Is it Him?"

"Nope. It's a Random. A freak mutation. Highly dangerous."

"Well, He does like to play around with the variables. I've never seen the fascination myself. I prefer to leave nothing to chance. Still, how bad can it be?"

"Erm," said Malvolian.

"*Erm?*" said Meed, raising an eyebrow.

"I had a PSGG. I, um, lost it along with the body."

"Oh dear. Naughty, naughty. Always said the GGs would be your downfall. Heh heh. Well, please yourself. You'd best tell me all about it."

Malvolian sat with Yasmine and Jonathon and told them all about it. They looked at his shadowy form but refrained from comment. Without a corporeal body, he was not going to be much of a player but neither felt particularly sorry for him. He'd brought it on himself. Malvolian dabbled in these games more than any other Aesir and was a famously bad loser. By the end of his tale, Meed's frown had deepened.

"You really should know better than to play with those things," he sighed. "If there's ever an investigation . . ."

"Look, I'm not here for a lecture. If I get found out, we're all for it. From what I can tell, you're as guilty as I am of breaking the rules. No wonder Gi-Darven's recent factory produce has been so crap. If he finds out you've been sabotaging his favourite nursery, you might actually see him lose his cool. Trust me, that can be unpleasant!"

"I've heard all about the little spats you two have had," said Meed. "They don't interest me. Stopping Gi's work is my number one priority – and it should be yours too. I take it you'd like me to put your little toy out of harm's way?"

"Don't worry about that, I'm not a complete dork. It's gone. Trouble is I can't get another."

"You rely too much on that technology crap. Use your brain!" snapped Meed angrily. Malvolian glowered at him then flounced off.

"You hurt his feelings," observed Yasmine cheerfully.

Wearing an unreadable expression, Meed floated into the sky.

Helios Gaste ran through long grass, mentally stimulating the body to still further improvements.

In a clearing, a large wooden man rose out of the earth. The man had three arms, three legs and a torso of varnished oak; its head was of thick, unbreakable glass. As Gaste approached, the head turned slowly to greet him.

He attacked at once, a flying side-kick, perfectly posed, complete with cry.

"Rog-ah!"

Gaste's right foot pounded the thick upper body of the dummy who stepped back, arms flailing in large, circular movements. The dummy wasted no time and thrust both an arm and a leg at Helios, the arm arcing downwards towards the Aesir's head while the leg thrust out fast and low at knee height. With breathtaking speed, Gaste parried the blow to the head with a left-handed *bon sau*, rolling the attack downwards with a spin of his elbow and controlling it with his right hand that dropped into *fook sau*. At the same time, his whole body swerved, the right leg sweeping behind the left and away from the kick. The dummy launched another attack with its central arm – an uppercut that Gaste had no option but to meet directly, his left arm falling as softly as possible to nullify the murderous punch.

He cupped his hand over the dummy's arm and, bringing his right hand into play too, spun around, throwing the dummy hard to the left, sweeping his leg and turning his entire body to complete the movement. The dummy hurtled away into the grass, rolled and vanished from sight.

Gaste stood silent, waiting and listening. Then he threw himself forwards just as a rain of arrows passed over where he had been standing. A single arrow clipped his leg and he swore, looking deep within the reaction subroutines for unnecessary lines to delete and claw back a few microseconds. By giving the dummy much of his energy, he was fighting at reduced speed anyway but Gaste liked to make it as hard as possible on himself. Unlike the others, he had little interest in role playing. Instead he simply liked to do what he was not ordinarily allowed to. He liked to fight and he liked to hurt and to be hurt. He didn't care if this poxy universe spawned a million Aesir potentials. Let Meed worry about that.

Not a second too late, he rolled quickly through the grass and a large, metal boot smacked silently into the ground at the edge of the clearing where he paused. It had landed precisely where his head had been.

The wooden dummy strode out of the tall grass, sunlight glinting on the rounded features of its glass head. Its two outer hands had become spears; the middle arm held a large axe. Its shiny, honey-coloured body was scored by dents and cuts from previous battles but it moved swiftly and without hesitation. Gaste threw himself forwards, feeling the adrenalin pumping. He let out a loud cry and, turning his body, threw an uppercut at the glass jaw. His knuckles took the full impact and he threw all his strength, all his body into the punch. The head split from the body with a huge crack but, at the same time, the axe swept along at the height of his stomach whilst one of the spears was thrust towards his eye.

Gaste seized the spear, just managing to avoid the axe blow and thrust his foot against the polished torso. With a flick of his whole body, he launched into a stomach throw, hurling the dummy into the air with his foot, rolling over backwards and thrusting upwards at the same time.

The dummy flew high into the air and Gaste, from nowhere, produced a hammer, which he threw from his prone position and at lightning speed. Dummy and hammer collided with a huge wrenching explosion and, for a moment, the sky flickered and stars showed through, darkness replacing the sky-blue. Then the scene returned to normal and Gaste lay for a while wishing there were clouds. Or a tougher challenge. Noticing that his hand was damaged slightly, he directed repairs.

He was restless and had been ready for days. Or weeks, it was hard to be sure.

"Not bad, but I think you're planning for the wrong sort of opponent," said a voice.

"Pinky?"

"Fuck off, I really wish folks wouldn't call me that!"

"I know," replied Gaste. "Why do you think we do it?" Malvolian had, once, returned from an adventure holiday locked into the semblance of a pink-fleshed human. It had been a joke played by Gi-Darven, apparently. The body had made him a laughing stock and he was highly embarrassed when Gi-Darven explained, at length, the roles Malvolian enjoyed best amongst the lower life-forms. He smiled and laughed along with everyone else but, underneath, decided that Gi-Darven had been a thorn in his side for too long and was ripe for a fall. Nobody loves a smartass.

"I hope you've done some work on the mental side of things. There's a few quirks in this one and I think your lack of imagination might be a problem."

"Want to try your luck?" snarled Gaste. "This body against your . . . what *is* that you're wearing? A *Temporary*?"

"Yes, well," began Malvolian. "I had a teensy accident. I broke the body I was using. But I'll have a new one when the time comes."

"Pretty risky. You're not leaving yourself much time to get acclimatised," said Gaste.

"I hardly think I need pointers from you!" said Malvolian with contempt. "Anyway, I have an excellent vehicle already. I've been working it remotely as a backup for a few days. I still have a few tricks up my sleeve."

"Hah! You still relying on all that dodgy tech?" Malvolian looked uncomfortable but didn't reply. "You'll make a big hole and then where will we be?"

"Right back where we started but – hey – such is life!"

When the mirth subsided, they walked back to join the others and make final arrangements. Anticipation was high. Ragnarok was always fun, whichever way it turned out.

Chapter Twenty Four

Genius hath electric power which earth can never tame.   *Lydia A Childe*

In the dimly-lit apartment, Barry McGarry sat and watched over a sleeping female form. Monica's physical charms held no attraction for him and her mental powers, if she had any, were either totally masked or inaccessible. It was highly frustrating. He reached for the phone and dialled a long number from memory. It was a number he rarely used but never forgot.

***

As the sun fell, at last, below Preston's erratic skyline, Fred Hartley paced up and down the aisle of the Minster. Outside the mob cheered and hooted. He dared not even guess why. There was no chance to control them and he found he didn't care. The best he could hope was that they eventually got fed up and went off home to sleep it off. As he wanted to.

He had nobody left to call on; the station was practically empty, just a few glassy-eyed individuals trying to cope with the madness. And failing. Sundays were supposed to be quiet!

Exhausted, Hartley had been ready to pack in about an hour ago when Father Stilton shuffled in looking dazed. His face had been as white as a teenager's panties – and a fraction less interesting. Hartley mentally rebuked himself for that deviant thought and tried to concentrate. But images of naked nuns danced behind his eyelids whenever he as much as blinked.

It had been a long, strange day.

Earlier, several men were sent to ask for *outside* help since none of the regular lines of communication were working. None had returned. More were sent and they too failed to report back. *Hardly a good sign,* commented the desk Sergeant in a rare moment of insight.

Now, standing over Marjorie MacManaman's child-like corpse, Hartley realised he had nothing left, no feelings, no ideas, no interest. It made no difference that he knew this woman very slightly. His care circuits were burned out, his analysis routines turned to mush. He resumed pacing. A generous observer might have given him the benefit of the doubt, assuming he was weighing up possible stratagems, or examining the scene for vital clues.

Hartley's mind drifted.

Marjorie was – *had been* – a regular visitor to the station, always wanting to report terrible crimes: students smoking pot, kids in the park drinking, her next door neighbour's tax disk being out of date, lewdness in the woods. Somehow she never saw the real crimes but fixated on a catalogue of pettiness. Still, thought Hartley, she might have been a sour old busybody but she didn't deserve this. He sighed and picked his nose, burying his index finger deeply and wiggling it around. For some reason he kept whistling excerpts from the Sound of Music, which he had never much liked.

In a day like today, Marjorie would be just another statistic in the ongoing *situation.* He felt sure there were more victims yet to be accounted for. But where were all his men?

He felt light-headed and realised he hadn't eaten a thing since breakfast. He peered at the glistening tip of his finger but resisted the temptation for an impromptu snack. Instead, he casually leaned against a pillar of pale sandstone and wiped it there. He sighed again, more heavily this time. "Look, I don't think anyone from forensics will be here until tomorrow. Can you lock the place up until then?"

"Well, I don't think we should just leave her here," said Stilton doubtfully. His eyes bore a haunted look and his lower lip trembled as if tears were only moments away.

"Oh . . ." said Hartley. He was finding it impossible to think. All day he had been battling a headache – a light, buzzing, annoying headache that would not go away. "I'm going to have to go home and get some sleep," he said, a note of pleading entering his voice.

"Oh," echoed Stilton, vacantly. He seemed lost – a boy with a man's problems, desperately wishing an adult would come and make everything alright. He didn't become a priest for this kind of shit, he told himself.

Stilton had always been a shy, cautious man. In his youth there had been a girl he felt sure he loved. But his mother had stepped in and reminded him sternly of his calling. She had her heart set on her only son being a priest. He had cried for a few days - but had then started to hear the voice. It called to him as he lay in his bed at night, proving his mother to be correct. God *did* want him after all.[9]

He had been much puzzled by Marjorie. Always an extreme, intolerant person, recently these traits were magnified until she became a veritable caricature. He wanted to say or do something holy but found he couldn't. He wondered how the good Lord could inspire followers such as her – and then remembered a little history. The good Lord very *often* inspired followers such as Marjorie – and far worse. It was perplexing. And how had she risen from being a frail old church cleaner to the Mouthpiece of the Minster – in a matter of days? How had he let it happen? Something was clearly very wrong and, as he did each time he had such thoughts, Stilton felt queasy and close to vomiting. Sometimes he felt he was within reach of a great truth, only to find it scampering away like a rat into a sewer.

Solemnly, he approached the body. She lay, her head twisted at an extreme angle to the right, her face a picture of . . . surprise. There was no fear, indeed a rather unpleasant snarl was frozen into the death mask. The morphed image of snarl and surprise was

---

[9] His mother went to her grave happy, believing earnestly that the cassette tape recorder was the finest invention ever.

both unsettling and mesmerising. Hartley peered over his shoulder, his breath stinking of whisky but Stilton seemed not to notice.

"What could do that to her face?" Hartley muttered to himself.

"Maybe she saw Satan," said Stilton. "She's been talking about him non-stop all day. I never expected anything like this. But I . . ."

"Yes?" said Hartley.

"I've seen some strange things around her. Very strange. I'm not sure they were entirely holy things. Not what I'd expect to feel in the presence of, well, of God's servants."

"You've lost me," said Hartley.

"Maybe it's nothing. I haven't been feeling well of late you see. But I was starting to sense, er, well, that there was . . . a dark underbelly to Marjorie MacManaman. In the last few days she's behaved very oddly. *Intensely* so. Yesterday she was positively burning with passion for all things righteous. Today she's all for burning people at the stake. I have to admit, she, she frightens me. Frightened," he quickly corrected.

"You serious? Forgive me but *was* she the cleaner, or . . . what did you call her earlier – the Mouthpiece of the Minster?"

"Um, it sounds like madness doesn't it?" Stilton appeared to be sweating although the church was cold. "Things are out of kilter here. I mean, I probably shouldn't tell you this but -"

"What?"

"Well, I came across a couple of the young nuns earlier . . ."

"You *too*?" Hartley felt distinctly uncomfortable and watched the young priest's face closely.

"Sorry, what? I was going to say they were having the most lewd conversation. Using language I wouldn't have believed. Foul, sexual language!"

"Oh," said Hartley. "I mean, I'm shocked, obviously." He tried to look like it but his mind was reliving a recent adventure. He closed his eyes and sighed.

"It's crazy. I've known one of those girls for quite some time. She was totally innocent in the ways of the world. What could have corrupted one as sweet as that?" Stilton hesitated. He wanted to say more but seemed to have lost the inspector's attention.

He wanted to mention how there were a great number of gaps in his day – time that he couldn't account for. He wanted to say how truly scared he was about the visions he had been having. Terrifying visions. Lustful visions. Visions of pain. He wanted to make a confession – but could not find the words.

Hartley groaned and felt his collar grow tight. He unfastened a few buttons but his eyes started to droop almost immediately. "Look, I'm sorry but I have to go. Maybe some of this will make sense in the morning. And she's not going anywhere. Sorry to be blunt Father but Preston's in a mess and goodness only knows what will happen overnight . . ." He began to wander towards the door, then turned. "Just one last thing. I hear you were addressing the crowd earlier. What on earth did you say to them?"

"Me? Was I? I don't . . ." Stilton looked bewildered. Then his gaze went blank. "I think perhaps if you haven't got the message now, it is not intended for you," he said.

"What?"

"Hum?" murmured Stilton. "Sorry, drifted off there. Where were we? I'll lock up shall I? I think I'll turn in too. Yes, a good night's sleep will sort everything."

Hartley regarded him strangely for a moment then rubbed his eyes with both hands. The naked nun flashbacks were starting to take creep into his ordinary vision and pretty much eliminated all natural, background thought processes. As the inspector resumed his journey to the door, Stilton spoke again in a cold monotone: "Oh, I forgot to say – I hope it's useful – a white-haired gentleman with a pony tail was around here earlier. One of my nuns said he was seen leaving in a hurry."

"*What?*" cried Hartley, his eyes opening wider than they had for some hours. "Why didn't you tell me this sooner?"

"Oh, well," said Stilton in the same flat voice. "It must have slipped my mind. Does it help at all?"

Hartley was already through the door.

Grinning broadly, Stilton blew a few candles out and left, humming.

***

Hartley fumbled for his car keys. The comforting weight of his replenished hip flask rested against his ribs, inside his coat. It seemed there was one last thing he ought to do.

He thought back over the day's incidents, struggling to comprehend them. There was one in particular that had left him stunned. A young woman had been burned alive in her home. All the exits had been blocked off and petrol had been poured through the letterbox. The worst part was that everyone they questioned on the estate where she lived said the girl was either a prostitute or a drug dealer. Or both. Either way, they remarked, she deserved to die. *It would be one less heathen to destroy when the time came.*

That last phrase bothered Hartley a lot. During the afternoon, he had heard many variations on it.

***

A slow knock on Arthur's door. As the door swung inwards, Hartley was revealed, stowing away something in his coat. In the hallway stood Arthur and Julie.

"Come in Inspector," said Art. "We've been half-expecting you."

Saying nothing, Hartley walked into the front room – a tidy, middle-class front room of malignant primness. He crouched on a small flowery settee in a room of white doilies, surrounded by vases of flowers and lavender scented cushions. Photographs of a striking-looking woman adorned most of the walls and there was neither TV set nor fire. The windows were hung with white lace and around the mirror was a garland of dried poppies and tulips. In the fireplace, a large brass chest held a dazzling array of fresh, wild flowers. A shrine of some kind.

Arthur and Julie sat, side by side, on the other settee facing him.

"You've come about the old woman?" asked Arthur.

"You're going to confess?" Hartley was baffled. As soon as the door had opened he had instantly regretted coming alone. Arthur had quite a reputation in his day. And *she* was here too! That was unexpected. Something about her was ringing an alarm bell furiously in his mind but the connections remained unmade. He wished for another sip of whisky - its taste lingered in his mouth like a promise. His flask was already near empty and he had no idea how. Sucking a super-duper-strong mint, he eyed the visible exits. Or exit, rather.

"I want you to promise you'll listen to what we have to say," said Arthur. Julie nodded.

"I'll listen. But if you're going to tell me you're a killer, don't expect a slugging match. I'm not that kind of copper."

Arthur rose, patting Julie's knee, and walked to the mantelpiece. He idly ran his fingers over one of the photographs and spoke, softly. "There's something really wrong in progress and it's all coming to a head. Tomorrow. Dinner time."

"Well, that wasn't quite what I thought you were going to say," said Hartley. "Can we start with Marjorie MacManaman?"

"If you like." Arthur turned and, framed against the bright light of a tall, free-standing lamp, set his hair free of its pony tail. The silver and white strands fell, straight and glossy about his shoulders. He had a halo of light and flowers; the rich smell and warmth enveloped the room. For a moment, everything was . . . perfect.

It is well-known that Life has only a limited number of perfect moments reserved for each of us. Often they fly by too fast, or we recognise them too late to savour them. This particular one was Julie's. Without knowing it, she had waited all her life to meet a man like this. A man she could respect and trust.

That afternoon, they had spoken at length and she had learned more about Art than he had intended to reveal. Here was a man who had loved his wife so much he had changed his entire life. He had tamed his nature because of love and was not embarrassed to talk about it. As Julie saw him bathed in light, tears streamed down her cheeks.

Unaware, Art continued.

"Something evil entered Marjorie MacManaman and, today, I killed it. Should I carry on or are you already thinking of calling for backup?"

"Carry on," urged Hartley, wondering how he was going to call for backup.

"I think I killed a couple of people today too," added Julie brightly. "Oh shit, did I say that out loud?" she stammered. Then she sniggered.

Arthur looked gravely at her, noticing the tears. "She is going to need some help," he said quietly. "She's been through a lot."

"Can I ask you something . . . Arthur?" said Hartley.

"Sure."

"They said you gave up crime after you got married?"

"That's right."

"You weren't involved in the Post Office job then?"

"He's stalling," hissed Julie. "He doesn't give a shit about what we say, I told you."

Arthur sat down again, next to her. She stroked his hair and gazed at him like a puppy at its master. "I killed an evil creature," he said. "There is something terrible coming and it's going to be worse than anything you've seen so far. Put it all together man. Think!"

"Is Jim Cavanah involved?" said Hartley. "And his pal?"

"Who?"

"Tall bloke. Pony tail and terrible dress sense first time I saw him. The second time he had smartened up and chopped his hair off. A bit of a nutter. His mate had an earring, a gold tooth, a skinhead and looks like a bit of a rogue. If you ask me it's all a front. Druggies both, certainly. Probably into minor trouble, but mostly harmless."

"Oh, them," said Arthur. "It wouldn't surprise me if they know something." He seemed reluctant to say any more.

Julie came to his aid. "Today, there were hundreds of people who wanted to burn a girl alive. I could tell. They were eager. Something is happening that's bigger than two guys."

"What do *you* believe will happen?" said Hartley.

"I think it might be the end of everything," she replied. "Would be just bloody typical of my luck! Tomorrow din-dins. Is there a God, do you suppose?"

"I'm pretty sure there isn't," said Hartley. "But I'd like to hedge my bets."

"There's something else," said Arthur.

"What?" Fred Hartley didn't want to hear anything more. He had heard way too much already.

"You can't leave Preston."

"*What?*"

"We tried. You can't leave. Nobody can get in and, somehow, nobody wants to. We're walled off from the rest of the world." Arthur reached over to brush a speck of dust off one of the photographs of his wife before continuing. "I don't drive any more so we looked at getting a train. Thing is, there *are* no trains stopping at Preston today. No staff at the station either. The whole place is deserted. It's the same at the bus station! There's not a bus in sight. And it hadn't occurred to anyone else in Preston to travel out of Preston this afternoon. We were the only would-be passengers."

"I have a car outside. Do you want me to prove I can leave Preston? I'll go now and do it." Hartley began to edge towards the door, a little too quickly.

"Haven't you heard a word we've said?" said Julie. "This is Apocalypse Time! Imagine that! Tell you what," she said, a sly expression creeping across her scrawny features. "Let's *all* take your car and you can see for yourself. If you can drive beyond a few miles out of town without being stopped, you can arrest us and lock us up somewhere. As long as you promise it will be safe. Of course you can't do that because nowhere will be safe!"

Hartley looked at them both and wondered. It was odd, but then everything was.

Hell, why not? "Come along then," he said.

They headed towards the motorway via the nearest route. As they drove down New Hall Lane, few people could be seen – and all made themselves scarce as they saw the lights of the car.

"They're out there," said Julie. "Watching us."

Hartley grunted and stomped on the accelerator.

They saw no other moving vehicles, not one. Randomly dotted about, small fires burned unattended, casting flickering shadows. In the windows of houses and shops only a very occasional light suggested anyone might be indoors. Generally, thick curtains were drawn tightly together, giving the impression that no one was home.

Up ahead, they saw a blanket of thick black smoke spreading towards them. As they drew nearer, they recognised the smouldering remains of the "Private" shop – purveyor of sex aids, tubes of lubricant and piles of mucky mags and films[10]. Someone had taken special care to burn it to the ground.

As they continued towards the M6, Hartley cursed as he saw the speed camera – seconds too late. It flashed smugly in the way that they do. The bastards. *Ching*, went the sound of a distant cash register.

The road sloped steeply downwards at this point and the tall hedges that bordered it gave way to fields. *Not far to the motorway now,* thought Hartley. Up ahead they saw a white transit van parked in the middle of the road, slewed untidily across both

---

[10] Or so I imagine.

sides of the carriageway.

"Take it easy," said Art. "We're close to the edge. You should probably stop just behind that van."

When they reached it, they saw that it was not, in fact, parked at all. It had been involved in some kind of accident. Some kind of very unusual, very nasty accident. The front of the van was *missing*, as if it had been sheared off. Or melted away by phasers.

They stopped the car and clambered out to take a closer look. Art watched Hartley's reaction closely. Curiously, the keys were still in the lock. But of White Van Man there was no sign.

A short distance ahead, a fuzzy transparent wall ran along the land, a deep, regular groove extending through fields and hedgerows for as far as the eye could see[11]. Beyond it, the road continued. They could see the row of tall orange lights that marked the motorway in the distance – and also the blurred lights of cars passing at speed.

The image shimmered, as if viewed through a dark mirror. Or through the thick glass wall of an aquarium. The wall extended upwards, forming a barely-visible transparent dome that reflected back a few stray orange beams from the street lights. A few faint stars shone through.

They guessed that the dome extended back towards the city centre. Looking at it generated all kinds of strange optical sensations; dancing Will O' The Wisp lanterns that blurred the vision. They surmised that the van had run into *whatever it was* (luckily for them) and bounced off. The wall was practically invisible until you were within a few yards.

Standing by the smooth, sliced metal of the ruined vehicle, Hartley felt like a man waking from a dream only to find himself in another that was even worse. He approached the wall but, as he reached out to touch it, his hand was driven back by a high-intensity buzz, as if it were made of electricity.

---

[11] Which, admittedly, wasn't very far.

"Probably not a good idea," said Art quietly.

"How is this possible?" Hartley gaped. "It feels like a million volts would zap me if I made contact."

"I don't know," said Art. "But I don't think we're leaving Preston in a hurry. Do you?"

"You knew this was here?"

"We found something similar at Bamber Bridge. We took a stroll this afternoon after . . . after returning from town. Of course it was daylight then and you could see it easier. Slightly. We walked back via the old tram road and found it practically slices Lostock Hall in half before curving away towards Penwortham. It's as if it is deliberately measured to chop us neatly out of the motorway network. I'm guessing it loops past Penwortham and maybe extends as far as Fulwood to the north, assuming it's roughly circular. Julie reckons someone placed a gigantic soup bowl over us. But you know what's weirder still?" He paused, waiting, but the Inspector was staring vacantly. Art continued, "I don't see anyone knocking on the outside, trying to get in and save us. Do you?"

He was right. Throughout the time they had stood there, not a single vehicle left the motorway and tried to enter Preston.

"Jesus," said Hartley under his breath.

"Yeah. You had to see it for yourself."

"Watch this," said Julie. She threw a rock towards the glassy wall. It disintegrated. The rock, that is.

A few minutes later, subdued, they climbed into the car once more and turned around. Then they retreated - back towards Preston. Hartley went along with their assumption that the wall would surely be the same in all directions. He felt numb and horribly sober.

During the drive, Art and Julie chattered about the strange events they had witnessed. In several places, they explained, the line of the soup bowl seemed to warp slightly. It mostly avoided buildings, taking lengthy diversions around many. And, here and there, the image beyond the wall looked distorted, as if seen through a fairground mirror.

Hartley was clearly shaken but tried to master his emotions. "OK, I admit that was a strange experience," he began. "We're locked in somehow. Right. And the phones don't work either. There's no radio or TV. Right. Okey dokey. And nobody outside seems to be hammering on . . . what would you say that thing was?"

"I don't know," said Julie. "I tried to break through but it's impossible."

Hartley noted she didn't say *they* had tried to break through.

"So we're sealed in," concluded Arthur. "Now why do you suppose that is?"

Hartley was struggling. "I don't understand how we could just walk up to the end of a road and be unable to go any further."

"We think that the bad people who are coming have something against Preston. Maybe they want to kill everyone," said Julie in a voice laced with excitement. "Then . . . who knows after that? I think it's our *quest* to stop them. Or it. Whatever. Us three here."

"You've tried throwing things high over, erm, over *it*?" said Hartley as if he didn't hear her.

Art sighed but his patience held. "Yes we did. And if you could get near, you could find out if it's possible to dig a tunnel underneath. The real question is, what do we do next? And why, other than White Van Man, are we the only ones to come out here and see this? Why is it so quiet everywhere?"

And so it was. Hartley looked from left to right and began to sweat profusely, fogging the windscreen. Wiping it hurriedly with his hand, he said, "have you seen the Omega Man?"

"The book was better," replied Arthur who had a passion for horror novels, sci-fi, escapism and fantasy. Anything but real life. "You think they're all going to come back later tonight – as zombie stroke vampires?"

"Limping vampires?" Hartley was desperate for a drink.

"You think they're hiding?"

"Or incubating. I don't know. Everyone but us must be under a weird spell. Even my officers have succumbed."

"How do we know you're not under it too?" mocked Julie.

"Relax, she's pulling your chain," said Arthur. "Let's drive around. There must be someone else for goodness' sake!"

They drove around in silence, threading through side-streets, stopping occasionally to investigate light or movement. Art banged his fist on the door of several houses where he spotted curtains rustling, but each time there was no answer. At the last of these, he shouted through the letter box. The only reply was a restless silence. Frustrated, he returned to the car, banging his head roughly as he did so. Sensing his pain, Julie touched him lightly on the shoulder and he smiled his gratitude as it melted away.

"I'll try knocking at the next one," she said. "Maybe you're scaring them you big monster you."

Art looked faintly uncomfortable at this, but then he pointed off to his right.

"There," he pointed. "A kid."

Sure enough, a boy of about ten could be seen playing in a doorway down one of the gloomy side streets. His tracksuit was bright – almost luminous – and he was bouncing a bright yellow football between his knees as if he didn't have a care in the world. All the street lamps had been put out and all of the houses were dark. The child appeared quite unconcerned as they turned in and drove up close.

Julie got out of the car slowly and approached him wearing a big, friendly smile. When she was within a few feet, the boy looked up, calmly rose to his feet and howled like a wolf. Then he kicked the football high into the night sky, turned and ran down the street.

"Oh, for fuck's sake," said Julie. "Stop!" The boy stopped in his tracks instantly. In no particular hurry, she caught up with him and tried a beaming smile. The boy smiled back.

"Hey kid," said Julie. "What's the rush?"

The boy appeared to be composed way beyond his years. His expression was calm and thoughtful.

"Everything OK?" called Hartley. "Need any help?"

Julie shook her head, but wondered if she did, indeed, need any help. The boy winked at her.

"Goblins," he whispered. "Goblins gonna get you."

"Where?" she said. "I don't see anyone except us. Where's your mum?"

"Goblins," repeated the boy. "And tomorrow, much worse than goblins."

"Who are you?"

"I AM WHO AM," said the boy, smirking. Then he vanished.

After that odd exchange, they headed into the city centre. Conversation seemed to have dried up somewhat. They didn't discuss the boy's words. Or his disappearance. They didn't look for anyone else.

When they neared the Preston Minster, they saw an array of radiant lights. Tangible expectation poured out in all directions. Drawing up, they saw a sight that made Art and Hartley gasp in horror. Nailed to the huge wooden door was the crucified form of Father Stilton. He was screaming.

"Jesus!" said Hartley. Then realised what he had said and blushed. "We've got to get him down."

"There are people around," said Arthur. "Probably the people who, you know, did it!" Sure enough, at the edges of the brilliant floodlights, a sizeable crowd was gathered. There were at least fifty, possibly more. They lurked on the edge of shadows, watching.

"They don't matter. And you don't have to come with me," said Hartley haughtily.

The old policeman had no intention of bending his rules. Deal with the immediate to the best of your ability then handle the consequences afterwards, was his way.

Getting out of the car, he looked around uncertainly. Then he leaned back in again. "How do I cut a man down who's being crucified?"

"Believe it or not, I've never done it," sighed Arthur, opening his own door. Julie joined them. Some of the crowd, seeing her, backed off even further, whispering. Soon only their eyes could be seen, glinting and wraith like.

The three walked to the impaled figure of Father Stilton, starkly aware of every step. Art's gaze remained unfocussed, his peripheral vision ready to warn of any sudden movement. Surely the crowd would not let them simply stroll up and take down the priest?

Stilton had been severely beaten and pinned to the door by huge bolts through his wrists and feet. A long, red and white striped spear protruded from his body beneath the ribcage and from his shoulder. His white dog collar was stained with blood. Up close, they saw dark blood had soaked heavily through his jacket and trousers. Somehow he held himself up, taking the weight on his feet despite the agony but he was weakening and would soon collapse.

Suddenly Father Stilton felt a burst of heat at his wrists and ankles.

Is my strength returning? he thought. *Fascinating.*

Gently, Julie took him down. First, she countered his weight as if he were an object she was lifting with her mind. Then she dissolved the bolts that held him. The spear melted into nothingness too as she lowered him easily to the ground with but a gesture. Then she laid her hands upon him.

"Wow," said Arthur. "You're amazing!" Hartley merely opened his mouth then shut it again like a goldfish demonstrating its full repertoire of engaging traits.

"I am," said Julie, running fingers through her hair self-consciously. Her gift felt clean and wholesome and she was glad to give it. Better still, *he* was pleased with her. She saw it in his eyes. Under her touch, Father Stilton lay, already healing fast.

"Goodness," he said. "You! You saved me! You truly *are* a saint!"

"I don't know about that," replied Julie modestly.

"What happened?" said Hartley to the priest. "I thought you were going to turn in?"

The young man looked at him in puzzlement. "Turn in? I, um, turned into . . . oh, I see. I haven't been very well today. And then things turned rather ugly. You arrived just in time," he added.

"Where to now?" said Art. "I mean, I think we should get away from here and decide what to do next." This seemed like common sense so they piled into the car once more. Stilton seemed positively chipper and grinned rather more than the situation warranted. Or so it appeared to Hartley. Driving with no particular direction in mind, he watched nervously via the mirror as the Minster lights dwindled into the distance. Father Stilton smiled at him from the back seat and winked.

They drove down Church Street, past rows of derelict shops, towards the Ring Road. Although the tall street lamps were working, casting a ghostly glow over the scene, all the traffic lights were out. Hartley pulled up sharp, tugged roughly on the handbrake and got out.

"What's up?" asked Art. Hartley didn't reply. He was motionless, his head turned towards the south. In minutes, they all saw what he was watching.

"Now that's what I call observation!" laughed Stilton. "My, what big eyes you have Inspector!"

A man jogged along the middle of the road at a leisurely pace in their direction. He wore a dark blue tracksuit that was slightly too small for him and a pair of white trainers.

"How on earth did you know . . .?" asked Art. Again Hartley remained silent as if transfixed. In a matter of minutes, Jim

Cavanah reached them, breathing lightly.

"Heyup!" he announced, nodding at Hartley. Then at Art. When he looked at the girl, he frowned a little and when he saw the state of Father Stilton, he was visibly shaken. Although Julie continued to work her magic on the priest, his face was badly cut and bruised. And, from what Jim could see, he was literally drenched in blood. Yet despite this he smiled bravely. Jim whispered something quietly to Hartley and suddenly the policeman became animated.

"You!" he said, redundantly.

"Aye, it's a fair cop," agreed Jim.

"Did you find your, er . . . Miss Vincent?"

"I did. Look, there's a bit of a problem."

"End of the world type problem?" asked the young priest, leaning forward, wincing in pain.

"Er, possibly," said Jim. "Do you all want to come to my mate's house and we can, you know, confer? I take it none of you has gone raving bonkers yet?"

"Um," said Hartley. "Is there a chance of something to eat and . . . drink?"

"There'll be something to keep you going, no worries. And, frankly, you don't want to be roving about tonight. Lucky I happened by, eh? I'll tell you all about it when we get there."

"Let's confer," said Art. "Unless anyone has a better idea?"

"Peachy," said Jim, leaning into the car. "Room for a little un? Want me in the back or the front, if you pardon the expression?"

As if in answer, Art clambered into the back between Julie and the priest. He was bulkier than Jim but none of them suggested an alternative seating arrangement. Julie's stricken expression told him to keep close. He parked the questions for later but flexed his muscles protectively.

Jim sniffed his armpits. "Sorry," he said, as he climbed in. Then he looked back over his shoulder and asked: "say, lass, do I know you?"

"I . . .," said Julie. "I'm not sure . . . I think . . . not . . ." She was clearly unhappy about something but Jim let it pass. He couldn't shake the feeling that he recognised her, though.

"Well, we'll do the complicated explanations when we get there shall we? Over a tinny and a plate of toast," Jim intoned happily. "Right, you want to drive down London Road . . ."

They headed for Dave and Sheila's house, arriving in the nick of time. It was starting to become a habit.

Outside the house, about a hundred people were gathered: a silent, brooding crowd[12]. They projected hostility and menace and were, therefore, not dissimilar to other dark, scary mobs lurking in scattered groups across the city. It was that kind of night[13].

As the car drew up, Jim saw Sheila peering nervously through her front room window, past the blinds and through the branches of the monkey-puzzle tree. Jim waved and saw her shoulders sag in relief.

The crowd continued staring at the house as if spellbound. Then, responding to some invisible command, they all began twitching and juddering as if a Mexican Wave of electricity was passing through them. Dave and Sheila's neighbours jerked about in excitement, possessed of a primal vigour.

The frequency of the spasms increased, the individual bursts becoming shorter. As the wave passed through them, every man, woman and child groaned as if in orgasm. They started to sway and grope each other. Clothes were loosened and a kind of rapture enveloped them all. They certainly looked happy and were obviously too pre-occupied to be a threat. Art wrinkled his nose in disgust.

"Golly," said Jim. He stepped through the writhing bodies,

---

[12] Yes, another one.

[13] i.e. nothing on the telly, demonic alien thoughts of murder and debauchery filling everyone's minds whilst they mentally counted down to Armageddon. You know the sort of thing.

followed by Arthur and Julie. Father Stilton hung back, his eyes wide in disbelief, fear and, occasionally, wonder. "Dear God, what is happening to these people?" he said. "There are children amongst them. Isn't anyone going to do something?"

"Like what?" said Hartley. "They're doing pretty much everything without assistance. They look possessed to me. So that would be your area, Father."

He locked the car and plodded along, bringing up the rear. "This the kind of thing your nuns were bringing to your attention, was it?"

Stilton's expression was blank.

"This afternoon. Our conversation."

The moment of puzzlement passed and the young priest sighed, "oh, of course, this afternoon. Sorry." His eyes drifted back and lingered on the mound of writhing, naked people as he entered the house. Hartley gave him a hard stare.

Once everyone was inside, they locked the door.

"Who's for tea?" said Sheila. "And in answer to your question Jim, I feel great!"

"Did your jog help you think things through?" said Dave.

"I hope you can do more than think," said Arthur.

"Let's see," said Jim distantly.

The goblins came at midnight.

Chapter Twenty Five

Every child is an artist. The problem is how to remain an artist once he grows up.
Pimlo Picarino

Monica awakened. A voice was speaking, a deep, theatrical voice, laced with undiluted *luvvyness*. Keeping her eyes closed, she listened. Her mind felt clear at last.

"She was heavily infected with something; at possession level or over. I've done what I can but I'm not sure I got it all."

"What do you mean?" said a voice she recognised. Barry McGarry, Tim's new agent (!). He was someone she had instantly disliked in their brief meeting prior to the show. *Smarmy little creep!*

"I can't be absolutely sure where her mind is concerned," said the man. "It's very odd in there." The speaker was in his mid forties, dressed in black, had hair that was dyed ink black and he sported a magnificent, intricately fashioned black beard (not that Monica knew any of this, of course).

"I was sure there was something more," said Barry. "Can't you open her up?"

"I already expended considerable effort in the attempt old boy and got precisely nowhere. The plain truth of the matter is you need somebody with more poke than I. Unfortunately, there aren't many in that particular club. Sorry Barry, dear heart. There might indeed be all manner of wonders within this lady, but I can conceive of no way to reach them. There could be nothing at all. It's frightfully difficult to talk in absolutes. At least I instilled a general feeling of well-being towards your good self. Should be helpful, ahem, depending on what you wish to *do* with her." He crossed his legs and brushed away an imaginary speck of dust from his trousers[14]. Under the PR maestro's keen glance, his composure sometimes withered but fortunately Barry appeared satisfied on this occasion.

"Well, I know you did your best. Once again you've earned my gratitude old friend. It was good of you to try. Oh and I meant to ask, that role is all sorted out as we agreed, yes? My girl was so anxious."

"Absolutely," said the man in black, wiping a bead of sweat from his brow. He left shortly afterwards, relieved to do so. Giving him no further thought, Barry McGarry wondered what he was going to do with Monica.

"Who was he?" she asked, opening her eyes. McGarry beamed at her like a kindly uncle.

"Just an acquaintance. A professional gentleman. I wanted his expert opinion on you."

"Me? What is it with *me* all of a sudden? I mean . . . nobody in the world has ever been interested in me in the slightest bit. Well, apart from a psychotic, obsessive weirdo. Anyway, the next thing I know everyone wants a piece of me!"

"Deary me," sighed McGarry, "I hope you aren't prone to tantrums. Or I'll never be able to release you!"

Monica glared at him and wondered where she was, what had happened to Tim and what the hell was happening generally. Mostly she wondered if it would all turn out to be Jim's fault. She had spent far too much time tied up recently and was getting fed up of it. Looking around, they appeared to be in a plush flat, expansive, tastefully lit and with no hint of menace whatsoever. She relaxed and went to Defcon 3[15].

Barry started to sit down next to her when – suddenly – there was a shift like a minor earthquake. For a moment it seemed entirely plausible that the sofa had quickly been swapped for

---

[14] they were black incidentally, or did you guess that already?
[15] The jailbirds in question merely said "what?" and fumbled with their hearing aids.

another. "Did you feel *that*?" he asked.

"Jim," she said. "Suddenly I can't feel him anymore."

"You could *feel* him?"

"Until just now. Say, does the name Preston mean anything to you?"

"Preston?" repeated Barry McGarry slowly. "Now isn't that curious? I was just thinking that very word but it seems my memory is playing tricks on me. I have hundreds of cross-referenced links to the word Preston but each one leads to a dead end. How can that be?" This last question was more to himself than to her. His smooth face harvested a frown that didn't stack easily.

As temporal shifts go, this one was fairly slick[16].

"It's in the north, I know that much. At the split second Jim vanished, I felt a hole there. Where he should be." She paused, looked around and then down at her handcuffed wrists. "Why the hell are you holding me prisoner? How did I get here?"[17]

"My dear, don't be so melodramatic. You have been behaving irrationally and I was afraid you would come to some harm. These are violent times and with Tim being attacked and you picked up raving and delirious on the motorway, I wanted to do the right thing. This wasn't my idea but the alternative was the police keeping you in a holding cell."

"Tim *attacked*?"

"I didn't want to bring it up yet," said Barry, abashed. "Tim's absolutely fine, don't worry. He's getting the best care in a private hospital and we shall be going to visit him very soon. I expect you would like to come along? We might even consider a round trip, taking in, er, what was that place called again?" Privately, Barry was baffled that this word appeared impossible to retain in his memory: a phenomenon he had never experienced before.

---

[16] *Nice one*, congratulated Yasmine, far, far away. Meed preened himself then attempted to generate a low level modesty field. It failed to materialise.

[17] It's like I've discovered footnotes all over again. Really sorry, OK?

537

Monica hesitated. "Preston, wasn't it? And if I'm not a prisoner, remove these handcuffs."

"Of course," said Barry. "They were left on from when the police handed you into my protective custody. Since you're calm now, we needn't keep you locked up. I do apologise if they mishandled you." He extracted a silver key from his pocket and released Monica. She had a sudden urge to hit him but held off for the time being. She dropped her alert status to Defcon 2 and wondered what feeble joke Jim would make of the analogy.

The apartment was luxurious and discerningly decorated. Barry had expensive and surprisingly subtle tastes. Paintings - modern ones – hung everywhere, carefully chosen and positioned. Many were originals. Many were Pollocks.

"So I can go?" asked Monica.

"If you like. But why not stay here for now? *Please*? I feel sort of responsible for you and the police were so worried you might damage yourself. You were found wandering on the moors in a pitiful state."

"I was? I don't remember." Monica's fever had abated but she still felt light-headed.

"We can go together in my car and in the meantime please enjoy the flat. There's food in the fridge, drinks, anything you like. The shower's through there and the TV remote is here. I just have to check up on a few things before we leave. Once again, I do apologise for any misunderstandings." Monica shrugged non-committally. She would rest, eat and relax. McGarry seemed charming enough – and not a threat. What was there to worry about?

"Right," said Barry. "I'm popping into my study for a short while. Shout if you need me. Make yourself at home. The phone's here if you need to call anyone. We'll go to see Tim first then on to . . . damn, what was that name? Anyway, my men will take us. Don't thank me, I insist! It's the least I can do considering all you've been through." Barry oozed charm and sincerity like pus from an overripe pimple.

Monica located a pen and wrote on her hand one word: Preston.

***

Outside Dave and Sheila's house, the crowd dispersed eventually after much grunting and sweaty perversity. They had made an awful mess of several immaculate, if boring and regimented, gardens. Fortunately, the spikes of Dave's Monkey Puzzle tree had kept their flabby nakedness at bay. Father Stilton reluctantly drew himself away from the window, trembling.

For several hours, they had swapped stories whilst Jim had subtly fired probes at each of them, trying to ascertain the levels of mental infection. Having 'cured' Sheila, with no apparent repercussions, he was feeling more confident at the old brain snooping lark. If she were still fine in the morning, he resolved to attempt his first multiple-vaccination. Even if that worked, the girl Julie was a potential problem. She had effortlessly resisted his attempts to poke into her mind. However, it was hearing how she had rescued and then revived the priest that worried him most. There was more to her than he could hope to discover in the available time. It also freaked him out that some recognition had passed between them but its nature remained elusive.

That was, until a voice in his head piped up.

"Course you've seen her before," said Spike. "Well, Max did. And quite intimately. A Clune moment, you know."

"I archived Clune along with his memories," said Jim. "I don't really have time to fiddle with them. How about a refresher?"

Spike told him what he knew and Jim felt sick to the stomach. He hated coincidences and this one felt just too . . . unlikely. And each time he glanced in Julie's direction, the old guy – Art – gave him a non-too-friendly stare. He had clearly taken it upon himself to be her custodian, but was there more to it than that? How did this puzzle fit together?

Frustrated, Jim digested the remainder of their news. The bulk of it he already knew. The sealing of Preston merely confirmed details he had received in a dream that afternoon shortly after cleansing Sheila's mind. He was interested in Julie yet she steadfastly refused to engage in idle chat. Knowing why was scant comfort.

My chickens came home to roost, he reflected miserably.

Nobody felt the need to venture out again that night. Jim needed to spend some time alone and Dave and Sheila wanted a night together. The gloomy feeling that it might be their last pervaded, although Jim remained maddeningly upbeat. On the surface.

Hartley stood on the patio for quite a while, alone, until his glass of whisky was drained. His flask was fully recharged – a sneaky funnel job when nobody was watching. For the emergencies that tomorrow would bring, was his excuse. He always gave himself an excuse. He watched a hedgehog snuffling about for a while then re-entered the house, slightly unsteady on his feet. He headed resolutely towards where Father Stilton sat quietly, reading a magazine.

Julie and Arthur sat in the garden talking quietly over a glass of wine.

Sitting down next to the priest, Hartley helped himself to toast, left there by a thoughtful Dave.

"You can't tell me that you believe my, er, situation today was not significant?" said Stilton, snacking on Sheila's cookies. "Crucified and then restored. What do you think about that?"

"That you shouldn't leap to conclusions," said Hartley, munching. *Nice toast*. He bid a silent goodnight to Dave who, having raided the fridge, was heading upstairs with can of beer, a tub of ice cream and a leery expression.

"I think the crowd were driven insane," he continued. "Like that lot out there. I also think that your so-called *saint* has a remarkable ability. But don't try to tell me there's anything godly going on because that's simply crap," he said.

"Well, you're welcome to disagree. Until tomorrow lunchtime anyway. That's when you'll have to make up your mind which side you're on. Make sure you don't come to the wrong decision."

"Father, it's like you're not the same man I spoke to this afternoon," said Hartley.

"I was afraid you were going to say that," said the priest.

***

"Something's wrong!" said Julie. She rose quickly and turned towards the house. The old policeman stared at her through the window in horror. His face sagged; he slumped in a chair. As she rushed in, Art a few strides behind, a cold draught told them the front door was open. Hartley's body was cold and he wasn't moving. His neck had been broken. Of the priest there was no sign.

Julie and Arthur stood over Hartley's body and held each other, stunned. In a few moments, Jim joined them from upstairs. After a moment's silence, he closed the front door. When he returned, he spoke softly but earnestly.

"I'd like to do something for you two now. I thought it could wait but I was wrong. It's the only way to be safe - I'm going to need to enter your minds."

"You can fuck off!" snapped Julie.

"It's the only way," said Jim. "Father Stilton was obviously not what he appeared to be. If we don't do this, others amongst us might also be, well, possessed . . ."

"And we should just trust you?" said Julie. "No way. I saw you. When you had your long hair."

"What?"

"I was there that night. I know it was you. And then . . ." she flicked a nervous eye at Art and her voice trailed off.

"Hmmm," he said. Did that happen a week ago or was it a lifetime?

"You are the one," she said. "I recognise you. They wanted me to kill you."

"*They?*"

"The voices," she said quietly.

"But you didn't?"

"Catch on quick, don't you. Of *course* I didn't."

"Why not?" asked Jim.

"Because I learned I could do things. I reckoned I must be worth something after all. I can do things that nobody else can. Anyway, I know what I have to do now whenever I meet Evil. Just don't get in my way!"

Jim sat down slowly and closed Hartley's eyes with a surprising tenderness. "What's that noise?" he said.

A small goblin leaped through the open back door. Art, automatically, crushed it against the wall with his boot. Its green blood smeared down the wallpaper like a slug-trail.

"Something's starting!" he cried. "Something bloody weird."

"Diversionary tactics," said Jim. "But perfectly timed! Bugger!"

For the next four hours, the house was under constant assault – as were other houses that did not display The Sign on their door. Daubed in blood, the Faithful marked their territory and awaited the dawn. They believed that at noon their prayers would be answered.

Finally, between skirmishes, Jim constructed an impermeable protective tent, mirroring (had he but known it) the barrier that currently separated Preston from the rest of the known universe. It took a great deal of effort and left him weary. Goblins, trolls, dwarves and gnolls pounded against the boundary. None could pass.

Afterwards, everyone in the house slept – some fitfully, others peacefully. Small bodies, green and twisted or blue or purple and twisted, littered the place. Jim and Arthur promised to clean them all up but eventually decided to throw them out of the back door to deal with in the morning. Julie had slain many with flashing razor blades that materialised in her hands. She moved like lightning and on several occasional, Jim spotted her hovering above the tiny goblins, then swooping down effortlessly. None could touch her. *Scary!*

Jim himself had used a pair of nunchaku – his favourite weapon – although far from practical in an enclosed space (as some of Sheila's broken ornaments testified). Dave and he had seen all the Bruce Lip films many times. They had both bought the weapons, but only Jim had learnt to use them – especially the double 'nunchaks' as portrayed in Way of the Gorgon. Having learned to fight, he found he could appreciate combat as an art form in its own right.

Julie, nervous about the task ahead, could not sleep and lay staring at the ceiling. Arthur lay on the sofa opposite, also awake, his strong arms folded around his body but starkly aware of the girl's presence. He sensed her, smelled her and wanted to get closer to her. Thinking of Peg felt good too. There was no guilt. Peg had loved him utterly and would have wanted him to find happiness if possible. Those memories secure and for the first time, he contemplated moving on. The past was the past. Sighing, Art cast himself into the chasm of sleep. Tomorrow would be a challenging day and he intended to prove his worth, whatever that entailed.

In their room, Dave and Sheila were talking quietly, their lovemaking interrupted, the mood understandably lost. Neither had taken any part in the fighting.

Jim returned to the spare room, alone, regretting his stupidity in not guessing what would happen. He was too easily hoodwinked and that was a bad sign. Poor Hartley hadn't deserved to die either. His face registered terror to test the resolution of the most dedicated martyr. He now lay in the kitchen murdered and draped in an old duvet. A stupid resting place for a good man. It would have to do.

Stilton was gone and whoever – or whatever – he was, he

remained a danger. Jim decided to tell them everything in the morning. They deserved that much. He hoped it would be enough to convince them to allow him access to their minds. He didn't fancy trying to force Julie to undergo anything she didn't agree to. She scared him. And more than slightly.

As he began to slumber, his thoughts turned to Monica. He tried again to locate her but the barrier blocked him. Worse, his dream theatre remained shut, its curtains drawn. Jim was isolated and he hated it. But he knew what he had to do. And, finally, who he was.

Chapter Twenty Six

Everything that is really great and inspiring is created by the individual who can labour in freedom.   Alfred Einsbatenn

Armageddon Part 1 (or, as it is more commonly known, Monday morning, March 24th 2003[18]) dawned lethargically. It was grey and overcast and found an irritated Barry McGarry in his car on the hard shoulder of a gridlocked M6, barking instructions into a mobile phone.

Overnight, over the whole area and for reasons unknown, a blanket of confusion had descended[19]. Drivers became mysteriously prone to leaving the motorway then rejoining immediately, as if searching for something. Every roundabout for miles was littered with even more broken glass than is usual.

By five that morning, both carriageways of the M6 had become impossibly busy, with most vehicles travelling at snail's pace, heads scanning to and fro Wimbledon-fashion. Tailbacks extended for twenty miles.

It was then that an elderly lady, who had been looping around bewildered for hours, finally slumped at the wheel, exhausted. The consequences of this impromptu nap wouldn't have been quite so disastrous had she not just rejoined the motorway, travelling in the *wrong* direction. Her tiny car slammed headlong into an equally confused trucker who was driving with a map on his lap and a complaining hooker in the passenger seat (the exact reverse of how he preferred).

The truck slewed across both carriageways; the messiest of many accidents since midnight. An oncoming police Range Rover swerved to miss it and hammered into a Minibus full of nuns that

---

[18] Correct, you missed it.
[19] It was a moist, smelly blanket - more of a cowpat than a blanket, if I'm striving for metaphorical harmony (which I never have).

had stopped in the inside lane to ask directions, distribute leaflets and bang tambourines. The resulting pileup was the last straw. The police, as perplexed as the motorists, felt they had no choice but to take the radical step of shutting the motorway between junctions 28 and 32. They would investigate. Or, at least, have a cup of tea and read the paper until the answer presented itself. Both on and off the motorway, this resulted in absolute chaos. Obviously.

When questions were asked later that morning, there were no clues to why things became pear-shaped between Leyland and Fulwood, merely blank faces. The local roads were similarly congested with a great multitude of the angry, the lost and the silly. And nobody knew why the trains terminated in all directions around that particular part of the country either. Most thought it had always been that way but became vague when pressed for reasons. Thinking about the whole issue seemed to cause frowns and headaches.

A few miles south of the roadblock, Barry scrutinised maps, tracing his finger up the blue line of the motorway until he encountered an area of inexplicable fuzziness. A pounding migraine threatened as he peered closely at the page. He forced himself to focus but still could not see the name Preston anywhere. Yet he knew it was there. He had gathered a lot of conflicting information that pointed to a cover-up on a national scale. Tellingly, the police now prevented him from investigating further. Based on Monica's intuition, he had approached from the east at first light, getting as far as Bolton before the traffic simply ground to a halt. They had driven around for hours, eventually finding their way onto the M6 at Wigan despite advice from various traffic centres to leave it well alone. As a man of influence, McGarry had no qualms about driving up the hard shoulder – but even that only got him so far. Now he stood under a large sign upon which Preston was clearly marked. His brain refused to process the information.

Monica knew something was badly wrong. She got out of the car and set off walking determinedly northwards. Seeing no other option, Barry McGarry and his two large associates abandoned the car where it stood and followed. Horns honked loudly in protest until Barry's men bit off a few aerials and wing mirrors.

"Hold on," he called after her.

Monica didn't reply. She was still silently fuming and remained suspicious about Barry's motives. Any artificially-implanted well-being she had for him had dissipated shortly after the admission that Tim was not, actually, fine. As such.

The visit to his bedside yesterday evening had not gone well and Monica found herself plunged into a cold bath of guilt and remorse. Barry, it seemed, had genuinely done all in his power to provide absolutely top-notch facilities but the prognosis remained uncertain. Worn out, she had slept there overnight and had agreed to go with Barry in the morning. To Preston. She had held Tim's hand for hours, whispering to him, talking to him but there had been not a flicker of recognition.

Striding along, they nipped past several police patrols who barely noticed them, occupied as they were in heated debate with those unfortunates who remained in their cars, desperate to get somewhere but unable to say where, exactly.

Eyes flashing dangerously, Monica marched hurriedly in search of her former husband.

***

"Ah, smell the coffee!" laughed Jonathon Meed. "I love this stuff. I'm starting to see why you're never off this rock Pinky!"

"You don't see shit!" said Malvolian. "And you're hardly doing it for the thrill, are you?"

Meed shrugged. "We're here now and totally committed. That's all that matters. I am looking forward to the resolution. Especially given your recent intelligence. It should all pan out nicely, I think."

"Well, after we do the horsemen gig, I return to my own agenda, OK? I mean, whatever's left of this place is my domain, right? Assuming you can take lock Him out. I want to see that sucker go down!"

"Whatever," said Yasmine, examining her nails. "And why should we care about your games with these animals? Why don't you grow your own playpen if that's what gets you off?"

"Shut up will you!" interrupted Gaste unexpectedly. "This is going to be fun. We're here. Loosen up and let yourself enjoy it!"

"Ooh, look at you!" she said, hands on hips, pouting. "Well, big boy, are you going to fork me before we go, or what?"

"Oh, sod it, why not?" shrugged Gaste. "Might as well try everything. I don't think we'll be coming back!"

After the laughs subsided, Meed returned to his meditation and Malvolian left them, returning to the body of Father Stilton. There was much to be done.

***

Jim arose and tumbled across the landing blearily. Voices downstairs told him everyone else was already awake, unless they were dead. He grabbed a few things from the floor of the spare room and went to freshen up. The light in the bathroom was not working and a small candle illuminated a basin full of cold water. This (the water) he splashed on his face before striding confidently downstairs, pulling on a t-shirt that bore the hand-written message "Prepare to Meet Thy Maker!" Noting the continuing inky blackness outside and the dark mood inside, he pulled a rose from behind his ear and presented it to Sheila.

"You won't let anything happen to him, will you?" she asked, the strain visible despite her efforts.

"I promise." He said it.

Oblivious, Dave stood at the window. His face was pale as he tried to muster the courage that would be needed. Art had removed Hartley's body and those of the goblins but none of them had the heart to ask for any details.

As the power was still off, breakfast was courtesy of a Calor gas camping stove. Jim poured himself some coffee. Although instant, the smell was hauntingly good. Gazing into the dark, aromatic liquid, his thoughts were a million miles away. A wave of sentimentality washed over him as he tried to come to terms with the reality that lay ahead. Regardless of the outcome, he knew this would be his last day on Earth. And Monica was lost. Again. Today, Jim knew, would be a microscopic version of what would spread across the planet. And, unless he got his act together sharpish, it wouldn't stop there.

In the early hours, he had let himself silently out of the house and through his protective force-field. He took a last walk, visited his flat and sat in the park to reflect.

Only Arthur had observed him leave and later marked his return with a nod. Jim's face had been grim but he had seemingly shed the indecision that had plagued him throughout the previous day. Their brief conversation helped Arthur reach an important decision too.

The final hour ticked by. Candles flickering, Arthur sat calmly in the semi-darkness, his eyes unfocussed. A faint smile played across his lips; he might have been a kindly grandfather in his favourite armchair. He was scrubbed and shaved, his still-wet hair loose and splendid. At his feet, cross-legged on the floor and leafing through a book, was Julie. Transformed, radiant, blooming. Overnight, her flesh had drained of what little colour it possessed until she resembled a statue carved in milky white marble. Her small chin was set, her manner self-assured and her eyes shone faintly. A pale glow spread from her eyes under the flesh of her cheeks. The effect was most unsettling and Jim was impressed to the point of anxiety.

Dave and Sheila were in the garden looking up at the stars, holding hands and talking softly. Seeing them, Jim felt incredibly, impossibly sad. He made a decision and, without a pause, muttered a few words under his breath. Then he closed his eyes, and gritted his teeth. Wiping away a bead of sweat, he sighed. His shoulders sagged as if already weary. In his hand, a small golden charm appeared.

"Right gang," he announced. "Brain washing time. Then we have an end of the world party to attend."

Chapter Twenty Seven

*Freedom hath a thousand charms to show,
That slaves however contented never know.*
Cowpie

Dawn had not come. Darkness remained. The sky (a velvety black) was dotted with unblinking stars. The protective dome sealing off Preston from the traditional four dimensions of the universe was now clear and utterly transparent.

The stage was set.

Fires burned across the city and many buildings were ablaze. Dense black smoke streamed from them. Abandoned cars were tossed around, some having been rammed through shop windows, others simply left in the middle of the road or pavement. Here and there, corpses lay, partially burnt, crushed or dismembered. From time to time shadowy figures walked by on missions unknown.

At 11:00 on that murky Monday, the massive sandstone wall of the Harris Library began to glow orange. Shortly afterwards, silently and magically, a hole appeared: an open doorway as tall as an upended bus.

It was one of those faintly embarrassing holes, the type nobody wants to look into. And yet, like an empty eye socket or your granny's deliberately exposed pantaloons[20], it lured the gaze and commanded unwilling fascination. At its edges, light shimmered and sparkled in a rainbow of colours. Indeed it might have been reasonable to suppose the whole thing was an optical illusion except that, over the next hour, pigeons flew into the hole. In their hundreds. They did not return.

Beyond the doorway was darkness - a deep, purply-brown kind

---

[20] For our American readers, pantaloons are a species of small, beige vole kept exclusively by Preston pensioners for reasons that are veiled in secrecy.

of darkness with occasional red flashes. It could have been a monstrous mouth floating before the towering wall. Viewed from the side, it might have not been there at all.

Preston was a mess. Even by its own low standards. The blanket of gloom appeared to be the final encouragement for all manner of warped excursions. When the sun did not rise, the minority who remained unaffected, and who had managed to survive through the night, lost all hope.

Small green-skinned men and strange, misshapen creatures wandered around at will, unremarked upon by others abroad. They ate flesh, they urinated against lampposts and they leapt out at children crying, "boo". Until the early hours, disparate groups had patrolled the streets, hunting like packs of binge drinkers, breaking into any house that did not bear the Sign. There was blood and there was death and there was no remorse. Many had driven their flabby bodies beyond endurance. It was weary, sweaty faces that turned towards the gaping hole in surprise, temporarily suppressing (due to sheer exhaustion) the compulsion to run amok.

As the gate materialised, the crowd held off killing and screwing (or killing *then* screwing), sensing, even through the fog of insanity, that a momentous event was in progress. Also, it was a welcome breather. Within minutes of the hole appearing, they felt the frenzy rising greater than before, threatening to envelope them, They held firm, excited and full of anticipation.

An old man fell to the ground, his heart unable to cope with the constant pumping of adrenalin around his body. Those around him watched as he clawed at the flagstones, gasped in pain then died. Their faces portrayed no emotion – only vague curiosity. They had seen far worse deaths under their own feet.

Finally, out of the darkness, four horsemen rode. Well, one of them was an oriental-looking chick in black leather, to be strictly accurate.[21]

Leading, on a magnificent white horse, rode Father Stilton, possessed by the demon known as Malvolian and who was, today, playing the role of Pestilence. He smiled contentedly. It was days like these that bestowed upon his ancient life a fleeting semblance of purpose.

Next came War – a barrel-chested, fiery-red hunter carrying him with pride. Helios Gaste's bronzed form, encased in light leather armour, was heavily oiled and stained with dark berries he'd pinched from somebody's garden. He sat astride the horse, excitement in his eyes, waving a long curved sword and whooping in delight.

Following him, the figure of Famine. Frost-eyed Yasmine, her dark hair tied back tightly, her already deathly-pale face painted like a geisha. At her back hung a huge black, skeletal flag of the carrion crow, picking flesh from a skull. And her armpits smelled of marzipan.

Finally, on a corpse-green horse, pale and luminous, rode Jonathon Meed. As he passed the threshold of the wormhole, it shimmered and he grinned like a fox eating shit out of a wire brush[22]. Meed had considerably altered the once-human body he occupied. He'd stretched it over a process of a thousand years, magnifying it in both size and power. Having improved basic bodily functions and performance, it was in brain extension that he'd concentrated the bulk of his efforts. Not afraid to cheat if he thought he could get away with it, Meed had spent a decade expanding the cranial cavity and accelerating tissue growth. He had also discovered a way to overclock its cumbersome organ without penalty. Meed felt ready for any challenge. And yet, careful to the last, he took nothing for granted. He fully expected this day to be far more challenging than the full blown 1,000 year

---

[21] There's a first time for everything.
[22] Bill me, OK?

Apocalypse he'd fancied running, a week on Tuesday after the golf.

Meed's mind was running so fast he was scarcely aware he only operated in four dimensions. He knew the effect of his work re-engineering the body would be quickly fatal, but also knew it only needed to last for a day. At the most. Once the scenario was played out, he'd let Malvolian finish off alone. The only thing that mattered now was winning. And there were no guarantees. Fortunately, if Pinky was right, Gi-Darven was still not playing with a full deck. That helped considerably.

Meed's black armour was a dull matt, its surface covered in living flies that buzzed fiercely. His horse's dead eyes were glassy and rather yellow; its flesh hung loosely at its neck and haunches. It snarled, foamed at the mouth and skittered about at the rear as if eager to get on with it.

Uncertain what the best response should be, the crowd cheered the emerging, god-like figures. A whistler put two fingers in his mouth and began to shriek loudly, deafening those around him. He was one of those people who always did this when in a crowd. Today, somebody stabbed him quietly but firmly in the back with a cheese knife, and his shrill whistle rose quickly in pitch before gargling into silence.

The Four Horsemen of the Apocalypse spread out silently across the flagged square. Lights fell on them from a source unseen and their nostrils glowed with power. As they dragged out the moment of tension, Gaste's horse took a major crap. It had clearly not been enjoying fresh green grass, judging by the smell, and had the good grace to look faintly embarrassed.

Meed surveyed the crowd with satisfaction. His viruses had done their work well. The mob was confused, angry, murderous, desperate and afraid. They were utterly terrified of death and the unknown, yet clearly willing to sacrifice their lives and those of others at a stroke. All these were normal, predictable, *desirable* reactions. They watched each other nervously, scrutinising faces, postures and eyes and listening keenly to any vocalisations for signs of the Enemy. None were quite sure who the Enemy *was* but there was a definite Us and Them thing swelling. A rage building. Fear reigned.

In the Market Square several thousand of the Faithful were gathered, called together because of an overwhelming urge. Elsewhere, other groups – seemingly unconnected but of like mind – hung around, their heads cocked as if listening. It was as if each had a synchronised internal clock counting down to a cataclysmic event. For example.

Father Stilton looked markedly different to how his parishioners remembered him. The ultra-short haircut suited him. Some commented on the glowing halo that hung over his head, illuminating his face with ghostly, beige light. He smiled and waved at someone he recognised from his flock then he cleared his throat. In a flash he was clothed in a gold jacket and twirling bow tie. His skin was deepest olive and his teeth glowing ochre. When he spoke, his voice was oily, like tinned fish.

"OK, the time has come. Ta daaaaaa! We've got an hour of God's tests to get through before it's all over. Glory be, eh? As God's right hand man, I have some little challenges for you all. You know the kind of thing I expect, yes? Without further ado, I'll get the ball rolling shall I?" He coughed.

"SHALL I?" he repeated.

"Yes! YES!" they exclaimed, having no idea what he was talking about.

"That's better! I'm not doing this for the good of my health you know!" He snorted.

"Now then, where was I? . . . . Oh yes, you'll like *this* one - not a lot. Ho ho. Anyway, it's a trial I've used a few times before (praise be) and it always separates the men from the boys. So, listen carefully campers." He coughed harshly for a moment then spat a gob of yellow phlegm onto the floor. It sizzled a bit. *The body is breaking down too quickly*, he thought. He then spoke in a low, cold voice that everyone – thousands of haggard, glazed-eyed people within the bubble that isolated Preston – could hear perfectly. In their minds. Those few who retained some hope of a return to sanity shuddered. And finally lost it.

"Here it is guys and gals - a starter for ten! The first person to bring me six severed heads cut directly from members of his (or her) *immeeeeediate* family, shall return through the Gate safely with me and avoid the nastiness of the Final Conflict!" He saw their gaping uncertainty and found it irritated him hardly at all.

The virus had all but finished off their higher cognitive abilities and unstoppable madness would erupt within minutes. It always happened this way. "Anyway, we'll be getting out of here at twelve sharp so All Things can be *resolved*. Once we give the word, I wouldn't dawdle if you want to avoid, you know, *everlasting agony*! Did I mention that part yet?" He grinned and many pools of pee appeared spontaneously, indicating some level of comprehension.

The crowd murmured, shuffled and looked generally fraught. Thousands of blank minds waited to be told what to do. Then they realised this was it. After a few moments, wives started to back away slightly from husbands. Children, dirty and feral, skulked deeper into the flickering shadows and began to search for better weapons. All kept their attention fixed on the four creatures before them, as if waiting for a starter's pistol.

Malvolian's special trigger words boosted virus intensity tenfold. In Moor Park, where two thousand Pagans assembled to attach sprigs of holly to their private parts, the words echoed into a distorted mush. The red mist descended. Outside the Deepdale Temple, nine hundred Islamic warriors in full battle dress beat their swords against their shields. Inside, huddled quietly together, women gulped collectively. If they had ever dared to doubt before that Allah was a bloke, those doubts were forgotten today.

As it was his turn next, Helios Gaste nudged his horse forward and spoke, his voice grating and dissonant. "To please *me*, I simply want to see violence. By this I mean beautiful, extreme violence. I don't care who dies, I don't care who suffers, I just want to see action and energy! As a bit of light relief, the best bare-knuckle fighters amongst you may compete for the right to fight *me*. Any who lands even a single punch on my body will return safely through the gate. Before the world is laid waste! So you will be spared, won't that be nice? My associate here didn't go into it but you *really* don't want to still be around when the gate shuts! Remember that. Soon I shall come amongst you so prepare yourselves!" He sheathed his sword and flexed his muscles meaningfully.

Some amongst the crowd sat on the floor and began to weep. Others clenched their fists and began to line up easy, scrawny targets.

Seeing her cue, Yasmine rolled her eyes and sighed, but played her part all the same.

"The first of you to bring me the *eyes* of your children is saved the horrors of Judgement Day!" Her voice droned, as if reading the words off an autocue. "The tiny catch is you have to do it with your bare hands *and* you have to tell them what you're going to do! So no cheating now! Who will be first? Golly goshkins! Oh, and I should tell you I haven't made up my mind yet whether *only* the first set of eyeballs will count. So once we give the signal, there's no time to lose!" She probed herself with her right middle finger and sniffed it curiously. Then she added. "None of you worms will want to experience The End Of All Things, trust me on this! I've seen it before - *and you haven't*! It's a hoot! For us!"

Yasmine Carrion guffawed. Her black horse resembled a hole in the fabric of space rather than a genuine colour. It was sooty, matt, a total lack of light. Blackest black. Yasmine gave the horse a garlic chew. "Your breath is a bit rank old lad," she said, stroking his mane and flicking a few lice away with her freshly scented finger.

The shiny insects scuttled across the flagstones until they

found human hosts, where they chomped deep into flesh and began to burrow. The lice were no ordinary critters and within seconds of being bitten, their new hosts began to grin wolfishly as they felt the strange chewings at their insides. It didn't take long for the little monsters to spread their own particular brand of psychosis.

Jonathon Meed sprang from a horse that stood, steaming and shivering. It appeared to be breathing, yet was infinitely frosty and lifeless. He floated gently to the ground, walked to the centre of the flag market and projected a huge image of Jim Cavanah into the air. His voice boomed into every enslaved mind, drowning out everything else.

His message was a command.

"Bring me *this* man. Alive if possible but if you absolutely have to kill him, do so. It will be almost as good and I won't be too cross. I will take up to *fifty* of you (for collaboration will be necessary) safely out with me as a reward for catching him. I'm sure you'll agree this is terribly nice of me. So work together eh? And mark this well: it's one hour until noon and the doorway is only passable if you accompany *us*. Some of you are going to survive today but (and I have to be honest here) not many. So a sense of urgency please, we score points for style. And to remind you one final time, if you don't please us you have no *future*. So distinguish yourselves. I am talking about hitherto forbidden acts that, even now, are growing in your imagination. Don't worry, it's supposed to be this way. Trust me on this! I can tell you officially that morality is over. There is no right and wrong; these things are done with, their purpose served. They stopped when those doors opened a few minutes ago!" He pointed a finger and a young, rather attractive woman fell to the ground, her flesh sliced into small chunks. Green liquid oozed from the remains, illuminated in the flickering flames of a nearby police car. Meed nodded, as if satisfied, then spoke again.

"The counting up is complete. Now there's just a narrow

window of opportunity for a few of you lucky souls to continue to exist. Avoid the Reckoning by giving spectacular entertainment to me! To us! Oh, and there is, I should add, a *special* prize for the single individual who becomes the biggest taker of life in the fifty something minutes remaining. Kill, kill, kill boys and girls! Awarding *that* prize always gives me the most pleasure of all. This really is Reality TV, as far as I'm concerned! And it's your very last chance to buy your fifteen minutes of fame!!"

"Your last *ever* chance."

"Ever!"

"Cappuccino? Er, capiche? Comprendez?"

The crowd looked stupidly at him.

"You have less than an hour to live you total twats! Are you fucking getting this or am I wasting my *fucking* time!?" He clapped his hands and the sound echoed like a gunshot. "I want to see you abase yourself before us – your Gods – and I want to see you amaze me as imaginatively as your feeble monkey brains can manage. I want to see you fuck like animals and I want to see you hurt each other in devilishly ingenious ways. Finally, ladies and gentlemen, boys and girls, there will be all kinds of special spot prizes in extreme categories we'll make up on the spot! We're going to be wandering all over this poxy town observing you. Marking you!"

"It's a city," corrected one well-dressed man automatically. Everyone looked at him. "Oops," he said, seeking a friendly face but not finding one. A space appeared around him as people backed away, hands in pockets, whistling.

Meed made a fist and the man began to grow. His body expanded outwards, going red, darker and darker. His bloated face was too surprised to register the pain. Then, with a loud bang, he exploded. Bits of goo rained down over the crowd who stood there, shaking in unholy unison, as if an awful transformation were taking place.

There was a brief moment of silence. Then one middle-aged

woman snapped, threw off her clothes, howled, and began rubbing the gore all over her body.

"That's the spirit, the first Special Prize is hereby awarded," chuckled Meed. The stars went out at his words and the madness began its final phase, as if by magic.

In the small bubble that was Preston, absolute blackness spread across the sky.

From nowhere, towering braziers formed, fires burning in them and lighting the city. Through the dancing shadows, the horsemen rode, each in their own direction.

Less than one hour remained.

Chapter Twenty Eight

Our hope of immortality does not come from any religions, but nearly all religions come from that hope.
Ralph G. Gribble

Monica peered through the strange, hard air in an effort to see Preston.

"Why can't we get through here?" Barry McGarry wanted to know. His man Carl was scratching his head, mystified. An all-too familiar sight. Having a mighty mental power didn't always equate to intelligence. It happened quite rarely, in fact. Barry's second henchman wandered away, seeking an entrance. In a few moments he was out of sight and neither Barry nor Carl would ever see him again.

"It's like bullet-proof glass," said Carl, reaching towards the invisible surface of the barrier and recoiling.

"You have a point there Carl," said Barry, "but how do you break through bullet proof glass?"

"A very big gun?" suggested Carl, delighted at the amount of dialogue he was suddenly getting. "You can get us through can't you?" he said to Monica.

"I don't think so. What does everyone think I am?"

"We don't know. That's why you're so interesting," said Barry. "There's just something about you."

"Oh bog off. This is hopeless isn't it? Maybe I should return to Tim in case he comes round." She was starting to feel light-headed and had an overwhelming impulse to scream and tear into Barry's smug face with her nails.

"Tim is going to be exactly the same whether we go back there now or in an hour's time," said Barry, sweating slightly, an uncomfortable, alien feeling for him. "It's a long drive, even assuming the roads clear up, so why don't we just wait here a bit longer and see what happens? Patience is a virtue, you know." He felt unusually hot and flustered, possibly because his rigidly maintained brain structures were, at last, falling under influence of the virus. Its field grew more potent at this proximity to the source.

Monica pushed against the wall and her hand met invisible resistance. Inside, she was certain, lay Preston, Jim, and a whole bunch of strangeness and answers. It was obviously strange because, if she looked closely through the glass, she could see the other side miles away, like a curving dome. The roof of the dome appeared to be a window onto the night sky yet beyond were the pale clouds of morning.

If it was an optical illusion, it was a good one! The enclosed land was flat and shrouded by a hazy fog that lay flat against the ground. There were no sign of buildings, roads, trees, anything. Occasional shifts in the darkness generated ripples of maroon smoke that spread upwards and outwards moving in what Monica could only describe as a *surreal* way. The ripples were accompanied by a loud rumbling from deep below. If she rested her hand against the surface, she felt a growling pulse that was so low in frequency it shook the very molecules in her skin.

"How come you can touch it?" asked Carl.

"What's that?" she said suddenly. A dark shape was walking through the smoke. One moment nothing; the next there it was, striding along, driving the smoke from under its – his – feet.

A priest.

Suddenly, he was there with his face against the darkening glass, his arms raised as if in supplication.

"Help me," he mouthed. They could hear nothing but could see intense pain in his eyes. There was blood splashed over his face and hands and his clothes bore many tiny gashes, like small teeth had chewed him.

He pushed his face to the glass, towards Monica and suddenly they felt a weird shifting sensation. The sphere expanded by approximately ten feet; it now included Monica, Carl and Barry![23]

"How did you do that?" asked Stilton. It appeared he was trying to contain a grimace and not managing it terribly well.

"What's going on?" asked Barry McGarry.

"Oh, you know. Stuff," said Stilton smiling slightly. "Hell, I'm crap at pretending." He drew a sword from a fold in space right in front of him and held up his left hand where a small, blue light pulsed. As he moved his hand in circles, the pulses quickened noticeably as it neared Monica. "I'm not really supposed to have this," he said. "It's a bit rascally but as long as we stay sealed in here, it's absolutely safe. Good isn't it?"

Barry ignored the light and eyed the sword warily. Clearing his throat, he said, "Carl here would prefer not to have to take the pointy thing away from you Father. Why don't you relax, lay it down and tell us all about it?" McGarry simultaneously launched a subtle probe that crept towards the priest under his words.

Stilton eyed him curiously.

"Clever," he remarked. "Not bad at all, considering. It's just as well we're shutting you lot down. Way too many anomalies. Anyway, for your information, I perceived something unusual in this direction. Took a stroll out of the maelstrom for a nosey. Trouble is I'm confused now."

"In what way?" asked Barry cautiously. Carl waited, poised for the signal to attack.

"Well, let's accept you have done tremendously well, you're still only a worm. I came in search of a mind altogether more impressive. And, no, I don't mean your pet troll."

"Er," said McGarry.

"Anyway, since I'm here would you like to be on my team? We kicked off an end of the Universe party and if you'd like a ticket to

---

[23] And a couple of birds, a cat who had been stalking them and an unfortunate Railtrack engineer. All had been accidentally too close to the edge. Or (in the case of the engineer) puzzling over a track that simply stopped.

the afterlife, I suggest you make with the extreme behaviour." The priest stuck his thumbs in his ears, poked his tongue out and wiggled his fingers.

"Really?" said McGarry, mopping his brow. "And should any of this make sense to me?"

"All I'm saying is: let your hair down. The Gods are watching and those who provide the most wacko entertainment can avoid the nastiness to come. Between you and me, later on we unleash demons and they eat the survivors. It's great. But only from a certain perspective. So what do you say – does it sound good? You may as well join in since you're here."

"Who *are* you?" said McGarry, his breath coming in ragged gasps.

"You really want to know?" Stilton was enjoying himself enormously. His voice dropped several semitones, became sibilant and scratchy. It resonated across the audio spectrum like claws on polystyrene. "My name is Legion. Actually, that's a mite confusing. You can call me Pestilence today. I rejoice in every sickness of body and soul. I've been known as B. L. ZeeBub and I am the bringer of corruption. Oh, and I am the thing most feared of all: I am old age. And I am hopelessness and I am spite and -"

Monica yawned loudly, interrupting his flow.

Stilton glared at her and his face changed, the flesh expanding and reddening. His body shuddered and his legs began to grow and twist. As he warped and distorted, the once genial catholic priest grew several horns that ran in a line down the centre of his head and down his spine. A tail broke free of his trousers that split apart with the rest of his clothes, leaving him naked. In the eerie half-light, pale, trembling flesh was exposed along with a winkie the size of a prawn. His legs continued to stretch and bend into nightmare shapes; his feet curving into huge claws.

Then, in a flash, he was Stilton again albeit with all the blood magically wiped away.

"I'll get that right later," he said brightly. "Just experimenting, you know. Trying to be creative. Think I might ditch the speech, what do you think?"

At that moment, Barry McGarry made a decision. He quietly took control of Carl, slaving his mind to his own. Carl didn't protest; he'd been expecting it. Barry aimed identical control commands at Monica but there was no response. The girl remained closed to him. Marshalling his mental forces, he wondered whether an all-out attack would be wise. His plans were interrupted by Monica's voice.

"What happened in Preston?" she asked. Stilton frowned and cocked his head to one side, squinting like Quasimodo.

"El? Is that *you* in there?" he said.

"I need to find Preston. All I can see is smoke."

She was clammy with sweat, her mind swamped with a dose of the virus that was at war with her natural immune system. In the rarefied atmosphere of the Preston Bubble, the virus was winning.

"I can take you there if you like," he said slowly, as if weighing a decision. "The geography has changed a bit but you can still get in. All of you can. For a short time." He looked at his watch and frowned. Something nagged at him. He had been sure that the thin girl posed the largest threat of all. Yet his Sensor device had led him here. It pulsed rapidly as he approached Monica – but not nearly so rapidly as it would if she was . . . *significant*.

Malvolian was a maverick - but he was no fool. Chancing across His legendary other half at this stage would be an astonishing development. *Could this be a monster stroke of luck?* he wondered. Curious, biting his lower lip until he drew blood, he began to explore the girl's mind.

It was unremarkable.

As he turned away from her, bored, Carl punched him.

"Oh thank God!" Stilton snorted blood and fell to his knees.

Carl waded in with two more blows, using his own fighting skills but with McGarry's mind directing, enhancing his body's innate speed. Malvolian rolled backwards and landed in a heap.

He got to his knees quickly and spat on the ground. A dark, bloody lump, like an exploded cyst steamed on the smoky earth. He felt the pain and glowered.

Abruptly, Carl was hurled backwards as if he had been struck. Instead of hitting the ground, he hung in the air, motionless, face upwards, hardly even breathing. Beneath him, a tiny hole formed. The hole sucked at the air; greedy spirals of it were drawn inside. There were wisps of smoke everywhere throughout this strange nowhere place and the wisps began to form patterns as if an elaborate spider's web were being spun. The web centred on the tiny whirlpool.

Malvolian rubbed his index finger around a silver disk grasped in his palm. The hole widened to about four inches in diameter and Carl's back was pulled towards it and then clamped tightly against it. He began to scream and to writhe. They realised in dismay the screams were related to the large amount of bodily tissue being forcibly dragged into the hole. His body began to tear apart – agonisingly slowly. Blood that oozed from the wounds simply floated around his torso and looped back again as if awaiting its turn to pass through the opening.

Carl was almost cut in half by this time; a huge chunk of flesh and bone having been lost from the base of his spine and stomach. The bare bones of his spine and ribs were visible for a few seconds before disintegrating and being drawn into darkness.

It took almost three minutes for the entire body to pass through. Barry and Monica stood, mute, forced to watch Carl die gradually and noisily. Before he passed on, Malvolian plundered his abundant mental reservoir and sighed with the pleasure of it. When Carl's screaming head was finally dragged through, the hole zipped up neatly and closed without a trace. Stilton turned to Barry.

"So, woddya reckon? Do you fancy jogging down to good old Preston and picking up some marvellous experiences? Some once-in-a-lifetime experiences to boost your precious databank?"

By the dark light from the priest's empty eyes, McGarry knew he was finished. Usually, whatever life threw in his direction, he managed to find a way to prevail. Today he foresaw only death. Carl had been a worthy associate – practically a friend – and had enormous wells of latent power that had served the McGarry empire faithfully. Witnessing his agony, Barry found emotions welling up from deep inside. Emotions he hadn't believed he still possessed. As Stilton turned away, releasing him, dismissing him as insignificant, a barrier melted away. Barry cast off the virus with the aid of nothing more than a deep breath.

Stilton punched Monica in the stomach.

"You know something don't you?" he raved unexpectedly. "Damn, I can sense it. Tell me! Is it *you* in there? Can it be?"

In the uncomfortable pause that followed, Barry hesitated. Time seemed to slow and he considered the options with his amazing computer of a brain. Then, arriving at the only logical conclusion, he threw it out. Hardly believing he was doing so, he launched himself physically at Stilton. Carl's punch had landed on target so perhaps the priest was vulnerable. The Barry of yesterday would never have understood what he was doing now – especially given what had happened to Carl. But he was committed, a man not accustomed to half measures. Despite being smooth and well presented, Barry had never forgotten his tough roots. He never forgot anything! Gripping Stilton around the throat, he pushed his thumbs into the windpipe and jugular vein.

"Run," he cried to Monica. "I'm sorry for everything, OK? Get out of here!"

"Well, well, you surprise me!" croaked Stilton, bending back Barry's perfectly manicured fingers with glee.

"And me," gasped Barry, trying not to pass out with the pain as each finger was snapped in turn.

"There's a Special Prize for surprising me!" laughed the crazed Priest. "But it's not one you're going to like!"

To echoes of scornful laughter, Monica fled. Ahead, she saw a dark opening in the ground and quickly descended rough-hewn steps into shadow. For a second she glanced back to see Barry McGarry and the Priest locked in a bitter grappling match. Then her head ducked below the line of smoke and into a twilight world. She ran and ran, descending into darkness. The stairs were worn, chipped marble and, here and there, items had fallen by the wayside. A necklace here, a ring there, a lock of hair, a heavily-scented t-shirt, a battered book. They were strange mementoes from other timelines and all of the items were hers.

At the base of the stairs, grass extended into the gloom. Monica stepped onto it, arriving in Winkley Square, in a small park amongst the trees. It felt like slipping backwards in time.

The steps rose out of the grass and could, she realised, only be seen from one angle. If she moved her head even a few inches, they vanished from sight.

The sky was dark although it was the middle of the day. Despite her heart hammering and her knees complaining, she ran. She headed towards what appeared to be a flickering bonfire at the northern end of the park. Behind her and from a place high above, she heard Malvolian's voice, its tone mocking.

"I seeeeee you!" he hollered. "Coo-ee! I can find you anywhere!" Then his voice switched and became a perfect copy of Barry McGarry's.

"I've just obtained some delicious information courtesy of my new host. I really can't wait for us to get together again! It's been so long."

Chapter Twenty Nine

The fact that some geniuses were laughed at does not imply that all who are laughed at are geniuses. They laughed at Columbus, they laughed at Fulton, they laughed at the Wright brothers. But they also laughed at Bozo the Clown.

Carl Sago

A long moment of silence descended over Dave and Sheila's starlit patio as our heroes made their last, lingering preparations. The sky darkened and the temperature dropped. And when the Apocalypse Gate opened far away, they felt it happen. They glanced skywards nervously but Jim's anti-virus held their minds together.

"It's time," said Jim. "Dave, mate, are you absolutely sure you want to be part of this?"

"I always expected the end of the world to be on a Monday," his friend replied. "Of course. I *have* to be part of it." Sheila was troubled but she kissed him lightly in resignation.

"Whatever happens, I love you," she said then faced Jim for the final time. "What *is* going to happen?"

"I can't really tell you," he replied in a voice laden with whimsy. "In a nutshell, things have gone screwy and we three – four," he hastily corrected, "are going to put it right. Like, destiny or something."

"Like Super Heroes!" said Dave, beaming.

"So why -" she began.

"I *need* you to stay here," he said. "It's important, OK? There must be something left at the end. Please hold on to this." He handed her a small, golden charm – a medallion on which the entwined fish shapes of Yin and Yang were carved. "Nothing can get at you in here. And as long as this is safe, no harm will come to Dave. You'll be connected at all times. Have faith in me."

"But what about you?"
Jim lowered his head and turned away.

Sheila gave Dave a lingering kiss and spoke in his mind.
I love you Dave Scofield. You sort it all out. Put the world to rights and come back in time for tea!
"Thanks babe," he said, aloud.

Earlier, Jim had transmitted his virus cure to them all. He was relieved to discover no adverse effects. All traces of the Aesir programs were purged. Arthur seemed largely unchanged and, after some persuasion, allowed Jim to take a brief journey on the inside to ensure the fix was irrevocable. Deeply dubious about the whole thing, he took little comfort from Julie's assurance that if his mind 'got fucked up', she'd take revenge on his behalf. Jim discovered that Art was most definitely a non-believer and, interestingly, this had shielded him from the worst effects of the virus.

Then there had been a rather strained moment with Julie. He had seen it coming, of course. She adamantly refused him access to her mind, threatening dire consequences should he try to employ force. Reluctantly she allowed Art to convince her that it was both painless and necessary. But there would be no intrusion – of that she was adamant. Eventually, Jim agreed to transmit the program into a point in space before her. From there, she reached forwards and engulfed it – nearly barfing with nausea as it whirled around her mind, cleaning and purging. A tense pause followed in which she glared at Jim as if ready to pounce. Then the tension eased and an expression of puzzlement, quickly replaced by wonder, washed over her.

They listened to Jim's plan and agreed to follow his guidelines, although Julie made a big show of not taking it very seriously.
I don't need you to tell me what to do, she muttered.

***

The front door slowly swung open, apparently under its own steam. Julie grinned in triumph.

"Nice," Jim conceded.

In the gloomy street outside, flaming braziers – some as tall as houses – began to materialise. Towering, made of charred black metal and lit with god-knows-what fuel, they gradually faded into existence. The braziers cast criss-crossing, sinister shadows, that danced over the road, the houses, the hedgerows, and the tree branches in a hellish orange glow. Figures slouched at the edges of visibility; pale people, zombie-like, dazed. Most were feral, naked and covered in filth. Many were plainly injured, dripping blood from untreated wounds. They carried weapons and their mouths hung open. Blankly, they listened as into their minds poured the edicts of returning ancient Gods. And finally, awfully, they grasped what was about to occur.

"Can't you help them?" asked Dave.

"Not yet," said Jim.

The party bid farewell to Sheila who watched them leave anxiously.

As they headed into town, some of Dave's neighbours became reanimated. Slowly, at first, they stretched; they rubbed grubby hands over faces; they gazed at their surroundings as if for the first time.

"Er," said Dave apprehensively.

"Let's crack on," said Jim. "They can't see us but try not to look at them. It won't be pleasant."

Art and Julie needed no such advice. A few paces behind, they walked arm in arm, occasionally giving each other soppy, dreamy looks. Jim wanted to slap them or throw a Mills & Boon in their direction. Wrapped in a brick.

"What it is with those two?" whispered Dave. "Anyone would think it was the end of the world."

"Dude," began Jim. It was a tone of voice Dave recognised well.

"Oh right," he said. "Here it comes. I've been waiting for you to start off exactly like that for the past hour or so."

"Look man, there's some things I already know about today – about the things that will come to pass. Unfortunately, I don't know how reliable they are. With each decision we make, entire futures change. Fresh possibilities are generated and, sometimes, whole universes are spawned. If you wanted to – or if you had lost yourself – you could wander through them forever."

Jim's voice faltered. When he spoke again, his words were thick with emotion. "Dude, the thing about life is . . . there are some really big decisions to make. By avoiding the hard ones you risk ending up as a waste of . . . space. And," Jim's voice began to rise in pitch and tempo, "important choices that affect the future are frightening. Aren't they?" Dave nodded dumbly. Their pace increased but Art and Julie lagged further behind.

He continued, "Fear freezes us. It makes life's biggest choices harder so what do we do?" Jim didn't wait but answered his own question. "I'll tell you what: We invent a mythology to comfort and guide us! You see, I've been contemplating God again . . ."

"Did you find some of that temple ball?" Dave ventured.

"What? Oh, well, a bit, yeah. Thing is with God, right . . . "Jim continued, ". . . people are so afraid he doesn't exist. But suppose we're truly alone? Ultimately, who will tell us if we made the wrong choices? Who will pick up the pieces?"

Dave didn't reply and Jim didn't appear to require one. "Obviously, we've always deluded ourselves that some super-wise dude will step in if we cock up badly enough. It's like an insurance policy – and we've paid without thinking. Trouble is man, the price has been too high."

They reached the bridge over the river. Stars were reflected in the dark water and fires raged in the distance, blotting out the sky over the city.

"Dude, what the *fuck* are you talking about?" Dave reckoned Jim must have smoked his entire temple ball stash. That couldn't be sensible under the circumstances.

"God and stuff. The Supreme Being. The Creator. Jah Doobie."

"Right. All of which you don't believe in, or do you?"

Jim slowed down, allowing the others to catch up. As if activated by a hidden switch, his aura suddenly became electrifying. Julie felt her skin tingle; the tiny hairs on the back of her hands sprang upright. She hadn't been listening but now she paid close attention and clasped Art's hands tightly. The one she had once thought amazing was talking about God. His presence called to her. A compulsion in her mind told her to concentrate. A voice told her to remember. And she did. The faint glow behind her eyes dimmed and a tiny frown danced a brief pirouette across her brow.

Jim clapped his hands together, startling them all, as if from sleep.

"Gang, today is Judgement Day. Somehow. And if there were a God, ideally he's a Good Caring Father who loves us, correct? I mean, he wants to look after us in heaven like some glorified petting zoo, right? We worship him and he keeps on being invisible and ineffable – that's the general deal, whatever version of the story was rammed into you as kids?"

"Jeez dude, I dunno about all that shit," said Dave. "Lots of people *don't* believe in God. You, for example."

But Jim was in full flow. Even Arthur listened intently.

"I think there *is* a grain of truth in it! Except the Afterlife isn't quite what you think." Before they could question this, he was off again. "And what about science? Science should one day have all the answers – no grey areas, yes? However, so far all it can suggest is that death equals nothingness. It *might* discover a spirit or soul one day – but it's a long way off matching the religion's tempting offers. A man hears what he wants to hear and disregards the rest, don't you know."

"I always have," agreed Dave.

"We live under a yoke of fear – fear we manufactured ourselves. Paradoxically, this fear holds back the advances in enlightened thinking. Jesus, some people build barriers between science and art, or between music and mathematics. But do you know the astonishing truth? Even with things wonky, broken and misdirected, we were *still* making progress. Despite external interference of a most insidious kind, Mankind *was* learning. Some from each generation were breaking free from the mob.

"It pisses me off that so many stupid arseholes gain positions of power. Arseholes prepared to commit terrible crimes because they say they *believe* something. Maybe these tossers would not have prevailed in the end, who knows? A growing number of ordinary folks *have* abandoned blind faith. They want to *see*! They want the truth – and they are willing to search for it! If God is to survive, it won't be by keeping a low profile, eh?"

"Um," said Dave. "You're leaving me behind man."

"I know. You're more right than you know. Dude, the Aesir *are* Gods – of a sort. They're a higher stage of evolution but they arose out of lower species in the same way as humans did. Of course, that's a gross simplification but do you get it man?"

"Oh sure."

Jim got like this sometimes, usually after a fresh delivery of Bubble Gum or White Widow.

Dave's attention switched to a lone child sitting by the side of the road. The child studiously poked a stick into the corpse of a dog until its intestines squeezed out onto the pavement. "Shouldn't we do something, man?" he said.

"And what would you suggest? The only way we can end this is by being in the right place at the right time. Look mate," Jim continued as was his wont, "the Aesir, for all their progress, fight amongst themselves just as we do. Some of them want to exclude us from taking that next step. They don't want their immortal club tainted. Strikes me that, for the Next Step in evolutionary terms, they don't seem a very *big* step. And I don't think they are the final step either . . ."

"Man, how long have you . . . where did you get all this stuff?" Dave wondered out loud.

"Meditation mostly. But, Dave, there's something else – something even bigger from our point of view. I've been wondering how to broach the subject because it's going to freak you out. Sorry in advance. You two also," he added, noting the continuing silence from Art and Julie.

"Tell us mate, you might as well. Hey, we're nearly there. I can see zillions of people and some weird shit is transpiring! Weird*er* shit," he corrected.

It was true - as they entered Church Street, masses of raging humanity – men, women and children – surged into view, emptying from side-streets, from deserted shops and from alleyways. They swarmed like insects, as if no individuals remained, just a huge, raging, conjoined entity on the path of self-destruction. It fought against itself, heedless of the terrible damage it inflicted. It was desperate and insane.

"Weirder shit, truly. Dave, there isn't much time so I'll come out with it. The thing is . . . *I'm* one of them. The Aesir."

"You're a God Jim. Always knew that."

"No, really."

"No... *Really*?" said Dave, warily.

"Aye."

Dave considered this for a moment and pulled on his luck earring. "Well, buggerations. Hey – looks like the party is in full swing! So, do we stick to the plan your Doobieness?"

"Unless I think of a better one."

"You can't just smite them then?"

"Not really, no."

A brick flew through the air and bounced close to Dave's feet; he jumped back in surprise. A gang of pensioners raced past, chasing a shrieking child. As they ran, they punched themselves.

One white-haired woman repeatedly stabbed her arm with a kitchen knife. Dave gulped.

"Can I ask you something?"

"Course you can."

"What happens when we die?"

Jim grinned. And for a moment, the years rolled away from him to reveal just Jim, Dave's old mate from those aimless, endless college days. "I've died many times," he said. "Doesn't appear to be the end, does it? If you want the longer explanation, you'll have to work it out for yourself. Assuming we manage to postpone the end of all things, of course."

There was nothing more left to say.

In silence, each went about their appointed tasks.

***

Meed was having a ball. He felt he'd been very creative so far and had seen some incredible spectacles – and even a monocle worn by a keen Patrick Moone fan. The pale-faced amateur astronomer had proved inventive enough to earn a Special Prize by painfully inserting a telescope into his rectum. The screaming man had used an entire tub of lard, a hammer and a shoe-expander plus a great deal of patience. But time had no meaning in this, the last hour of existence. It stretched into countless virtual hours. Time ran in the traditional direction, albeit at varying speeds.

Meed, of the immortal Aesir, sometimes known as Loki, at other times Herod, Ravana and others, laughed until he wet his pants. Had the telescope been a refractor it would have been an impressive stunt, but a Newtonian reflector of such proportions required true commitment.

Content, he rode on, randomly stopping to chat with folks crawling in the dirt but who were most willing to please him with any atrocity they could dream up.

Whenever he ran into Carrion, she was giggling uncontrollably as she crouched, pecking over the dead. All her misery and whining was cast off, as he had known it would be. Her Special Prizes had been awarded quickly and carelessly. Very few of the beneficiaries would survive and those who did would be made to fight it out to the death anyway. The Gods could be cruel. Indeed, they usually were.

Angry to see Meed winking at her so knowingly, Carrion dashed off down the dark streets seeking further diversion.

An elderly couple, seeing Meed's passage, told him to put some trousers on. If they hoped this would amuse him, they quickly realised it had not. He chopped their legs off and left them twitching in the ground, like the frogs they used to carve up, still alive, in their restaurant. It was good to deal out Justice. *Justice once*, Meed snickered.

A mob of perhaps twenty young men gang-raped an elderly woman and her poodle, then each other. Bored, Meed prepared to ride by. They were reaching the limits of their primitive imaginations.

Seeing his yawn, one of the men desperately produced a gun. From where, you couldn't imagine. Soon there were several more. The men shot each other at point blank range until only one was left standing. "Oh go on then, Special Prize," Meed sighed wearily to the victor. "Now go and do something really interesting before I change my mind!"

As he rode past the grim Avenham flats in the direction of Winkley Square, a familiar-looking figure stepped into the road far ahead and began warming his hands on a burning brazier. The man resembled Rama. Or Jesus. Or Zeno.

Curious, Meed nudged the horse ahead, his spurs tearing the dead flesh of the horse's flanks.

***

A squad of girl guides accompanied by a dozen shaven-headed brutes carrying bats, axes and knives marched purposefully towards Jim and Dave. Ignoring Dave as if he weren't there, they seized Jim roughly.

"It's you," said the leader – a swarthy youth in a loincloth and boots. He was smeared all over in blood. A gaping wound on his cheek revealed a selection of bad molars. If he was in any pain, he hid it well.

"Looks like my masking program doesn't work so near to the Gate," observed Jim as they wrenched his arms behind his back. "That's a pisser." Dave hesitated and was about to leap into action when his friend spoke again. "Don't sweat it dude. I'm not being a victim this time. Tried that before – didn't like it. Watch!"

Within Jim's flesh, a white light began to shine. It revealed his body, glowing, through his jeans and t-shirt. The effect on the skinheads was startling and instant. Each of them fell to his knees, weeping and begging for forgiveness.

Jim moved his shoulder experimentally and, once satisfied there was no damage, addressed them.

"Best you hide. Lay low until this is all over. Save anyone you can. I'll be watching. Those Four are liars. Get as far away from the Gate as you can and maybe you'll make it."

The leader, his cheeks streaked with blood and tears, grovelled at Jim's feet. "I'm so sorry," he said. "Forgive me."

Jim sighed deeply. "Do good things," he said. "Now, fuck off, I'm busy."

"Wow," said Dave as they backed away, turned and ran.

"Don't start," said Jim. "It gets harder from here and I should conserve my strength. So this is your absolute, final, last chance to go home. You don't have to do this."

"You said you needed four."

"Technically I do. But it's going to get nasty. I don't -"

"I'm not leaving. You wouldn't in my place, would you?"

Jim shook his head sadly. "I wish things could have been different," he said. "Let's get this over with, shall we?"

***

In the Dog And Partridge pub, Helios Gaste smiled as a large, overweight biker hurtled towards him. The clumsy oaf was drunk and lurched like a cow in a canoe. With his thick beard, bloodshot eyes and heavy leathers, he resembled a warrior of old although, plainly, his best days were behind him. Everyone had drunk ale and played pool for a while – on Gaste's behest – but now it was time for the serious business of the day. Hundreds jammed the doors as they tried to gain entrance, desperate for a chance to impress the least intimidating of the Four. Eventually, most of the front of the pub was torn open to reveal the contests taking place inside.

The powerful Aesir casually side-stepped and was about to deliver a lightning punch to the base of the guy's skull, when the biker dropped like a stone, at the same time thrusting out a leg in a speedy snap kick. It caught Gaste by surprise on the side of the knee and he definitely heard a sharp crack.

"Shit, that hurt!" he said.

"I'm in, right?" said the biker from the floor.

"Yes, you're in," said Gaste, rubbing his leg better. "Next!" He wouldn't underestimate these people again.

He ruthlessly killed the next five challengers without letting them move a muscle. Then he started to relax again. There was no point leaving without some spoils. The growing black market in lower races had reached the edges of Aesir society. Gaste couldn't see the fascination with flesh though and was looking forward to dumping the body he now wore. He'd pushed it to its limits and beyond, but still wasn't satisfied.

A bell rang loudly, disturbing his thoughts. Most of the surviving Prestonians had gathered as close to the centre as possible and were in the final stages of insanity. It was like a scene from hell. Ditch the simile, it *was* a scene from Hell.

Blood and excrement flowed everywhere, was daubed on the pavements, onto walls, onto the few surviving shop windows. Every pale, flabby body was exposed or decorated garishly. Many carried a weapon or souvenir body part from a loved one. Most of the aggression seemed to have dissipated and they looked vaguely numb, as if drugged. The final hour had lasted perhaps a whole exhausting day.

Gaste knew the time was near. Disappointed, he headed for the Gate. Behind him, silent and unseen, an old man with a tightly-bound ponytail followed.

***

A golden altar in the shape of a bull rose thirty feet high where the cenotaph once stood. All the sacrifices had long since been made and blood dripped over its monstrous belly. The mound of corpses was mute witness to the acts that one man can do to another if he believes them to be in his best interest.

The survivors awaited the final moments with acceptance, cattle who have arrived at the slaughter house to be greeted by the stench of their future. Above them hovered Holy Father Stilton – a man who currently wore the body of a monstrous bluebottle – but whom they recognised nevertheless. Nobody knew what was supposed to happen next, nor were they sure which side they had been on. Not that it mattered. Theirs minds and their wills were broken. That, ultimately, was the point.

***

The crowd parted to allow Helios Gaste to enter the square. He was now dressed like a Roman gladiator and carried a net, a trident and wore a cheer-leading skirt.

"I told you to practise," hissed Meed angrily, materialising next to him.

"Whatever," said Gaste. "This hasn't been what I expected. Whatever happened to all the super-heroes and all the incredible battles we were to have? I've met nobody worth my efforts."

Meed was feeling a little unsettled. He was sure he'd seen Jim Cavanah a few minutes ago but the man had turned out to be a lone weirdo. Meed hadn't even bothered to kill him.

He looked at his watch – more because the body seemed to

enjoy the habit – and swore.

A minute to go.

Malvolian buzzed down to the pile of bodies and began sucking up fluid. Yasmine sidled up behind Meed and heckled.

"It's fucked up, isn't it?"

Meed scanned the empty faces and prepared to call forth demons.

G.D. had never left it so late in any previous contest. What had gone wrong?

And then, in his peripheral vision, he saw the crowd open up once again. Four figures converged on the assembled Aesir. Meed sighed in relief and Gaste cracked his knuckles. The girl Yasmine Carrion sauntered forward, wearing nothing but black leather boots and gauntlets. Her body was purest white and all her bodily hair had gone. She was so ready for this.

Malvolian scuttled down from the pile of bodies and was transformed. He became a bland-faced man wearing an immaculately tailored black suit. But his hands remained as large, razor-sharp pincers bearing thick black hairs. He waved them about for effect and found he rather liked it. He'd always enjoyed taking the form of the Lord of the Flies.

A tall human female with thick, dark hair broke away from the mob and walked slowly, unnoticed, behind Jim.

The survivors gaped and waited to see what would happen next.

Chapter Thirty

Life is what happens to you while you're busy making other plans.   Jimmie Lemon

Jim came within a few yards of Jonathon Meed when everything changed. To the stunned and terrified crowd, the two men simply faced each other and ceased to move. Time flowed like chicken soup down a rusty grate.

The Gods and their challengers, apparently, had departed, leaving behind only their images.

"I told you they wouldn't hold it in this dump," a goblin commented.

"Can we start?" asked another, licking its lips.

"Nope. Door's still open," replied the first.

"Time out then. Hey ho."

Nobody – human – moved. Well, much. There was some general shuffling and fidgeting as the unhappy humans noticed that a legion of orcs, trolls, demons and chimerae surrounded them. It seemed a final period of contemplation was granted but unfortunately, nobody saw a way to capitalise on it. A purple-skinned demon sharpened its wicked sword against a flagstone and hummed a happy tune.

"Do I tell you about my Special Prize?" asked a matronly woman, nervously.

"Absolutely," grinned the demon. "And then I'll tell *you* about mine!"

***

In a remote temple on a stony hillside, Jim and Dave waited patiently whilst Jonathon Meed argued with the ageing abbot. Of the others, there was no sign.

In this place, wherever it was, the sky was yellow. The rocks and stones of the temple wall were orange with whitewashed borders, painted with no lack of precision along the uppermost sections of wall and around the lintels of each door. Yellow and black flags hung limply on iron poles hammered high into the walls, dragon and tiger patterns being prevalent upon them.

Whatever the argument was about, Meed eventually gave in and angrily turned his back on the old man. Still shaking his head, he approached Jim and Dave, kicking the ground like a petulant child. He seemed relieved to see Dave and patted him companionably on the shoulder.

"Come on," said Jim. He led and Meed followed, into the innermost courtyard of the temple. Dave lagged behind, absorbing everything and giving himself a running commentary. Jim had been deliberately vague about the role he should play but Dave had reverted to his default unworried state. Jim could be in charge. He liked that.

They entered the courtyard. Purple clouds drifted through the air in friendly clumps. In an adjacent courtyard, a bonsai tree played chess with a goblin.

The abbot watched them go and then glanced through a window, down the dusty track where, he presumed, they had come from. He frowned a fleeting, mystified frown, scratched his bottom and vanished.

inside, under a dome of eerie lemon sky, Meed smiled cordially and slapped his thighs in anticipation. Jim blew gently and the purple clouds dispersed but his countenance was grim and his heart heavy. For a moment only, he hesitated, as if considering another path. And in that instant of indecision, his mask slipped and the anguish etched into his face was clear.

Dave observed the scene with interest until he noticed that there were some rather interesting nipple-headed mushrooms growing in the shadows. He started filling his pockets with them.

Meed cleared his throat theatrically. "Good of you to come. You cut it a bit fine though." Despite his complaints, the Head Horseman of the Four Norsemen seemed relaxed. Relieved, even.

Jim sighed, "I remembered it all at last," he said.

"You usually do Gi. Usually long before this I have to say. What rules apply this time?"

Jim told him.

A small bell sounded from somewhere high above and twelve monks in white robes and carrying deckchairs filed into the courtyard. The goblin was heard to whoop triumphantly from nearby and the chess game ended with the tree's king toppled by the unexpected appearance of twin queens. Several of the monks struggled to assemble their deckchairs correctly but most managed it. They sat down to patiently watch what would soon unfold, munching fig biscuits, drinking ginseng tea or smoking from an ornate *Shisha* pipe (from which multiple curly tubes sprouted). The monks chatted excitedly amongst themselves while the two men prepared for battle.

Dave grabbed a spare *Shisha* nozzle and took an experimental lungful. He offered a handful of his mushrooms to one of the monks who politely refused, so he munched a few of them speculatively himself then blew down the tube, sniggering as several of the monks leaped back, spitting out foul water with a curse.

In the yellow corner, Jim Cavanah was resplendent in loose black trousers, white socks, a white vest and black training shoes. His body was in surprisingly good fettle and the flab of recent years had conveniently melted off in the night. He'd shaved, leaving all the little hairs in a bucket on the patio as a souvenir for Sheila. He'd briefly considered leaving an imprint of his face in a towel or something but deduced it wouldn't be appreciated. Stroking his head, he thought he might keep his hair short for a while, but not this short. Clune had rather overdone it – but once you let your dark side take over, you must live with the consequences. Anyway, Monica liked it short, he recalled, aware his mind should probably focus.

He performed a few gentle stretches while the sun rose over

the rooftops and peeped into the courtyard, obligingly flooding the scene with a wash of dreamy yellow light. The delicate mosaic floor was inlaid with pictures of stars, planets, signs of the zodiac and the magic herb. The physical exercise helped, as it always did. Jim felt resolved and at peace.

He breathed slowly and drank deeply. The air was fresh and invigorating and shockingly chill inside his expanding lungs. Slow, circular motions of his arms exercised the joints and loosened his shoulders and arms. He stretched his arms backwards and behind his body, again working the shoulders. Jim was methodical, aware that the body was a fine machine and, as such, required knowledgeable care and attention. He slowly rotated his hands, working the wrists then bent each of his hands backwards in turn. All the time he kept his mind empty, his eyes narrow slits against the light.

He didn't think. He felt.

"For an old bastard, you're quite supple," observed Dave from the sidelines, drawing on the pipe with a loud gurgle. Grey smoke drifted slothfully from the *hubbly-bubbly* laced with a dusky scent akin to roasting strawberries. One of the monks poked at it inexpertly with a set of silver tongs and it hissed and sparked in response.

Jim bent forwards and put his hands flat on the ground – no easy matter for a tall man. His legs felt tighter at the back of his knees than he'd have liked and he gently ran his hands over the area, flooding it with warmth.

"Man, this is some seriously sweet smoke. Not strong but euphoric, if you know what I mean. You sure I can't do anything to help?" said Dave. "Cos if not I can see myself getting pleasantly hammered."

"No sweat mate, you stay put," said Jim. He proceeded to work his hips then his knees and tried out a round of speed-punching. Watching from his vantage point in Jim's head, Spike nodded in encouragement. A lot was riding on this.

You're as ready as you'll ever be.

In contrast, Meed's preparations were minimal. He simply sat on the floor in the red corner and tried to pry out some of the pretty tiles in the mosaic with a penknife. As he did this, he spied on Jim out of the corner of his eye, an expression of curious surprise on his face.

The small bell sounded three times in quick succession, its clear, high tones cutting through the haze.

Finally it was time.

They squared up. As they had done many times before.

This time it felt different.

Jim held out his right fist and touched his left palm with it, bowing solemnly.

"Fuck you!" snorted Jonathon Meed. His anger had been growing since Jim mentioned the rules of the encounter. Unconventional as ever! His former good mood evaporated entirely as his immortal enemy struck a few flowery poses.

A silent mutual appraisal followed. The contest had started but neither of them moved an inch. Meed spat on the ground.

Quicker than a ray of light, Jim closed and hit him very, very fast.

"Ouch, you bastard!" said Meed.

"Hurt did it? Wing Chun snap punch. Good eh?"

"You bloody *hit* me! I can't believe you're doing it like this!"

"Beautiful wasn't it?"

"My dose!" Meed was upset.

"Fighting as an art form. Who would have believed it possible?"

"Well, I wouldn't call it beautiful! You punched me you twat! You've never done *that* before! We're supposed to be higher beings. Are you absolutely sure you've remembered *everything*?" He touched the tip of his nose with a finger and was horrified to see a spot of blood.

"A random chance played its part. Bruce Lip. I bet you've

never even heard the name."

"You learned how to fight!" Meed was aghast. Helios was too, but elsewhere. We'll catch up with him shortly.

Jim slipped into preaching mode, to the echoes of Dave's chortles from a short distance. "I loved the Bruce Lip films as a kid. Took up Wing Chun myself. The other students talked about him like he was some kind of God, which was weird. But I was impressionable and soon got hooked on Kung Fu. Imagine, Meed, if you can, fighting done with care and imagination but not with hate and uncontrolled destruction."

"You're having me on," said Meed.

Jim circled around, his trainers sliding easily over the hard mosaic tiles, his feet twitching with excitement. He felt loose but ready to act and to react.

"You're . . . serious about . . . fighting me, *physically*?" Meed whined. He clearly wasn't getting it.

"Don't call me Shirley," drawled Jim predictably. "The way I see it, Lip demonstrated that fighting was also Art. Indeed anything can be. He raised the bar for everyone though we didn't know it at the time. I started to think about all the facets of Art and I started with Art and Science. Why do humans perceive them as separate entities or, worse, opposites? Leonardo knew better but for some reason we miss all the important lessons of history. You'd know all about that, of course."

Meed simply glared because he knew his enemy was far from finished talking.

"You know the weird thing?" Jim continued. "I realised it only last night. I remembered that, whenever we meet, our confrontations are always mental, intense and draining. But they are never *beautiful*. Hey Meed, I can do the noises too!" Jim did a few screams, waved his arms and beckoned with his fingertips.

"Good noises dude", encouraged Dave. "There is no spoon, right? Hey man, any chance of some munchies? I don't know how we got here, but I can't get any mental vibes going on. Can't hear

Sheila any more. I'm bloody starving though." Some chilli crisps appeared in his hands and a can of Chocomel by his side. "Thanks mate!" he grinned. "Now gob that twat and let's get out of here!"

Jim nodded and simultaneously launched a side thrust kick towards his unsuspecting arch-enemy. It connected with him above the pelvis and bent him almost sideways. He stood upright again holding his side in pain.

"Ow!" he said. "I refuse to descend to this primitive level! You know it's not my style!"

"My style?" drawled Jim. "You can call it the art of fighting without fighting!"

"Foiding widaht foiding!" joined in Dave from the sidelines, in his best imitation Aussie accent.

With a flurry of short, direct punches, Jim's hard knuckles pounded Jonathon's borrowed cheeks and nose. If the original owner's mental processes had not been destroyed aeons ago by Meed's forced invasion, they were surely jelly by now. The body was strong – but Meed had never planned to use it for fighting.

After six lightning fast strikes, Jim stepped backwards, smartly, to observe the damage.

"Right!" snarled Meed and transformed the creaking body into a large, troll-like creature, about nine feet high. His cells positively creaked with the abuse and his muscles bulged dangerously. "If you want to revert to the ancient ways it's fine by me. *She* used to like a bit of the primitive too – and look where it got Her!"

Furiously, Jim threw himself at the troll, slamming into its body like a car into a wall. He fell awkwardly and then quickly got to his feet. Meed watched contemptuously.

"Why do you keep torturing yourself? Not even you could put Her mind back together – even if you ever found it."

"We need emotional content," Jim muttered quietly. "Not anger." With that he relaxed and adopted a loose, boxing stance.

From his vantage point squatting in the dust, Dave gawped at the giant, its blue-green scaly flesh glinting in the sunshine. "Mortal Kombat!" he cried but his voice seemed distant. He was surprised to see his hands were slightly translucent. A trick of the light, perhaps.

Jim took a flying kick at Meed's surprised gargoyle face, slightly enhancing his reactions to add extra speed and height. Meed fell like a stone and Jim was on top of him in seconds applying a solid arm lock to the troll.

"Did Ju Jitsu in later life. You should never stop learning. Beowulf could have used a bit of this, eh?"

"I still don't believe we're doing this!" said Meed, beginning to laugh in spite of himself as he strained to get free.

"Admit it. You're loving it," demanded Jim and released him. "You should never be too old to learn something new."

Meed shook his head but grinned broadly.

"You're a card, Gi, I'll give you that. And you've always been a good loser. Weapons!" he shouted. His troll body shrank back into its previous human form. He ached a little from the exertion but it was too late to master such transformations.

Twin butterfly knives appeared in his gnarled hands. The knives were long with a straight back, the blade curving from the tip to a handle that continued in a smooth arc. It was designed to protect the hands from cuts all the way round. A gold, black and red tassel hung from each handle. Meed hadn't quite grasped the full functionality though. The blades were too long for some of the wrist-spinning, close-in Wing Chun movements they were supposed to be compatible with. Each was huge and very sharp.

Jim brandished nunchaku – because it felt right. He was marginally less accomplished with weapons than with fists and feet, but content to have a go. The knives flicked in, mirroring Jim's earlier attack. Meed picked things up fast. His lunges were a little more sluggish and far less polished than Jim's – but unlike

Jim he was holding 8 pounds of metal. As the blades swirled before his eyes, he backed off frantically across the courtyard.

An eerie stillness descended. The watching monks froze, some with half-raised cups en route to their lips. They halted without so much as a flicker, as if in a movie that had been paused. The only animation (outside the fight) came from Dave who sat cross-legged in the bright sunlight, munching, and also from the monk sitting next to him. This was the shiny-headed fellow who, earlier, had refused the mystical mushroom but who now offered Dave an impressive Y-shaped joint with both hands. The monk was drawing patterns in the dirt with his feet and saying "Glook glook."

Taking the artistic reefer carefully, seeing it bend under its own weight, Dave offered his wooden pipe in return. "No tobacco in this I hope?" he asked.

"Do I look stupid?" asked the monk. Dave started to reply but then thought better of it. Who was he to comment, really? The herbal aroma was rising and the sun was shining. If this were truly the momentous occasion Jim had prophesied, they had nice weather for it.

Meed was less impressed. "I don't reckon much to the set and the extras."

"It's not perfect. I didn't have much time. And before you ask, you're not getting a Hollywood ending speech off me either. You tried to screw my work, so let's fight!"

The nunchaku swung straight through Meed's guard, between the knives and caught him on the tip of the chin. Jim caught it again under his right armpit and stood there, posing.

"How'd you get rid of the beer gut dude?" said Dave re-lighting one end of the prodigious doobie. The monk sniffed at the pipe cautiously and peered closely into it before asking to borrow Dave's lighter.

"Time out?" said Jim, seeing them and smelling the magic weed.

Meed snorted. "You know I never touch that crap. Turns you psycho, correct?"

"Ah, you've really done your research, haven't you?" said Jim. "Half an hour with the Daily Mail, I bet. You have no fecking idea what makes my Creation so special, do you? We can do this either way – easy or hard. We can chill for a bit and then do the final stage or we can press on. Up to you."

"I'm not going to smoke that shit if that's what you're hinting at. How would we ever fight afterwards?"

Jim sighed. "Quite. Oh well, if you really want to finish this, let's do it!"

He leaped forward, ducking under a sweeping left hand blow. Butterfly knives are much used in advanced Wing Chun practice and Meed's knowledge of this was limited to what he could glean from his databanks. As Jim guessed, they were woefully incomplete on such topics. Having to fight like an animal was bound to catch him on the hop.

Meed flushed red to realise that both Gaste and Carrion would have been better equipped for this particular shindig! In his anger he threw a mental blast in Jim's direction. Jim glared at him, his eyes ablaze.

"Desperation setting in already? Outmanoeuvred again – go on, admit it! You can leave in one piece. Quit and promise not to come back. I'll clean up. There will be *some* fallout though. Pinky's used one forbidden gadget too many, as I'm sure you know."

"If you have gained knowledge from the Outside then your stewardship will be revoked," said Meed. "You have to obey the rules in here – more than *anyone*! Wouldn't it hurt you to be banished while I remain? Imagine what I would do amongst your little play-creatures! And your . . . friends."

"Not from the Outside, from the Future!" laughed Jim. "Ever hear of prescience?"

"Of course. Enough to know it's not possible here. This is one of the absolutes, the constants. You can view the past but if you enter the future you can't come back. I'm quoting from the LTU Absolutes and everybody knows how they work!"

"Well, if I told you how I did it, I'd have to kill you," laughed Jim. "Which, by coincidence, is exactly what I'm going to do. The kill you part," he added, unnecessarily.

Meed lunged, spittle flying from his lips. Jim, standing side on, swayed slightly backwards to avoid the blow. His right hand parried with the nunchaku held tightly together. At the same time his body was in motion, turning, bringing in his left arm that went, elbow first under Meed's armpit. Jim's right hand encircled the lunging arm, thrusting it downwards and driving Meed over his body. He hit the floor flat on his back and Jim stood over him, satisfied.

"We'll call that sorted shall we?" he said.

"You honestly call this beautiful?" Meed crawled stiffly to his knees. "It's ridiculous! This isn't Art. It's brawling with set pieces."

"Nice description. And yes, I admit you're not very pretty," said Jim. "But your shortcomings are your own responsibility. It's not up to me to show you how to appreciate Art. You need the cultural references, the bigger picture. In my own construction, I set the challenges! I know what you did. And why!"

Meed rose to his feet and beat off the dust.

"You're a fool to think these apes deserve a future," he said. And threw one of the knives at Dave.

It hammered into his chest with unexpected accuracy. Certainly Dave looked surprised as it pinned him to one of the hundred or so wooden struts encircling the courtyard and supporting the roof of the buildings beyond. Dave coughed and slumped without a word.

"I left him at home," said Jim. "I thought it best." He snapped his fingers and Dave vanished. For an instant, a golden Yin Yang symbol hung in the air where he had been.

"Pointless theatricals as ever. So you're only three after all? And the other two were the best you could find? You're well and truly finished this time. This could be the end of your LTU recruitment projects!" Meed snarled. Clearly, he was very angry. His face flushed. Twisty red blood vessels swelled and darkened on his nose as if ready to burst.

"You'll never be a match for me without *Her*. It's over for you but you can't accept it. Elea-Mira is gone. You are alone and you always will be. Now, do you want to continue to brawl like a beast or do you want to finish this contest like an Aesir?"

"As you wish," said Jim without enthusiasm. He clapped his hands and the courtyard faded.

They floated in a pale ultramarine sea with endless miles of water above. And below, as far as they could see, there was only blue-green shimmering water illuminated by faint light from the unseen depths. There was almost no resistance as they moved, no apparent gravity and no sense of time passing. For a while, each guided their illusory bodies through the water, experimenting.

Free of the limitations of flesh (their physical shells were parked nearby in stasis) the battle would now be held in the traditional Aesir manner: as a trial of mental strength.

Meed felt confident. It was a relief to finally turn to the fighting skills in which he had no equal. He fixed his attention on the one the Aesir called the Dreamer, and worse. Before it began, he overclocked the meat in which his consciousness currently resided, forcing it to run at dangerous speeds. The inevitable tissue damage was of no concern.

Jim's projection stroked a fish and pulled faces at it.

"Ready?" he said, without glancing in Meed's direction.

***

Helios Gaste was disappointed. *Just an old man.* They faced each other on a barren hillside near a small copse. The sky was a flawless blue and distant mountains poked through the earth like teeth, grey and shimmering through the heat haze. A dirt trail snaked upwards, winding carelessly through a mixture of rocks, shale and dry tussocks. It could have been a Mediterranean summer's day and Art wistfully recalled a time when he and Peg had taken a package holiday to Spain. The sun burned the refreshment from what little wind blew.

The man he faced seemed to be a native, at ease in the climate.

"I bloody knew it. I suppose you're the powerful mind freak?" said Gaste. "Just my luck to come up against a wizard or something. The hair gives you away." He looked crestfallen.

"Nope," said Art. "The powerful mind freak will be kicking the shit out of your Smoke Demon ally about now! And I'll be kicking the shit out of you!"

"Oh thank you G.D., thank you!" said Gaste throwing his shirt to the ground with gusto.

Art adjusted his ponytail and removed his jacket to reveal a lean body that, although past its best, was nevertheless powerful. His feet swelled and groaned in his boots and he even contemplated stripping down to his boxers for a bit more freedom, but a latent streak of English reserve held him back. Already his legs were feeling sticky with the heat and he wished he'd taken Jim's advice to don some of Dave's tracksuit bottoms rather than his traditional fighting garb of white shirt and suit.

The old bouncer was in good shape; fine fettle, as they say in Lancashire. His shirt was pasted to his body, revealing more muscle than fat. His thick torso, huge neck and powerful upper arms promised a worthwhile diversion to an eager Helios Gaste.

They loosened up a little, Art rolling his head round slowly, only faintly disconcerted by the crunchings of age. He turned his neck to the extremes of left and right, fighting to release the tightness and the tension. Then he rotated his hands at the wrists, alternately stretched them backwards against his arms and pushed the tips of his fingers as far back as they would go. Then he slowly rotated his arms, turning his whole body at the waist in a large circle. He threw a few punches at the air, slow, lazy, powerful, concealing his true speed but giving his body the silent cue to be ready. His fingers tingled, there was a slight ache in his left hand.

Not too bad, considering.

Art felt better than he had for years. Thanks, presumably, to Jim and Julie's earlier attention.

Without word or further preamble, they fought.

**

As Julie crossed the flag market towards Malvolian, she was aware of hundreds of pairs of eyes following her. In jeans, t-shirt and strapless sandals she was petite and innocuous, something like a grenade in the precious seconds after its pin is pulled. To some of the witnesses, her face seemed familiar but their addled brains were making every kind of synaptic connection. Very few recognised her as The Girl Who Battled Against Evil, or the Saint of Preston Minster, or any of a selection of bizarre titles conceived and spewed forth by Marjorie MacManaman.

It seemed impossible that so many weird events had occurred in so short a time. But nobody appreciated time in quite the same way. The hapless onlookers were in sync with a common clock source hidden inside a program – a program lurching towards its final termination stage.

Reality shifted and Julie found herself facing Malvolian across a fragrant garden, as if beamed in by a faithful Scotty. It was perpetual night and hundreds of moths flocked and fluttered around candles set in small earthenware pots in every corner of the garden. Marking the perimeter, an ivy-engulfed wall of red brick towered over a land of shrubs, trees and water features. The flickering light from the candles lent the place a magical air, like a fairy glen. Or a pixie glenda.

From every corner, the mist of competing scents was

overwhelming. Intoxicated, Julie ignored her enemy and went to sit on a wooden bench beside a rock-pool. Into it bubbled a stream of purest water.

Malvolian sat quietly next to her and folded his arms. He had shed the Stilton body when Barry McGarry made an unfixable hole in it with his neatly-manicured thumbs. McGarry himself provided a worthy alternate host.

Julie cocked her head slightly and examined him. This new form was one she didn't recognise: a small man in expensive clothes, although his shirt hung loose and his trousers were dubiously stained around the groin. More striking was his completely blank expression. His face was smooth, unlined; a face unbreached by emotion. They sat silently together – as they had in the Minster only a short time ago. Yet a lifetime away. And (in his case) in an entirely different body.

The idea that the 'self' could be reduced to a series of electro-magnetic impulses was not one Julie cared to entertain. She wasn't *that* type of girl. Nor had she given much thought to terms such as 'soul' or 'spirit'. But Jim's words had touched her. He, she realised, was the source of it all. These people had used trick voices ordering her to kill him. They had failed.

Life, Julie realised, was too short to try to understand the complicated things that Jim had talked about. Such topics had remained unresolved by geniuses for centuries so why waste her time with them! With a mind bruised and damaged, Julie had struggled to hold herself together through adult life. She'd avoided deeper thoughts in exactly the same way she avoided treading in dog dirt. Emotion had been nothing but a hindrance. What was the term? She had been comfortably numb. Over the course of a single week, Julie had changed. There was no going back.

Of them all (Jim had said) only she could hope to take on Malvolian and prevail. Julie wasn't worried for herself, only for Art. But the decision was made. Art was on his own journey and if he returned it would be to her.

The look in his eyes as they parted was one that Julie had hoped to see all her life. His parting expression, although Art could not know it, melted the seals on innermost vaults. The good things and the bad flooded out. In a microsecond, she understood. It was clear and obvious, a chance for redemption.

The demon had to die.

Malvolian cleared his throat noisily. The girl was woolgathering. "I was the Devil, you know. I encouraged every one of those men who hurt you."

"Doesn't matter," she spat. "They chose to do what they did, just as I am going to choose how you suffer."

Malvolian spluttered and contorted Barry McGarry's face with unfamiliar commands. The facial muscles did their best to comply but were simply not accustomed to laughter. The effect was disturbing and would have unnerved anyone else.

"I have already broken your life child. Your old hero will die very soon – and you will join him. It's nothing to worry about, however, no great failure. It happens all the time actually. You insects plop back in the cauldron, get a quick reinitialise and you're good as new. You might get reloaded a million times without ever knowing it. It's so marvellous!"

Julie ignored the babbling. A purple flower, glowing as if reflecting ultra-violet light, had caught her eye. She stood up and walked slowly towards some rhododendron bushes. The garden was beautifully maintained and contained an eclectic mixture of plants. Some she recognised but there were other, stranger flowers.

"I like this place," she said, plucking off the largest flower with her mind alone. It floated in the air and swooped gently under her nose. Disappointingly, there was no scent.

She turned to face him, ripping the petals off and shredding their atoms. Falling to the lush, moist grass, they vanished, gluons pouring everywhere and dribbling into the structure of the underlying soil.

"He loves me, he loves me not," she said, as if preoccupied. Malvolian watched, fascinated, keenly observing the sub-molecular destruction and the casual strength she employed to mask the fallout. He shuddered inwardly.

"It's nice here," she said. "Can I stay when I've killed you?"

"Forever," he replied, but his words sounded hollow.

"I'm much stronger than you," she said. "I can tell. I'm stronger than anyone. Even the . . . even Jim. *And* he knew it!"

"Good job I have help then", said Malvolian. With his accumulated mental powers and the small, pulsing machine in his pocket, he had no grounds for worry. Yet he was, at heart, a coward. It would have been, he reflected, better to find the *other*. He believed he understood the power she concealed yet she had eluded him, somehow. Uneasy, he nevertheless launched into action.

He hit Julie with a falling pillar of air. It weighed as much as a moderately sized landslide and caught her hard on the shoulder. She fell under it, rolling backwards into the bushes, landing on her bottom, only catching the weight with the power of her mind at the last possible moment. From a well-tended flowerbed she pushed against monumental forces and began to rise to her feet.

"Give me it as hard as you can big boy," she challenged. Flustered, she drew on phrases from her former life, automatically. "Go on, find out how much I can take. I dare you! Don't worry that I'll break. I'm tougher than I look!"

Malvolian *did* bring forth all his strength. And Carl's. And Barry McGarry's. And a host of extra juice from those he had destroyed. He brought some naughty extra power too – piped in via his secret machine. The illegal (for many good reasons) device funnelled strength from the Outside, piercing the impenetrable forcefield in time and space. Malvolian had cheated in many previous incarnations and had often been lucky. He hoped to be so again.

With more clout than he'd had at his disposal over countless millennia, Malvolian crushed his enemy. Julie fell back, her face pressed sideways into the dirt, her hair strangling her, worming into her nose and mouth. Grass, daisies and small primroses swirled and began to grow at an accelerated rate, winding round her, grasping, alive.

He sighed as she continued to buckle under the enormous yet invisible force. Her whole body was pressed backwards, flat to the ground. Twisting vegetation curled around her tiny frame and after a few minutes of frantic effort, her resistance finally began to fade. Raging, she tried to speak but her mouth was clogged with dirt.

Malvolian felt her life force weaken as her heart stopped and her lungs emptied. But he maintained the pressure until he was sure she was truly extinguished. Feeling her ribs snap, piercing her organs many times, he allowed himself a relieved whistle.

That was scary! Julie's corpse was so tiny yet it concealed power of an awesome magnitude. The *potential* of these creatures! No wonder Meed felt it vital to stop them.

Then, unexpectedly she looked up, a cheeky smile creasing her face. The plants sprang aside, her hair stood on end and her tongue wiggled mischievously. As Malvolian looked on in horror, her chest expanded and her lungs rasped. Suppressing the pain, she scowled and increased the rate of internal repairs.

Her fingers worked the black soil like writhing tendrils, muscles tightening on thin arms.

"It that it?" I said, is that *it*? Surely that isn't the absolute best you can do?"

A spiny anteater of doubt snuggled against Malvolian's sphincter and shook its quills. The slender human was way beyond any of the Aesir assembled, he now knew for sure. An anomaly. Worse, she was a winking anomaly slowly getting to its feet and dusting off its tiny hands.

"Going to kill you know," she said, cheerily, brushing soil from her face.

***

"I guessed you'd find your way here. I'm glad I get to deal with you!" Yasmine Carrion clapped her hands in delight.

Monica walked slowly over, her face drained, her hands trembling. One minute they were in Preston – she was a few steps behind Jim – the next she found herself on a grey, empty road through moorlands and in thick mist. Once again she had to deal with one of her kidnappers – the woman, naked, painted white and obviously quite mad. Monica felt she was losing her mind too. No, she corrected. She felt like she had already lost everything.

"Who the fuck are you people?" she demanded. "And where are we? Where's Jim?"

"Don't you know anything? Even now?"

"What is going on?" Monica wiped the tears from her face, angry at their presence but unable to stem the flow. Mascara had run down her cheeks earlier, leaving a grey-blue residue. She probably looked as crazy as everyone else.

Wandering the streets, eluding the roaming mobs and hiding from a madman who taunted her had been a waking nightmare. Even her mental shield had been hard pressed and, worse, she had totally failed to find Jim despite calling his name for hours. Once she thought she heard him but it seemed so far, far away. Like a sample played back too slowly, its cry was deep, familiar but unreachable.

When Jim and his companions pushed out from the crowd, she knew she must follow. But as she made to catch up, she was transported here. Somehow. With this naked bitch!

A trap!

With a furious snarl, Monica drew herself to her full height, no longer ashamed of it, no longer stooping slightly in an effort to be less intimidating. Her thick, black hair was everywhere, stuck in clumps, strands glued to her face and neck. It was shifted only slightly by the cold wind that tore, wailing, through thin grass, reeds and heather. She screamed, repeating her question with fearsome passion.

"What the HELL is going ON???" Now she resembled some elemental Xena, Warrior Princess (a hint for you would-be film makers out there).

Yasmine raised an eyebrow, her pupils narrowed as if seeing Monica afresh. "Well, you piece of nothing, *this* is what we call the Final Battle. Raganarok we used to call it in the old days. I've heard all about you – who hasn't? – but it's obvious you're faulty goods. My part will be no fun at all!"

Monica simply stood and glared at her enemy. Her hands dangled limply by her side, her head hung low, her thoughts starting to drift away.

"Whatever," she said eventually. And blanked her. Literally. With all her might.

***

In darkness and in pain, Tim floated. Fully conscious, he regarded his beaten-up shell as it lay inert on the bed below, with a detachment that was too real for comfort. Somehow a wall had been built around his mind, either protecting or imprisoning it. Via a thin lifeline, his consciousness was a dangling prisoner outside the wall.

He was locked out of his own brain!

Tim could not understand what had happened - or why he remained aware yet totally out of his mind.

For countless hours – or perhaps years – he floated. His thoughts were free; they soared and he searched for something or someone familiar before returning to his body. But he didn't know where to look and couldn't understand the terrain.

Through sepia vision, he surveyed a world of blurred shapes. Life-forces of humans and even animals, shone like silver. Even plant life pulsed with a pure white that both dazzled and elated his mind's eye. It was apparent he was in some kind of private institution or clinic. Every patient had their own room; there were extensive grounds and facilities. And other things were going on, unpleasant things for selected residents.

Back in his own room, Tim considered the situation and for the thousandth time pushed against the base of the slender cord binding him to his body, reasoning that this could be the one weakness of the wall. The cord was the only thing maintaining his connection; it must be possible to pass back through and take control.

At that moment, Tim thought he heard something. Most of the voices he'd heard in the last hour or two had an echoing, unreal quality. They were somehow *out of phase*, he knew, although he had no idea where the knowledge originated. Almost all of his memories were inaccessible, locked away in the meat of his brain.

Now he heard a voice, very distant, calling. It was Monica.

Like a flash he was moving, faster than electricity, as fast as thought itself.

I'm coming.

***

Yasmine Carrion laughed until she peed herself.

"You honestly thought that little trick would work *here*?" She continued to snort until the tears ran down her neck.

The wind increased in volume, the bluest of noise, the kiss of a spider on dry, brittle skin. Mist hung at the borders of vision, a grey constant, a dirty window steamed by sour breath.

Monica's confident barrier fell to the ground, broke into tiny pieces and scampered away like startled rats. Yasmine had switched to a white suit of armour upon which was painted a black and red skeleton. Her eyes glowed like traditional demonic coals and green fire poured from her mouth. In her hands was a whip of man-flesh, its dark strips dried amongst glass and disease, its donors having been skinned alive for the sheer hell of it. Carrion cracked the whip into Monica's face.

Monica screamed and stepped back, narrowly avoiding the

lash. Quick as a flash, the whip cracked a second time and tore into her side and ripped her left arm. The agony was intense and she knew that death was before her.

And then Tim arrived in her head.

Trust me? he asked, gently.

With my life, she replied without hesitation.

Tim then did the thing that Monica couldn't. He accessed her staggeringly huge reservoir of power and built first a shield and then a sword. With them, he attacked the shocked Yasmine Carrion and, with one sweep, cut off the arm that held the whip.

Carrion, far from giving up, hurled herself at Monica, howling like a particularly howly banshee determined to demonstrate its prowess in the howling department. Pinning the shield arm underneath her body, Yasmine held Monica down. Her mouth expanded grotesquely, the flesh in her cheeks ripping apart as her jaws broke free of their hinges. Fangs thrust through her gums like a JCB tearing soil. She bit deeply into Monica's shoulder and neck.

Gripping Monica's wrist tightly, she held the sword at bay, laying beside her like a lover. Her fangs grew so long that they shredded the flesh of her lips so that blood now flowed freely over the lower part of her face. The stump of her arm flapped madly, spraying dark goo over them both. Red, glowing coals burned into Monica as she whispered softly in her ear.

"Nice try but this is the way it had to end. Well, except for this hiccough," (she peered at the stump with disdain.) "You had me going for a minute there. But then there's a first time for everything"

"Sure is bitch," said Tim with Monica's voice and dislocated her shoulder pulling the trapped arm free. The stump couldn't block the blow as Monica took over, delivering the flat of her palm to her enemy's chin. Living with Jim, you picked a few things up. Especially as he had been most insistent she learn something about self-defence.

Between panting breaths, the process of remembering the times training with Jim switched on a tiny light in Monica's consciousness. This, in turn, triggered a flood of thoughts that began to pour in at random. Soon there was no doubt that something was happening to her mind.

Then, with a sharp click, an image of R2D2 appeared in her head next to a hovering remote control. The diminutive robot began projecting moving pictures, accompanied by a faint whirring sound. Monica activated the "pause" button, being rather too busy fighting for her life to concentrate on it.

It was a creepy feeling though, knowing there was a message (obviously from Jim). She guessed it was one she would not wish to hear.

Momentarily stunned by the palm heel strike, Yasmine fell sideways and Monica followed up her advantage with a mental blast, primed and aimed by Tim. It completely fried the brain stem and dispersed Carrion's personality.

She shrieked like the wicked witch of the west as she died.

"Not all smoke and mirrors," whispered Tim.

Monica spoke to the presence sharing her head-space. "How did you get here?"

"I heard your call and followed until I hit a wall. But for me all walls have a way in, sorry love but they do. I think I surprised some guy though. Couldn't see his face but I'm sure it was . . . oh, never mind. He was getting the shit beaten out of him by a blonde chick. I only saw the scene for a nanosecond as I was drawn into his pants."

"Pants?" said Monica doubtfully.

"Yeah, I didn't expect that either," said Tim. "He had some kind of device in them. Look I can't stay. I'll tell you the rest when . . . damn, my body's pulling me back. The hole is closing. I love you." He was gone.

"Love you too," said Monica, not sure if he heard, as the mist did, finally, begin to clear.

***

Malvolian's human form was helpless, battered, bleeding. Julie's lips curled back in triumph and her hands, with their concealed razor blades, were covered in thick, sticky blood. Mental power was fine for holding and manipulating. But for killing, only real blades offered a satisfactory connection between life and death. The body of Barry McGarry had not, on the whole, fared well. Malvolian, in desperation, cranked up the input amplitude of the *Grimatron* device way beyond safety. And the *Grimatron* was notoriously unsafe anyway. It didn't actually *have* a safety setting – merely a selection of progressively unsafe ones. At its maximum, things were so unsafe that pretty much anything could happen.

A small sub-routine, hovering undetected in the air over Julie's head, fell into the *Grimatron's* field and flashed briefly before it disappeared.

The Lord Malvolian, weary and wounded, felt something enter the protective bubble. Meed would be furious but Malvolian had worries of his own and bubble penetration was was way down the list. The girl appeared to be applying tension to the bonding that his consciousness relied upon. They'd always known that, whilst limited by an organic brain, even the Aesir were vulnerable. It was supposed to add excitement to their adventures, apparently.

The energy required to tear apart a personality such as his, even in this universe, was considerably more than that needed to destroy mere atoms. Yet she appeared to be making progress.

Which was Bad.

Julie casually quashed every attack from the demon using automated defence systems. The few bombs, mental or physical, that got through, were rendered inert by instant healing. With wild abandon, she tore through Malvolian's mind, noticing with some satisfaction how he cried out in pain from time to time.

The battle had stretched to perhaps twenty minutes. Julie did nothing in particular to bring about a speedy conclusion, although she could have done it at any time. She relished the amazed and desperate expression on the demon's face as he realised he was outgunned and outclassed. Occasionally he attempted to flee, but there was nowhere to go.

With surprising clarity, Malvolian felt a blood vessel burst in his brain. He set about scanning the body schematics to see if he could heal it using psychokinesis to hold the torn tissue together. If the body died, he would be banished and out of the game – but his personality would escape intact. In fact, that was now the best outcome to hope for.

The blood rushed into his cranial cavity and held it back with an instinctive effort of will. Bored, Julie stepped up the pace. With a blast of searing mental radiation, she toasted the battered shell that had been Barry McGarry. Inside, the spirit of the demon Malvolian shrieked.

It was then that Julie located the personality core.

She sniffed, briefly, at a gorgeous purple flower before beginning to tear his mind apart.

"He loves me. He loves me not," she whispered.

Malvolian grasped for a tiny silver device – his panic switch – and, using all his remaining strength, pushed its single button. The machine began to suck and he felt his mind drawn from the body towards the secure backup device. If the others survived, they'd find and release him.

He was furious.

This was just not cricket!! In fact it was a complete absence of turgid tedium involving blokes in white jumpers.

Not having been born yesterday (despite some of the sicker fantasies of certain punters) Julie twigged that her adversary was escaping. Feeling his consciousness draining away at speed into a bulge in his trousers, she followed the trail, not unamused by the irony.

As Malvolian uploaded himself, he felt the rush of a space

tadpole sneakily borrowing his resources. Seizing its opportunity, it flew out via the very force field breach that supplied power to the machine. Malvolian, despite his predicament, was horrified.

Julie discovered the device on the borders of several intersecting dimensions (not that she understood it in those terms). It proved impossible to hit so instead, she froze the brain and dispersed the remaining electromagnetic pulses to the four winds.

Malvolian saw only darkness. He decided that it was really quite dark indeed. Very soon, sardonic laughter greeted him, which he had kind of expected.

***

Tim's core escaped. The last image he took from inside the sphere was of a slight girl splattered in gore and standing over Barry McGarry's body. Using her fingers she was examining the ruined head with fascination, as if in a laboratory. Or an abattoir.

***

Julie cast aside Malvolian's empty vessel, which made no sound. His mind had been dispersed, its many fragments floating at the very edges of reality. Then, as if sucked in by a cosmic Dyson, the particles spiralled and vanished.

Her gloating turned to fear in a matter of seconds as she remembered Arthur.

The garden shimmered and grew insubstantial.

Chapter Thirty One

Faith is a cop-out. If the only way you can accept an assertion is by faith, then you are conceding that it can't be taken on its own merits.
                                  Dan Faker

Helios Gaste knew great joy. The ageing human fought well and, despite being slow, weak and inferior, he had frustrated every attack for approaching 30 minutes. They were surprisingly evenly matched and Gaste couldn't help but admire the way his opponent fought silently, sealing his emotions and pain away. He felt it made everything worthwhile and his respect for the elderly pugilist grew with each passing moment.

For his part, Arthur was desperately tired. He varied his movements and pace, bobbed and weaved and used the space wisely and with ingenuity. Only years of experience kept him inches from humiliation.

Impassive to the last, he knew it was hopeless. The man he faced was an oiled, muscled fighting machine with lightning-fast reactions, a staggering array of skills and the staying power of a buffalo on Viagra. Worse, from Art's point of view, his opponent was completely engrossed in the fight, seemingly hoping it could last forever. Art, on the other hand, had taken too much punishment and saw his last three punches fly wildly off-target. The guy had moved faster than he could sense, let alone see.

"You are a worthy champion that Gi-Darven has chosen," commented Helios in his guttural voice. "You need not resist further. We both know how this will end."

"It's been my curse to always know how I will die and at whose hand," said Arthur, improvising. "And I haven't met the man yet!"

"Marvellous!" said Gaste. "Well said! You certainly are something old man. Maybe Meed is wrong and some of you people deserve a future. I will kill you cleanly and with honour!"

Can't wait! muttered Arthur under his breath, sweat running into his eyes and over his balls.

Gaste lurched forward, a blur of fists and feet. Retreating, Art found himself backing into a tree and, as he took his bearings, was caught by a solid punch on the jaw. The world swam and he dispelled the nausea using one of the mental pills Jim had donated. There were precious few left and, it seemed, each bestowed its gifts in lesser measure than its predecessor. No more repair pills remained and just a single speed pill. He took it – by blinking at its icon, as instructed, in his mind's eye.

Ducking, Arthur elbowed Gaste in the groin. Gaste had quickly learned this was a vulnerable area and had protected it with extensive shielding. Even so, Arthur's blow resonated through his lower body and shook him to the bone. The Aesir unleashed an angry rain of extravagant blows that Arthur had been hoping for. His final repair pill would run for a few minutes more and he intended to make best use of it. *Rumble in the Jungle*, he thought.

When Julie found the trail, Art was having the crap kicked out of him. Punches and kicks were tearing into her love and his arms flailed around wildly in a feeble attempt to ward them off. It seemed he had lost control.

She was about to step in when she saw his flailing hands sweep purposefully towards Gaste and, at the last minute, change direction. In a fluid motion, Art came in close and poked out Gaste's eyes with his thumbs, pushing them in deep and hard. This drove the demon into a bellowing rage and the ferocity of his attacks increased still further. He didn't seem to feel the pain. Worse, having two gaping pits where his eyes had been was evidently less of a disadvantage than Arthur had expected. And hoped for.

Those dark, bloody holes fascinated Julie. She stood, transfixed. Once, when a young girl, she had found a kitten thus maimed and the memory of its face haunted her. It was then that her mind discovered the first clues that it could retreat within itself and hide or reshape some aspects of reality.

Arthur was on the floor by the time the trance ended and she realised what was happening. The man with the black eyes was kicking him repeatedly and Julie saw death was near.

"My God, Art!" she cried. Gaste stopped kicking for a moment, snarling, his face contorted and ugly.

"Who is it?" he said, mentally probing but finding no one.

Ignoring him, Julie concentrated on Art. He was still conscious – but barely and close to passing out. She gave him *auto-heal* – better than those stupid pills – and fed him energy so he would recover even faster. *Cavanah should have done this*, she thought.

Cavanah was near, she could sense him. And someone else too – but there was no time for that. Gaste had finally located her and thrust a feeble mental bolt in her direction. Its intention may have been to put her out of the way until the fight was over but Julie shrugged it off scornfully. She was about to rip his head off when Arthur kicked out from the ground, catching Gaste in a knee not long since broken in the same place. The kick tore through the temporary repairs and the leg snapped like a twig.

"Ow!" said Gaste and hit the ground. "Not fair!"

Arthur was on him and in a few seconds had a tight lock on his neck. Powerful fingers dug into Art's forearm and mighty muscles strained, but the ageing bouncer's strength was restored and his will unassailable. He cut off the blood supply to the brain, throttling the life out of his enemy. As the body expired, Julie caught its fleeing essence and tore it into a million pieces. As before, the pieces fizzled into a hole in space, as if sucked down an invisible plughole.

Then she rushed over, kissed Art and stroked his hot, battered body, feeling the recovery well underway. He removed his shoes and socks, his sodden shirt and trousers and lay in his boxer shorts, breathing heavily. Pale flesh began to redden immediately in the harsh light. At Julie's touch, the deep gouges in his arm faded completely.

"We should go up here a short distance," she said, indicating the dust trail. "There's something we need to witness. You going to be OK?"

Arthur smiled. Yes, he was quite sure of it. Wiping the sweat from his brow, he regarded his dead adversary at his feet and shook his head.

"I wish I understood," he said to himself.

"Don't worry, it'll soon be over," she told him. "And we're going to be fine. I can do anything, you know."

Art's smile faded a tiny bit but he kissed her forehead and then her lips with a passion he struggled to control.

"It's going to be alright," he agreed, hoping with all his heart that it would be.

***

Monica discovered a garden and paused for a moment beside Barry McGarry. He was undeniably dead.

Inside the garden it was deepest night but as she passed through its wrought iron gate, the stars faded. Outside, the sky began to fill with early morning light. And the further she followed the dusty path that wound up the hillside, the lighter it became. Until, soon, the sun was at its highest point, a fiery orb in a deep blue ocean-sky.

Further up the path another corpse sprawled next to a pile of bloody clothes. This one she also recognised – as the swarthy Greek who had kidnapped her! It seemed he'd been working out, but it hadn't done him any good.

She *knew* it would all turn out to be Jim's fault. Somehow.

And then she remembered. Jim had left her a message.

Jogging a few hundred yards to put the – strangely flyless – corpse well behind her, Monica sat by the side of the road on a flat rock sheltered by a cherry tree. There she closed her eyes and pushed 'play' on the remote still floating in her head. She never once questioned how she could do this. It was way too late for doubt and questions.

R2D2 began to project a short film presented by her ex-husband, the man who, it turned out, had created everything – and with a bigger Bang than he'd ever seemed capable of.

When the film was over, Monica stared into the distance for a long time. She was far, far beyond surprise but at least she knew what she was meant to do. How it could possibly help was beyond her wildest guesses.

She knew Jim (now better than ever) and knew also that it would turn out OK. He'd promised – and for all his faults Jim never lied.

The path continued to rise and she followed it, at peace. The sky became yellow. Ahead, at the summit, was a temple. Intuition told her this was not a place of worship or of prayer but of study. At the door stood the elderly abbot, waiting for her.

"We've been expecting you," he confirmed, bowing low. "And may I say that you are indeed the most beautiful creature ever to grace this place. It could have been created to reflect your beauty."

"You've been smoking dope with Jim and Dave," accused Monica. "I know those corny lines, I've heard them a hundred times before!"

"Not guilty, please," said the abbot. "I only have a very small knowledge base. Mostly I'm here to look venerable and add an air of mystery. Don't dawdle now. You best get on, er, grasshopper. He needs you."

Monica breezed past him without another word and the abbot, content at last, ceased to exist.

She headed for the bright courtyard instinctively. Several figures sat as if in frozen meditation, but on inspection were actually moving, albeit incredibly slowly. Her feet carried her, effortlessly, where they needed to go, almost as if they had tread the same path before.

Monica marched boldly into the bright sunlight. In the

courtyard, the air hummed and crackled. Electricity crawled over her skin.

She saw visions in the air. Some she recognised, some she did not. In one, Jim lay naked, staring wistfully across a pillow and reaching out to stroke her hair. There was fear in his gesture – a fear that she had not understood at the time. Jim always seemed to be reaching out to her, as if he needed something he could never vocalise.

There followed other images of Jim in various costumes. Seemingly he had appeared in many historical dramas and had made a collage video of the most heroic scenes. Oddly, images of torture then followed and she gaped in disgust at Roman Arenas, the Inquisition, the Crusades and so many Holy Wars. How these events fitted in, she couldn't begin to guess but, as quickly as they appeared, they were replaced by an image she *did* recognise. It was, painfully, the last night they had tried to save their marriage. Jim had had a ridiculous idea to meet on neutral territory – for one last night in a hotel. He'd arrived with chocolates, champagne, pizza and eyes like a baby calf. She had honestly tried – but it was not to be. At the last, it descended into another sad attempt to seize a happiness they both knew was gone forever. Jim's desperation was all-too evident and his disappointment infectious.

Some things when broken can never be repaired, they learned that night. He'd pushed too hard for a response she could not give. She realised then that theirs would never be a happy ending.

Visions danced before her upturned eyes revealing other scenes from his life and scenes involving her, although she did not recall ever experiencing them. Then, as clear as if he was right next to her, Jim's voice reverberated through her head.

"Elea-Mira, whatever happens remember that I'll always love you. You are the most beautiful thing I've ever seen, touched, smelt or kissed and I've loved you from the first time I saw you. But if you love someone, you must set them free. Think of me sometimes – and kindly if you can – as you gaze upon those different stars in a different sky. Think of me as Jim, if that's all you can remember. I'll catch you next time around, my love, and I swear I'll put things right."

Strange words, she thought.

A final vision flickered before her eyes – of another man. He might have been a younger version of Jim and wore a black leather jacket. This man leaned on the prow of a ship – a large, ugly, rusting ship. His eyes scanned the horizon but his expression was unreadable. Then the image faded.

Monica could weep no more. She raised her arms, knowing it was time to obey Jim's last request.

A spark of love, with its dying breath, called out to its mate over vast tracts of space. And, suddenly, she found herself adrift in an endless sea. Ahead, two great monsters were locked in mortal combat, teeth and tentacles tearing into each other, dark blood staining the water. One was pale green and covered in gaping wounds. The other was a dark purple and howling in delight.

"Jim?" she called. The uncertainty was gone. For a moment, she thought there was something else. She thought she *was* someone else. And, as quickly as it came, the thought dissipated like a dream on waking. There was a task to complete before returning to her life.

The green beast turned an eye the size of a dinner plate towards her. It was dying and the eye was filled with an infinity of sadness. It closed.

Without hesitation, Monica held her arms out like a spear. This caused her to fly through the water towards the creature. She rammed into its side, merging with it for a moment. The flesh was soft and yielding and gave her a mild shock over her whole body.

The monstrous fish tried to speak but in a language she could not understand. Shaking with urgency, it opened its huge mouth but no more words came. The great eye dimmed and it died.

Despite counting on it, Jonathon Meed was amazed at his victory. He took control of the watery scene and allowed it to melt away.

Who says the bad guys always lose?

Standing in the courtyard once more, he discarded his illusory fishy body for that of a pervy hill farmer. Jim's corpse was nowhere to be seen. Monica stood there, hands still outstretched, clasped, her expression haunted.

"How the hell did you get here?" Meed spoke, despite being speechless with anger.

"I'm here too," said Art, stepping from behind a pillar. He walked from the shadows into sunshine like a god.

"And me," said Julie, dramatically closing from the other side. She couldn't quite remember what should happen next but fortunately Art had paid more attention.

"You all won?" said Meed feeling his victory snatched away. "That's impossible!"

"#CSISKIL XYZZY PURGE-ALL" said Monica precisely as Jim had instructed her.

"Execute," said Julie happily.

"Delete," said Art, completing the spell.

Chapter Thirty Two

Laws alone can not secure freedom of expression; in order that every man present his views without penalty there must be spirit of tolerance in the entire population.   Alfred Einsbatenn

Being immortal isn't as easy as you might think. For a start, it has challenges I bet you haven't even considered.

It has long been argued, amongst the wise[24], that immortals should keep busy, have goals and purpose just like everyone else. I hope I don't sound like a pompous twat, but trust me when I confirm this is true. Of course, we disagree amongst ourselves about what is worthwhile and what it's all about generally. However, one thing is certain – a Prime Directive exists. And it is this: all beings are programmed to procreate. Give them a choice of screw or eat and they'll screw. Offer screw or die and they'll definitely screw. But ask them whether they'd rather screw or win a million pounds and some humans wouldn't be quite so sure. I'm afraid it gets complicated when you introduce elements that interferes with the basic "screwing is tops" tenet. Not to labour the point too much but you know there is summat up when that goes wrong. Of course, if it's got to that stage, there will have been other signs too.

How do we immortals procreate? Well, I'm glad you asked. It shows an inquisitive nature and that's always good. You should know that the Aesir are a special case: We aren't drawn from a single stock. Anyway, we have long struggled to decide if there's a need for more of us. There was never any hurry because we live outside time and mostly outside everything else too. Being pure energy, we don't even wear watches. It could be tea-time and not one of us would feel peckish. Not having stomachs is another

---

[24] That's us by the way. The Aesir.

factor there. But I digress.

Certainly procreation could never occur by animal coupling! We're too far past all that flesh and squirting juices nonsense. I personally thought it was worth a look but there you go, It's no secret that I'm in the pro-Darven camp. I'm fairly sure that, amongst the juveniles, there are those who indulge. But I don't want to drop anyone in it.

Anyway, important questions started to be asked: can a mega-advanced society decay? Can we cease to exist? Should we sublime and join with the Great Universal Carbuncle? An investigation was scheduled but I can't tell you how it's getting on.

Now I should relate something about the hero of this tale. Well, hero isn't quite the right word. His name is Gi-Darven – also known as Gilgamesh Ozymandeus Darven. He's always been regarded as a little peculiar but, along with his mate Elea-Mira, he was quite a bright star amongst us.

Their tale is long and rather sad so this isn't the place for a lengthy summary. Suffice it to say that they were tasked with twin projects. The rest of us carried on having a good time and they went off to enjoy themselves in the dark, throwing strange particles around and so on. Gi was supposed to investigate alternative means of procreation and, naturally, he combined it with his hobby, which was the growing and nurturing of universes. To Elea, we entrusted the question of whether we could ever cease to exist, which seemed the more important of the two. I must stress there was no urgency to either of these. However, they got well and truly stuck in.

Gi began by constructing and tending a series of plain, linear universes. Although long regarded as somewhat quaint, in his hands they often produced interesting results. His innovative idea was that individuals – rather than entire civilisations – could graduate and join us. How that would upset the Vanir if they knew! They've been trying, like, forever!

Foul play was suspected early on, particularly after the loss of a string of Gi's favourites, notably a certain Wolfang Amadeus Mozart at a tragically early age. But generally things seemed to be progressing with promise.

However, there were dark times ahead on many systems across this universe, not just Gi's favourite hunting ground. Creatures of power and wealth imposed their special brand of constricting freedom on those with less power. Science was ridiculed and Art, instead of flourishing, floundered. I'm told an unmade bed was passed off – with a straight face – as the Real Thing. Art was delegated, reduced, simplified and, frankly, lost its mojo. He almost closed the whole project down.

In parallel, Elea-Mira was busy exploring the nature of our people and began making radical suggestions to reverse a trend she named *Reverse Evolutionary Personality Decay*. I admit that probably wasn't the exact phrase but then nobody took her findings very seriously. Except Gi.

Some say it was to prove the seriousness of her warnings, others that she was merely careless; anyway, something bad happened. Elea vanished. We looked everywhere – and Gi-Darven became quite frantic. But she had achieved the impossible. She had ceased to be.

"She wouldn't go without me," GD bleated, touchingly at first. He could be a bit of a whiner though and started to get obsessive and, frankly, a bore about the whole thing.

As his mood darkened, he again became convinced that his projects were being sabotaged, that someone was tampering with the developing universes. He discovered that Elea had last been seen in a particular greenhouse, next to a flowering universe that was special to them both. To cut a long story short, Gi-Darven began to make trips into his own Creation, claiming to be on the trail of Elea. By all accounts, he spent much of his time in a particular galaxy and on a particular planet – perhaps because the sentient creatures bore a vague resemblance to our own distant origins.

I think we all felt sorry for him. Certainly we humoured him. After all, he'd either get over it or he wouldn't.

And so it was that, on one occasion, he went native, full term and became Jim Cavanah. This was a man who behaved as if he had all the answers but harboured a secret even he could not know[25].

Unfortunately, some amongst us did not agree with G.D.'s plans for boosting and revitalising our numbers. In private, they sneered, calling it Quantitative Easing and even worse names. Their leader was, as you may have guessed, Meed. If you ask me, he was probably driven by jealousy.

It transpires that Meed and several others were slipping in, dabbling, and quietly slipping out again. The production line at the Future Art Factory faltered, turning out fewer worthy artists, composers and thinkers each year.[26] Eventually there were none.

Fortunately, Jim Cavanah found the solution. Never a modest man, he reasoned that only GOD himself could do what he was doing. Normally he would have bathed in smugness at his great achievements but the final realisation only dawned as he tiptoed past Dave and Sheila's room to raid the fridge, a matter of hours before the final battle. By the other sounds they were making, they weren't calling for him specifically anyway.

Having awakened as himself, he knew he did not have long. Rules are rules and he wrote most of them. Annoyingly, he had discovered his true love at long last. Well *most* of her. Yet, frustratingly he was trapped in a Ragnarok Scenario. We do love contests – they're useful to show if a civilisation is on track. Anyway, is that enough explanation do you suppose?

***

---

[25] There are rules of self-awareness relating to our own creations. Think about it! I mean, if you think we're arrogant now . . .

[26] This occurred on all planets in all galaxies, although our story has mercifully concentrated on just one.

You might find it interesting to know of the conversation Jim Cavanah had that last night with Art, while Julie the mad hooker slept. Sorry, is that insensitive? It's just that she scares us, I'll admit. Anyway, Jim told Art as much as he felt necessary, and quite a bit more than he intended. It's another reason we don't really permit this sort of thing. Art asked him the question he most wanted answered.

"Do we have a soul mate?"

"Sure we do mate," said Jim, trying to keep a straight face. "It's a little tadpoley thing."

Art waited patiently. He drummed his fingers.

"OK, in my opinion yes," said Jim at last.

"And when together you feel . . . happy? Complete?"

Jim squirmed on the settee and looked uncomfortable. "I don't know about happy," he said. "There's a unique feeling when you're with the one you love. Complete seems a good way to put it. It's amazing luck if you both feel the same way. You know what I mean, Art?"

Art stroked Julie's hair but said nothing.

Jim continued. "You can love others too, of course. Spread it around, I've always said. You can love a dozen women but only one will make you the best you can be. Very few people meet their soul mate, Art. Very few. The fact that you did should make you rejoice."

"What about her?" he asked, meaning Julie.

"She's special that's for sure. And I reckon only you can save her," said Jim. "If you do what I suggest, there's a chance."

Jim then told him how he was going to wipe Meed's code from humanity, allowing religion and other mental cancers to wither away naturally.

Art listened[27].

---

[27] So there you go. You didn't think I was going to tell you everything, right?

Chapter Thirty Three

Time is an illusion. Lunchtime doubly so
Dougie Adama

In the smoking, dazed centre of Preston, a wormhole opened briefly. From it stepped a broad, silver-haired man in boxer shorts and a thin, blonde girl. A tall, dark-haired woman followed silently; she walked into the centre of the market place and fulfilled the last of Jim's requests.

"#CSISINT BANG SETTAWIT!"

The force field folded into nothingness. The survivors slumped to the ground. All the demons, gargoyles, trolls and frost giants were banished. A subtle vibration roared, beeping like Morse code, into the earth. It resonated through every atom of the planet, and many nearby, before continuing its journey to the outermost reaches of the cosmos.

It took just a few seconds for all Jim's remaining energy to be pass from Monica's mind and be spent.

Smoke from burning wrecks drifted around, flurries of sooty blackness filling the sky. Monica observed Art and Julie walk off, hand in hand, without looking back. They seemed an odd couple and she wondered what they would do together and whether it would be enough in the long run. She hoped so. Sometimes you have to settle for less and make the best of it.

Her memories of Jim seemed to be fading. He was still alive in a sense. She knew that much. But he was . . . removed. He didn't even belong in this universe, he merely wandered in from time to time. Always an arrogant son of a bitch, his claim that he'd grown the universe from a seed was beyond her comprehension.

He had set her free, he said.

He would catch her later, he said.

His eyes had been moist and it seemed as if there was going to be something more. Perhaps he would return with her after all and they could live happily ever after.

It was not to be and secretly she was relieved. Living with Jim had not been easy when he thought he was God. But when he *knew* it?!

In the haze, alone and unnoticed, Monica surveyed a new world. She wondered whether things could have worked out any better. It seemed an unsatisfactory ending. And as each second ticked by, her memories of Jim faded a little more. His last gift.

At length, she sensed Tim's mind and set out to help him, immune to the groans of the dying and the mutilated.

***

"I'll never be like her," said Julie. She held a faded photo of Peg in her tiny hands. Art was clearing the room that had been a shrine, storing its contents lovingly in boxes bound for the attic.

"No," said Art. "But look at me. I am a different man now. Somebody worked their magic and I'll be damned if I'm going to waste it. Stay here, with me!"

Somebody had indeed worked their magic. Although old enough to be her grandfather, Art now resembled a much younger man.

"What will we do?" she asked, breathlessly.

"Everything we ever wanted," he said. "Jim said there were things he'd like me to tackle. He hoped we'd do them together."

"That Jim was a funny one wasn't he?" she said.

"You could say that," agreed Art.

"Do you know what he said to me, just before I went to kill the smoke demon?"

"No."

"He said to go away and sin no more," said Julie, smiling. "Then he patted me on the bottom. I almost hit him but I changed my mind."

"He's got a weird sense of humour alright," said Art.

Chapter Thirty Four

Freedom is not worth having if it does not connote freedom to err. It passes my comprehension how human beings, be they ever so experienced and able, can delight in depriving other human beings of that precious right.   *Gimpy*

Three days had passed since the Apocalypse. Relief workers were still wandering around Preston in dismay, trying to distinguish the new mess from the old. A national disaster had been proclaimed for which National Lottery funds were being hastily allocated. There was talk of a charity single involving Roman Cheating and/or Wylie Minnow.

"Psssst!" said a voice at Dave's kitchen window. The electricity was still off but Dave was doing the dishes to some ghetto-blasted Pavaroti. Every so often he stopped to examine intricate patterns and colours in the bubbles.

"Jim?" he said, looking up from a particularly shiny bubble.

"Need a quick word."

"Wow, I thought you'd left us for good. Hold on, I'll call Sheila."

"Don't do that mate," said Jim. "It's only a flying visit."

Dave wiped his hands on a tea towel and took a couple of tinnies from the fridge. He opened the back door and the cat rushed in through his legs. Stupid beast refused to use the flap.

They stood under a tree in the garden like the old days. Jim wore sandals and was dressed in a flowing blue robe with *Gandalf* sleeves. He looked faintly insubstantial and wore an enigmatic, wistful smile. Dave offered the can and his old pal took it and held it before him in a toast. They clicked tinnies as they had done on so many occasions. This would be the last.

"I suppose I can drink. I made this vessel – copied an idea of

Julie's – with a few tweaks of my own. Looks like my old one, don't you think? Jesus, that girl's powerful!"

"Are they going to be alright?" asked Dave. "Art and Julie. They seem fine on the surface but I still wonder if she's a bit nutso underneath."

"Art can handle her," said Jim. "Don't you worry. Good Art can fix anything, did you know that?"

"Had a smoke already dude? Sounds like one of your half-arsed wisecracks disguised as philosophy."

Jim looked up at the clear starry night and, as if on cue, a shooting star cut a fiery trail and was lost behind the trees.

"Ah, man, I'm always high now. Kinda by definition when you think about it. It's one more reason I can't stay."

Jim wandered to the fence and gazed into the small wood that bordered Dave's garden. The noises and scents of the night drifted lazily by and the fence was dry and crumbly under his fingers. It would be a long hot summer. Dave joined him and, silently, they observed a toad as it mumbled about, seeking slugs.

"I thought you wanted to live happily ever after?" said Dave at length. "I wish you could. We were going to grow into two grumpy old men, going to Amsterdam a few times a year, getting trashed, having a laugh. It's not much of an ambition but I was looking forward to it."

"Me too man, but I can't reverse reality. Now I'm connected to the full catalogue of my thoughts, no meat brain can contain them. And one has to obey the rules. Hopefully we'll see what humanity is really capable of as the cure spreads."

"I think we'll get there," said Dave. "You might have cleared everyone's noggins but it still takes time to walk without a crutch. People aren't used to thinking for themselves."

An owl hooted nearby, startling them. Dave was secretly pleased to note that Jim was as surprised by the sound as he was.

"Well, I'll watch with interest," mumbled Jim who lapsed into silence.

Dave suddenly remembered a question. "Did you win your big contest? I mean, I guess you did but what *happened*?"

For a moment, his old friend's mask slipped to reveal – what was it – anguish? Despair? He gave a long sigh.

"No, actually But then yes, kinda. The greater the sacrifice, the greater the effect. Let's just say I prioritised the repair job and leave it at that. Amongst my folk there was pressure to close this whole universe but I persuaded them otherwise. Something precious to me remains here after all. Meed and his allies are out of the way – for now. But I can't promise they won't try again one day. We don't go in for punishment and revenge, you see. Cycle of hate and all that. And we accept the cyclic nature of things."

For a time there was a pleasant silence between them.

"I based this universe on the principles of Linear Time," said Jim at last. "You do stuff once then you move on and do something else. You remember the previous thing but have no knowledge of the next thing. The framework is elegant and challenging for us but it contains a neat little trick if you can find it. They say that time is as stubborn as a camel – you can't make it back up. Which is my long-winded way of saying . . . make the most of what you've got my friend. You don't come by this way again."

"Deep shit dude. Are you sure I can't go get Sheila? She'd love to see you and talk bollocks again."

"I don't want any fuss. I wanted to chat one last time. I said goodbye to Monica already. Broke my heart."

"We saw her too, briefly. She's gone back to that Tim. He's big news, apparently. In America though. Too much competition over here now."

"I thought it was best. Despite his flaws he does love her."

"Don't *you*?" Dave sipped deeply from his tinny then burped. The toad shuffled off into the darkness, away from the prattling creatures.

"Of course I do. But things have changed. I could no more hang out here than you could move in with a bucket of bacteria. Think of the logistics!"

"That's a fecking weird concept. You *sure* you're not off your face?"

"I told you, I'm always High now. It's how we are. Stoneliness is next to Godliness. Being with Monica now would be impossible for both of us. That's why when we Gods do, you know, mingle, we always have a handicap. At least I didn't come as a bull. Never really got all that animal stuff." He paused for a while before adding, quietly, "and I was too late to get everything I wanted."

"That sounds real sad," said Dave. "Is that just in your reality then or everywhere?"

Jim considered this for a moment and then broke into a wide grin. In spite of the slightly ethereal cast to his features, it was unmistakably the Jim of old. "Thanks mate, *that's* the perspective I needed," he said. Something in his mood had shifted.

"I don't get it," said Dave.

"You might just have helped me see something that was right in front of my nose. I'm going to miss that. Look, unfortunately I have to leave very soon. I still have tons to say but there's never enough time is there? Some rapid advice: Learn to use your nice clean brain and remember that minds are fragile things. Don't peer too closely into them. And this isn't me trying to hold you back. It's just that the more detail you leech the more you disturb. Some stuff you know without knowing it. Probing can change the past or redirect how consciousness copes with the future. And there are futures spawned every minute. Don't be afraid to explore them."

"Trippy shit dude," gurgled Dave happily.

Jim shook his head, smiling. "Alright," he said. "I'll bugger off. But before I go, don't you have any earth-shattering final questions? *I* might not come back. In fact I don't propose to."

Dave pondered.

"What's the point? I mean, why do it, why make this universe – or others?" he asked. "And where do you go from here?"

"The first one's easy: to give birth to God. Or gods, anyway." Jim grinned. "We got fed up waiting for races to catch us up so this was an idea of mine. And as you probably realise by now, the point of it all is creation for its own sake. Art, in other words. Art in all its forms, that's the route to godhood that works best. I'm not talking copy and paste bling-encrusted bullshit either! I'm talking real, honest art, something unique, personal, greater than itself."

"Coo," said Dave.

"Interacting with reality very, very, very, very deeply will generate changes. General Reality shifts to accommodate the new, worthy thing it accepts from Local Reality – like squeezing up to make room on a bus. And that, my dear friend, is what my universes are about. When working properly, they produce output beyond the imagination of their Creator. Let there be light, etcetera, etcetera. Should be a blast of trumpets about now don't you reckon?"

Jim was now speaking without drawing breath. He continued in the same vein. "As for where I'm going, well, who knows? Shame it's too late to start a new religion. Always got great art from them, oddly enough. Hopefully you'll fill the hole with wonder and be inspired by that instead, much healthier in the long run. Oh, and I meant to say earlier, it goes without saying that just being lovely and cool and mellow and harmless can earn celestial promotion too. The Buddhists weren't far off there and it'd be unfair not to give them a round of applause or something. Do you think the universe is fair now?"

"If you planted it dude, deffo! And cheers for the deep and quality reply what I will surely ponder. One more quickie from your Dudeness, while you're giving me the High Tiddly Eye Tie?" He didn't wait for a reply. "Can we learn to travel in time? Without a camel."

"Ooh, not bad. The short answer is yes, you can. On my hairy, scarry knee I promise. I'll even offer a clue: start by counting very, very, very fast," drawled Jim with not entirely a straight face. "Oh, and you've got to change something unchangeable and discover something sitting right under your nose. Humanity has a long way to go. And now so have I."

There was definitely a tear. Possibly two.

"I love you man," Jim said at the last. He began to fade as if beaming up to a distant Scotty.

"I love you too!! In a blokey way, of course," Dave added. The old joke. As they embraced, he saw Jim's face become suddenly more substantial. It rippled and became real flesh. Jim's clothing morphed from the hippyish ethereal robes to a black leather jacket, jeans and boots.

Spike drained the tinny, patted Dave on the head and, without a word, leaped over the fence and vanished into the woods. As he began to run, he roared with laughter, life and potential.

Dave watched after him for a long time.

THE END

Printed in Poland
by Amazon Fulfillment
Poland Sp. z o.o., Wrocław